THE LADY OF THE LAKE

Also by Andrzej Sapkowski from Gollancz:

The Last Wish
Blood of Elves
Time of Contempt
Baptism of Fire
Sword of Destiny
The Tower of the Swallow
The Lady of the Lake
Season of Storms

THE LADY OF
THE LAKE

ANDRZEJ SAPKOWSKI

Translated by David French

This edition first published in Great Britain in 2018 by Gollancz

First published in Great Britain in 2017 by Gollancz
an imprint of the Orion Publishing Group Ltd
Carmelite House, 50 Victoria Embankment
London EC4Y 0DZ

An Hachette UK Company

3 5 7 9 10 8 6 4 2

Originally published as *Pani Jeziora*

Published by arrangement with Literary Agency 'Agence de l'Est'

Original text Copyright © Andrzej Sapkowski 1999
English translation Copyright © David French 2017

A CIP catalogue record for this book is
available from the British Library.

ISBN 978 1 473 21160 5

Typeset by Input Data Services Ltd, Somerset

Printed and bound by CPI Group (UK) Ltd, Croydon, CR0 4YY

MIX
Paper from
responsible sources
FSC® C104740

www.gollancz.co.uk

CHAPTER ONE

The lake was enchanted. There was absolutely no doubt about it.

Firstly, it lay right beside the mouth of the enchanted Cwm Pwcca valley, permanently veiled in mist and famed for witchcraft and magical phenomena.

Secondly, it was enough to look.

The lake was deep, a vivid, pure blue, just like polished sapphire. It was as smooth as a looking glass, so smooth the peaks of the Y Wyddfa massif gazing into it seemed more stunning reflected than in reality. A cold, bracing wind blew in from the lake and nothing disturbed the dignified silence, not even the splash of a fish or the cry of a water bird.

The knight shuddered in amazement. But instead of continuing to ride along the ridge he steered his horse towards the lake, as though lured by the magical power of the witchcraft slumbering down there, at the bottom, in the depths. The horse trod timidly across broken rocks, showing by a soft snorting that it also sensed the magical aura.

After descending to the very bottom of the valley, the knight dismounted. Leading his steed by the bridle, he neared the water's edge, where faint ripples were playing among colourful pebbles.

He kneeled down, his chain mail rustling. Scaring away fry, fish as tiny and lively as needles, he scooped up water in his cupped hands. He drank slowly and gingerly, the ice-cold water numbing his lips and tongue and stinging his teeth.

As he stooped again, a sound, carried over the surface of the water, reached his ears. He raised his head. His horse snorted, as though confirming it had also heard.

He listened. No, it was no illusion. What he had heard was singing. A woman singing. Or, more likely, a girl.

The knight, like all knights, had been raised on stories of bards and tales of chivalry. And in them – nine times out of ten – girlish

1

airs or wailing were bait, and the knights that followed them usually fell into traps. Often fatal ones.

But his curiosity got the better of him. The knight, after all, was only nineteen years old. He was very bold and very imprudent. He was famous for the first and known for the second.

He checked that his sword slid well in the scabbard, then tugged his horse and headed along the shore in the direction of the singing. He didn't have to go far.

On the lakeside lay great, dark boulders – worn smooth to a shine. You might have said they were the playthings of giants carelessly tossed there or forgotten after a game. Some of the boulders lay in the lake, looming black beneath the crystalline water. Some of them protruded above the surface. Washed by the wavelets, they looked like the backs of leviathans. But most of them lay on the lakeside, covering the shore all the way to the treeline. Some of them were buried in the sand, only partly sticking out, leaving their true size to the imagination.

The singing that the knight could hear came from just behind the rocks near the shore. And the girl who was doing the singing was out of sight. He led his horse, holding it by the bit and nostrils to stop it whinnying or snorting.

The girl's garments were spread on a perfectly flat boulder lying in the lake. She, naked and waist-deep in the water, was washing and singing the while. The knight didn't recognise the words.

And no wonder.

The girl – he would have bet his life – was not flesh-and-blood. That was evident from her slim figure, the strange colour of her hair and her voice. He was certain that were she to turn around he would see huge, almond-shaped eyes. And were she to brush aside her ashen hair he would surely see pointed ears.

She was a dweller of Faërie. A spirit. One of the Tylwyth Têg. One of those creatures the Picts and Irish called Daoine Sidhe, the Folk of the Hill. One of those creatures the Saxons called elves.

The girl stopped singing for a moment, submerged herself up to the neck, snorted and swore very coarsely. It didn't fool the knight, though. Fairies – as was widely known – could curse like humans. Oftentimes more filthily than stablemen. And very often the oath preceded a spiteful prank, for which fairies were famous. For example, swelling someone's nose up to the size of a cucumber or shrinking another's manhood down to the size of a broad bean.

Neither the first nor the second possibility appealed to the knight. He was on the point of a discreet withdrawal when the noise of hooves on the pebbles suddenly betrayed him. No, not his own steed, which – being held by the nostrils – was as calm and quiet as a mouse. He had been betrayed by the fairy's horse, a black mare, which at first the knight hadn't noticed among the rocks. Now the pitch-black animal churned up the pebbles with a hoof and neighed a greeting. The knight's stallion tossed its head and neighed back politely. So loudly an echo sped across the water.

The fairy burst from the water, for a moment presenting herself to the knight in all her alluring splendour. She darted towards the rock where her clothing lay. But rather than seizing a blouse and covering up modestly, the she-elf grabbed a sword and drew it from its scabbard with a hiss, whirling it with admirable dexterity. It lasted but a short moment, after which she sank down, covering herself up to her nose in the water and extending her arm with the sword above the surface.

The knight shook off his stupefaction, released the reins and genuflected, kneeling on the wet sand. For he realised at once who was before him.

'Hail,' he mumbled, holding out his hands. 'Great is the honour for me . . . Great is the accolade, O Lady of the Lake. I shall accept the sword . . .'

'Could you get up from your knees and turn away?' The fairy stuck her mouth above the water. 'Perhaps you'd stop staring? And let me get dressed?'

He obeyed.

He heard her splash out of the water, rustle her clothes and swear softly as she pulled them over her wet body. He examined the black mare, its coat as smooth and lustrous as moleskin. It was certainly a horse of noble blood, certainly enchanted. And undoubtedly also a dweller of Faërie, like its owner.

'You may turn around.'

'Lady of the Lake—'

'And introduce yourself.'

3

'I am Galahad, of Caer Benic. A knight of King Arthur, the lord of Camelot, the ruler of the Summer Land, and also of Dumnonia, Dyfneint, Powys, Dyfedd . . .'

'And Temeria?' she interrupted. 'Redania, Rivia, Aedirn? Nilfgaard? Do those names mean anything to you?'

'No. I've never heard them.'

She shrugged. Apart from her sword she was holding her boots and her blouse, washed and wrung out.

'I thought so. What day of the year is it today?'

'It is,' he opened his mouth, utterly astonished, 'the second full moon after Beltane . . . Lady . . .'

'Ciri,' she said dully, wriggling her shoulders to allow her garments to lie better on her drying skin. She spoke strangely. Her eyes were large and green.

She involuntarily brushed her wet hair aside and the knight gasped unwittingly. Not just because her ear was normal, human, and in no way elven. Her cheek was disfigured by a large, ugly scar. She had been wounded. But could a fairy be wounded?

She noticed his look, narrowed her eyes and wrinkled her nose.

'That's right, it's a scar!' she repeated in her extraordinary accent. 'Why do you look so scared? Is a scar such a strange thing for a knight to see? Is it so ugly?'

He removed his chainmail hood with both hands and brushed aside his hair.

'Indeed it isn't,' he said, not without youthful pride, displaying a barely healed scar of his own, running from temple to jaw. 'And only blemishes on one's honour are ugly. I am Galahad, son of Lancelot du Lac and Elaine, daughter of King Pelles, lord of Caer Benic. That wound was dealt me by Breunis the Merciless, a base oppressor of maidens, before I felled him in a fair duel. In sooth, I am worthy of receiving that sword from your hands, O Lady of the Lake.'

'I beg your pardon?'

'The sword. I'm ready to receive it.'

'It's *my* sword. I don't let anyone touch it.'

'But . . .'

'But what?'

4

'The Lady of the Lake always . . . always emerges from the waters and bestows a sword, doesn't she?'

She said nothing for some time.

'I get it,' she finally said. 'Well, every country has its own customs. I'm sorry, Galahad, or whatever your name is, but I'm clearly not the Lady I'm meant to be. I'm not giving away anything. And I won't let anyone take anything from me. Just to make things clear.'

'But,' he ventured, 'you must come from Faërie, don't you, m'lady?'

'I come . . .' she said a moment later, and her green eyes seemed to be looking into an abyss of space and time. 'I come from Rivia, from the city of the same name. From Loch Eskalott. I sailed here by boat. It was foggy. I couldn't see the shore. I only heard the neighing. Of Kelpie . . . My mare, who followed me.

She spread out her wet blouse on a stone, and the knight gasped again. The blouse had been washed, but perfunctorily. Patches of blood were still visible.

'The current brought me here,' the girl began again, either not seeing what he had noticed or pretending not to. 'The current and the spell of a unicorn . . . What's this lake called?'

'I don't know,' he confessed. 'There are so many lakes in Gwynedd—'

'In Gwynedd?'

'Naturally. Those mountains are Y Wyddfa. If you keep them on your left hand and ride through the forests, after two days you'll reach Dinas Dinlleu, and then on to Caer Dathal. And the river . . . The nearest river is . . .'

'Never mind what the nearest river's called. Do you have anything to eat, Galahad? I'm simply dying of hunger.'

*

'Why are you watching me like that? Afraid I'll disappear? That I'll fly off with your hard tack and smoked sausage? Don't worry. I got up to some mischief in my own world and confused destiny, so I shouldn't show my face there for the moment. I'll stay a while in yours. In a world where one searches the sky in vain for the

5

Dragon or the Seven Goats. Where right now it's the second full moon after Belleteyn, and Belleteyn is pronounced 'Beltane'. Why are you staring at me like that, pray?'

'I didn't know fairies could eat.'

'Fairies, sorceresses and she-elves. They all eat. And drink. And so on.'

'I beg your pardon?'

'Never mind.'

The more intently he observed her, the more she lost her enchanting aura, and the more human and ordinary – common, even – she became. Though he knew she wasn't, couldn't be that. One didn't encounter common wenches at the foot of Y Wyddfa, in the region of Cwm Pwcca, bathing naked in mountain lakes and washing bloodstained blouses. Never mind what the girl looked like, she couldn't be an earthly being. In spite of that, Galahad was now gazing quite freely and without fear at her ashen hair, which, now it was dry, to his amazement gleamed grey. At her slender hands, petite nose and pale lips, at her masculine outfit of somewhat outlandish cut, sewn from delicate stuff of extremely dense weave. At her sword, of curious construction and ornamentation, but by no means resembling a ceremonial accoutrement. At her bare feet caked with the dried sand of the beach.

'Just for clarity,' she began, rubbing one foot against the other, 'I'm not a she-elf. And as for being an enchantress, I mean a fairy . . . I'm a little unusual. I don't think I'm one at all.'

'I'm sorry, I really am.'

'Why exactly?'

'They say . . .' he blushed and stammered. 'They say that when fairies meet young men, they lead them to Elfland and there . . . Beneath a filbert bush, on a carpet of moss, they order them to render—'

'I understand.' She glanced at him quickly, then bit down hard on a sausage. 'Regarding the land of Elves,' she said, swallowing, 'I fled from there some time ago and am in no hurry to return. Regarding, however, the rendering of services on mossy carpets . . . Truly, Galahad, you've happened upon the wrong Lady. All the same, I thank you kindly for your good intentions.'

'M'lady! I did not wish to offend—'

'You don't have to apologise.'

'Only because,' he mumbled, 'you're enchantingly comely.'

'Thank you, once again. But still, nothing's going to happen.'

They were silent for a time. It was warm. The sun, standing at its zenith, warmed the stones pleasantly. A faint breeze ruffled the surface of the lake.

'What does . . .' Galahad began suddenly in a strangely enraptured voice. 'What does the spear with the bloody blade mean? Why does the King with the lanced thigh suffer and what does it mean? What is the meaning of the maiden in white carrying a grail, a silver bowl—?'

'And besides that,' she interrupted him. 'Are you feeling all right?'

'I merely ask.'

'And I merely don't understand your question. Is it some previously agreed password? Some signal by which the initiated recognise each other? Kindly explain.'

'But I cannot.'

'Why then, did you ask?'

'Because . . .' he stammered. 'Well, to put it briefly . . . One of our number failed to ask when he had the chance. He grew tongue-tied or was embarrassed . . . He didn't ask and because of that there was great unpleasantness. So now we always ask. Just in case.'

*

'Are there sorcerers in this world? You know, people who practise the magical arts. Mages. Knowing Ones.'

'There's Merlin. And Morgana. But Morgana is evil.'

'And Merlin?'

'Average.'

'Do you know where to find him?'

'I'll say! In Camelot. At the court of King Arthur. I am presently headed there.'

'Is it far?'

'From here to Powys, to the River Hafren, then downstream to Glevum, to the Sea of Sabina, and from there to the flatlands of the Summer Land. All in all, some ten days' ride . . .'

7

'Too far.'

'One may,' he stammered, 'take a short-cut by riding through Cwm Pwcca. But it is an enchanted valley. It is dreadful there. One hears of Y Dynan Bach Têgdwell there, evil little men—'

'What, do you only carry a sword for decoration?'

'And what would a sword achieve against witchcraft?'

'Much, much, don't worry. I'm a witcher. Ever heard of one? Pshaw, naturally you haven't. And I'm not afraid of your little men. I have plenty of dwarf friends.'

Of course you do, he thought.

*

'Lady of the Lake?'

'My name's Ciri. Don't call me Lady of the Lake. Brings up bad, unpleasant, nasty associations. That's what they called me in the Land of . . . What did you call that place?'

'Faërie. Or, as the druids say: Annwn. And the Saxons say Elfland.'

'Elfland . . .' She wrapped a tartan Pictish rug he had given her around her shoulders. 'I've been there, you know? I entered the Tower of the Swallow and bang! I was among the elves. And that's exactly what they called me. The Lady of the Lake. I even liked it at the start. It was flattering. Until the moment I understood I was no Lady in that land, in that tower by the lake – but a prisoner.'

'Was it there,' he blurted out, 'that you stained your blouse with blood?'

She was silent for a long while.

'No,' she said finally, and her voice, it seemed to him, trembled a little. 'Not there. You have sharp eyes. Oh well, you can't flee from the truth, can't bury your head in the sand . . . Yes, Galahad. I've often become stained lately. With the blood of the foes I've killed. And the blood of the friends I tried hard to rescue . . . And who died in my arms . . . Why do you stare at me so?'

'I know not if you be a deity or a mortal . . . Or one of the goddesses . . . But if you are a dweller on this earth of ours . . .'

'Get to the point, if you would.'

'I would listen to your story,' Galahad's eyes glowed. 'Would you tell it, O Lady?'

'It is long.'

'We have time.'

'And it doesn't end so well.'

'I don't believe you.'

'Why?'

'You were singing when you were bathing in the lake.'

'You're observant.' She turned her head away, pursed her lips and her face suddenly contorted and became ugly. 'Yes, you're observant. But very naive.'

'Tell me your story. Please.'

'Very well,' she sighed. 'Very well, if you wish . . . I shall.'

She made herself comfortable. As did he. The horses walked by the edge of the forest, nibbling grass and herbs.

'From the beginning,' asked Galahad. 'From the very beginning . . .'

'This story,' she said a moment later, wrapping herself more tightly in the Pictish rug, 'seems more and more like one without a beginning. Neither am I certain if it has finished yet, either. The past – you have to know – has become awfully tangled up with the future. An elf even told me it's like that snake that catches its own tail in its teeth. That snake, you ought to know, is called Ouroboros. And the fact it bites its own tail means the circle is closed. The past, present and future lurk in every moment of time. Eternity is hidden in every moment of time. Do you understand?'

'No.'

'Never mind.'

Verily do I tell you that whoever believes in dreams is as one trying to catch the wind or seize a shadow. He is deluded by a beguiling picture, a warped looking glass, which lies or utters absurdities in the manner of a woman in labour. Foolish indeed is he who lends credence to dreams and treads the path of delusion.

Nonetheless, whoever disdains and does not believe them at all also acts unwisely. For if dreams had no import whatsoever why, then, would the Gods, in creating us, give us the ability to dream?

The Wisdom of the Prophet Lebioda, 34:1

CHAPTER TWO

A light wind ruffled the surface of the lake, which was steaming like a cauldron, and drove ragged wisps of mist over it. Rowlocks creaked and thudded rhythmically, the emerging oar-blades scattering a hail of shining drops.

Condwiramurs put a hand over the side. The boat was moving at such a snail's pace the water barely foamed or climbed up her hand.

'Oh, my,' she said, packing as much sarcasm into her voice as she could. 'What speed! We're hurtling over the waves. It's making my head spin!'

The rower, a short, stocky, compact man, growled back angrily and indistinctly, not even raising his head, which was covered in a grizzly mop of hair as curly as a caracul lamb's. The novice had put up with quite enough of the growling, hawking and grunting with which the boor had dismissed her questions since she had boarded.

'Have a care,' she drawled, struggling to keep calm. 'You might do yourself a mischief from such hard rowing.'

This time the man raised his face, which was as swarthy and weather-beaten as tanned leather. He grunted, hawked, and pointed his bristly, grey chin at the wooden reel attached to the side of the boat and the line disappearing into the water stretched tight by their movement. Clearly convinced the explanation was exhaustive, he resumed his rowing. With the same rhythm as previously. Oars up. A pause. Blades halfway into the water. A long pause. The pull. An even longer pause.

'Aha,' Condwiramurs said nonchalantly, looking heavenwards. 'I understand. What's important is the lure being pulled behind the boat, which has to move at the right speed and the right depth. Fishing is important. Everything else is unimportant.'

What she said was so obvious the man didn't even take the trouble to grunt or wheeze.

'Who could it bother,' Condwiramurs continued her monologue, 'that I've been travelling all night? That I'm hungry? That my backside hurts and itches from the hard, wet bench? That I need a pee? No, only trolling for fish matters. Which is pointless in any case. Nothing will take a lure pulled down the middle of the current at a depth of a score of fathoms.'

The man raised his head, looked at her foully and grumbled very – very – grumblingly. Condwiramurs flashed her little teeth, pleased with herself. The boor went on rowing slowly. He was furious.

She lounged back on the stern bench and crossed her legs, letting her dress ride up.

The man grunted, tightened his gnarled hands on the oars, and pretended only to be looking at the fishing line. He had no intention of rowing any faster, naturally. The novice sighed in resignation and turned her attention to the sky.

The rowlocks creaked and the glistening drops fell from the oar blades.

The outline of an island loomed up in the quickly dispersing mist. As did the dark, tapering obelisk of the tower rising above it. The boor, though he was facing forwards and not looking back, knew in some mysterious way that they had almost arrived. Without hurrying, he laid the oars on the gunwales, stood up and began to slowly wind in the line on the reel. Condwiramurs, legs still crossed, whistled, looking up at the sky.

The man finished reeling in the line and examined the lure: a large, brass spoon, armed with a triple hook and a tassel of red wool.

'Oh my, oh my,' said Condwiramurs sweetly. 'Haven't caught anything? Oh dear, what a pity. I wonder why we've had such bad luck? Perhaps the boat was going too fast?'

The man cast her a look which expressed many foul things. He sat down, hawked, spat over the side, grasped the oars in his great knotty hands and bent his back powerfully. The oars splashed, rattled in the rowlocks, and the boat darted across the lake like an arrow, the water foaming with a swoosh against the prow, eddies seething astern. He covered the quarter arrow shot that separated them from the island in less than a grunt, and the boat came up onto the pebbles with such force that Condwiramurs lurched from the bench.

The man grunted, hawked and spat. The novice knew that meant – translated into the speech of civilised people – *get out of my boat, you brash witch*. She also knew she could forget about being carried ashore. She took off her slippers, lifted her dress provocatively high, and disembarked. She fought back a curse as mussel shells pricked her feet.

'Thanks,' she said through clenched teeth, 'for the ride.'

Neither waiting for the answering grunt nor looking back, she walked barefoot towards the stone steps. All of her discomforts and problems vanished and evaporated without a trace, expunged by her growing excitement. She was there, on the island of Inis Vitre, on Loch Blest. She was in an almost legendary place, where only a select few had ever been.

The morning mist had lifted completely and the red orb of the sun had begun to show more brightly through the dull sky. Squawking gulls circled around the tower's battlements and swifts flashed by.

At the top of the steps leading from the beach to the terrace, leaning against a statue of a crouching, grinning chimera, was Nimue.

The Lady of the Lake.

*

She was dainty and short, measuring not much more than five feet. Condwiramurs had heard that when she was young she'd been called 'Squirt', and now she knew the nickname had been apt. But she was certain no one had dared call the little sorceress that for at least half a century.

'I am Condwiramurs Tilly.' She introduced herself with a bow, a little embarrassed as she was still holding her slippers. 'I'm glad to be visiting your island, Lady of the Lake.'

'Nimue,' the diminutive sorceress corrected her. 'Nimue, nothing more. We can skip titles and honorifics, Miss Tilly.'

'In that case I'm Condwiramurs. Condwiramurs, nothing more.'

'Come with me then, Condwiramurs. We shall talk over breakfast. I imagine you're hungry.'

'I don't deny it.'

*

There was white curd cheese, chives, eggs, milk and wholemeal bread for breakfast, served by two very young, very quiet serving girls, who smelt of starch. Condwiramurs ate, feeling the gaze of the diminutive sorceress on her.

'The tower,' Nimue said slowly, observing her every movement and almost every morsel she raised to her mouth, 'has six storeys, one of which is below ground. Your room is on the second floor above ground. You'll find every convenience needed for living. The ground floor, as you see, is the service area. The servants' quarters are also located here. The subterranean, first and third floors house the laboratory, library and gallery. You may enter and have unfettered access to all the floors I've mentioned and the rooms there. You may take advantage of them and of what they contain, when you wish and however you wish.'

'I understand. Thank you.'

'The uppermost two storeys contain my private chambers and my private study. Those rooms are absolutely private. In order to avoid misunderstandings: I am extremely sensitive about such things.'

'I shall respect that.'

Nimue turned her head towards the window, through which the grunting Ferryman could be seen. He had already dealt with Condwiramurs' luggage, and was now loading rods, reels, landing nets, scoop nets and other fishing tackle into his boat.

'I'm a little old-fashioned,' she continued. 'But I've become accustomed to having the exclusive use of certain things. Like a toothbrush, let's say. My private chambers, library and toilet. And the Fisher King. Do not try, please, to avail yourself of the Fisher King.'

Condwiramurs almost choked on her milk. Nimue's face didn't express anything.

'And if . . .' she continued, before the girl had regained her

16

speech, 'if he tries to avail himself of you, decline him.'

Condwiramurs finally swallowed and nodded quickly, refraining from any comment whatsoever. Though it was on the tip of her tongue to say she didn't care for anglers, particularly boorish ones. With heads of dishevelled hair as white as curds.

'Good,' Nimue drawled. 'That's the introductions over and done with. Time to get down to business. Doesn't it interest you why I chose precisely *you* from among all the candidates?'

If Condwiramurs pondered the answer at all, it was only so as not to appear too cocksure. She quickly concluded, though, that with Nimue, even the slightest false modesty would offend by its insincerity.

'I'm the best dream-reader in the academy,' she replied coolly, matter-of-factly and without boastfulness. 'And in the third year I was second among the oneiromancers.'

'I could have taken the number one.' Nimue was brutal, frank. 'Incidentally, they suggested that high-flyer somewhat insistently, as it happens, because she was apparently the important daughter of someone important. And where dream-reading and oneiromancy are concerned, you know yourself, my dear Condwiramurs, that it's a pretty fickle gift. Fiascos can befall even the best dream-reader.'

Condwiramurs kept to herself the riposte that she could count her fiascos on the fingers of one hand. After all, she was talking to a master. *Know your limits, my good sir*, as one of her professors at the academy, a polymath, used to say.

Nimue praised her silence with a slight nod of her head.

'I made some enquiries at the academy,' she said a moment later. 'Hence, I know that you do not boost your divination with hallucinogens. I'm pleased about that, for I don't tolerate narcotics.'

'I divine without any drugs,' confirmed Condwiramurs with some pride. 'All I need for oneiroscopy is a hook.'

'I beg your pardon?'

'You know, a hook,' the novice coughed, 'I mean an object in some way connected to what I'm supposed to dream about. Some kind of thing or picture . . .'

'A picture?'

'Uh-huh. I divine pretty well from a picture.'

17

'Oh,' smiled Nimue. 'Oh, since a painting will help, there won't be any problem. If you've satisfactorily broken your fast, O first dream-reader and second-among-oneiromancers. I ought to explain to you without delay the other reasons why it was you I chose as my assistant.'

Cold emanated from the stone walls, alleviated neither by the heavy tapestries nor the darkened wood panelling. The stone floor chilled her feet through the soles of her slippers.

'Beyond that door,' she indicated carelessly, 'is the laboratory. As has been said before, you may make free use of it. Caution, naturally, is advised. Moderation is particularly recommended during attempts to make brooms carry buckets of water.'

Condwiramurs giggled politely, although the joke was ancient. All the lecturers regaled their charges with jokes referring to the mythical hardships of the mythical sorcerer's apprentice.

The stairs wound upwards like a sea serpent. And they were precipitous. Before they arrived at their destination Condwiramurs was sweating and panting hard. Nimue showed no signs of effort at all.

'This way please.' She opened the oak door. 'Mind the step.'

Condwiramurs entered and gasped.

The chamber was a picture gallery. The walls were covered from floor to ceiling with paintings. Hanging there were large, old, peeling and cracked oils, miniatures, yellowed prints and engravings, faded watercolours and sepias. There were also vividly coloured gouaches and temperas, clean-of-line aquatints and etchings, lithographs and contrasting mezzotints, drawing the gaze with distinctive dots of black.

Nimue stopped before the picture hanging nearest the door, portraying a group gathered beneath a great tree. She looked at the canvas, then at Condwiramurs, and her mute gaze was unusually eloquent.

'Dandelion.' The novice, realising at once what was expected, didn't make her wait. 'Singing a ballad beneath the oak Bleobheris.'

Nimue smiled and nodded, and took a step, stopping before the next painting. A watercolour. Symbolism. The silhouettes of two women on a hill. Gulls circling above them, and below a procession of shadows on the hillside.

'Ciri and Triss Merigold, the prophetic vision in Kaer Morhen.'

A smile, a nod, a step, the next painting. A rider at gallop on a horse down an avenue of misshapen alders extending the arms of their boughs towards him. Condwiramurs felt a shudder running through her.

'Ciri . . . Hmm . . . It's probably her ride to meet Geralt on the farm of the halfling Hofmeier.'

The next painting, a darkened oil. A battle scene.

'Geralt and Cahir defending the bridge on the Yaruga.'

Then things went more quickly.

'Yennefer and Ciri, their first meeting in the Temple of Melitele. Dandelion and the dryad Eithne, in Brokilon Forest. Geralt's company in a blizzard on the Malheur pass—'

'Bravo, splendid,' interrupted Nimue. 'Excellent knowledge of the legend. Now you know the other reason it's you that's here and not anybody else.'

*

A large canvas portraying the Battle of Brenna overlooked the small ebony table they sat down at. It showed a key moment of the battle; that is, somebody's vulgarly heroic death. The painting was beyond a doubt the work of Nikolai Certosa, which could be ascertained by the atmosphere, the perfect attention to detail and the lighting effects typical for that artist.

'Indeed, I know the legend of the Witcher and the witcher girl,' replied Condwiramurs. 'I know it, I have no hesitation in saying, thoroughly. I loved that story when I was a young girl. I became engrossed in it. I even dreamed of being Yennefer. I'll be frank, though, even if it was love at first sight, even if it was explosively torrid . . . my love wasn't everlasting.'

Nimue raised her eyebrows.

'I first became acquainted with the story,' continued Condwiramurs, 'in popular abridgements and versions for young people, *précis* cut and cleaned up *ad usum delphini*. Later, naturally, I studied the so-called serious and complete versions. Extensive to the point of superfluity, and at times also beyond. Then passion was replaced by cool reflection and wild desire by something like marital duty. If you know what I mean.'

Nimue confirmed she did with a barely perceptible nod.

'Summing up, I prefer legends that cleave more strongly to legendary convention, do not mix fables with reality, and don't try to integrate the simple, elegant morality of the story with deeply immoral historical truth. I prefer legends to which encyclopaedists, archaeologists and historians don't add epilogues. I prefer it when a prince climbs to the top of the Glass Mountain, kisses the sleeping princess, she wakes up and they both live happily ever after. A legend should end like that and no other way . . . Who painted that portrait of Ciri? That full-length one?'

'There isn't a single portrait of Ciri.' The voice of the little sorceress was so matter-of-fact it was almost cold. 'Not here, nor anywhere in the world. Not a single portrait has survived, not a single miniature painted by anybody who could have seen, known or even remembered Ciri. That full-length portrait shows Pavetta, Ciri's mother, and it was painted by Ruiz Dorrit, court artist to the Cintran monarchs. It is known that Dorrit painted Ciri's portrait at the age of nine, also full-length, but the canvas, called *Infanta with a Greyhound*, was lost, regrettably. Let us, though, return to the legend and your attitude to it. And to how, in your opinion, a legend ought to end.'

'It ought to end happily,' said Condwiramurs with conviction. 'Good and righteousness should triumph, evil should be punished exemplarily, and love should unite the lovers until the end of their days. And none of the heroes should bloody die! And the legend of Ciri? How does that end?'

'Precisely. How?'

Condwiramurs was struck dumb for a moment. She hadn't expected a question like that; she sensed a test, an exam, a trap. She said nothing, not wanting to be caught out.

How does the legend of Ciri end? But everybody knows that.

She looked at a dark-hued watercolour which depicted an amorphous barge gliding over the surface of a mist-shrouded lake, a barge being plied with a long pole by a woman visible only as a black shape.

That's exactly how the legend ends. Just like that.

Nimue read her thoughts.

'It isn't so certain, Condwiramurs. By no means is it certain.'

*

'I heard the legend,' began Nimue, 'from the lips of a wandering storyteller. I'm a country child, the fourth daughter of the village wheelwright. The times the storyteller Pogwizd, a wandering beggar, dwelled in our village were the most beautiful moments of my childhood. One could take a break from the daily toil, see those fabulous wonders, see that far-distant world with the eyes of the soul. A beautiful and marvellous world . . . More distant and marvellous even than the market in the town nine miles away from us . . .

'I was about six or seven then. My oldest sister was fourteen and was already twisted from stooping over her labours. A peasant woman's lot! In our village, girls were prepared for that from childhood! To stoop! Endlessly to stoop, to stoop and bend over our work, over a child, under the weight of a swollen belly, forced on you by your man the moment you'd risen from childbed.

'Those beggar's tales made me begin to wish for something more than a stoop and the daily grind, to dream for something more than the harvest, a husband and children. The first book I bought from the takings of selling brambles gathered in the forest was the legend of Ciri. The cleaned-up version, as you nicely described it, for children, the précis *ad ursum delphini*. That version was just right for me. I was a poor reader. But already by then I knew what I wanted. I wanted to be like Philippa Eilhart, like Sheala de Tancarville, like Assire var Anahid . . .'

They both looked at a gouache depicting a castle chamber, a table and some women sitting around it, in subtle chiaroscuro. Legendary women.

'In the academy where I was admitted – at the second attempt, actually,' Nimue continued, 'I only studied the myth with respect to the Great Lodge during lessons on the history of magic. At first I simply didn't have time to read for pleasure. I had to focus, in order to . . . keep up with the darling daughters of counts and bankers to whom everything came easily, who laughed at lasses from the country . . .'

She fell silent and cracked her knuckles.

'I finally found time for reading,' she continued, 'but then I realised that the vicissitudes of Geralt and Ciri entertained me much less than they had during my childhood. A similar syndrome to yours occurred. What did you call it? Marital duties? It was like that until . . .'

She fell silent and rubbed her face. Condwiramurs noticed in amazement that the hand of the Lady of the Lake was trembling.

'I suppose I was eighteen, when . . . when something happened. Something that made the legend of Ciri live in me again. That made me begin to involve myself with it seriously, as a scholar. Made me begin to devote my life to it.'

The novice remained silent, although curiosity was raging inside her.

'Don't pretend you don't know,' Nimue said tartly. 'Everyone knows that the Lady of the Lake is possessed by a literally pathological obsession about the legend of Ciri. Everybody gossips about how an initially harmless fad transformed into something like an addiction to narcotics, or simply a mania. There is a good deal of truth to those rumours, my dear Condwiramurs, a good deal! And you, since I chose you as my assistant, will also descend into mania and dependency. For I shall demand it. At least for the time of your apprenticeship. Do you understand?'

The novice nodded.

'You think you understand.' Nimue regained control of herself and calmed down. 'But I shall explain it to you. Gradually. And when the time comes I shall explain everything to you. For the time being—'

She broke off and looked through the window, at the lake, at the black line of the Fisher King's boat clearly standing out from the shimmering golden surface of the water.

'For the time being, rest. Look at the gallery. You will find in the cupboards and display cases albums and boxes of engravings, all thematically linked to the tale. In the library are all the legend's versions and adaptations, and also most of the scholarly treatises. Devote some time to them. Have a good look, read and concentrate.

I want you to have some material for your dreams. A hook, as you called it.'

'I will. Madame Nimue?'

'Yes.'

'Those two portraits . . . Hanging beside each other . . . Aren't they of Ciri either?'

'Not a single portrait of Ciri exists,' Nimue repeated patiently. 'Later artists only painted her in scenes, each according to their own imagination. As far as those portraits are concerned, the one on the left is more likely a free variation on the subject, since it depicts the she-elf, Lara Dorren aep Shiadhal, a person the artist couldn't have known. For the artist is Lydia van Bredevoort, who's certainly familiar to you from the legend. One of her surviving oils still hangs in the academy.'

'I know. And the other portrait?'

Nimue looked long at the picture, at the image of a slender girl with fair hair and a sad expression wearing a white dress with green sleeves.

'It was painted by Robin Anderida,' she said, turning around and looking Condwiramurs straight in the eyes. 'And who it portrays . . . You tell me, dream-reader and oneiromancer. Explain it. And tell me about your dream.'

*

Master Robin Anderida was the first to see the emperor approaching and bowed. Stella Congreve, Countess of Liddertal, stood up and curtseyed, gesturing to the girl seated on a carved armchair to do the same.

'Greetings, Ladies.' Emhyr var Emreis inclined his head. 'Greetings to you, too, Master Robin. How goes the work?'

Master Robin coughed in embarrassment and bowed again, nervously wiping his fingers on his smock. Emhyr knew that the artist suffered from acute agoraphobia and was pathologically shy. But whose concern was that? What mattered was how well he painted.

The emperor, as was customary when he was travelling, was wearing an officer's uniform of the Impera guards' brigade: black armour and a cloak with an embroidered silver salamander. He walked over and looked at the portrait. First at the portrait and only afterwards at the model: a slender girl with fair hair and a wistful gaze. She was wearing a white dress with green sleeves, with a slight décolletage decorated with a peridot necklace.

'Excellent,' he said intentionally into space, so they wouldn't know who he was praising. 'Excellent, Master. Please continue, without paying attention to me. A word, if you would, Countess.'

He walked away, towards the window, making her follow him.

'I ride,' he said quietly. 'State affairs. Thank you for your hospitality. And for her. For the princess. Good work, indeed, Stella. Truly deserving of praise. Both for you and her.'

Stella Congreve curtseyed low and gracefully.

'Your Imperial Majesty is too good to us.'

'Don't speak too soon.'

'Oh . . .' She pursed her lips slightly. 'Has it come to that?'

'It has.'

'What will become of her, Emhyr?'

'I don't know,' he replied. 'In ten days I renew the offensive in the North. And it promises to be an exacting, a very exacting war. Vattier de Rideaux is monitoring plots and conspiracies aimed at me. Reasons of state may force on me very extreme acts.'

'That child is not to blame for anything.'

'I said reasons of state. Reasons of state have nothing in common with justice. In any case . . .' He waved a hand. 'I want to talk to her. Alone. Come closer, Princess. Closer, closer, look lively. Your emperor commands.'

The girl curtseyed low. Emhyr looked her up and down, returning in his memory to that momentous audience in Loc Grim. He was full of appreciation, nay admiration, for Stella Congreve, who in the course of the six months that had passed since that moment had managed to transform the ugly duckling into a little noblewoman.

'Leave us,' he commanded. 'Take a break, Master Robin. To clean your brushes, let's say. While I would ask you, Countess, to wait in the antechamber. And you, Princess, follow me onto the terrace.'

The wet snow which had fallen in the night was melting in the

24

first rays of the morning sun, and the roofs of the towers and pinnacles of Darn Rowan Castle were still wet and glistened as though on fire.

Emhyr went over to the balcony's balustrade. The girl – in keeping with protocol – hung back three paces. He gestured impatiently for her to come closer.

The emperor said nothing for a long time, resting both hands on the balustrade, staring at the hills and the evergreen yews covering them, clearly distinct from the white limestone of the rocky faults. The river glinted, a ribbon of molten silver winding through the valley.

Spring was in the air.

'I reside here too seldom,' said Emhyr. The girl said nothing. 'I come here too seldom,' he repeated, turning around. 'And it's a beautiful place, exuding calm. A beautiful region . . . Do you agree with me?'

'Yes, Your Imperial Majesty.'

'Spring is in the air. Am I right?'

'Yes, Your Imperial Majesty.'

From below, in the courtyard, came the sound of singing disturbed by clanking, rattling and the clattering of horseshoes. The escort, informed that the emperor had ordered his departure, was hurriedly making ready for the road. Emhyr remembered that among the guardsmen was one who sang. Often. And regardless of circumstances.

> Look on me graciously
> With eyes of cornflower blue
> Grant me mercifully
> Your fondness so true
> Think on me mercifully
> And at this night hour
> Decline me not graciously
> But receive me to your bower

'A pretty ballad,' he said ponderously, touching his heavy, gold, imperial necklace with his fingers.

'It is, Your Imperial Majesty.'

25

Vattier assures me he is on Vilgefortz's trail. That finding him is a question of days, at most weeks. The traitors' heads will fall, and the real Cirilla, Queen of Cintra, will be brought to Nilfgaard.

And before the authentic Cirilla, Queen of Cintra, comes to Nilfgaard, something will have to be done with her look-alike.

'Raise your head.'

She obeyed.

'Do you have any wishes?' he asked, suddenly and harshly. 'Any complaints? Requests?'

'No, Your Imperial Highness. I do not.'

'Indeed? Interesting. Ah well, but I can't exactly order you to have any. Raise your head, as befits a princess. Stella has taught you manners, I trust?'

'Yes, Your Imperial Majesty.'

Indeed, they have taught her well, he thought. *First Rience, and then Stella. They've taught her the roles and lines well, no doubt threatening her with torture and death for a slip or mistake. They warned her she would have to perform before a cruel audience, unforgiving of errors. Before the awe-inspiring Emhyr var Emreis, Emperor of Nilfgaard.*

'What's your name?' he asked abruptly.

'Cirilla Fiona Elen Riannon.'

'Your real name.'

'Cirilla Fiona—'

'Do not try my patience. Your name!'

'Cirilla . . .' The girl's voice broke like a twig. 'Fiona . . .'

'That will do, by the Great Sun,' he said between clenched teeth. 'That will do!'

She sniffed loudly. Contrary to protocol. Her mouth trembled, but protocol did not forbid that.

'Calm yourself,' he commanded, but in a soft and almost gentle voice. 'What do you fear? Are you ashamed of your own name? Are you afraid to disclose it? If I ask, it is only because I'd like to address you by your rightful name. But I have to know what it sounds like.'

'It sounds dull,' she answered, and her huge eyes suddenly gleamed like emeralds lit by a flame. 'For it is a dull name, Your Imperial Majesty. A name just right for somebody who's a nobody.

26

As long as I am Cirilla Fiona I mean something . . . As long as . . .'

Her voice stuck in her throat so abruptly that she involuntarily brought her hands up to her neck as though what was around it was not a necklace but a garrotte. Emhyr continued to measure her with his gaze, still full of appreciation for Stella Congreve. At the same time, he felt anger. Unjustified anger. Unjustified and therefore very infuriating.

What do I want from this child? he thought, feeling the anger rising in him, seething in him, frothing up like soup in a pot. *What do I want from a child, whom . . ?*

'Know that I had nothing to do with your abduction, girl,' he said sharply. 'I didn't have anything to do with your kidnapping. I didn't issue any such orders. I was deceived . . .'

He was furious with himself, aware he was making a mistake. He ought to have ended the conversation much earlier, ended it haughtily, arrogantly, menacingly, as befitted an emperor. He ought to have forgotten about this girl with the green eyes. This girl that did not exist. She was a double. An imitation. She didn't even have a name. She was nobody. *The emperor does not ask for forgiveness, does not demean himself before someone who . . .*

'Forgive me,' he said, and the words were unfamiliar, clung unpleasantly to his lips. 'I committed an error. Yes, it's true, I'm guilty of what happened to you. I was at fault. But I give you my word that you are in no danger. Nothing ill will befall you. No harm, no discredit, no woe. You needn't be afraid.'

'I'm not.' She raised her head and looked him straight in the eyes, contrary to protocol. Emhyr shuddered, moved by the honesty and trust of her gaze. He immediately stood erect, imperious and repellently supercilious.

'Ask me for whatever you wish.'

She looked at him again, and he involuntarily recalled the innumerable occasions when he had so easily bought himself ease of conscience for the harm or pain he'd caused somebody. Secretly and reprehensibly pleased that he was paying so little.

'Ask me for whatever you wish,' he repeated, and because he was already weary his voice suddenly gained in humanity. 'I'll make your every wish come true.'

If only she wouldn't look at me, he thought. *I can't bear her gaze.*

27

Apparently people are afraid to look at me, he thought. *So what then am I afraid of?*

Vattier de Rideaux can shove his 'reasons of state'. If she asks, I'll have her taken home, where she was snatched from. I'll order her taken there in a golden carriage and six. All she need do is ask.

'Ask me for whatever you wish,' he repeated.

'Thank you, Your Imperial Majesty,' said the girl, lowering her eyes. 'Your Imperial Majesty is very noble and generous. If I might make a request . . .'

'Speak.'

'I'd like to be able to stay here. Here, in Darn Rowan. With Lady Stella.'

He wasn't surprised. He'd sensed something like that.

Tact restrained him from asking questions that would have been humiliating for them both.

'I gave my word,' he said, coldly. 'Let your wish come true.'

'Thank you, Your Imperial Majesty.'

'I gave my word,' he repeated, trying hard to avoid her gaze, 'and I shall keep it. I think, nonetheless, that you've made a bad choice. You gave voice to the wrong wish. Were you to change your mind . . .'

'I shall not,' she said, when it became clear that the emperor was not going to complete his sentence. 'Why should I? I've chosen Lady Stella, I've chosen things I have known so little of in my life . . . A home, warmth, goodness . . . kindness. You can't make a mistake by choosing something like that.'

Poor, naive creature, thought Emperor Emhyr var Emreis, Deithwen Addan yn Carn aep Morvudd, the White Flame Dancing on the Barrows of his Enemies. *By choosing something like that one can make the most awful mistakes.*

But something – perhaps a distant memory – stopped the emperor from saying it aloud.

*

'Interesting,' said Nimue, after listening to the account. 'An interesting dream, indeed. Were there any others?'

'And some!' Condwiramurs cut off the top of her egg with a

swift, sure movement of her knife. 'My head's still spinning from that pageant! But that's normal. The first night always brings deranged dreams. You know, Nimue, they say about us dream-readers that our talent isn't about being able to dream. If you pass over visions during trances or under hypnosis, our dreams don't differ from other people's in intensity, richness or pro-cognitive content. Something quite different distinguishes us and determines our talent. We remember the dreams. We seldom forget what we have dreamed—'

The Lady of the Lake cut her off. 'Because your endocrine glands function in some abnormal way. Your dreams, to trivialise them somewhat, are nothing more than endorphin released into the body. Like most native, magical gifts yours is also mundanely organic. But why am I talking about something you know perfectly well yourself? Go on, what other dreams do you remember?'

'A young lad.' Condwiramurs frowned. 'Wandering among desolate fields, with a bundle over his shoulder. The fields are barren, it's spring. Willows by the roads and on the baulks. Willows, twisted, full of hollows, spreading their branches . . . Naked, not yet in leaf. The lad is walking, looking around. Night falls. Stars appear in the sky. One of them is moving. It's a comet. A reddish, twinkling spark, cutting slantways across the horizon.'

'Well done,' Nimue smiled. 'Although I have no idea who you were dreaming about, we can at least precisely determine the date of the event. The red comet was visible for six days in the spring of the year the Cintran Peace was signed. To be more precise, in the first days of March. Did any date markers appear in the other dreams?'

'My dreams,' snapped Condwiramurs, salting her egg, 'are not a farmer's calendar. They don't have charts with dates! But, to be precise, I dreamed a dream about the Battle of Brenna, after having a good look at the canvas of Nikolai Certosa in your gallery. And the date of the Battle of Brenna is also known. It's the same date as the year of the comet. Am I wrong?'

'You aren't. Was there anything special in the dream about the battle?'

'No. A seething mass of horses, people and weapons. Soldiers were fighting and yelling. Someone, probably a bit dim, was wailing, "Eagles! Eagles!"'

'What else? You said it was a whole pageant of dreams.'

'I don't remember . . .' Condwiramurs broke off.

Nimue smiled.

'Oh, all right.' The novice lifted up her nose haughtily, not letting the Lady of the Lake make a spiteful remark. 'I occasionally forget, naturally. No one's perfect. I repeat, my dreams are visions, not library cards—'

'I know,' interrupted Nimue. 'This isn't a test of your dream-reading abilities; it's an analysis of a legend. Of its mysteries and gaps. We're doing pretty well, as a matter of fact. In the first dreams you already identified the girl in the portrait, Ciri's double, with whom Vilgefortz tried to hoodwink Emperor Emhyr.'

They stopped, because the Fisher King had entered the kitchen. After bowing and grunting he took a loaf of bread, a tureen and a small, linen bundle. He went out, not forgetting to bow and grunt.

'He's limping badly,' said Nimue, seemingly offhandedly. 'He was seriously wounded. A wild boar gashed open his leg during a hunt. That's why he spends so much time in the boat. When he's rowing and catching fish the wound doesn't bother him. In the boat he forgets about his disability. He's a very decent and good man. And I . . .'

Condwiramurs remained politely silent.

'Need a man,' explained the small sorceress bluntly.

Me too, thought the novice. *Dammit, as soon as I get back to the academy I'll let someone take me. Celibacy is good, but for no longer than a semester.*

Nimue cleared her throat.

'If you've broken your fast and finished daydreaming, let's go to the library.'

*

'Let's get back to your dream.'

Nimue opened a portfolio, flicked through several sepia watercolours and took one of them out. Condwiramurs recognised it at once.

'The audience at Loc Grim?'

'Of course. The double is being presented at the imperial court. Emhyr pretends he's been tricked, puts a brave face on it. Here, look, the ambassadors of the Northern Kingdoms, for whom the charade is being played out. Here, in turn, we see the Nilfgaardian dukes who have suffered an affront: the emperor spurned their daughters, disregarding their dynastic proposals. Greedy for revenge, they whisper, leaning towards each other. They're hatching a plot and a murder. The double stands with her head bowed, and the artist, to underscore the mystery, has even decorated her with a handkerchief to hide her facial features.

'And we know nothing more about the bogus Ciri,' continued the sorceress a moment later. 'None of the legend's versions tell us what became of the double afterwards.'

'It's safe to guess, though,' said Condwiramurs sadly, 'that the girl's fate was unenviable. When Emhyr obtained the original – and we know he did, don't we? – he got rid of the counterfeit. When I dreamed, I didn't sense tragedy, and actually I ought to have sensed something, if . . . On the other hand, what I see in dreams is not necessarily the real truth. Like anybody, I dream dreams. Desires. Longings . . . and fears.'

'I know.'

*

They talked until lunchtime, looking through portfolios and fascicles of prints. The Fisher King had been lucky with his catch, because there was grilled salmon for lunch. For supper too.

Condwiramurs slept badly that night. She had overeaten.

She didn't dream anything. She was a little downhearted and embarrassed about that, but Nimue wasn't at all concerned. *We have time*, she said. *There are plenty of nights ahead of us.*

*

The tower of Inis Vitre had several bathrooms, truly luxurious, shining with marble and glistening with brass, heated by a hypocaust located somewhere in the cellars. Condwiramurs had no problem occupying the baths for hours, but every now and again would meet Nimue in the sweathouse, a tiny wooden hut with a jetty leading out towards the lake. They would sit on benches, wet, inhaling the steam that belched from stones sprinkled with water, swishing themselves lazily with birch twigs, as salty sweat dripped into their eyes.

'If I understood right,' Condwiramurs wiped her face, 'my practice here in Inis Vitre is meant to explain all the gaps in the legend of the Witcher and the witcher girl?'

'That's right.'

'During the day, by looking at the prints and discussing them, I'm meant to charge myself up before sleep, in order at night to be able to dream the real, unknown version of a given event.'

This time Nimue didn't even consider it necessary to concur. She just beat herself a few times with the whisk, stood up and splashed water on the hot stones. The steam billowed and the heat stopped their breath for a moment.

Nimue poured the rest of the water on herself from a small wooden pail. Condwiramurs admired her figure. Although petite, the sorceress was extremely well-proportioned. A woman in her twenties would have envied her curves and firm skin. Condwiramurs, for example, was twenty-four. And was envious.

'Even if I explain anything,' she continued, wiping her sweaty face again, 'how will we be certain I'm dreaming the true version? I truly didn't know—'

'We'll discuss that outside,' interrupted Nimue. 'I've had enough of sitting in this heat. Let's cool off. And then we'll talk.'

That was also part of the ritual. They ran from the sweathouse, bare feet slapping on the planks of the jetty, and then leaped into the lake, yelling wildly. After splashing around they climbed out onto the jetty, squeezing their hair.

The Fisher King, alarmed by the splashes and squeals, looked around from his boat and glanced at them, shielding his eyes with a hand. But he turned around at once and scrutinised his fishing tackle.

Condwiramurs considered behaviour like that insulting and reprehensible. Her opinion of the Fisher King had improved greatly when she noticed that he devoted the time he wasn't angling to reading. He even took a book with him to the privy, and it was no less than *Speculum Aureum*, a serious and demanding work. So, even if during the first days of her stay in Inis Vitre Condwiramurs had been somewhat surprised at Nimue keeping him around, she had stopped long since. It became clear that the Fisher King was only seemingly a lout and a boor. Or it was a mask he hid behind.

All the same, thought Condwiramurs, it was an insult and unforgivable affront to turn back towards one's rods and spinners when two naked women with bodies like nymphs, to whom one's eyes should have been glued, were parading on a jetty.

'If I dream something,' she said, going back to the subject and drying herself with a towel, 'what guarantee is there I've dreamed the true version? I know all the literary versions of the legend, from Dandelion's *Half a Century of Poetry* to Andrei Ravix's *The Lady of the Lake*. I know the Honourable Jarre; I know all the scholarly treatments, not to mention popular editions. Reading all those texts has left a mark, had an influence. I'm unable to eliminate them from my dreams. Is there any chance of breaking through the fiction and dreaming the truth?'

'Yes, there is.'

'How great?'

'The same chance the Fisher King has.' Nimue nodded towards the boat on the lake. 'As you can see, he keeps on casting his hooks. He catches waterweed, roots, submerged tree stumps, logs, old boots, drowned corpses and the Devil knows what else. But from time to time he catches something worthwhile.'

'So I wish us good hunting,' sighed Condwiramurs, dressing. 'Let's cast the bait and fish. Let's search for the true versions of the legend, let's unstitch the upholstery and lining, and let's tap the chest for a false bottom. And what will happen if there isn't a false bottom? With all due respect, Nimue, we aren't the first in these fishing grounds. What chance is there that any detail or particular has escaped the attention of the hordes of scholars who fished it before us? That they've left us even a single fish?'

'They have,' stated Nimue with conviction, combing out her wet hair. 'What they didn't know, they plastered over with confabulation and purple prose. Or drew a veil over it.'

'For instance?'

'The sojourn of the Witcher in Toussaint, to give the first example that comes to mind. All the versions of the legend dismiss that episode with a curt sentence, "The protagonists wintered in Toussaint." Even Dandelion, who devoted two chapters to his exploits in that county, is astonishingly enigmatic on the subject of the Witcher. Would it not then be worth finding out what happened that winter? After the flight from Belhaven and the meeting with the elf Avallac'h in the subterranean complex of Tir ná Béa Arainne? After the skirmish in Caed Myrkvid with the druids? What did the Witcher do in Toussaint from October to January?'

'What did he do? He wintered!' snorted the novice. 'He couldn't cross the pass before the thaw, so he wintered and got bored. No wonder later authors treated that boring fragment with a laconic "The winter passed". Well, since I must, I'll try to dream something. Do we have any pictures or drawings?'

Nimue smiled.

'We even have a drawing on a drawing.'

*

The cave painting depicted a hunting scene. A large, purple bison was being pursued in wild leaps by skinny human figures with bows and spears, painted with careless brushstrokes. The bison had tiger stripes and something resembling a dragonfly was hovering above its lyre-shaped horns.

'So this,' Regis nodded, 'is that wall painting. Executed by the elf Avallac'h. The elf who knew a great deal.'

'Yes,' Geralt confirmed dryly. 'That's the painting.'

'The problem is that we've thoroughly explored these caves, but there are no traces of any elves, or the other creatures you mentioned.'

'They were here. Now they've hidden themselves. Or decamped.'

'That's an indisputable fact. Don't forget, you were only given an audience after the flaminika's intercession. It was clearly decided that one audience would suffice. Now that the flaminika has refused cooperation quite categorically, I truly know not what else you can do. We've been dragging ourselves through these caves all day. I can't help feeling it's pointless.'

'Me too,' the Witcher said bitterly, 'I can't either. I've never understood elves. But at least I know why most people aren't fond of them. Because it's difficult not to feel that they're mocking us. The elves mock us, deride us, in everything they do, say and think. Scoff at us.'

'It's your anthropomorphism talking.'

'Perhaps a little. But the impression remains.'

'What do we do?'

'We return to Caed Myrkvid and Cahir. The druidesses have probably patched up his scalped pate. Then we mount our horses and take advantage of Princess Anna Henrietta's invitation. Don't make faces, vampire. Milva has a few broken ribs, Cahir's nut has been split open, so a little rest in Toussaint will do both of them good. We also have to untangle Dandelion from this business, because it looks like he's well and truly caught up.'

'Very well,' sighed Regis. 'Let it be. I'll have to steer clear of looking glasses and dogs, watch out for sorcerers and telepaths . . . and if in spite of that they unmask me, I'm counting on you.'

'You can,' Geralt responded gravely. 'I won't abandon you in need. Comrade.'

The vampire smiled, and because they were alone, showed his full set of fangs.

'Comrade?'

'It's my anthropomorphism talking. On we go, let's get out of these caverns, comrade. Because all we'll find here is rheumatism.'

'I agree. Unless . . . Geralt? Tir ná Béa Arainne, the elven necropolis, according to what you saw, is behind the cave painting, right behind that wall. We could get there if we . . . you know. Smashed it. Haven't you thought about that?'

'No. I haven't.'

*

The Fisher King had been lucky again, because there was smoked char for supper. Fish so tasty that the lesson wasn't learned. Condwiramurs stuffed herself again.

*

Condwiramurs burped and tasted the smoked char. *Time for bed*, she thought, for the second time catching herself mechanically turning a page in the book without registering the content at all. *Time for bed*.

She yawned and put the book aside. She rearranged the pillows, changing their positions from reading to repose. She magicked the lamp off. The chamber was immediately plunged into darkness as opaque and viscous as molasses. The heavy velour curtains were tightly drawn – the novice had long known from experience that she dreamed better in the darkness. *What to choose*, she thought, stretching and wriggling about on the sheets. *Let it run its oneiric course or try to anchor myself?*

In spite of widespread assurances, dream-readers didn't remember even half of their prophetic dreams, a significant proportion of which remained in the oneiromancers' memory as a muddle of images, changing colour and shape like a kaleidoscope, a child's toy of mirrors and pieces of glass. Not so bad if the images were random and without even a semblance of meaning, then one could calmly wave them aside on the basis of *I can't remember, so it's not worth remembering*. Dreams like that were called 'crap' by dream-readers.

Worse and slightly shameful were 'apparitions' – dreams of which dream-readers only remembered fragments, only snatches of meaning, dreams after which all that remained the next morning was a vague sense of a signal having been received. If an 'apparition' repeated itself too often one could be certain one was dealing with a dream of significant oneiric value. Then the dream-reader – through concentration and auto-suggestion – tried hard to force herself to re-dream the specific 'apparition' exactly. The best results occurred by making oneself re-dream it immediately on waking – which was called 'snagging'. If the dream couldn't be 'snagged' all that remained was an attempt at evoking a given dream vision during one of the next periods of sleep, by concentrating and meditating before falling asleep. That method of programming dreams was called 'anchoring'.

After twelve nights spent on the island Condwiramurs already had three lists, three sets of dreams. There was a list of successes worth boasting about – a list of 'apparitions' which the dream-reader had successfully 'snagged' or 'anchored'. That included the dreams about the rebellion on the Isle of Thanedd and the journey of the Witcher and his company through the blizzard on the Malheur pass, through the spring downpours and soft roads in the Sudduth valley. There was also – the novice hadn't admitted to Nimue – a list of failures, dreams that in spite of her efforts still remained enigmas. And there was a list of works in progress – a list of dreams that were waiting for their turn.

And there was one dream, strange, but very pleasant, which kept returning in snatches and flashes, in elusive sounds and silky touches.

A nice, tender dream.

Very well, thought Condwiramurs, closing her eyes. I'm ready.

*

'I think I know what occupied the Witcher while he wintered in Toussaint.'

'Well, well.' Nimue raised her eyes from above her spectacles and the leather-bound grimoire she was leafing through. 'Have you finally dreamed something?'

'I'll say!' Condwiramurs said cockily. 'I've dreamed it! The Witcher Geralt and a woman with short black hair and green eyes. I don't know who it could have been. Perhaps that duchess Dandelion writes about in his memoirs?'

'You must have been reading inattentively.' The sorceress cooled her novice's enthusiasm somewhat. 'Dandelion describes Duchess Anarietta precisely, and other sources confirm that she had – and I quote – "hair of chestnut tones, blazing like gold itself."'

'And so it isn't her,' the novice agreed. 'My woman had black hair. Like coal itself. And the dream was . . . Hmmm . . . interesting.'

'I'm all ears.'

'They conversed. But it wasn't an ordinary conversation.'

'Was there something extraordinary about it?'

'For most of it she had her legs slung over his shoulders.'

37

*

'Tell me, Geralt, do you believe in love at first sight?'

'Do you?'

'I do.'

'Now I know what brought us together. The attraction of opposites.'

'Don't be cynical.'

'Why not? Cynicism is meant to be proof of intelligence.'

'Not true. Cynicism – in spite of all its pseudo-intelligent aura – is repulsively insincere. I can't stand insincerity of any kind. Since we're on the subject . . . Tell me, Witcher, what do you love most about me?'

'This.'

'You're descending from cynicism into triviality and banality. Try again.'

'The thing I love most about you is your mind, your intelligence and your spiritual profundities. Your independence and freedom, your—'

'I don't understand where all this sarcasm in you comes from . . .'

'It wasn't sarcasm; it was a joke.'

'I can't bear jokes like that. Especially not at the wrong time. Everything, my dear, has its time and a time is set for all matters under the sun. There is a time for silence and a time for speech, a time for weeping tears and a time for laughter, a time for sowing and a time for groping, I mean reaping, a time for jokes and a time for gravity . . .'

'A time for carnal caresses and a time for refraining from them?'

'Hey, don't take it so literally! Accept, rather, that there's a time for compliments. Love-making without compliments smacks of physiology and physiology is shallow. Pay me compliments.'

'No one, from the Yaruga to the Buina, has such a gorgeous behind as you.'

'Blast it, now for a change you've compared me to some barbaric little northern rivers. Passing over the various metaphors, couldn't you have said from the Alba to the Velda? Or from the Alba to Sansretour?'

'I've never seen the Alba. I try hard to avoid judgements when they aren't backed up by hard experience.'

'Ooh! Truly? Then I think you've seen and experienced enough bums – for that's what we're talking about – to be able to judge. Well, White Hair? How many women have you had before me? Eh? I asked you a question, Witcher! No, no, let go, hands off, you won't wriggle out of it like that. How many women have you had before me?'

'None. You're my first.'

'At last.'

*

Nimue stared for a long time at a painting depicting ten women sitting at a round table in subtle chiaroscuro.

'Pity,' she finally said, 'that we don't know what they really looked like.'

'The Great Sorceresses?' snorted Condwiramurs. 'There are dozens of portraits of them! In Aretuza alone—'

'I said *really*,' interrupted Nimue. 'I didn't mean flattering likenesses painted on the basis of other flattering likenesses. Don't forget there was a time when the reputations of sorceresses were maligned. As were the sorceresses themselves. And later there was the time of propaganda when the Great Sorceresses must have aroused respect, admiration and reverential fear by their very appearance. The *Meetings of the Lodge*, *The Conspiracies* and *The Convents* all date from that time, canvasses and engravings showing a table and around it ten magnificent, enchantingly beautiful women. And there aren't any real, authentic portraits. Apart from two exceptions. The portrait of Margarita Laux-Antille that hangs in Aretuza on the Isle of Thanedd and which miraculously survived the fire is authentic. And the portrait of Sheala de Tancarville in Ensenada, Lan Exeter is authentic.'

'And the portrait of Francesca Findabair painted by elves hanging in the Vengerberg gallery?' asked Condwiramurs.

'A forgery. When the Door was opened and the elves departed, they took away with them or destroyed every work of art, leaving not a single painting. We don't know if the Daisy of the Valleys was really as comely as the tales have it. We have no idea at all what Ida Emean looked like. And since in Nilfgaard images of sorceresses were destroyed very diligently and thoroughly, we don't have any idea about the true appearances of Assire var Anahid or Fringilla Vigo.'

'Let's suppose and agree that they all looked exactly as they were later portrayed,' sighed Condwiramurs. 'Dignified, imperious, good and wise, foresighted and noble. And beautiful, captivatingly beautiful . . . Let's suppose that. Then it's somehow easier to live.'

*

The daily activities on Inis Vitre took on the character of a somewhat tiresome routine. The analysis of Condwiramurs' dreams, beginning at breakfast, usually dragged on all the way to midday. The novice spent the time between noon and their next meal taking walks – which also quickly became habitual and quite boring. No wonder. In the course of an hour one could go around the island twice, feasting one's eyes all the while on such engrossing things as granite, a dwarf pine, pebbles, freshwater mussels, water and gulls.

After lunch and a long siesta followed discussions, the inspection of tomes, scrolls and manuscripts, the study of pictures, prints and maps. And long debates about the mutual inter-relationships between legend and truth extending into the night . . .

And then the nights and dreams. Various dreams. Celibacy made itself felt. At times, instead of the mysteries of the Witcher legend, Condwiramurs dreamed of the Fisher King in all sorts of situations, from extremely non-erotic to extremely erotic. In an extremely non-erotic dream The Fisher King was dragging her behind his boat on a rope. He was rowing slowly and languidly, so she was sinking, drowning, spluttering, and on top of that a terrible fear was tormenting her – she felt that something had pushed off the lake bottom and was swimming up towards her, something awful, something that wanted to swallow the bait – her – being pulled behind the boat. That something was on the point of seizing her when the Fisher King leaned more heavily on the oars, pulling her out of range of the invisible predator's jaws. As she was dragged along she choked on water and at that moment she awoke.

In an unambiguously erotic dream she was kneeling on the bottom of the rocking boat, hanging over the side, and The Fisher King was holding her by the shoulders and fucking her exuberantly, grunting, hawking and spitting as he did so. Apart from the physical pleasure, Condwiramurs felt gut-wrenching terror – what would happen if Nimue caught them at it? She suddenly saw the face of the little sorceress rocking in the lake. . . and she awoke, soaked in sweat.

Then she got up and opened the window, luxuriated in the night air, the light of the moon and the mist rolling off the lake.

And dreamed on.

*

The tower of Inis Vitre had a terrace supported on columns, suspended over the lake. At the beginning, Condwiramurs did not pay any attention to the matter, but finally began to wonder. The terrace was strange, because it was totally inaccessible. It was impossible to get onto the terrace from any of the rooms she knew.

Aware that the abodes of sorceresses were sure to have such secret anomalies, Condwiramurs did not ask any questions. Even when – as she took a walk along the lake shore – she saw Nimue watching her from the terrace. It was inaccessible, it turned out, only to the unauthorised and the profane.

Piqued that she was thought of as profane, she dug her heels in and pretended that nothing was the matter. But it wasn't long before the secret of the terrace was revealed.

It was after she had been visited by a series of dreams, triggered by the watercolours of Wilma Wessely. Clearly fascinated by that fragment of the legend, the artist devoted all her works to Ciri in the Tower of the Swallow.

'I'm having strange dreams after those paintings,' the novice complained the next morning. 'I'm dreaming of . . . paintings. Always the same paintings. Not situations, not scenes, but paintings. Ciri on the tower's battlements . . . An unmoving picture.'

'And nothing else? No sensations apart from visual ones?'

Nimue knew, of course, that a dream-reader as able as Condwiramurs dreamed with all her senses – she didn't only experience

41

the dream with sight, like most people, but also with her hearing, touch, smell – even taste.

'No.' Condwiramurs shook her head. 'Only . . .'

'Yes, yes?'

'A thought. A stubborn thought. That by this lake, in this tower, I'm not the mistress at all, but a captive.'

'Follow me.'

Just as Condwiramurs had guessed, the way to the terrace was only possible through the sorceress's private chambers, which were utterly clean, pedantically tidy, smelling of sandalwood, myrrh, lavender and naphthalene. They had to use a tiny door and a winding staircase leading downwards.

This chamber, unlike the others, didn't have wood panelling or tapestries. It was simply painted white and was thus very bright. It was all the brighter since there was a huge triptych window, or rather a glass door, leading straight onto the terrace perched above the lake.

The only pieces of furniture in the chamber were two armchairs, an immense looking glass in an oval, mahogany frame and a kind of rack with a horizontal bar and a tapestry draped over it. The tapestry measured about five foot by seven and its tassels rested on the floor. It showed a rocky cliff over a tarn, and a castle carved into the cliff, which seemed to be part of the rock wall. A castle Condwiramurs knew well from numerous illustrations.

'Vilgefortz's citadel, Yennefer's place of imprisonment. The place where the legend ended.'

'That is so.' Nimue nodded, apparently indifferently. 'The legend ended there, at least in its known versions. It's those versions we know, so we think we know the ending. Ciri fled from the Tower of the Swallow, where, as you dreamed it, she had been a prisoner. When she realised what they wanted to do to her, she escaped. The legend gives many versions of her flight—'

'The one I like most,' cut in Condwiramurs, 'is the one where she threw objects behind her. A comb, an apple and a neckerchief. But—'

'Condwiramurs.'

'I beg your pardon.'

'As I said, there are myriad versions of the escape. But it is still

42

none too clear how Ciri reached Vilgefortz's castle straight from the Tower of the Swallow. You couldn't dream the Tower of the Swallow, could you? Try dreaming the castle. Examine that tapestry carefully . . . Are you listening to me?'

'That looking glass . . . It's magical, isn't it?'

'No. I squeeze my pimples in front of it.'

'I beg your pardon.'

'It's Hartmann's looking glass,' explained Nimue, seeing the novice's wrinkled nose and sullen expression. 'Look into it, if you wish. But please be cautious.'

'Is it true,' asked Condwiramurs in a voice trembling with excitement, 'that from Hartmann's looking glass you can pass into other—'

'Worlds? Indeed. But not at once, not without preparation, meditation, concentration and a whole host of other things. When I recommended caution I was thinking about something else.'

'What?'

'It works both ways. Something may also emerge from Hartmann's looking glass.'

*

'Know what, Nimue . . . When I look at that tapestry—'

'Have there been dreams?'

'Yes. But strange ones. From a bird's eye view. I was a bird . . . I saw the castle from the outside. I couldn't go inside. Something barred my way.'

'Look at the tapestry,' commanded Nimue. 'Look at the citadel. Look at it carefully; focus your attention on every detail. Concentrate hard; etch that image deeply into your memory. I want you to get there in your dream, to go inside. It's important for you to go inside.'

*

A truly devilish gale must have been raging outside, beyond the castle walls. The fire was roaring in the grate, quickly consuming the logs. Yennefer was delighting in the warmth. Her current

43

prison was, admittedly, much, much warmer than the dank dungeon where she had spent the last two months, but despite her delight her teeth still chattered. She had completely lost track of time, and no one had hurried to inform her about the date, but she was certain it was December, or perhaps even January.

'Eat, Yennefer,' said Vilgefortz. 'Don't be shy, tuck in.'

The sorceress had no intention of being shy. If, though, she was coping quite slowly and awkwardly with the chicken, it was only because her barely healed fingers were still clumsy and stiff. It was hard work to hold a knife and fork in them. And she didn't want to eat with her fingers – she wanted to show Vilgefortz and the other diners, the sorcerer's guests, that she was stronger than they believed. She didn't know any of them.

'I'm truly sorry to have to inform you,' said Vilgefortz, caressing the stem of his wine glass, 'that Ciri, your ward, has departed this life. You only have yourself to blame, Yennefer. You and your senseless obstinacy.'

One of the guests, a short, dark-haired man, sneezed loudly, and blew his nose on a cambric handkerchief. His nose was red and swollen, and clearly completely blocked up.

'Bless you,' said Yennefer, not at all bothered by Vilgefortz's portentous words. 'Where did you catch such an awful chill, good sir? Did you stand in a draught after bathing?'

Another guest, old, huge, thin, with hideously pale eyes, suddenly cackled. The one with the cold, although his face contorted in anger, thanked the sorceress with a bow and a brief catarrhal sentence. Not brief enough for her not to detect a Nilfgaardian accent.

Vilgefortz turned his face towards her. He was no longer wearing on his head the golden scaffolding or the crystal lens in his eye socket, but he looked even more horrible than when, during the summer, she had first seen his mutilated face. His regenerated left eyeball was now functioning, but was much smaller than his right. The sight took her breath away.

'You, Yennefer,' he drawled, 'no doubt think I'm lying, think I'm trying to ensnare you, trick you. To what end would I do that? I was as distressed as you at the news of Ciri's death. What am I saying? Even more than you. After all, I had pinned very specific hopes on the maid, had made plans which were to have determined my future. Now the girl is dead, and my plans are ruined.'

'Good.' Yennefer, trying hard to hold the knife in her stiff fingers, was slicing a pork cutlet stuffed with plums.

'You, though,' continued the wizard, paying no attention to her remark, 'are merely connected to Ciri by sentimental attachment, which consists in equal measure of regret caused by your own barrenness and a sense of guilt. Yes, yes, Yennefer, guilt! For, after all, you participated in the cross-breeding, in the animal husbandry that resulted in little Ciri's birth. And then transferred your affection onto the fruit of a genetic experiment, an unsuccessful one, which failed anyway. Because the experimenters lacked in knowledge.'

Yennefer raised her glass to him in silence, praying it wouldn't fall from her fingers. She was slowly coming to the conclusion that at least two of them would be stiff for a long time. Possibly permanently.

Vilgefortz snorted at her gesture.

'Now it's too late, it's happened,' he said through clenched teeth. 'But know this, Yennefer, that I possess knowledge. If I'd had the girl as well I would have made use of that knowledge. Indeed, it was bad luck for you, for I would have given you a reason for your crippled excuse of a maternal instinct. Although you're as dry and sterile as a stone, you'd not only have had a daughter, but a granddaughter too. Or, at least, an excuse for a granddaughter.'

Yennefer snorted contemptuously, although inside she was seething with fury.

'With the greatest regret I'm compelled to further spoil your splendid mood, my dear,' the sorcerer said coldly. 'Because I imagine you'll be saddened to hear that the Witcher, Geralt of Rivia, is also dead. Yes, yes, the same Witcher Geralt, with whom, as with Ciri, you were bound by an ersatz emotion, a ridiculous, foolish and sickly sweet fondness. Know, Yennefer, that our dear Witcher departed from this world in a truly ardent and spectacular fashion. In this case you don't have to reproach yourself. You're not to blame in the slightest for the Witcher's death. I'm responsible for the entire fracas. Try the marinated pears, they are simply delicious.'

Cold hatred lit up Yennefer's violet eyes. Vilgefortz burst out laughing.

'I prefer you like this,' he said. 'Indeed, were it not for the dimeritium bracelet you'd reduce me to ashes. But the dimeritium is working, so you can only scorch me with your gaze.'

The man with the cold sneezed, blew his nose and coughed until tears trickled from his eyes. The tall man scrutinised the sorceress with his unpleasant, fishy gaze.

'And where is Mr Rience?' asked Yennefer, drawing out her words. 'Mr Rience, who promised me so much, told me so much about what he'd do to me? Where is Mr Shirrú, who never passed up a chance to shove or kick me? Why have the guards, until quite recently boorish and brutal, begun to behave with timid respect? No, Vilgefortz, you don't have to answer. I know. What you've been talking about is one big lie. Ciri escaped you and Geralt escaped you, taking the time, I expect, to give your thugs a bloody good hiding. And what now? Your plans have fallen through, turned to dust. You admitted it yourself, your dreams of power have vanished like smoke. And the sorcerers and Dijkstra are fixing your position, oh yes. Not without reason and not from mercy have you stopped torturing me and forcing me to scan for information you need. And Emperor Emhyr is tightening his net, and is no doubt very, very angry. Ess a tearth, me tiarn? A'pleine a cales, ellea?'

'I use the Common Speech,' said the one with the runny nose, holding her gaze. 'And my name is Stefan Skellen. And by no means, by no means at all, have I filled my britches. Why, I still have the impression that I'm in a much better situation than you, Madam Yennefer.'

The speech tired him, he coughed hard again and blew his nose into the sodden cambric handkerchief.

Vilgefortz struck the table with his hand.

'Enough of this game,' he said, grotesquely swivelling his miniature eye. 'Know this, Yennefer. You are no longer of use to me. In principle I ought to have you shoved in a sack and drowned in the lake, but I use that kind of method with the utmost reluctance. Until the time circumstances permit or compel me to make another decision, you shall remain in isolation. I warn you, however, that I shan't allow you to cause me problems. If you decide to go on hunger strike again, know this, that I shall not – as I did in October – waste time feeding you through a straw. I shall simply let you starve to death. And in the case of escape attempts the guards' orders are explicit. And now, farewell. If, naturally, you have satisfied your—'

'No.' Yennefer stood up and hurled her napkin down onto the table. 'Perhaps I would've eaten something more, but the company spoils my appetite. Farewell, gentlemen.'

Stefan Skellen sneezed and coughed hard. The pale-eyed man measured her with an evil look and smiled hideously. Vilgefortz looked to one side.

As usual when she was led to or from the prison, Yennefer tried to work out where she was, obtain even a scrap of information that might help her to plan her escape. And each time she met with disappointment. The castle didn't have any windows through which she could see the surrounding terrain, or even the sun to try to orient herself. Telepathy was impossible, and the two heavy dimeritium bracelets on her arms and the collar around her neck effectively prevented all attempts at magic.

The chamber in which she was being held was as cold and austere as a hermit's cell. Nonetheless, Yennefer recalled the joyous day when she was transferred there from the dungeon. From the dungeon, on whose floor stood a permanent puddle of stinking water and on whose walls efflorescence and salting erupted. From the dungeon where she'd been fed on scraps that the rats easily tore from her lacerated fingers. When after around two months she had been unshackled and dragged out of there, allowed to bathe and change, Yennefer had been beside herself with happiness. The small room to which she had been transferred seemed like a royal boudoir to her, and the thin gruel they brought her like bird's nest soup, fit for the imperial table. Naturally, after some time, however, the gruel turned out to be dishwater, her hard pallet a hard pallet and the prison a prison. A cold, cramped prison, where after four paces you reached the wall.

Yennefer swore, sighed, and sat down on the scissor chair which was the only furniture she could use apart from the pallet. He entered so quietly she almost didn't hear him.

'The name's Bonhart,' he said. 'I'd advise you to remember that name, witch. Imprint it deeply in your memory.'

'Go fuck yourself, you swine.'

'I'm a man hunter.' He ground his teeth. 'Yes, yes, listen carefully, witch. In September, three months ago, I hunted down your little brat in Ebbing. That Ciri of yours, about whom so much is said.'

Yennefer listened attentively. *September. Ebbing. Caught her. But she isn't here. Perhaps he's lying?*

'An ashen-haired witcher girl, schooled at Kaer Morhen. I ordered her to fight in the arena, to kill people to the screams of the public. Slowly, slowly, I transformed her into a beast. I prepared her for that role with whip, fist and boot heel. The training process was lengthy. But she escaped from me, the green-eyed viper.'

Yennefer gasped imperceptibly.

'She escaped into the beyond. But we shall meet again. I'm certain that we shall meet again one day. Yes, witch. And if I regret anything it's only that they roasted your witcher lover, Geralt, in the fire. I'd have loved to let him taste my blade, the accursed freak.'

Yennefer snorted.

'Well, listen, Bonhart, or whatever your name is. Don't make me laugh. You're no match for the Witcher. You can't compare yourself to him. In any way. You are, as you admitted, a dogcatcher. But only good for little curs. For very little curs.'

'Look here then, witch.'

He tore open his jerkin and shirt and took out three silver medallions, tangling up their chains. One was shaped like a cat's head, the next an eagle or a gryphon. She couldn't see the third one well, but it was probably a wolf.

'Country fairs,' she snorted again, feigning indifference, 'are full of stuff like that.'

'They aren't from a fair.'

'You don't say.'

'Once upon a time,' Bonhart hissed, 'decent people feared witchers more than monsters. Monsters, after all, hid in forests and the undergrowth, while witchers had the audacity to hang around temples, chanceries, schools and playgrounds. Decent people rightly considered that a scandal. So they looked for somebody to bring the impudent witchers to order. And they found someone. Not easily, not quickly, not nearby, but they did. As you can see I've bagged three. No more freaks have appeared in the area or annoyed decent citizens by their presence. And were one to appear, I'd do away with him just like I did with the previous ones.'

'In your dreams?' Yennefer's face became contorted. 'With a crossbow, from hiding? Or perhaps with a draught of poison?'

Bonhart put the medallions back under his shirt and took two paces towards her.

'You vex me, witch.'

'That was my intention.'

'Oh, yes? I'll soon show you, bitch, that I can compete with your witcher lover in any way. Why, that I'm even better than him.'

*

The guards standing outside the door started at the thudding, banging, crashing, howling and wailing. And if the guards had ever happened to hear before the yelling of a panther caught in a trap, they would have sworn there was a panther in the cell.

Then a dreadful roar reached their ears. It was the exact sound of a wounded lion. Although the guards actually hadn't ever heard that, either, only seen one on coats of arms. They looked at each other. They nodded to each other. Then they rushed inside.

Yennefer was sitting in the corner of the chamber among the remains of her pallet. Her hair was dishevelled, her dress and blouse were torn from top to bottom, and her small breasts were rising in the rhythm of heavy breathing. Blood dripped from her nose, her face was quickly swelling, and welts from fingernails were also growing on her right arm.

Bonhart was sitting on the other side of the chamber amongst pieces of a stool, holding his crotch in both hands. Blood was dripping from his nose too, staining his grey whiskers a deep carmine. His face was criss-crossed with bloody scratch marks. Yennefer's barely healed fingers were a poor weapon, but the padlocks on the dimeritium bracelets had splendidly sharp edges.

Both tines of the fork that Yennefer had swiped from the table

49

during supper were rammed deep and evenly into the bone of Bonhart's swelling cheek.

'Only little curs, you dogcatcher,' gasped the sorceress, trying to cover up her breasts with the remains of her dress. 'And stay away from bitches. You're too weak for them, pipsqueak.'

She couldn't forgive herself for not striking where she had aimed –his eye. But why, the target was moving, and besides, nobody's perfect.

Bonhart roared, stood up, pulled out the fork, howled and staggered from the pain. He swore hideously.

Meanwhile, two more guards looked inside the cell.

'Hey, you!' roared Bonhart, wiping blood from his face. 'In here! Drag that harlot into the middle of the floor, spread-eagle her and hold her down.'

The guards looked at each other. Then at the floor. And then at the ceiling.

'You'd better be going, sir,' said one. 'There won't be any spread-eaglin' or holdin' here. It's not among our duties.'

'And apart on that,' muttered the other, 'we don't mean to end up like Rience or Schirrú.'

*

Condwiramurs put aside the painted board, which depicted a prison cell. And, in the cell, a woman sitting with head bowed, manacled to the stone wall.

'They imprisoned her,' she murmured. 'And the Witcher was taking his pleasure in Toussaint with some brunette.'

'Do you condemn him?' Nimue asked severely. 'Knowing practically nothing?'

'No. I don't condemn him, but—'

'There are no "buts". Be quiet, please.'

They sat in silence for some time, leafing through engravings and watercolours.

'All the versions of the legend—' Condwiramurs pointed to one of the engravings '—give Rhys-Rhun castle as the place of the ending, the finale, the conclusive battle between Good and Evil. Armageddon. All of the versions. Aside from one.'

'Aside from one,' nodded Nimue. 'Aside from an anonymous, not very popular version, known as the Black Book of Ellander.'

'The Black Book states that the ending of the legend played out in Stygga citadel.'

'Indeed. And the Book of Ellander presents matters that describe the legend in a way that differs significantly from the canon.'

'I wonder—' Condwiramurs raised her head '—which of those castles is portrayed in the illustrations? Which one is shown on your tapestry? Which likeness is true?'

'We shall never know. The castle that witnessed the ending of the legend doesn't exist. It was destroyed. Not a trace of it remains. All the versions agree on that, even the one given by the Book of Ellander. None of the locations given in the sources is convincing. We do not know and shall not know what that castle looked like and where it stood.'

'But the truth—'

'But the truth means nothing whatsoever,' Nimue interrupted sharply. 'Don't forget, we don't know what Ciri really looked like. But look at this figure here, on this piece of parchment drawn on by Wilma Wessely, in a heated conversation with the elf, Avallac'h, against a background of figurines of macabre children. It's her. Ciri. There isn't any doubt about it.'

'But,' Condwiramurs soldiered on pugnaciously, 'your tapestry—'

'Depicts the castle where the legend's climax was played out.'

There was a long silence. The sheets of parchment rustled as they were turned over.

'I don't like the version of the legend from the Black Book,' Condwiramurs began again. 'It's . . . It's—'

'Brutally authentic.' Nimue finished her novice's sentence, nodding.

*

Condwiramurs yawned, put down an edition of *Half a Century of Poetry* with an afterword by Professor Everett Denhoff Jr. She plumped up her pillow, changing the arrangement for reading to one suitable for sleeping. She yawned, stretched and blew out the lamp. The chamber was plunged into darkness, lit only by needles of moonlight squeezing through chinks in the curtains. *What should I choose tonight?* wondered the novice, wriggling on the sheets. *Take pot luck? Or anchor myself?*

After a brief moment she decided on the latter.

It was a vague, repeating dream that she couldn't see through to the end. It evaporated, vanished among other dreams, like a thread of the weft vanishes and gets lost among the pattern of a coloured fabric. A dream that vanished from her memory, but which in spite of that stubbornly remained in it.

She fell asleep immediately, the dream engulfing her at once. As soon as she closed her eyes.

A night sky, cloudless, bright from the moon and the stars. Hills, and on their slopes vineyards dusted with snow. The black, angular outline of a building: a wall with battlements, a keep, a lonely corner watchtower.

Two horsemen. The two of them ride beyond the outer wall, they dismount, they both enter the portal. But only one of them enters the opening to a dungeon gaping in the floor.

The one with utterly white hair.

Condwiramurs moaned in her sleep, tossing around on her bed.

The white-haired man descends the stairs, deep, deep into the cellar. He walks along dark corridors, from time to time illuminating them by lighting brands held in cast-iron cressets. The glow from the torches casts ghastly shadows on the walls and vaulting.

Corridors, stairs, and again corridors. A dungeon, a huge crypt, barrels by the walls. Piles of rubble, heaps of bricks. Then a corridor which forks into two. Darkness both ways. The white-haired man lights another torch. He unsheathes the sword on his back. He hesitates, not knowing which fork to take. He finally decides on the one to the right. It's very dark, winding and full of rubble. Condwiramurs groans in her sleep. Fear grips her. She knows that the way chosen by the white-haired man leads towards danger.

She knows at the same time that the white-haired man seeks danger.

For it is his profession.

The novice thrashes around in the sheets, moaning. She's a dream-reader, she's dreaming, she's in an oneiric trance, she suddenly knows what is about to happen. *Beware!* She wants to scream, though she knows she's unable to. *Look out, behind you!*

Beware, Witcher!

The monster attacked from the darkness, from an ambush, silently and horrendously. It suddenly materialised in the darkness like a flame flaring up. Like a tongue of flame.

No matter how much he hurried, urged, fumed and stormed, the Witcher remained in Toussaint almost the whole winter. What were the reasons? I shall not write about them. It is all over. There is no point dwelling on it. Anyone who would condemn the Witcher I would remind that love has many names and not to judge less they themselves are judged.

Dandelion, *Half a Century of Poetry*

CHAPTER THREE

The monster attacked from the darkness, from an ambush, silently and horrendously. It suddenly materialised in the darkness like an exploding flame flaring up. Like a tongue of flame.

Geralt, though taken by surprise, reacted instinctively. He dodged, brushing the dungeon wall. The beast flew past, rebounded off the dirt floor like a ball, flailed its wings and leaped again, hissing and opening its awful beak. But this time the Witcher was ready.

He jabbed from the elbow, aiming at the crop beneath the crimson dewlap, which was large, twice as big as a turkey's. He found the target, and felt his blade slice the body open. The blow's force knocked the beast to the ground, against the wall. The skoffin screamed, and it was almost a human scream. It thrashed around among broken bricks, writhed and fluttered its wings, splashing blood and lashing its whip-like tail around. The Witcher was certain the battle was over, but the monster surprised him unpleasantly. It unexpectedly lunged for his throat, croaking horribly, talons outstretched and beak snapping. Geralt dodged, pushed off from the wall with his shoulder and smote with great force from below, taking advantage of the momentum he'd generated. The wounded skoffin tumbled among the bricks again, and stinking gore splashed on the dungeon wall, describing fanciful patterns. Wounded, the monster stopped thrashing around and was only trembling, croaking, extending its long neck, swelling its crop and shaking its dewlap. Blood flowed swiftly between the bricks it lay on.

Geralt could easily have finished it off, but didn't want to damage its hide too much. He waited calmly for the skoffin to bleed to death. He moved a few steps away, turned around to the wall, undid his trousers and pissed, whistling a sad song. The skoffin stopped croaking, lay still and went quiet. The Witcher moved closer and poked it gently with the point of his sword. Seeing it was done, he seized the monster by the tail and picked it up. He held it by the base of its tail at hip height. The skoffin's vulture-like beak reached the floor and its wingspan measured more than four feet.

'You're light, kurolishek.' Geralt shook the beast, which indeed didn't weigh much more than a well-fattened turkey. 'You're light. Luckily they're paying me by the piece, not the pound.'

*

'It's the first time,' Reynart de Bois-Fresnes whistled softly through his teeth, which, as Geralt knew, he did to express the highest admiration. 'It's the first time I've ever seen anything like it. An absolute oddity, by my troth, an oddity to end all oddities. Does that mean it's the infamous basilisk?'

'No.' Geralt raised the monster higher so the knight could examine it better. 'It isn't a basilisk. It's a kurolishek.'

'Is there a difference?'

'A crucial one. A basilisk, also known as a regulus, is a reptile; but a kurolishek, also known as a skoffin or cockatrice, is neither a reptile nor a bird. It's the only member of an order that scholars called ornithoreptiles, for after lengthy debate they found—'

'And which one,' interrupted Reynart de Bois-Fresnes, clearly uninterested in the scholars' motives, 'can kill or petrify with a look?'

'Neither of them. That's fiction.'

'Why do people fear them both so much then? This one here isn't all that big. Can it really be dangerous?'

'This one here—' the Witcher shook his quarry '—usually attacks from the rear and aims unerringly between the vertebrae or below the left kidney, at the aorta. One blow of its beak usually suffices. And as regards the basilisk it doesn't matter where it strikes. Its venom is the most powerful known neurotoxin. It kills in a few seconds.'

'Ugh . . . And which one, do tell, can be despatched with the help of a looking glass?'

'Either of them. If you whack it over the head.'

Reynart de Bois-Fresnes chortled. Geralt didn't laugh. The joke about the basilisk and the looking glass had stopped amusing him in Kaer Morhen, for the teachers had flogged it to death. The jokes about virgins and unicorns were just as unamusing. The record for idiocy and primitivism was achieved in Kaer Morhen by the numerous versions of the joke about the she-dragon the young witcher shook hands with for a bet.

He smiled. At the memories.

'I prefer you when you smile,' said Reynart, scrutinising him very closely. 'I prefer you much more, a hundredfold more like you are now. Compared to how you were back then in October, after that scrap in the Druids' Forest when we were riding to Beauclair. Back then, let me tell you, you were sullen, embittered and as sour as a usurer who's been swindled, and as irritable as a man who hasn't had any luck the whole night. Or even in the morning.'

'Was I really like that?'

'Really. Don't be surprised that I prefer you the way you are now. Changed.'

'Occupational therapy.' Geralt shook the kurolishek he was holding by the tail. 'The salutary influence of professional activity on the psyche. And so, to continue my cure, let's get down to business. There's a chance of making a little more money on the skoffin than the fee agreed for its killing. It's almost undamaged. If you have a customer for a whole one, to be stuffed or prepared, don't take less than two hundred. If you have to flog it in portions, remember that the most valuable feathers are from just above the rump, specifically, those ones, the central tail feathers. You can sharpen them much thinner than goose feathers, they write more prettily and cleanly, and are harder-wearing. A scribe who knows his stuff won't hesitate to give five apiece.'

'I have customers wanting to stuff a corpse,' smiled the knight. 'The coopers' guild. They saw that vile creature stuffed in Castel Ravello. You know, that giant water flea, or whatever it's called . . . You know the one. The one they clubbed to death in the dungeons under the ruins of the old castle the day after Samhain . . .'

'I remember.'

'Well, so the coopers saw the stuffed beast and asked me for something equally rarefied to decorate their guild chambers. The kurolishek will be just right. The coopers in Toussaint, as you can

59

guess, are a guild who can't complain of a shortage of orders and thanks to that are wealthy. They're bound to give two hundred and twenty. Perhaps even more, I'll try to haggle. And as far as the feathers are concerned . . . The barrel bodgers won't notice if we pull a few pieces from the kurolishek's arse and sell them to the ducal chancery. The chancery doesn't pay out of its own pocket, but from the ducal coffers, so they'll pay not five but ten for a feather without a quibble.'

'I take my hat off to your shrewdness.'

'*Nomen est omen.*' Reynart de Bois-Fresnes grinned more broadly. 'Mamma must have sensed something, christening me with the name of the sly fox from the well-known cycle of fables.'

'You ought to have been a merchant, not a knight.'

'I ought,' agreed the knight. 'But, well, if you're born the son of a noble lord, you'll live a noble lord and die a noble lord, having first begat further, ho, ho, noble lords. You won't change anything, no matter what. Anyway, you reckon up pretty decently, Geralt, but you don't make a living from merchandising.'

'I don't. For similar reasons to you. But with the single difference that I won't begat anything. Let's get out of these dungeons.'

Outside, at the foot of the castle walls, they were enfolded by the cold and wind from the hills. The night was bright, the sky cloudless and starry. The moonlight sparkled on the swathes of fresh, white snow lying on the vineyards.

Their tethered horses greeted them with snorts.

'We ought to meet the customer at once and collect the money,' said Reynart, looking meaningfully at the Witcher. 'But you are surely hurrying back to Beauclair, what? To a certain bedchamber?'

Geralt did not reply, as he didn't answer questions like that on principle. He hauled the kurolishek's remains onto the pack horse and then mounted Roach.

'Let's meet the customer,' he decided, turning back in the saddle. 'The night is young, and I'm hungry. And I fancy a drink. Let's ride to town. To The Pheasantry.'

Reynart de Bois-Fresnes laughed, adjusted a shield with a red and gold chequerboard pattern hanging from the pommel, and climbed up into the high saddle.

'As you wish, my good fellow. The Pheasantry it is. Yah, Bucephalus!'

They went at a walk down the snow-covered hillside towards the highway, which was clearly marked by a sparse avenue of poplars.

'You know what, Reynart,' Geralt suddenly said. 'I also prefer you as you are now. Talking normally. Back in October you were using infuriating, moronic mannerisms.'

''Pon my word, Witcher, I'm a knight errant,' chortled Reynart de Bois-Fresnes. 'Have you forgotten? Knights always talk like morons. It's a kind of sign, like this shield here. You can recognise the fraternity, like by the arms on the shield.'

*

''Pon my word,' said the Chequered Knight, 'you needlessly bother yourself, Sir Geralt. Your beloved is surely hale, for she has doubtless utterly forgotten about her infirmity. The duchess retains excellent court medics, fully capable of curing any malaise. 'Pon my word, there's no need to distress yourself.'

'I'm of the same opinion,' said Regis. 'Cheer up, Geralt. After all the druidesses treated Milva too—'

'And druidesses are expert healers,' interjected Cahir, 'the best proof of which is my very own noggin which was cut open by a miner's axe, and which is now, take a look, almost good as new. Milva is sure to be well too. There's no need to worry.'

'Let's hope.'

'She's hale, your Milva, and hearty,' repeated the knight. 'I'll wager she's already cavorting at wedding balls! Cutting a caper. Feasting! In Beauclair, at the court of Duchess Anarietta, balls alternate with banquets. Ha, 'pon my word, now that I've fulfilled my vows, I also—'

'You've fulfilled your vows?'

'Fortune shone on me! For you ought to know that I made my vows, and not just any vows, but on a flying crane. In the spring. I vowed to fell fifteen marauders before Yule. I was lucky; I'm now free of my vows. Now I can drink and eat beef. Aha, I don't have to conceal my name. I am, if you will, Reynart de Bois-Fresnes.'

'It's our pleasure.'

'Regarding those balls,' said Angoulême, urging her horse on to catch up with them. 'I hope platter and goblet won't pass us by either? And I'd also love to shake a leg!'

''Pon my word, there'll be everything at Beauclair,' Reynart de Bois-Fresnes assured them. 'Balls, feasts, banquets, revels and poetry evenings. You're friends of Dandelion's, for heaven's sake . . . Of Viscount Julian's, I meant to say. And the Lady Duchess is most fond of the latter.'

'I'll say! He was bragging about it,' said Angoulême. 'What was the truth about that love? Do you know the story, sir knight? Do tell!'

'Angoulême,' said the Witcher, 'do you have to know?'

'I don't. But I want to! Don't whinge, Geralt. And stop being sullen, for at the sight of your mush, roadside mushrooms pickle. And you, sir knight, say on.'

Other knights errant riding at the head of the procession were singing a knightly refrain with a repeating chorus. The words of the song were quite unbelievably foolish.

'It occurred these six summers past,' began the knight. 'The poet tarried with us all winter and spring, he played his lute, sang romances and declaimed poetry. Duke Raymund was actually staying in Cintra, at a council. He didn't hurry home, it was no secret he had a paramour in Cintra. And the Duchess and Lord Dandelion . . . Ha, Beauclair is strange indeed and spellbinding, full of amatory enchantment . . . You shall see for yourselves. As the Duchess and Lord Dandelion learned then. They noticed not, from verse to verse, from word to word, from compliment to compliment, posies, glances, sighs . . . To put it briefly: both came to an intimate understanding.'

'How intimate?' chortled Angoulême.

'One was not an eye witness,' said the knight coolly. 'And it is not seemly to repeat rumours. Besides, as my good lady undoubtedly knows, love has many faces, and it is a most relative thing how intimate was the understanding.'

Cahir snorted softly. Angoulême had nothing to add.

'The Duchess and Lord Dandelion,' continued Reynart de Bois-Fresnes, 'trysted in secret some two months from Belleteyn to the summer Solstice. But they disregarded caution. News got out, evil rumours began to spread. Lord Dandelion, without hesitating, mounted his horse and rode away. He acted prudently, as it turned out. For as soon as Duke Raymund returned from Cintra, an accommodating serving lad informed him of everything. As soon as the duke found out what an insult he had suffered and how he had been cuckolded, he was seized by yellow bile, as you may imagine. He overturned a tureen of broth on the table, cleft the informer lad with a hatchet, and uttered scabrous words. He then punched the marshal's face and smashed a great Koviran looking glass before witnesses. Then he imprisoned the duchess in her chambers and, having threatened her with torture, extracted everything from her. At which point he sent after Lord Dandelion, ordered him put to death without clemency and his heart torn from his breast. For, having read something similar in an ancient ballad, he meant to fry his heart and force Duchess Anarietta to eat it in front of the entire court. Uurgh, what an abomination! Luckily, Lord Dandelion managed to flee.'

'Indeed. And the duke died?'

'He did. The incident, as I said, caused him great ill humour. His blood became so heated from it that apoplexy and palsy seized him. He lay like a plank for nigh on a year. But recovered. Even began to walk. Only he winked one eye, ceaselessly, like this.'

The knight turned around in the saddle, squinted his eye and screwed up his face like a monkey.

'Although the duke had always been an incurable fornicator and stallion,' he continued a moment later, 'that winking made him even more *pericolosus* in love-making, for every dame thought he was winking at her out of fondness and giving her amorous signs. And dames are most covetous of such homage. I in no way impute that they are all wanton and dissolute, by no means, but the duke, as I said, winked much, almost endlessly, so on the whole he got what was coming to him. His cup ran over in his frolics and one night he was struck again by the apoplexy. He gave up the ghost. In his bedchamber.'

'Atop a dame?' guffawed Angoulême.

'In truth . . .' The knight, until then deadly serious, smiled under his whiskers. 'In truth beneath one. The details are unimportant.'

'Verily,' nodded Cahir seriously. 'Duke Raymund wasn't

63

greatly mourned, was he? During the tale I had the impression—'

'That you were fonder of the inconstant wife than the betrayed husband,' the vampire interrupted in mid-sentence. 'Perhaps for the reason that she now reigns?'

'That is one reason,' replied Reynart de Bois-Fresnes disarmingly frankly. 'But not the only one. For Duke Raymund, may the earth lie lightly on him, was such a good-for-nothing rogue and, excuse my language, whoreson, that he would have given the very Devil stomach ulcers in half a year. And he reigned for seven years in Toussaint. While everyone adored and adores Duchess Anarietta.'

'May I then venture,' said the Witcher tartly, 'that Duke Raymund didn't leave many inconsolable friends who were ready to waylay Dandelion with daggers?'

'You may.' The knight glanced at him and his eyes were quick and intelligent. 'And, 'pon my word, you won't be wide of the mark. I said, did I not? Lady Anarietta dotes on the poet and everyone here would walk through fire for Lady Anarietta.'

> *The good knight returned*
> *To find he'd been spurned*
> *His love had not tarried*
> *But swiftly been married*
> *A chevalier's woe!*
> *With a hey, nonny, no!*

Crows, disturbed by the knights' singing, took flight, cawing, from the roadside thicket.

They soon rode out of the trees straight into a valley among hills on which the white towers of small castles were framed strikingly against the sky, which was coloured with dark blue streaks. Wherever they looked the gentle hillsides were covered with neat avenues of evenly trimmed bushes like columns of soldiers. The ground was carpeted with red and gold leaves.

'What is it?' asked Angoulême. 'Vines?'

'Grapevines, yes,' said Reynart de Bois-Fresnes, 'They're the famed valleys of Sansretour. The finest wines of the world are pressed from the grapes that mellow here.'

''Tis true,' agreed Regis, who as usual was an expert on everything. 'The crux is the volcanic earth and the microclimate here which ensures every year a simply ideal combination of sunny and rainy days. If we add traditions, expertise and the utmost care of the vinedressers, it yields a result in the form of a product of the highest class and distinction.'

'Well said,' the knight smiled. 'Distinction indeed. Look over there, say, at the hillside below that castle. Here the castle gives the distinction to the vineyard and the cellars deep beneath it. That one is called Castel Ravello, and from its vineyards come such wines as Erveluce, Fiorano, Pomino and the celebrated Est Est. You must have heard of it. One pays the same for a keg of Est Est as for ten kegs of wine from Cidaris or the Nilfgaardian vineyards by the Alba. And there, look, as far as the eyes can see, other castles and other vineyards, and the names are surely no strangers to you either. Vermentino, Toricella, Casteldaccia, Tufo, Sancerre, Nuragus, Coronata, and finally Corvo Bianco – Gwyn Cerbin in the elven tongue. I trust the names are familiar to you?'

'They are, ugh.' Angoulême contorted her face. 'Particularly by learning the hard way to check if some rascal of an innkeeper hadn't poured us one of those famous wines by chance instead of the usual cider, because then you might have to leave your horse with him, so costly Castel or Est Est. Yuck. I don't understand, it might be quality gear to those great lords, but we, ordinary folk, can get plastered just as well on the cheap stuff. And I'll tell you this, because I've experienced it: you puke after Est Est just the same as you do after scrumpy.'

*

'Caring not for Angoulême's vulgar October jests,' Reynart leaned back from the table, his belt loosened, 'today we drink a fine label and a fine vintage, Witcher. We can afford it, we've made some money. We can revel.'

'That's right,' Geralt beckoned to the innkeeper. 'After all, as Dandelion says, perhaps there are other motivations for earning money, but I just don't know any. So let's eat whatever's behind those appetising smells wafting from the kitchen. Incidentally, it's extremely crowded in The Pheasantry today, though the hour's quite late.'

'Why, it's Yuletide Eve,' explained the innkeeper, overhearing him. 'Folk are wassailing. Making merry. Telling fortunes. As tradition demands, and tradition here—'

'I know,' interrupted the Witcher. 'And what did tradition demand from the kitchen today?'

'Cold tongue with horseradish. Capon broth with brain meatballs. Beef roulade served with dumplings and cabbage . . .'

'Keep it coming, good fellow. And to accompany it . . . What should we drink with it, Reynart?'

'If it's beef,' said the knight after a moment's thought, 'then red Côte-de-Blessure. And the vintage? It was the year old Duchess Caroberta turned up her toes.'

'That's the year,' the innkeeper nodded. 'At your service, sire.'

A mistletoe wreath, clumsily thrown behind her by a wench from the next table, almost fell into Geralt's lap. The wench's companions whooped with laughter. And she blushed prettily.

'You're out of luck!' The knight picked up the wreath and threw it back. 'He won't be your future husband. He's spoken for, noble maiden. He's already been ensnared by a pair of green orbs—'

'Be quiet, Reynart.'

The innkeeper brought the order. They ate and drank in silence, listening to the revellers' merriment.

'Yule,' said Geralt, putting down his cup. 'Midinvaerne. The winter solstice. I've been hanging around here for two months. Two wasted months!'

'One month,' Reynart corrected him coolly and soberly. 'If you've lost anything, it's but a month. Then the snows covered up the mountain passes and you couldn't have left Toussaint, no matter what. You've waited until Yule, so you'll surely wait till spring too. It's force majeure, thus your grief and sorrow are in vain. While as far as your sorrow goes, don't overdo the pretence. For I don't believe you regret it that much.'

'Oh, what do you know, Reynart? What do you know?'

'Not much,' agreed the knight, pouring the wine. 'Not much more than what I see. And I saw your first encounter; yours and

66

hers. In Beauclair. Do you remember the Feast of the Vat? The white knickers?'

Geralt did not reply. He remembered.

'A charming place, Beauclair Palace, full of amatory enchantment,' muttered Reynart, savouring the wine's bouquet. 'The very sight is bewitching. I recall how you were all dumbstruck when you saw it in October. What was the expression Cahir used then? Let me think.'

*

'An elegant little castle,' Cahir said in admiration. 'Well I'll be, an elegant and pleasing little castle, indeed.'

'The duchess lives well,' said the vampire. 'You have to admit it.'

'Fucking nice gaff,' added Angoulême.

'Beauclair Palace,' repeated Reynart de Bois-Fresnes proudly. 'An elven edifice, only slightly modified. Allegedly by Faramond himself.'

'Not allegedly,' objected Regis. 'Beyond any doubt. Faramond's style is apparent at first glance. It suffices to look at those small towers.'

The slender white obelisks of the red-roofed towers referred to by the vampire soared into the sky, rising up from the castle's delicate construction which grew wider towards the ground. The sight evoked the image of candles with festoons of wax flowing over the intricately carved base of a candlestick.

'The town spreads out at the foot of Beauclair,' explained Sir Reynart. 'The walls, naturally, were added later. After all, as you know, elves don't wall their towns. Spur on your horses, noble comrades. We have a long road ahead of us. Beauclair only seems close, but the mountains distort perspective.'

'Let us ride on.'

They rode swiftly, overtaking wanderers and goliards, wagons and carts loaded with dark, seemingly mouldy grapes. Then there were the town's busy narrow streets, smelling of fermenting grape juice, then a gloomy park full of poplars, yews, barberries and boxwood. Then there were rose beds, mainly containing multiflora and centifolia. And further still there were the carved columns, portals and archivolts of the palace, liveried servants and flunkeys.

The man who greeted them was Dandelion, coiffured and arrayed like a prince.

*

'Where's Milva?'

'She's well, don't worry. You'll find her in the chambers that have been prepared for you. She doesn't want to leave them.'

'Why not?'

'You'll find out later. Now follow me. The duchess awaits.'

'In our travelling things?'

'Such were her wishes.'

The hall they entered was full of people, dressed as colourfully as birds of paradise. Geralt did not have time to look around. Dandelion shoved him towards a marble staircase, beside which were two women who stood out from the crowd, being assisted by pages and courtiers.

It was quiet, but it became even quieter.

The first woman had a pointed, turned-up nose, and her blue eyes were piercing and seemed a little feverish. Her chestnut hair was pinned up into an elaborately, truly artistic coiffure, supported by velvet ribbons, complete down to the tiniest nuances, including an unerringly geometric, sickle-shaped curl on her forehead. The upper part of her dress had a plunging neckline shimmering with a thousand blue and lilac stripes on a black background. The skirt was black, densely strewn with tiny, gold chrysanthemums in a regular pattern. The neckline and décolletage – something like a complicated scaffolding or cage – held captive in its intricate coils a necklace of lacquer, obsidian, emeralds and lapis lazuli ending in a jade cross which almost plunged between her small breasts, which were supported by a close-fitting bodice. The diamond-shaped neckline was large and plunging, baring the woman's delicate shoulders, and seemed not to offer adequate support – Geralt was expecting the dress to slide from her bust at any moment. But it didn't and was held in its proper place by the mysterious arcana of dressmaking and the buffers of puffed sleeves.

The second woman equalled the first in height. She was wearing the same lipstick. And there the similarities ended. This woman wore a net cap on her short, black hair, which metamorphosed at the front into a veil extending to the tip of her petite nose. The veil's floral motif didn't mask her beautiful, sparkling eyes set off by green eye-shadow. An identical floral veil covered the modest décolletage of her long-sleeved black dress, which in several places was scattered with an apparently random pattern of sapphires, aquamarines, rock crystals and gold openwork stars.

'Her Enlightened Ladyship Duchess Anna Henrietta,' someone whispered behind Geralt's back. 'Kneel, sire.'

I wonder which of the two, thought Geralt, bending his painful knee clumsily into a ceremonial bow. *Both look just as bloody high-born. Not to say regal.*

'Arise, Sir Geralt,' said the one with the intricate chestnut coiffure and pointed nose, dispelling his doubts. 'We welcome you and your friends to Beauclair Palace in the Duchy of Toussaint. We are delighted to be able to offer lodging to people on such a noble mission. People, furthermore, being bonded in friendship with Viscount Julian, who is so dear to our heart.'

Dandelion bowed deeply and vigorously.

'The viscount,' continued the duchess, 'has disclosed your names to us, revealed the nature of your expedition, and said what brings you to Toussaint. The tale touched our heart. We shall be glad to converse with you at a private audience, Sir Geralt. That matter must, however, be somewhat postponed, since state duties make their demands upon us. The grape harvest is over and tradition demands our participation in the Festival of the Vat.'

The other woman, the one in the veil, leaned over towards the duchess and quickly whispered something. Anna Henrietta looked at the Witcher, smiled, and licked her lips.

'It is our will,' she raised her voice, 'that Geralt of Rivia shall serve us in the Vat alongside Viscount Julian.'

A murmur ran through the group of courtiers and knights like the whisper of pines struck by the wind. Duchess Anarietta shot the Witcher another smouldering glance and left the hall with her companion and a retinue of pages.

'By thunder,' whispered the Chequered Knight. 'I'll be damned! Quite some honour has befallen you, Witcher, sir.'

'I don't quite understand what this is about,' Geralt admitted. 'In what way am I to serve Her Highness?'

'Her Grace,' broke in a portly gentleman with the appearance of a confectioner, approaching. 'Forgive me, sire, for correcting you, but in the given circumstances I must do so. We greatly respect tradition and protocol here in Toussaint. I am Sebastian Le Goff, Chamberlain and Marshal of the Court.'

'My pleasure.'

'Lady Anna Henrietta's official and protocolary title—' the chamberlain not only looked like a confectioner but even smelt of icing '—is "Her Enlightened Ladyship". Her unofficial one is "Her Grace". Her familiar one, beyond the court, is "Lady Duchess". But one should always address her as "Your Grace".'

'Thank you, I shall remember. And the other woman? How should I entitle her?'

'Her official title is: "The Honourable",' the chamberlain informed him gravely. 'But addressing her as "Ma'am" is permissible. She is kin to the duchess and is called Fringilla Vigo. In accordance with Her Grace's will, you are to serve her, Madam Fringilla, in the Vat.'

'And what does this service consist of?'

'Nothing difficult. I shall explain soon. As you see, we've used mechanical presses for years, but nonetheless tradition . . .'

*

The courtyard resounded with a hubbub and frenetic squealing of pipes, the wild music of recorders and the demented jingling of tambourines. Tumblers and buffoons dressed in garlands cavorted and somersaulted around a vat placed on a platform. The courtyard and cloisters were full of people – knights, ladies, courtiers and richly attired burghers.

Chamberlain Sebastian Le Goff raised up a staff twisted around with green vines, and struck it three times against the podium.

'Hear ye, hear ye!' he cried. 'Noble ladies, lords and knights!'

'Yea, yea!' replied the crowd.

'Yea, yea! Welcome to our ancient custom! May the grape prosper! Yea, yea! May it mellow in the sun!'

'Yea, yea! May it mellow!'

'Yea, yea! May the trod grape ferment! May it gather strength and taste in the barrel! May it flow tastily to goblets and thence to heads, to the glory of majesty, comely ladies, noble knights and vinedressers!'

'Yea, yea! May it ferment!'

'Let the Beauties step forward!'

Two women – Duchess Anna Henrietta and her black-haired companion – emerged from damask tents on opposite sides of the courtyard. They were both wrapped tightly in scarlet capes.

'Yea, yea!' the chamberlain struck his cane on the ground. 'Let the Youths step forward!'

The "Youths" had been instructed and knew what to do. Dandelion approached the duchess, and Geralt, the black-haired woman. Who, he now knew, was called the Honourable Fringilla Vigo.

The two women cast off their capes as one, and the crowd greeted them with thunderous applause. Geralt swallowed.

The women were wearing tiny, white, gossamer-thin blouses with shoulder straps, revealing their midriffs. And clinging frilly knickers. And nothing else. Not even jewellery.

They were also barefoot.

Geralt picked Fringilla up and she quite eagerly put an arm around his neck. She smelled faintly of ambergris and roses. And femininity. She was warm and her warmth penetrated him like an arrowhead. She was soft and her softness scalded and nettled his fingers.

They carried them to the vat – Geralt, Fringilla, and Dandelion, the Duchess – and helped them alight on the grapes, which burst and spurted forth juice. The crowd roared.

'Yea, yea!'

The duchess and Fringilla placed their hands on each other's shoulders, and by supporting one another more easily kept their balance on the grapes into which they had sunk up to their knees. The must squirted and sprayed around. The women, turning, trod the grapes, giggling like schoolgirls. Fringilla winked at the Witcher, quite against protocol.

'Yea, yea!' shouted the crowd. 'Yea, yea! May it ferment!'

The crushed grapes splashed juice, the cloudy must bubbled and foamed copiously around the treaders' knees.

The chamberlain struck his cane against the planks of the platform. Geralt and Dandelion moved closer, helping the women out of the vat. Geralt saw Anarietta pinch Dandelion's ear as he carried her, and her eyes shone dangerously. It seemed to him that Fringilla's lips brushed his cheek, but he couldn't be certain whether intentionally or not. The smell of the must was heady and intoxicating.

He stood Fringilla on the podium and wrapped her in the scarlet cape. Fringilla squeezed his hand quickly and powerfully.

'These ancient traditions,' she whispered, 'can be arousing, can't they?'

'They can.'

'Thank you, Witcher.'

'The pleasure's all mine.'

'Not all yours. I assure you, not all yours.'

*

'Pour the wine, Reynart.'

More Yuletide prophecies were being carried out at the next table. A strip of apple peel cut into a long spiral was thrown down and the initial letter of one's future partner's name was divined from the shape it arranged itself into. Each time, the peel formed itself into a letter 'S'. In spite of that there was no end to the mirth.

The knight poured.

'It turned out that Milva was well,' said the Witcher pensively, 'although she still had a bandage around her ribs. She remained in her chamber, though, and refused to leave, not wanting at any cost to put on the dress she'd been presented with. It looked as though there would be a protocolary scandal, but the omniscient Regis pacified the situation. After quoting a good dozen precedents he made the chamberlain bring a male outfit to the archer. Angoulême, for a change, joyfully discarded her trousers, riding boots and footwraps, and soap, a dress and a comb turned her into quite a pretty lass. All of us, let's face it, were cheered up by the

72

bathhouse and the clean clothes. Even me. We set off for the audience in a very decent mood—'

'Stop for a moment,' Reynart gestured with his head. 'Business is heading towards us. Ho, ho, and not one, but two vineyards! Malatesta, our customer, is bringing a comrade . . . and a rival. Wonders will never cease!'

'Who's the other one?'

'Pomerol vineyard. We're drinking their wine, Côte-de-Blessure, right now.'

Malatesta, the steward of the Vermentino vineyard, had noticed them, waved, and approached, leading his companion, an individual with a black moustache and a bushy, black beard, who resembled a brigand more than an official.

'Gentlemen,' Malatesta introduced the bearded man, 'Mr Alcides Fierabras, steward of Pomerol vineyard.'

'Sit you down.'

'We're here for but a moment. To talk to Master Witcher regarding a beast in our cellars. I conclude from seeing your good selves here that the monster is killed?'

'Dead.'

'The agreed sum,' Malatesta assured them, 'will be transferred to your account at the Cianfanellis' bank tomorrow at the latest. Oh, thanking you, Master Witcher. Thanks a hundredfold. Such a gorgeous cellar, vaulted, north-pointing, not too dry, not too damp, just what's needed for wine, and owing to that vile brute it couldn't be used. You saw yourselves, we needs must brick up all that part of the cellar, but the beast managed to find a way through . . . Where it came from is anyone's guess . . . Probably from hell itself . . .'

He spat on the floor.

'Caves hollowed out in volcanic tuff always abound in monsters,' instructed Reynart de Bois-Fresnes wisely. He had been accompanying the Witcher for over a month, and being a good listener, had managed to learn a great deal. 'It goes without saying. Where there's tuff, there's sure to be a monster.'

'Very well, perhaps it was Tuff.' Malatesta glared at him. 'Whoever that Tuff happens to be. But folk are saying it's because our cellars are connected to deep caverns that are said to lead to the very centre of the earth. There are many similar dungeons and caves like that around here . . .'

'Like under our cellars, to give the first example that springs to mind,' said the black-bearded Pomerol vineyard. 'Those dungeons go on for miles, but no one knows to where. The men who wanted to unravel the matter didn't return. And a dreadful monster was also seen there. They say. I'd therefore like to suggest—'

'I can guess what you want to propose,' said the Witcher, dryly, 'and I consent to the proposition. I will explore your cellars. We shall set the fee depending on what I find there.'

'You won't do badly,' the bearded man assured him. 'Hem, hem . . . One more thing . . .'

'Pray speak . . .'

'That succubus that haunts men at night and torments them . . . Which Her Enlightened Ladyship the Duchess has ordered killed . . . I believe there's no need. For the ghoul doesn't bother anyone, in truth . . . Yes, it occasionally haunts . . . Bedevils a little—'

'But nobbut adults,' Malatesta quickly interrupted.

'You took the words out of my mouth, friend. All in all, the succubus doesn't harm anyone. And recently there's been no word about it at all. Doubtless, it would be scared of you, Master Witcher. What, then, is the point of tormenting it? Why, you aren't lacking ready cash, sire. And were you to be short . . .'

'Something could be transferred to my account at Cianfanellis' bank,' Geralt said with stony countenance. 'To the witcher's pension fund.'

'So be it.'

'Then not a single blond hair on the succubus' head will be harmed.'

'Farewell, then.' The two vineyards stood up. 'Feast in peace, we shan't disturb. It's a holiday today. A tradition. Here, in Toussaint, tradition—'

'Is sacred,' said Geralt. 'I know.'

*

The party at the next table were making another noisy Yuletide prophecy, carried out with the help of balls fashioned from the soft inside of cakes and bones left over from a carp. The wine was flowing as they did so. The innkeeper and his serving girls were rushed off their feet, hurrying to and fro with jugs.

'The famous succubus,' remarked Reynart, serving himself more cabbage, 'began the memorable series of witcher contracts that you took on in Toussaint. Then things speeded up and you couldn't keep the customers away. Funny, I don't remember which vineyard gave you the first contract . . .'

'You weren't present. It happened the day after the audience with the duchess. Which you didn't attend either, as a matter of fact.'

'No wonder. It was a private audience.'

'Private, huh,' snorted Geralt. 'It was attended by some twenty people, not counting the motionless lackeys, youthful pages and a bored jester. Among that number was Le Goff, the chamberlain with the appearance and smell of a confectioner, and several magnates bowing under the weight of their golden chains. There were several coves in black: councillors, or perhaps judges. There was the baron with the Bull's Head coat of arms I met in Caed Myrkvid. There was, naturally, Fringilla Vigo, a person evidently close to the duchess.

'And there were we, our entire gang, including Milva in male costume. Ha, I was wrong to speak of the *entire* company. Dandelion was not with us. Dandelion, or rather Viscount What's-His-Name, sat sprawled in a curule seat on Her Pointy-Nosed Highness Anarietta's right hand and postured like a peacock. Like a real pet.

'Anarietta, Fringilla and Dandelion were the only people seated. No one else was permitted to sit down. And anyway I was glad they didn't make me kneel.

'The duchess listened to my tale, seldom interrupting, fortunately. When, however, I briefly related the results of the conversations with the druidesses, she wrung her hands, in a gesture suggesting worry as sincere as it was exaggerated. I know that sounds like some sort of bloody oxymoron, but believe me, Reynart, in her case that's how it was.'

*

'Oh, oh,' said Duchess Anna Henrietta, wringing her hands. 'You have sorely worried us, Master Geralt. Truly do we tell you that sorrow fills our heart.'

She sniffed through her pointed nose, held out her hand, and Dandelion at once pressed a monogrammed cambric handkerchief into it. The duchess brushed both her cheeks with the handkerchief so as not to wipe the powder off.

'Oh, oh,' she repeated. 'So the druidesses knew nothing about Ciri? They were unable to help you? Was all your effort then wasted and your journey in vain?'

'Certainly not in vain,' Geralt answered with conviction. 'I confess I'd counted on obtaining some concrete information or hints from the druids that would at least explain in the most general way why Ciri is the object of such a relentless pursuit. The druids, though, couldn't or didn't want to help me, and in this respect I indeed gained nothing. But . . .'

He paused for a moment. Not for dramatic effect. He was wondering how frank he could be in front of the entire auditorium.

'I know that Ciri's alive,' he finally said dryly. 'She was probably wounded. She's still in danger. But she's alive.'

Anna Henrietta gasped, applied the handkerchief again and squeezed Dandelion's arm.

'We pledge you our help and support,' she said. 'Stay in Toussaint as long as you wish. You ought to know that we have resided in Cintra, and we knew and were fond of Pavetta, we knew and liked little Ciri. We are with you with all our heart, Master Geralt. If needs be you shall have the assistance of our scholars and astrologers. Our libraries and book collections stand open before you. You are certain, we deeply trust, to find some track, sign or spoor that will indicate the right way. Do not act hastily. You need not hurry. You may stay here as you like; you are a most welcome guest.'

'Thank you, Your Grace.' Geralt bowed. 'Thank you for your kindness and favour. We must, nonetheless, set off as soon as we have rested a little. Ciri is still in danger. When we stay in one place too long the threat not only grows, but begins to endanger the people who show us kindness. And unrelated strangers. I wouldn't want to allow that to happen for anything.'

The duchess was silent for some time, stroking Dandelion's forearm with measured movements, as you would a cat.

'Your words are noble and virtuous,' she said at last. 'But you have nothing to fear. Our knights routed the ne'er-do-wells pursuing you so that none escaped with his life. Viscount Julian told us about it. Anyone who dares to trouble you will meet the same fate. You are under our care and protection.'

'I value that.' Geralt bowed again, under his breath cursing his knee – but not only his knee. 'Nonetheless I cannot omit to mention something Viscount Dandelion forgot to tell Your Enlightened Ladyship. The ne'er-do-wells from the mine who pursued me to Belhaven, and whom your valiant knighthood vanquished in Caed Myrkvid, were indeed ne'er-do-wells of the first water, but they bore Nilfgaardian livery.'

'And what of it?'

It was on the tip of his tongue to say that if the Nilfgaardians had captured Aedirn in twenty days, they would need just twenty minutes to capture her little duchy.

'There is a war on,' he said instead. 'What happened in Belhaven and Caed Myrkvid may be regarded as a diversion at the rear. That usually results in repression. In wartime—'

'The war,' the duchess interrupted him, raising her pointy nose, 'is definitely over. We wrote to our cousin, Emhyr var Emreis, regarding this matter. We sent a memorandum to him, in which we demanded that he put an end forthwith to the senseless bloodletting. The war is sure to be over, peace is sure to have been concluded.'

'Not exactly,' replied Geralt coldly. 'Fire and sword are wreaking havoc on the far side of the Yaruga, blood is flowing. There's nothing to indicate that it's about to end. Quite the contrary, I'd say.'

He immediately regretted what he'd said.

'What?' The duchess's nose, it appeared, became even pointier, and a nasty, grindingly snarling note sounded in her voice. 'Did I hear right? The war is still raging? Why wasn't I informed of this? Minister Tremblay?'

'Your Grace, I . . .' mumbled one of the golden chains, genuflecting. 'I didn't want to . . . concern . . . worry . . . Your Grace . . .'

'Guard!' Her Majesty howled. 'To the tower with him! You are in disfavour, Lord Tremblay! In disfavour! Lord Chamberlain! Mister Secretary!'

'At your service, Your Enlightened Ladyship . . .'

'Have the chancellery immediately issue a severe note to our cousin, the Emperor of Nilfgaard. We demand that he immediately, and I mean immediately, stops warring and makes peace. For war and discord are evil things! Discord ruins and accord builds!'

'Your Grace,' mumbled the chamberlain-confectioner, as white as castor sugar, 'is absolutely right.'

'What are you still doing here, gentlemen? We have issued our orders! Be off with you, this instant!'

Geralt looked around discreetly. The courtiers had stony expressions, from which he concluded that similar incidents were nothing new at the court. He made a firm resolution only to say 'yes' to the Lady Duchess in future.

Anarietta brushed the tip of her nose with her handkerchief and then smiled at Geralt.

'As you see,' she said, 'your anxieties were unfounded. You have nothing to fear and may rest here as long as you like.'

'Yes, Your Grace.'

In the silence, the tapping of a death watch beetle in one of the pieces of antique furniture could be heard distinctly. As could the curses being hurled by a groom in a distant courtyard.

'We also have a request for you, Master Geralt,' Anarietta interrupted the silence. 'In your capacity as a witcher.'

'Yes, Your Grace.'

'It is the request of many noble ladies of Toussaint, and ours at the same time. A nocturnal monster is plaguing local homesteads. This devil, this phantom, this succubus in female form, so lewd that we daren't describe it, torments our virtuous and faithful husbands. She haunts bedchambers at night, committing lewd acts and disgusting perversions, which modesty forbids us to speak of. You, as an expert, surely know what the matter is.'

'Yes, Your Grace.'

'The ladies of Toussaint ask you to put an end to this abomination. And we add our voice to this request. And assure you of our generosity.'

'Yes, Your Grace.'

*

Angoulême found the Witcher and the vampire in the palace grounds, where they were enjoying a walk and a discreet conversation.

'You won't believe me,' she panted. 'You won't believe me when I tell you . . . But it's the honest truth . . .'

'Spit it out.'

'Reynart de Bois-Fresnes, the Chequered Knight errant, is standing in a queue before the ducal treasurer with the other knights errant. And do you know for what? For his monthly salary! The queue, I'm telling you, is half an arrow-shot long, and it's sparkling with coats of arms. I asked Reynart what it's all about and he said errant knights also get hungry.'

'So what's the problem?'

'You must be joking! It's a knight errant's noble vocation to wander. Not for a monthly salary!'

'The one does not preclude the other,' said the vampire Regis very gravely. 'Truly. Believe me, Angoulême.'

'Believe him, Angoulême,' said Geralt dryly. 'Stop running around the palace looking for scandal and go and keep Milva company. She's in a dreadful state, she oughtn't to be alone.'

'True. I think auntie's got her period, because she's as angry as a wasp. I think—'

'Angoulême!'

'I'm going, I'm going.'

Geralt and Regis stopped beside a bed of slightly wilted centifolia roses. But they were unable to talk any longer. A very thin man in an elegant cloak the colour of umber emerged from behind the orangery.

'Good day,' he bowed, brushing his knees with a marten kalpak. 'May I ask which of you gentlemen is the witcher, known as Geralt, and renowned for his craft?'

'I am he.'

'I am Jean Catillon, steward of the Castel Toricella vineyards. The fact is that a witcher would serve us very well in the vineyard. I wished to find out if you would not consider . . .'

'What is it about?'

'It is thus,' began steward Catillon. 'Owing to this damned war, merchants visit more seldom, our reserves are growing, and there is less and less space for the barrels. We thought it was a small problem, for beneath the castles the cellars go on for miles, ever deeper. I think the cellars extend to the centre of the earth. We also found a little cellar under Toricella, beautiful, if you please, vaulted, not too dry, not too damp, just right for the wine to mature—'

'What of it?' the Witcher interrupted.

'It turned out that some kind of monster prowls in the cellar, if you please, which probably came from the depths of the earth. It burned two people, melted their flesh to the bone, and blinded another, because, he, I mean the monster, sire, spits and pukes some sort of caustic lye—'

'A solpuga,' Geralt stated bluntly. 'Also called a venomer.'

'Well, well,' smiled Regis. 'You can see for yourself, Lord Catillon, that you're dealing with an expert. This expert, one might say, is a godsend. And have you turned to the renowned local knights errant in this matter? The duchess has an entire regiment of them, and missions like these are, let's face it, their speciality, their raison d'être.'

'Not at all.' Steward Catillon shook his head. 'Their raison d'être is to protect the roads and passes, for if the merchants couldn't get here, we'd all be reduced to beggary. What's more, the knights are bold and valiant, but only on horseback. None of them would venture under the ground. What's more, they're expen—'

He broke off and fell silent. He had the expression of a person who, if he could, would kick himself. And greatly regretted it.

'They're expensive,' Geralt finished off the sentence, without excessive spitefulness. 'So you ought to know, good sir, that I'm *more* expensive. It's a free market. And there's free competition. If we sign a contract, I'll dismount and head underground. Think it through, but don't ponder too long, for I'm not staying long in Toussaint.'

'You astonish me,' said Regis, as soon as the steward had gone. 'Has the witcher in you suddenly revived? Are you accepting contracts? Going after monsters?'

'I'm astonished myself,' replied Geralt frankly. 'I reacted instinctively, prompted by an inexplicable impulse. I'll weasel out of it. I'll treat every quote they offer as too low. Always. Let's get back to our conversation . . .'

'Hold on.' The vampire gestured with his eyes. 'Something tells me you have more clients.'

Geralt swore under his breath. Two knights were walking towards him down the cypress-lined avenue.

He recognised the first at once; the huge bull's head on a snow-white tabard couldn't have been confused with any other crest. The other knight – tall, grey-haired, with nobly angular physiognomy, as though carved from granite – had five gold demi fleurs-de-lis on his blue tunic.

Having stopped at the regulation distance of two paces, the knights bowed. Geralt and Regis returned the bows, after which the four of them observed a silence of ten heartbeats as decreed by chivalric custom.

'Gentlemen,' said Bull's Head, 'may I introduce Baron Palmerin de Launfal. My name is, as you may recall—'

'Baron de Peyrac-Peyran. How could we not?'

'We have an urgent matter for Master Witcher.' Peyrac-Peyran got down to business. 'Regarding, so to speak, a professional undertaking.'

'Yes.'

'In private.'

'I have no secrets from Master Regis.'

'But the noble gentlemen undoubtedly do,' the vampire smiled. 'For which reason, with your permission, I shall go to look at that charming little pavilion, probably a temple of quiet and private contemplation. Lord de Peyrac-Peyran . . . Lord de Launfal . . .'

They exchanged bows.

'I'm all ears.' Geralt interrupted the silence, having no intention of waiting for the tenth heartbeat to die away.

'The matter,' Peyrac-Peyran lowered his voice and looked around timidly, 'concerns this succubus . . . Well, this nocturnal phantom, the one that haunts. Which the duchess and the ladies have commissioned you to destroy. Have they promised you much for the killing of the spectre?'

'I beg your pardon, but that's a trade secret.'

'But of course,' responded Palmerin de Launfal, the knight with

81

the fleur-de-lis cross. 'Your conduct is commendable. Indeed, I greatly fear that I shall be insulting you with this proposal, but in spite of that I submit it. Relinquish the contract, Master Witcher. Don't go after the succubus, leave it in peace. Saying nothing to the ladies or the duchess. And 'pon my word, we, the gentlemen of Toussaint, will outbid the ladies' offer. Bewildering you with our generosity.'

'A proposal,' said the Witcher coldly, 'that is indeed not very far from an insult.'

'Sir Geralt,' Palmerin de Launfal's face was hard and grave. 'I shall tell you what emboldened us to make the offer. It was the rumour about you that said you only kill monsters that represent a danger. A real danger. Not an imagined one, stemming from ignorance or prejudice. Permit me to say that the succubus doesn't threaten or harm anybody. It haunts people's dreams. From time to time . . . And bedevils a little . . .'

'But exclusively adults,' Peyrac-Peyran added quickly.

'The ladies of Toussaint,' said Geralt looking around, 'would not be happy to learn of this conversation. The duchess likeways.'

'We agree absolutely with you,' mumbled Palmerin de Launfal. 'Discretion is recommended in every respect. One should let sleeping bigots lie.'

'Open me an account in one of the local dwarven banks,' Geralt said slowly and softly. 'And astonish me with your generosity. I nonetheless warn you that I'm not easily astonished.'

'And we shall nonetheless do our best,' promised Peyrac-Peyran proudly.

They exchanged farewell bows.

Regis, who had naturally heard everything with his vampirish hearing, returned.

'Now,' he said without a smile, 'you may also naturally claim that that was an involuntary reaction and an inexplicable impulse. But you'll be hard pressed to explain away the open bank account.'

Geralt looked somewhere high up, far away, above the tops of the cypresses.

'Who knows,' he said, 'perhaps we'll spend a few days here, after all. Bearing in mind Milva's ribs, perhaps even more than a few days. Perhaps a few weeks? So it won't hurt if we gain financial independence for that time.'

*

'Hence the account at the Cianfanellis',' nodded Reynart de Bois-Fresnes. 'Well, well. If the duchess learned about this there would certainly be a reshuffle, a new distribution of patents of nobility. Ha, perhaps I would be promoted? I give my word, I truly regret not having the makings of an informer. Tell me about the famous feast I was so looking forward to. I so wished to be at that banquet, to eat and drink! But they sent me abroad, to the watchtower, in the cold, foul weather. Eh, what a blight, the doom of a knight . . .'

'The great and grandiosely heralded feast,' began Geralt, 'was preceded by serious preparations. We had to find Milva, who'd hidden in the stables, and convince her that the fate of Ciri and almost the entire world depended on her participation in the banquet. We almost had to force her into a dress. Then we had to make Angoulême promise she would avoid saying "fuck" and "arse". Once we'd finally achieved everything and intended to relax with a glass of wine, Chamberlain Le Goff appeared, smelling of icing sugar and puffed up like a swine's bladder.'

*

'In the given circumstances, I must stress,' began Chamberlain Le Goff nasally, 'that there are no inferior places at Her Grace's table. No one has the right to feel piqued by the place assigned to him or her. We in Toussaint, nonetheless, avidly observe ancient traditions and customs, and according to those customs—'

'Get to the point, sir.'

'The feast is tomorrow. I must execute a seating plan according to honour and rank.'

'Naturally,' said the Witcher gravely. 'I'll tell you what's what. The most noble of us, both in rank and honour, is Dandelion.'

'Viscount Julian,' said the chamberlain, putting on airs, 'is an extraordinarily honoured guest. And thus will sit at Her Grace's right hand.'

83

'Naturally,' the Witcher repeated, as grave as death itself. 'And regarding us, he didn't reveal our ranks, titles and honours, did he?'

'He only revealed—' the chamberlain cleared his throat '—that my lords and ladies are incognito on a knightly mission, and he was not able to betray its details or your true names, coats of arms and titles, since they are protected by vows.'

'Precisely. So what's the problem?'

'Why, I must seat you! You are guests, and moreover the viscount's comrades, so in any case I will place you nearer the head of the table . . . among the barons. But, of course, it cannot be that you are all equal, lords and ladies, for it is never thus that everyone is equal. If by rank or birth one of you is more superior, he ought to sit at the top table, near the duchess . . .'

'He,' the Witcher unhesitatingly pointed at the vampire, who was standing close by, raptly admiring a tapestry that took up almost the whole wall, 'is a count. But hush! It's a secret.'

'Understood,' the chamberlain almost choked in amazement. 'In the given circumstances . . . I shall put him on the right of Countess Notturna, nobly born aunt of the Lady Duchess.'

'Neither you nor the aunt will regret it.' Geralt was poker-faced. 'He has no equal either in comportment or in the conversational arts.'

'I'm glad to hear it. You meanwhile, Lord of Rivia, will sit beside the Esteemed Lady Fringilla. As tradition dictates. You bore her to the Vat, you are . . . hmmm . . . her champion, as 'twere . . .'

'Understood.'

'Very well. Ah, Your Grace . . .'

'Yes?' the vampire said in surprise. He had just moved away from the tapestry, which depicted a fight between giants and cyclopes.

'Nothing, nothing,' smiled Geralt. 'We're just chatting.'

'Aha.' Regis nodded. 'I don't know if you've noticed, gentlemen . . . But that cyclops in the tapestry, the one with the club . . . Look at his toes. He, let's be frank, has two left feet.'

'Verily,' Chamberlain Le Goff confirmed without a trace of amazement. 'There are plenty of tapestries like that in Beauclair. The master who wove them was a true master. But he drank an awful lot. As artists do.'

'It's time we were going,' said the Witcher, avoiding the eyes of the girls tipsy on wine who were glancing at him from the table, where they'd been amusing themselves with fortune-telling. 'Let's be off, Reynart. Let's pay, mount up and ride to Beauclair.'

'I know where you're hurrying,' the knight grinned. 'Don't worry, your green-eyed lady is waiting. It's only just struck midnight. Tell me about the feast.'

'I'll tell you and we'll ride.'

'And we'll ride.'

*

The sight of the table, arranged in a gigantic horseshoe, signalled emphatically that autumn was passing and winter was coming. Game in all possible forms and varieties dominated the delicacies heaped on great serving dishes and platters. There were huge quarters of boar, haunches and saddles of venison, various forcemeats, aspics and pink slices of meat, autumnally garnished with mushrooms, cranberries, plum jam and hawthorn berry sauce. There were autumn fowls – grouse, capercaillie, and pheasant, decoratively served with wings and tails, there was roast guinea fowl, quail, partridge, garganey, snipe, hazel grouse and mistle thrush. There were also genuine dainties, such as fieldfare, roasted whole, without having been drawn, since the juniper berries with which the innards of these small birds are full form a natural stuffing. There was salmon trout from mountain lakes, there was zander, there was burbot and pike's liver. A green accent was given by raiponce, late-spring salad, which, if such a need arose, could even be dug up from under the snow.

Mistletoe took the place of flowers.

The evening's ornament was placed on a large silver tray in the middle, forming the centrepiece of the high table at which Duchess Anarietta and the most distinguished guests were seated. Among truffles, flowers cut from carrots, quartered lemons and artichoke hearts lay a huge sturgeon, and on its back was a whole roast heron, standing on one leg, holding a gold ring in its upraised beak.

'I vow on the heron,' cried Peyrac-Peyran, the baron with the bull's head in his arms whom the Witcher knew well, standing and lifting up his goblet. 'I vow on the heron to defend knightly honour and the virtue of ladies and I vow never, ever to yield the field to anyone!'

The oath was rewarded with thunderous applause. And the eating began.

'I vow on the heron!' yelled another knight, with bushy whiskers pointing pugnaciously upwards. 'I promise to defend the borders and Her Grace Anna Henrietta to the last drop of my blood! And in order to prove my loyalty, I vow to paint a heron on my shield and fight incognito for a year, concealing my name and arms, calling myself the Knight of the White Heron! I wish Her Grace good health!'

'Good health! Happiness! Viva! Long live Her Grace!'

Anarietta thanked them with a faint nod of her head, decorated with a diamond-encrusted tiara. She had so many diamonds on her that she could have scratched glass just by passing. Beside her sat Dandelion, smiling foolishly. A little further away, between two matrons, sat Emiel Regis. He was dressed in a black, velvet jacket, looking like a vampire. He was waiting on the ladies and entertaining them with his conversation. They listened with fascination.

Geralt took the platter with the zander garnished with parsley and served Fringilla Vigo, who sat on his left, and was dressed in a gown of mauve satin and a gorgeous amethyst necklace, which sat prettily on her breast. Fringilla, watching him from beneath her black eyelashes, raised her goblet and smiled enigmatically.

'Your good health, Geralt. I'm glad they put us together.'

'Don't count your chickens,' he replied with a smile, for he was actually in decent humour. 'The feast has only just begun.'

'On the contrary. It has lasted long enough for you to have complimented me. How long must I wait?'

'You are enchantingly beautiful.'

'Slowly, slowly, with restraint!' She laughed – he would have sworn – entirely sincerely. 'At this rate I'm afraid to think where we might end up by the end of the banquet. Start with . . . Hmm . . . Say that I have a tasteful dress and that mauve suits me.'

'Mauve suits you. Although I confess I like you most in white.'

He saw a challenge in her emerald eyes. He was afraid to take it up. He was in such good humour.

Cahir and Milva had been seated opposite. Cahir was sitting between two very young and ceaselessly twittering noblewomen, perhaps the barons' daughters. The archer, meanwhile, was accompanied by an older, gloomy knight with a pockmarked face, who was as quiet as a stone.

A little further away, meanwhile, sat Angoulême, calling the tune – and making a racket – among some young knights errant.

'What's this?' she yelled, picking up a silver knife with a rounded end. 'Without a point? Are they afraid we'll start stabbing each other or what?'

'Such knives,' explained Fringilla, 'have been used in Beauclair since the times of Duchess Carolina Roberta, Anna Henrietta's grandmamma. It infuriated Caroberta when during banquets the guests used the knives to pick their teeth. And you can't pick your teeth with a knife with a rounded end.'

'You cannot,' agreed Angoulême, contorting her face roguishly. 'Luckily they've also given us forks!'

She pretended to put the fork in her mouth, but stopped on seeing Geralt's menacing look. The young knightling on her right chuckled shrilly. Geralt picked up a dish of duck in aspic and served Fringilla. He saw Cahir doing his uttermost to satisfy the barons' daughters' whims, while they gazed at him. He saw the young knights buzzing around Angoulême, vying with each other to pass her dishes and chuckling at her foolish jokes.

He saw Milva crumbling bread, staring at the tablecloth.

Fringilla seemed to read his thoughts.

'She's done poorly, your taciturn companion,' she whispered, leaning towards him. 'Why, it can happen when a seating plan is being drawn up. Baron de Trastamara isn't blessed with courtliness. Or eloquence.'

'Perhaps that's better,' Geralt said softly. 'A courtier drooling graciousness would've been worse. I know Milva.'

'Are you sure?' She glanced at him swiftly. 'You aren't measuring her according to your own standards, are you? Which, incidentally, are quite cruel.'

He didn't reply, but instead served her, pouring her wine. And decided it was high time to clear up a few matters.

'You're a sorceress, aren't you?'

'I am,' she admitted, masking her surprise extremely deftly. 'How did you know?'

'I can sense the aura,' he said without going into details. 'And I'm skilled.'

'To be quite clear,' she said a moment later, 'it wasn't my intention to deceive anybody. I have no obligation to flaunt my profession or put on a pointed hat and black cloak. Why use me to frighten children? I have the right to remain incognito.'

'Undeniably.'

'I'm in Beauclair because the largest, best-stocked library in the known world is here. Apart from university libraries, naturally. But universities are jealous of giving access to their shelves, and here I'm a relation and good friend of Anarietta and can do as I wish.'

'I envy you.'

'During the audience, Anarietta hinted that the book collection may conceal a clue which may be useful to you. Don't be put off by her theatrical gushiness. That's just the way she is. And it really is likely that you'll find something in the library. Why, it's quite probable. It's enough to know what to look for and where.'

'Indeed. Nothing more.'

'The enthusiasm of your answers truly lifts my spirits and encourages me to talk.' She narrowed her eyes slightly. 'I can guess the reason. You don't trust me, do you?'

'A little more grouse, perhaps?'

'I vow on the heron!' A young knight from the end of the horseshoe stood up and blindfolded himself with a sash given him by the lady sitting next to him. 'I vow not to take off this sash until the marauders from the Cervantes pass are entirely wiped out.'

The duchess gave her acknowledgement with a gracious nod of her diamond-sparkling head.

Geralt hoped Fringilla wouldn't continue on the subject. He was mistaken.

'You don't believe me and you don't trust me,' she said. 'You've given me a doubly painful blow. You don't only doubt that I sincerely want to help, but neither do you believe I can. Oh, Geralt! You've cut my pride and lofty ambition to the quick.'

'Listen—'

'No!' She raised her knife and fork as though threatening him. 'Don't try to apologise. I can't bear men who apologise.'

'What kind of men *can* you bear?'

She narrowed her eyes, and continued to hold her cutlery like daggers about to strike.

'The list is long,' she said slowly. 'And I don't want to bore you with the details. I merely state that men who are ready to go to the end of the world for their beloved, dauntlessly, scorning risk and danger, occupy quite a high position. And those that don't quit, even though there seems to be no chance of success.'

'And the other positions on the list?' he blurted out. 'The other men to your taste? Also madmen?'

'And what is true manliness—' she tilted her head playfully '—if not class and recklessness blended together in the correct proportions?'

'Lords and ladies, barons and knights!' shouted Chamberlain Le Goff loudly, standing up and raising a gigantic cup in both hands. 'In the given circumstances I shall take the liberty of offering a toast: to Her Enlightened Ladyship, Duchess Anna Henrietta.'

'Health and happiness!'

'Hurrah!'

'Long live the duchess! Vivat!'

'And now, lords and ladies . . . .' The chamberlain put the cup down and nodded solemnly towards the liveried servants. 'Now . . . The Magna Bestia!'

An enormous roast on a dish, filling the hall with its marvellous aroma, was carried in by four servants on something resembling a sedan chair.

'The Magna Bestia!' roared the revellers as one. 'Hurrah! The Magna Bestia!'

'What bloody beast is that?' Angoulême expressed her anxiety loudly. 'I'm not going to eat it until I find out what it is.'

'It's an elk,' Geralt explained. 'A roast elk.'

'Not just any elk,' said Milva, after clearing her throat. 'That bull weighed seven hundredweight.'

'With a fine six-point rack. Seven hundredweight and forty pounds,' gruffly commented the tight-lipped baron sitting beside her. They were the first words he'd uttered from the start of the banquet.

Perhaps it would have been the beginning of a conversation, but the archer blushed, fixed her gaze on the tablecloth and resumed her crumbling of bread.

But Geralt had taken Fringilla's words to heart.

'Did you, my lord baron,' he asked, 'bring down that magnificent bull?'

'Not I,' said the tight-lipped baron. 'My son-in-law. He's an excellent shot. But that's a male topic, if I may say so . . . I beg for forgiveness. One shouldn't bore the ladies . . .'

'With what bow?' asked Milva, still staring at the tablecloth. 'No doubt nothing weaker than a seventy-pounder.'

'A laminate. Layers of yew, acacia and ash, glued together with sinews,' the baron slowly responded, visibly surprised. 'A double-bent zefar. Seventy-five pounds draw.'

'And the draw length?'

'Twenty-nine inches.' The baron was speaking slower and slower and he seemed to be spitting out each word.

'A veritable ballista,' Milva said calmly. 'You could down a stag at even a hundred paces with a bow like that. If the archer was genuinely able.'

'Aye,' wheezed the baron, as though somewhat piqued. 'I can hit a pheasant from five and twenty paces, if I may say so.'

'From a score and five,' Milva raised her head, 'I can hit a squirrel.'

The baron, disconcerted, gave a slight cough and quickly served the archer with food and drink.

'A good bow,' he muttered, 'is half the success. But no less important as the quality, if I may say so, of the shot. So you see, my lady, according to me an arrow—'

'Good health to Her Grace Anna Henrietta! Good health to Viscount Julian de Lettenhove!'

'Cheers! *Vivant!*'

'. . . and she fucked him!' Angoulême finished another foolish anecdote. The young knights roared with laughter.

The barons' daughters, called Queline and Nique, listened to Cahir's tales open-mouthed, their eyes sparkling and their cheeks flushed. At the top table the entire upper aristocracy were listening to Regis's disquisitions. Only isolated words reached Geralt's ears – despite his witcher's hearing – but he worked out that the talk was of spectres, strigas, succubuses and vampires. Regis waved a silver fork and demonstrated that the best remedy against vampires is silver, a precious metal the barest touch of which is absolutely fatal to them. And garlic, asked the ladies? Garlic is also effective, admitted Regis, but socially troublesome, since it stinks awfully.

The band on the gallery played fiddles and pipes, and the acrobats, jugglers and fire-eaters showed off their artistry. The jester tried to amuse the guests, but what chance did he have against Angoulême? Then a bear tamer appeared with a bear, which – to general delight – did a dump on the floor. Angoulême became morose and subdued – it was difficult to compete with something like that.

The pointy-nosed duchess suddenly fell into a fury, and one of the barons fell out of favour and was escorted to the tower for some imprudent word. Few – apart from those directly involved – seemed bothered by the matter.

'You won't be leaving here in a hurry, you doubter,' said Fringilla Vigo, swinging her glass. 'Although you'd leave at once if you could, nothing will come of it.'

'Don't read my thoughts, please.'

'I'm sorry. They were so strong I couldn't help it.'

'You've no idea how many times I've heard that.'

'You've no idea how much I know. Eat some artichokes, please, they're good for you, good for the heart. The heart's a vital organ in a man. The second most important.'

'I thought the most important things were class and recklessness.'

'The qualities of the spirit ought to go hand in hand with the attributes of the body. From that comes perfection.'

'No one's perfect.'

'That's not an argument. One ought to try. Do you know what? I think I'll have those hen grouse.'

She cut the bird up on her plate so quickly and violently it made the Witcher shudder.

91

'You won't be leaving here in a hurry,' she said. 'Firstly, you have no reason to. Nothing's threatening you—'

'Nothing at all, indeed,' he interrupted, unable to stop himself. 'The Nilfgaardians will take fright at the stern note issued by the ducal chancellery. And even if they risked it they would be driven from here by the knights errant taking vows on the heron with their eyes blindfold.'

'You're not in danger,' she repeated, paying no attention to his sarcasm. 'Toussaint is generally regarded as an insignificant fairy-tale duchy, ridiculous and unreal, and in a state of permanent intoxication and unending bacchic joy owing to the production of wine. It isn't really treated seriously by anybody, but enjoys privileges. After all, it supplies wine, and without wine, as everyone knows, there's no life. For which reason no agents, spies or secret services operate in Toussaint. And there's no need for an army, it's enough to have blindfolded knights errant. No one will attack Toussaint. I can see from your face I haven't thoroughly convinced you?'

'Not thoroughly.'

'Pity,' Fringilla squinted. 'I like doing things thoroughly. I don't like anything that's incomplete, and neither do I like half measures. Or anything left unsaid. Thus I will add: Fulko Artevelde, the Prefect of Riedburne, thinks you're dead. He was informed by fugitives that the druidesses burned you all alive. Fulko is doing what he can to cover up the issue, which bears the hallmarks of a scandal. It's in his interest to do so; he has his career in mind. Even when he finds out you're alive it'll be too late. The version he gave in his reports will be binding.'

'You know a great deal.'

'I've never concealed that. So the argument about being pursued by Nilfgaard can be eliminated. And there aren't any other arguments in favour of a rapid departure.'

'Interesting . . .'

'But true. One can leave Toussaint via four mountain passes, leading towards the four points of the compass. Which pass will you choose? The druidesses told you nothing and refused to cooperate. The elf from the mountains has vanished . . .'

'You really do know a great deal.'

'We've already established that.'

'And you wish to help me.'

'But you reject that help. You don't believe in the sincerity of my intentions. You don't trust me.'

'Listen, I—'

'Don't explain yourself. And eat some more artichokes.'

Someone else had made a vow on the heron. Cahir was paying the barons' daughters compliments.

Angoulême, now tipsy, could be heard throughout the entire hall. The tight-lipped baron, excited by the discourse on bows and arrows, had begun to dance attendance on Milva.

'Please, won't you try some wild boar, miss. Oh, if I may say so . . . There are fields of crops on my estates dug up by whole herds of them, if I may say so.'

'Oh.'

'You can come across some fine animals, three-hundredweight specimens . . . Height of the season . . . If, miss, you'd express a desire . . . We could, so to speak, go hunting together . . .'

'We shan't be staying here so long.' Milva looked strangely enquiringly at Geralt. 'For we have more serious tasks than hunting, if you excuse me, sir.

'Although,' she added quickly, seeing that the baron was looking gloomy, 'I would most eagerly go hunting game with Your Lordship if there is time.'

The baron's face lit up at once.

'If not the chase,' he declared enthusiastically, 'then at least I must invite you to my residence. I will show you my antler, trophy, pipe and sabre collections, so to speak . . .'

Milva fixed her eyes on the tablecloth.

The baron seized a tray of fieldfares, served her and then filled her wine glass.

'Forgive me,' he said. 'I am no courtier. I don't know how to entertain. I'm pretty wretched at courtly discourse.'

'I was raised in the forest.' Milva cleared her throat. 'I esteem silence.'

Fringilla found Geralt's hand under the table and squeezed it hard. Geralt looked her in the eyes. He couldn't guess what was hidden in them.

'I trust you,' he said. 'I believe in the sincerity of your intentions.'

'You aren't lying?'

'I swear on the heron.'

*

The town sentry must have had a few too many Yuletide tipples, for he was swaying. He banged his halberd against a signboard and loudly, though incoherently, announced it was ten of the clock, although it was actually well after midnight.

'Go to Beauclair by yourself,' Reynart de Bois-Fresnes said unexpectedly as soon as they'd left the tavern. 'I'm staying in town. Until tomorrow. Farewell, Witcher.'

Geralt knew the knight had a lady-friend in town whose husband travelled a lot on business. They'd never talked about it, for men don't talk about such matters.

'Farewell, Reynart. Deal with the skoffin. Don't let it go off.'

'There's a frost.'

There was a frost. The narrow streets were empty and tenebrous. The moonlight shone on the roofs, gleamed brilliantly on the icicles hanging from the eaves, but didn't reach the streets. Roach's horseshoes rang on the cobblestones.

Roach, thought the Witcher, heading towards Beauclair Palace. *A shapely chestnut mare, a present from Anna Henrietta. And Dandelion.*

He spurred his horse on. He was in a hurry.

*

After the feast everybody met for breakfast, which they had become accustomed to taking in the servants' hall. They were always welcome there, God only knew why. Something hot was always found for them, straight from the saucepan, skillet or spit, and there was always bread, dripping, bacon, cheese and pickled mushrooms. A jug or two of some white or red produce of the famous local vineyards was never lacking.

They always went there. Since they had arrived at Beauclair two weeks before. Geralt, Regis, Angoulême and Milva. Only Dandelion broke his fast elsewhere.

'They serve him his dripping and scratchings in bed!' commented Angoulême. 'And they pay obeisance to him!'

Geralt was inclined to believe it was like that. And that day he decided to investigate.

*

He found Dandelion in the knights' hall. The poet was wearing a crimson beret, as big as a loaf of sourdough rye bread, and a matching doublet richly embroidered with golden thread. He was sitting on a curule seat with his lute in his lap and reacting with careless nods to the compliments of the ladies and courtiers surrounding him.

Anna Henrietta, fortunately, wasn't in sight. So Geralt without hesitation broke protocol and went boldly into action. Dandelion saw him at once.

'Lords and ladies,' he said pompously, waving a hand just like a real king, 'if you could leave us alone? The servants may also absent themselves!'

He clapped and before the echo had died away they were alone in the knights' hall with suits of armour, paintings, panoplies and the intense, lingering smell of the ladies' powder.

'What fun,' Geralt remarked without excessive malice. 'You shoo them away like that, do you? It must feel nice to issue orders with one lordly gesture, one clap, one regal frown. Watch as they scuttle backwards like crayfish, bending over towards you in a bow. What fun. Eh? My Lord Favourite?'

Dandelion grimaced.

'Is it about anything particular?' he asked sourly. 'Or just to talk for the sake of it?'

'Something particular. So particular, it couldn't be more so.'

'Say on, if you please.'

'We need three horses. That's for me, Cahir and Angoulême. And two unmounted packhorses. Together, three good steeds and two hacks. Hacks, well, as a last resort, mules, laden with vittles and feed. Your duchess must consider you worth that much, what? You've earned at least that, I trust?'

'There won't be a problem with it.' Dandelion, not looking at Geralt, got down to tuning his lute. 'I'm only surprised by your haste. I'd say it surprises me to the same degree as your foolish sarcasm does.'

'My haste surprises you?'

'You'd better believe it. October is ending, and the weather is visibly worsening. Snow will fall in the passes any day now.'

'And you're surprised by my haste.' the Witcher nodded. 'But I'm glad you reminded me. Sort out some warm clothing. Some furs.'

'I thought,' Dandelion said slowly, 'that we'd sit out the winter here. That we'd stay here—'

'If you want to stay,' Geralt blurted out, 'then stay.'

'I do.' Dandelion stood up suddenly and put down his lute. 'And I will.'

The Witcher audibly sucked in air and said nothing. He looked at a tapestry depicting a fight between a titan and a dragon. The titan, standing solidly on two left legs, was trying hard to break the dragon's jaw, and the dragon looked none too pleased about it.

'I'm staying,' Dandelion repeated. 'I love Anarietta. And she loves me.'

Geralt still said nothing.

'You'll have your horses,' continued the poet. 'I'll order them to prepare you a thoroughbred mare called Roach, naturally. You'll be equipped, well-stocked with food and warmly dressed. But I sincerely advise you to wait till the spring. Anarietta—'

'Am I hearing right?' The Witcher finally regained his voice. 'Or do my ears deceive me?'

'Your intellect,' snapped the troubadour, 'is certainly blunt. I can't speak for your other senses. I repeat: we love one another, Anarietta and I. I'm staying in Toussaint. With her.'

'In what role? Lover? Favourite? Or perhaps ducal consort?'

'I'm indifferent in principle to our formal and legal status,' Dandelion admitted frankly. 'But one cannot rule anything out. Including marriage.'

Geralt was silent again, contemplating the titan fighting the dragon.

96

'Dandelion,' he said finally. 'If you've been drinking, sober up. If you haven't taken a drink, do so. Then we'll talk.'

'I don't quite understand why you're talking like this.' Dandelion frowned.

'Then have a little think.'

'What about? Does my relationship with Anarietta shock you so much? Perhaps you'd like to appeal to my good sense. Skip it. I've thought the matter through. Anarietta loves me—'

'And do you know the saying "the favours of duchesses are uncertain"?' Geralt interrupted, 'Even if your Anarietta isn't flighty, and if you'll excuse the frankness she looks that way to me, then—'

'Then what?'

'Duchesses only marry musicians in fairy tales.'

'Firstly—' Dandelion puffed himself up '—even a boor like you must have heard of morganatic marriages. Must I give you examples from ancient and modern history? Secondly, it'll probably surprise you, but I'm not from the hoi-polloi. My people, the de Lettenhoves, come from—'

'I'm listening to you and I'm amazed,' Geralt interrupted again, losing his temper. 'Is my friend Dandelion really spouting such balderdash? Has my friend Dandelion really gone completely mad? Is Dandelion, whom I know as a realist, now beginning all of a sudden to live in the sphere of illusion? Open your bloody eyes, you dolt.'

'Aha,' Dandelion said slowly, tightening his lips. 'What a curious reversal of roles. I'm a blind man, and you meanwhile have suddenly become an attentive and astute observer. It was usually the other way around. And, out of interest, what don't I notice that you can see? Eh? What, according to you, should I open my eyes to?'

'For instance,' drawled the Witcher, 'the fact that your duchess is a spoiled child that has grown up into a spoiled and arrogant turkey cock. That fact she – fascinated by the novelty – has graced you with her charms, and will dump you immediately when a new busker with a newer and more beguiling repertoire comes along.'

'What you're saying is very base and vulgar. You're aware of that, I hope?'

'I'm aware of your lack of awareness. You're a lunatic, Dandelion.'

The poet said nothing and stroked the neck of his lute. Some time passed before he spoke.

'We set off from Brokilon on a deranged mission,' he began slowly. 'Taking a lunatic risk, we launched ourselves on an insane quest for a mirage without the slightest chance of success. A quest for a phantom, a daydream, an absolutely impossible ideal. We set off in pursuit like idiots, like madmen. But I didn't utter a word of complaint, Geralt. I didn't call *you* a madman. I didn't ridicule you. For you had hope and love in you. You were being guided by them on this reckless mission. I was too, as a matter of fact. But I've caught up with the mirage, and I was lucky enough that the dream came true. My mission is over. I've found what is so difficult to find. And I intend to keep it. Is that insanity? It would be insanity to give it up and let it slip through my fingers.'

Geralt was silent for as long as Dandelion had been earlier.

'Pure poetry,' he finally said. 'And it's difficult to rival you at that. I won't say another word. You've destroyed my arguments. Helped, I admit, by your quite apposite ones. Farewell, Dandelion.'

'Farewell, Geralt.'

*

The palace library really was immense. Its dimensions were at least twice those of the knights' hall. And it had a glass roof. Owing to which it was light. Although Geralt suspected it was bloody hot during the summer.

The aisles between the bookshelves were narrow and cramped so he walked cautiously, in order not to knock any books off. He also had to step over volumes piled up on the floor.

'I'm here.'

The centre of the library was lost among the books, which were arranged in piles and columns. Many were lying quite chaotically, individually or in picturesque heaps.

'Here, Geralt.'

He ventured among the canyons and ravines between the books. And found her.

She was kneeling among scattered incunables, leafing through and categorising them. She had on a modest grey dress, hitched up a little for convenience. Geralt found the sight extremely seductive.

'Don't be horrified by the mess,' she said, wiping her brow with her forearm, because she was wearing thin, dust-stained silk gloves. 'The books are being inventoried and catalogued. But the work was stopped at my request so I could be alone in the library. I can't bear strangers' eyes on me while I'm working.'

'I'm sorry. Shall I leave?'

'*You're* not a stranger.' She narrowed her eyes slightly. 'I enjoy . . . having your eyes on me. Don't stand like that. Sit here, on the books.'

He sat down on *A Description of the World* published in folio.

'This shambles—' Fringilla indicated around her with a brisk gesture '—has unexpectedly made my work easier. I was able to get to books that are normally lying somewhere at the bottom of a heap that's impossible to shift. The ducal librarians moved the mounds – a titanic effort! – thanks to which some literary treasures and rarities saw the light of day. Look. Ever seen anything like this?'

'*Speculum Aureum*? Yes, I have.'

'I apologise, I forgot. You've seen plenty. That was meant to be a compliment, not sarcasm. And take a glance at that. It's *Gesta Regum*. We'll start with that so you'll understand who your Ciri really is, whose blood flows in her veins . . . Your expression's sourer than usual, did you know? What's the reason?'

'Dandelion.'

'Tell me.'

He did. Fringilla listened, sitting cross-legged on a pile of books.

'Well,' she sighed, after he'd finished. 'I admit I expected something of the kind. I noticed long ago that Anarietta was betraying symptoms of lovesickness.'

'Love?' he snorted. 'Or a lordly whim.'

'You seem not to believe—' she looked at him piercingly '—in sincere and pure love?'

'My beliefs,' he said, 'aren't the subject of debate and are beside the point. It's about Dandelion and his stupid—'

He broke off, suddenly losing confidence.

'Love,' Fringilla said slowly, 'is like renal colic. Until you have an attack, you can't even imagine what it's like. And when people tell you about it you don't believe them.'

'There's something in that,' the Witcher agreed. 'But there are also differences. Good sense can't protect you from renal colic. Or cure it.'

'Love mocks good sense. That's its charm and beauty.'

'Stupidity, more like.'

She stood up and walked towards him, taking off her gloves. Her eyes were dark and profound beneath the curtains of her eyelashes. She smelled of ambergris, roses, library dust, decayed paper, minium and printing ink, oak gall ink, and strychnine, which was being used to poison the library mice. The smell had little in common with an aphrodisiac. So it was all the stranger that it worked on him.

'Don't you believe,' she said in a changed voice, 'in sudden impulses? In unforeseen attractions? In the impacts of fireballs flying along collision trajectories? In cataclysms?'

She held out a hand and touched his arms. He touched her arms. Their faces moved closer, still hesitantly, vigilantly, as though they were afraid of scaring away some very, very timid creature.

And then the fireballs collided and a cataclysm ensued.

They fell onto a pile of folio volumes which scattered in all directions under their weight. Geralt pushed his nose into Fringilla's cleavage, seized her powerfully and grabbed her by the knees. Various books impeded him from pulling her dress up above her waist, including *The Lives of the Prophets*, which was resplendent with intricate initials and illustrations, and *De Haemorrhoidibus*, a fascinating but controversial medical treatise. The Witcher pushed the volumes to one side, impatiently tugging at her skirt. Fringilla raised her hips enthusiastically.

Something was chafing her shoulder. She turned her head. *A Study of the Midwife's Art*. She quickly looked the other way so as not to tempt fate. *On Hot, Sulphurous Waters*. The temperature was rising indeed. Out of the corner of her eye she saw the frontispiece of the book her head was resting on. *Remarks on Inevitable Death*. Even better, she thought.

The Witcher was fighting with her underwear. She lifted her

hips, but this time gently, so it would look like an accidental movement and not provocative assistance. She didn't know him and didn't know how he reacted to women. Whether he didn't, perhaps, prefer the kind that pretend they don't know what they want, to those that do. And whether it would discourage him if her knickers were hard to take off.

The Witcher, however, wasn't betraying any signs of discouragement. On the contrary, one might say. Seeing that it was high time, Fringilla spread her legs enthusiastically and vigorously, knocking over a tower of books and fascicles, which slid down on them like an avalanche. A copy of *Mortgage Law* bound in embossed leather came to rest against her buttock and a copy of *Codex Diplomaticus* decorated with brass edgings against Geralt's wrist. Geralt assessed and exploited the situation at once, placing the bulky tome where it belonged. Fringilla squealed, because the edgings were cold. But only for a moment.

She sighed loudly, let go of the Witcher's hair, spread her arms and seized a book in each hand, her left grabbing *Descriptive Geometry*, her right *An Outline Study of Reptiles and Amphibians*. Geralt, holding her hips, knocked over another pile of books with an unwitting kick, but was nonetheless too occupied to worry about the volumes falling on him. Fringilla, moaning spasmodically, thrashed her head from side to side over the pages of *Remarks on Inevitable* . . .

The books subsided with a rustle, the sharp scent of old dust making their noses tingle.

Fringilla screamed. The Witcher didn't hear it, because her thighs were clenched against his ears. He threw off the bothersome *History of Wars* and *The Journal of All the Arts Necessary for a Happy Life*. Impatiently fighting with the buttons and fastenings of her bodice, he wandered from the south to the north, unintentionally reading the inscriptions on covers, spines, frontispieces and title pages. Under Fringilla's waist was *The Exemplary Farmer*. Under her armpit, not far from her small, charming, jauntily pert breast, *On Ineffective and Recalcitrant Shire Reaves*. Under her elbow *Economics; or, a Simple Exposition on how to Create, Divide up and Consume Wealth*.

He read *Remarks on Inevitable Death* with his mouth on her neck and his hands near *Shire Reaves* . . . Fringilla emitted a difficult to classify sound; neither a scream, a moan nor a sigh.

The bookshelves shook, piles of books trembled and tumbled down, arranging themselves like rocky inselbergs during a severe earthquake. Fringilla screamed. A rare book, the first edition of *De larvisscenicis et Figuriscomicis*, fell from its shelf with a crash, followed by *A Collection of General Horsemanship Commands*, taking down with it John of Attre's *Heraldry*, embellished with beautiful prints.

The Witcher groaned, kicking over more volumes as he jerked a leg straight. Fringilla screamed once again, long and loudly, knocking over *Contemplations; or, Meditations for Every Day of the Year*, an interesting anonymous work which had ended up on Geralt's back for no apparent reason. Geralt trembled and read above her shoulder, learning – like it or not – that *Remarks* . . . had been written by Dr Albertus Rivus, had been published by the Academia Cintrensis, and had been printed by the master typographer Johann Froben Jr in the second year of the reign of HM King Corbett.

All was silent, save only the rustle of books slipping down and pages turning over.

What to do? thought Fringilla, touching Geralt's side and the hard corner of *Deliberations on the Nature of Things* with lazy strokes of her hand. *Should I suggest it? Or wait until he does? As long as he won't think me flighty and immodest . . .*

What will happen if he doesn't suggest it?

'Let's go and find a bed somewhere,' the Witcher suggested, a little hoarsely. 'It doesn't do to treat books like this.'

*

We found a bed, thought Geralt, letting Roach gallop down an avenue in the castle grounds. *We found a bed in the alcove in her chambers. We made love like mad things, voraciously, greedily, ravenously, as though following years of celibacy, as though storing it up for later, as though at risk of celibacy again.*

We told each other many things. We told each other very trivial truths. We told each other very beautiful lies. But those lies, although they were lies, weren't calculated to deceive.

Excited by the gallop, he steered Roach straight at a snow-covered rose bed and made the mare jump it.

We made love. And talked. And our lies became more and more mendacious.

Two months. From October to Yule.

Two month of furious, greedy, wild love.

Roach's horseshoes thudded on the flags of the courtyard at Beauclair Palace.

*

He passed through corridors quickly and soundlessly. No one saw or heard him. Not the guardsmen with halberds, killing time on their sentry duty by chatting and gossiping, nor the slumbering lackeys and pages. Even the candle flames didn't flicker when he passed by the candelabras.

He was near the palace kitchen. But he didn't go in, didn't join the company, who were inside, disposing of a small cask and something fried. He remained in the shadows, listening.

Angoulême was speaking.

'There's something bewitched about this place, this fucking Toussaint. Some kind of charm hangs over the whole valley. Especially over the palace. I was surprised at Dandelion, I was surprised at the Witcher, but now I'm nauseous and I've got a weird feeling in the pit of my stomach. Shit, I even caught myself . . . Eh, I'm not going to tell you that. Seriously, let's get out of here. Let's get out of here as fast as possible.'

'Tell that to Geralt,' said Milva. 'It's him you should tell.'

'Yes, talk to him,' said Cahir somewhat sarcastically. 'During one of those brief moments when he's free. Between the two activities he's been engaging in for two months to help him forget.'

'As for you,' snorted Angoulême, 'you're mainly available in the park, playing at hoops with the barons' daughters. Pshaw, no two ways about it, there's something bewitched about this bloody Toussaint. Regis disappears somewhere at night, aunty has her tight-lipped baron—'

'Shut it, you brat! And don't call me aunty!'

'Come, come,' Regis interjected placatingly. 'Girls, take it easy. Milva, Angoulême. Let there be concord. United we stand, divided we fall. As Her Grace the Duchess, lady of this country, this palace, this bread, dripping and gherkins, says: *Another drop, anyone?*'

Milva sighed heavily.

'We've stayed here too long! Too long, I tell you, too long we've sat here in idleness. It's driving us mad.'

'Well said,' said Cahir. 'Very well said.'

Geralt cautiously withdrew. Soundlessly. Like a bat.

*

He passed through corridors quickly and soundlessly. No one saw or heard him. Neither the guards, nor the liveried servants nor the pages. Not even the candle flames flickered as he passed by the candelabras. The rats heard him, raised their whiskered snouts, and stood up on their hind legs. But they didn't take fright. They knew him.

He often went that way.

In the alcove it smelled of charms and witchcraft, ambergris and roses, and woman's sleep. But Fringilla wasn't asleep.

She sat up in bed, threw off the eiderdown, enthralling him with the sight and taking possession of him.

'You're here at last,' she said, stretching. 'You neglect me dreadfully, Witcher. Get undressed and come here quickly. Very, very quickly.'

*

She passed quickly and soundlessly through the corridors. No one saw or heard her. Neither the guardsmen, idly gossiping at their posts, nor the slumbering liveried servants, nor the pages. Not even the candle flames flickered as she passed by the candelabras. The rats heard her, raised their whiskered snouts, stood up on their hind legs, and followed her with their black beady eyes. They didn't take fright. They knew her.

She often went that way.

*

There was a corridor in Beauclair Palace, and at the end a chamber, the existence of which no one knew about. Neither the current lady of the castle, the Duchess Anarietta, nor the first lady of the castle, her great-grandmamma, the Duchess Ademarta. Nor the architect, the celebrated Peter Faramond, who made extensive modifications to the building, nor the master masons who worked according to Faramond's plans and guidelines. Hell, even Chamberlain Le Goff, who was thought to know everything about Beauclair, didn't know about the existence of that corridor.

The corridor and the chamber, disguised by a powerful illusion, were known only to the palace's original elven builders. And later – when the elves had gone, and Toussaint became a duchy – to the small number of sorcerers linked to the ducal house. Including Artorius Vigo, a master of magical arcana and great specialist in illusions. And his young niece, Fringilla, who had a special talent for illusions.

Having passed quickly and noiselessly through the corridors of Beauclair Palace, Fringilla Vigo stopped in front of a fragment of wall between two columns decorated with acanthus leaves. A softly spoken spell and rapid gesture made the wall – which was illusory – vanish, revealing a corridor, apparently blind. At the end of the corridor, though, was a door, disguised by another illusion. And beyond the door a dark chamber.

Once inside, not wasting time, Fringilla launched a telecommunicator. The oval looking glass became cloudy and then cleared, lighting up the room, illuminating in the darkness the ancient, dust-laden tapestries on the walls. A large room plunged in subtle chiaroscuro, a round table with several women sitting around it appeared in the looking glass. Nine women.

'Greetings, Miss Vigo,' said Philippa Eilhart. 'What's new?'

'Nothing, unfortunately,' replied Fringilla, after clearing her throat. 'Nothing since the last telecommunication. Not a single attempt at scanning.'

'That's bad,' said Philippa. 'Frankly speaking, we'd counted on you uncovering something. Please at least tell us . . . has the

Witcher calmed down now? Are you capable of keeping him in Toussaint at least until May?'

Fringilla Vigo said nothing for some time. She didn't have the slightest intention of mentioning to the lodge that only in the last week the Witcher had called her 'Yennefer' twice, and both at a moment when in every respect she was entitled to hear her own name. But the lodge, in turn, was entitled to expect the truth. Honesty. And a legitimate conclusion.

'No,' she answered at last. 'Probably not until May. But I'll do everything in my power to keep him here as long as possible.'

Korred, *a monster of the large Strigiformes family (q.v.), also called by local people a corrigan, rutterkin, rumpelstiltskin, fidgeter or mesmer. One thing can be said about him; he is dreadfully beastly. He is such a devil's spawn and scoundrel, such a bitch's tail, that we shall not write anything about his appearance or habits, since in sooth I tell you: we shall not waste breath on the whoreson.*

Physiologus

CHAPTER FOUR

An odour that was a mixture of the smells of old wooden panelling, melting candles and ten kinds of perfume hung in the columned hall of Montecalvo Castle. Ten specially selected blends of scent used by the ten women seated at a round oak table in armchairs carved in the shape of sphinxes' heads.

Fringilla Vigo regarded Triss Merigold, was sitting opposite her in a light blue dress buttoned high up to the neck. Beside Triss, remaining in the shadows, sat Keira Metz. Her large, eye-catching earrings of many-facetted citrines sparkled every now and then with a thousand reflections.

'Please continue, Miss Vigo,' urged Philippa Eilhart. 'We're in a hurry to learn the end of the story. And to take urgent steps.'

Philippa – exceptionally – wasn't wearing any jewellery apart from a large sardonyx cameo brooch pinned to her vermilion dress. Fringilla had already heard the rumour and knew whose present the cameo brooch had been, and whose profile it depicted.

Sheala de Tancarville, sitting beside Philippa, was all in black, diamonds twinkling subtly. Margarita Laux-Antille wore heavy gold without stones on claret-coloured satins, while Sabrina Glevissig had her favourite onyxes – matching the colour of her eyes – in her necklace, earrings and rings.

Nearest to Fringilla sat the two elves – Francesca Findabair and Ida Emean aep Sivney.

The Daisy of the Valleys was, as usual, regal, though today neither her coiffure nor her crimson dress were extraordinarily splendid and the red of her diadem and necklace was that of modest – though tasteful – garnets, not rubies. Ida Emean, meanwhile, was dressed in muslins and tulles in autumn tones, so delicate and gauzy that they swayed and undulated like anemones even in the barely perceptible drafts triggered by the movement of the centrally heated air.

As usual of late, Assire var Anahid's modest but distinguished elegance aroused admiration. The Nilfgaardian sorceress wore a single emerald cabochon in a gold setting on a gold chain resting in the high décolletage of her close-fitting, dark-green dress. Her manicured fingernails, painted very dark green, gave the composition a flavour of truly magical extravagance.

'We're waiting, Miss Vigo,' reminded Sheala de Tancarville. 'Time's passing.'

Fringilla cleared her throat.

'December came,' she began her story. 'Yule came, then the New Year. The Witcher calmed down sufficiently to stop mentioning Ciri in every conversation. The expeditions against monsters that he regularly undertook seemed utterly to absorb him. Well, perhaps not quite utterly . . .'

She paused. It seemed to her she could detect a flash of hatred in Triss Merigold's azure eyes. But it might just have been the gleam of flickering candle flame. Philippa snorted, playing with her brooch.

'Don't overdo the modesty, Miss Vigo. This is a closed circle. A circle of women who know what, apart from pleasure, sex can serve. We all use that tool when the need arises. Please go on.'

'Even if during the day he maintained the appearance of secretiveness, superiority and pride,' continued Fringilla, 'at night he was completely in my power. He told me everything. He paid homage to my femininity, which considering his age was extremely generous, I must admit. And then he fell asleep. In my arms, with his mouth on my bosom. Searching for a surrogate for the maternal love he never experienced.'

This time, she was certain, it wasn't the gleam of candlelight. *Very well, I pray you, envy me*, she thought. *Envy me. There's plenty to envy.*

'He was,' she repeated, 'completely in my power.'

*

'Come back to bed, Geralt. The sky's still bloody grey!'

'I'm meeting someone. I have to ride to Pomerol.'

'I don't want you to ride to Pomerol.'

'I'm meeting someone. I've given my word. The manager of the vineyard will be waiting for me by the gate.'

'This monster hunting of yours is stupid and pointless. What are you trying to prove by killing another monster from the caverns? Your masculinity? I know better ways. Come on, back to bed. You aren't going to any Pomerol. At least not so quickly. The steward can wait, and anyway, what is a steward? I want to make love with you.'

'Forgive me. I don't have time. I've given my word.'

'I want to make love with you!'

'If you want to join me for breakfast, start getting dressed.'

'I don't think you love me, Geralt. Don't you love me anymore? Answer me!'

'Put on that grey and pearl dress, the one with the mink trimming. It suits you very much.'

*

'He was completely under my spell, he fulfilled my every wish,' repeated Fringilla. 'He did everything I demanded of him. That's how it was.'

'And we believe you,' said Sheala de Tancarville, extremely dryly. 'Please continue.'

Fringilla coughed into her fist.

'The problem was his troop,' she went on. 'That strange assemblage he called a company. Cahir Mawr Dyffryn aep Ceallach, who watched me and flushed with effort trying to remember me. But he couldn't recall, because when I stayed at Darn Dyffra, his grandparents' family castle, he was six or seven. Milva, an apparently swashbuckling and haughty girl, and whom I happened to catch crying twice hiding in a corner of the stable. Angoulême, a flighty whelp. And Regis Terzieff-Godefroy. A character I was unable to fathom. That entire gang had an influence on him I couldn't eradicate.'

Very well, very well, she thought, *don't raise your eyebrows so high, don't sneer. Wait. That's not the end of the story yet. You're yet to hear of my triumph.*

'Every morning,' she continued, 'the whole company would

meet in the kitchen in the basement of Beauclair Palace. The royal chef was fond of them, God knows why. He always cooked something up for them, so ample and tasty that breakfast usually lasted two, and occasionally even three, hours. Geralt and I ate with them many times. Which is how I know what absurd conversations they used to have.'

*

Two hens, one black, the other speckled, were walking around the kitchen, stepping timidly on their clawed feet. Glancing at the company breaking their fast, the hens pecked crumbs from the floor.

The company had gathered in the palace kitchen, as they did every morning. The royal chef was fond of them, God knows why, and always had something tasty for them. Today it was scrambled eggs, sour rye soup, stewed aubergine, rabbit forcemeat, goose breasts and sausage with beetroot, with a large circle of goat's cheese on the side. They all ate briskly and in silence. Apart from Angoulême, who was talking nonsense.

'And I tell you we should set up a brothel here. When we've done what we have to do, let's return and open a house of ill repute. I've looked around in town. There's everything here. There are ten barber's shops alone, and eight apothecaries. But there's only one knocking shop and it's more like a seedy shithouse than a proper cathouse, I tell you. There's no competition. We'll open a luxury bordello. We'll buy a big house with a garden—'

'Angoulême, have mercy.'

'—just for respectable punters. I'll be the madam. I tell you, we'll make a fortune and live like kings. Finally they'll elect me councillor, and then I won't let you die for sure, because when they elect me, I'll elect you and before you can say Jack Robinson—'

'Angoulême, we've asked. There, eat some bread and forcemeat.'

It was quiet for a while.

'What are you hunting today, Geralt? Tough job?'

'Eyewitnesses give conflicting descriptions.' The Witcher raised his head from his plate. 'So it's either a pryskirnik, i.e. a fairly hard job, or a drelichon, i.e. a fairly hard job, or a nazhempik, i.e. a

112

fairly easy one. It might turn out the job's extremely easy, because they last saw the monster before Lammas last year. It might have bolted from Pomerol over the hills and far away.'

'I hope it has,' said Fringilla, gnawing at a goose bone.

'And how's Dandelion doing?' the Witcher suddenly asked. 'I haven't seen him for such a long time that I get all my information about him from lampoons sung in the town.'

'We aren't any better off,' smiled Regis with pursed lips. 'All we know is that our poet is on such intimate terms with Lady Duchess Anarietta that she's allowed him, even before witnesses, to use quite a familiar *cognomen*. He calls her Little Weasel.'

'That's very apt!' Angoulême said with her mouth full. 'That lady duchess really does have a weaselly nose. Not to mention her teeth.'

'No one's perfect.' Fringilla narrowed her eyes.

'How very true.'

The hens, the black and the speckled one, had become audacious enough to begin pecking at Milva's boots. The archer drove them away with a brisk kick and an oath.

Geralt had been scrutinising her for some time. Now he made up his mind.

'Maria,' he said gravely, almost harshly, 'I know our conversations can't be considered serious or our jokes sophisticated. But you don't have to pull such sour faces. What's the matter?'

'Something must be the matter,' said Angoulême. Geralt silenced her with a fierce look. Too late.

'What do you know?' Milva stood up suddenly, almost knocking over her chair. 'What do you know, eh? The Devil take you! You can kiss my arse, all of you, get it?'

She grabbed her cup from the table, drained it and smashed it on the floor without a second thought. And ran out, slamming the door.

'Things are serious—' Angoulême began a moment later, but this time the vampire silenced her.

'The matter is very serious,' he confirmed. 'I hadn't expected such an extreme reaction from our archer. One usually reacts like that when one is jilted, not when one jilts another.'

'What the bloody hell are you talking about?' said Geralt,

annoyed. 'Eh? Perhaps someone will finally explain what this is all about?'

'It's about Baron Amadis de Trastamara.'

'The tight-lipped hunter?'

'The very same. He proposed to Milva. Three days ago on a hunting trip. He'd been inviting her to go hunting for a month . . .'

'One hunt—' Angoulême flashed her teeth impudently '—lasted two days. With the night spent in his hunting lodge, get it? I swear—'

'Shut up, girl. Speak, Regis.'

'He formally and ceremoniously asked for her hand. Milva declined, it appears, in quite a harsh way. The baron, though he looks level-headed, was upset by the rejection, sulked like a jilted stripling and immediately left Beauclair. And since then Milva has been walking around downcast.'

'We've been here too long,' muttered the Witcher. 'Too long.'

'Now who's talking?' said Cahir, who had said nothing up until then. 'Who's talking?'

'Forgive me.' The Witcher stood up. 'We'll talk about it when I return. The steward of Pomerol vineyard is waiting for me. And punctuality is part of the witchers' code.'

*

After Milva's abrupt exit and the Witcher's departure the rest of the company ate in silence. The two hens, one black, the other speckled, walked around the kitchen, stepping timidly on their clawed feet.

'I have a small problem . . .' said Angoulême, raising her eyes towards Fringilla from over the plate she was wiping with a crust.

'I understand,' nodded the sorceress. 'It's nothing dreadful. When was your last period?'

'What do you mean?' Angoulême leaped to her feet, frightening the chickens. 'It's nothing of the sort. It's something completely different!'

'Tell me.'

'Geralt wants to leave me here when he goes back on the road.'

'Oh.'

'He says,' Angoulême snapped, 'that he can't put me at risk, and similar rubbish. And I want to go with him—'

'Oh.'

'Don't interrupt me, will you? I want to go with him, with Geralt, because it's only when I'm with him I'm not afraid that One-Eyed Fulko will catch me. And here in Toussaint—'

'Angoulême,' Regis interrupted her, 'your words are in vain. Madam Vigo is listening, but can't hear. Only one thing horrifies her: the Witcher leaving.'

'Oh,' Fringilla repeated, turning her head towards him and screwing up her eyes. 'What are you hinting at, Mr Terzieff-Godefroy? The Witcher leaving? And when might that be? If one might ask?'

'Maybe not today, maybe not tomorrow,' the vampire replied in a soft voice. 'But one day, for certain. No offence intended.'

'I don't feel offended,' responded Fringilla coldly. 'If you had me in mind, naturally. Returning to you, Angoulême, I assure you that I shall discuss the matter of leaving Toussaint with Geralt. I guarantee you that the Witcher will hear my opinion on the subject.'

'Why, naturally,' snorted Cahir. 'How did I know you'd say that, Madam Fringilla?'

The sorceress looked long and hard at him.

'The Witcher,' she said finally, 'ought not to leave Toussaint. No one who wishes him well should encourage him to do that. Where will he have it so good as here? He's living in the lap of luxury. He has his monsters to hunt, he's earning a pretty penny from it. His friend and comrade is the favourite of the reigning duchess, and the duchess herself is also favourably disposed to him. Mainly owing to the succubus that was haunting people's bedchambers. Yes, yes, gentlemen. Anarietta, like all the noble ladies of Toussaint, is inordinately well-disposed towards the Witcher. For the succubus has suddenly stopped haunting. The ladies of Toussaint have thus clubbed together to pay him a special bonus, which they will deposit in the Witcher's account in the Cianfanellis' bank any day now. Increasing the small fortune that the Witcher has already stored up there.'

'A pretty gesture from the ladies.' Regis didn't lower his gaze.

'And a well-deserved bonus. It isn't easy to stop a succubus from haunting. You may believe me, Madam Fringilla.'

'I do. And while we're on the subject, one of the palace guards claims he saw it. At night, on the battlements of Caroberta's Tower. In the company of another spectre. Some kind of vampire. The two demons were taking a stroll, the guard swore, and they looked as though they were friends. Do you perhaps know anything about this, Mr Regis? Are you able to explain it, sir?'

'No, I'm not, madam.' Regis didn't even bat an eyelid. 'There are things in heaven and earth that even philosophers have never dreamed about.'

'Without doubt there are such things,' said Fringilla, nodding her black hair. 'Regarding, nonetheless, whether the Witcher is preparing to depart, do you know anything else? For you see, he hasn't mentioned any such plan, and he usually tells me everything.'

'Of course he does,' Cahir grunted. Fringilla ignored him.

'Mr Regis?'

'No,' the vampire said after a moment's silence. 'No, Madam Fringilla, please worry not. The Witcher doesn't show us any greater affection or confidence than you. He doesn't whisper into our ears any secrets he would keep from you.'

'Where, then—' Fringilla was as composed as granite '—do these revelations about departing come from?'

'Well, it's like our darling Angoulême's catchphrase, which brims with youthful charm.' The vampire didn't bat an eyelid this time either. 'There comes a time when you've either got to shit or free up the shithouse. In other words—'

'Spare the other words,' Fringilla interrupted sharply. 'Those charming ones will suffice.'

Silence reigned for quite some time. The two hens, the black and the speckled one, walked around pecking whatever they could. Angoulême wiped her beetroot-stained nose with her sleeve. The vampire toyed pensively with the wooden peg from the sausage.

'Thanks to me,' Fringilla broke the silence, 'Geralt has come to know Ciri's lineage, the complexities and secrets of her genealogy, known only to a few. Thanks to me he knows what he had no idea about a year ago. Thanks to me he has information, and information is a weapon. Thanks to me and my magical protection he is safe from enemy scanning, and thus also from assassins. Thanks to me and my magic his knee doesn't hurt him now and he can bend it. Around his neck is a medallion, made by my magical art, possibly not as good as his original witcher one, but powerful anyway. Thanks to me – and only me – in the spring or summer he will be able to face his enemies in combat, equipped with information, protected, fit, prepared and armed. If anyone present here has done more for Geralt, given him more, may they step forward. I'd be happy to honour them.'

No one said anything. The hens pecked Cahir's boots, but the young Nilfgaardian paid no attention. 'Verily,' he said with a sneer, 'none of us has given Geralt more than you, m'lady.'

'How did I know you'd say that?'

'That's not the point, Madam Fringilla—' began the vampire. The sorceress didn't let him finish.

'What is the point then?' she asked aggressively. 'That he's with me? That we are joined by affection? That I don't want him to leave now? That I don't want a sense of guilt to destroy him? That same sense of guilt, that atonement, which drove you all onto the road?'

Regis said nothing. Cahir didn't speak either. Angoulême watched, clearly not understanding very much.

'If it is written in the scrolls of destiny,' the sorceress said after a moment, 'that Geralt will win Ciri back, then it shall happen. Irrespective of whether the Witcher goes into the mountains or whether he stays in Toussaint. Destiny catches up with people. And not the other way around. Do you understand that? Do you understand that, Lord Regis Terzieff-Godefroy?'

'Better than you think, Madam Vigo.' The vampire twiddled the wooden peg from the sausage. 'But for me – please forgive me – destiny isn't a scroll written on by a Great Demiurge, nor the will of heaven, nor the inevitable verdict of some providence or other, but the result of many apparently unconnected facts, events and occurrences. I would be inclined to agree with you that destiny catches up with people . . . and not just people. But the view that it can't be the other way around doesn't convince me. For such a view is facile fatalism, a paean praising torpor and indolence, a warm eiderdown and the beguiling warmth of a woman's loins. In short, life in a dream. And life, Madam Vigo, may be a dream, may also finish as a dream . . . But it's a dream that has to be dreamed actively. Which is why, Madam Vigo, the road awaits us.'

'Suit yourselves.' Fringilla stood up, almost as suddenly as Milva a moment earlier. 'As you wish! Blizzards, frost and destiny await you in the mountain passes. And the expiation you so sorely search for. Suit yourselves! But the Witcher shall stay here. In Toussaint! With me!'

'I think,' the vampire said calmly, 'that you are wrong, Madam Vigo. The dream that the Witcher is dreaming, I humbly submit with respect, is an enchanting and beautiful one. But every dream, if dreamed too long, turns into a nightmare. And we awake from such dreams screaming.'

*

The nine women sitting around the great round table in Monte-calvo Castle were looking fixedly at Fringilla Vigo. At Fringilla, who suddenly began to stammer.

'Geralt left for the Pomerol vineyard on the morning of the eighth of January. And returned . . . at eight in the evening . . . or nine in the morning . . . I don't know . . . I'm not sure . . .'

'Organise your thoughts,' Sheala de Tancarville said gently. 'Please speak more coherently, Madam Vigo. And if part of the story discomfits you, you may simply pass over it.'

*

The speckled hen, treading cautiously on its clawed feet, was walking around the kitchen. The smell of chicken broth was in the air.

The door slammed open. Geralt rushed into the kitchen. He had a bruise and a purple and red scab on his windburned face.

'Come on, company, get packed,' he announced without unnecessary introductions. 'We're riding out! In an hour, and not a moment longer, I want to see you all on the hillock outside the town, by that post. Packed, in the saddle, ready for a long ride and a difficult one.'

That was enough. It was as though they'd been waiting for this

118

news for a long time, as though they'd been in readiness for a long time.

'I'll be ready in a flash!' yelled Milva, leaping up. 'I'll be ready in half an hour!'

'I will too.' Cahir stood up, discarded a spoon and looked closely at the Witcher. 'But I'd like to know what it is. A whim? A lovers' tiff? Or are we really leaving?'

'We really are. Angoulême, why are you making faces?'

'Geralt, I—'

'Don't worry, I'm not leaving you. I've changed my mind. You need looking after, my girl, I can't let you out of my sight. To horse, I said, get packed and fasten on your saddlebags. And singly, so as not to raise suspicion, outside the town, by the post on the hillock. We'll meet there in an hour.'

'Without fail, Geralt!' yelled Angoulême. 'At fucking last!'

In the blink of an eye all that was left in the kitchen were Geralt and the speckled hen. And the vampire, who went on calmly slurping chicken broth and dumplings.

'Are you waiting for a special invitation?' the Witcher asked coldly. 'Why are you still sitting here? Rather than loading up Draakul the mule? And saying goodbye to the succubus?'

'Geralt,' Regis said calmly, giving himself a second helping from the tureen. 'I need as long to say goodbye to the succubus as you do to your raven-haired beauty. Assuming you have any intention of saying goodbye to her. And just between you and I, you can send the youngsters to get packed by shouting, hastening and making a fuss. I deserve something else, if only for reasons of age. A few words of explanation, please.'

'Regis—'

'An explanation, Geralt. The quicker you begin the better. Yesterday morning, in accordance with your agreement, you met the steward of Pomerol vineyard at the gate . . .'

*

Alcides Fierabras, the black-bearded steward of the Pomerol vineyard he'd met in The Pheasantry on Yule Eve, was waiting for the Witcher at the gate, with a mule, and he in turn was dressed and equipped as though planning to journey far, far away, to the ends of the earth, beyond the Solveiga Gate and the Elskerdeg pass.

'It's close, but as a matter of fact it isn't,' he responded to Geralt's sour remark. 'You are, sire, a visitor from the wide world. Our little Toussaint may seem a backwater to you, you think you can toss a hat from one border to the other, and a dry one, to boot. Well, you're mistaken. It's quite a long way to Pomerol vineyard, which is where we're headed, and if we arrive by noon it'll be a success.'

'So it's a mistake,' the Witcher said dryly, 'for us to be setting off so tardily.'

'Well, maybe it is.' Alcides Fierabras glowered at him and blew into his whiskers. 'But I knew not that you were the kind who was inclined to start at daybreak. For that's rare among grand lords.'

'I'm not a grand lord. Let's be off, steward, sir, let's not waste time on idle chatter.'

'You took the words right out of my mouth.'

They took a shortcut through the town. At first Geralt wanted to protest, afraid of getting stuck in the familiar crowded back-streets. But Steward Fierabras, it turned out, knew better both the town and the times when the streets wouldn't be crowded. They rode quickly and without difficulty.

They entered the town square and passed the scaffold. And the gallows, displaying a hanged man.

'A perilous thing,' the steward nodded, 'to make rhymes and sing airs. Particularly in public.'

'Judgements are harsh here,' said Geralt, realising what it was about. 'Elsewhere you're pilloried at most for a lampoon.'

'Depends who the lampoon's about,' commented Alcides Fierabras soberly. 'And on the rhymes. Our Lady Duchess is good and endearing, but when she's irritated . . .'

'You can't stifle a song, as a friend of mine says.'

'Not a song. But a singer you can, sir.'

They crossed the town and left through the Coopers' Gate straight into the valley of the Blessure, whose rapids were briskly splashing and foaming. The snow in the fields was only in furrows and hollows, but it was quite cold.

They were passed by a detachment of knights, heading no

doubt towards the Pass of Cervantes, to the border watchtower of Vedette. Suddenly all they could see were colourful gryphons, lions, hearts, lilies, stars, crosses, chevrons and other heraldic trifles painted on shields and embroidered on cloaks and caparisons. Hooves drummed, pennants flapped, and a song resounded about the fortunes of a knight and his beloved who married another instead of waiting for him.

Geralt followed the detachment with his eyes. The sight of the knights errant reminded him of Reynart de Bois-Fresnes, who'd just returned from service and was recuperating in the arms of his townswoman, whose husband, a merchant, didn't return morning or night, probably having been held up somewhere on his journey by swollen rivers, forests full of beasts and other turmoil of the elements. The Witcher wouldn't have dreamed of tearing Reynart away from his lover's embrace, but sincerely regretted not postponing the contract with Pomerol vineyard to a later date. He'd grown fond of the knight and missed his company.

'Let's ride, Master Witcher.'

'Let us ride, Master Fierabras.'

They rode upstream along the highway. The Blessure wound and meandered, but there was an abundance of small bridges so they didn't have to go out of their way.

Steam belched from the nostrils of Roach and the mule.

'What do you think, Mr Fierabras, will the winter last long?'

'There were frosts at Samhain. And the saying goes, "When at Samhain there's ice, dress warm and nice".'

'I see. And your vines? Won't the winter damage them?'

'It's been colder.'

They rode on in silence.

'Look there,' said Fierabras, pointing. 'There in the valley lies the village of Fox Holes. Pots grow in the fields there, wonder of wonders.'

'I beg your pardon?'

'Pots. They grow in the bosom of the earth, just like that, a pure trick of nature, without any human help at all. Like spuds or turnips grow elsewhere, in Fox Holes pots grow. Of all shapes and kinds.'

'Indeed?'

'As I live and breathe. For which reason Fox Holes has an agreement with the village of Dudno in Maecht. Because there, so the stories go, the earth bears forth pot lids.'

'Of all shapes and kinds?'

'Precisely, Master Witcher.'

They rode on. In silence. The Blessure sparkled and foamed on the rocks.

*

'And look over yonder, Master Witcher, the ruins of the ancient burgh of Dun Tynne. That burgh was the witness to dreadful scenes, if one is to believe the stories. Walgerius, who they called the Cuckold, killed his faithless wife, her lover, her mother, her sister and her brother. Cruelly and bloodily. And then sat down and cried, no one knows why . . .'

'I've heard about that.'

'Have you been here before?'

'No.'

'Ah. Meaning the story has travelled widely.'

'Precisely, Master Steward.'

*

'And that slender tower, beyond that burgh, over there?' The Witcher pointed. 'What is it?'

'Over there? That's a temple.'

'To which godhead?'

'Who'd remember that?'

'Very true. Who would?'

*

Around noon they saw the vineyard, hillsides gently falling towards the Blessure, bristling with evenly pruned vines, now misshapen and woefully leafless. At the top of the highest hill, lashed by the wind, were the soaring towers, squat keep and barbican of Pomerol Castle.

Geralt was interested to see that the road leading to the castle was well-used, no less furrowed by hooves and wheel rims than the main highway. It was evident that people often turned off the highway towards Pomerol Castle. He stopped his questions until he noticed at the foot of the castle a dozen or so wagons with horses and covered in tarpaulins, sturdy and well-made vehicles used for transporting goods long distances.

'Merchants,' explained the steward when asked. 'Wine merchants.'

'Merchants?' Geralt was surprised. 'How's that? I thought the mountain passes were covered in snow, and Toussaint cut off from the world. How could the merchants get here?'

'There are no bad roads for a merchant,' said steward Fierabras gravely. 'At least not for those who treat their trade seriously. They observe the principle, Master Witcher, that since the end is justified, the means must be found.'

'Indeed,' Geralt said slowly. 'An apposite principle worthy of imitation. In any situation.'

'Without doubt. But in truth, some of the traders have been stuck here since autumn, unable to leave. But they don't lose heart. They say, "Why, who cares, in the spring of the year we'll be here first, before the competition shows up." With them they call it positive thinking.'

'It would be hard to fault that principle either,' nodded Geralt. 'One thing still interests me, Master Steward. Why do the merchants stay here, in the middle of nowhere, and not in Beauclair? Isn't the duchess keen on putting them up? Perhaps she disdains merchants?'

'Not at all,' answered Fierabras. 'The Lady Duchess always invites them, while they graciously decline. And stay among the vineyards.'

'Why?'

'Beauclair, they say, is naught but feasts, balls, junkets, boozing and amour. A fellow, they say, only grows idle and stupid, and wastes time, instead of thinking about trade. And one should think about what's really important. About the goal guiding us. Without let up. Not distract your thinking on mere bagatelles. Then, and only then, is the intended goal achieved.'

'Indeed, Mr Fierabras,' the Witcher said slowly. 'I'm content with our shared journey. I've gained a great deal from our conversations. Truly a great deal.'

*

Contrary to the Witcher's expectations they didn't ride to Pomerol Castle, but a little further, to a prominence beyond the valley, where another castle rose, somewhat smaller and much more neglected. The castle was called Zurbarrán. Geralt was thrilled at the prospect of the upcoming work. Zurbarrán, dark and toothed with crumbling crenellations, looked the epitome of an enchanted ruin, and was no doubt teeming with witchcraft, marvels and monsters.

Inside, in the courtyard, instead of marvels and monsters he saw around a dozen people preoccupied with tasks as enchanted as rolling barrels, planing planks and nailing them together. It smelled of fresh timber, fresh lime, stale cat, sour wine and pea soup. The pea soup was served out soon after.

Made hungry by the journey, the wind and the cold, they ate briskly and in silence. They were accompanied by steward Fierabras's subordinate, introduced to Geralt as Szymon Gilka. They were served by two fair-haired women with plaits two ells long. They both sent the Witcher such suggestive glances he decided to hasten to his work.

Szymon Gilka hadn't seen the monster. He only knew of its appearance second-hand.

'It was as black as pitch, but when it crawled across the wall, the bricks could be seen through it. Like jelly it was, see, Master Witcher, or some sort of snot, if you'll excuse me. And it had long thin limbs, and a great number of them, eight or even more. And Yontek stood, stood and watched until at last he had a brainwave and shouted out loud "Die, perish!" and then threw in an exorcism: "Croak, you bastard, by God!" Then the beastie hop, hop, hop! Hopped away and that's all we saw of it. Bolted into the cave mouth. Then the lads said, "If there's a monster, give us a bonus for toiling in dangerous conditions, and if you don't we'll complain to the guild." And I says, your guild can kiss my—'

'When was the monster first seen?' Geralt interrupted.

124

''Bout three days since. Bit before Yule.'

'You said—' the Witcher looked at the steward '—before Lammas.'

Alcides Fierabras blushed in the places not covered by his beard. Gilka snorted.

'Aye, aye, Master Steward, if you want to steward you should come here more often and not just polish a chair with your arse in your office in Beauclair. That's what I think—'

'I'm not interested in what you think,' interrupted Fierabras. 'We're talking about the monster.'

'But I've already said it. Everything what happened.'

'Weren't there any victims? Was no one attacked?'

'No. But last year a farmhand disappeared without trace. Some say a monster dragged him into the chasm and finished him off. Others, meanwhile, say it weren't no monster, but that the farmhand made a cowardly escape off his own bat, because of debts and alley money and main tents. Because he, mark you, played the bones hard, and on top of that was shafting the miller's daughter, and that miller's daughter rushed to the courts, and the courts ordered the farmhand to pay main tents—'

'Did the monster attack anyone else?' Geralt unceremoniously interrupted his discourse. 'Did anyone else see it?'

'No.'

One of the serving women, pouring Geralt more of the local wine, brushed his ear with her breast, then winked encouragingly.

'Let's go,' said Geralt quickly. 'No point idling time away talking. Take me to these cellars.'

*

Fringilla's amulet, unfortunately, didn't live up to the hopes pinned on it. Geralt didn't believe for a moment that the polished chrysoprase mounted in silver would replace his witcher's wolf medallion. In any case, Fringilla hadn't given any such promises. She had assured him, however – with great conviction – that after melding with the psyche of the wearer the amulet was capable of various things, including warning of danger.

Nonetheless, either Fringilla's spells hadn't worked, or Geralt and the amulet differed in the matter of what constituted danger. The chrysoprase perceptibly twitched when, as they walked to the cellars, they crossed the path of a large, ginger cat sauntering across the courtyard with its tail in the air. Indeed, the cat must have received some kind of signal, for it fled, meowing dreadfully.

When, though, the Witcher went down into the cellars it kept vibrating annoyingly, but in dry, well-ordered and clean vaults where the only danger was the wine in huge barrels. Someone who had lost their self-control and was lying with their mouth open under the spigot would be in danger of serious over-drinking. And nothing else.

The medallion didn't twitch, however, when Geralt abandoned the service part of the cellars and descended down a series of steps and drifts. The Witcher had worked out long before that there were ancient mines under most of the vineyards in Toussaint. When the vines had been planted and started to bear fruit and generate better profits, exploitation of the mines must have ceased, and the mines abandoned, their corridors and galleries partly modified into wine cellars and stores. Pomerol and Zurbarrán castles stood over a disused slate mine. It was riddled with drifts and holes, and a moment's inattention would have been enough for one to end up at the bottom of one of them with a compound fracture. Some of the holes were covered by rotten planks covered with slate powder and thus hardly differed from the floor. An incautious step onto something like that would have been dangerous – so the medallion ought to have given him a warning. It didn't.

It also didn't give a warning when a vague, grey shape sprang out of a heap of slate waste about ten paces in front of Geralt, scratched the mine floor with its claws, pranced, howled piercingly, then uttered a squeal and a snicker, before tearing off down the corridor and ducking into one of the niches gaping in the wall.

The Witcher swore. The magical trinket reacted to ginger cats, but not to gremlins. He'd have to talk to Fringilla about that, he thought, as he approached the opening into which the creature had vanished.

The amulet twitched powerfully.

About time, he thought. But right away he pondered matters more deeply. The medallion couldn't have been that stupid, after all. The standard, favourite tactic of the gremlin was to flee and then slash its pursuer from an ambush with a surprise blow of its sickle-sharp talons. A gremlin might be waiting there in the darkness and the medallion had signalled it.

He waited a long time, holding his breath, intently focusing his hearing. The amulet lay placid and inert on his chest. A musty, disagreeable stench drifted from the hole. It was deadly silent. And no gremlin could have endured being quiet for so long.

Without a second thought he entered the hole on hands and knees, scraping his back against the jagged rock. He didn't get far.

Something rustled and cracked, the floor gave way, and the Witcher tumbled downwards along with a few hundredweight of sand and stones. Fortunately, it didn't last long, and there wasn't a bottomless chasm under him but an ordinary corridor. He flew like shit off his shovel and smashed with a crunch at the foot of a pile of rotten wood. He shook the dirt from his hair and spat sand, swearing very coarsely. The amulet was twitching ceaselessly, fluttering on his chest like a sparrow inside his jacket. The Witcher stopped just short of tearing it off and flinging it away. First of all, Fringilla would have been livid. Second of all, the chrysoprase was supposed to have other magical abilities. Geralt hoped they would be less unreliable.

When he tried to stand up, he laid a hand on a rounded skull. And realised that what he was lying on wasn't wood at all.

He stood up and quickly inspected the pile of bones. They belonged to people. At the moment of their deaths they had all been manacled and were most probably naked. The bones were crushed, with bite marks. The victims might not have been alive when they were being bitten. But he couldn't be certain.

He was led out of the drift by a long corridor, which headed onwards as straight as a die. The slate wall had been worked to a smooth finish. It no longer looked like a mine.

He suddenly emerged into an immense cavern whose ceiling vanished into the darkness. In the centre of the cavern was a huge, black, bottomless hole, over which was suspended a dangerously fragile-looking stone bridge.

The jingle of water dripping from the walls echoed. Coldness and unidentifiable stenches drifted up from the chasm. The amulet hung motionless. Geralt set foot on the bridge, intent and focused, trying hard to stay well away from the crumbling balustrade.

There was another corridor on the far side of the bridge. He noticed rusted cressets in the smoothly carved walls. There were also niches, some of which contained small sandstone figures, but the ceaseless dripping of water had melted and eroded them into amorphous lumps. There were also tiles bearing reliefs set into the walls. The tiles were made of more a durable material so the reliefs were still recognisable. Geralt made out a woman with crescent horns, a tower, a swallow, a wild boar, a dolphin and a unicorn.

He heard a voice.

He stopped, holding his breath.

The amulet twitched.

No. It wasn't an illusion, it wasn't the murmur of shifting slate or the echo of dripping water. It was a human voice. Geralt shut his eyes and looked hard. Searching for the source.

The voice, the Witcher could have sworn, was coming from another niche, from behind another small figure, also eroded, but not enough to remove its shapely female curves. This time the medallion did its job. It flashed, and Geralt suddenly saw a reflection of metal in the wall. He grasped the eroded woman in a powerful embrace and twisted hard. There was a grating, and the entire niche revolved on steel hinges, revealing a spiral staircase leading upwards.

The voice again sounded from the top of the stairs. Geralt didn't think twice.

At the top he found a door that opened smoothly and without any grating. Beyond the door was a tiny vaulted room. Four enormous brass pipes with their ends flared like trumpets protruded from the wall. A chair stood in the middle between the trumpet-like openings, and on the chair sat a skeleton. On its pate it had the remains of a biretta slumped down beyond its teeth. It was wearing the rags of fine garments, around its neck was a golden chain, and on its feet curled-toed cordovan slippers, much gnawed by rats.

The sound of a sneeze erupted from one of the horns, so loud and unexpected that the Witcher started. Then someone blew their nose and the sound – intensified by the brass tube – was simply unbearable.

'Bless you,' the pipe sounded. 'Why, how your nose is running, Skellen.'

Geralt shoved the skeleton off the chair, not forgetting to remove and pocket the golden chain. Then he sat down at the surveillance post. At the end of the horn.

*

One of the men being eavesdropped on had a deep, rumbling bass voice. When he spoke, the brass tube vibrated.

'Why, how your nose is running, Skellen. Where did you catch such a chill? And when?'

'Not worth mentioning,' answered the man with the runny nose. 'I caught the damned illness and now it won't subside. As soon as it lets up, it returns. Even magic doesn't help.'

'Perhaps you ought to change your sorcerer?' came another voice, grating like a rusty old hinge. 'For at the moment that Vilgefortz can't boast of much success, can he? I'd say—'

'Leave it,' interjected someone speaking with characteristic long-drawn-out syllables. 'That wasn't why we organised this meeting, here, in Toussaint. At the world's end.'

'At the end of the bloody world!'

'This world's end,' said the man with the cold, 'is the only country I know that doesn't possess its own security service. The only corner of the empire that isn't crawling with Vattier de Rideaux's agents. They regard this endlessly merry and fuddled duchy as ridiculous, and no one takes it seriously.'

'Little countries like this,' said the one who stretched out his syllables, 'have always been a paradise for spies, and favourite locations for rendezvous. So they also attract counter-intelligence and narks, diverse professional snoopers and eavesdroppers.'

'Perhaps it was like that long ago. But not during the distaff governments, that have prevailed in Toussaint for almost a hundred years. I repeat, we are safe here. No one will track us down or eavesdrop on us. We can, in the guise of merchants, calmly discuss matters so vital to Your Ducal Majesties. So vital to your private fortunes and estates.'

'I despise self-interest, it's as simple as that!' said the one with the grating voice, annoyed. 'And I'm not here for self-interest! I'm concerned only with the good of the empire. And the good of the empire, gentlemen, is a strong dynasty! It will be detrimental and most evil for the empire if some mongrel, rotten fruit of bad blood, the spawn of the corporally and morally sick northern kinglets, ascends to the throne. No, gentlemen. I, de Wett of the de Wetts, shall not look on passively, by the Great Sun, at something like this! Particularly since my daughter had almost been promised—'

'Your daughter, de Wett?' roared the thundering bass. 'What am I to say? I, who supported that pup Emhyr in the fight against the usurper? Indeed, the cadets set off from my residence to storm the palace! Afterwards, the little sneak looked benignly at my Eilan, smiled, paid her compliments, while he was squeezing her tittles behind a curtain, I happen to know. And now what . . . A fresh empress? Such an affront? Such an outrage? The Emperor of the Eternal Empire, who prefers a stray from Cintra to the daughters of ancient houses! What? He's on the throne by my grace, and he dares insult my Eilan? No, I will not abide that!'

'Nor I!' shouted another voice, high and gushing. 'He also maligned me! He discarded my wife for that Cintran stray!'

'As luck would have it,' said the man who drawled his syllables, 'the stray has been dispatched to the next world. So it would appear from Lord Skellen's account.'

'I listened to that account attentively,' said the grating-voiced man, 'and I've come to the conclusion that nothing is certain apart from that the stray vanished. If it has vanished it may reappear once more. It has vanished and reappeared several times since last year! Indeed, Lord Skellen, you have disappointed us greatly, it's as simple as that. You and that sorcerer, Vilgefortz!'

'This is not the time, Joachim! Not the time to accuse and blame each other, driving a wedge into our unity. We must be a strong, unified force. And a decisive one. For it's not important if the Cintran is alive or not. An emperor who has once abused the ancient families with impunity will do it again! The Cintran is no more? Then he's liable in a few months to present us with an empress from Zerrikania or Zangvebar! No, by the Great Sun, we shall not allow it!'

'We shall not allow it, it's as simple as that! Well said, Ardal! He has dashed the hopes of the Emreis family. Every moment Emhyr is on the throne he damages the empire, simple as that. And there *is* someone to put on the throne. Young Voorhis . . .'

A loud sneeze and then the sound of someone blowing their nose boomed out.

'A constitutional monarchy,' said the sneezer. 'It's high time for a constitutional monarchy, for a progressive political system. And afterwards democracy . . . The government of the people . . .'

'Imperator Voorhis,' repeated the deep voice with emphasis. 'Imperator Voorhis, Stefan Skellen. Who will be married to my Eilan or one of Joachim's daughters. And then I, as the Grand Chancellor of the Crown, and de Wett as the Marshal of Internal Affairs. Unless, as an advocate of some hoi-polloi, you declare your resignation from the title and the position. What?'

'Let's leave aside historical processes,' said the one with the cold, in a conciliatory tone. 'Nothing can stop them anyhow. But for today, Your Grace Grand Chancellor aep Dahy, if I have any reservations about Prince Voorhis it's chiefly because he is a man of iron character, proud and unyielding, whom it is difficult to sway.'

'If one may say something,' said the drawling voice. 'Prince Voorhis has a son, little Morvran. He is a much better candidate. Firstly, he has a more compelling right to the throne, both on the spear and the distaff side. Secondly, he's a child, on whose behalf a council of regents shall govern. Which means us.'

'Foolishness! We shall cope with his father too! We shall find a way!'

'We could plant my wife on him!' suggested the gushing one.

'Be silent, Lord Broinne. Now is not the time. Gentlemen, it behoves us to debate something else, it's as simple as that. For I would like to observe that Emhyr var Emreis still reigns.'

'I'll say,' agreed the man with the cold, trumpeting into a handkerchief. 'He lives and reigns, is well in body and in mind. The second, in particular, cannot be questioned after he expelled from Nilfgaard both Your Graces and your armies – which may have been loyal to you. How do you plan to stage a coup, Duke Ardal, when at any moment you may have to go into battle at the head of the East Army Group? And by now Duke Joachim should probably also be with his army and the Verden Special Operations Group.'

'Give the acerbity a miss, Stefan Skellen. And don't make faces that only you think make you look like your new paymaster, the sorcerer Vilgefortz. And know this, Tawny Owl, since Emhyr suspects something, it is you and Vilgefortz who shoulder the blame. Admit it, you'd like to capture the Cintran and trade her to gain favour with Emhyr, wouldn't you? Now that the girl is dead, there's nothing to trade with, is there? Emhyr will tear you apart with horses, simple as that. You must accept it with humility. You, and the sorcerer you've allied with against us!'

'We must all accept it, Joachim,' interjected the bass. 'It's time to face facts. We aren't at all in a better position than Skellen. The circumstances have put us all in the same boat.'

'But it was Tawny Owl who put us in that boat! We were supposed to act in secret, and now what? Emhyr knows everything! Vattier de Rideaux's agents are hunting Tawny Owl throughout the empire. And we've been sent to war to get rid of ourselves, quite simply!'

'I'd be pleased about that,' said the drawling one. 'I'd take advantage of it. Everyone has had enough of this current war, I can assure you, gentlemen. The army, the common folk, and above all merchants and entrepreneurs. News of a cessation of hostilities will be greeted throughout the empire with great joy, irrespective of the result. And you, gentlemen, as commanders of the armies, have an influence on the result of the war permanently within arm's reach, so to speak, don't you? What could be easier than to don a laurel wreath in the event of the victory that ends the war? Or, in the event of defeat, to step forward as men of the moment, intercessors of the negotiations that'll put an end to the bloodshed?'

'True,' said the one with the grating voice a moment later. 'By the Great Sun, it's true. You talk sense, Lord Leuvaarden.'

'By sending you to the front,' said the bass, 'Emhyr put a noose around his own neck.'

'Emhyr is still alive, Your Grace,' said the gushing one. 'Is alive and well. Let's not sell the bear's skin before catching the bear.'

'No,' said the bass. 'First let's kill the bear.'

There was a long silence.

'Assassination, then. Death.'

'Death.'

'Death!'

'Death! It's the only solution. As long as he's alive, Emhyr has supporters. When he dies, everyone will support us. The aristocracy will be on our side, for we are the aristocracy and the aristocracy's strength is in its solidarity. A significant part of the army will be with us, particularly the part of the officer corps that remembers Emhyr's purges after the defeat at Sodden. And the people will be on our side—'

'Because the people are ignorant, stupid and easily manipulated,' finished Skellen, blowing his nose. 'It's enough to shout "Hurrah!", make a speech from the steps of the senate, open the prisons and lower taxes.'

'You are absolutely right, Count,' said the one who extended his syllables. 'Now I know why you clamour so for democracy.'

'I warn you, gentlemen,' grated the one called Joachim, 'that it won't go off without a hitch. Our plan depends on Emhyr dying. And we can't close our eyes to the fact that Emhyr has many henchmen, has a corps of internal troops, and a fanatical guard. It won't be easy to hack our way through the Impera Brigade, and they – let's not delude ourselves – will fight to the last man.'

'And here,' declared Skellen, 'Vilgefortz can offer us his help. We won't have to besiege the palace or fight our way through the "Impera". The issue will be solved by one assassin with magical protection. As it was in Tretogor just before the rebellion of the mages on Thanedd.'

'King Radovid of Redania.'

'That's right.'

'Does Vilgefortz have such an assassin?'

'He does. In order to prove our reliability, gentlemen, I'll tell you who it is. The sorceress Yennefer, who we're holding in prison.'

'In prison? I heard that Yennefer was Vilgefortz's accomplice.'

'She's his prisoner. She will carry out the assassination like a golem, bewitched, hypnotised and programmed. And then commit suicide.'

'A bewitched hag doesn't especially suit me,' said the one who drew out his syllables, and his reluctance made him draw them out even more. 'Better would be a hero, an ardent idealist, an avenger—'

'An avenger,' Skellen interrupted. 'That fits perfectly here, Lord Leuvaarden. Yennefer will be avenging the harm caused her by the tyrant. Emhyr tormented and caused the death of her ward, an innocent child. That cruel dictator, that deviant, instead of taking care of the empire and the people, persecuted and tortured a child. For that he won't escape vengeance . . .'

'I very much approve,' Ardal aep Dahy declared.

'I do, too,' grated Joachim de Wett.

'Splendid!' gushed the Count of Broinne. 'For outraging other men's wives the tyrant and degenerate will receive his just deserts. Splendid!'

'One thing.' Leuvaarden drawled out his syllables. 'In order to establish trust, Count Stefan, please reveal to us Lord Vilgefortz's current place of abode.'

'Gentlemen, I . . . I'm forbidden . . .'

'It will be a guarantee. A safeguard of your sincerity and devotion to the cause.'

'Don't be afraid of betrayal, Stefan,' added aep Dahy. 'None of those present here will betray us. It's a paradox. Under other conditions perhaps among us there'd be one who would buy his life by betraying the others. But all of us know only too well that we won't buy anything with perfidy. Emhyr var Emreis doesn't forgive. He is incapable of forgiving. He has a lump of ice in place of his heart. Which is why he must die.'

Stefan Skellen didn't hesitate for long.

'Very well,' he said. 'Let it be a safeguard of my sincerity. Vilgefortz is hiding in . . .'

*

The Witcher, sitting at the openings of the trumpets, clenched his fists so hard they hurt. He pricked up his ears. And racked his memory.

*

The Witcher's doubts regarding Fringilla's amulet were misplaced and were dispelled in a flash. When he entered the large cavern and approached the stone bridge above the black chasm, the medallion jerked and fluttered on his neck, now not like a sparrow, but like a large, strong bird. A rook, for example.

Geralt froze. The amulet calmed down. He didn't make the smallest movement, in order that not a single rustle or even loud breath would confuse his ears. He waited. He knew that on the other side of the chasm, beyond the bridge, was whatever was lurking in the darkness. He couldn't rule out that something might also be hiding behind his back, and that the bridge was meant to be a trap. He had no intention of being caught in it. He waited. Until something happened.

'Greetings, Witcher,' he heard. 'We've been waiting here for you.'

The voice emerging from the gloom sounded strange. But Geralt had heard voices like that before, and he knew them. The voices of creatures not accustomed to communicating using speech. Able to use the apparatus of the lungs, diaphragm, windpipe and voice box, these creatures weren't in complete control of their articulatory apparatus, even when the construction of their lips, palates and tongues were quite similar to those of humans. The words spoken by creatures like that, apart from their strange accent and intonation, were full of sounds unpleasant to the human ear – from hard and nastily barking to hissing and slimily soft.

'We've been waiting for you,' repeated the voice. 'We knew you'd come, lured by rumours. That you'd crawl in here, under the ground, to stalk, pursue, torment and murder. You won't leave here now. You won't see the sun you've come to love so much again.'

'Show yourself.'

Something moved in the darkness on the far side of the bridge. In one place the gloom seemed to thicken and assume a more or less human form. The creature, it seemed, never remained in the same position or place for a moment, but shifted with the help of swift, nervous and shimmering movements. The Witcher had seen such creatures before.

'A korred,' he stated coldly. 'I might have expected somebody like you here. It's a wonder I haven't happened upon you before.'

'Well, well.' Derision sounded in the restless creature's voice. 'It's dark, but he recognised me. And do you recognise him? And him? And him?'

Three more creatures emerged from the darkness, as noiselessly as ghosts. One of them, lurking behind the korred's back, was also humanoid in shape and general appearance, but was shorter, more hunched and more simian. Geralt knew it was a kilmulis.

The two other monsters, as he had rightly suspected, were skulking in front of the bridge, ready to cut off his retreat if he stepped onto it. The first, on the left, scrabbled its claws like a huge spider, stopped moving and shuffled its numerous legs. It was a pryskirnik. The last creature, roughly resembling a candelabra, seemed to slip straight out from the cracked slate wall. Geralt couldn't guess what it was. A monster like that didn't feature in any witcher tomes.

'I don't want to fight,' he said, counting a little on the fact that the creatures had begun by talking instead of simply leaping on his back from the darkness. 'I don't want to pick a fight with you. But if it comes to it I'll defend myself.'

'We've taken that into account,' hissed the korred. 'Which is why there are four of us. Which is why we lured you here. You've driven us to a dog's life, O roguish witcher. The most beautiful holes in this part of the world, a wonderful place for wintering. We've been wintering here almost since the dawn of time. And now you've come here hunting, you good-for-nothing. Chasing us, stalking us, killing us for money. We're putting an end to it. And to you too.'

'Listen, korred—'

'Be polite,' the creature snapped. 'I can't stand boorishness.'

'How should I address—'

'Mister Schweitzer.'

'And so, Mister Schweitzer,' continued Geralt, apparently obediently and meekly, 'it's like this. I came here, I admit, as a witcher, with a witcher task. I suggest we pass over the matter. Something has occurred in these vaults, however, which has changed the situation diametrically. I've learned something extremely important to me. Something that may change my entire life.'

'And what results from that?'

'I must immediately get onto the surface.' Geralt was a model of calm and patience. 'I must immediately set off on a long journey, without a moment's delay. A road which may turn out to be one from which I won't return. I doubt if I'll ever be back in these parts—'

'You want to buy your life like that, witcher?' hissed Mr Schweitzer. 'Nothing doing. Your begging is in vain. We have you in our grasp and we won't let you out of it. We'll kill you not just for our own sake, but for the sake of our other comrades. For our freedom and your freedom, so to speak.'

'I won't just never return here,' Geralt continued patiently, 'but I shall cease my witcher activities. I shall never kill any of you again—'

'You lie! You lie from fear!'

'But—' Geralt wasn't to be interrupted this time either '—I must, as I've said, get out of here right away. So you have two alternatives to choose from. Firstly, you'll believe in my sincerity, and I leave you here. Or secondly, I leave here over your dead bodies.'

'Or thirdly,' the korred rasped, 'you'll be the dead body.'

The Witcher's sword rasped as he drew it from the scabbard on his back.

'Not the only one,' he said unemotionally. 'Certainly not the only one, Mister Schweitzer.'

The korred was silent for some time. The kilmulis was rocking and rasping behind his back. The pryskirnik was bending and straightening its limbs. The candelabra was changing its shape. Now it looked like a misshapen Christmas tree with two huge glowing eyes.

'Give us some proof,' the korred said at last, 'of your sincerity and good will.'

'What?'

'Your sword. You claim you'll give up being a witcher. A witcher is his sword. Throw it into the chasm. Or break it. Then we'll let you out.'

For a moment Geralt stood without moving. The water dripping from the walls and ceiling could be heard in the silence. Then slowly, without hurrying, he jammed his sword vertically and deeply into a rocky cleft. And broke the blade with a powerful blow of his boot. The blade shattered with a whine whose echo sounded in the caverns.

Water dripped from the walls, dribbling down them like tears.

'I can't believe it,' the korred said slowly. 'I can't believe anyone would be that stupid.'

They all fell on him, instantly, without any shouting, noises or commands. Mister Schweitzer was the first to lope across the bridge, his claws extended and baring fangs that wouldn't have shamed a wolf.

Geralt let him come closer, then twisted his hips and slashed, hacking through his throat and lower jaw. The next moment he was on the bridge and cutting open the kilmulis with a powerful blow. He crouched and fell to the ground, just in time, and the attacking candelabra flew over his head, barely scratching his jacket with its talons. The Witcher dodged away from the pryskirnik, from its thin legs flashing like scythes. A blow from one of them hit him on the side of the head. Geralt danced, making a feint and encircling himself with a sweeping slash. The pryskirnik leaped again, but missed. It crashed against the barrier and smashed it, tumbling into the chasm with a hail of stones. Until that moment it hadn't emitted the merest sound, but now it howled as it hurtled into the chasm. The howling gradually faded.

They attacked him from two sides – from one the candelabra, from the other the kilmulis, which, although wounded and gushing blood, had managed to stand up. The Witcher jumped onto the balustrade of the bridge, felt shifting stones grinding against each other and the whole bridge shuddering. He balanced, slipped out of reach of the candelabra's clawed feet and found himself behind the kilmulis's back. The kilmulis didn't have a neck, so Geralt slashed it in the temple. But the monster's skull was like iron, so he had to hack it a second time. He lost too much time doing it.

He was hit in the head, the pain exploded in his skull and eyes. He whirled around, defending himself with a parry, feeling blood pouring from under his hair, trying hard to understand what had happened. He dodged another blow of the claws and understood.

The candelabra had changed shape – it was now attacking with its improbably extended legs.

That had a flaw. Now its centre of gravity and balance was disrupted. The Witcher ducked under the legs, drawing closer. The candelabra, seeing what was afoot, fell on its back like a cat, sticking out its rear legs, which were just as taloned as its fore legs. Geralt jumped over it, slashing mid-leap. He felt the blade cut flesh. He hunched up, turned and cut once more, dropping to his knee. The creature screamed and threw its head forward violently, savagely snapping its massive teeth just in front of the Witcher's chest. Its huge eyes shone in the darkness. Geralt shoved it back with a powerful blow of the sword pommel and cut from close range, removing half its skull. Even without that half the strange creature, which didn't feature in any witcher tomes, still snapped its teeth for a good few seconds. Then it died, with a terrible, almost human sigh.

The korred was twitching convulsively in a pool of blood.

The Witcher stood over it.

'I cannot believe,' he said, 'that someone could be so stupid as to be taken in by such a simple illusion as the one with the broken sword.'

He wasn't certain if the korred was conscious enough to understand. But actually he didn't care.

'I warned you,' he said, wiping off the blood that was pouring down his cheek. 'I warned you I had to get out of here.'

Mister Schweitzer trembled violently, wheezed, whistled and gnashed his teeth. Then fell silent and stopped moving.

Water dripped from the walls and ceiling.

*

'Are you satisfied, Regis?'

'I am now.'

'In that case . . .' The Witcher stood. 'Go on. Run off and pack. And be quick.'

'It won't take me very long. *Omnia mea mecum porto.*'

'What?'

'I have very little luggage.'

'So much the better. Outside the town in half an hour.'

'I'll be there.'

*

He'd underestimated her. She caught him in the act. He only had himself to blame. Rather than rushing, he could have ridden around the back of the palace and left Roach in the larger stables there, the one for the errant knighthood, staff and servants, and where his company also kept their horses. He hadn't done that, but had used the ducal stables owing to haste and habit. And he might have guessed there would be somebody in the stable who would inform on him.

She was walking from stall to stall, kicking the straw. She was wearing a short lynx-skin coat, a white satin blouse, a black equestrian skirt and high boots. The horses snorted, sensing the anger emanating from her.

'Well, well,' she said on seeing him, flexing the riding crop she was holding. 'We're bolting! Without saying goodbye. For the letter which is probably lying on my table is no farewell. Not after what we had. I imagine some extremely important arguments explain and justify your behaviour.'

'They do. Sorry, Fringilla.'

'"Sorry, Fringilla",' she repeated, sneering furiously. 'How curt, how economical, how unpretentious, with such attention to style. The letter you left for me, I'm absolutely certain, is doubtless edited just as elegantly. Without excess lavishness as regards ink.'

'I must ride,' he uttered. 'You can guess why. And for whose sake. Please forgive me. I intended to flee stealthily and silently, because . . . I didn't want you to try and come after me.'

'Your fears were groundless,' she drawled, bending the crop. 'I wouldn't have gone after you even if you'd asked me, grovelling at my feet. Oh, no, Witcher. Ride alone, die alone, freeze alone in the mountain passes. I have no obligations towards Ciri. And towards you? Do you know how many have begged for what you had? And for what you're now contemptuously rejecting, tossing away?'

'I'll never forget you.'

'Oh,' she hissed. 'You don't know how much I feel like making sure you really won't. Even if not using magic, then using this whip!'

'You won't do it.'

'You're right, I won't. I wouldn't be able to. I shall behave as befits a scorned and spurned lover. Classically. I shall walk away with my head high. With dignity and pride. Swallowing back the tears. Then I'll howl into a pillow. And then I'll bed another!'

By the end she was almost screaming.

He said nothing. Neither did she.

'Geralt,' she said finally, in quite a different voice. 'Stay with me.

'I think I love you,' she said, seeing he was delaying his answer. 'Stay with me. I implore you. I've never asked anyone nor thought I ever would. But I ask you.'

'Fringilla,' he answered after a while. 'You're a woman a man can only dream about. My fault, my only fault, is that I don't have the nature of a dreamer.'

'You are,' she said a moment later, biting her lip, 'like an angler's hook, which once it's stuck in, can only be pulled out with blood and flesh. Well, I've only got myself to blame. I knew what I was doing, playing around with a dangerous toy. Luckily, I also know how to cope with the effects. In that respect I have an advantage over the rest of the female species.'

He didn't comment.

'In any case,' she added, 'a broken heart, although it hurts greatly, a lot more than a broken arm, heals much, much more quickly.'

He didn't comment that time, either. Fringilla contemplated the bruise on his cheek.

'How was my amulet? Does it work well?'

'It's quite simply wonderful. Thank you.'

She nodded.

'Where are you riding to?' she asked in a completely different voice and tone. 'What did you find out? You know where Vilgefortz is hiding, don't you?'

'Yes. Don't ask me to tell you where that is. I won't.'

'I'll buy that information. Quid pro quo.'

'Oh, yes?'

'I have information,' she repeated, 'that is valuable. And to you quite simply invaluable. I'll sell it to you in exchange for—'

'For peace of mind,' he finished, looking her in the eyes. 'For the trust I placed in you. A moment ago there was talk of love. And now we're starting to talk of trade?'

She was silent for a long while. Then she hit her boot violently, hard, with the riding crop.

'Yennefer,' she quickly recited, 'the one whose name you called me several times in the night, in moments of ecstasy, never betrayed you, nor Ciri. She was never an accomplice of Vilgefortz. In order to rescue Cirilla, she fearlessly took an exceptional risk. She suffered a defeat, and fell into Vilgefortz's hands. She was certainly tortured into the attempts at scanning that took place last autumn. It's not known if she's alive. I don't know any more. I swear.'

'Thank you, Fringilla.'

'Now go.'

'I trust you,' he said, without moving. 'And I shall never forget what was between us. I trust you, Fringilla. I won't stay with you, but I think I loved you too . . . In my own way. Please keep utterly secret what you are about to find out. Vilgefortz's hideout is in—'

'Wait,' she interrupted. 'You'll tell me later, you'll disclose it later. Now, before you leave, say goodbye to me. The way you ought to say goodbye. Not with paltry letters, not with mumbled apologies. Say goodbye to me the way I desire.'

She took off her lynx fur coat and tossed it down on a pile of straw. She violently tore off her blouse, beneath which she was naked. She fell onto the fur, pulling him after her, onto her. Geralt caught her by the nape of her neck, lifted up her skirt, and suddenly realised there would be no time to take his gloves off. Fringilla was fortunately not wearing gloves. Or knickers. Even more fortunately she wasn't wearing spurs either, for soon after the heels of her riding boots were literally everywhere. It doesn't bear thinking what might have happened had she been wearing spurs.

When she screamed he kissed her. Stifling the scream.

The horses, scenting their furious passion, neighed, stamped and thumped against their stalls until hay and dust fell from the ceiling.

'Rhys-Rhun citadel, in Nazair, by Lake Muredach,' Fringilla Vigo ended triumphantly. 'That's where Vilgefortz's hide-out is. I got it out of the Witcher before he rode away. We have enough time to overtake him. He has no chance of getting there before April.'

The nine women gathered in the columned chamber of Montecalvo Castle nodded, favouring Fringilla with looks of great appreciation.

'Rhys-Rhun,' repeated Philippa Eilhart, baring her teeth in a predatory smile and playing with the sardonyx cameo brooch fastened to her dress. 'Rhys-Rhun in Nazair. Well, see you soon, Master Vilgefortz . . . See you soon!'

'When the Witcher gets there,' hissed Keira Metz, 'he'll find rubble which by then won't even be stinking of ash.'

'Or dead bodies.' Sabrina Glevissig smiled enchantingly.

'Well done, Miss Vigo,' nodded Sheala. 'Over three months in Toussaint . . . But it was probably worth it.'

Fringilla Vigo's eyes swept over the sorceresses sitting at the table. Over Sheala, Philippa and Sabrina Glevissig. Over Keira Metz, Margarita Laux-Antille and Triss Merigold. Over Francesca Findabair and Ida Emean, whose eyes, ringed with garish elven makeup, expressed absolutely nothing. Over Assire var Anahid, whose eyes expressed anxiety and concern.

'It was,' she admitted.

Quite sincerely.

*

The sky slowly changed from dark blue to black. An icy gale blew among the vineyards. Geralt fastened his wolf-skin cloak and wrapped a woollen scarf around his neck. And felt wonderful. As usual, love expressed had raised him up to the peak of his physical, psychological and moral powers, had erased all traces of doubt, and his thinking was clear and intense. He only regretted he would be deprived of that wonderful panacea for a long time.

The voice of Reynart de Bois-Fresnes startled him out of his reverie.

'Bad weather's coming,' said the knight errant, looking east-wards, from where the gale was blowing. 'Make haste. If snow comes with that wind, if it catches you on the Malheur pass, you'll be stuck in a trap. And then pray for a thaw to all the gods you venerate, know and understand.'

'We understand.'

'The Sansretour will guide you for the first few days. Keep to the river. You'll pass a trapper's manufactory and reach a place where a right-bank tributary flows into the Sansretour. Don't forget: a right-bank tributary. Its course will indicate the way to the Mal-heur pass. Should you with God's will conquer Malheur, don't hurry too much, for you'll still have the Sansmerci and Mortblanc passes ahead of you. Should you conquer both of them, you'll de-scend into the Sudduth valley. Sudduth has a warm microclimate, almost like Toussaint. Were it not for the poor soil they would plant vines there.'

He broke off, embarrassed by the reproachful gazes.

'Indeed,' he hemmed. 'To the point. At the mouth of the Sudduth lies the small town of Caravista. My cousin, Guy de Bois-Fresnes, lives there. Visit him and mention me. Should it turn out my cousin's died or gone insane, remember the direction of your journey is the Mag Deira plain, the valley of the River Sylte. Further on, Geralt, it's according to the maps you copied at the town cartographer's. Since we're on the subject of cartography, I don't exactly understand why you asked me about some castles or other—'

'Better forget about that, Reynart. Nothing like that took place. You heard nothing, saw nothing. Even if they torture you. Understand?'

'I do.'

'A rider,' warned Cahir, getting his unruly stallion under con-trol. 'A rider's galloping towards us from the palace.'

'If there's only one,' Angoulême grinned, stroking the battle-axe hanging from her saddle, 'it's small beer.'

The rider turned out to be Dandelion, riding like a bat out of hell. Astonishingly the horse turned out to be Pegasus, the poet's gelding, which didn't like galloping and was not in the habit of doing so.

'Well,' said the troubadour, panting as though *he* had been carrying the gelding and not the other way around. 'Well, I made it. I was afraid I wouldn't catch you.'

'Just don't say you're finally riding with us.'

'No, Geralt.' Dandelion lowered his head. 'I'm not. I'm staying here in Toussaint with my Little Weasel. I mean with Anarietta. But I couldn't not say farewell to you. Or wish you a safe journey.'

'Thank the duchess for everything. And make excuses as to why it's so sudden and without a farewell. Explain it somehow.'

'You took a knightly vow and that's that. Everybody in Toussaint, including the Little Weasel, will understand, and here . . . Have it. Let it be my contribution.'

'Dandelion.' Geralt took a heavy pouch from the poet. 'We aren't suffering from a shortage of money. It's not necessary . . .'

'Let it be my contribution.' Repeated the troubadour. 'Cash always comes in useful. And besides, it isn't mine, I took those ducats from the Little Weasel's private coffer. Why are you looking like that? Women don't need money. I mean what for? They don't drink, they don't play dice, and they're bloody women themselves. Well, farewell! Be off, because I'll burst into tears. And when it's all over you're to stop by Toussaint on your way back and tell me everything. And I want to hug Ciri. Do you promise, Geralt?'

'I promise.'

'So, farewell.'

'Wait.' Geralt wheeled his horse around and rode closer to Pegasus. He took a letter surreptitiously from his bosom. 'Make sure this letter reaches—'

'Fringilla Vigo?'

'No. Dijkstra.'

'Are you serious, Geralt? And how do you propose I do it?'

'Find a way. I know you will. And now farewell. Give us a hug, you old fool.'

'Give us a hug, comrade. I'll be looking out for you.'

They watched him ride away and saw him trotting towards Beauclair.

The sky darkened.

'Reynart.' The Witcher turned around in the saddle. 'Ride with us.'

'No, Geralt,' replied Reynart de Bois-Fresnes a moment later. 'I'm errant. But not asinine.'

*

There was unusual excitement in the great columned chamber of Montecalvo Castle. The subtle chiaroscuro of candelabras that usually predominated there was replaced by the milky brightness of a huge, magical screen. The image on the screen shimmered, flickered and vanished, intensifying the excitement and tension. And anxiety.

'Ha,' said Philippa Eilhart, smiling predatorily. 'Pity I can't be there. A little action would do me good. And a little adrenaline.'

Sheala de Tancarville looked at her sarcastically, but didn't say anything. Francesca Findabair and Ida Emean magically stabilised the image, and enlarged it to fill the entire wall. They clearly saw black mountain peaks against a dark blue sky, stars reflecting in the surface of a lake, and the dark and angular shape of a castle.

'I still can't be sure,' said Sheala, 'if it wasn't a mistake to entrust the command of the strike force to Sabrina and young Metz. They broke Keira's ribs on Thanedd, she may want to get revenge. And Sabrina . . . Why, she loves action and adrenaline a little too much. Right, Philippa—'

'We've discussed that already.' Philippa cut her off, and her voice was as acidic as plum pickle. 'We've established what there was to establish. No one will be killed without an absolute need. Sabrina and Keira's force will enter Rhys-Rhun as quiet as mice, on tiptoe, hush-hush. They'll take Vilgefortz alive, without a single scratch, without a single bruise. We agreed on that. Although I still think we ought to make an example. So that those in the castle who survive the night will awake screaming to the end of their days when they dream of this night.'

'Revenge,' said the sorceress from Kovir, 'is the delight of mediocre, weak and petty minds.'

'Perhaps,' agreed Philippa, with an apparently indifferent smile. 'But that doesn't stop it being a delight.'

'Let's drop it.' Margarita Laux-Antille raised a goblet of sparkling wine. 'I suggest we drink to the health of Madam Fringilla

Vigo, thanks to whose efforts Vilgefortz's hide-out was discovered. Solid, exemplary work indeed, Madam Fringilla.'

Fringilla bowed, responding to the salutes. She noticed something like mockery in Philippa's black eyes, and dislike in the azure gaze of Triss Merigold. She couldn't decipher the smiles of Francesca and Sheala.

'They are beginning,' said Assire var Anahid, pointing at the magical image.

They settled themselves more comfortably. Philippa dimmed the lights with a spell in order for them to see better. They saw swift, black shapes peeling off from the rocks, as silent and agile as bats. Saw them flying low and then plummeting onto the battlements and machicolations of Rhys-Rhun Castle.

'I probably haven't had a broom between my legs for a century,' murmured Philippa. 'I'll soon forget how to fly.'

Sheala, staring at the screen, quietened her with an impatient hiss.

Fire flashed briefly in the windows of the black castle complex. Once, twice, thrice. They knew what it was. The bolted doors and hasps splintered asunder under the impact of ball lightning.

'They're inside,' said Assire var Anahid softly. She was the only one not observing the screen on the wall, but was staring at a crystal ball on the table. 'The strike force is inside. But something's not right. Not how it's meant to be . . .'

Fringilla felt the blood flowing from her heart to her belly. She now knew what wasn't right.

'Madam Glevissig,' reported Assire, 'is opening the direct telecommunicator.'

The space between the columns in the hall suddenly lit up. In the materialising oval they saw Sabrina Glevissig in male attire, her hair tied on her forehead with a chiffon scarf and her face blackened with stripes of camouflage pigment. Behind the sorceress's back could be seen dirty stone walls, and on them shreds of rags, once tapestries. Sabrina extended a gloved hand hung with long strands of cobwebs towards them.

'The only thing there's plenty of here,' she said, gesticulating wildly, 'is this! Just this! Bloody hell, what stupidity . . . What a fiasco . . .'

'Make yourself clearer, Sabrina!'

'Make what clearer?' yelled the Kaedwenian witch. 'What could be clearer here? Can't you see? This is Rhys-Rhun Castle! It's empty! Empty and dirty! It's a sodding empty ruin! There's nothing here! Nothing!'

Keira Metz emerged from behind Sabrina's shoulder, looking like a hellish fiend in her facial camouflage.

'There isn't and there hasn't been anyone in this castle,' she said calmly, 'for at least fifty years. For fifty years there hasn't been a living soul here, not counting the spiders, rats and bats. We made the landing in completely the wrong place.'

'Have you made sure it isn't an illusion?'

'Do you take us for children, Philippa?'

'Listen, both of you.' Philippa Eilhart nervously ran her fingers through her hair. 'Tell the mercenaries and novices they were on manoeuvres. Pay them and return. Return at once. And put a brave face on it, do you hear? Put a brave face on it!'

The oval of the communicator went out. Only the image on the wall screen remained. Rhys-Rhun Castle against the black sky, twinkling with stars. And the lake, with the stars reflected in it.

Fringilla Vigo looked down at the table. She felt as though the pounding blood would soon burst her cheeks.

'I . . . really,' she said at last, unable to bear the silence in the columned hall of Montecalvo Castle. 'I . . . really don't understand . . .'

'But I do,' said Triss Merigold.

'That castle . . .' said Philippa deep in thought, not paying any attention to her comrades. 'That castle . . . Rhys-Rhun . . . will have to be destroyed. Utterly annihilated. And when legends and tales begin to be made up about this whole debacle, it will be necessary to subject them to scrupulous censorship. Do you understand what I mean, ladies?'

'Only too well,' nodded Francesca Findabair, who had been silent up until that moment. Ida Emean, also silent, took the liberty of making quite an ambiguous snort.

'I . . .' Fringilla Vigo still seemed stunned. 'I truly can't comprehend . . . how it could have happened . . .'

'Oh,' said Sheala de Tancarville after a very long silence. 'It's nothing serious, Miss Vigo. No one's perfect.'

Philippa snorted softly. Assire var Anahid sighed and raised her eyes towards the plafond.

'After all,' added Sheala, pouting her lips, 'it's befallen all of us at some time. Each of us, sitting here, has been cheated, taken advantage of, and made a laughing stock of by some man, at some time.'

'I love you, I'm charmed by your lovely form:
And if you're not willing, I'll have to use force.'
'Father, my Father, he's gripped me at last!
The Erlkönig's hurting me, holding me fast! –

Johann Wolfgang Goethe

Everything has been, everything has happened. And everything has
already been written about.

Vysogota of Corvo

CHAPTER FIVE

A scorching, stuffy afternoon fell on the forest, and the lake surface, which had been as dark as jade shortly before, now flashed gold and lit up with reflections. Ciri had to shield her eyes with her hand. The glare reflected in the water blinded her, and she felt pain in her eyeballs and temples.

She rode through the lakeside thicket and urged Kelpie into the lake, deep enough for the water to reach above the mare's knees. The water was so clear that even from the height of the saddle Ciri could see the colourful mosaic of the bottom, the mussels and the swaying, feathery pond weed in the shadow cast by the horse. She saw a small crayfish striding proudly among the pebbles.

Kelpie whinnied. Ciri jerked the reins and rode into the shallows, but not onto the bank, because it was sandy and covered in rocks, and that ruled out riding fast. She led the mare right to the water's edge so she could walk on the hard gravel at the bottom. And almost at once urged Kelpie into a trot. She was as fleet as a real trotter, trained not to be ridden but to pull a gig or a landau. But she soon found that trotting was too slow. A kick of Ciri's heels and a shout urged the mare into a gallop. They raced among splashes of water flying all around, sparkling in the sun like drops of molten silver.

When she saw the tower, she didn't slow down yet not even the merest snort was audible in Kelpie's breathing, and her gallop was still light and effortless.

She hurtled into the courtyard at full speed, with a clatter of hooves, and pulled the mare up so suddenly that for a moment Kelpie's horseshoes slid over the flags with a long-drawn-out grinding sound. She stopped just before the elf-women waiting at the foot of the tower. Right in front of their noses. She felt satisfaction, for two of them, usually unmoving and dispassionate, now stepped back involuntarily.

'Never fear,' she snorted. 'I won't ride you down! Unless I mean to.'

The elves recovered quickly, their faces once more smoothed by calm, and nonchalant indifference returned to their eyes.

Ciri dismounted, or rather flew from the saddle. There was defiance in her eyes.

'Bravo,' said a fair-haired elf with a triangular-shaped face, emerging from the shadow under an arcade. 'A nice display, Loc'hlaith.'

He had greeted her like that the first time, when she had entered the Tower of the Swallow and found herself among the blooming spring. But that was long ago and things like that had stopped making any impression on her at all.

'I'm no Lady of the Lake,' she barked. 'I'm a prisoner here! And you're my gaolers! And I may as well speak bluntly! There you go!' She threw the reins to one of the elves. 'The horse needs rubbing down. Water her when she cools. And above all she must be looked after!'

The fair-haired elf smiled slightly.

'Indeed,' he said, watching the elf-women wordlessly lead the mare to the stable. 'You're a wronged prisoner here, and they are your harsh gaolers. It's quite plain.'

'Let them have a taste of their own medicine!' She stood akimbo, stuck up her nose and looked him boldly in the eyes, which were pale blue like aquamarines and quite gentle. 'I'm treating them as they treat me! And a prison's a prison.'

'You astonish me, Loc'hlaith.'

'And you treat me like a fool. And you haven't even introduced yourself.'

'I apologise. I am Crevan Espane aep Caomhan Macha. I am, if you know what it means, Aen Saevherne.'

'I do.' She looked at him with an admiration that she was unable to hide in time. 'A Knowing One. An elven sorcerer.'

'I could be called that. For convenience I use the alias Avallac'h, and you may address me as such.'

'Who told you—' she became sullen '—that I wish to address you at all? Knowing One or not, you're a gaoler, and I'm—'

'—a prisoner,' he finished sarcastically. 'You mentioned it. A badly treated prisoner to boot. You're probably forced to take rides around here, you wear a sword on your back as a punishment, likewise the elegant and quite rich apparel, so much more elegant and clean than what you arrived here in. But in spite of these dreadful conditions you haven't given in. You get your revenge for the harm you've received with brusqueness. With great courage and enthusiasm you also smash looking glasses which are works of art.'

She blushed, very cross with herself.

'Oh,' he said quickly, 'you may smash looking glasses to your heart's content. After all, they're only objects, and who cares if they were made seven hundred years ago? Would you like to promenade with me along the lake shore?'

The wind that rose slightly tempered the heat. Furthermore, the tall trees and the tower cast shadows. The water in the bay was a dull green; densely garlanded by water lilies and piled up with spherical yellow flowers, it almost resembled a meadow. Moorhens, gargling and nodding their red beaks, cruised briskly among the leaves.

'That mirror . . .' Ciri mumbled, twisting a heel in the wet gravel. 'I'm sorry about that. I lost my temper. And that's that.'

'Ah.'

'They disrespect me. Those elf-women. When I talk to them they pretend they can't understand. And when they do talk to me, they speak incomprehensibly on purpose. They humiliate me.'

'You speak our tongue fluently,' he explained calmly. 'But it's still a foreign language to you. Besides, you use *hen llinge*, and they use *ellylon*. The differences are slight, but do nonetheless exist.'

'I understand *you*. Every word.'

'When I talk to you I use *hen llinge*. The language of the elves from your world.'

'And you?' She turned around. 'What world are you from? I'm not a child. It's enough to look up at night. There isn't a single constellation I know. This world isn't mine. It isn't my place. I entered it by accident. And I want to leave. To get away.'

She bent over, picked up a stone and made a movement as though meaning to throw it absent-mindedly into the lake, towards the moorhens. She abandoned her plans under his gaze.

'Before I've ridden a furlong,' she said, not hiding her resentment, 'I'm at the lake. And I can see the tower. Regardless of which direction I ride, when I turn around there's always the lake and the tower. Always. There's no way of getting away from it. So it's a prison. Worse than a dungeon, than an oubliette, than a chamber with a barred window. Do you know why? Because it's more humiliating. *Ellylon* or not, it angers me when I'm sneered at and shown disrespect. Yes, yes, there's no sense making faces. You've also slighted me, you also mock me. And you're surprised that I'm furious?'

'As a matter of fact I am.' He opened his eyes wide. 'Inordinately.'

She sighed and shrugged.

'I entered the tower long ago,' she said, trying to stay calm. 'I happened upon another world. You were waiting for me, sitting and playing the pipes. You were even astonished at how long I'd delayed my arrival. You called me by my name, and only afterwards began that "Lady of the Lake" nonsense. Then you vanished without a word of explanation. Leaving me in prison. Call it what you like. I call it spiteful and malicious contempt.'

'Zireael, it's only been eight days.'

'Ah,' she scowled. 'You mean I'm lucky? Because it might have been eight weeks? Or eight months? Or eight . . .'

She fell silent.

'You've strayed far from Lara Dorren,' he said softly. 'You've lost your inheritance, you've lost the bond with your blood. No wonder the women don't understand you, nor you them. You don't just talk differently, you *think* differently. With quite different frames of reference. What is eight days or eight weeks? Time means nothing.'

'Very well!' she screamed in anger. 'I agree I'm not a wise elf, I'm a stupid human. To me time does mean something. I count the days, I even count the hours. And I've reckoned that many of both the first and the second have passed. I don't want anything from you now, I'll make do without explanations, it doesn't bother me why it's spring here, why there are unicorns here, and different constellations in the night sky. I'm not at all interested how you know my name and how you knew I'd turn up here. I only want one thing. To return home. To my world. To people!

People who think like me! Using the same frames of reference!'

'You'll return to them. In some time.'

'I want to go now!' she yelled. 'Not in some time! For time here is an eternity! What right do you have to hold me here? Why can't I leave this place? I came here myself! Of my own will! You don't have any right!'

'You came here yourself,' he calmly confirmed. 'But not of your own will. You were led here by destiny, helped a little by us. For you have been long awaited. Very long. Even according to our reckoning.'

'I don't understand any of that.'

'We've waited long.' He paid no attention to her. 'Fearing but one thing: whether you'd be able to enter here. You were. You proved your blood, your lineage. And that means that your place is here, not among the Dh'oine. You are the daughter of Lara Dorren aep Shiadhal.'

'I am Pavetta's daughter! I don't even know who your Lara is!'

He snorted, but very slightly, almost imperceptibly.

'In that case,' he said, 'it'd be best if I explained to you who "my" Lara is. Since time is short, I'd prefer to begin the explanations en route. But why, for the sake of a foolish demonstration you've almost run the mare into the ground—'

'Into the ground? Ha! You don't yet know how much that mare can endure. Where are we going?'

'If you permit I'll also explain that en route.'

*

Ciri halted Kelpie, who was now wheezing, recognising that a breakneck gallop was senseless and of no use at all.

Avallac'h hadn't lied. Here, on open ground, on meadows and moors dotted with menhirs, the same force was active as around Tor Zireael. You could try riding at full speed in any direction, but after a furlong or so an invisible force made you ride around in a circle.

Ciri patted the wheezing Kelpie on her neck, and looked at the small group of elves who rode at an easy pace. A moment earlier, when Avallac'h had finally told her what they wanted from her, she had launched into a gallop, to escape from them, to leave them as far as possible behind her – they and their impudent, unthinkable task.

Now, though, they were in front of her again. At a distance of more or less a furlong.

Avallac'h hadn't lied. There was no escape.

The only good thing the gallop had brought was that it had cooled her head, chilled her rage. She was now much calmer. But nonetheless she was still shaking with anger.

What a mess I'm in, she thought. *Why did I go into the Tower?*

She shuddered, thinking back. Recalling Bonhart riding after her across the ice on his grey horse, muzzle foaming.

She shuddered even more intensely. And calmed down.

I'm alive, she thought, looking around. *It's not the end of the battle. Death will end the fight, everything else only interrupts it. They taught me that at Kaer Morhen.*

She urged Kelpie to a walk and then, seeing the mare was gamely raising her head, to a trot. She rode down an avenue of menhirs. The grass and heather reached her stirrups.

She quite quickly caught up with Avallac'h and the three elf-women. The Sage, smiling slightly, turned his aquamarine eyes enquiringly on her.

'Please, Avallac'h.' She cleared her throat. 'Tell me it was a dismal joke.'

Something like a shadow passed over his face.

'I'm not accustomed to joking,' he said. 'And since you consider it a joke, I'll take the liberty repeating it with due gravity: we want to have your child, O Swallow, daughter of Lara Dorren. Only when you bear it will we permit you to leave here, to return to your world. The choice, naturally, is yours. I presume your reckless dash helped you to reach a decision. What is your answer?'

'My answer is no,' she replied firmly. 'Categorically and absolutely no. I don't agree and that's that.'

'Tough luck,' he shrugged. 'I admit I am disappointed. But why, it's your choice.'

'How can you demand something like that at all?' she cried in a trembling voice. 'How could you dare? By what right?'

He looked at her calmly. Ciri also felt the gaze of the elf-women on her.

'I believe,' he said, 'that I told you the story of your family in detail. You seemed to understand. Thus your question astonishes me. We have the right to demand, and we can, O Swallow. Your father, Cregennan, took a child from us. You will give us one back. You will repay the debt. It seems just and logical to me.'

'My father . . . I don't remember my father, but he was called Duny. Not Cregennan. I've already told you!'

'And I replied that those few ridiculous human generations are meaningless to us.'

'But I don't want to!' yelled Ciri so loudly that the mare skittered beneath her. 'I don't want to, understand? I don't waaaant tooooooo! The thought of a bloody parasite being implanted in me is sickening. I feel nauseous when I think that that parasite will grow inside me, that—'

She broke off, seeing the faces of the elf-women. Two of them expressed boundless atonishment. The third boundless odium. Avallac'h coughed meaningfully.

'Let's ride on a little and talk in private,' he said coolly. 'Your views, O Swallow, are a little too radical to be expressed in front of witnesses.'

She did as he asked. They rode on silence for a long while.

'I'll escape from you.' Ciri spoke first. 'You won't keep me here against my will. I escaped from the Isle of Thanedd, I escaped from the Trappers and the Nilfgaardians, I escaped from Bonhart and Tawny Owl. And I'll escape from you. I'll find a way to outwit your witchcraft.'

'I thought,' he replied a moment later, 'that you cared more about your friends. About Yennefer. And Geralt.'

'You know about that?' she gasped in amazement. 'Well, yes. True. You are a Knowing One! So you ought to know I'm thinking about them. There, in my world, they're in danger now, at this moment. And yet you want to imprison me here . . . Well, for at least nine months. You see for yourself I don't have a choice. I understand it's important for you – a child, that Elder Blood – but I cannot. I simply cannot.'

The elf said nothing for a while. He rode so close he was touching her knee.

'The choice, as I said, belongs to you. You ought, however, to know something. It would be dishonest to conceal it from you. You can't escape from here, O Swallow. So if you refuse to co-operate you will stay here forever, and will never see your friends or your world again.'

'That's despicable blackmail!'

'If, though,' he continued, unconcerned by her yelling, 'you agree to what we ask, we'll prove to you that time is meaningless.'

'I don't understand.'

'Time passes differently here than there. If you do us this favour, we shall return the favour. We shall enable you to regain the time you will lose among us here. Among the Folk of the Alder.'

She said nothing, her eyes fixed on Kelpie's black mane. *Use delaying tactics*, she thought. As Vesemir said in Kaer Morhen *when they're about to hang you, ask for a glass of water. You never know what might happen before they bring it.*

One of the elf-women suddenly screamed and whistled.

Avallac'h's horse neighed, and danced on the spot. The elf brought it under control and shouted something to the elf-women. Ciri saw one of them draw a bow from a leather quiver hanging from her saddle. She stood up in the stirrups and shielded her eyes with a hand.

'Keep calm,' said Avallac'h sharply. Ciri gasped.

Some unicorns were galloping over the moor about two hundred paces from them. An entire herd, at least thirty head.

Ciri had seen unicorns before. Sometimes, particularly at dawn, they came up to the lake at the foot of the Tower of the Swallow. They had never let her approach them, though. But had vanished like ghosts.

The leader of the herd was a great stallion with a strange, reddish coat. He suddenly stopped, neighed piercingly and reared up. He trotted on his hind hooves, waving his fore hooves in the air in a way that would have been absolutely impossible for any horse.

Ciri noted in amazement that Avallac'h and the three elf-women were humming, singing in chorus some strange, monotonous tune.

Who are you?

She shook her head.

Who are you? The question sounded again in her skull, pounded in her temples. The elves' song suddenly rose a tone in pitch. The ruddy unicorn neighed and the entire herd answered in kind. The earth trembled as they galloped away.

The song of Avallac'h and the elf-women broke off. Ciri saw the Knowing One furtively wiping the sweat from his brow. The elf glanced at her out of the corner of his eye, understanding that she had seen.

'Not everything here is as pretty as it looks,' he said dryly. 'Not everything.'

'Are you afraid of unicorns? But they're wise and friendly.'

He didn't answer.

'I heard,' she went on, 'that elves and unicorns loved one another.'

He turned his head.

'Then accept,' he said coldly, 'that what you saw was a lovers' tiff.'

She didn't ask any more questions.

She had enough of her own concerns.

*

The tops of the hills were decorated by cromlechs and dolmens. The sight of them reminded Ciri of the stone near Ellander, beside which Yennefer taught her what magic is. *That was so long ago*, she thought. *Ages . . .*

One of the elf-women shouted again. Ciri glanced to where she was pointing. Before she had time to note that the herd being led by the ruddy stallion had returned, the second elf-woman shouted. She stood up in the stirrups.

Another herd emerged from the opposite side, from behind a hill. The unicorn leading it was bluish-grey and dappled.

Avallac'h quickly said a few words. It was the *ellylon* language that Ciri found so difficult, but she understood, particularly since the elf-women reached for their bows in unison. Avallac'h turned his face towards Ciri, and she felt a buzzing growing in her head.

It was a buzzing quite similar to what a conch shell emits when pressed to the ear. But much stronger.

'*Do not resist,*' she heard a voice. '*Do not fight. I must leap, I must transport you to another place. You are in mortal danger.*'

A whistle and a long, drawn-out cry reached them from far away. And a moment later the earth shuddered under iron-shod hooves.

Riders emerged from behind the hill. An entire troop.

The horses were wearing caparisons, the riders crested helmets, and the cloaks around their shoulders fluttered in the gallop. Their vermilion-amaranth-crimson colour brought to mind the glow of a fire in the sky illuminated by the blaze of the setting sun.

A whistling and a cry. The horsemen raced towards them en masse.

Before they had ridden half a furlong the unicorns had vanished. They disappeared, leaving a cloud of dust behind them.

*

The riders' leader, a black-haired elf, sat on a dark bay stallion as huge as a dragon. It was adorned, like all the horses in the troop, in a caparison embroidered with dragon's scales, and wore on its head a truly demonic horned bucranium. Like all the elves, the black-haired one wore beneath his cloak of a myriad shades of red a mail shirt made of unbelievably tiny rings, thanks to which it fit his body snugly, like knitted woollen cloth.

'Avallac'h,' he said, saluting.

'Eredin.'

'You owe me a favour. You will pay it back when I demand it.'

'I'll pay it back when you demand it.'

The black-haired elf dismounted. Avallac'h also dismounted, gesturing to Ciri to do the same. They walked up the hill between white rocks with peculiar shapes covered in spindle and dwarf shrubs of flowering myrtle.

Ciri looked at them. They were of equal height, meaning they were both extremely tall. But Avallac'h's face was gentle, while the black-haired elf's face brought to mind a bird of prey. *Fair and black*, she thought. *Good and evil. Light and dark . . .*

162

'Zireael, let me introduce you to Eredin Bréacc Glas.'

'I'm pleased to meet you.' The elf bowed and Ciri returned the bow. Not very gracefully.

'How did you know,' Avallac'h asked, 'that we were in danger?'

'I had no idea.' The elf scrutinised Ciri. 'We patrol the plain, for news has got out that the one-horns have become anxious and aggressive. No one knows why. I mean, now I know why. It's because of her, naturally.'

Avallac'h neither confirmed nor denied it. Meanwhile, Ciri countered the black-haired elf's gaze with a haughty expression. For a moment they looked at each other, neither of them wanting to be the first to look away.

'So that's the supposed Elder Blood,' remarked the elf. 'Aen Hen Ichaer. The inheritance of Shiadhal and Lara Dorren? One isn't inclined to believe it. For it's simply a young Dh'oine. A human female.'

Avallac'h said nothing. His face was motionless and indifferent.

'I assume you aren't mistaken,' the black-haired elf continued. 'Why, I take it for granted, for you, as rumour has it, never err. Hidden deep in this creature is the Lara gene. Yes, when one examines her more closely, one can see certain traits testifying to the young one's lineage. She indeed has something in her eyes that brings to mind Lara Dorren. Doesn't she, Avallac'h? Who, if not you, is more entitled to judge?'

Avallac'h didn't speak this time either. But Ciri noticed a faint blush on his pale face. She was very surprised. And pondered it.

'Summing up—' the black-haired elf grimaced '—there is something precious, something beautiful, in this little Dh'oine female. I see it. And I have the impression I've seen a gold nugget in a pile of compost.'

Ciri's eyes flashed furiously. Avallac'h slowly turned his head.

'You talk just like a human, Eredin,' he said slowly.

Eredin Bréacc Glas bared his teeth in a smile. Ciri had seen teeth like that before: very white, very small and very inhuman, as straight as a die, and lacking canines. She'd seen teeth like that on the dead elves lying in a row in the courtyard of the Kaedwen watchtower. She had delighted in teeth like that on Iskra. But the teeth in Iskra's smile looked pretty, while on Eredin they were ghastly.

'Does this lass,' he said, 'who is trying hard to kill me with her stare, already know the reason she's here?'

'Indeed.'

'And is prepared to cooperate?'

'Not completely.'

'Not completely,' he repeated. 'Ha, that's not good. Since the nature of the cooperation demands that it be complete. It's simply not possible if it's less than complete. And, because we are separated from Tir ná Lia by half a day's ride, it'd be worth knowing where we stand.'

'Why be impatient?' Avallac'h pouted his lips slightly. 'What can we gain by haste?'

'Eternity.' Eredin Bréacc Glas became serious. Something shone briefly in his green eyes. 'But that's your speciality, Avallac'h. Your speciality and your responsibility.'

'You have spoken.'

'Indeed I have. And now forgive me, but duty calls. I'll leave you an escort, for safety. I advise you to overnight here, on this hill. If you set off tomorrow at daybreak, you'll be in Tir ná Lia at the right time. *Va faill*. Aha, one more thing.'

He leaned over, broke and then tore off a twig of flowering myrtle. He brought it close to his face, then handed it to Ciri.

'My apologies,' he said briefly, 'for the hasty words. *Va faill, luned.*'

He walked away quickly and a moment later the earth shuddered beneath hooves, as he rode off with the entire troop.

'Just don't tell me,' she growled, 'that I would have to . . . That it's him . . . If it's him, then I'll never, ever.'

'No,' Avallac'h slowly corrected her. 'It's not him. Be calm.'

Ciri brought the myrtle up to her face. In order for him not to see the excitement and fascination that had seized her.

'I am calm.'

*

The dry thistles and heather of the steppe were replaced by lush green grass and damp ferns. The marshy ground was yellow and violet with buttercups and lupins. Soon they saw a river, which

164

although it was crystal clear had a brown tinge. It smelled of peat.

Avallac'h was playing various lively tunes on his pipes. Ciri, glum, was thinking intensely.

'Who,' she finally said, 'is to be the father of the child that matters so much to you? Or perhaps it is of no importance?'

'It is important. Am I to understand you've made your decision?'

'No, you aren't. I'm simply clearing up certain matters.'

'May I help? What do you want to know?'

'You know very well what.'

They rode on in silence for a time. Ciri saw some swans sailing elegantly down the river.

'The child's father,' Avallac'h spoke calmly and to the point, 'will be Auberon Muircetach. Auberon Muircetach is our ... How do you say ... Our highest leader?'

'King? King of all the Aen Seidhe?'

'Aen Seidhe, the People of the Hills, are the elves of your world. We are Aen Elle, the Folk of the Alder. And Auberon Muircetach is indeed our king.'

'The Alder King?'

'One could call him that.'

They rode on in silence. It was very warm.

'Avallac'h.'

'Yes.

'If I agree, then afterwards ... Later ... will I be free?'

'You'll be free and may go wherever you wish. Assuming you don't decide to stay. With the child.'

She snorted contemptuously, but said nothing.

'So you've decided?' he asked.

'I'll decide when we arrive.'

'We have arrived.'

Ciri saw the palaces from behind the weeping willows which hung down towards the water like green curtains. She had never seen anything like them in her entire life. The palaces, although built of marble and alabaster, were like fragile bowers. They seemed so delicate, light and airy, as though they weren't buildings but apparitions of buildings. Ciri expected at any moment that the wind would blow and the little palaces would vanish along with the mist rising from the river. But when the wind blew, when the mist vanished, when the willow branches moved and ripples appeared on the river, the little palaces didn't vanish and had no intention of vanishing. They only gained in beauty.

Ciri looked in admiration at the little terraces, at the little towers resembling water lilies sticking up from water, at the little bridges suspended above the river like festoons of ivy, at the staircases, steps, balustrades, at the arcades and cloisters, at the peristyles, at the tall and short columns, at the large and small domes, at the slender pinnacles and towers resembling asparagus spears.

'Tir ná Lia,' Avallac'h said softly.

The closer they went, the more the beauty of the place seized her powerfully by the heart, more powerfully squeezed her throat, making tears well up in the corners of her eyes. Ciri looked at the fountains, at the mosaics and terracotta, and at the sculptures and monuments. At lacy constructions of whose purpose she couldn't conceive. And at constructions she was certain served no purpose. Beside aesthetics and harmony.

'Tir ná Lia,' repeated Avallac'h. 'Have you ever seen anything like it?'

'I have.' She felt the pressure on her throat. 'I once saw something like this. In Shaerrawedd.'

Now it was the elf's turn to say nothing for a long while.

*

They crossed over the river on an openwork bridge, which seemed so fragile that Kelpie danced and snorted a long time before she was brave enough to step on it.

Although agitated and tense, Ciri looked around attentively, not wanting to overlook anything, no sight that the fairy-tale city of Tir ná Lia offered. Firstly, she was simply consumed by curiosity, and secondly she couldn't stop thinking about escaping and so looked out watchfully for an opportunity.

She saw long-haired elves in close-fitting jerkins and short cloaks embroidered with fanciful leaf-shaped motifs walking on small bridges and terraces, along avenues and peristyles, on balconies and cloisters. She saw coiffured and provocatively made-up elf-women in gauzy dresses or in outfits resembling male costume.

Eredin Bréacc Glas greeted them outside the portico of one of the palaces. At his curt order, small, grey-attired elves swarmed around, quickly and silently taking care of their horses. Ciri looked on somewhat amazed. Avallac'h, Eredin and all the other elves she had met before were extremely tall. She had to crane her neck to look them in the eye. The small grey elves were much shorter than her. *A different race*, she thought. *A race of servants. Even here, in this fairy-tale world, there must be someone to do the work for the idle.*

They entered the palace. Ciri gasped. She was an infanta of royal blood, raised in palaces. But she had never seen such marble and malachite, such stuccos, floors, mosaics, mirrors and candelabras. She felt uncomfortable, awkward in that dazzling interior, out of place, dusty, sweaty and unwashed after her journey.

Avallac'h, quite the opposite, wasn't at all concerned. He brushed his breeches and boots with a glove, ignoring the fact that the dust was settling on a looking glass. Then he tossed his gloves grandly to the grey elf-woman bowing before him.

'Auberon?' he asked curtly. 'Is he waiting?'

Eredin smiled.

'Yes. He's in a great hurry. He demanded that the Swallow go to him immediately, without a moment's delay. I talked him out of it.'

Avallac'h raised his eyebrows.

'Zireael,' Eredin explained very calmly, 'ought to go to the king free of cares, unburdened, rested, composed and in a good mood. A bath, a new outfit, hairstyle and makeup will ensure that good mood. Auberon will probably be able to hold out that long, I think.'

Ciri sighed deeply and looked at the elf. She was positively amazed at how kind he seemed. Eredin smiled, revealing his even teeth.

'Only one thing arouses my reservations,' he declared. 'And that is the aquiline glint in our Swallow's eyes. Our Swallow is flashing her eyes left and right, quite like a stoat looking for holes in a cage. The Swallow, I see, is still far from unconditional surrender.'

Avallac'h didn't comment. Ciri, naturally, didn't either.

'I'm not surprised,' continued Eredin. 'It cannot be any other way, since it's the blood of Shiadhal and Lara Dorren. But listen to me very attentively, Zireael. There is no escape from here. There is no possibility of breaking Geas Garadh, the Spell of the Barrier.'

Ciri's gaze said clearly that she wouldn't believe it until she had tested it.

'Even if you were by some miracle to force the Barrier—' Eredin didn't take his eyes off her '—then know that it would mean your doom. This world only looks pretty. But it carries death, particularly to the inexperienced. Even magic can't heal a wound from a one-horn's spike.

'Know also,' he continued, not waiting for a comment, 'that your wild talent won't help you at all. You won't make the leap, so don't even try. And even if you managed, know that my Dearg Ruadhri, my Red Riders, can catch up with you even in the abyss of times and places.'

She didn't quite understand what he was talking about. But it puzzled her that Avallac'h had suddenly become sullen and was frowning, very evidently unhappy about Eredin's speech. As though Eredin had said too much.

'Let us go,' he said. 'Come this way, Zireael. We'll hand you over to the ladies. It's necessary for you to look beautiful. The first impression is most important.'

*

Her heart was pounding in her breast, the blood thrummed in her temples, her hands were shaking a little. She brought them under control by clenching her fists. She calmed herself with the help of deep breaths. She loosened her shoulders, and moved her neck, stiff with nervousness.

She observed herself once again in the large looking glass. The sight didn't especially please her. Her hair, still damp from bathing, was trimmed and combed so it at least partly concealed her scar. Her makeup nicely emphasised her eyes and mouth, the silver-grey skirt slit to halfway up her thigh, and black waistcoat with sheer blouse of pearl crepe looked very presentable. The silk scarf around her neck highlighted it all compellingly.

Ciri adjusted and straightened the scarf, then reached between her thighs and adjusted what was necessary. And she had on some truly sensational things beneath the skirt – panties as delicate as gossamer and stockings almost reaching the panties, which in some incredible way stayed up without garters.

She reached for the handle. Hesitantly, as though it wasn't a handle but a sleeping cobra.

Spet! she thought involuntarily in the elven tongue, *I've fought against men with swords. I'll take on one man with* . . .

She closed her eyes and sighed. And entered the chamber.

There was no one inside. A book and a carafe lay on the malachite table. There were strange reliefs on the walls, which were draped with heavy curtains and flowery tapestries. In one corner stood a statue. In another a four-poster bed. Her heart began to pound again. She swallowed.

She saw a movement out of the corner of one eye. Not in the chamber. On the terrace.

He was sitting there, turned towards her in half-profile.

Although by now somewhat aware that among elves everything looked different to what she was accustomed to, Ciri experienced a slight shock. All the time the king had been talked about, God knows why, she had had in mind Ervyll of Verden, whose daughter-in-law she had almost once become. Thinking about that king, she saw a large man immobilised by rolls of fat, breath stinking of onions and beer, with a red nose and bloodshot eyes visible above an unkempt beard. Holding a sceptre and orb in his swollen hands, flecked with liver spots.

But a completely different king was sitting by the balustrade of the terrace.

He was very slim, and it was also apparent that he was very tall. His hair was as ashen as hers, shot with snow-white streaks, long, and falling down onto his shoulders and back. He was dressed in a black velvet jerkin. He was wearing typical elven boots with numerous buckles running all the way up the leg. His hands were slender and white, with long fingers.

He was busy blowing bubbles. Holding a small bowl of soapy water and a straw, which he was blowing through. The iridescent, rainbow bubbles floated down towards the river.

She cleared her throat softly.

King Alder turned his head. Ciri was unable to suppress a gasp.

His eyes were extraordinary. As bright as molten lead, bottomless. And full of unimaginable sadness.

'Swallow,' he said. 'Zireael. Thank you for agreeing to come.'

She swallowed, not knowing at all what to say. Auberon Muircetach put the straw to his lips and sent another bubble into space.

She locked her fingers in order to stop them trembling, cracking her knuckles. Then she nervously combed her hair. The elf was apparently only paying attention to the bubbles.

'Are you anxious?'

'No,' she lied arrogantly. 'I'm not.'

'Are you hurrying somewhere?'

'Indeed I am.'

She must have put a little too much nonchalance into her voice, and felt she was balancing on the edge of good manners. But the elf wasn't paying attention. He blew a huge bubble through the end of the straw, making it resemble a cucumber by rocking it. He admired his handiwork for a long time.

'Would I be a nuisance if I asked you where you're in such a rush to get to?'

'Home!' she snapped, but at once corrected herself, adding in a calm tone. 'To my world.'

'To what?'

'To my world!'

'Ah. Forgive me. I'd have sworn you said "To my quirk". And I was indeed very amazed. You speak our language splendidly, but you could still work on your pronunciation and accent.'

'Is my accent important? After all, you don't need me for conversation.'

'Nothing should stop us striving for excellence.'

Another bubble sprang up at the end of the straw. When it broke away it drifted up and burst as it touched a willow branch. Ciri gasped.

'So you're in a hurry to get back to your world,' Auberon Muircetach said a moment later. 'To yours! Indeed, you humans aren't overly blessed with humility.'

He dipped the straw in the bowl, and with a seemingly careless blow encircled himself in a swarm of rainbow bubbles.

'Humans,' he said. 'Your hirsute forebear on the spear side

appeared in the world much later than the hen. And I've never heard of any hens laying claim to the world ... Why are you fidgeting and hopping on the spot like a little monkey? What I'm saying ought to interest you. After all, it's history. Ah, let me guess. History doesn't interest you and bores you.'

A huge iridescent bubble floated towards the river. Ciri said nothing, biting her lip.

'Your hirsute forebear,' the elf continued, stirring the mixture with the straw, 'quickly learned how to use his opposable thumb and rudimentary intelligence. With their help he did various things, usually as amusing as they were woeful. That is, I meant to say that if the things your forebear did hadn't been woeful, they would have been amusing.'

Another bubble, and, immediately after, a second and a third.

'We, the Aen Elle, were little concerned what foolishness your ancestor got up to. We, unlike our cousins, the Aen Seidhe, left that world long ago. We chose another, more interesting universe. For at that time – you'll be astonished by what I say – one could move quite freely between the worlds. With a little talent and skill, naturally. Beyond all doubt you understand what I have in mind.'

Ciri was dying of curiosity, but remained stubbornly silent, aware that the elf was teasing her a little. She didn't want to make his task any easier.

Auberon Muircetach smiled and turned around. He had on a golden necklace, a badge of office called a *torc'h* in the Elder Speech.

'*Mire, luned.*'

He blew softly, moving the straw around nimbly. Instead of one large bubble, as before, several of them hung from the end.

'A bubble beside a bubble, and another beside another,' he crooned. 'Oh, that's how it was, that's how it was ... We used to say to ourselves, what's the difference, we'll spend some time here, some time there, so what if the Dh'oine insist on destroying their world along with themselves? We'll go somewhere else ... To another bubble ...'

Ciri nodded and licked her lips under his burning gaze. The elf smiled again, shook the bubbles, blew once again, this time

171

creating a single large bunch from a myriad of small bubbles joined to each other at the end of the straw.

'The Conjunction came—' the elf raised the straw, hung with bubbles '—and even more worlds were created. But the door is closed. It is closed to all apart from a handful of chosen ones. And time is passing. The door ought to be opened. Urgently. It's imperative. Do you understand that word?'

'I'm not stupid.'

'No, you aren't.' He turned his head. 'You can't be. For you are Aen Hen Ichaer, of the Elder Blood. Come closer.'

When he reached out his hand towards her she clenched her teeth involuntarily. But he only touched her forearm, and then her hand. She felt a pleasant tingling. She dared to look into his extraordinary eyes.

'I didn't believe it when they said it,' he whispered. 'But it's true. You have Shiadhal's eyes. Lara's eyes.' She lowered her gaze. She felt insecure and foolish.

The Alder King rested his elbow on the balustrade and his chin on his hand. For a long time, he seemed only to be interested in the swans swimming in the river.

'Thank you for coming,' he finally said, without turning his head. 'And now go away and leave me alone.'

*

She found Avallac'h on the terrace by the river just as he was boarding a boat in the company of a gorgeous elf-woman with straw-coloured hair. The elf-woman was wearing lipstick the colour of pistachios and flecks of golden glitter on her eyelids and temples.

Ciri was about to turn around and walk away when Avallac'h stopped her with a gesture. And invited her into the boat with another. Ciri hesitated. She didn't want to talk in front of witnesses. Avallac'h said something quickly to the elf-woman and blew her a kiss. The elf-woman shrugged and went away. She only turned around once, to show Ciri with her eyes what she thought of her.

'If you could, refrain from comment,' said Avallac'h when she sat down on the bench nearest the bow. He also sat down, took out his pipes and played, utterly unconcerned about the boat. Ciri looked around apprehensively, but the boat was sailing perfectly down the centre of the current, not deviating by even an inch towards the steps, pillars and columns extending into the water. It was a strange boat. Ciri had never seen one like it, even on Skellige, where she had spent a long time examining everything that was capable of floating on the water. It had a very high, slender prow, carved in the shape of a key. It was very long, very narrow and very unstable. Indeed, only an elf could sit in something like that and play his pipes instead of holding the tiller or the oars.

Avallac'h stopped playing.

'What troubles you?'

He heard her out, watching her with a strange smile.

'You're saddened,' he stated rather than asked. 'Saddened, disappointed, but above all indignant.'

'Not at all! I'm not!'

'And you shouldn't be.' The elf became serious. 'Auberon treated you with reverence, like a born Aen Elle. Don't forget, we, the Alder Folk, never hurry. We have time.'

'He told me something quite different.'

'I know what he told you.'

'And what it's all about, do you also know that?'

'Indeed.'

She had already learned a great deal. Not by sighing, not even by flickering an eyelid, did she betray her impatience or anger, when once again he put the pipes to his mouth and played. Melodiously, longingly. For a long time.

The boat glided along and Ciri counted the bridges passing over their heads.

'We have,' he said right after the fourth bridge, 'more than serious grounds to suppose that your world is in danger of destruction. By a climactic cataclysm of immense scale. As a scholar you have certainly encountered Aen Ithlinne Speath, Ithlinne's Prophecy. There is talk of the White Frost in the prophecy. According to us it concerns extensive glaciation. And because it so happens that ninety per cent of the land of your world is in the northern hemisphere, this glaciation may endanger the existence of most living creatures. They will simply perish from the cold. Those that

173

survive will fall into barbarism, will destroy each other in merciless battles for food, or become prey to predators insane with hunger. Remember the text of the prophecy: The Time of Contempt, the Time of the Battle Axe, the Time of the Wolfish Blizzard.'

Ciri didn't interrupt, fearing he would begin playing again.

'The child that matters so much to us,' continued Avallac'h, fiddling with the pipes, 'the descendant and bearer of the Lara Dorren gene, the gene that was specially constructed by us, may save the denizens of that world. We have reason to believe that the descendant of Lara – and of you, naturally – will possess abilities a thousandfold more powerful than that which we, the Knowing Ones, possess. And which you possess in rudimentary form. You know what this is about, don't you?'

Ciri had come to learn that in the Elder Speech such rhetorical devices, although apparently questions, not only did not demand, but quite simply did not brook, a response.

'In short,' Avallac'h continued, 'it concerns the possibility of transferring between worlds not only oneself, one's own – indeed – insignificant person. It concerns the opening of Ard Gaeth, the great and permanent Gateway, through which everyone would pass. We managed to do it before the Conjunction, and we want to achieve it now. We will evacuate from the dying world the Aen Seidhe residing there. Our brothers, to whom we owe it to help. We wouldn't be able to live with the thought that we had abandoned anything. And we shall rescue, evacuate from that world, everyone who is in danger. Everyone, Zireael. Humans too.'

'Really?' She couldn't hold it back. 'Dh'oine too?'

'Dh'oine too. Now you see for yourself how important you are, how much depends on you. How important a thing it is for you to remain patient. How important a thing it is for you to go to Auberon this evening and stay all night. Believe me, his behaviour wasn't a demonstration of enmity. He knows that this isn't an easy matter for you, that he might hurt and discourage you by being importunately hasty. He knows a great deal, O Swallow. I don't doubt you've noticed.'

'I have,' she snapped. 'I've also noticed that the current has borne us quite far from Tir ná Lia. Time to take up the oars. Which I can't see here, as a matter of fact.'

'Because there aren't any.' Avallac'h raised an arm, twisted his hand and snapped his fingers. The boat stopped. It rested for a while in place, and then began to move against the current.

The elf made himself more comfortable, put his pipes to his lips and gave himself over entirely to his music.

*

In the evening the Alder King entertained her to supper. When she entered, rustling silk, he invited her to the table with a gesture. There were no servants. He served her himself.

The supper consisted of over a dozen kinds of vegetables. There were mushrooms, boiled and simmered in a sauce. Ciri had never eaten mushrooms like them before either. Some of them were as white and thin as dainty leaves, tasted delicate and mild, and others were brown and black, fleshy and aromatic.

Auberon was also generous with the rosé wine. Seemingly light, it went to her head, relaxed her, and loosened her tongue. The next thing she knew she was telling him things she never thought she would.

He listened. Patiently. And then, when she suddenly remembered why she was there. She turned gloomy and fell silent.

'As I understand it—' he served her quite new mushrooms, greenish and smelling of apple pie '—you think that destiny connects you to this Geralt?'

'Precisely so.' She raised a cup now marked with numerous smudges of lipstick. 'Destiny. He, I mean Geralt, is linked to me by destiny, and I am to him. Our destinies are conjoined. So it would be better if I went away from here. Right away. Do you understand?'

'I confess that I don't quite.'

'Destiny!' She took a sip. 'A force which it's better not to get in the way of. Which is why I think . . . No, no thank you, don't serve me any more, please, I've eaten so much I think I'll burst.'

'You mentioned thinking.'

'I think it was a mistake to lure me here. And force me to . . . Well, you know what I mean. I must get away from here, and hurry to help him . . . Because it's my destiny—'

175

'Destiny,' he interrupted, raising his glass. 'Predestination. Something that is inevitable. A mechanism which means that a practically unlimited number of unforeseeable events must end with the same result and no other. Is that right?'

'Certainly!'

'Then whence and wherefore do you wish to go? Drink your wine, enjoy the moment, delight in life. What is to come will come, if it's inevitable.'

'Like hell. It's not that easy.'

'You're contradicting yourself.'

'No, I'm not.'

'You're contradicting your contradiction, and that's a vicious circle.'

'No!' She tossed her head. 'You can't just sit and do nothing! Nothing comes by itself!'

'Sophistry.'

'You can't waste time unthinkingly! You might overlook the right moment . . . That one right, unique moment. For time never repeats itself.'

'Permit me.' He stood up. 'Look at that, over there.'

On the wall he was pointing at was a protruding relief portraying an immense, scaly snake. The reptile, curled up in a figure of eight, was sinking its great teeth into its own tail. Ciri had once seen something like it, but couldn't remember where.

'There,' said the elf. 'The ancient snake Ouroboros. Ouroboros symbolises eternity and is itself eternal. It is the eternal going away and the eternal return. It is something that has no beginning and no end.

'Time is like the ancient Ouroboros. Time is fleeting moments, grains of sand passing through an hourglass. Time is the moments and events we so readily try to measure. But the ancient Ouroboros reminds us that in every moment, in every instant, in every event, is hidden the past, the present and the future. Eternity is hidden in every moment. Every departure is at once a return, every farewell is a greeting, every return is a parting. Everything is simultaneously a beginning and an end.

'And you too,' he said, not looking at her at all, 'are at once the beginning and the end. And because we are discussing destiny, know that it is precisely *your* destiny. To be the beginning and the end. Do you understand?'

She hesitated for a moment. But his glowing eyes forced her to answer.

'I do.'

'Get undressed.'

He said it so casually, so indifferently, she almost yelled in anger. Instead, she began to unfasten her waistcoat with trembling hands.

Her fingers were disobedient; the hooks and eyes, little buttons and ribbons awkward and tight. Though Ciri hurried as much as she could, wanting to get everything over as quickly as possible, the undressing lasted an annoyingly long time. But the elf didn't give the impression of being in a hurry. As though he really had the whole of eternity at his disposal.

Who knows, she thought, *perhaps he has?*

Now, completely undressed, she shuffled from foot to foot, the floor chilling her feet. He noticed it and pointed wordlessly to the bed.

The bedclothes were made of mink. Of mink pelts sewn into great sheets. Wonderfully soft, warm and pleasantly ticklish.

He lay down beside her, fully dressed, even in his boots. When he touched her, she tensed up, involuntarily, a little angry at herself, for she had decided to act proud and impassive. Her teeth, whether she liked it or not, were chattering somewhat. His touch thrilled her, however, and his fingers taught her and commanded her. Guided her. Once she had begun to understand the suggestions so well that she was almost anticipating them, she closed her eyes and imagined it was Mistle. But she was unable to. For he was so unlike Mistle.

He instructed her with his hand. She obeyed. Willingly. Urgently.

He didn't hurry at all. He made her soften beneath his caresses like a silk ribbon. He made her moan. Made her bite her lips. Made her whole body jerk in a sudden, shocking spasm.

What he did then, she hadn't expected at all.

He stood up and walked away. Leaving her aroused, panting and trembling.

He didn't even look back.

177

The blood struck Ciri's face and temples. She curled up in a ball on the mink sheets and sobbed. From rage, shame and humiliation.

*

In the morning she found Avallac'h in the peristyle behind the palace, among an avenue of statues. The statues – most peculiarly – portrayed elven children. In various – mainly playful – poses. The one Avallac'h was standing by was particularly interesting: it depicted a young elf standing on one leg with its face contorted in anger, fists clenched.

Ciri couldn't tear her gaze away for a long time, and she felt a dull ache in her belly. Only when urged by Avallac'h did she tell him everything. In general terms and stammering.

'He,' Avallac'h said gravely after she had finished, 'has watched the smokes of Samhain more than six hundred times. Believe me, Swallow, that is a lot even for the Alder Folk.'

'What do I care?' she snapped. 'I made an agreement! You must have learned from the dwarves, your comrades, what a contract is? I'm keeping my side of it! I'm giving myself! What do I care that he can't or doesn't want to? What do I care if it's senile impotence, or if I don't attract him? Perhaps Dh'oine repulse him? Perhaps like Eredin he only sees in me a nugget in a heap of compost?'

'I hope . . .' Avallac'h's face, exceptionally, changed and contorted. 'I hope you didn't say anything like that to him?'

'No, I didn't. Though I felt like it.'

'Beware. You don't know what you're risking.'

'It's all the same to me. I entered into a contract. Take it or leave it! Either you keep your side of the bargain, or we nullify the contract and I'll be free.'

'Beware, Zireael,' he repeated, pointing at the statue of the upset child. 'Don't be like this one here. Consider every word. Try to understand. And if you don't understand something, don't act rashly under any circumstances. Be patient. Remember, time means nothing.'

'Yes, it does!'

'Please, don't be an unruly child. I repeat again: be patient with Auberon. Because he's your only chance of regaining your freedom.'

'Really?' she almost screamed. 'I'm beginning to have my doubts! I'm beginning to suspect you of cheating me! That you've all cheated me—'

'I promised you—' Avallac'h's face was as lifeless as a stone statue '—you will return to your world. I've given my word. Doubting someone's word is a serious insult to the Aen Elle. In order to keep you from doing it, I suggest we end this conversation.'

He was about to go, but she barred his way. His aquamarine eyes narrowed and Ciri understood she was dealing with a very, very, dangerous elf. But it was too late to withdraw.

'That's very much in the elven style,' she hissed like a viper. 'To insult someone and then not let them get even.'

'Beware, O Swallow.'

'Listen.' She lifted her head proudly. 'Your Alder King won't fulfil the task, that's more than clear. It isn't important if he's the problem or if I am. That's trivial and meaningless. But I want to fulfil the contract. And get it over with. Let someone else impregnate me to beget the child you care so much about.'

'You don't know what you're talking about.'

'And if I'm the problem—' she didn't change her tone or expression '—it means you're mistaken, Avallac'h. You lured the wrong person to this world.'

'You don't know what you're talking about, Zireael.'

'If, though,' she screamed, 'you're all repulsed by me, use the hinny breeders' method. What, don't you know? You show the stallion a mare, and then you blindfold it and put the jenny in front of it.'

He didn't even deign to reply. He passed her by unceremoniously and walked off along the avenue of statues.

'Or you, perhaps?' she yelled. 'If you want I'll give myself to you! Well? Won't you sacrifice yourself? I mean, they say I've got Lara's eyes!'

He was in front of her in two paces. His hands shot towards her neck like snakes and squeezed like steel pincers. She understood that if he'd wanted to, he could have throttled her like a fledgling.

179

He let her go. He leaned over and looked into her eyes from close up.

'Who are you,' he asked extremely calmly, 'to dare to defile her name in such a way? Who are you to dare to abuse me with such miserable charity? Oh, I know, I see who you are. You are not the daughter of Lara. You are the daughter of Cregennan. You are a thoughtless, arrogant, selfish Dh'oine, a simply perfect represent-ative of your race, who understands nothing, and must ruin and destroy, besmirch by touch alone, denigrate and defile by thought alone. Your ancestor stole my love from me, took her away from me, selfishly and arrogantly took Lara from me. But I shall not permit you, O his worthy daughter, to take the memory of her from me.'

He turned around. Ciri overcame the lump in her throat.

'Avallac'h.'

A look.

'Forgive me. I behaved thoughtlessly and shabbily. Forgive me. And, if you can, forget it.'

He went over to her and embraced her.

'I've already forgotten,' he said warmly. 'No, let us not return to that ever again.'

*

When she entered the royal chambers that evening – bathed, perfumed and coiffured – Auberon Muircetach was sitting at the table, bent over a chessboard. He instructed her to sit opposite without a word.

He won in nine moves.

The second time, she played white and he won in eleven moves.

Only then did he raise his eyes, his extraordinary, clear eyes.

'Get undressed, please.'

He deserved credit for one thing – he was delicate and didn't hurry at all.

When – as before – he got up from the bed and walked away without a word, Ciri accepted it with calm resignation. But she couldn't fall asleep until almost the very break of day.

And when the windows brightened from the dawn, and she finally fell asleep, she had a very strange dream.

Vysogota, stooping, was cleaning duckweed from a muskrat trap. Reeds blown by the wind rustled.

I feel guilty, Swallow. It was I who suggested the idea of this insane escapade. I showed you the way to that accursed Tower.

'Don't reproach yourself, Old Raven. Had it not been for the tower, Bonhart would have caught me. At least I'm safe here.'

You are not safe there.

Vysogota straightens up.

Behind him Ciri sees hills, bare and rounded, sticking up from the grass like the bent back of a monster lurking in ambush. A huge boulder is lying on the hill. And two figures stand beside it. A woman and girl. The wind yanks and tugs the woman's black hair.

The horizon blazes with lightning.

Chaos extends a hand towards you, daughter. O Child of the Elder Blood, O girl entangled in Movement and Change, Destruction and Rebirth. Both destined and destiny. From behind a closed door Chaos holds its talons out to you, not knowing yet if you will become its tool, or a hindrance in its plans. Not knowing if you will by chance play the role of a grain of sand in the works of the Clock of Destiny. Chaos fears you, O Child of Destiny. And wants to make you feel fear. Which is why it sends you dreams.

Vysogota stoops and cleans the muskrat trap. *But he's dead,* Ciri thinks clear-headedly. *Does that mean that in the spirit world the dead have to clean muskrat traps?*

Vysogota straightens up. The sky burns with the glow of fires behind his back. Thousands of horsemen gallop across the plain. Horsemen in red cloaks.

Dearg Ruadhri.

Listen to me carefully, Swallow. The Elder Blood you have in your veins gives you great power. You are the Master of Places and Times. You have a mighty Power. Don't let criminals and rogues take it from you and use it for dishonourable purposes. Defend yourself! Flee out of reach of their vile hands.

'That's easy to say! They've ensnared me with some kind of magical barrier or tether . . .'

You are the Master of Places and Times. You cannot be tethered.

Vysogota straightens up. Behind his back is a plateau, a rocky plain, and on it shipwrecks. Dozens of shipwrecks. And beyond them a castle; black, ominous, toothed with battlements, rising up above a mountain lake.

They will perish without your help, O Swallow. Only you can save them.

Yennefer's mouth, cut and bloodied, moves noiselessly, gushing blood. Her violet eyes shine, burn in her face; gaunt, contorted, blackened by torture, covered by a shock of unkempt, dirty black hair. A foul-smelling puddle in a hollow of the floor, rats scurrying all around. The horrifying cold of the stone walls. The cold of shackles on her wrists, on her ankles . . .

Yennefer's hands and fingers are a mass of dried blood.

'Mummy! What have they done to you?'

A marble staircase leading downwards. A staircase with three landings.

Va'esse deireadh aep eigean . . . Something ends . . . What?

A staircase. Fire blazing in iron cressets at the bottom. Burning tapestries.

Let's go, says Geralt. Steps leading downwards. *We have to. We must. There's no other way. Just this staircase. I want to see the sky.*

His lips aren't moving. They're blue and there's blood on them. Blood, blood everywhere . . . The stairs are totally covered in blood.

There's no other way. No other way, Star-Eye.

'How?' she cries. 'How can I help them? I'm in another world! Imprisoned! And powerless!'

You cannot be imprisoned.

Everything has been written, says Vysogota. *Even this. Look beneath your feet.*

Ciri sees in horror that she's standing in a sea of bones. Among skulls, shinbones and ribs.

Only you can prevent it, Star-Eye.

Vysogota straightens up. Behind him is winter, snow, a blizzard. The wind blows and whistles. Before her, in the snowstorm, on a horse, is Geralt. Ciri recognises him, although he has a fur hat on his head, and his face is shrouded in a woollen scarf. Behind him in

182

the blizzard loom other riders, their silhouettes vague, so muffled up are they that there is no way to identify them.

Geralt looks straight at her. But doesn't see her. Snow falls into his eyes.

'Geralt! It's me! Here!'

He can't see her. Or hear her among the wailing of the gale.

'Geraaalt!'

It's a moufflon, says Geralt. *Only a moufflon. Let's go back.* The riders disappear, dissolving in the snowstorm.

'Geraaalt! Nooooo!'

*

She woke up.

*

Next morning she went at once to the stables without even eating breakfast. She didn't want to meet Avallac'h, didn't want to talk to him. She preferred to avoid the intrusive, curious, questioning, clinging looks of the other elves and elf-women. On every other occasion studiously indifferent, now the elves were betraying their curiosity on the subject of the royal bedchamber, and the palace walls, Ciri was certain, had ears.

She found Kelpie in her stall, found her saddle and harness. Before she managed to saddle the mare the servants were already beside her; those little grey elves, short, a head shorter than ordinary Aen Elle. They assisted her with the mare, bowing and smiling ingratiatingly.

'Thank you,' she said. 'I'd cope by myself, but thank you. It's sweet of you.'

The nearest girl smiled and Ciri shuddered.

For she had canine teeth.

Ciri was by her so fast the girl was almost dumbfounded. Ciri brushed the hair back from her ear. An ear that didn't end in a point.

'You're human!'

The girl – and all the others with her – knelt down on the freshly

183

swept floor. She bowed her head. Expecting to be punished.

'I . . .' Ciri began, kneading the reins. 'I . . .'

She didn't know what to say. The girls continued to kneel. The horses nervously snorted and stamped in their stalls.

Outside, in the saddle, trotting, she still couldn't gather her thoughts. Human girls. Working as servants, but that was unimportant. What was important was that there were Dh'oine in this world . . .

People, she corrected herself. *I'm thinking like them.*

She was startled out of her reverie by Kelpie neighing loudly and starting. She raised her head and saw Eredin.

He was sitting on his dark bay stallion, now without its demonic bucranium and most of the other battle paraphernalia. He was, though, wearing a mail shirt beneath a cloak shimmering in many shades of red.

The stallion neighed a husky welcome, shook its head and bared its yellow teeth at Kelpie. Kelpie, in accordance with the principle that one settles matters with the master and not with the servant, reached for the elf's thigh with her teeth. Ciri jerked the reins sharply.

'Careful,' she said. 'Keep your distance. My mare doesn't like strangers. And she bites.'

'Biters—' the elf glared at her evilly '—should be tamed with an iron bit. Tight enough to draw blood. A splendid method for eradicating bad habits. In horses too.'

He jerked the stallion's bridle so hard that the horse snorted and took several paces backwards, foam trickling from its muzzle.

'Why the mail shirt?' Now Ciri was glaring at the elf. 'Are you preparing for war?'

'Quite the opposite. I desire peace. Does your mare, apart from being skittish, have any other virtues?'

'What kind?'

'May I challenge you to a race?'

'If you wish, why not.' She stood up in the stirrups. 'There, towards those cromlechs—'

'No,' he interrupted. 'Not there.'

'Why not?'

'That's off limits.'

'For everyone, naturally.'

'Not everyone, naturally. Your company is too precious to us, Swallow, for us to risk being deprived of it by you or anyone else.'

'Anyone else? You can't be thinking about the unicorns?'

'I don't want to bore you with what I think. Or be frustrated by your not understanding my thoughts.'

'I don't understand.'

'I know you don't. Evolution didn't give you a sufficiently folded brain to enable you to understand. Listen, if you want a race I suggest along the river. That way. To the Porphyry Bridge, the third one along. Then across the bridge to the other side, then along the bank, downstream, finishing at the stream that flows into the river. Ready?'

'Always.'

He urged on his stallion with a cry, and the horse set off like a hurricane. Before Kelpie could start he was well ahead. He made the earth tremble, but he couldn't match Kelpie. She caught up with him quickly, even before the Porphyry Bridge. The bridge was narrow. Eredin yelled, and the stallion, incredibly, picked up speed. Ciri understand immediately what was happening. Not for all the world would two horses fit on the bridge. One had to yield.

Ciri had no intention of slowing. She pressed herself to Kelpie's mane, and the mare shot ahead like an arrow. She brushed against the elf's stirrup and hurtled onto the bridge. Eredin yelled again. The stallion reared up, hit its side against an alabaster figure, knocking it from its plinth and smashing it into pieces.

Ciri, sniggering like a ghoul, galloped across the bridge. Without looking back.

She dismounted by the stream and waited.

He trotted up a moment later. Smiling and composed.

'My compliments,' he said curtly, dismounting. 'Both to the mare and to the Amazon.'

Although she was strutting like a peacock she snorted carelessly.

'Aha! Won't you brutally tame us now?'

'Not unless you permit me,' he smiled suggestively. 'Some mares like rough caresses.'

'Not so long ago—' she looked at him haughtily '—you compared me to compost. And now we're talking about caresses?'

He went closer to Kelpie, stroked and patted the mare's neck and shook his head on finding it was dry. Kelpie tossed her head and neighed at length. Eredin turned towards Ciri. *If he pats me too*, she thought, *he'll regret it.*

'Follow me.'

Moss-covered steps made of sandstone blocks stood alongside the stream, which flowed down from a steep, thickly wooded hillside into the river. The steps were ancient, cracked, split by tree roots. They zig-zagged upwards, occasionally crossing the stream over footbridges. All around was a forest, a wild forest, full of old ash and hornbeam, yew, maple and oak, the floor carpeted with a thicket of hazel, tamarisk and bramble. It smelled of wormwood, sage, nettles, wet stones, the spring and mould.

Ciri walked in silence, not hurrying, and controlling her breathing. She was also trying to control her nerves. She had no idea what Eredin might want from her, but she had her misgivings.

There was a stone terrace beside another cascade, falling with a roar from a rocky cleft, and on it, overshadowed by wild lilac, was an old bower, wound around with ivy and spiderwort. The ribbon of the river, roofs, peristyles and the terraces of Tir ná Lia could be seen below the crowns of the trees.

They stood a while, looking.

'No one told me—' Ciri was the first to interrupt the silence '—what that river's called.'

'The Easnadh.'

'The Sigh? Pretty. And that stream?'

'The Tuathe.'

'The Whisper. That's pretty too. Why did no one tell me that there are humans living in this world?'

'Because it's irrelevant information and totally meaningless to you. Let's go into the bower.'

'What for?'

'Let's go in.'

The first thing she noticed after entering was a bare wooden divan. Ciri felt her temples beginning to throb. *Of course*, she thought, *I should have seen that coming. I read a romance written by Anna Tiller in the temple, didn't I? About an old king, a young queen and a pretender prince greedy for power. Eredin is ruthless, ambitious*

and determined. He knows that whoever has a queen is the real king,
a real ruler. A real man. Whoever possesses a queen, possesses the
kingdom. Here, on this couch, will begin the coup d'état . . .

The elf sat down on a marble table, and gestured at a chair for
Ciri. The view from the window seemed to interest him more than
she did, and he wasn't looking at the couch at all.

'You'll remain here forever,' he said, surprising her, 'my
Amazon, as light as a little butterfly. To the end of your butterfly
life.'

She was silent, looking him straight in the eye. There was nothing in those eyes.

'They won't let you leave,' he repeated. 'They won't accept that,
contrary to the prophecy and myths, you're no one and nothing,
a meaningless creature. They won't believe it and they won't let
you leave. They hoodwinked you with a promise to ensure your
submission, but they never intended to keep that promise. Never.'

'Avallac'h gave me his word,' she said hoarsely. 'Allegedly it's
an insult to doubt the word of an elf.'

'Avallac'h is a Knowing One. Knowing Ones have their own
code of honour in which every second sentence there's mention of
the end justifying the means.'

'I don't understand why you're telling me all this. Unless . . .
you want something from me. Unless I have something you desire.
And you want to bargain. Well? Eredin? My freedom for . . . for
what?'

He looked at her for a long while. And she vainly searched in
his eyes for some indication, some signal, some sign. Of anything.

'You've no doubt managed to get to know Auberon a little,' he
began slowly. 'You've certainly noticed already that he is simply
unimaginably ambitious. There are things he'll never accept, that
he'll never concede. He'd sooner die.'

Ciri was silent, biting her lips and glancing at the couch.

'Auberon Muircetach,' continued the elf, 'will never use magic
or other measures which might change the current situation. And
such measures exist. Good, powerful, guaranteed measures. Much
more effective than the aphrodisiacs that Avallac'h's servants sat-
urate your cosmetics with.'

He moved his hand quickly over the dark, veined table top.

When he withdrew it a tiny flacon of grey-green nephrite was lying on the table.

'No,' said Ciri hoarsely. 'Absolutely not. I won't agree to that.'

'You didn't let me finish.'

'Don't treat me like a fool. I won't give him what's in that flacon. You won't use me for things like that.'

'You draw very hasty conclusions,' he said slowly, looking her in the eye. 'You're trying to outrun yourself in the race. And things like that always end with a fall. A very painful fall.'

'I said no.'

'Think it over well. Regardless of what the vessel contains, you always win. You always win, Swallow.'

'No!'

With a movement just as dextrous as before, truly worthy of a conjuror, he swept the flacon from the table. Then he stayed silent for a long while, looking at the River Easnadh glinting among the trees.

'You'll die here, little butterfly,' he said finally. 'They won't let you leave. But it's your choice.'

'I made a deal. My freedom for—'

'Freedom,' he snorted. 'You keep talking about freedom. And what would you do if you finally regained it? Where would you make for? Get it into your head that at this moment not only places but time separate you from your world. Time passes differently here than there. Those you knew as children are now decrepit, those who were your peers died long ago.'

'I don't believe you.'

'Think back to your legends. Legends about people who mysteriously disappeared and returned years later, only to gaze on the overgrown graves of their loved ones. Do you think they were fantasies, fabrications? You're mistaken. For whole centuries people have been kidnapped, carried away by horsemen whom you call the Wild Hunt. Kidnapped, exploited, and then discarded like the shell of a sucked-out egg. But not even that will befall you, Zireael. You will die here. You won't even have the chance of seeing your friends' graves.'

'I don't believe what you're saying.'

'Your beliefs are your own private matter. And you chose your own fate yourself. Let's go back. I have a request, Swallow. Would you like to consume a light meal with me in Tir ná Lia?'

For several heartbeats hunger and a reckless fascination fought in Ciri against anger, fear of poison and general antipathy.

'With pleasure.' She lowered her eyes. 'Thank you for the offer.'

'No, I thank you. Let's go.'

As they were exiting the bower she glanced at the divan once again. And thought that Anna Tiller was actually a stupid and gushing hack.

They descended to the River Sigh slowly, in silence, amidst the aroma of mint, sage and nettle. Down the steps. Along the bank of a stream called the Whisper.

*

When that evening, perfumed, with hair still damp after an aromatic bath, she entered the royal chambers, she found Auberon on a sofa, bent over a large book. Without a word, with only a gesture, he ordered her to sit beside him.

The book was richly illustrated. To tell the truth, there was nothing in it apart from illustrations. Although she tried to play the sophisticated lady, the blood rushed to Ciri's cheeks. She'd seen several such works in the temple library in Ellander. But they couldn't compete with the book of the Alder King, neither in the richness and variety of the positions, nor in the artistry of their depiction.

They looked at it for a long time, in silence.

'Please get undressed.'

This time he also got undressed. His body was slender and boyish, downright skinny like Giselher, like Kayleigh, like Reef, whom she'd seen many times when they bathed in streams or mountain lakes. But vitality exuded from Giselher and the Rats, life exuded from them, the desire to live, blazing among the silver drops of water spraying around.

But from him, from the Alder King, the cold of eternity exuded.

He was patient. Several times it seemed it was about to happen. But nothing came of it. Ciri was angry at herself, certain that it was because of her ignorance and paralysing lack of skill. He noticed and calmed her. As usual, very effectively. And she fell asleep in his arms.

But in the morning he wasn't with her.

*

The next evening, for the first time, the Alder King betrayed his impatience.

She found him hunched over the table where a looking glass framed in amber was lying. White powder had been sprinkled on it.

It's beginning, she thought.

Auberon used a small knife to gather the fisstech and form it into two lines. He took a silver tube and sniffed up the narcotic, first to the left, then to the right nostril. His eyes, usually sparkling, dimmed slightly and became cloudy, began to water. Ciri knew at once it wasn't his first dose.

He formed two fresh lines on the glass, then invited her over with a gesture, handing her the tube. *Oh, who cares*, she thought. *It'll be easier.*

The drug was extremely powerful.

A short while later they were both sitting on the bed, hugging, and staring at the moon with their eyes watering.

Ciri sneezed.

'An uncharted night,' she said, wiping her nose with the sleeve of her silk blouse.

'Enchanting,' he corrected her, wiping an eye. 'Ensh'eass, not en'leass. You need to work on your pronunciation.'

'I will.'

'Get undressed.'

At first it seemed it would be good, that the drug would stimulate him as much as it was her. And its effect on her was to make her active and adventurous, why, she even whispered a few extremely indecent – in her opinion – words into his ear. It must have got to him a little – the effect was, hmm, tangible, and at one moment Ciri was certain it was about to happen. But it didn't. At least not all the way.

And once again he became impatient. He stood up and threw

a sable fur over his shoulders. He stood like that, turned away, staring at the window and the moon. Ciri sat up and wrapped her arms around her knees. She was disappointed and cross, and at the same time she felt strangely wistful. It was doubtless the action of the powerful fisstech.

'It's all my fault,' she mumbled. 'That scar blights me, I know. I know what you see when you look at me. There's not much elf left in me. A gold nugget in a pile of compost—'

He turned around suddenly.

'You're extremely modest,' he drawled. 'I would say rather: a pearl in pig shit. A diamond on the finger of a rotting corpse. As part of your language training you can create even more comparisons. I'll test you on them tomorrow, little Dh'oine. O human creature in whom nothing, but nothing, remains of an elven woman.'

He walked over to the table, picked up the tube and leaned over the looking glass. Ciri sat as though petrified. She felt as if she'd been spat on.

'I don't come here out of love!' she barked furiously. 'I'm being held and being blackmailed, as you well know! But I'm reconciled to it, I'm doing it for—'

'For whom?' he interrupted heatedly, quite unlike an elf. 'For me? For the Aen Seidhe imprisoned in your world? You foolish maid! You're doing it for yourself. You come here for yourself and vainly try to give yourself to me. For it's your only hope, your only chance. And I'll tell you one more thing. Pray, pray zealously to your human idols, godheads and totems. Because it'll either be me, or Avallac'h and his laboratory. Believe me, you wouldn't want to end up in the laboratory and become acquainted with the alternative.'

'It's all the same to me,' she said softly, huddling up in bed. 'I'll agree to anything, as long as I regain my freedom. To finally free myself from you. To depart. To my world. To my friends.'

'Your friends!' he sneered. 'Here are your friends!'

He turned around and abruptly tossed the fisstech-strewn looking glass to her.

'Here are your friends,' he repeated. 'Have a look.'

He went out, the tails of the fur flapping behind him.

At first she only saw her own, blurred reflection in the dirtied glass. But almost immediately the looking glass brightened up milkily, filled up with smoke. And then with an image.

Yennefer suspended in a chasm, back arched, with hands raised. The sleeves of her dress are like the outstretched wings of a bird. Her hair undulates, little fishes dart among it. Whole shoals of shimmering, busy little fish. Some of them are nibbling the sorceress's cheeks and eyes. A rope runs towards the bottom of the lake from Yennefer's leg, and the end of the rope, trapped in the sludge and waterweed, is a large basket of stones. High above, the surface of the water shines and sparkles.

Yennefer's dress undulates in the same rhythm as the waterweed.

The surface of the looking glass, smudged with fisstech, becomes enveloped in smoke.

Geralt, glassily pale, with closed eyes, sits under long icicles extending from a rock, motionless, covered in ice and quickly being buried in snow being blown over him by a blizzard. His white hair has already become white tangles of ice, white icicles hang from his eyebrows, eyelashes and lips. The snow keeps falling and falling. The snowdrift covering Geralt's legs grows, the fluffy piles on his shoulders grow. The blizzard howls and whistles . . .

Ciri leapt up from the bed, and hurled the looking glass at the wall with great force. The amber frame smashed and the glass shattered into a million splinters.

She recognised, knew, remembered that kind of vision. From her earlier dreams.

'It's all false!' she yelled. 'Do you hear, Auberon? I don't believe it! It's not true! It's just your anger, which is as impotent as you are! It's your anger . . .'

She sat on the floor and burst into tears.

*

She suspected the palace walls had ears. The next day she couldn't rid herself of the ambiguous looks. She felt sneers behind her back, listened out for whispers.

Avallac'h was nowhere to be found. *He knows*, she thought, *he knows what happened and is avoiding me. In advance, before I got up, he sailed or rode somewhere far away with his gilded elf-woman. He doesn't want to talk to me, doesn't want to admit his entire plan has come to nothing.*

Eredin was nowhere to be found either. But that was to be expected. He often went riding with his Dearg Ruadhri, the Red Horsemen.

Ciri led Kelpie out of the stable and rode to the far side of the river, frantically thinking the whole time, not noticing anything around her.

To escape is what matters. It doesn't matter if all those visions were false or true. One thing is certain – Yennefer and Geralt are there in my world and my place is there, with them. I have to escape from here, escape without delay! After all, there must be a way. I entered it alone, I ought to be able to leave alone. Eredin said I have an untamed talent, and Vysogota suspected the same thing. There was no way out of Tor Zireael; I explored it thoroughly. But perhaps there is some other tower . . .

She looked into the distance, at the far-off hill, at the silhouette of the cromlech visible there. *Forbidden territory*, she thought. *Ha, I see it's too far. The barrier probably won't allow me to go there. Not worth the effort. I'll ride upstream instead. I haven't ridden there yet.*

Kelpie neighed, tossed her head, and broke into a hard run. She wouldn't let herself be turned. Instead she trotted hard towards the hill. Ciri was so dumbstruck that for a moment she didn't react and let the mare run. Only a moment later did she yell and tug at the reins. The result was that Kelpie reared up, kicked, jerked her rump and galloped away. Continuing in the same direction.

Ciri didn't stop her, didn't try to control her. She was utterly amazed. But she knew Kelpie too well. The mare could be disobedient, but not to this extent. Behaviour like this must mean something.

Kelpie slowed to a trot. She continued straight ahead towards the hill topped with the cromlech.

More or less a furlong, Ciri thought. *At any moment the barrier will come down.*

The mare ran into the stone circle, amidst crowded, moss-covered and lopsided monoliths growing out of a thicket of thorny brambles, and stopped dead. The only thing Kelpie moved was her ears, which she pricked up attentively.

Ciri tried to rein her around and then set off. Without success. Were it not for the blood vessels throbbing on Kelpie's neck, Ciri would have sworn she was sitting not on a horse, but on a statue. Suddenly something touched her back. Something sharp, something that penetrated her clothing and pricked painfully. She didn't have time to turn around. Then a ruddy-coloured unicorn emerged from behind the rocks without the slightest noise and thrust its horn under her arm. Hard. Roughly. She felt a trickle of blood running down her side.

Yet another unicorn emerged from the other side. This one was completely white, from the tips of its ears to the end of its tail. Only its nostrils were pink, and its eyes were black.

The white unicorn approached. And slowly, very slowly, placed its head in her lap. The excitement was so powerful Ciri moaned.

I've grown, resounded in her head. *I've grown, Star-Eye. Back then, in the desert, I didn't know how to behave. Now I know.*

'Little Horse?' she moaned, still almost hanging from the two horns piercing her.

My name is Ihuarraquax. Do you remember me, Star-Eye? Do you remember treating me? Saving me?

He stepped back and turned around. She saw the mark of a scar on his leg. She recognised him. Remembered.

'Little Horse! It's you! But your coat was a different colour . . .'

I've grown up.

In her head came a sudden confusion, whispers, voices, cries and neighing. The horns withdrew. She noticed that the second unicorn, the one behind her back, was dappled blue-grey.

The elders are learning you, Star-Eye. They are learning you through me. Just a moment longer and they'll be able to talk by themselves. They'll tell you themselves what they want from you.

The cacophony in Ciri's head burst in an eruption of savage tumult. And almost immediately abated, before it flowed into a stream of comprehensible and clear thoughts.

We want to help you escape, Star-Eye.

She was silent, though her heart pounded hard in her chest.

Where is the tremendous joy? Where are the thanks?

'And why,' she asked aggressively, 'this desire to help me all of a sudden? Do you love me so much?'

194

We don't love you at all. But this is not your world. This is no place for you. You cannot stay here. We don't want you to stay.

She clenched her teeth. Although excited by the prospect, she shook her head. Little Horse – Ihuarraquax – pricked up his ears, pawed the ground with a hoof and glanced at her with his black eye. The ruddy unicorn stamped so hard the ground shook, and twisted its horn menacingly. It snorted angrily, and Ciri understood.

You don't trust us.

'I don't,' she confessed cheerfully. 'Everybody here is playing a game of their own, and trying to exploit me in my ignorance. Why exactly should I trust you? There's clearly no love lost between you and the elves. I saw for myself on the steppe how there was almost a fight. I can easily assume you want to use me to annoy them. I'm not fond of them either, after all they've imprisoned me and are forcing me to do something I don't want to do at all. But I won't allow myself to be taken advantage of.'

The ruddy unicorn shook his head, and his horn made a threatening movement again. The blue-grey one neighed. Ciri's head thundered like the inside of a well, and the thought she picked up was unpleasant.

'Aha!' she cried. 'You're just like them! Either subservience and obedience, or death? I'm not afraid! And I won't let myself be abused!'

She felt confusion and chaos in her head again. It was some time before a clear thought emerged.

It's good, Star-Eye, that you don't like being taken advantage of. That is precisely what concerns us. That is precisely what we want to guarantee to you. To ourselves. And to the whole world. To all worlds.

'I don't understand.'

You are a dangerous weapon, a fell weapon. We can't allow that weapon to fall into the hands of the Alder King, the Fox or the Sparrowhawk.

'Who?' she stammered. 'Ah . . .'

The Alder King is old. But the Fox and the Sparrowhawk cannot seize power over Ard Gaeth, the Gateway to the Worlds. They captured it once. They lost it once. Now they can do nothing more than wander, roam among the worlds taking tiny steps, alone, like spectres, powerless. The Fox to Tir ná Béa Arainne, the Sparrowhawk and his horsemen around the Spiral. They can go no further, they don't have the strength. Which is why they dream of Ard Gaeth and power. We shall show you how they have already abused such power. We shall show you, Star-Eye, when you leave here.

'I can't leave here. They've put a spell on me. A barrier. Geas Garadh . . .'

You cannot be imprisoned. You are now Master of the Worlds.

'Like hell. I don't have any natural talent, I can't control anything. And I relinquished the Power in the desert, a year ago. Little Horse was a witness.'

In the desert you relinquished conjuring. The Power you have in your blood cannot be relinquished. You still have it. We shall teach you how to use it.

'And isn't it, perhaps,' she shouted, 'that you want to capture that power, this power over the worlds that I reputedly have?'

It is not. We do not have to capture that power. For we have always had it.

Trust them, requested Ihuarraquax. *Trust, Star-Eye.*

'Under one condition.'

The unicorns jerked up their heads and flared their nostrils. You would have sworn sparks were shooting from their eyes. *They don't like it*, thought Ciri, *when conditions are imposed on them. They don't even like the sound of the word.* Spet, *I don't know if I'm doing the right thing . . . Let's hope it doesn't end tragically . . .*

Speak. What is the condition?

'Ihuarraquax will be with me.'

*

In the evening it clouded over, became close. A thick, sticky mist rose from the river. And when darkness fell over Tir ná Lia, a storm sounded with a dull, distant growl. Every now and then the glow of lightning lit the horizon.

Ciri had been ready a long time. Dressed in black, with sword on her back, anxious and tense, she waited impatiently for dusk.

She passed quietly through the empty vestibule, stole through the colonnade and onto the terrace. The River Easnadh sparkled in the darkness, willows soughed.

196

Distant thunder rolled across the sky.

Ciri led Kelpie out of the stable. The mare knew what was expected of her. She trotted obediently towards the Porphyry Bridge. For a moment Ciri followed her tracks, then glanced at the terrace beside which the boats stood.

I can't, she thought. *I'll appear before him once more. Perhaps I'll manage to delay the pursuers by doing it? It's risky, but there's no other way.*

*

In the first moment she thought he wasn't there, that the royal chambers were empty. Because they were silent and lifeless.

She only noticed him after a moment. He was sitting in an armchair in the corner, a white shirt gaping open on his skinny chest. The shirt was made of stuff so fine it clung to his body as though wet.

The Alder King's face and hands were almost as white as his shirt.

He raised his eyes towards her, and there was a void in them.

'Shiadhal?' he whispered. 'I'm glad you are here. You know, they told me you had died.'

He opened his hand and something fell onto the carpet. It was the flacon of grey-green nephrite. 'Lara.' The Alder King moved his head, and touched his neck as though his royal torc'h was garrotting him. *'Caemm a me, luned.* Come to me, daughter. *Caemm a me, elaine.'*

Ciri sensed death in his breath.

'Elaine blath, feainne wedd . . .' he sang. *'Mire, luned,* your ribbon has come undone . . . Allow me . . .'

He tried to lift his hand, but he was unable to. He sighed deeply, raised his hand abruptly, and looked her in the eyes. This time lucidly.

'Zireael,' he said. *'Loc'hlaith.* You are indeed destiny, O Lady of the Lake. Mine too, as it transpires.

Va'esse deireadh aep eigean . . .' he said a moment later, and Ciri observed with dread that his words and movements had begun to slow down horribly.

'But,' he finished with a sigh, 'it's good that something is beginning.'

They heard a long-drawn-out peal of thunder outside the window. The storm was still far away. But it was approaching fast.

'In spite of everything,' he said, 'I very much don't want to die, Zireael. And I'm so sorry that I must. Who'd have thought it? I thought I wouldn't regret it. I've lived long, I've experienced everything. I've become bored with everything . . . but nonetheless I feel regret. And do you know what else? Come closer. I'll tell you in confidence. Let it be our secret.'

She bent forward.

'I'm afraid,' he whispered.

'I know.'

'Are you with me?'

'Yes, I am.'

'*Va faill, luned.*'

'Farewell, O Alder King.'

She sat with him, holding his hand, until he went completely quiet and his delicate breath faded. She didn't wipe away the tears. She let them flow.

The storm was coming closer. The horizon blazed with lightning.

*

She ran quickly down the marble staircase to the terrace with the small columns, beside which the boats were rocking. She untied one, the outermost, which she had selected the evening before. She pushed off the terrace with a long mahogany pole she had had the foresight to remove from a curtain rod. She doubted whether the boat would be as obedient to her as it had to Avallac'h.

The boat glided noiselessly with the current. Tir ná Lia was quiet and dark. Only the statues on the terrace followed her with their dead gaze. Ciri counted the bridges.

The sky above the forest was lit up by a flash of lightning. A moment later there was a long grumble of thunder.

The third bridge.

Something stole across the bridge, softly, as nimble as a great black rat. The boat rocked as he jumped onto the bow. Ciri threw down the rod and drew her sword.

'And so,' hissed Eredin Bréacc Glas, 'you wish to deprive us of your company?'

He also drew a sword. In a brief flash of lightning she managed to size up the weapon. The blade was single-edged, slightly curved. The edge of the blade was shining and undoubtedly sharp, the hilt was long and the pommel was in the shape of a circular, openwork plate. It was apparent at once that the elf knew how to use it.

He unexpectedly rocked the boat, pressing a foot down hard on the side. Ciri kept her balance with ease, and righted the boat with a powerful tilt of her body, then almost immediately tried the same trick by jumping on the side with both feet. He wobbled but kept his balance and lunged at her with his sword. She parried the blow, blocking instinctively, for she could see little. She retaliated with a rapid, low cut. Eredin parried and struck, and Ciri deflected the blow. A stream of sparks flew from the blades as though from flint and steel.

He rocked the boat again, hard, almost knocking her over. Ciri danced, balancing with arms outstretched. He retreated towards the bow and lowered his sword.

'Where did you learn that, Swallow?'

'You'd be astonished.'

'I doubt it. Was it your idea that the barrier can be overcome by sailing along the river, or did someone reveal it to you?'

'It doesn't matter.'

'It does. And let's get to the bottom of it. There are methods for doing that. Now drop your sword and we'll go back.'

'Like hell.'

'We're going back, Zireael. Auberon's waiting. Tonight, I guarantee, he'll be lively and full of vigour.'

'Like hell,' she repeated. 'He overdosed on that invigorating draught you showed me. The one you gave him. Or perhaps it wasn't for vigour at all.'

'What are you talking about?'

'He's dead.'

Eredin quickly overcame his astonishment and suddenly went

for her, rocking the boat. Balancing, they traded several ferocious blows, the water carrying the resonant clang of steel.

Lightning lit up the night. A bridge slid past above their heads. One of the last bridges of Tir ná Lia. Or maybe the last?

'You must understand, Swallow,' he rasped, 'that you're only delaying the inevitable. I can't let you leave here.'

'Why not? Auberon's dead. And I'm nobody and mean nothing, after all. You told me so yourself.'

'Well, it's true.' He raised his sword. 'You mean nothing. You're a tiny clothes moth that can be crushed in the fingers into shining dust, but which, perhaps, if it's allowed, can cut out a hole in a precious fabric. You're a grain of pepper, despicably small, but which when inadvertently chewed spoils the most exquisite food, forces one to spit it out, when one wanted to savour it. That is what you are. Nothing. An irritating nothing.'

Lightning. In its light Ciri saw what she wanted to see. The elf raised his sword and swung, leaping onto the bench of the boat. He had the advantage of height. He was sure to win the next clash.

'You ought not to draw a weapon on me, Zireael. It's too late now. I won't forgive you that. I won't kill you, oh, no. But a few weeks in bed, in bandages, will certainly do you good.'

'Wait. First, I want to tell you something. Disclose a certain secret.'

'And what could you tell me?' he snorted. 'What can you tell me that I don't know? What truth can you reveal to me?'

'That you won't fit under the bridge.'

He had no time to react, struck the bridge with the back of his head and shot forward, losing his balance completely. Ciri could have simply pushed him out of the boat, but was afraid that wouldn't be enough, that it wouldn't stop her being pursued. Besides, he, whether deliberately or not, had killed the Alder King. And he deserved pain for that.

She stabbed him in the thigh, right at the edge of his mail shirt. He didn't even scream. He flew overboard and splashed into the river, the water closing over him.

She turned around and looked. It was a long time before he surfaced. Before he dragged himself out onto some marble steps descending into the river. He lay still, dripping water and blood.

'It'll do you good,' she muttered. 'A few weeks in bed in bandages.'

She grabbed the pole, and pushed off powerfully. The River Easnadh became more and more rapid. The boat was moving more quickly. The final buildings of Tir ná Lia soon lay behind her.

She didn't look back.

First it became very dark, for the boat had passed into an old forest, among trees whose boughs touched each other over the river, forming a vault. Then it brightened up as the forest came to an end, and on both banks there were alder wetlands, reeds and bulrushes. Tussocks of weed, floating water plants and tree trunks appeared in the previously clear river. When the sky brightened up from the lightning she saw rings on the water, and after the thunder rumbled she heard the splash of startled fish. Something was splashing and plopping, squelching and smacking its lips. Several times, not far from the boat, she saw large glowing eyes. Several times the boat shuddered upon hitting something large and alive. *Not everything here is beautiful. For the unaccustomed this world means death.* She repeated the words of Eredin in her mind.

The river broadened considerably, spreading out wide. Islands and channels appeared. She let the boat float randomly, wherever the current took her. But she began to worry. What would happen if she made a mistake and took the wrong branch?

She had barely thought that when the neighing of Kelpie and a strong, mental signal from the unicorn came from the rushes by the bank.

'It's you, Little Horse!'

Hurry, Star-Eye. Follow me.

'To my world?'

First, I must show you something. The elders ordered me to.

They rode, first through a forest, then across a steppe densely furrowed with ravines and gorges. Lightning flashed, thunder bellowed. The storm was coming closer. A wind was getting up.

The unicorn led Ciri to one of the ravines.

It's here.

'What's here?'

Dismount and see.

She obeyed. The ground was uneven. She tripped. Something crunched and slipped under her foot. Lightning flashed and Ciri cried hollowly.

She was standing among a sea of bones.

The ravine's sandy slopes had subsided, probably washed away by downpours. And that revealed what had been concealed. A burial ground. A boneyard. A huge heap of bones. Shinbones, hip bones, ribs and thigh bones. And skulls.

She picked up one of them.

The lightning flashed and Ciri screamed. She understood whose remains they were.

The skull, which bore the marks of a blade, had canine teeth.

Now you understand, she heard in her head. *Now you know. They did it, the Aen Elle. The Alder King. The Fox. The Sparrowhawk. This world was not their world at all. It became their world. After they had conquered it. When they opened Ard Gaeth, having deceived and taken advantage of us, just as they have tried to deceive and take advantage of you.*

Ciri threw the skull away.

'Murderers!' she shouted into the night. 'Scoundrels.'

Thunder rolled across the sky with a clatter. Ihuarraquax neighed loudly, in warning. She understood. She leaped into the saddle, and urged Kelpie into a gallop with a cry.

Pursuers were on their trail.

*

This has happened before, she thought, gulping air as she galloped. *This has happened before. A ride like this, reckless, in the darkness, on a night full of dread, ghosts and apparitions.*

'Forward, Kelpie!'

A furious gallop, eyes watering from the speed. Lightning split the sky in two. Ciri sees alders lit up on both sides of the road. From all sides misshapen trees reach out towards her the long, knobbly arms of their boughs, snap the black jaws of their hollows, and hurl curses and threats in her tracks. Kelpie neighs piercingly, hurtles along so fast her hooves seem only to brush the earth. Ciri flattens herself against the mare's neck. Not just to minimise the drag, but also to avoid the alder branches, trying to knock or pull her from the saddle. The branches swish, lash, and whip, trying to latch onto her clothes and hair. The misshapen trunks sway, the hollows snap and roar.

Kelpie neighs wildly. The unicorn replies. There is a snow-white dot in the gloom. It points the way.

Hurry, Star-Eye! Ride with all your might!

There are more and more alders, it's getting more and more difficult to dodge their boughs. Soon they'll bar the entire road . . .

A cry behind. The voice of the pursuers.

Ihuarraquax neighs. Ciri receives his signal. She understands its significance. She presses herself to Kelpie's neck. She doesn't have to urge her on. The mare, chased by fear, flies in a breakneck gallop.

Again a signal from the unicorn, clearer, penetrating her brain. It's an instruction, quite simply an order.

Leap, Star-Eye. You must leap. Into another place, into another time.

Ciri doesn't understand, but she fights to. She tries hard to understand, she focuses, she focuses so hard that the blood buzzes and pulses in her ears . . .

Lightning. And after it a sudden darkness, darkness soft and black, black darkness that nothing can lighten.

A buzzing in her ears.

*

The wind on her face. A cool wind. Drops of rain. The scent of pine in her nostrils.

Kelpie prances, snorts and stamps. Her neck is hot and wet.

Lightning. Soon after it thunder. In the light Ciri sees Ihuarraquax shaking his head and horn, powerfully pawing the ground with his hoof.

'Little Horse?'

I'm here, Star-Eye.

The sky is full of stars. Full of constellations. The Dragon. The Winter Maiden. The Seven Goats. The Pitcher.

And almost just above the horizon – the Eye.

'We did it,' she gasped. 'We made it, Little Horse. This is my world!'

His signal is so clear that Ciri understands everything.

No, Star-Eye. We've fled from one world. But it still isn't your place, not your time. There are still many worlds ahead of us.

'Don't leave me alone.'

I will not. I am in debt to you. I must pay it off. Entirely.

*

Along with the growing wind, the sky darkens from the west. The clouds, coming in waves, extinguish the constellations in turn. The Dragon goes out, the Winter Maiden goes out, then the Seven Goats and the Pitcher. The Eye, which shines brightest and longest, goes out.

The line of the horizon is lit up by the short-lived brightness of lightning. Thunder rolls with a dull rumble. The wind abruptly intensifies, blowing dust and dry leaves into their eyes.

The unicorn neighs and sends a mental signal.

There's no time to lose. Our only hope is in a quick escape. To the right place, and the right time. We must hurry, Star-Eye.

I am the Master of Worlds. I am the Elder Blood.

I am of the blood of Lara Dorren, the daughter of Shiadhal.

Ihuarraquax neighs, urges them on. Kelpie echoes it with a long-drawn-out snort. Ciri puts on her gloves.

'I'm ready,' she says.

A buzzing in her ears. A flash and brightness. And then darkness.

The trial, sentence and execution of Joachim de Wett is usually ascribed by most historians to the violent, cruel and tyrannical nature of Emperor Emhyr, and neither is there any shortage either – particularly amongst authors of a literary bent – of allusive hypotheses about revenge and the settling of wholly private scores. It is high time the truth were told: the truth, which for every attentive scholar is more than obvious. Duke de Wett commanded the Verden Group in such a way that the term 'inept' is much too mild. Having against him forces twice as weak as his own, he delayed the offensive to the north, and directed all his efforts towards a fight against the Verdanian guerrillas. The Verden Group committed unspeakable atrocities against the civilian population. The result was easy to predict and was inevitable. If, in the winter, the forces of the insurgents had numbered less than half a thousand, by spring almost the entire country had risen up. King Ervyll, who had been devoted to the Empire, was eliminated, and the insurrection was led by his son, Prince Kistrin, who sympathised with the Nordlings. Having on his flank a landing force of pirates from Skellige, to the fore an offensive of Nordlings from Cidaris, and at the rear a rebellion, de Wett became entangled in piecemeal engagements, suffering defeat after defeat. In the process he delayed the offensive of the Centre Army Group – instead of, as had been planned, engaging the Nordlings' wing, the Verden Group tied down Menno Coehoorn. The Nordlings immediately exploited the situation and went on the counter-attack, breaking through the encirclement near Mayena and Maribor, and thwarting the chances of those vital forts being swiftly captured a second time.

The ineptitude and stupidity of de Wett also had a psychological significance. The myth of Nilfgaard's invincibility was broken. Scores of volunteers began to flock to the army of the Nordlings . . .

Restif de Montholon
The Northern Wars. Myths, Lies and Half-truths.

CHAPTER SIX

Jarre – what else can be said? – was very disappointed. An upbringing in a temple and his own open nature made him believe in people, in their goodness, kindness and selflessness. Not much remained of that faith.

He had already slept two nights in the open, among the remains of hay ricks, and now it looked like he would be spending a third night in a similar fashion. In every village where he asked for a bed or a piece of bread he was answered with either a weighty silence, or insults and threats from behind securely locked gates. It didn't help when he said who he was and why he was travelling.

He was very, very disappointed in people.

It was quickly growing dark. The boy marched jauntily and briskly along a path between some fields. He spotted a hay rick, resigned and downcast at the prospect of another night under the open sky. March was, admittedly, extremely warm, but it got cold at night. And very frightening.

Jarre looked up at the sky, where, as it had been every night for almost a week, the gold and red bee of a comet was visible, crossing the sky from the west to the east, dragging in its wake a flickering plait of fire. He wondered what this strange phenomenon, mentioned in many prophecies, might actually auger.

He started walking again. It was growing darker and darker. The track led downwards, into an avenue of dense undergrowth that assumed terrifying shapes in the semi-darkness. From below, where it was even darker, drifted the cold, foul smell of rotting weed and something else. Something very unpleasant.

Jarre stopped. He tried to persuade himself that what was crawling over his back and shoulders was not fear, but cold. Unsuccessfully.

A low footbridge connected the banks of a canal overgrown with osiers and misshapen willows, black and shining like freshly pared pitch. Long holes gaped in the footbridge in places where the timbers had rotted and caved in, and the handrail was broken, its spindles submerged in the water. The willows grew more thickly beyond the bridge. Although it was still a long way to the actual night, although the distant meadows beyond the canal were still glowing with a yarn of mist hanging on the top of the grass, darkness reigned among the willows. Jarre saw the vague ruins of a building in the gloom – probably a mill, sluice or eel smokery.

I must cross that footbridge, thought the lad. *There's nothing to be done! Although I feel in my bones that something evil is lurking in the darkness, I must get to the other side of this canal. I must cross this canal, like that mythical leader or hero I read about in yellowed manuscripts in the Temple of Melitele. I'll traverse this canal and then . . . What was it? The cards will have been dealt? No, the dice will have been cast. Behind me lies my past, before me stretches my future . . .*

He stepped onto the bridge and at once knew that his sense of foreboding hadn't been mistaken. Before he even saw them. Or heard them.

'Well?' rasped one of the men who now blocked his way. 'Didn't I say? I said, just wait a tick and someone'll appear.'

'Exackly, Okultich,' another of the characters armed with clubs lisped slightly. 'Verily we'll 'ave to make you a fortune-teller or a wise-man. Well, gentle passer-by, walking all alone! Will you give us what you have of your own free will, or will it have to come to a struggle?'

'I don't have anything!' yelled Jarre at the top of his voice, although he didn't have much hope that anybody would hear and rush to help. 'I'm a poor wanderer! I don't have a groat to my name! What can I give you? This cane? These garments?'

'Not only that,' said the lisping one, and something in his voice made Jarre tremble. 'For you ought to know, poor wanderer, that in truth we, being in urgent need, were looking out for a wench. Well, night's just around the corner, no one else is coming now, so beggars can't be choosers. Grab 'im, boys!'

'I have a knife,' yelled Jarre. 'I'm warning you!'

He had a knife indeed. He'd swiped it from the temple kitchen the day before his flight and hidden it in his bundle. But he didn't reach for it. He was paralysed – and terrified – by the realisation that it was pointless and that nothing would help him.

'I have a knife!'

'Well, prithee,' sneered the lisping one, approaching. 'He has a knife. Who'd have thought it?'

Jarre couldn't run away. Terror turned his legs into two posts stuck into the ground. Adrenaline seized him by the throat like a noose.

'Hi there!' a third character suddenly shouted, in a young and strangely familiar voice. 'I think I know him! Yes, yes, I know him! Let him be, I say, he's a pal! Jarre? Do you recognise me? I'm Melfi! Hey, Jarre? Do you recognise me?'

'Yes . . . I do . . .' Jarre fought against the hideous, overwhelming, previously unfamiliar sensation with all his strength. Only when he felt a pain in his hip, which had smashed against a timber of the bridge, did he understand what the sensation was.

The sensation of losing consciousness.

*

'Oh, this is a surprise,' said Melfi. 'Why, a fluke among flukes! Why, coming across a fellow-countryman. A pal from Ellander. A mate! Eh, Jarre?'

Jarre swallowed a bite of the hard, rubbery piece of fatback that his strange company had given him and ate a bit of roasted turnip. He didn't reply, but only nodded towards the whole group of six surrounding the campfire.

'And which way are you going, Jarre?'

'To Vizima.'

'Ha! We're heading to Vizima too! Why, a fluke among flukes! What, Milton? Remember Milton, Jarre?'

Jarre didn't. He wasn't certain if he had ever seen him. As a matter of fact, Melfi was exaggerating a little in calling him a pal. He was the cooper's son from Ellander. When the two of them used to attend the temple school, Melfi would regularly and severely beat Jarre and call him a 'bastard-without-a-mother-or-father-begotten-in-the-nettles'. This went on for about a year, after which the cooper took his son out of school, since it had been proved

209

that his offspring was only fit for barrels. Thus Melfi, rather than toiling to learn the arcana of reading and writing, toiled to whittle staves in his father's workshop. And after Jarre had completed his studies and on the strength of a recommendation from the temple became an assistant scribe in the magistrates' court, the cooper's son – following the example of his father – bowed to him, gave him presents and declared his friendship.

'—we're going to Vizima,' Melfi continued his tale. 'To join up. All of us here, to a man, are going to join the army. These here, look, Milton and Ograbek, peasant boys, have been selected for the acreage duty, why, you know. . .'

'I do.' Jarre cast his eyes over the peasant sons, fair-haired and as alike as brothers, chewing some unrecognisable food roasted in the cinders. 'One for each two score and ten acres. The acreage levy. And you, Melfi?'

'With me,' sighed the cooper's son, 'it's like this, see: the first time the guilds had to supply a recruit my father got me out of trouble. But when poverty came, we had to draw lots a second time, because the town so decided . . . Well, you know . . .'

'I do,' nodded Jarre again. 'An additional lottery for the levy was decreed by a resolution of Ellander town council on the day of the sixteenth of January. It was necessary owing to the Nilfgaardian threat—'

'Just listen to 'im talk, Pike,' raspingly interjected the thickset and shaven-headed fellow, the one called Okultich, who had hailed him on the bridge not long before.

'Fop! Know-it-all!'

'Smart alec!' drawled another huge farmhand with a dopey smile permanently plastered onto his round face. 'Know-all!'

'Shut it, Klaproth,' slowly lisped the one called Pike, the oldest of the company, sturdy, with a drooping moustache and a shaved nape. 'Since he's a know-it-all, it's worth listening when he talks. There may be a benefit from it. Facts. And facts never harmed anyone. Well, almost never. And almost no one.'

'I'll second that,' announced Melfi. 'He, I mean Jarre, is indeed clever, knows his letters . . . A scholar! I mean he works as a court scribe in Ellander, and at the Temple of Melitele the whole book collection is under his care—'

'What then, I wonder,' interrupted Pike, staring at Jarre through the smoke and sparks, 'is a sodding court-temple librarian doing on the highway to Vizima?'

'Just like you,' said the boy, 'I'm going to join the army.'

'And what—' Pike's eyes shone, reflecting the glow like the eyes of a real fish in the light of a torch on the bow of a boat '—what is a court-temple scholar hoping to find in the army? For he can't be going to join up. Eh? Why, any fool knows that temples are exempt from the levy, they don't have to supply recruits. And any fool knows that every single court is capable of defending its scribe and wangling him out of joining the army. So what's it all about, master clerk?'

'I'm joining the army as a volunteer,' declared Jarre. 'I'm signing up myself, of my own free will, not from the levy. Partly for personal reasons, but mainly from patriotic duty.'

The company roared with loud, thunderous, general laughter.

'Heed, boys,' Pike finally said, 'what contractions sometimes lurk in a body. Two natures. Here we have a young shaver, it would seem, educated and worldly, and undoubtedly clever by nature on top of all that. He ought to know what's happening in the war, know who's fighting whom and who will soon utterly defeat whom. And he, as you've heard, without being forced, of his own free will, out of paterotic duty, wants to join the losing party.'

No one commented. Jarre included.

'Such a paterotic duty,' Pike finally said, 'is usually only the mark of the feeble-minded. Why, perhaps it even befits temple-court alumni. But there was talk here of some sort of personal reasons. I'm awful curious as to what those personal reasons might be.'

'They're so personal—' Jarre cut him off '—that I'm not going to talk about them. All the more so since you, good sir, are in no hurry to talk about your reasons.'

'Now heed,' said Pike a moment later. 'Were some boor to talk to me like that, he'd get a punch in the mush right off. Well, if he's a learned scribe . . . I'll forgive him . . . just this once. And say: I'm also going to join up. And also as a volunteer.'

'In order, like one of the feeble-minded, to join the losers?' It surprised Jarre himself where so much insolence had suddenly come from. 'Fleecing travellers on bridges en route?'

'He,' chortled Melfi, anticipating Pike, 'he's still mad at us for that ambush on the footbridge. Let it go, Jarre, it was only a prank! Just innocent tricks. Right, Pike?'

'Right.' Pike yawned and snapped his teeth so loud it echoed. 'Just innocent tricks. Life is sad and glum, just like a calf being led to the slaughter. Then only tricks or pranks can cheer it up. Don't you think so, scribe?'

'I do. By and large.'

'That's good.' Pike didn't lower his shining eyes from him. 'For otherwise you'd be a miserable companion for us and it would be better if you walked to Vizima by yourself. Right away, for instance.'

Jarre said nothing. Pike stretched.

'I've said what I meant to say. Well, mates, we've fooled around, frolicked, had our fun, and now it's time. If we're to be in Vizima by suppertime, we ought to set off with the sun.'

*

The night was very cold, and Jarre couldn't sleep despite his tiredness. He was curled up in a ball under his mantle, with his knees almost touching his chin. When he finally fell asleep, he slept badly, his dreams constantly waking him up. He couldn't remember most of them. Apart from two. In the first dream, the witcher, Geralt of Rivia, was sitting beneath long icicles hanging from a rock, motionless, covered in ice and being quickly buried under drifting snow. In the other dream, Ciri was galloping on a black horse, hugging its mane, along an avenue of misshapen alders that were trying hard to seize her with their crooked boughs.

Oh, and just before dawn he dreamed of Triss Merigold. After her stay in the temple the year before the boy had dreamed about the sorceress several times. The dreams had made Jarre do things which he was very ashamed of afterwards.

This time, naturally, nothing shameful happened. It was too cold.

*

All seven of them set off in the morning, barely after the sun rose. Milton and Ograbek, the peasant sons from the acreage duty, fortified themselves by singing a soldiers' song.

> *Here rides the warrior, armour glinting bright.*
> *Flee young lass, he'll steal a kiss this night.*
> *And wherefore not; who will stay his hand?*
> *For his keen blade defends the motherland.*

Pike, Okultich, Klaproth and Melfi the cooper's son – who had attached himself to them – were telling each other anecdotes and stories; extremely funny ones. In their opinion.

'—and the Nilfgaardian asks: "What stinks around here?" And the elf says: "Shit". Haaa, haa, haaa!'

'Ha, ha, ha, ha! And do you know this one? A Nilfgaardian, an elf and a dwarf are walking along. They look: a mouse is scampering . . .'

The longer the day went on, the more other wanderers, peasants' carts, bailiffs and small squads of marching soldiers they encountered on the highway. Some of the carts were crammed with goods. Pike's gang followed them with their noses almost touching the ground, like pointers, gathering whatever fell – here a carrot, there a potato, a turnip, occasionally even an onion. Some of the loot they cleverly put away for a rainy day, and some they greedily devoured without even interrupting their joke-telling.

'—and the Nilfgaardian goes: fluuub! And shits himself right up to the ears! Ha, ha, ha, ha, ha, ha!'

'Haa, haaa, haa! O Gods, I can't bear it . . . Shat himself . . . Haaaa, haaa, haaa!'

Jarre was waiting for an opportunity and a pretext to wander off. He wasn't keen on Pike, he wasn't keen on Okultich. He wasn't keen on the glances which Pike and Okultich were casting at the passing merchants' wagons, peasants' carts and the women and girls sitting on them. He wasn't keen on Pike's sneering tone, since he kept talking about the usefulness of signing up as a volunteer when defeat and extermination were certain and self-evident.

There was a smell of ploughed earth. And smoke. They saw the roofs of buildings in the valley, among a regular patchwork of fields, groves and fishponds gleaming like mirrors. Sometimes the distant barking of a dog, the lowing of an ox, or the crowing of a cock reached their ears.

'You can see these villages are wealthy,' Pike lisped, licking his lips. 'Tmall but fanthy.'

'Halflings live and farm here in the valley,' Okultich hurried to explain. 'Everything about them's fancy and pretty. A thrifty little nation, those midgets.'

'Damned inhumans,' rasped Klaproth. 'Bloody kobolds! They farm here, and poverty and misery befalls real people because of creatures like them. Even war doesn't harm such as them.'

'For now.' Pike stretched his mouth in an ugly smile. 'Remember this village, lads. The outermoft one, among those birches, right in the forest. Remember it well. If I ever dethire to visit here again, I wouldn't want to go astray.'

Jarre turned his head away. He pretended he couldn't hear. That all he could see was the highway in front of him.

They walked on. Milton and Ograbek, the peasant sons from the acreage duty, sang a new song. Less soldierly. Perhaps a little more pessimistic. Which could – particularly after Pike's earlier allusions – be considered a bad omen.

> *Hark and think on what I say,*
> *I shall speak of death today,*
> *For no matter how old you be,*
> *You'll not escape its misery,*
> *Be ever mindful of your due;*
> *Death will surely throttle you!*

*

'He,' judged Okultich morosely, 'must have cash. If he doesn't have cash, may me balls be cut off.'

The individual about whom Okultich had made such a ghastly bet was a wandering trader, hurrying beside a donkey-drawn cart.

'Dosh or no dosh,' lisped Pike, 'the donkey must be worth something. Hasten your steps, boys.'

'Melfi.' Jarre seized the cooper's son by his sleeve. 'Open your eyes. Can't you see what's being planned?'

'Oh, they're only jokes, Jarre.' Melfi wrenched himself free. 'Just jokes . . .'

The trader's cart – it was evident from close up – was at the same time a stall, and could be set up within a few moments. The whole donkey-drawn construction was covered in garishly and picturesquely sprawling writing, in which the goods on sale included balsams and remedies, protective talismans and amulets, elixirs, magical philtres and poultices, cleaning agents, and furthermore detectors of metals, ores and truffles and fail-safe baits for fish, ducks and wenches.

The trader, a thin old man weighed down by the burden of his years, looked around, saw them, cursed and drove his donkey on. But the donkey, like all donkeys, had no intention of going any faster.

'Fine robes on that one,' judged Okultich quietly. 'And we'll certainly find a little something on the cart . . .'

'Very well, boys,' said Pike. 'Chop, chop! We'll deal with this matter while there are few witnesses on the road.'

Jarre, astonished at his courage, pulled ahead of the company in a few swift paces and turned around, standing between them and the merchant.

'No,' he said, fighting to get a word out of his tight throat. 'I won't allow it . . .'

Pike slowly opened his coat and displayed a long knife shoved into his belt, clearly as sharp as a razor.

'Out of the road, scribbler,' he lisped malevolently. 'If you respect your neck. I thought you'd fit into our company, but no, your temple, I see, has made you overly sanctimonious. You stink overly of pious incense. So out of the way, for otherwise—'

'And what's going on here? Eh?'

Two strange shapes emerged from behind the stout and spreading willows which flanked the highway and were the most common feature of the Ismena valley's scenery.

The two men wore waxed and upwardly twisted moustaches, colourful puffed breeches, quilted short jackets decorated with ribbons and huge, soft velvet berets with bunches of feathers. Apart from the sabres and daggers hanging from their broad belts, the two men carried on their backs double-handed swords, probably two yards long, with hilts measuring two feet and large, curved cross guards.

These landsknechts were hopping up and down, and fastening their trousers. Neither of them made even a movement towards the hilts of their terrible swords, but in any case, Pike and Okultich immediately became more docile, and the huge Klaproth shrank like a deflated goatskin.

'We're . . . we're doing nothing . . .' lisped Pike. 'Nothing we shouldn't . . .'

'Just pranks!' squealed Melfi.

'No one's been harmed,' unexpectedly piped up the stooping trader. 'No one!'

'We,' Jarre quickly interjected, 'are going to Vizima, to join up. Perhaps you're going the same way, noble sirs?'

'Indeed we are,' the landsknecht snorted, realising at once what this was about. 'We head for Vizima. Whoever wishes may go with us. It will be safer.'

'Safer, I swear,' added the other one, knowingly, eyeing Pike up and down. 'It behoves me to add, indeed, that not long ago we saw a mounted patrol in the vicinity of the Vizimian bailiwick. They are most inclined to hang, and miserable will be the fate of any marauder whom they catch in the act.'

'And it's most good—' Pike had regained his aplomb, and grinned a gap-toothed smile '—my lords, it's good, gentlemen, that there is law and punishment for rogues, that is the correct order of things. Thus let us set off to Vizima, to the army, for our paterotic duty summons us.'

The landsknecht looked at him long and quite contemptuously, then shrugged, straightened his great sword on his back and set off down the road. His companion, Jarre, as well as the merchant with his donkey and cart set off after him, and at the rear, some distance away, shambled Pike's rabble.

'Thank you, sir knights,' the merchant said some time later, driving his donkey with a withy. 'And thank you, young master.'

'It's nothing.' The landsknecht waved a hand. 'We're accustomed to it.'

216

'Various characters are drawn to the army.' His companion looked back over his shoulder. 'The order comes to a village or small town to supply a recruit for every five hundred acres, and sometimes that method is used to rid themselves right away of the worst sort of scoundrel. And then the roads are full of nuisances like that lot there. Well, in the army the lance-corporal's rod will teach them obedience. Those rascals will learn discipline when they've run the gauntlet once or twice, faced the rows of lashes—'

'I,' Jarre hurried with an explanation, 'am signing on as a volunteer, not compulsorily.'

'Commendable, commendable.' The landsknecht glanced at him and twisted the waxed ends of his moustaches. 'And I see you are moulded from somewhat different clay than those men. Why are you with them?'

'Fate brought us together.'

'I've seen such chance encounters and fraternising before.' The soldier's voice was grave. 'It led the fraternisers to the same gibbet. Learn a lesson from that, lad.'

'I shall.'

*

Before the cloud-darkened sun had stood at the zenith, they reached the main road. Here a forced break in their journey awaited them. As it did a large group of wanderers who also had to stop – for the main road was packed full of marching soldiers.

'Southwards,' one of the landsknechts commented knowingly on the direction of the march. 'To the front. To Maribor and Mayena.'

'Heed their standards,' the other one indicated with his head.

'Redanians,' said Jarre. 'Silver eagles on crimson.'

'You've guessed right.' The landsknecht slapped him on the back. 'You're a truly smart youngster. That's the Redanian Army, which Queen Hedwig has sent to aid us. Now we are strong in unity. Temeria, Redania, Aedirn and Kaedwen. Now we're all allies, supporters of one cause.'

'A bit late,' said Pike with a pronounced sneer from behind their backs. The landsknecht looked back, but said nothing.

'So let's sit down,' suggested Melfi, 'and give our pins a rest. There's no end in sight of that army. It will be ages before the road frees itself up.'

'Let's sit down,' said the merchant, 'yonder, on that hill. The view will be better from there.'

The Redanian cavalry rode by and, after them, raising dust, marched crossbowmen and pavisiers. After them a column of heavy cavalry trotted past.

'And they,' Melfi pointed to the armoured troops, 'are marching under different colours. They have black standards, flecked with something white.'

'Ah, the ignorant provinces.' The landsknecht glanced at him contemptuously. 'They don't know their own king's arms. They are silver lilies, blockhead . . .'

'Field sable with lilies argent,' said Jarre, who all of a sudden felt a desire to prove that of all people he wasn't from the ignorant provinces.

'In the kingdom of Temeria's former coat of arms,' he began, 'there was a lion passant. But the Temerian royal dukes used a different one. To be precise, they added an extra field to the shield, containing three lilies. Since in heraldic symbolism the lily flower is a sign of the successor to the throne, the royal son, the heir to the throne and sceptre—'

'Sodding know-it-all,' barked Klaproth.

'You can shut your gob, cloth-head,' said the landsknecht menacingly. 'And you, lad, go on. This is interesting.'

'And when Prince Goidemar, the son of old King Gardik, went to fight against the insurgents of the she-devil Falka, the Temerian Army, under his standard, under the emblem of the lily, fought and won decisive victories. And when Goidemar inherited the throne from his father, he established three lilies argent on a field sable as the kingdom's coat of arms as a memento of those victories and for the miraculous escape of his wife and children from the hands of the enemy. And later King Cedric changed the state coat of arms by a special decree so that it's a black shield aspersed with silver lilies. And the Temerian coat of arms has been like that ever since. Which you may all easily confirm for yourself, since the Temerian lancers are riding along the main road right now.'

'You have worked it out very elegantly, young master,' said the merchant.

'Not I,' Jarre sighed, 'but John of Attre, a heraldic scholar.'

'And you are no worse schooled, I see.'

'Perfect for a recruit,' added Pike under his breath. 'To be clubbed to death under the standard of those silver lilies, for the king and Temeria.'

They heard singing. Menacing, soldierly, booming like a sea wave, like the growl of an approaching storm. Following the Temerians passed other soldiers in close and even array. Grey, almost colourless cavalrymen, over which neither standards nor pennants fluttered. A pole with a horizontal bar decorated with horses' tails and three human skulls nailed to it was being borne in front of the commanders riding at the head of the column.

'The Free Company.' The first landsknecht subtly indicated the grey riders. 'Mercenaries. Soldiers of fortune.'

'They're clearly stout-hearted,' gasped Melfi. 'Every man! And they're marching in step, as though on parade . . .'

'The Free Company,' the landsknecht repeated. 'Take a good look, O peasants and striplings, at a genuine soldier. They've been in battle before. It was they, those mercenaries, the companies of Adam Pangratt, Molla, Frontin and Abatemarco, who tipped the scales at Mayena. Thanks to them the Nilfgaardian encirclement was broken. We owe it to them that that the fortress was liberated.'

'Brave and doughty folk indeed, those mercenaries,' added the other, 'as unyielding in battle as a rock. Though the Free Company serves for coin, as you can easily mark from their song.'

The troop approached at a walk, their thunderous song sounding a strong and booming, but strangely gloomy, bitter, note.

> Ne'er in thrall of sceptre or throne
> Ne'er allied with queen or king
> No league or union do we own
> 'Cept with the ducat gaily sparkling!
>
> We kiss not a monarch's hand
> Nor take an oath most stirring

For we're a valiant hired band!
Swearing only on the ducat sparkling

'Eh, to serve with them,' sighed Melfi again. 'To fight together with such as them . . . A man would know glory and spoils . . .'

'Do my eyes fail me or what?' Okultich screwed up his face. 'At the head of the second regiment . . . A woman? Do those soldiers of fortune fight under the command of a woman?'

'She's a woman,' confirmed the landsknecht. 'But not just any woman. That's Julia Abatemarco, who they call Pretty Kitty. She's some warrior! Under her command the mercenaries demolished the Black Cloaks and elven troops at Mayena, even though only twice five hundred of them assailed three thousand.'

'I've heard,' said Pike in a strange, repulsively obsequious, but at the same time malicious, tone, 'that the victory didn't count for much, that the ducats spent on the mercenaries went down the drain. Nilfgaard regrouped and gave our boys a thrashing, and a sound one. And encircled Mayena again. And perhaps they've already captured the stronghold? And perhaps they're already heading here? Perhaps they'll be here any day? Perhaps those corrupt mercenaries were bribed with Nilfgaardian gold long ago? And perhaps—'

'And perhaps,' interrupted the landsknecht, enraged, 'you want a punch in the face, you churl? Beware, for running down our army is punished by the noose! So shut your trap, while I'm in a good mood!'

'Oooh!' The bruiser Klaproth, mouth wide open, defused the situation. 'Oooh, look! Look at those funny short-arses!'

An infantry formation armed with halberds, guisarmes, battle-axes, flails and morning stars marched along the road, to the dull thud of drums, the fierce hooting of bagpipes and the shrill whistling of fifes. Dressed in fur cloaks, mail shirts and pointed pot helmets, the soldiers were indeed extremely short.

'Dwarves from the mountains,' explained the first landsknecht. 'One of the Mahakam Volunteer Foot.'

'I thought,' said Okultich, 'that the dwarves weren't with us, but against us. That those foul short-arses had betrayed us and were in league with the Black Cloaks—'

220

'You thought?' The landsknecht glanced at him piteously. 'Using what, I wonder? If you swallowed a cockroach with your soup, dolt, you'd have more intelligence in your guts than in your head. Those marching there are one of the dwarven foot regiments that Brouver Hoog, the headman of Mahakam, has sent us as succour. Most of them have also seen action, suffered great losses, so they've been withdrawn to Vizima to regroup.'

'The dwarves are a valiant folk,' confirmed Melfi. 'When one of them thumped me in the ear in the tavern in Ellander at Samhain it rang until Yule.'

'The dwarven regiment is the last in the column.' The landsknecht shaded his eyes with a hand. 'That's the end of the march. The road will soon be empty. Let's prepare to set off, for it's almost noon.'

*

'So many military folk are marching south,' said the seller of amulets and remedies, 'that there's surely going to be a great war. Great misfortune will fall on the people! Great defeats on the armies! Thousands of folk will die from fire and sword. So consider, gentlemen, that this comet, which can be seen in the sky every night, trails a fiery red tail behind it. If a comet's tail is blue or pale, it heralds cold ailments: chills, pleurisy, phlegm and catarrh, and such aquatic misfortunes as floods, downpours or long periods of rainy weather. While a red colour indicates that it's a comet of fevers, blood and fire, and also of the iron which springs from the fire. Dreadful, dreadful defeats will befall the people! Great pogroms and massacres will happen. As it says in the prophecy: corpses will pile up to a height of a dozen ells, wolves shall howl on the desolate ground, and men will kiss other men's footsteps . . . Oh woe to us!'

'Why to us?' the landsknecht interrupted coolly. 'The comet is flying high. It can also be seen from Nilfgaard, not to mention the Ina valley, whence, they say, Menno Coehoorn is approaching. The Black Cloaks are also looking at the sky and also see the comet. Why, then, should we not assume that it foretells their defeat and not ours? That their corpses will be piled up?'

'That's right!' snapped the other landsknecht. 'Woe to them, to the Black Cloaks.'

'You've worked it out elegantly, gentlemen.'

'Certainly.'

*

They passed by the forest surrounding Vizima and entered meadows and pastures. Entire herds of horses were grazing there, of various kinds: cavalry, harness, and draught horses. There was next to no grass on the meadows, it being March, but there were wagons and barracks full of hay.

'See that?' Okultich licked his lips. 'Eh, fine little horses! And no one's guarding them! There for the taking—'

'Shut your trap,' hissed Pike and obsequiously directed his gap-toothed grin at the landsknechts. 'He, gentlemen, has always dreamed of serving in the cavalry, which is why he looks at those steeds so greedily.'

'In the cavalry!' snorted the first landsknecht. 'What fantasies has the churl! He'll sooner be a stable boy, gathering muck from under the horses with a pitchfork and wheeling it out on a barrow.'

'That's right, sire!'

They went on, and soon reached a causeway running beside ponds and ditches. And suddenly they saw the red tiles of the towers of Vizima castle looming over the lake above the tops of alders.

'Well, we're almost there,' said the merchant. 'Can you smell it?'

'Uurgh!' Melfi grimaced. 'What a stench! What's that?'

'Probably soldiers on the royal coin who died of hunger,' muttered Pike behind their backs, making sure the landsknechts didn't hear.

'Almost makes your eyes water, doesn't it?' laughed one of them. 'Aye, thousands of military folk have wintered here, and military folk have to eat, and when they eat they defecate. Nature has ordered things thus and there's nothing you can do about it! And what's been shat out is carted to these ditches and dumped, without even being buried. In the winter, while the frost kept the

222

shit frozen, you could stand it, but from the spring . . . Ugh!'

'And more and more fresh soldiers are arriving and adding to the old heap.' The other landsknecht also spat. 'And can you hear that great buzzing? It's flies. There are swarms of them, an uncommon thing for early spring! Cover your gobs with whatever you can, for they'll get into your eyes and mouths, the bastards. And briskly. The quicker we pass by, the better.'

*

They passed the ditches, but didn't manage to lose the stench. On the contrary, Jarre would have sworn that the closer to the town they were, the worse the fug was. Except it was more varied, richer in scale and hue. The military camps and tents surrounding the castle stank. The huge field hospital stank. The crowded and busy suburbs stank, the embankment stank, the gate stank, the berm stank, the small squares and streets stank, the walls of the great castle towering over the town stank. Fortunately, the nostrils quickly became accustomed and it soon made no difference to them if it was dung, or rotten meat, or cat's piss, or another field kitchen.

There were flies everywhere. They buzzed annoyingly, getting into the eyes, ears and nose. They couldn't be driven away. It was easier to squash them on the face. Or chew them up.

When they had just exited the shadow of the gatehouse, their eyes were struck by a huge mural depicting a knight with his finger aimed at them. The writing beneath the mural asked in huge letters: WHAT ABOUT YOU? HAVE YOU SIGNED UP?

'All right, all right,' mumbled the landsknecht. 'Unfortunately.'

There were plenty of similar murals. You could have said there was a mural on every wall. It was generally the knight with his finger, but there was also often a solemn Mother Country with grey hair blowing around, against a background of burning villages and babies on Nilfgaardian pikes. There were also images of elves with bloodied knives in their teeth.

Jarre suddenly looked around and found they were alone: he, the landsknechts and the merchant. There wasn't any sign of Pike, Okultich, the peasants from the draft or Melfi.

'Yes, yes,' the first landsknecht confirmed his speculation, eyeing him closely. 'Your comrades scrammed at the first opportunity, they scarpered around the first corner. And do you know what I'll tell you, lad? It's good that your paths have diverged. Don't strive for them to converge again.'

'Shame about Melfi,' muttered Jarre. 'He's a good lad at heart.'

'Everyone chooses his destiny. And you, come with us. We'll show you where to sign up.'

They entered a square in the middle of which stood a pillory on a stone platform. Townspeople and soldiers greedy for amusement were gathered around the pillory. A handcuffed convict, who had just been hit in the face with a lump of mud, spat and wept. The crowd roared with laughter.

'Hey!' yelled the landsknecht. 'Look who they've put in the stocks. Why, it's Fuson! I wonder what for?'

'For farming,' a fat burgher in a wolf skin and felt cap hurried to explain.

'For what?'

'For farming,' the fat man repeated with emphasis. 'For what he sowed.'

'Ha, now, if you'll excuse me, you've dropped a clanger like a bull dumping on a threshing floor,' laughed the landsknecht. 'I know Fuson, he's a shoemaker, the son of a shoemaker, and the grandson of a shoemaker. He's never ploughed, nor sown, nor harvested in his life. You're exaggerating, I say, with that sowing, you really are.'

'That's the bailiff's own words!' said the burgher crossly. 'He's to stand in the pillory until twilight for sowing! For the villain sowed after being goaded on by Nilfgaard and for Nilfgaardian silver pennies . . . He sowed some strange crops, in truth. Foreign, I'll warrant . . . Let me think . . . Aha! Defeatism!'

'Yes, yes!' called the vender of amulets. 'I've heard tell of it! Nilfgaardian spies and elves are spreading the plague, spoiling wells, springs and brooks with various poisons and using devil's trumpet, hemlock, lepra and defeatism.'

'Aye,' the burgher in the wolf skin nodded. 'They hung two elves yesterday. Most probably for poisoning.'

'Round that corner—' the landsknecht pointed '—is the tavern where the conscription committee sits. A big canvas sheet is stretched out there with the Temerian lilies on it, which you know, of course, lad. You'll find it without any difficulty. Look after yourself. May we meet again in better times, God willing. Farewell to you, too, merchant, sir.'

The merchant cleared his throat loudly.

'Noble gentlemen,' he said, rooting around in his chests and boxes, 'let me, as proof of my gratitude . . . for your help. . .'

'Don't trouble yourself, good fellow,' said the landsknecht with a smile. 'We helped and that's that, don't mention it . . .'

'Perhaps a miraculous ointment against lumbago?' The merchant dug something out from the bottom of a box. 'Perhaps a universal and reliable medicine for bronchitis, gout, paralysis, dandruff and scrofula? Perhaps a resinous balsam for bee, viper and vampire bites? Perhaps a talisman to protect you from the effects of the stare of the evil eye?'

'And do you have, perhaps,' the landsknecht asked seriously, 'something to protect one from the effects of bad vittles?'

'I do!' beamed the merchant. 'This is a most effective remedy made from magical roots, flavoured with aromatic herbs. Three drops after a meal should suffice. Please, take it, noble gentlemen.'

'Thanks. Farewell, sir. Farewell to you, too, lad. Good luck!'

'Honest, politic and courteous,' commented the merchant, when the soldiers had disappeared into the crowd. 'You don't encounter such as them every day. Well, but you turned out al right too, young master. What then can I give you? An amulet against lightning? A bezoar? A turtle's shell effective against witches' spells? Ha, I also have a corpse's tooth for fumigation and a bit of dried devil's dung, it's good to wear it in your right shoe . . .'

Jarre tore his gaze away from some people doggedly cleaning a slogan from the wall of a building: DOWN WITH THE SODDING WAR.

'Leave it, sir,' he said. 'Time I went . . .'

'Ha,' cried the merchant, taking a small, heart-shaped brass medallion from the box. 'This ought to suit you, young man, it's just right for young people. It's a great rarity, the only one I have. It's a magical amulet. It makes the wearer never forget his love, even though time and countless miles separate them. Look, it opens here, and inside is a leaf of thin papyrus. Suffice to write on the leaf the name of your beloved in magical red ink, which I have, and she will not forget, not change her heart, not betray you or cast you aside. Well?'

'Hmfff . . .' Jarre blushed slightly. 'I don't really know . . .'

'What name—' the merchant dipped a stick in the magical ink '—am I to write?'

'Ciri. I mean, Cirilla.'

'There. Take it.'

'Jarre! What are you doing here, by a hundred devils?'

Jarre whirled around. *I had hoped,* he thought mechanically, *that I was leaving my whole past behind me, that everything would now be new. But I almost unceasingly keep bumping into old acquaintances.*

'Mr Dennis Cranmer . . .'

A dwarf in a heavy overcoat, cuirass, iron vambraces and tall fox fur hat with a tail cast a crafty glance over the boy, the merchant and then again over the boy.

'What are you,' he asked again sharply, ruffling his eyebrows, beard and moustache, 'doing here, Jarre?'

For a moment the boy considered lying, and to lend credence entangling the kind merchant into the false version. But he almost immediately rejected the idea. Dennis Cranmer, who had once served in the guard of the Duke of Ellander, enjoyed the reputation of a dwarf whom it was hard to deceive. And it wasn't worth trying.

'I want to join up.'

He knew what the next question would be.

'Did Nenneke give you permission?'

He didn't have to answer.

'You bolted.' Dennis Cranmer nodded his beard. 'You simply fled from the temple. And Nenneke and the priestesses are tearing their hair out . . .'

'I left a letter,' muttered Jarre. 'Mr Cranmer, I couldn't . . . I had to . . . It wasn't right to stay there idly, when the enemy are in the marches . . . At a dangerous moment for the fatherland

'... And what's more she ... Ciri ... Mother Nenneke didn't want to agree at all, although she's sent three quarters of the girls from the temple to the army, she didn't allow me ... And I couldn't ...'

'So you did a runner.' The dwarf frowned sternly. 'By a hundred bloody demons, I ought to tie you up with a stick under your knees and send you to Ellander by courier post! Order you locked up in the oubliette under the castle until the priestesses come to collect you! I ought to ...'

He panted angrily.

'When did you last eat, Jarre? When did you last have hot vittles in your gob?'

'Really hot? Three ... No, four days ago.'

'Come with me.'

*

'Eat slower, son,' Zoltan Chivay, one of Dennis Cranmer's comrades cautioned him. 'It isn't healthy to guzzle your food so quickly, without chewing properly. Where are you rushing to? Believe me, no one's going to take it away from you.'

Jarre wasn't so sure about that. A fist-fight duel was taking place right then in the main room of The Shaggy Bear inn. Two stocky dwarves, as wide as stoves, were punching each other so loudly it thudded, amidst the roars of their comrades from the Volunteer Regiment and the applause of the local prostitutes. The floor was shaking, furniture and pots were falling, and drops of blood from smashed noses were spraying around like rain. Jarre was just waiting for one of the fighters to sprawl across the officers' table and bang into the wooden plate of pork knuckle, the great bowl of steamed peas and the earthenware mugs. He quickly swallowed a piece of fatty meat he had bitten off, assuming that what he swallowed was his.

'I don't really get it, Dennis.' Another dwarf, called Sheldon Skaggs, didn't even turn his head when one of the fighters almost caught him with a right hook. 'Since this boy's a priest, how can he join up? Priests aren't allowed to shed blood.'

'He's a student at the temple, not a priest.'

'I've never been bloody able to understand those tortuous human superstitions. Well, but it doesn't do to mock other people's beliefs. The conclusion, though, is that this young man here, although brought up in a temple, has nothing against spilling blood. Particularly Nilfgaardian blood. Eh, what, young man?'

'Let him eat in peace, Skaggs.'

'I'm happy to answer . . .' Jarre swallowed a mouthful of pork knuckle and shoved a handful of peas into his mouth. 'It's like this: you can spill blood in a just war. In the defence of higher reasons. That's why I'm signing up . . . The motherland is calling . . .'

'You can see for yourselves—' Sheldon Skaggs swept his gaze over his companions '—how much truth there is in the statement that humans are a race similar to and related to us, that we come from a common root, both us, and them. The best proof is, here, sitting before us, wolfing down peas. In other words: you can come across loads of similar stupid zealots among young dwarves.'

'Especially after the Mayena battle,' remarked Zoltan Chivay coolly. 'Tons more volunteers always sign up after a victorious battle. The rush will stop when news spreads of Menno Coehoorn's army marching up the Ina, leaving behind only earth and water.'

'As long as a rush in the other direction doesn't start,' muttered Cranmer. 'I somehow don't trust volunteers. Interesting that every second deserter is a volunteer.'

'How can you . . .' Jarre almost choked. 'How can you suggest something like that, sir? I'm joining up for ideological reasons . . . To fight a just and legitimate war . . . The motherland . . .'

One of the fighting dwarves fell from a blow that, it seemed to the boy, shook the very foundations of the building, the dust rising a yard in the air from gaps in the floorboards. This time, the fallen dwarf, rather than leaping up and whacking his adversary, lay, clumsily twitching his limbs, prompting associations of a huge beetle flipped on its back.

Dennis Cranmer stood up.

'The matter is settled!' he declared loudly, looking around the inn. 'The position of commander of the troop made vacant after the heroic death of Elkana Foster, who fell on the battlefield at Mayena, is taken up by . . . What's your name, mate? Because I've forgotten.'

'Blasco Grant!' The victor of the fist fight spat a tooth onto the floor.

'Blasco Grant takes up the position. Are there any other contentious issues regarding promotions? There aren't? Well and good. Innkeeper! Beer!'

'Where were we. . . ?'

'A just war.' Zoltan Chivay began to count, bending his fingers back. 'Volunteers. Deserters—'

'Exactly,' Dennis interrupted. 'I knew I wanted to refer to something, and the matter concerned deserting and treacherous volunteers. Remember Vissegerd's former Cintran corps? The whoresons, it turns out, didn't even change their standard. I know that from the mercenaries of the Free Company, from the gang of Julia "Pretty Kitty". Julia's gang quarrelled with the Cintrans at Mayena. They marched in the vanguard of the Nilfgaardian troop, under the same standard with the lions—'

'The Mother Country summoned them,' Skaggs interjected morosely. 'And Empress Ciri.'

'Quiet,' Dennis hissed.

'That's true,' said a fourth dwarf, Yarpen Zigrin, who'd said nothing until then. 'Quiet. Quieter than quietness itself. And not for fear of snoopers, but because you don't talk about things you have no idea about.'

'While you, Zigrin—' Skaggs stuck out his chin '—*do* have an idea, eh?'

'I do. And I'll say one thing: no one, whether it's Emhyr var Emreis or the rebellious sorcerers from Thanedd, or even the devil himself, could make that girl do anything. They couldn't break her. I know that. Because I know her. That bloody marriage with Emhyr is a hoax. A hoax various asses have been taken in by . . . That girl, I tell you, has a different destiny. Quite a different one.'

'You talk,' muttered Skaggs, 'as though you really knew her, Zigrin.'

'Drop it,' snapped Zoltan Chivay unexpectedly. 'He's right about that destiny. I believe it. I also have reason to.'

'Eh.' Sheldon Skaggs waved a hand. 'Why waste breath. Cirilla, Emhyr, destiny . . . They're distant matters. While a closer matter, gentlemen, is Menno Coehoorn and the Centre Army Group.'

'Aye,' sighed Zoltan Chivay. 'Something tells me a huge battle won't pass us by. Perhaps the biggest history has ever seen.'

'A great deal,' mumbled Dennis Cranmer. 'Truly a great deal will be decided . . .'

'And put an end to even more.'

'Everything . . .' Jarre belched, decorously covering his mouth with his hand. 'Everything will end.'

The dwarves eyed him up for a moment, keeping silent.

'I don't quite understand you, young man,' Zoltan Chivay finally said. 'You wouldn't like to explain what you have in mind, would you?'

'In the ducal council . . .' Jarre stammered. 'In Ellander, I mean, it was said that victory in this great war is so important, because . . . because it's the great war to end all wars.'

Sheldon Skaggs snorted and spat beer down his beard. Zoltan Chivay burst out laughing.

'Don't you believe so, gentlemen?'

Now it was Dennis Cranmer's turn to snort. Yarpen Zigrin remained serious, looking intently and seemingly with concern at the boy.

'Look, son,' he said at last, very seriously. 'Evangelina Parr is sitting at the bar. She is, one must admit, large. Why, even enormous. But in spite of her size, beyond all doubt, she isn't a whore to end all whores.'

*

Turning into a narrow and deserted alley, Dennis Cranmer stopped.

'I must praise you, Jarre,' he said. 'Do you know what for?'

'No.'

'Don't pretend. You don't have to in front of me. It's praiseworthy that you didn't blink when Cirilla was being talked about. It's even more praiseworthy that you didn't open your trap then . . . Hey, hey, don't make faces. I knew a lot of what went on behind Nenneke's temple walls, a lot, you can believe me. And if that's too little for you, then know that I heard what name the merchant wrote on that medallion for you.

230

'Keep it up.' The dwarf tactfully pretended he hadn't noticed the crimson blush that suffused the boy's face. 'Keep it up, Jarre. And not only in the case of Ciri . . . What are you staring at?'

On the wall of a granary visible at the end of the lane was a lopsided, whitewashed slogan reading MAKE LOVE NOT WAR. Just under that somebody had scribbled in much smaller letters AND TAKE A SHIT EVERY MORNING.

'Look somewhere else, idiot,' Dennis Cranmer barked. 'Just for looking at graffiti like that you can get into trouble, and if you say something at the wrong time, they'll flog you at the post, they'll flay the skin off your back. The judgments are swift here! Extremely swift!'

'I saw the shoemaker in the pillory,' muttered Jarre. 'Reputedly for sowing defeatism.'

'His defeatism,' the dwarf stated seriously, pulling the boy by his sleeve, 'probably lay in the fact that when he took his son to his troop he wept, instead of cheering patriotically. They punish differently for more serious sowing. Come, I'll show you.'

They entered a small square. Jarre stepped back, covering his mouth and nose with his sleeve. About a dozen corpses were hanging from a large, stone gallows. Some of them – their appearance and smell betrayed it – had been hanging there a long time. 'That one,' pointed Dennis, simultaneously driving flies away, 'wrote stupid graffiti on walls and fences. That one claimed that war is a matter for lords and that the Nilfgaardian drafted peasants aren't his enemies. And that one told the following anecdote when he was drunk: "What's a spear? It's a nobleman's weapon, a stick with a poor man on each end." And there, at the end, do you see that woman? She was the madam of the military brothel on wheels, which she decorated with the words "Soldier, get your leg over today! You might not be able to tomorrow".'

'And just for that . . .'

'Furthermore, one of the girls had the clap, as it turned out. Which contravenes the law concerning sabotage and the undermining of military readiness.'

'I understand, Mr Cranmer.' Jarre stood up straight in a position he considered soldierly.

'But don't worry about me. I'm no defeatist . . .'

'You haven't understood shit and don't interrupt me, because I haven't finished. That last hanged man, the one stinking to high heaven, was only guilty of reacting to the chatter of a provocateur-snooper with the shout "You were right, sir, it's like that and not otherwise, as two plus two makes four!" Now tell me if you understand.'

'I do.' Jarre looked around furtively. 'I shall be careful. But . . . Mr Cranmer . . . What's it really like . . . ?'

The dwarf also looked around.

'It's like this,' he said softly. 'Marshal Menno Coehoorn's Centre Army Group is marching north with a force of around a hundred thousand men. Indeed, were it not for the insurrection in Verden, they'd already be here. Indeed, it would be better if negotiations were to take place. Indeed, Temeria and Redania don't have the forces to stop Coehoorn. Indeed, not before the strategic border of the Pontar.'

'The River Pontar,' whispered Jarre, 'is north of here.'

'That's exactly what I wanted to say. But remember: keep your trap shut about that.'

'I'll beware. When I'm in my unit will I also have to? May I also encounter a snooper?'

'In a frontline unit? Near the front? Not really. Snoopers are so ardent behind the front, because they're afraid of ending up on it. Furthermore, if they hung every soldier what grumbles, complains and swears there'd be no one left to fight. But, like you did with the matter of Ciri, Jarre, always keep your trap shut. Mark my words, no dung fly ever flew into a trap that was shut. Now go, I'll take you to the committee.'

'Will you put in a good word for me?' Jarre looked at the dwarf hopefully. 'Eh? Mr Cranmer?'

'Dear me, you're an ass, Mr Scribe. This is the army! If I put in a good word for you and tried pulling strings it would be as though I'd embroidered "lemon" on your back in gold thread! You'd have a hard time in your troop, laddie.'

'What about if I joined . . .' blinked Jarre, 'your unit . . .'

'Don't even think about it.'

'Because there's only room for dwarves in it, right?' the boy said bitterly. 'And not for me?'

'Right.'

Not for you, thought Dennis Cranmer. *Not for you, Jarre. Because I still have unpaid debts with Nenneke. Which is why I'd prefer you to return from the war in one piece. And the Mahakam Volunteer Regiment, consisting of dwarves, specimens of a foreign and inferior race, will always be sent to do the lousiest tasks, to the worst sectors. The ones you don't come back from. The ones you don't send humans to.*

'So how can I make sure,' Jarre continued, downcast, 'that I'll end up in a good troop?'

'And which one, according to you, is so first-rate it's worth trying to get into?'

Jarre turned around on hearing singing, swelling like a breaking wave, growing like the thunder of an approaching storm. Loud, powerful, swaggering singing, as hard as steel. He'd heard singing like that before.

The mercenary troop, formed up into threes, walked their horses along the narrow street leading from the castle. At their head, on a grey stallion, beneath a pole decorated with human skulls, rode the commander, a grey-haired man with an aquiline nose and hair plaited into a queue falling down onto his armour.

'Adam "Adieu" Pangratt,' mumbled Dennis Cranmer.

The singing of the mercenaries thundered, roared and rumbled. Counterpointed by the ringing of horseshoes on cobbles, it filled the narrow street way up to the tops of the houses, and into the blue sky above the town.

> *No lover or wife'll shed a tear*
> *When comes our time for dying*
> *With a ready step and a lusty cheer*
> *Our prize is the ducat sparkling!*

'You ask what troop . . .' said Jarre, unable to tear his eyes from the cavalrymen. 'Why, one like that! In one such as that I'd like to—'

'Each has his song,' the dwarf interrupted quietly. 'And each bites the blood-soaked earth his own way. Just as it befalls him. And they either cry for him or not. In a war, scribbler, you only sing and march as one, you stand in the ranks as one. And later in

233

battle everyone gets what is written for him. Whether in "Adieu" Pangratt's Free Company, or in the infantry, or in the convoys ... Whether in a shining suit of armour with a glorious crest, or in bast shoes and a flea-ridden sheepskin coat ... Whether on a fleet steed, or behind a shield ... Something different comes to each one. As it befalls him! Well, and there's the commission, do you see the sign above the entrance? That's your way, since you've thought to become a soldier. Go, Jarre. Farewell. We'll meet again when it's all over.'

The dwarf's gaze followed the boy until he disappeared into the door of the tavern occupied by the recruiting commission.

'Or we won't meet again,' he added softly. 'No one knows what's written for anybody. Or what will befall them.'

*

'Can you ride? Can you shoot a longbow or crossbow?'

'No, sir. But I can write and calligraph, ancient runes, too ... I know the Elder Speech ...'

'Can you wield a sword? Are you trained in lanceplay?'

'... I've read *The History of Wars*. The work by Marshal Pelligram ... And Roderick de Novembre ...'

'Or perhaps you know how to cook?'

'No, I don't ... But I reckon up well ...'

The recruiting officer grimaced and waved a hand.

'A well-read smart-alec! You're not the first today. Write him out a chitty for the pee-eff-eye. You'll be serving in the pee-eff-eye, lad. Run with this chitty to the southern end of the town, then beyond the Maribor Gate, down by the lake.'

'But ...'

'You'll find it for sure. Next!'

*

'Hey, Jarre! Hey! Wait!'

'Melfi?'

'Who else?' The cooper's son staggered, holding on to the wall. 'It's me, right here, tee-hee!'

'What's wrong with you?'

'Wrong with me? He, he! Nothing! We've had a bit to drink! We drank to Nilfgaard's confusion! Ugh, Jarre, I'm glad to see you, for I thought I'd lost you somewhere . . . My comrade. . .'

Jarre stepped back as though someone had hit him. For the cooper's son's breath didn't only smell of second-rate beer and third-rate vodka, but also of onions, garlic and God knows what else. Very intensively.

'And where,' Jarre asked sneeringly, 'is your eminent company?'

'You asking about Pike?' Melfi grimaced. 'Then I'll tell you: to hell with him! Do you know, Jarre, I think he was a bad man.'

'Bravo. You saw through him quickly.'

'Didn't I just!' Melfi strutted, not noticing the mockery. 'He hid it, but whoever cheats me can eat the devil! I tell you I know what he was planning! What drew him here to Vizima! You probably think, Jarre, that he and his miscreants came to sign up like us? Ha, well you're seriously mistaken! Do you know what he had planned? You wouldn't believe it!'

'I would.'

'He needed horses and uniforms,' Melfi finished triumphantly. 'He meant to steal them from round here. For he meant to go to war in disguised as a soldier!'

'Let him end his days on the gallows.'

'The quicker the better!' The cooper's son staggered slightly, stopped by the wall and undid his breeches. 'I'm just sorry that Ograbek and Milton, those stupid village idiots, were taken in. They followed Pike, so they're liable to meet the hangman too. Well, bollocks to them, effing bumpkins! And how goes it with you, Jarre?'

'Regarding?'

'Did the recruiting officers post you anywhere?' Melfi sent a stream of piss down the whitewashed wall. 'I asked because I'm already recruited. I'm to go through the Maribor Gate, to the southern end of the castle. And where do you have to go?'

'To the south side too.'

'Ha!' The cooper's son jumped up and down a few times, shook, and fastened his trousers. 'So we're going to fight together?'

235

'I don't think so.' Jarre looked at him condescendingly. 'I was assigned in accordance with my qualifications. To the pee-eff-eye.'

'Well, naturally.' Melfi hiccupped and breathed his dreadful mixture over him. 'You're book-learned! They probably assign smart alecs like you to important matters, not any old ones. Well, what to do. But for now, we'll be travelling a little longer together. For our route's to the southern end of the castle.'

'Looks like it.'

'Let's go then.'

'Let's go.'

*

'I don't think it's here,' judged Jarre, looking at a parade square surrounded by tents, where a troop of scruffs with long sticks on their shoulders were kicking up dust. Every scruff, as the boy observed, had a bunch of hay attached to his right leg and a bunch of straw attached to his left.

'I think we've come to the wrong place, Melfi.'

'Straw! Hay!' the roar of the lance corporal directing the scruffs could be heard from the parade square. 'Straw! Hay! Even it up, for fuck's sake!'

'A standard's fluttering over the tents,' said Melfi. 'See for yourself, Jarre. Those same lilies, what you were talking about on the road. Is there a standard? There is. Is there an army? There is. That means it's here. We've come to the right place.'

'You, maybe. Not me, for sure.'

'Ah, some officer or other is standing there by the fence. Let's ask him.'

It moved fast after that.

'New recruits?' yelled the sergeant. 'From the conscription office? Papers! Why the fuck are you standing one behind the other? March on the spot! Don't fucking stand there! Left turn! About-turn, right-fucking-turn! Quick march! About-fucking-turn! Listen and remember. First-of-fucking-all, get to the quartermaster! Get your kit! Mail shirt, boots, pike, helmet and sword, for fuck's sake! Then to the drill ground! Be ready for the fucking muster, at dusk! Quiiiick maaarch!'

'Just a minute.' Jarre looked around hesitantly. 'Because I think I have a different posting—'

'Whaaaaaaaat?'

'I beg your pardon, officer, sir.' Jarre blushed. 'I only want to prevent a possible error . . . For the commissioner clearly . . . He distinctly spoke of a posting to the pee-eff-eye, so I—'

'You're at home, my lad,' snorted the sergeant, somewhat disarmed by the 'officer'. 'This is your posting. Welcome to the Poor Fucking Infantry.'

*

'And why,' repeated Rocco Hildebrandt, 'and for what reason, are we to pay you gentlemen tax? We've already paid everything we were supposed to.'

'Blow this, look at 'im, the smart-arsed halfling.' Pike, sprawled on the saddle of a stolen horse, grinned at his comrades. 'He's already paid! And he thinks that's all. Really, 'e's the spitting image of that turkey what were thinking about Sunday. But they chopped 'is 'ead off on Saturday!'

Okultich, Klaproth, Milton and Ograbek cackled in unison. The joke was excellent, after all. And the amusement promised to be even more excellent.

Rocco noticed the revolting, clammy gazes of the marauders, and looked back. On the threshold of his cottage stood Incarvilia Hildebrandt, his wife, and Aloë and Yasmin, his two daughters.

Pike and his company looked at the hobbit girls, smiling lecherously. Yes, assuredly, the amusement promised to be first-class.

Impatientia Vanderbeck, Hildebrandt's niece, normally called by the pet name 'Impi', approached the hedge on the other side of the highway. She was a very pretty girl. The bandits' smiles became even more lecherous and revolting.

'Well, shorty,' Pike hurried him, 'hand over the penny to the royal army, give us your vittles, give us your horses, and lead the cows from the cowshed. We aren't going to stand here till sundown. We must get round a few more villages today.'

'Why must we pay and hand over our food?' Rocco Hildebrandt's voice trembled slightly, but determination and doggedness still resounded in it. 'You say it's for the army, that it's for our defence. And who, I ask, will defend us against hunger? We've already paid the winter levy, and the geld, and the poll tax, and the land tax, and the animal tax, and the devil only knows what else! If that wasn't enough, four halflings from this hamlet, my son included in that number, are coach drivers in the army convoys! And no one else but my brother-in-law, Milo Vanderbeck, known as Rusty, is a field surgeon, an important personage in the army. That means we've paid our acreage with interest. . . For what reason are we to pay more? Wherefore and what for? And why?'

Pike gave a long look at Incarvilia Hildebrandt, née Biberveldt, the halfling's wife. At their plump daughters, Aloë and Yasmin. At the gorgeous Impi Vanderbeck, dressed in a green frock. At Sam Hofmeier and his grandfather, old grandpa Holofernes. At Granny Petunia, doggedly picking at a flowerbed with a hoe. At the other halflings from the hamlet, mainly womenfolk and youngsters, apprehensively peeping out from their households and from behind fences.

'You ask why?' he hissed, leaning over in the saddle and looking into the halfling's terrified eyes. 'I'll tell you why. Because you're a mangy halfling, a foreigner, a stranger, and whoever robs you, you repulsive brute, delights the gods. Whoever vexes you, non-human, is carrying out a good and paterotic deed. And also because I feel sick with the desire to send your non-human nest up in smoke. Because I feel a yen coming on to fuck your midget women. And because we're five burly fellows, and you're a handful of short-arsed wretches. Now do you know why?'

'Now I know,' said Rocco Hildebrandt slowly. 'Off with you, Big Folk. Begone, you good-for-nothings. We shan't give you anything.'

Pike straightened up, and reached for the short sword hanging from his saddle.

'Have at them!' he yelled. 'Kill them!'

With a movement so fast it was almost imperceptible, Rocco Hildebrandt stooped down towards his barrow, took out a crossbow concealed under a rush mat, brought it to his cheek and sent a bolt straight into Pike's mouth, which was wide open in a yell. Incarvilia Hildebrandt, née Biberveldt, swung her arm powerfully and a sickle spun through the air, slamming into Milton's throat. The peasant's son puked blood and somersaulted backwards over his horse's rump, swinging his legs comically. Ograbek, moaning, tumbled beneath the horse's hooves, with grandpa Holofernes' secateurs buried in his belly up to the handles' wooden facings. The strongman Klaproth aimed a club at the old man, but flew from the saddle, squealing inhumanly, caught right in the eye with the spike of a dibber flung by Impi Vanderbeck. Okultich reined his horse around and hoped to flee, but granny Petunia sprang at him and jabbed the teeth of her rake into his thigh. Okultich cried out and fell, his foot caught in the stirrup, and the frightened horse dragged him across the sharp poles of the wattle fence. The brigand yelled and wailed as he was dragged and Granny Petunia – with her rake – and Impi – with her curved pruning knife – followed him like two she-wolves. Grandpa Holofernes blew his nose loudly.

The entire incident – from Pike's shout to grandpa Holofernes blowing his nose – took more or less the same time it would to rapidly utter the sentence 'Halflings are incredibly fast and can throw all sorts of missiles unerringly'.

Rocco sat down on the cottage steps. His wife, Incarvilia Hildebrandt, née Biberveldt, planted herself beside him. Their daughters, Aloë and Yasmin, went to help Sam Hofmeier finish off the wounded and strip the dead.

Impi returned in her green frock with the sleeves spattered up to the elbows with blood. Granny Petunia also returned, walking slowly, panting, grunting, leaning on her blood-spattered rake and holding her lower back. *Oh, she's getting old, our granny*, thought Hildebrandt.

'Where should we bury the brigands, Mr Rocco?' asked Sam Hofmeier.

Rocco Hildebrandt put his arm around his wife and looked up at the sky.

'In the birch copse,' he said. 'Next to the other ones.'

The sensational adventure of Mr Malcolm Guthrie of Braemore took the pages of many newspapers by storm. Even The Daily Mail *of London devoted several lines to it in its column 'Bizarre'. However, because very few of our readers read the press south of the Tweed, and if they do, then only newspapers more serious than* The Daily Mail, *let us remind you what happened. On the day of the 10th March last year Mr Malcolm Guthrie went fishing to Loch Glascarnoch. While there Mr Guthrie happened upon a young woman with an ugly scar on her face (sic!), riding a black mare (sic) in the company of a white unicorn (sic), who were emerging from the fog and darknes (sic). The girl spoke to the dumbstruck Mr Guthrie in a language which Mr Guthrie was so kind as to describe as, we quote: 'probably French, or some other dialect from the continent'. Because Mr Guthrie does not speak French or any other dialect from the continent, a conversation was not possible. The girl and the accompanying menagerie vanished, to quote Mr Guthrie again: 'like a golden dream'.*

Our comment: Mr Guthrie's dream was undoubtedly as golden as the colour of the single malt whisky Mr Guthrie customarily drinks, as we learned, drinking often and in such quantities that would explain the seeing of white unicorns, white mice and monsters from lochs. And the question we would like to pose runs thusly: What did Mr Guthrie think he was doing with a fishing rod by Loch Glascarnoch four days before the angling season began?

The Inverness Weekly, 18 March 1906 edition

CHAPTER SEVEN

Along with the intensifying wind the sky darkened from the west, and the clouds, approaching in waves, extinguished the constellations one after the other. The Dragon went out, the Winter Maiden went out and the Seven Goats went out. The Eye, which shines brightest and longest, went out.

The edge of the horizon lit up with a short-lived flashes of lightning. Thunder rolled with a dull rumble. The wind abruptly intensified, blowing dust and dry leaves into their eyes.

The unicorn neighed and sent a mental signal. Ciri understood immediately what he wanted to say.

There's no time to lose. Our only hope is in a quick escape. To the right place, and the right time. We must hurry, Star-Eye.

I am the Master of Worlds, she recalled. I am of the Elder Blood, I have power over time and place.

I am of Lara Dorren's blood.

Ihuarraquax neighed, urged them on. Kelpie echoed him with a long-drawn-out snort. Ciri put on her gloves.

'I'm ready,' she said.

A buzzing in her ears. A flash and brightness. And then darkness.

*

The water in the lake and the early-evening silence bore the curses of the Fisher King, who sat on his boat jerking and tugging the line, trying to free a lure caught on the lake bottom. A dropped oar thudded.

Nimue cleared her throat impatiently. Condwiramurs turned away from the window, and then bent over the etchings. One of the boards in particular caught her eye. A girl with windswept hair, riding a black mare rearing up. Beside her a white unicorn, also rampant, its mane blown around like the girl's.

'I think that's the only fragment of the legend that historians have never quibbled about,' commented the novice, 'unanimously regarding it as a fabrication and a fairy-tale embellishment, or a delirious metaphor. And painters and illustrators, spiting the scholars, took a liking to the episode. Look, prithee: each picture is Ciri and the unicorn. What do we have here? Ciri and the unicorn on a cliff above a sea beach. And here, if you please: Ciri and the unicorn in a landscape like something from a drug-induced trance, at night, beneath two moons.'

Nimue said nothing.

'In a word—' Condwiramurs tossed the boards onto the table '—everywhere it's Ciri and the unicorn. Ciri and the unicorn in the labyrinth of the worlds, Ciri and the unicorn in the abyss of times—'

'Ciri and the unicorn,' interrupted Nimue, looking at the window, at the lake, at the boat and the Fisher King thrashing around in it. 'Ciri and the unicorn emerge from nothingness like apparitions, suspended over some lake or other . . . And perhaps it's constantly the same lake, one that spans times and places like a bridge, at once different, but nonetheless the same?'

'I beg your pardon?'

'Apparitions.' Nimue wasn't looking at her. 'Visitors from other dimensions, other planes, other places, other times. Apparitions that change someone's life. That also change their own life, their own fate . . . Unbeknownst to them. For them it's simply . . . another place. Not that place, not that time . . . Once again, one more time in a row, not that time—'

'Nimue,' Condwiramurs interrupted with a forced smile. 'It's me who's the dream-reader, let me remind you. I'm the expert on dream visions and oneiroscopy. And all of a sudden you begin to prophesy. As though you saw what you're talking about . . . in a dream.'

The Fisher King, judging by the sudden intensity of his voice and his cursing, had failed to unhitch the lure and the line had snapped. Nimue said nothing, and looked at the engravings. At Ciri and the unicorn.

'I really have seen in a dream what I've been talking about,' she finally said, very calmly. 'I saw it many times in my dreams. And once while awake.'

*

As it is known, the journey from Człuchów to Malbork may in certain conditions take even five days. And since the letters from the Człuchów Commander to Winrych von Kniprode, Grand Master of the Order, had without fail to reach the addressee no later than on the day of Pentecost, the knight Heinrich von Schwelborn didn't delay and set off the day after Sunday *Exaudi Domine*, in order to travel peacefully and with no risk of being late. *Langsam, abersicher*. The knight's attitude greatly pleased his escort, which consisted of six mounted crossbowmen, commanded by Hasso Planck, a baker's son from Cologne. The crossbowmen and Planck were more accustomed to noble gentlemen who swore, yelled, urged and ordered them to gallop at breakneck speed, and afterwards, when they didn't make it in time anyway, put all the blame on the poor infantry, by lying in a way unbefitting a knight, not to mention one from a religious military order.

It was warm, though overcast. It drizzled from time to time, and the ravines were enveloped in fog. The hills, overgrown by lush greenery, reminded Sir Heinrich of his native Thuringia, his mother, and the fact that he hadn't had a woman for over a month. The crossbowmen riding at the rear were languidly singing a ballad by Walther von der Vogelweide. Hasso Planck was dozing in the saddle.

Wer guter Fraue Liebe hat
Der schämt sich aller Missetat . . .

The journey was proceeding peacefully and who knows, perhaps it would have been peaceful all the way, had Sir Heinrich not noticed the glistening surface of a lake down below around noon. And because the following day was Friday and it behove them to get in holy-day food in advance, the knight ordered his men to ride down to the water and look around for a fisherman's homestead.

The lake was large, and there was even an island on it. No one knew its name, but it was probably called Holy Lake. In this pagan land – as if in mockery – every second lake was called 'holy'.

Their horseshoes crunched on the shells lying on the shore. Fog hung over the lake, but it was obvious it was uninhabited. There was no sign of a boat, nor a net, nor any living soul. *We'll have to search elsewhere,* thought Heinrich von Schwelborn. *And if not, too bad. We'll eat what we have in our saddlebags, even if that means smoked bacon, and in Malbork we'll make our confession, the chaplain will demand a penance and the sin will be absolved.*

He was about to issue an order when something buzzed in his head under his helmet, and Hasso Planck yelled horrifyingly. Von Schwelborn looked and was struck dumb. And crossed himself.

He saw two horses: one white and the other black. A moment later, though, he noticed in horror that the white horse had a spirally twisted horn on its domed forehead. He also saw that a girl was sitting on the black, her ashen hair combed so as to obscure her cheek. The group apparition seemed not to be touching either the ground or the water – it looked as though it were suspended above the fog trailing over the surface of the lake.

The black horse neighed.

'Whoops . . .' said the girl with the grey hair quite distinctly, 'Ire lokke, ire tedd! Squaess'me.'

'Saint Ursula, O my patron . . .' mumbled Hasso, white as a sheet. The crossbowmen froze open-mouthed, and made the sign of the cross.

Von Schwelborn also crossed himself, after which with a trembling hand he drew a sword from a scabbard strapped under his saddle flap.

'Heilige Maria, Mutter Gottes!' he roared. 'Steh mir bei!'

That day Sir Heinrich didn't shame his valiant ancestors, the von Schwelborns, including Dietrich von Schwelborn, who had fought bravely at Damietta and was one of the few not to run away when the Saracens conjured up and set a demon on the crusaders. After spurring his horse and having recalled his fearless forebear, Heinrich von Schwelborn charged the apparition among the freshwater mussels splashing up from under his horse's hooves.

'For the Order and Saint George!'

The white unicorn reared up like a heraldic emblem, the black mare danced, and the girl was alarmed, it was clear at first glance. Heinrich von Schwelborn rode on. Who knows how it all would have ended if the fog hadn't suddenly been blown towards him

246

and the image of the strange group dissolved, disintegrating into a myriad of colours like a stained-glass window smashed by a stone. And everything vanished. Everything. The unicorn, the black horse and the strange girl . . .

Heinrich von Schwelborn's steed rode into the lake with a splash, stopped, tossed its head, neighed, and ground its teeth on the bit.

Hasso Planck, struggling to control his unruly horse, rode over to the knight. Von Schwelborn was huffing and puffing, almost wheezing, goggled-eyed like a fast-day fish.

'On the bones of Saint Ursula, Saint Cordula and all the eleven thousand virgin martyrs of Cologne . . .' Hasso Planck stammered out. 'What was it, noble Herr Ritter? A miracle? A revelation?'

'Teufelswerk!' von Schwelborn grunted, only now blanching horrifyingly and chattering his teeth. 'Schwarze Magie! Zauberey! A damned, pagan, devilish matter . . .'

'We ought to get out of here, sire. As quickly as possible . . . It's not far from Pelplin, anything to get within the sound of church bells . . .'

Sir Heinrich looked back for the last time on a rise just outside the forest. The wind had blown away the fog and the shining surface of the lake had grown dull and rippled in the places not obscured by the wall of trees.

A great osprey circled above the water.

'Godless, pagan land,' muttered Heinrich von Schwelborn. 'Much, much work, much hardship and labour await us before the Order of the Teutonic Knights will finally drive the Devil from this nest of Slavs.'

*

'Little Horse,' said Ciri, reproachfully and sneeringly at once. 'I don't want to be intrusive, but I'm in a bit of a hurry to get back to my world. My friends and family need me, you know that, don't you? And first we end up by some lake with a ridiculous boor in chequered clothes, then run into a pack of filthy, yelling shaggy heads with clubs, and finally on a madman with a black cross on his cloak. They're the wrong times, the wrong places! Please, do try a bit harder. I beg you.'

247

Ihuarraquax neighed, nodded his horned head and communicated something to her, a clever thought. Ciri didn't quite understand. She didn't have time to ponder, since the inside of her skull was filled with cool brightness, her ears buzzed and her nape tingled.

And black and very soft nothingness engulfed her again.

*

Nimue, laughing joyously, dragged the man by the hand. The two of them ran down to the lake, winding their way among the young birches and alders, among stumps and blown down trees. After running onto the sandy beach, Nimue threw off her sandals, lifted up her dress and splashed around in bare feet in the water by the shore. The man also took off his boots, but was in no hurry to enter the water. He removed his cloak and spread it out on the sand.

Nimue ran over, threw her arms around his neck and stood on tiptoes to kiss it. The man had to lean over a long way in any case. Not without reason was Nimue called Squirt – but now that she was eighteen and was a novice of the magical arts, the privilege of using that epithet was exclusively reserved for her closest friends. And some men.

The man, his mouth clamped on Nimue's, put his hand down the front of her dress.

It moved fast after that. The two of them ended up on the cloak spread out on the sand, Nimue's dress up above her waist, her thighs powerfully gripping the man's hips, and her hands digging into his back. When he took her – too impatiently as usual – she clenched her teeth, but quickly caught up with him in excitement, drew level, and kept up with him. She was skilled.

The man was uttering amusing sounds. Nimue observed fantastic shapes of the cumuli slowly gliding across the sky over his shoulder.

Something rang, as a bell submerged at the bottom of the ocean rings. There was a sudden buzzing in Nimue's ears. *Magic*, she thought, turning her head, freeing herself from under the cheek and shoulder of the man lying on her.

A white unicorn stood by the lake shore – literally suspended above the surface. Beside it was a black horse. And in the saddle of the black horse was sitting . . .

But I know that legend, the thought flashed through Nimue's head. *I know that fairy tale! I was a child, a little child, when I heard that tale.* The wandering storyteller, the beggar Pogwizd, had told it to her. *The witcher Ciri . . . with a scar on her cheek . . . The black mare Kelpie . . . Unicorns . . . The land of the elves . . .*

The movements of the man, who hadn't noticed the phenomenon at all, became more and more urgent, and the sounds he was uttering more and more amusing.

'Whooops,' said the girl on the black mare. 'Another mistake! It's not this place, not this time. And what's more, I see, it's a bad time. I'm sorry.'

The image blurred and shattered, as painted glass shatters, suddenly fell to pieces, disintegrated into a rainbow-coloured twinkling of sparkles, gleaming and gold. And then all of it vanished.

'No!' screamed Nimue. 'No! Don't disappear! I don't want you to go!'

She straightened her knees and tried to free herself from under the man, but she could not – he was stronger and heavier than her. The man groaned and moaned.

'Oooooh, Nimue . . . Ooooh!'

Nimue screamed and dug her teeth into his shoulder.

They lay on his sheepskin coat, quivering and hot. Nimue looked at the lake shore, at the caps of foam whipped up by the waves. At the reeds bent over by the wind. At the colourless, hopeless void, the void left by the disappearing legend.

A tear trickled down the novice's nose.

'Nimue . . . Is something the matter?'

'Yes.' She cuddled up to him, but carried on looking at the lake. 'Don't say anything. Hold me and don't say anything.'

The man smiled proudly.

'I know what happened,' he said boastfully. 'Did the earth move?'

Nimue smiled sadly.

'Not just the earth,' she replied after a moment's silence. 'Not just the earth.'

A flash. Darkness. The next place.

The next place was tenebrous, baleful and foul.

Ciri involuntarily hunched over in the saddle, shaken – both in the literal and the metaphorical sense of the term. For Kelpie's horseshoes had thudded against something as painfully hard, flat and unyielding as rock. After a long time of gliding in very soft limbo, the impression of hardness was so astonishing and unpleasant that the mare neighed and suddenly lunged aside, beating out a staccato rhythm on the ground that made Ciri's teeth chatter.

The second shock, the metaphorical one, was supplied by the smell. Ciri groaned and covered her mouth and nose with her sleeve. She felt her eyes immediately filling with tears.

All around rose a sour, acrid, thick and glutinous stench, a smell of burning both choking and dreadful, impossible to define, resembling nothing Ciri had ever smelled. It was – she was certain of it – the stench of decay, a corpselike reek of final degradation and degeneration, the odour of disintegration and destruction; in addition, there was the impression that whatever was decaying hadn't smelled any more pleasantly when it was alive. Not even when it had been in its salad days.

She bent over in a nauseous reflex she was unable to control. Kelpie snorted and shook her head, contracting her nostrils. The unicorn, which had materialised beside them, leaned back on his haunches, jumped up and kicked. The hard ground answered with a shock and a loud echo.

All around was the night, the dark and filthy night, muffled by the sticky and reeking tatters of darkness.

Ciri glanced upwards, searching for the stars, but there was nothing above her, only an abyss, lit up in places by an indistinct, red glow, like a distant fire.

'Whooops,' she said and grimaced, feeling the sour and rotten mist settling on her lips. 'Yuuuckk! Not this place, not this time! Under no circumstances!'

The unicorn snorted and nodded his head, his horn describing a short and dynamic arc.

The ground grinding beneath Kelpie's hooves was rock, but strange, unnaturally smooth, emitting an intensive stench of burning and dirty ash. It took some time for Ciri to realise that what she was looking at was a road. She had had enough of that unpleasant and annoying hardness. She guided the mare to the side of the road, marked by something that had once been trees, but were now hideous and naked skeletons. Corpses hung with shreds of rags, quite like the remains of rotten shrouds.

The unicorn gave a warning by neighing and sending a mental signal. Too late.

Just beyond the strange road and the dead trees a heap of scree began, and further away, at its edge, a steep slope running downwards, almost a precipice. Ciri yelled, stuck her heels into the sides of the mare as she slipped down. Kelpie jerked, crushing whatever the heap was made of under her hooves. And it was waste. Mostly some kind of strange pots. The vessels didn't crumble under the horseshoes, didn't crunch, but burst repulsively softly and stickily, like great fishes' bladders. Something squelched and gurgled, and the odour belching forth almost knocked Ciri from the saddle.

Kelpie, neighing wildly, trampled through the rubbish dump, struggling back upwards towards the road. Ciri, choking from the stench, grabbed the mare's neck.

They managed to get up. And greeted the weird road's disagreeable hardness with joy and relief.

Ciri, trembling all over, looked down onto the rubbish dump which ended in a black lake filling the bottom of the basin. The surface of the lake was lifeless and gleaming, as it wasn't water but solidified pitch. Beyond the lake, beyond the rubbish dumps, the piles of ash and heaps of cinders, the sky was red from distant glows, and was marked by trails of smoke.

The unicorn snorted. Ciri was about to wipe her watering eyes with her cuff, when she suddenly noticed her entire sleeve was covered in dust. The flecks of dust also covered her thighs, the pommel of her saddle and Kelpie's mane and neck.

The stench was stifling.

'Disgusting,' she muttered. 'Repulsive . . . I feel like I'm sticky all over. Let's get out of here . . . Let's get out of here with all haste, Little Horse.'

The unicorn pricked up his ears and snorted.

Only you can make it happen. Act.

'Me? All alone? Without your help?'

The unicorn nodded his horned head.

Ciri scratched her head, sighed and shut her eyes. She focused.

At first there was only disbelief, resignation and fear. But a cool brightness – the brightness of knowledge and power – quickly came over her. She had no idea where the knowledge and power were coming from, where their roots and source originated. But she knew she could do it. That she *would* do it if she wanted.

Once more she cast a glance at the hardened and lifeless lake, the smoking heap of refuse and the skeletons of trees. The sky was lit up by a distant glow.

'I'm glad it's not my world.' She leaned over and spat. 'Very glad!'

The unicorn neighed meaningfully. She understood what he wanted to say.

'Even if it's mine,' she wiped her eyes, mouth and nose with a handkerchief, 'it's at once not mine, because it's far away in time. It's the past, or—'

She broke off.

'The past,' she repeated softly. 'I deeply believe it's the past.'

*

They greeted the heavy rain, the proper downpour they fell under in the next place, as a blessing. The rain was warm and aromatic, smelling of summer, weeds, mud and compost. The rain washed the filth from them, purged them. The rain was quite simply a catharsis.

Like any catharsis, it also became monotonous, excessive and unbearable after a short while. After some time, the water she was washing herself in began to wet her annoyingly, run down her neck and chill her unpleasantly. So they got out of that rainy place.

For it wasn't that place either. Or that time.

252

*

The next place was very warm, the weather very hot, so Ciri, Kelpie and the unicorn dried off and steamed like three kettles. They found themselves on some sweltering moors at the edge of a forest. At once it could be deduced it was a very large forest, quite simply a dense, wild and inaccessible wilderness. Hope that it might be Brokilon Forest thumped in Ciri's heart, the hope that at last it might be a familiar and appropriate place.

They rode slowly along the edge of the forest. Ciri was looking out for something that might serve as a sign. The unicorn snorted, raised his head and horn, and looked around. It was anxious.

'Do you think, Little Horse,' she asked, 'that they might be following us?'

A snort – comprehensible and unambiguous even without telepathy.

'We haven't managed to flee far enough away yet?'

She didn't understand what he telepathically told her in answer. There was no far or near? A spiral? What spiral?

She didn't understand what he was talking about. But the anxiety infected her.

The scorching moors weren't the right place or the right time.

They understood it in the early evening, when the heat eased off, and instead of one, two moons rose in the sky above the forest. One large, the other small.

*

The next place was a seashore, a steep cliff, from which they saw breakers crashing against strangely-shaped rocks. They smelled the sea wind, and terns, black-headed gulls and petrels screeched, covering the ledges of the cliff in a restless white layer.

The sea reached all the way to the dark, cloudy horizon.

Down below, on the rocky beach, Ciri suddenly noticed the skeleton of a gigantic fish with a horrendously huge head partly buried in the shingles. Its great teeth, bristling in its sun-bleached jawbones, were at least three spans long, and it seemed one could have ridden a horse into its maw and easily paraded under

253

the portals of its ribs without knocking one's head against its spine.

Ciri wasn't certain if fish like that existed in her world and her time.

They rode along the edge of the cliff, and the seagulls and albatrosses weren't frightened at all, reluctantly moving out of their way. Why, they even tried hard to peck and pinch the feathers on Kelpie and Ihuarraquax's fetlocks! Ciri instantly understood that the birds had never seen a human or a horse. Or a unicorn.

Ihuarraquax snorted, shook his head and horn, clearly anxious. It turned out he had reason to be.

Something creaked, just like canvas being torn. The terns rose with a cry and a fluttering, for a moment covering everything in a white cloud. The air above the cliff suddenly vibrated and became blurred like glass with water spilled over it. And then it shattered like glass. And darkness poured out of the rupture, while riders spilled out of the darkness. Around their shoulders fluttered cloaks whose vermilion-amaranth-crimson colour brought to mind the glow of a fire in a sky lit up by the blaze of the setting sun.

Dearg Ruadhri. The Red Horsemen.

Even before the crying of birds and the neighing of the unicorn had died away, Ciri had reined her mare around and spurred her into a gallop. But the air also ruptured in another place, and from the rupture, cloaks fluttering like wings, rushed out more horsemen. The semicircle of the noose closed, pressing them against the cliff. Ciri cried out, jerking Swallow out of its scabbard.

The unicorn summoned her with a sharp signal that penetrated her brain like a needle. She understood at once this time. He was showing her the way. A gap in the circle. He meanwhile reared up, neighed piercingly and charged at the elves with his horn lowered menacingly.

'Little Horse!'

Save yourself, Star-Eye! Don't let them catch you!

She pressed herself against Kelpie's mane.

Two elves barred her way. They had lassos, nooses on long shafts. They tried to throw them over Kelpie's neck. The mare nimbly twisted her head out of reach of one, but didn't slow her gallop for a second. Ciri severed the other noose with a single flourish of her sword, and urged Kelpie with a cry to run quicker. The mare flew like a hurricane.

But others were now hard on their heels. She could hear their cries, the thud of their hooves, the flapping of their cloaks. *What about Little Horse*, she thought, *what have they done to him?*

There was no time for reflection. The unicorn was right; she couldn't let them capture her again. She had to dive into space, hide, and lose herself in the labyrinth of places and times. She focused, sensing with horror that all she had in her head was a void and a strange, ringing, quickly growing hubbub.

They're casting a spell on me, she thought. *They want to beguile me with witchcraft. Over my dead body! Spells have a range. I won't let them get close to me.*

'Run, Kelpie!'

The black mare stuck out her neck and flew like the wind. Ciri flattened herself on her neck to minimise air resistance.

The cries from behind her back, a moment earlier still loud and dangerously close, faded, drowned out by the screaming of frightened birds. Then they became harder and harder to make out. Remote.

Kelpie flew like a hurricane. So fast the sea wind howled in her ears.

A note of fury sounded in the distant shouts of the pursuers. They understood they couldn't keep up. That they had no chance of catching up with the black mare, who was running without any sign of fatigue, as light, soft and supple as a cheetah.

Ciri didn't look back. But she knew they continued to pursue her for a long time, even though it was futile. Until the moment their own horses began to wheeze and rasp, stumble and lower their foaming muzzles almost to the ground, teeth bared. Only then did they quit, sending after her nothing but curses and impotent threats she could no longer hear.

Kelpie flew like a gale.

*

The place she fled to was dry and windy. The keen, howling wind quickly dried the tears on her cheeks.

She was alone. Alone again. All alone.

A wanderer, a permanent vagabond, a sailor lost on the boundless sea among the archipelago of places and times.

A sailor losing hope.

The gale whistled and howled, rolling balls of dried weeds over the cracked earth.

The gale dried her tears.

*

Inside her skull cool lucidity, in her ears a buzzing, a monotonous buzzing, like from the twisted interior of a sea conch. A tingling in her nape. Black and very soft nothingness.

A new place. Another place.

An archipelago of places.

*

'This night,' said Nimue, wrapping herself up in a fur, 'will be a good night. I sense it.'

Condwiramurs didn't comment, although she had already heard similar assurances a good few times. For it wasn't the first evening they had sat on the terrace, the lake blazing with the sunset in front of them, and behind them the magical looking glass and magical tapestry.

The curses of the Fisher King reached them from the lake, multiplied by the echo rolling across the water. The Fisher King was often in the habit of using vivid language to emphasise dissatisfaction with his angling failures – the unsuccessful strikes, plays, landings and other techniques he used. It had gone particularly badly that evening, judging from the strength and repertoire of the oaths.

'Time,' said Nimue, 'has neither a beginning nor an end. Time is like the serpent Ouroboros, which bites its own tail with its teeth. Eternity is hidden in every moment. And eternity consists of the moments that create it. Eternity is an archipelago of moments. You may sail through that archipelago, although navigation is very difficult, and it is dangerous to get lost. It's good to have a lighthouse whose light can guide you. It's good to be able to hear someone calling among the fog . . .'

She fell silent for a while.

'How does the legend that interests us end? It seems to us – to you and me – that we know how it ends. But Ouroboros is still grasping its own tail in its teeth. Yes, how the legend ends is being settled now. At this moment. The ending of the legend will depend on whether and when the sailor lost among the archipelago of moments sees the lamp of the lighthouse. If she hears the calling.'

A curse, a splash and the banging of oars in the rowlocks could be heard from the lake.

'It will be a good night tonight. The last before the summer solstice. The moon is getting smaller. The sun is passing from the Third to the Fourth House, to the sign of the Goat-Fish. The best time for divination . . . The best time . . . Focus, Condwiramurs.'

Condwiramurs, as so many times before, obediently focused, slowly entering a state close to a trance.

'Search for her,' said Nimue. 'She is somewhere among the stars, among the moonlight. Among the places. She is there. She is awaiting help. Let's help her, Condwiramurs.'

*

Concentration, fists at her temples. A buzzing in her ears, as though from the inside of a conch. A flash. And abruptly soft and black nothingness.

*

There was a place where Ciri saw burning pyres. The women bound by chains to stakes howled wildly and horrifyingly for mercy, and the crowd gathered around roared, laughed and danced. There was a place where a great city was burning, roaring with fire and bursting with flames from collapsing roofs, and black smoke hooded the whole sky. There was a place where enormous two-legged lizards fought one another, and garish blood gushed from beneath fangs and claws.

257

There was a place where hundreds of identical white windmills threshed the sky with their slender sails. There was a place where hundreds of snakes hissed and squirmed on stones, scraping and rustling their scales.

There was a place where there was darkness, and in the darkness voices, whispers and terror.

There were even more places. But none of them was the right one.

*

She was finding moving from place to place so easy that she began to experiment. One of the few places she wasn't afraid of was those warm moors at the edge of the wild forest above which two moons rose. Calling forth in her memory the sight of those moons and repeating in her mind what she wanted, Ciri focused, strained and plunged into the nothingness.

She succeeded at the second attempt.

Now encouraged, she decided to attempt an even more daring experiment. It was obvious that aside from places, she also visited times. Vysogota had talked about that, as had the elves, and the unicorns had mentioned it. Why, she had managed – albeit unwittingly – to do it before! When she had been wounded in the face she had escaped from her persecutors into time, jumped forward four days, and then Vysogota couldn't account for those days. Nothing added up for him . . .

Perhaps that was her chance? A leap into time?

She decided to try. The burning city, for example, couldn't be burning permanently, could it? And if she were to get there before the fire? Or after it?

She landed almost in the centre of the fire, scorching her eyebrows and eyelashes and arousing horrendous panic amongst the victims of the fire fleeing from the blazing city.

She escaped to the friendly moors. *It probably wasn't worth taking a risk like that*, she thought, *the devil only knows how it might end. I do better with places, so I'll stick to places. Let's try to get to places. Familiar places, ones I remember well. And ones I have pleasant associations with.*

She began with the Temple of Melitele, imagining the gate, the building, the grounds and the workshop, the novices' dormitory, and the rooms where Yennefer lived. She concentrated with her fists against her temples, evoking in her memory the faces of Nenneke, Eurneid, Katje and Iola the Second.

Nothing came of it. She found herself in some swamps shrouded in mist and swarming with mosquitoes, resounding with the whistling of turtles and the deafening croaking of frogs.

She tried in turn – with no better result – Kaer Morhen, the Isles of Skellige, and the bank in Gors Velen where Fabio Sachs worked. She didn't dare to try Cintra, knowing that the city was occupied by Nilfgaardians. Instead of that she tried Vizima, the city where she and Yennefer used to go shopping.

*

Aarhenius Krantz, sage, alchemist, astronomer and astrologer, fidgeted on a hard stool with his eye stuck to the eyepiece of a telescope. The comet of great size and power, which it had been possible to observe in the sky for almost a week, merited observation and research. A comet like that, as Aarhenius Krantz knew, with a fiery red tail, usually heralded great wars, conflagrations and massacres. Now, to tell the truth, the comet had been a bit late with its prophecy, because the war with Nilfgaard was well underway, and one could already have prophesied conflagrations and massacres correctly, without hesitation, for not a day went by without them. Aarhenius Krantz, who was familiar with the movements of heavenly bodies, was however hoping to calculate when, in how many years or centuries, the comet would appear again, announcing another war, which, who knows, it would perhaps be possible to prepare for better than the present one.

The astronomer stood up, massaged his backside and went to relieve his bladder. From the terrace, through the small balustrade. He always pissed straight from the terrace onto a bed of peonies, not caring at all about the housekeeper's reprimands. It was quite simply too far to the privy. Wasting time walking a long way to relieve himself bore the risk of the loss of valuable reflections, which no scholar could afford to do.

He stood by the balustrade and undid his trews, looking at the lights of Vizima reflected in the lake. He sighed with relief and raised his eyes heavenwards.

Stars, he thought, *and constellations. The Winter Maiden, the Seven Goats, the Pitcher. According to some theories, they aren't just little twinkling lights, but worlds. Other worlds. Worlds from which time and space separate us . . . I believe deeply*, he thought, *that one day journeys to those other places, to those other times and universes, will be possible. Yes, it will certainly be possible one day. A way will be found. But it will demand utterly new thinking, a new, original idea that will tear apart the rigid corset called rational cognition that restricts it today . . .*

Ah, he thought, hopping, *if only it could be achieved . . . If only one could experience inspiration. If there could be one, unique opportunity . . .*

Something flashed below the terrace, the darkness of the night ruptured like a starburst, and a horse emerged from the flare. With a rider on its back. The rider was a girl.

'Good evening,' she greeted him politely. 'I'm sorry if it's a bad time. May one know what place this is? And what time?'

Aarhenius Krantz swallowed, opened his mouth and mumbled.

'The place,' the girl repeated patiently and clearly. 'The time.'

'Errrm . . . Iiii . . . Ummm . . .'

The horse snorted. The girl sighed.

'Well, it must be the wrong place again. The wrong place, the wrong time. But answer me, fellow! With at least one comprehensible word. For I can't be in a world where people have forgotten articulate speech!'

'Errr . . .'

'One little word . . .'

'Ummm . . .'

'Then bugger you, you stupid old goat,' said the girl.

And vanished. Along with the horse.

Aarhenius Krantz closed his mouth. He stood for a while by the balustrade, staring into the night, at the lake and the distant lights of Vizima reflected in it. Then he buttoned up his trousers and returned to his telescope.

The comet swiftly flashed across the sky. One ought to observe it, not let the eyepiece and eye lose sight of it. Track it until it disappeared into the chasms of the universe. It was an opportunity, and a scholar cannot waste such an opportunity.

*

Perhaps I could try from another direction, she thought, staring at the two moons above the moor, now visible as two crescents, one small, the other large and less crescent. *Perhaps not imagine places or faces*, she thought, *but strongly desire . . . Strongly wish for something, very strongly, right from my belly . . .*

What harm is there in trying?

Geralt. I want to go to Geralt. I very much want to go to Geralt.

*

'Oh, no,' she cried. 'Where have I bloody ended up now?'

Kelpie confirmed that she thought the same by whinnying, belching steam from her nostrils and scraping her snowbound hooves.

The blizzard whistled and moaned, blinding them. Sharp snowflakes stung her cheeks and hands. The cold chilled her to the marrow, nipped her joints like a wolf. Ciri trembled, hunching her shoulders and hiding her neck in the meagre, non-existent protection of her turned-up collar.

To the left and right rose majestic, menacing peaks, grey, glazed monuments whose summits vanished somewhere high up in the fog and blizzard. A swift, very swollen river, dense with frazil and lumps of ice, sped along the bottom of the valley. It was white all around. And cold.

So much for my abilities, thought Ciri, feeling the inside of her nose freezing. *So much for my power. A fine Master of the Worlds, well, well. I wanted to go to Geralt, and I ended up in the middle of some bloody wilderness, winter and blizzard.*

'Come on, Kelpie, move, or you'll go numb!' She grabbed the reins with fingers paralysed by the frost. 'Gee up, gee up, girl! I know it's not the place it's meant to be, I'll soon get us out of here, we'll soon return to our warm moor. But I have to concentrate, and that may take some time. So move yourself! Come on, ride!'

Kelpie belched steam from her nostrils.

The strong wind blew. Snow stuck to her face, melting on her eyelashes. The freezing snowstorm howled and whistled.

*

'Look!' called Angoulême, outshouting the blizzard. 'Look there! There are tracks. Someone rode that way!'

'What are you saying?' Geralt unwrapped the shawl he had wrapped around his head to protect his ears from frostbite. 'What are you saying, Angoulême?'

'Tracks! Hoof prints!'

'A horse, here?' Cahir also had to shout. The blizzard intensified, and the River Sansretour, it seemed, whooshed and roared even louder. 'How could a horse get here?'

'Look for yourselves!'

'Indeed,' commented the vampire, the only member of the company who wasn't displaying symptoms of being utterly frozen, since he was for obvious reasons just as insensitive to low as to high temperatures. 'Hoof prints. But are they a horse's?'

'It's impossible for it to be a horse.' Cahir massaged his cheeks and nose hard. 'Not in the middle of nowhere. The tracks must have been left by some wild animal. Most probably a moufflon.'

'Moufflon yourself!' yelled Angoulême. 'When I say a horse, I mean a horse!'

Milva, as usual, preferred practice to theory. She dismounted and bent over, pushing her fox-fur kalpak back on her head.

'The pup's right,' she decided after moment. 'It's a horse. I think it's even shod, but it's hard to say, the blizzard has covered the tracks. It rode over there, into that ravine.'

'Ha!' Angoulême banged her arms together briskly. 'I knew it! Somebody lives here! In the vicinity! Let's follow the trail, perhaps we'll find some warm cottage or other? Perhaps they'll let us get warm? Perhaps they'll treat us to something?'

'For certain,' said Cahir with a sneer. 'Most probably a crossbow bolt.'

'It would be most sensible to keep to our plan and the river,'

Regis decided in his most omniscient tone. 'Then we won't be at risk of getting lost. And further down the Sansretour there was meant to be a trapper's manufactory, there's a greater likelihood they'll put us up there.'

'Geralt? What do you say?'

The Witcher said nothing, and fixed his eyes on the snowflakes swirling in the blizzard.

'We'll follow the tracks,' he finally decided.

'Actually—' began the vampire, but Geralt immediately interrupted him.

'Follow the hoof prints! Ride!'

They spurred their steeds, but didn't get very far. They ventured not more than a quarter of a furlong into a gorge.

'That's it.' Angoulême stated a fact, looking at the quite smooth and virginal snow. 'Now you see it, now you don't. Like an elven circus.'

'What now, Witcher?' Cahir turned around in the saddle. 'The tracks have ceased. They've been covered up by the blizzard.'

'No they haven't,' Milva said. 'The blizzard doesn't reach here, in the canyon.'

'What happened to the horse then?'

The archer shrugged, huddled up in the saddle, pulling her head into her shoulders.

'Where's that horse?' Cahir wasn't giving up. 'Did it vanish? Evaporate? Or perhaps we imagined it? Geralt? What do you say?'

The gale howled above the ravine, whipping up and swirling the snow.

'Why,' asked the vampire, scrutinising the Witcher intently, 'did you order us to follow those tracks, Geralt?'

'I don't know,' he confessed a moment later. 'I . . . I felt something. Something touched me. Never mind what. You were right, Regis. Let's go back to the Sansretour and keep by the river, without any excursions or diversions that might end badly. According to what Reynart said, the real winter and bad weather only begin in the Malheur pass. When we get there we'll have to be sound in body. Don't just stand there, we're turning around.'

'Without having cleared up what happened to that strange horse?'

'What's there to explain?' the Witcher said bitterly. 'The tracks were swept away, and that's that. Anyway, maybe it really was a moufflon?'

Milva looked at him strangely, but refrained from comment.

When they returned to the river the mysterious tracks were no longer there either, for they had been covered up by wet snow. Frazil was floating densely, pieces of pack ice were swirling and turning around in the tin-grey current of the Sansretour.

'I'll tell you something,' Angoulême piped up. 'But promise you won't laugh.'

They turned around. In her woollen pompom hat pulled down over her eyes, with cheeks and nose red from the cold, wearing a shapeless sheepskin coat, the girl looked funny, a dead ringer for a small, plump kobold.

'I'll tell you something about those tracks. When I was with Nightingale, in the hanza, they said that during the winter the Mountain King, leader of the ice demons, rides on an enchanted horse in the passes. To meet him face to face is certain death. What do you say to that, Geralt? Is it possible that—'

'Anything,' he interrupted her. 'Anything's possible. On we go, company. Before us is the Malheur pass.'

The snow lashed and whipped, the wind blew, and ice demons whistled and wailed amidst the blizzard.

*

Except the moor she'd landed on wasn't the one she knew, Ciri realised at once. She didn't even have to wait until evening, she was sure she wouldn't see the two moons.

The forest along whose edge she rode was as wild and inaccessible as the other one, but differences could be seen. Here, for example, there were more birches and fewer beeches. She hadn't heard or seen any birds there, while there were great numbers of them here. There had only been sand and moss between the clumps of heather; here whole carpets of green clubmoss sprawled. Even the grasshoppers running from under Kelpie's hooves were somehow different here. Somehow familiar. And then . . .

Her heart began beating harder. She saw a track, overgrown and neglected. Leading into the forest.

Ciri looked around carefully and made sure the strange track didn't go on any further, that it ended here. That it didn't lead to the forest, but from it or through it. Without deliberating for long, she prodded the mare's sides with her heels and rode between the trees. *I'll ride south*, she thought. *If I don't come across anything to the south, I'll turn around and ride in the opposite direction, beyond the moor.*

She trotted beneath a canopy of boughs, looking around attentively, trying hard not to overlook anything important. Because of that she didn't overlook an old man peeping out from behind an oak tree.

The old man, who was very short, but not at all stooped, was dressed in a linen shirt and trews made from the same material. On his feet he had huge and very funny-looking bast slippers. In one hand he held a gnarled stick and in the other a wicker basket. Ciri couldn't see his face precisely, for it was hidden by the frayed and drooping brim of a straw hat, from under which protruded a sunburnt nose and a tangled grey beard.

'Fear not,' she said. 'I won't do you any harm.'

The grey-bearded man shifted his weight from one foot to the other and removed his hat. He had a round face flecked with liver spots, ruddy and not very wrinkled, thin eyebrows, and a small and very receding chin. His long grey hair was tied up on his nape in a queue, but the top of his head meanwhile was completely bald, as yellow and shiny as a pumpkin.

She saw him looking at her sword, at the hilt extending above her shoulder.

'Don't be afraid,' she repeated.

'Ho, ho!' he said, mumbling a little. 'Ho, ho, my young maiden. Forest Gramps isn't afraid. He ain't one of those fearful types, oh no.'

He smiled. He had large, very protruding teeth, because of a bad occlusion and receding jaw. It was because of that that he mumbled so much.

'Forest Gramps ain't afraid of wanderers,' he repeated. 'Or even brigands. Forest Gramps is poor, he's a poor thing. Forest Gramps is peaceful, he doesn't disturb no one. Hey!'

He smiled again. When he smiled he seemed to be all front teeth.

'And you, young lass, aren't you afraid of Forest Gramps?'

Ciri snorted.

'I'm not, just imagine. I'm not the fearful kind either.'

'Hey, hey, hey! Well I never!'

He took a pace towards her, resting on his stick. Kelpie snorted. Ciri tugged on the reins.

'She doesn't like strangers,' she warned. 'And she bites.'

'Hey, hey! Forest Gramps knows. Bad, unruly mare! Where are you riding from, miss? And where are you heading, may I ask?'

'It's a long story. Where does this road lead?'

'Don't you know that, miss?'

'Don't answer questions with questions, if you don't mind. Where will that road take me? What place is this, in any case? And what . . . time is it?'

The old man stuck his teeth out again, moving them like a coypu.

'Hey, hey!' he mumbled. 'Well I never. What time, you ask, miss? Oh, I see you've travelled from far away, from far away to Forest Gramps, miss!'

'From quite far away, indeed,' she nodded indifferently. 'From other—'

'Places and times,' he completed her sentence. 'Gramps knows. Gramps guessed.'

'What?' she asked, excited. 'What did you guess? What do you know?'

'Forest Gramps knows much.'

'Speak!'

'Miss must be hungry?' he stuck out his teeth. 'Thirsty? Fatigued? If you want, miss, Forest Gramps will take you to his cottage, feed you, give you drink. Take you in.'

For a long time Ciri hadn't had the time or the peace of mind to think about rest or food. Now the words of the strange old man tightened up her stomach, knotted up her guts, and tied up her tongue. The old man observed her from under the brim of his hat.

'Forest Gramps,' he mumbled, 'has meat in his cottage. Has spring water. And has hay for the mare, the bad mare that wanted

266

to bite good old Gramps! Hey! Everything is in Forest Gramps'
cottage. And we'll be able to talk about other places and times
. . . It's not far at all, oh no. Will the young traveller avail herself?
Won't disdain a visit to poor old Gramps?'

Ciri swallowed.

'Lead on.'

Forest Gramps turned around and shambled down a barely
visible path among the thicket, measuring off the road with energetic swings of his stick. Ciri rode behind him, dipping her head
under branches and reining Kelpie back. The mare was indeed
determined to bite the old man, or at least eat his hat.

In spite of his assurances it wasn't near at all. When they got
there, to a clearing, the sun was almost at its zenith.

Gramps' cottage turned out to be a picturesque shack on stilts,
with a roof that had clearly often been patched up using whatever
happened to be to hand. The shack's walls were covered with hides
resembling pigskin. In front of the cottage there was a wooden construction shaped like a gallows, a low table and a chopping stump
with an axe stuck in it. Behind the cottage was a hearth made of
stones and clay with a large, blackened cauldron on it.

'This is Forest Gramps' home,' the old man indicated with his
stick, not without pride. 'Forest Gramps lives here. He sleeps here.
He cooks vittles here. Should he have something to cook. It's a
hardship, a severe hardship to get vittles in the forest. Does miss
wanderer like pearl barley?'

'She does,' Ciri swallowed again. 'She likes everything.'

'With a bit of meat? With some grease? With scratchings?'

'Mhm.'

'And it don't look,' Gramps shot her an appraising glance, 'that
miss has lately tasted meat and scratchings often, oh no. You're
skinny, miss, skinny. Skin and bones! Hey, hey! And what's that?
Behind your back, miss?'

Ciri looked around, taken in by the oldest and most primitive
trick in the book. A terrible blow of the gnarled stick caught her
right in the temple. Her reflexes helped only in that she raised her
arm, and her hand partly cushioned a blow capable of smashing
her skull like an egg. But in any case, Ciri ended up on the ground,
stunned, bewildered and completely disorientated.

Gramps, grinning, leaped at her and struck her again with the stick. Ciri once again managed to shield her head with her hands, with the result that both flopped down inertly. The left one was definitely injured, the metacarpals probably shattered.

Gramps, leaping forward, attacked from the other side and whacked her in the stomach with his stick. She screamed, curling up into a ball. Then he stooped on her like a hawk, turned her over face downwards and pinned her down with his knees. Ciri tensed up, kicked back hard, missing, then delivered a vicious blow with her elbow, this time hitting the target. Gramps roared furiously and smashed her in the back of the head with his fist, so powerfully she lurched face-first into the sand. He seized her by the hair on her nape and pressed her mouth and nose against the ground. She felt herself suffocating. The old man kneeled on her, still pressing her head against the ground, tore the sword from her back and cast it aside. Then he began to fiddle with his trousers. He found the buckle and unfastened it. Ciri howled, choking and spitting sand. He pushed her down harder, immobilising her, entangling her hair in his fist. He tore her trousers off her with a powerful tug.

'Hey, hey,' he mumbled, wheezing. 'And hasn't Gramps got a nice bit of stuff. Ooh, ooh, Gramps hasn't had one like this for a long, long time.'

Ciri, feeling the repulsive touch of his dry, claw-like hand, yelled with her mouth full of sand and pine needles.

'Lie still, miss,' she heard him slavering, kneading her buttocks. 'Gramps isn't as young as he was, not right away, slowly . . . But never fear, Gramps will do what's to be done. Hey, hey! And then Gramps will eat his fill, hey, his fill! Lavishly—'

He broke off, roared, and squealed.

Feeling that his grip had eased off, Ciri kicked, jerked and leaped up like a spring. And saw what had happened.

Kelpie, creeping up noiselessly, had seized Forest Gramps in her teeth by his queue and almost lifted him into the air. The old man howled and squealed, struggled, kicked and wriggled his legs, finally managing to tear himself free, leaving the long, grey lock of hair in the mare's teeth. He tried to grab his stick, but Ciri kicked it out of range of his hands. She was about to treat him to another kick where he deserved it, but her movements were hindered by her trousers being halfway down her thighs. Gramps made good use of the time it took her to pull them up one-handed. He was by the stump in a few bounds and jerked the axe from it, driving the determined Kelpie away with a swing. He roared, stuck out his awful teeth and attacked Ciri, raising the axe to strike.

'Gramps is going to fuck you, miss!' he howled wildly. 'Even if Gramps has to chop you up into pieces first. It's all the same to Gramps if you're in one piece, or in portions.'

She thought she'd cope with him easily. After all he was a decrepit old geezer.

She was very much mistaken.

In spite of his enormous slippers he jumped like a spinning top, hopped like a rabbit, and swung the axe with the bent handle like a butcher. After the dark and sharpened blade had literally grazed her several times Ciri realised that the only thing that could save her was to run away.

But she was rescued by a coincidence. Stepping back, she knocked her foot against her sword. She picked it up in a flash.

'Drop the axe,' she panted, drawing Swallow from the scabbard with a hiss. 'Drop the axe onto the ground, you lecherous old man. Then, who knows, perhaps I'll spare your life. And not cut you into pieces.'

He stopped. He was panting and wheezing, and his beard was disgustingly covered in saliva. He didn't drop his weapon, though. She saw savage fury in his eyes.

'Very well!' she swung her sword in a hissing moulinet. 'Make my day!'

For a moment he looked at her, as though not understanding, then he stuck out his teeth, goggled, roared and lunged at her. Ciri had had enough of fooling around. She dodged him with a swift half-turn and cut from below across both his raised arms, above the elbows. Gramps released the axe from his bloodied hands, but immediately jumped at her again. She leaped aside and slashed him in the nape of the neck. More out of mercy than need; he would soon have bled to death from his two severed brachial arteries.

He lay, fighting unbelievably hard not to give up his life, still writhing like a worm in spite of his cloven vertebrae. Ciri stood over him. The last grains of sand were still grating in her teeth.

She spat them out straight onto his back. He was dead before she finished spitting.

*

The strange construction in front of the cottage resembling a gallows was equipped with iron hooks and a block and tackle. The table and chopping block were worn smooth, sticky with grease and reeked horribly.

Like a shambles.

In the kitchen, Ciri found a cauldron of the pearl barley he had offered her, swimming in grease, full of pieces of meat and mushrooms. She was very hungry, but something told her not to eat it. She only drank some water from a wooden pail and nibbled a small, wrinkled apple.

Behind the shack she found a cellar with steps, deep and cool. In the cellar stood pots of lard. Something was hanging from the ceiling. The remains of a side of meat.

She ran out of the cellar, stumbling on the steps, as though devils were pursuing her. Then fell over in some nettles, jumped up, and ran tottering over to the cottage, grabbing with both hands one of the stilts supporting it. Although she had almost nothing in her stomach, she vomited very spasmodically for a very long time.

The side of meat hanging in the cellar belonged to a child.

*

Led by the strong smell, she found a water-filled hollow in the forest, into which the prudent Forest Gramps would throw scraps of what it wasn't possible to eat. Looking at the skulls, ribs and pelvises sticking out of the ooze, Ciri realised with horror that she was only alive thanks to the ghastly old man's lecherousness, only owing to the fact that he had felt like frolicking. Had his hunger been more powerful than his despicable sexual urges he would have hit her treacherously with the axe, not the stick. Suspended by the legs from the wooden gallows he would have disembowelled and skinned her, dressed and divided her on the table, chopped her up on the chopping block . . .

Although she was unsteady on her feet from giddiness, and her left hand was swollen and pain was shooting through it, she dragged the corpse to the hollow in the forest and pushed it into the stinking slime, among the bones of his victims. She returned, covered up the entrance to the cellar with branches and twigs, and the yard and entire smallholding with brushwood. Then she meticulously set fire to it all from four sides.

She only rode away once it had thoroughly caught fire, when the fire was raging and roaring satisfactorily. When she was certain that no rain showers would interfere with all traces of that place being obliterated.

*

Her hand wasn't in such bad shape. It was swollen, indeed, it hurt awfully, but probably no bones were broken.

As evening approached only one moon indeed rose. But somehow, strangely, Ciri didn't feel like considering this world hers.

Nor staying in it longer than need be.

*

'It'll be a good night tonight,' murmured Nimue. 'I can sense it.'

Condwiramurs sighed.

The horizon blazed gold and red. There was a stripe of the same colour on the lake, from the horizon to the island.

They sat in armchairs on the terrace, with the looking glass in the ebony frame and the tapestry depicting the old castle hugging a rock wall behind them, looking at themselves in the mountain lake.

How many evenings, thought Condwiramurs, *how many evenings have we sat like this until dusk has fallen and later, in the dark? Without any results? Just talking?*

It was getting cool. The sorceress and the novice covered themselves with furs. From the lake they heard the creaking of the rowlocks of Fisher King's boat, but they couldn't see it – it was obscured by the brilliance of the sunset.

'I quite often dream,' Condwiramurs returned to their interrupted conversation, 'that I'm in an icy wasteland, where there's
nothing but the white of the snow and mounds of ice, glistening
in the sun. And there's a silence, a silence ringing in the ears. An
unnatural silence. The silence of death.'

Nimue nodded, as though to indicate she knew what was meant.
But she didn't comment.

'Suddenly,' continued the novice, 'suddenly I feel I can hear
something. That I feel the ice tremble beneath my feet. I kneel
down, rake aside the snow. The ice is as transparent as glass, as in
some clear, mountain lakes, when the pebbles at the bottom and
the fish swimming can be seen through a layer two yards thick.
In my dream I can also see, although the layer of ice is dozens or
perhaps hundreds of yards thick. It doesn't stop me seeing . . . and
hearing . . . people calling for help. At the bottom, deep beneath
the ice . . . is a frozen world.'

Nimue didn't comment this time either.

'Of course I know what the source of that dream is,' continued
the novice. 'Ithlinne's Prophecy, the infamous White Frost, the
Time of Frost and the Wolfish Blizzard. The world dying among
the snows and ice, in order, as the prophecy says, to be born again
centuries later. Cleansed and better.'

'I believe deeply,' said Nimue softly, 'that the world will be born
again. Whether into something better, not particularly.'

'I beg your pardon?'

'You heard me.'

'Didn't I mishear? Nimue, the White Frost has already been
prophesied thousands of times. Every time the winter is severe it's
been said that it has come. Right now even children don't believe
that any winter is capable of endangering the world.'

'Well, well. Children don't believe. But I, just imagine, do.'

'Based on any rational premises?' asked Condwiramurs with a
slight sneer. 'Or only on a mystical faith in the infallibility of elven
predictions?'

Nimue said nothing for a long while, picking at the fur she was
draped in.

'The earth,' she finally began in a slightly sermonising tone, 'has
a spherical shape and orbits the sun. Do you agree with that? Or

perhaps you belong to one of those fashionable sects that try to prove something utterly different.'

'No. I don't. I accept heliocentrism and I agree with the theory of the spherical shape of the earth.'

'Excellent. You are sure then to agree with the fact that the vertical axis of the globe is tilted at an angle, and the path of the earth around the sun doesn't have the shape of a regular circle, but is elliptical?'

'I learned about it. But I'm not an astronomer, so—'

'You don't have to be an astronomer, it's enough to think logically. The earth circles the sun in an elliptical-shaped orbit, and so during its revolution sometimes it's closer and sometimes further away. The further the earth is from the sun, the colder it is on it; that must be logical. And the less the world's axis deviates from the perpendicular the less light reaches the northern hemisphere.'

'That's also logical.'

'Both those factors, I mean the ellipticalness of the orbit and the degree of tilt of the world's axis, are subject to changes. As can be observed, cyclical ones. The ellipse may be more or less elliptical, that is stretched out and elongated, and the earth's axis may be less or more tilted. Extreme conditions, as far as climate is concerned, are caused by a simultaneous occurrence of the two phenomena: the maximum elongation of the ellipse and only an insignificant deviation of the axis from the vertical. The earth orbiting the sun receives very little light and heat at the aphelium, and the polar regions are additionally harmed by the disadvantageous angle of tilt of the axis.'

'Naturally.'

'Less light in the northern hemisphere means the snow lies longer. White and shining snow reflects sunlight, the temperature falls even more. The snow lies even longer because of that, it doesn't melt at all in greater and greater stretches or only melts for a short time. The more snow and the longer it lies, the greater the white and shining reflective surface . . .'

'I understand.'

'The snow's falling, it's falling and falling and there's more and more of it. So observe that masses of warm air drift with the sea currents from the south, which condense over the frozen northern land. The warm air condenses and falls as snow. The greater the temperature differences, the heavier the falls. The heavier the falls, the more white snow that doesn't melt for a long time. And the colder it is. The greater the temperature difference and the more abundant the condensation of the masses of air . . .'

'I understand.'

'The snow cover becomes heavy enough to become compacted ice. A glacier. On which, as we now know, snow continues to fall, pressing it down even more. The glacier grows, it's not only thicker and thicker, but it spreads outwards, covering greater and greater expanses. White expanses . . .'

'Reflecting the sun's rays,' Condwiramurs nodded. 'Becoming colder, colder and even colder. The White Frost prophesied by Ithlinne. But is a cataclysm possible? Is there really a danger that the ice that has lain in the north forever will all of a sudden flow south, crushing, compressing and covering everything? How fast does the ice cap spread at the pole? A few inches annually?'

'As you surely know,' said Nimue, eyes fixed on the lake, 'the only port in the Gulf of Praxeda that doesn't freeze is Pont Vanis.'

'Yes. I am aware.'

'Enriching your knowledge: a hundred years ago none of the Gulf's ports used to freeze. A hundred years ago – there are numerous accounts of it – cucumbers and pumpkins used to grow in Talgar, and sunflowers and lupins were cultivated in Caingorn. They aren't cultivated now, since their growth is impossible; it's simply too cold there. And did you know there were once vineyards in Kaedwen? The wines from those vines probably weren't the best, because it appears from the surviving documents that they were very cheap. But local poets sung their praises anyway. Today vines don't grow in Kaedwen at all. Because today's winters, unlike the former ones, bring hard frosts, and a hard frost kills vines. It doesn't just retard growth, it simply kills. Destroys.'

'I understand.'

'Yes,' Nimue reflected. 'What more is there to add? Perhaps that it snows in Talgar in the middle of November and drifts south at a speed of more than fifty miles a day. That at the end of

December and the beginning of January snowstorms occur by the Alba, where still a hundred years ago snow was a sensation? And that every child knows that the snows melt and the lakes thaw in April in our region, don't they? And every child wonders why that month is called April – the Opening. Didn't it surprise you?'

'Not especially,' admitted Condwiramurs. 'Anyway at home in Vicovaro we didn't say April, but Falsebloom. Or in the elven: Birke. But I understand what you're implying. The name of the month comes from ancient times when everything really did bloom in April . . .'

'Those distant times are all a hundred, a hundred and twenty years ago. That's virtually yesterday, girl. Ithlinne was absolutely right. Her prophecy will be fulfilled. The world will perish beneath a layer of ice. Civilisation will perish through the fault of the Destroyer, who could have, who had the opportunity, to open a path to hope. It is known from legend that she didn't.'

'For reasons that the legend doesn't explain. Or explains with the help of a vague and naive moral.'

'That's true. But the fact remains a fact. The White Frost is a fact. The civilisation of the northern hemisphere is doomed to extinction. It will vanish beneath the ice of a spreading glacier, beneath permanent pack ice and snow. There's no need to panic, though, because it'll take some time before it happens.'

The sun had completely set and the blinding glare had disappeared from the surface of the lake. Now a streak of softer, paler light lay down on the water. The moon rose over Inis Vitre, as bright as a gold sovereign chopped in half.

'How long?' Condwiramurs asked. 'How long, according to you, will it take? I mean, how much time do we have?'

'A good deal.'

'How much, Nimue?'

'Some three thousand years.'

On the lake, the Fisher King banged his oar down in the boat and swore. Condwiramurs sighed loudly.

'You've reassured me a little,' she said after a while. 'But only a little.'

*

The next place was one of the foulest Ciri had visited. It certainly appeared in the top ranking and at the top of that ranking.

It was a port, a port channel. She saw boats and galleys by jetties and posts, saw a forest of masts, saw sails, sagging heavily in the still air. Smoke, clouds of stinking smoke, were creeping and hanging all around.

Smoke also rose from behind crooked shacks by the channel. The loud, broken crying of a child could be heard from there.

Kelpie snorted, jerking her head sharply, and stepped back, banging her hooves on the cobbles. Ciri glanced down and noticed some dead rats. They were lying everywhere. Dead rodents contorted in agony with pale, pink paws.

Something's not right here, she thought, feeling horror gripping her. *Something's wrong here. Get out of here. Run from here as quickly as possible.*

A man in a gaping shirt was sitting under hanging nets and lines, his head resting on his shoulder. A few paces away lay another. They didn't look as if they were asleep. They didn't even twitch when Kelpie's horseshoes clattered on the stones right next to them. Ciri bowed her head, riding under the rags hanging from washing lines and giving off an acrid odour of filth.

There was a cross on the door of one of the shacks painted in whitewash. Black smoke left a trail in the air behind the roof. The child was still crying, somebody shouted in the distance, somebody closer coughed and wheezed. A dog howled.

Ciri felt her hand itching. She looked down.

Her hand was flecked with the black dots of fleas, like caraway seeds.

She screamed at the top of her voice. Shaking all over in horror and revulsion, she began to brush herself off, waving her arms wildly. Kelpie, alarmed, burst into a gallop, and Ciri almost fell off. Squeezing the mare's sides with her thighs she combed and ran her fingers through her hair, she shook her jacket and blouse. Kelpie galloped into a smoke-enveloped alleyway. Ciri screamed with terror.

She rode through hell, through an inferno, through the most nightmarish of nightmares. Among houses marked with white crosses. Among smouldering piles of rags. Among the dead lying singly and those who lay in heaps, one upon the other. And among living, ragged, half-naked spectres with cheeks sunken from pain, grovelling through dung, screaming in a language she didn't understand, stretching out towards her bony arms, covered in horrible, bloody pustules . . .

Run! Run from here!

Even in the black nothingness, in the oblivion of the archipelago of places, Ciri could still smell that smoke and stench in her nostrils.

*

The next place was also a port. There was also a quay here, with a piled canal busy with cogs, launches and other craft, and above them a forest of masts. But here, in this place, above the masts, seagulls were cheerfully screeching, and it stank in a normal, familiar way: of wet wood, pitch, sea water, and also fish in all its three basic varieties: fresh, rotten and fried.

Two men were arguing on the deck of a cog, shouting over each other in raised voices. She understood what they were saying. It was about the price of herrings.

Not far away was a tavern. The odour of mustiness and beer, and the sound of voices, clanking and laughter belched from the open door. Someone roared out a filthy song, the same verse the whole time:

> *Luned, v'ard t'elaine arse*
> *Aen a meath ail aen sparse!*

She knew where she was. Before she had even read on the stern of one of the galleys: *Evall Muire*. And its home port. Baccalá. She knew where she was.

In Nilfgaard.

She fled before anyone could pay more close attention to her.

But before she managed to dive into nothingness, a flea, the last of the ones that had crawled all over her in the previous place, that had survived the journey in time and space nestled in a fold of her jacket, leaped a great flea leap onto the wharf.

277

That same evening the flea settled into the mangy coat of a rat, an old male, the veteran of many rat fights, testified to by one ear chewed off right by its skull. That same evening the flea and the rat embarked on a ship. And the next morning set sail on a voyage. On a barge; old, neglected and very dirty.

The barge was called *Catriona*. That name was to pass into history. But no one knew that then.

*

The next place – difficult though it was to believe – was a truly astonishingly idyllic scene. A thatched tavern grown over with wild vines, ivy and sweet peas stood among hollyhocks by a peaceful, lazy river flowing among willows, alders and oaks bent over the water, right beside a bridge connecting the banks with its elegant, stone arch. A sign with gilded letters on it swung over the porch. The letters were completely foreign to Ciri. But there was quite a well-executed picture of a cat, so she assumed it was The Black Cat tavern.

The scent of food drifting from the tavern was simply captivating. Ciri did not ponder for long. She straightened her sword on her back and entered.

It was empty inside. Only one of the tables was occupied, by three men with the appearance of peasants. They didn't even look at her. Ciri sat down in the corner with her back to the wall.

The innkeeper, a corpulent woman in a perfectly clean apron and horned cap, approached and asked about something. Her voice sounded jangling, but melodic. Ciri pointed a finger at her open mouth, patted herself on the stomach, after which she cut off one of the silver buttons on her jacket and laid it on the table. Seeing a strange glance, she set to cutting off another button, but the woman stopped her with a gesture and a hissing, though nicely ringing, word.

The value of a button turned out to be a bowl of thick vegetable soup, an earthenware pot of beans and smoked bacon, bread and a jug of watered-down wine. Ciri thought she'd probably burst into tears at the first spoonful. But she controlled herself. She ate slowly. Delighting in the food.

The innkeeper came over, jingling questioningly, and laid her cheek on her pressed-together hands. Would she stay the night?

'I don't know,' said Ciri. 'Perhaps. In any case, thank you for the offer.'

The woman smiled and went out into the kitchen.

Ciri unfastened her belt and rested her back against the wall. She wondered what to do next. The place – particularly compared to the last few – was pleasant, and encouraged her to stay longer. She knew, though, that excessive trust could be dangerous, and lack of vigilance fatal.

A black cat, exactly like the one on the inn sign, appeared from nowhere and rubbed against her calf, arching its back. She stroked it, and the cat gently butted her palm, sat down and began licking the fur on its breast. Ciri gazed into space, her sight drifting elsewhere...

She saw Jarre sitting by the fireplace in a circle of some unattractive looking scruffs. They were all knocking over small vessels containing a red liquid.

'Jarre?'

'That's what you should do,' said the boy, looking into the flames of the fire. 'I read about it in *The History of Wars*, a work written by Marshal Pelligram. You should do that when the motherland is in need.'

'What should you do? Spill blood?'

'Yes. Precisely. The motherland is calling. And partly for personal reasons.'

'Ciri, don't sleep in the saddle,' says Yennefer. 'We're almost there.'

There are large crosses painted in whitewash on the houses of the town they are arriving in, on all the doors and gates. Thick, reeking smoke, smoke is billowing from pyres with corpses burning on them. Yennefer seems not to notice it.

'I have to make myself beautiful.'

A small mirror is floating in front of her face, over the horse's ears. A comb is dancing in the air, tugging through her black curls. Yennefer is using witchcraft, she doesn't use her hands at all, because . . .

Because her hands are a mass of clotted blood.

'Mummy! What have they done to you?'

'Stand up, girl,' says Coën. 'Master your pain, get up and onto the comb! Otherwise fear will seize you. Do you want to be dying of fear all your life?'

His yellow eyes shine unpleasantly. He yawns. His pointed teeth flash white. It's not Coën at all. It's the cat. The black cat . . .

A column of soldiers many miles long are marching. A forest of spears and standards sways and undulates over them. Jarre also marches, he has a round helmet on his head, and a pike on his shoulder so long he has to clutch it tightly in both hands, otherwise it would overbalance him. The drums growl, and the soldiers' song booms and rumbles. Crows caw above the column. A mass of crows . . .

A lake shore. On the beach whitecaps of whipped up foam, rotten reeds washed up. An island on the lake. A tower. Toothed battlements, a keep thickened by the protrusions of machicolations. Over the tower, in the darkening blue of the sky, the moon shines, as bright as a gold sovereign chopped in half. Two women wrapped in furs sit on the terrace. A man in a boat . . .

A looking glass and a tapestry.

Ciri jerks her head up. Eredin Bréacc Glas is sitting opposite, on the other side of the table.

'You can't not know,' he says, showing his even teeth in a smile, 'that you're only delaying the inevitable. You belong to us and we'll catch you.'

'Like hell!'

'You will return to us. You will roam a little around places and times, then you'll reach the Spiral and we'll catch you in it. You will never return to your world or time. It's too late, in any case. There's nothing for you to return to. The people you knew died long ago. Their graves are overgrown and have caved in. Their names have been forgotten. Your name also.'

'You're lying! I don't believe you!'

'Your beliefs are your private matter. I repeat, you'll soon reach the Spiral, and I'll be waiting there for you. You desire that secretly, don't you, *me elaine luned?*'

'You've got to be talking rubbish!'

'We Aen Elle sense things like that. You were fascinated by me, you desired me and feared that desire. You desired me and you still desire me, Zireael. Me. My hands. My touch . . .'

Feeling a touch, she leaped up, knocking over a cup, which was fortunately empty. She reached for her sword, but calmed down almost at once. She was in The Black Cat inn, she must have dropped off, dozing on the table. The hand that had touched her hair belonged to the portly innkeeper. Ciri wasn't fond of that kind of familiarity, but kindness and goodness simply radiated from the woman, which she couldn't pay back with brusqueness. She let herself be stroked on the head, and listened to the melodic, jingling speech with a smile. She was weary.

'I must ride,' she said at last.

The woman smiled, jingling melodiously. *How does it happen,* thought Ciri, *what can it be ascribed to, that in all worlds, places and times, in all languages and dialects that one word always sounds comprehensible? And always similar?*

'Yes. I must ride to my mamma. My mamma is waiting for me.'

The innkeeper led her out into the courtyard. Before she found herself in the saddle, the innkeeper suddenly hugged Ciri hard, pressing her against her plump breast.

'Goodbye. Thank you for having me. Forward, Kelpie.'

She rode straight for the arched bridge over the tranquil river. When the mare's horseshoes rang on the stones, she looked around. The woman was still standing outside the inn.

Concentration, fists at her temples. A buzzing in her ears, as though from the inside of a conch. A flash. And abruptly soft and black nothingness.

'*Bonne chance, ma fille!*' Thérèse Lapin, the innkeeper of the tavern Au Chat Noir in Pont-sur-Yonne cried after her by the highway running from Melun to Auxerre. 'Have a pleasant journey!'

*

Concentration, fists at her temples. A buzzing in her ears, as though from the inside of a conch. A flash. And abruptly soft and black nothingness.

A place. A lake. An island. The moon like a sovereign hacked

281

in half, its light lies down on the water in a luminous streak. In the streak a boat, on it a man with a fishing rod . . .

On the terrace of the tower . . . Two women?

*

Condwiramurs couldn't bear it and screamed in amazement, immediately covering her mouth with her hand. The Fisher King dropped the anchor with a splash, swore gruffly, and then opened his mouth and froze like that. Nimue didn't even twitch.

The surface of the lake, bisected by a streak of moonlight, vibrated and rippled as though having been struck by a gale. The night air above the lake ruptured, like a smashed stained-glass window cracks. A black horse emerged from the crack. With a rider on its back.

Nimue calmly held out her hands, chanting a spell. The tapestry hanging on the stand suddenly burst into flames, lighting up in an extravaganza of tiny multi-coloured lights. The tiny lights reflected in the oval of the looking glass, danced, teemed in the glass like coloured bees and suddenly flowed out like a rainbow-coloured apparition, a widening streak, making everything as bright as day.

The black mare reared up and neighed wildly. Nimue spread wide her arms violently, and screamed a formula. Condwiramurs, seeing the image forming and growing in the air, focused intently. The image gained in clarity at once. It became a portal. A gate beyond which was visible . . .

A plateau full of shipwrecks. A castle embedded in the sharp rocks of a cliff, towering over the black looking glass of a mountain lake . . .

'This way!' Nimue screamed piercingly. 'This is the way you must take! Ciri, daughter of Pavetta! Enter the portal, take the road leading to your encounter with destiny. May the wheel of time close! May the serpent Ouroboros sink its teeth into its own tail!

'Roam no more! Hurry, hurry to help your friends! This is the right way, O, witcher girl.'

The mare whinnied again, flailed the air with its hooves once more. The girl in the saddle turned her head, looking now at them, now at the image called up by the tapestry and the looking glass. She brushed her hair aside, and Condwiramurs saw the ugly scar on her cheek.

'Trust me, Ciri!' cried Nimue. 'For you know me! You saw me once!'

'I remember,' they heard. 'I trust you. Thank you.'

They saw the mare spurred on and running with a light and dancing step into the brightness of the portal. Before the image became blurred and dispersed, they saw the ashen-haired girl wave a hand, turned towards them in the saddle.

And then everything vanished. The surface of the lake slowly calmed, the streak of moonlight became smooth again.

It was so quiet they felt they could hear the Fisher King's wheezing breath.

Holding back the tears welling up in her eyes, Condwiramurs hugged Nimue tightly. She felt the little sorceress tremble. They remained in an embrace for some time. Without a word. Then they both turned around towards the place where the Gate of the Worlds had vanished.

'Good luck, witcher girl!' they cried in unison. 'Good luck!'

Close by that field where the fierce battle took place, where almost the whole force of the North clashed with almost the entire might of the Nilfgaardian invader, were two fishing villages. Old Bottoms and Brenna. Because, however, Brenna was burned down to the ground at that time, it caught on at first to call it the 'Battle of Old Bottoms'. Today, nonetheless, no one says anything other than the 'Battle of Brenna', and there are two reasons for that. Primo, after being rebuilt Brenna is today a large and prosperous settlement, while Old Bottoms did not resist the ravages of time and all trace of it was covered over by nettles, couch grass and burdock. Secundo, somehow that name did not befit that famous, memorable and, at the same time, tragic battle. For, just ask yourself: here was a battle in which more than thirty thousand men laid down their lives, and if Bottoms was not enough, they had to be Old as well.

Thus in all the historical and military literature it became customary only to write the Battle of Brenna – both in the North, and in Nilfgaardian sources, of which, nota bene, there are many more than ours.

The Venerable Jarre of Ellander the Elder.
Annales seu Cronicae Incliti Regni Temeriae

CHAPTER EIGHT

'Cadet Fitz-Oesterlen, fail. Please sit down. I wish to draw your attention to the fact that lack of knowledge about famous and important battles from the history of our fatherland is embarrassing for every patriot and good citizen, but in the case of a future officer is simply a scandal. I shall take the liberty of making one more small observation, Cadet Fitz-Oesterlen. For twenty years, that is since I've been a lecturer at this institution, I don't recall a diploma exam in which a question about the Battle of Brenna hasn't come up. Thus, ignorance in this regard virtually rules out any chances of a career in the army. Well, but if one is a baron, one doesn't have to be an officer, one can try one's luck in politics. Or in diplomacy. Which I sincerely wish for you, Cadet Fitz-Oesterlen. And let's return to Brenna, gentlemen. Cadet Puttkammer!'

'Present!'

'Please come to the map. And continue. From the point where eloquence gave up on the lord baron.'

'Yes sir. The reason Field Marshal Menno Coehoorn decided to execute a manoeuvre and a rapid march westwards were the reports from reconnaissance informing that the army of the Nordlings was coming to the relief of the besieged fortress of Mayena. The marshal decided to cut off the Nordlings' progress and force them into a decisive battle. To this end he divided the forces of the Centre Army Group. He left some of his men at Mayena, and set off at a rapid march with the rest of his troops—'

'Cadet Puttkammer! You aren't a novelist. You're to be an officer! What kind of expression is: "the rest of his troops"? Please give me the exact *ordre de bataille* of Marshal Coehoorn's strike force. Using military terminology!'

'Yes, Captain. Field Marshal Coehoorn had two armies under his command: The 4th Horse Army, commanded by Major General Markus Braibant, our school's patron—'

'Very good, Cadet Puttkammer.'

'Damn toady,' hissed Cadet Fitz-Oesterlen from his desk.

'—and the 3rd Army, commanded by Lieutenant General Rhetz de Mellis-Stoke. The 4th Horse Army consisted of, numbering over twenty thousand soldiers: the Venendal Division, the Magne Division, the Frundsberg Division, the 2nd Vicovarian Brigade, the 3rd Daerlanian Brigade and the Nauzicaa and Vrihedd Divisions. The 3rd Army consisted of: the Alba Division, the Deithwen Division and . . . hmmm . . . and the . . .'

*

'The Ard Feainn Division,' stated Julia 'Pretty Kitty' Abatemarco. 'If you haven't ballsed anything up, of course. They definitely had a large silver sun on their gonfalon?'

'Yes, Colonel,' stated the reconnaissance commander firmly. 'Without doubt, they did!'

'Ard Feainn,' murmured Pretty Kitty. 'Hmmm . . . Interesting. That would mean that not only the horse army but also part of the 3rd are coming for us in those columns you supposedly saw. No, sir! Nothing on faith alone! I have to see it with my own eyes. Captain, during my absence you command the company. I order you to send a liaison officer to Colonel Pangratt—'

'But, Colonel, is that wise, to go yourself—'

'That's an order!'

'Yes, sir!'

'It's sheer lunacy, Colonel!' the commander of the reconnaissance outshouted the rush of the gallop. 'We might run into some elven patrol—'

'Don't talk! Lead on!'

The small troop galloped hard down the gorge, flashed like the wind down the stream's valley and rushed into a forest. Here they had to slow down. The undergrowth impeded riding, and furthermore they were indeed in danger of suddenly happening upon reconnaissance troops or pickets, which the Nilfgaardians had undoubtedly sent. The party of mercenaries had admittedly stolen up on the enemy from the flank, not head on, but the flanks were certainly also guarded. The game was thus as risky as hell.

But Pretty Kitty liked games like that. And there wasn't a soldier in the entire Free Company who wouldn't have followed her. All the way to hell.

'It's here,' said the commander of the reconnaissance. 'The tower.'

Julia Abatemarco shook her head. The tower was crooked, ruined, bristling with broken beams forming a latticework through which the wind, blowing from the west, played as though on a tin whistle. It wasn't known who had built the tower here, in a wilderness, or why. But it was apparent it had been built a long time before.

'It won't collapse?'

'Certainly not, Colonel.'

'Sir' wasn't used among the mercenaries of the Free Company. Or 'madam'. Only rank. Julia climbed to the top of the tower, almost running up. The reconnaissance commander only joined a minute later, panting like a bull covering a heifer. Leaning on the crooked railing, Pretty Kitty surveyed the valley using a telescope, sticking her tongue between her lips and sticking out her shapely rear. The reconnaissance commander felt a quiver of excitement at the sight. He quickly controlled himself.

'Ard Feainn, there's no doubt.' Julia Abatemarco licked her lips. 'I can also see Elan Trahe's Daerlanians, there are also elves from the Vrihedd Brigade, our old friends from Maribor and Mayena . . . Aha! There are also the Death's Heads, the famous Nauzicaa Brigade. I can also see the flames on the pennants of the Deithwen armoured division. And a white standard with a black alerion, the sign of the Alba Division . . .'

'You recognise them,' murmured the reconnaissance commander, 'as though they were friends . . . Are you so well-informed?'

'I'm a graduate of the military academy,' Pretty Kitty cut him off. 'I'm a qualified officer. Good, I've seen what I wanted to see. Let's return to the company.'

*

'The 4th and 3rd Horse are making for us,' said Julia Abatemarco. 'I repeat, the whole of the 4th Horse and probably the whole of the cavalry of the 3rd Army. A cloud of dust was rising into the sky behind the standards that I saw. By my reckoning, forty thousand horse are heading this way in those three columns. And maybe more. Perhaps—'

'Perhaps Coehoorn has divided up the Centre Army Group,' finished Adam 'Adieu' Pangratt, leader of the Free Company. 'He only took the 4th Horse and the cavalry from the 3rd, without infantry, in order to move quicker . . . Ha, Julia, were I in the place of Constable Natalis or King Foltest—'

'I know,' Pretty Kitty's eyes flashed. 'I know what you'd do. Have you sent runners to them?'

'Naturally.'

'Natalis is nobody's fool. Perhaps, tomorrow—'

'Perhaps.' Adieu didn't let her finish. 'And I even think that will happen. Spur your horse, Julia. I want to show you something.'

They rode a few furlongs, quickly, pulling a long way ahead of the rest of the soldiers. The sun was almost touching the hills in the west, the wetland forests cloaked the valley in a long shadow. But enough could be seen for Pretty Kitty to guess at once what Adieu Pangratt had meant to show her.

'Here,' Adieu confirmed her speculation, standing up in the stirrups. 'I would engage the enemy here tomorrow. If the command of the army were mine.'

'Nice terrain,' agreed Julia Abatemarco. 'Level, hard, smooth . . . There's room to form up . . . Hmmm . . . From those hills to those fishponds there . . . It'll be some three miles . . . That hill, there, is a perfect command position . . .'

'You're right. And there, look, in the centre, there's one more small lake or fishpond. It's sparkling over there. It can be taken advantage of . . . That little river is suitable for a border, because although it's small, it's marshy . . . What's that river called, Julia? We rode that way yesterday, didn't we? Do you remember?'

'I've forgotten. I think it's the Halter. Or something like that.'

*

Whoever knows those parts can easily imagine the whole thing, while to those who are less well travelled I shall reveal that the left wing of the royal army reached the place where today the settlement of Brenna is located. At the time of the battle there was no settlement, for the year before it had been sent up in smoke by the Squirrel elves and had burned down to the ground. For there, on the left wing, stood the Redanian royal corps, which the Count of Ruyter was commanding. And there were eight thousand foot and frontline horse in that corps.

The centre of the royal formation stood beside a hill later to be named Gallows Hill. There, on the hill, stood with their detachment King Foltest and Constable Jan Natalis, having a prospect of the whole battlefield from high up. Here the main forces of our army were gathered – twelve thousand brave Temerian and Redanian infantrymen formed in four great squares, protected by ten cavalry companies, standing right at the northern end of the fishpond, called Golden Pond by local folk. The central formation, meanwhile, had a reserve regiment in the second line – three thousand Vizimian and Mariborian foot, over which Voivode Bronibor held command.

From the southern edge of Golden Pond, however, up to the row of fishponds and a bend in the River Chotla, to the marches a mile wide, stood the right wing of our army, the Volunteer Regiment formed of Mahakam dwarves, eight companies of light horse and companies of the eminent Free Mercenary Company. The condottiero Adam Pangratt and dwarf Barclay Els commanded the right wing.

Field Marshal Menno Coehoorn deployed the Nilfgaardian Army opposite them, about a mile or two away, on a bare field beyond the forest. Iron-hard men stood there like a black wall, regiment by regiment, company by company, squadron by squadron, endless it seemed, as far as the eye could see. And, from the forest of standards and spears, one could deduce that it was not just a broad but a deep array. For it was an army of six and forty thousand, which few knew about at that time, and just as well, because at the sight of that Nilfgaardian might many hearts sank somewhat.

And hearts started to beat beneath the breastplates of even the bravest, started to beat like hammers, for it became patent that a heavy and bloody battle would soon begin and many of those who stood in that array would not see the sunset.

Jarre, holding his spectacles which were sliding off his nose, read the entire passage of text once again, sighed, rubbed his pate, and then picked up a sponge, squeezing it a little and rubbing out the last sentence.

The wind soughed in the leaves of a linden tree and bees buzzed. The children, as children will, tried hard to outshout another.

A ball which had rolled across the grass came to rest against the foot of the old man. Before he managed to bend over, clumsy and ungainly, one of his grandchildren flashed past like a little wolf cub, grabbing the ball in full flight. He knocked the table, which began to rock, and Jarre saved the inkwell from falling over with his right hand, holding down the sheets of paper with the stump of his left.

The bees buzzed, heavy with tiny yellow balls of acacia pollen.

Jarre took up his writing again.

The morning was cloudy, but the sun broke through the clouds and its height clearly signalled the passing of the hours. A wind got up; pennants fluttered and flapped like flocks of birds taking flight. And Nilfgaard stood on, stood on, until everyone began to wonder why Marshal Menno Coehoorn did not give his order to march forward . . .

*

'When?' Menno Coehoorn raised his head from the maps and turned his gaze on his commanders. 'When, you ask, will I give the order to begin?'

No one said anything. Menno quickly looked his commanders up and down. The most anxious and nervous seemed to be those who were going to remain in reserve – Elan Trahe, commander of the 7th Daerlanian, and Kees van Lo of the Nauzicaa Brigade. Ouder de Wyngalt, the marshal's *aide-de-camp*, who had the least chance of active involvement in the fighting, was also nervous.

Those who were to strike first looked composed, why, even bored. Markus Braibant was yawning. Lieutenant General Rhetz de Mellis-Stoke kept sticking his little finger in his ear, pulling it out and looking at it, as though really expecting to find something worthy of his attention. Oberst Ramon Tyrconnel, the young commander of the Ard Feainn Division, whistled softly, fixing his gaze on a point on the horizon known only to him. Oberst Liam aep Muir Moss of the Deithwen Division turned the pages of his ever-present slim volume of poetry. Tibor Eggebracht of the Alba Heavy Lancers scratched the back of his neck with the end of a riding crop.

'We shall begin the attack,' said Coehoorn, 'as soon as the patrols return. Those hills to the north trouble me, gentlemen. Before we strike I must know what is behind them.'

*

Lamarr Flaut was afraid. He was terribly afraid, and the fear was creeping over his innards. It seemed to him he had at least twelve slimy eels covered in stinking mucus in his intestines, doggedly searching for an opening they would be able to escape through. An hour earlier, when the patrol had received its orders and set off, Flaut had hoped deep down that the cool of the morning would drive away the terror, hoped that routine, practised ritual, the hard and severe ceremony of service would quell the fear. He was disappointed. Only now, after an hour had passed and after travelling some five miles, far, dangerously far from his comrades, deep, hazardously deep in enemy territory, close, mortally close to unknown danger, had the fear showed what it was capable of.

They stopped at the edge of a fir forest, prudently not emerging from behind the large juniper bushes growing at the edge. A wide basin stretched out before them, beyond a belt of low spruces. Fog trailed over the tops of the grass.

'No one,' judged Flaut. 'Not a soul. Let's go back. We're a little too far already.'

The sergeant looked at him askance. *Far? We've barely ridden a mile. And crawling along like lame tortoises, at that.*

'It'd be worth,' he said, 'having a look beyond that hill, Lieutenant. I reckon the prospect will be better from there. A long way, over both valleys. If someone's heading that way, we can't not see them. Well then? Do we ride over, sir? It's no more than a few furlongs.'

A few furlongs, thought Flaut. *Over open ground, totally exposed.* The eels squirmed, violently searching for a way out of his guts. At least one, Flaut felt clearly, was well on its way.

I heard the clank of a stirrup. The snorting of a horse. Over there, among the vivid green of young pines on a sandy slope. Did something move there? A figure?

Are they surrounding us?

A rumour was going around the camp that a few days earlier the mercenaries of the Free Company, having wiped out a patrol of the Vrihedd Brigade in an ambush, had taken an elf alive. It was said they'd castrated him, torn his tongue out and cut off all his fingers . . . And finally gouged out his eyes. Now, they had jeered, you won't frolic with your elven whore in any fashion. And you won't even be able to watch her when she frolics with others.

'Well, sir?' the sergeant cleared his throat. 'Shall we nip up that hill?'

Lamarr Flaut swallowed.

'No,' he said. 'We cannot dally. We've ascertained it: there's no enemy here. We must give a dispatch on it to headquarters. Back we go!'

*

Menno Coehoorn listened to the dispatch and raised his head from the maps.

'To your companies,' he ordered briefly. 'Mr Braibant, Mr Mellis-Stoke. Attack!'

'Long live the Emperor!' yelled Tyrconnel and Eggebracht. Menno looked at them strangely.

'To your companies,' he repeated. 'May the Great Sun enlighten your glory.'

*

Milo Vanderbeck, halfling, field surgeon, known as Rusty, greedily breathed into his nostrils the heady blend of the smells of iodine, ammonia, alcohol, ether and magical elixirs hanging beneath the tent roof. He wanted to enjoy that aroma to the full now, while it was still healthy, pure, virginally uncontaminated and clinically sterile. He knew it wouldn't stay like that for long.

He glanced at the operating table – also virginally white – and at the surgical instruments, at the dozens of tools which inspired respect and confidence by the cool and menacing dignity of their cold steel, the pristine cleanliness of the metal sheen, the order and aesthetics of their arrangement.

His staff – three women – busied themselves around the instruments. Rusty spat and made a correction in his thoughts. One woman and two girls. He spat again. One old, though beautiful and young-looking, grandmother. And two children.

A sorceress and healer, called Marti Sodergren. And the volunteers. Shani, a student from Oxenfurt. Iola, a priestess from the Temple of Melitele in Ellander.

I know Marti Sodergren, thought Rusty, *I've already worked with that beauty more than once. A bit of a nymphomaniac, she's also prone to hysteria, but that's nothing, as long as her magic works. Anaesthetic, disinfectant and blood-staunching spells.*

Iola. A priestess, or rather a novice. A girl with looks as plain and dull as linen, with long, strong peasant hands. The temple had prevented those hands from becoming tainted by the ugly mark of heavy and dirty slogging on the soil. But it hadn't managed to disguise their descent.

No, thought Rusty, *I'm not afraid for her, by and large. Those peasant woman's hands are sure hands, trustworthy hands. Besides, girls from temples seldom disappoint, they don't cave in at moments of despair, but seek comfort in religion, in their mystical faith. Interestingly, it helps.*

He glanced at red-haired Shani, nimbly threading curved needles with catgut.

Shani. A child from reeking city backstreets, who made it to the Academy of Oxenfurt thanks to her own thirst for knowledge and the unimaginable sacrifices of her parents in paying her fees. A schoolgirl. A jester. A cheerful scamp. What does she know? How to thread needles? Put on tourniquets? Hold retractors? Ha, the question is: when will the little red-haired student faint, drop the retractors and tumble nose-first into the open belly of a patient being operated on?

People aren't very hardy, he thought. *I asked to be given an elf woman. Or somebody from my own race. But no. There's no trust.*

Not towards me either, as a matter of fact.

I'm a halfling. An unhuman.

A stranger.

'Shani!'

'Yes, Mr Vanderbeck?'

'Rusty. I mean, to you it's "Mr Rusty". What's this, Shani? And what's it for?'

'Are you testing me, Mr Rusty?'

'Answer, girl!'

'It's a raspatory! For stripping the periosteum during amputations! So that the periosteum doesn't crack under the teeth of the saw, to make the sawing clean and smooth! Satisfied? Did I pass?'

'Quiet, girl, quiet.'

He raked his fingers through his hair.

Interesting, he thought. *There are four of us doctors here. And each one's ginger! Is it fate or what?*

'Please step outside the tent, girls,' he beckoned.

They obeyed, though all of them snorted to themselves. Each in her own way.

Outside the tent sat a cluster of orderlies enjoying the last minutes of sweet idleness. Rusty cast a severe glance at them, and sniffed to check if they were already plastered.

A blacksmith, a huge fellow, was bustling around by his table which resembled a torture chamber, and organising his tools which served to pull the wounded out of suits of armour, mail shirts and bent visors.

'In a moment, over there,' began Rusty without introductions, indicating the field, 'people will start slaughtering each other. And a moment after that moment the first casualties will appear. Everyone knows what they're supposed to do, each one of us knows their duties and their place. If everyone obeys what they ought to obey nothing can go wrong. Clear?'

None of the 'girls' commented.

'Over there,' continued Rusty, pointing again, 'almost a hundred thousand soldiers will begin to wound each other. In very elaborate ways. There are, including the other two hospitals, twelve of us doctors. Not for all the world will we manage to help all those that are in need. Not even a scanty percentage of those in need. No one expects that.

'But we're going to treat them. Because it is, excuse the banality, our raison d'être. To help those in need. So we shall banally help as many as we manage to help.'

Once again no one commented. Rusty turned around.

'We won't manage to do much more than we're capable of,' he said more quietly and more warmly. 'But we shall all do our best to make sure it won't be much less.'

*

'They've set off,' stated Constable Jan Natalis, and wiped his sweaty hand on his hip. 'Your Majesty, Nilfgaard has set off. They're heading for us!'

King Foltest brought his dancing horse, a grey in a trapping decorated with lilies, under control. He turned his beautiful profile, worthy of featuring on coins, towards the constable.

'Then we must receive them with dignity. Constable, sir! Gentlemen!'

'Death to the Black Cloaks!' yelled the mercenary Adam 'Adieu' Pangratt and Graf de Ruyter in unison. The constable looked at them, then straightened up and breathed in deeply.

'To your companies!'

From a distance the Nilfgaardian war drums thundered dully, crumhorns, oliphants and battle horns wailed. The ground, struck by thousands of hooves, shuddered.

*

'Here they come,' said Andy Biberveldt, a halfling and the leader of the convoy, brushing the hair from his small, pointed ear. 'Any moment . . .'

Tara Hildebrandt, Didi "Brewer" Hofmeier and the other carters who were gathered around him nodded. They could also hear the dull, monotonous thud of hooves coming from behind the hill and forest. They could feel the trembling of the ground.

The roar suddenly increased, jumping a tone higher.

'The archers' first salvo.' Andy Biberveldt was experienced, and had seen – or rather heard – many a battle. 'There'll be another.'

He was right.

'Now they'll clash!'

'We'd beee . . . ttter, geee . . . ttt under the carts,' suggested William Hardbottom, known as Momotek, fidgeting anxiously. 'I'm ttttt . . . telling you.'

Biberveldt and the other halflings looked at him with pity. Under the carts? What for? Nearly a quarter of a mile separated them from the site of the battle. And even if a patrol turned up here, at the rear, by the convoys, would hiding under a cart save anyone?

The roaring and rumbling increased.

'Now,' Andy Biberveldt judged. And he was right again.

A distinct, macabre noise which made the hair on their heads stand up reached the ears of the victuallers from a distance of a quarter of a mile, from beyond the hill and the forest, through the roaring and the sudden thud of iron smashing against iron.

Squealing. The gruesome, desperate, wild squealing and shrieking of mutilated animals.

'The cavalry . . .' Biberveldt licked his lips. 'The cavalry have impaled themselves on the pikes . . .'

'I jjjjust,' stammered out the pale Momotek, 'ddddon't know . . . how the horses are to blame . . . the whoresons.'

*

Jarre rubbed out another sentence with a sponge. God only knew how many that made. He squinted his eyes, recalling that day. The moment the two armies clashed. When the two armies, like determined mastiffs, went for each other's throats, clenched in a mortal grip.

He searched for words he could use to describe it.

In vain.

*

The wedge of cavalry rammed into the square. Like the thrust of a gigantic dagger, the Alba Division crushed everything that was defending access to the living body of the Temerian infantry – the pikes, javelins, halberds, spears, pavises and shields. Like a dagger, the Alba Division thrust into the living body and drew blood. Blood, in which horses now splashed and slid. But the dagger's blade, though thrust in deep, hadn't reached the heart or any of the vital organs. The wedge of the Alba Division, instead of smashing and dismembering the Temerian square, thrust in and became stuck. Became lodged in the elastic horde of foot soldiers, as thick as pitch.

At first it didn't look dangerous. The head and sides of the wedge were made up of elite heavily-armoured companies, and the landsknechts' edges and blades rebounded from the shields and armour plate like hammers from anvils, and neither was there any way to get through the barding of the steeds. And although every now and then one of the armoured men would tumble from his horse or with his horse, the swords, battle-axes, hatchets and morning stars of the cavalrymen cut down the pressing infantrymen. Trapped in the throng, the wedge shuddered and began to drive in deeper.

'Albaaa!' Second Lieutenant Devin aep Meara heard the cry of Oberst Eggebracht soaring above the clanging, roaring, groaning and neighing. 'Forward, Alba! Long live the Emperor!'

They set off, hacking, clubbing and slashing. Beneath the hooves of the squealing and kicking horses was the sound of splashing, crunching, grinding and snapping.

'Aalbaaa!'

The wedge became caught again. The landsknechts, although thinned out and bloodied, didn't yield, but pressed forward and gripped the cavalry like pliers. Until they cracked. Under the blows of halberds, battle-axes and flails, the armoured troops of the front line caved in and broke. Jabbed by partizans and pikes, hauled from the saddle by the hooks of guisarmes and bear spears, mercilessly pounded by iron balls-and-chains and clubs, the cavalrymen of the Alba Division began to die. The wedge thrust into the square of infantry, which not long before had been menacing iron, cutting into a living body, was now like an icicle in a huge peasant fist.

'Temeriaaaa! For the king, boys! Kill the Black Cloaks!'

But neither was it coming easily to the landsknechts. Alba didn't let itself be broken up. Swords and battle-axes rose and fell, hacked

299

and slashed, and the infantry paid a grim price in blood for every horseman knocked from the saddle.

Oberst Eggebracht, stabbed through a slit in his armour by a pike blade as thin as a bodkin, yelled and rocked in the saddle. Before anyone could help him, an awful blow of a flail swept him to the ground. The infantry teemed over him.

The standard with a black alerion bearing a gold *perisonium* on its chest wobbled and fell.

The armoured soldiers, including also Second Lieutenant Devlin aep Meara, rushed over to it, hacking, hewing, trampling and yelling.

I'd like to know, thought Devlin aep Meara, tugging his sword out of the cloven kettle hat and skull of a Temerian landsknecht. *I'd like to know*, he thought, deflecting with a sweeping blow the toothed blade of a gisarme which was stabbing at him.

I'd like to know what all this is for. What's the point of it? And who's the cause of it?

*

'Errr . . . And then the convent of the great master sorceresses gathered . . . Our Esteemed Mothers . . . Errr . . . Whose memory will always live among us . . . For . . . Errr . . . the great master sorceresses of the First Lodge . . . decided to . . . Errr . . . Decided to . . .'

'Novice Abonde. You are unprepared. Fail. Sit down.'

'But I revised, really—'

'Sit down.'

'Why the hell do we have to learn about this ancient history?' muttered Abonde, sitting down. 'Who's bothered about it today? And what use is it?'

'Silence! Novice Nimue.'

'Present, mistress.'

'I can see that. Do you know the answer to the question? If you don't, sit down and don't waste my time.'

'Yes I do.'

'Go on.'

300

'So, the chronicles teach us that the convent of master sorceresses gathered at Bald Mountain Castle to decide on how to end the damaging war that the emperor of the South was waging with the kings of the North. Esteemed Mother Assire, the holy martyr, said that the rulers would not stop fighting until they had lost a lot of men. And Esteemed Mother Philippa, the holy martyr, answered: "Let us then give them a great and bloody, awful and cruel battle. Let us bring about such a battle. Let the emperor's armies and the kings' forces run in blood in that battle, and then we, the Great Lodge, shall force them to make peace". And this is precisely what happened. The Esteemed Mothers caused the Battle of Brenna to happen. And the rulers were forced to sign the Peace of Cintra.'

'Very good, novice Nimue. I'd have given you a starred A grade . . . Had it not been for that "so" at the beginning of your contribution. We don't begin sentences with "so". Sit down. And now, who'll tell us about the Peace of Cintra?'

The bell for the break rang. But the novices didn't react with immediate uproar and the banging of desktops. They maintained a peaceful and dignified silence. They weren't chits from the kindergarten now. They were third-formers! They were fourteen!

And that carried certain expectations.

*

'Well, there's not much to add here.' Rusty assessed the condition of the first wounded man who was right then sullying the immaculate white of the table. 'Crushed thighbone . . . The artery is intact, otherwise they would have brought us a corpse. It looks like an axe blow, and at the same time the saddle's hard pommel acted like a woodcutter's chopping block. Please look . . .'

Shani and Iola bent over. Rusty rubbed his hands.

'As I said, nothing to add. All we can do is take away. To work. Iola! Tourniquet, tightly. Shani, knife. Not that one. The double-bladed one. For amputations.'

The wounded man couldn't tear his restless gaze from their hands, tracked their movements with the eyes of a terrified animal caught in a snare.

'A little magic, Marti, if you please,' nodded the halfling, leaning over the patient so as to fill his entire field of vision. 'I'm going to amputate, son.'

'Nooooo!' yelled the injured man, thrashing his head around and trying hard to escape from Marti Sodergren's hands. 'I don't waant tooo!'

'If I don't amputate, you die.'

'I'd rather die . . .' The wounded man was speaking slower and slower under the effect of the healer's magic. 'I'd rather die than be a cripple . . . Let me die . . . I beg you . . . Let me die!'

'I can't.' Rusty raised the knife, looked at the blade, at the still shining, immaculate steel. 'I can't let you die. For it so happens that I'm a doctor.'

He stuck the blade in decisively and cut deeply. The wounded man howled. For a human, inhumanly.

*

The messenger reined in his horse so hard that turf sprayed from its hooves. Two adjutants clutched the bridle and calmed down the foaming steed. The messenger dismounted.

'From whom?' shouted Jan Natalis. 'From whom do you come?'

'From Graf de Ruyter . . .' the messenger panted. 'We've held the Black Cloaks. . . But there are severe casualties . . . Graf de Ruyter requests reinforcements . . .'

'There are no reinforcements,' the constable replied after a moment's silence. 'You must hold out. You must!'

*

'And here,' Rusty indicated with the expression of a collector showing off his collection, 'please look at the beautiful result of a cut to the belly . . . Someone has helped us somewhat by previously conducting an amateur laparotomy on the poor wretch. It's good he was carried carefully, none of his more important organs have been lost . . . I mean, I assume they haven't been. What's up with him, Shani, in your opinion? Why such a face, girl? Have you only known men from the outside before today?'

'The intestines are damaged, Mr Rusty . . .'

'A diagnosis as accurate as it is obvious! One doesn't even have to look, it's enough to sniff. A cloth, Iola. Marti, there's still too much blood, be so kind as to give us a little more of your priceless magic. Shani, clamp. Put on some arterial forceps, you can see it's pouring, can't you? Iola, knife.'

'Who's winning?' suddenly asked the man being operated on, quite lucidly, although he mumbled a little, rolling his goggling eyes. 'Tell me . . . who . . . is winning?'

'Son.' Rusty stooped over the open, bloody and throbbing abdominal cavity. 'That really is the last thing I'd be worrying about in your shoes.'

*

. . . Cruel and bloody fighting then began on the left wing and the centre of the line, but here, though great was Nilfgaard's fierceness and impetus, their charge broke on the royal army like an ocean wave breaks on a rock. For here stood the select soldiers, the valiant Mariborian, Vizimian and Tretorian armoured companies, and also the dogged landsknechts, the professional soldiers of fortune, whom cavalry could not frighten.

And thus they fought, truly like the sea against a rocky cliff, thus continued the battle in which you could not guess who had the upper hand, for although the waves endlessly beat against the rock, not weakening, and they only fell back to strike anew, the rock stood on, as it had always stood, still visible among the turbulent waves.

The battle unfolded in a different way on the right wing of the royal army.

Like an old sparrowhawk that knows where to stoop and peck its prey to death, so Field Marshal Menno Coehoorn knew where to aim his blows. Clenching in his iron fist his select divisions, the Deithwen lancers and the armoured Ard Feainn, he struck at the junction of the line above Golden Pond, where the companies from Brugge stood. Although the Bruggeans resisted heroically, they turned out to be more weakly accoutred, both in armour and in spirit, than their foes. They did not weather the Nilfgaardian advance. Two companies of the Free Company under the old condottiero Adam Pangratt went to their aid and held back Nilfgaard, paying a severe price in blood. But the awful threat of being surrounded stared the dwarves of the Volunteer Regiment standing on the right flank in the face, and the severing of the array imperilled the whole royal army.

Jarre dipped his quill pen in the inkwell. His grandchildren further away in the orchard were shouting, their laughter ringing like little glass bells.

Jan Natalis, nonetheless, attentive as a crane, had noticed the menacing danger, and understood in an instant which way the wind was blowing. And without delay sent a messenger to the dwarves with an order for Colonel Els . . .

*

In all his seventeen-year-old naivety, Cornet Aubry believed that to reach the right wing, deliver the order and return to the hill would take him ten minutes at most. Absolutely no more! Not on Chiquita, a mare as nimble and fleet as a hind.

Even before he had arrived at Golden Pond, the cornet had become aware of two things: there was no telling when he'd reach the right wing, and there was no way of telling when he'd manage to return. And that Chiquita's fleetness would come in very handy.

Fighting was raging on the battlefield to the east of Golden Pond. The Black Cloaks and the Bruggean horse protecting the infantry array were smiting each other. In front of the cornet's eyes figures in green, yellow and red cloaks suddenly shot out like sparks, like the glass of a stained-glass window, from the whirl of the battle, chaotically bolting towards the River Chotla. Nilfgaardians flooded like a black river behind them.

Aubry pulled his mare back hard, jerked the reins, ready to turn tail and flee, get out of the way of the fugitives and the pursuers. A sense of duty took the upper hand. The cornet pressed himself to his horse's neck and galloped at breakneck speed.

All around was yelling and hoof beats, a kaleidoscopic twinkling of figures, the flashes of swords, clanging and thudding. Some of the Bruggeans who were pressed against the fishpond were putting up desperate resistance, herding together around a standard bearing an anchored cross. The Black Cloaks were slaughtering the scattered and exposed infantry.

The view was obscured by a black cloak with the symbol of a silver sun.

'*Evgyr*, Nordling!'

Aubry yelled, and Chiquita, excited by the cry, give a truly deer-like bound, saving Aubry's life by carrying him out of range of the Nilfgaardian sword. Arrows and bolts suddenly howled over his head, figures flickered before his eyes again.

Where am I? Where are my comrades? Where is the enemy?

'*Evgyr morv*, Nordling!'

Thudding, clanking, neighing of horses, shouts.

'Stand, you little shit! Not that way!'

A woman's voice. A woman on a black stallion, in armour, with hair blown around, her face covered in spots of blood. Beside her armoured horsemen.

'Who are you?' The woman smeared the blood on her sword with a fist.

'Cornet Aubry ... Constable Natalis' Flügel-Adjutant ... With orders for Colonels Pangratt and Els—'

'You have no chance of getting to where Adieu is fighting. We'll ride to the dwarves. I'm Julia Abatemarco ... To horse, dammit! They're surrounding us! At the gallop!'

He didn't have time to protest. There was no point anyway.

After some furious galloping, a mass of infantry emerged from the dust, a square, encased like a tortoise in a wall of pavises, like a pincushion bristling with spear blades. A great gold standard with crossed hammers fluttered over the square and beside it rose up a pole with horsetails and human skulls.

The square was being attacked by Nilfgaardians, who were darting forwards and jumping back like dogs worrying a beggar swinging a cane. The Ard Feainn Division, owing to the great suns on their cloaks, could not be mistaken for any other.

'Fight, Free Company!' yelled the woman, whirling her sword around in a moulinet. 'Let's earn our pay!'

The horsemen – and with them Cornet Aubry – charged the Nilfgaardians.

The clash only lasted a few moments. But it was terrible. Then the wall of pavises opened before them. They found themselves inside the square, in a crush, amongst dwarves in mail shirts, basinets and pointed chichak helmets, amongst the Redanian infantry, light Bruggean horse and armoured condottieri.

Julia Abatemarco – Pretty Kitty, condottiero, Aubry only now recognised her – dragged him in front of a pot-bellied dwarf in a chichak helmet decorated with a splendid plume, sitting awkwardly on an armoured Nilfgaardian horse, in a lancer's saddle with large pommels, which he had clambered into to be able to see over the heads of the infantrymen.

'Colonel Barclay Els?'

The dwarf nodded his plume-helmeted head, noticing with evident appreciation the blood with which the cornet and his mare were sprayed. Aubry blushed involuntarily. It was the blood of the Nilfgaardians whom the condottieri had hacked down just beside him. He himself hadn't even managed to draw his sword.

'Cornet Aubry . . .'

'The son of Anzelm Aubry?'

'His youngest.'

'Ha! I know your father! What have you brought me from Natalis and Foltest, Cornet, my boy?'

'You are threatened by a breach in the centre of the line . . . The constable orders the Volunteer Regiment to pull back the wing as soon as possible, and retreat to Golden Pond and the River Chotla . . . In order to reinforce—'

His words were drowned out by roaring, clanging and the squealing of horses. Aubry suddenly realised how absurd the orders he had brought were. What little significance those orders had for Barclay Els, for Julia Abatemarco, for that dwarven square under a gold standard with hammers fluttering over the surrounding black sea of Nilfgaard, attacking them from all sides.

'I'm late . . .' he whimpered. 'I arrived too late . . .'

Pretty Kitty snorted. Barclay Els grinned.

'No, little cornet, son,' he said. 'It was Nilfgaard that came too soon.'

*

'Congratulations to you, ladies, and to me, on a successful segmentectomy of the small and large bowel, splenectomy, and a liver

306

suture. I draw your attention to the time it took to remove the consequences of what was done to our patient in a split second during the battle. I recommend that as material for philosophical reflections. Miss Shani will sew up the patient.'

'But I've never done it before, Mr Rusty!'

'You have to start sometime. Red to red, yellow to yellow, white to white. Sew like that and it's sure to be fine.'

*

'What the hell?' Barclay Els twisted his beard. 'What are you saying, little cornet? Anzelm Aubry's youngest son? That we're just loafing around here? We didn't even fucking budge in the face of the enemy! We didn't budge an inch! It ain't our fault the men from Brugge didn't hold out!'

'But the order—'

'I don't give a shit about the order!'

'If we don't fill the breaches,' Pretty Kitty shouted over the commotion, 'the Black Cloaks will break the front! They'll break the front! Open the array, Barclay! I'm going to strike! I'll get through!'

'They'll slaughter you before you get to the fishpond! You'll perish senselessly!'

'So what do you suggest?'

The dwarf swore, tore his helmet from his head and hurled it to the ground. His eyes were savage, bloodshot, dreadful.

Chiquita, frightened by the yells, danced beneath the cornet, as far as the crush permitted.

'Summon Yarpen Zigrin and Dennis Cranmer! Pronto!'

It was apparent at first glance that the two dwarves had come from the heaviest fighting. They were both bespattered with blood. The steel spaulder of one of them bore the mark of a cut so powerful it had bent the edges of the metal plating outwards. The head of the other dwarf was wrapped in a rag oozing blood.

'Everything in order, Zigrin?'

'I wonder,' panted the dwarf, 'why everyone's asking that?'

Barclay Els turned around, found the cornet's gaze and stared hard at him.

'So, Anzelm's youngest son?' he rasped. 'The king and the constable have ordered us to go to them and support them? Well, keep your eyes wide open, little cornet. This'll be worth seeing.'

*

'Sod it!' roared Rusty, springing back from the table and brandishing his scalpel. 'Why? Blast it, why does it have to be like this?'

No one answered him. Marti Sodergren just spread her arms. Shani bowed her head and Iola sniffed.

The patient who had just died was looking upwards, and his eyes were unmoving and glazed.

*

'Strike, kill! Confusion to the whoresons!'

'Keep in line!' Barclay Els roared. 'Keep an even step! Hold the line! And keep close! Close!'

They won't believe, thought Cornet Aubry. *They'll never believe me when I tell them about it. This square is fighting in a total encirclement . . . Surrounded on all sides by cavalry, being torn, hacked, pounded and stabbed . . . And the square is marching. It's marching in line, serried, pavise by pavise. It's marching, trampling and stepping over corpses, pushing the élite Ard Feainn Division in front of it . . . And it's marching.*

'Fight!'

'Even step! Even step!' bellowed Barclay Els. 'Hold the line! The song, for fuck's sake, the song! Our song! Forward, Mahakam!'

Several thousand dwarven throats yelled the famous Mahakam battle song.

> *Hooouuuu! Hooouuu! Hou!*
> *Just wait! Don't be hasty!*
> *Things will very soon get tasty!*
> *This shambles will fall apart*
> *Shaken to its very heart!*
> *Hoooouuuu! Hooouuu! Hou!*

'Fight! Free Company!' Julia Abatemarco's high-pitched soprano cut into the throaty roar of the dwarves, like the thin, keen edge of a misericorde. The condottieri, breaking free of the line, counter-struck the cavalry attacking the square. It was a truly suicidal stroke, as the entire momentum of the Nilfgaardian offensive turned onto the mercenaries, now deprived of the protection of the dwarven halberds, pikes and pavises. The thudding, yelling and squealing of horses made Cornet Aubry cringe involuntarily in the saddle. Someone struck him in the back and he felt himself drift with his mare, stuck in the crush, towards the greatest confusion and the most terrible slaughter. He tightly gripped his sword hilt which suddenly seemed slippery and strangely unwieldy.

A moment later, carried in front of the line of pavises, he was already hacking around himself like a madman and yelling like a madman.

'One more time!' he heard the wild cry of Pretty Kitty. 'One more shove! You'll do it, boys! Fight, kill! For the ducat, gaily sparkling! To me, Free Company!'

A helmetless Nilfgaardian rider with a silver sun on his cloak penetrated the line, stood up in his stirrups, and with a terrible blow of his battle axe felled a dwarf along with his pavise, and cleaved open the head of another. Aubry turned in the saddle and hacked backhanded. A sizeable fragment bearing hair flew from the head of the Nilfgaardian, who tumbled to the ground. At the same time the cornet was also struck in the head and fell from the saddle. The crush meant he didn't end up on the ground imme-diately, but hung for several seconds, screaming shrilly, between the sky, the earth and the sides of two horses. But although he had the fright of his life, he didn't have time to experience pain. When he fell, his skull was almost immediately crushed by iron-shod hooves.

*

Sixty-five years later, when asked about that day, about Brenna Field, about the square marching towards Golden Pond over the bodies of friends and enemies, the old woman would smile, wrin-kling up even more a face already as shrivelled and dark as a prune.

Impatient – or perhaps pretending to be impatient – she waved a trembling, bony hand, grotesquely contorted by arthritis.

'There was no way,' she mumbled, 'that either of the sides could gain the advantage. We were in the middle. In the encirclement. And they were on the outside. And we were simply killing one another. They us, and we them . . . Eck-eck-eeck . . . They us. We them . . .'

The old woman struggled to overcome a coughing fit. Those listeners who were closest saw on her cheek a tear, making its way with difficulty among the wrinkles and old scars.

'They were just as brave as us,' mumbled the old dear, who had once been Julia Abatemarco, Pretty Kitty of the Free Mercenary Company. 'Eck-eck . . . We were all just as brave. Us and them.'

The old woman fell silent. For a long time. Her audience didn't urge her on, seeing her smile at her recollections. At her glory. At the faces of those who gloriously survived, looming in the fog of oblivion, of forgetting. In order later to be shabbily killed by vodka, drugs and consumption.

'We were all just as brave,' finished Julia Abatemarco. 'Neither of the sides had the strength to be braver. But we . . . We managed to be brave for a minute longer.'

*

'Marti, I'd be very grateful if you could give us a little more of your wonderful magic! Just a little bit more, just a few ounces! The inside of this poor wretch's belly is one great goulash, seasoned, additionally, by loads of metal rings from a mail shirt. I can't do anything while he thrashes about like a fish being gutted! Shani, dammit, hold those retractors! Iola! Are you asleep, dammit? Clamp! Claaampp!'

Iola breathed out heavily, fighting to swallow the saliva filling her mouth. *I'm going to faint soon*, she thought. *I can't bear it, I can't bear this any longer, this stench, this ghastly mixture of blood, puke, excrement, urine, the content of intestines, sweat, fear and death. I can't bear these endless screams any longer, this moaning, these bloodied, slimy hands clinging to me as though I really was their hope, their escape, their life . . . I can't bear the pointlessness of what*

310

we're doing. Because it is pointless. It's one great, enormous pointless pit of pointlessness.

I can't bear the effort and the fatigue. They keep bringing new ones . . . And new ones . . .

I can't stand it. I'm going to vomit. I'm going to faint. I'll shame myself.

'Dressing! Compress! Bowel clamp! Not that one! Soft clamp! Mind what you're doing! Make another mistake and I'll smack you in that ginger head! Do you hear? I'll smack you in that ginger head!'

Great Melitele. Help me. Help me, O goddess.

'There! Better already! One more clamp, priestess! Clamp on the artery! Good! Good, Iola, keep it up! Marti, mop his eyes and face. And mine too . . .'

*

Where does that pain come from? thought Constable Jan Natalis. *What hurts so much?*

Aha.

My clenched fists.

*

'Let's finish them off!' yelled Kees van Lo, rubbing his hands. 'Let's finish them off, sir! The line's breaking along the formation, let's strike! Let's strike without delay, and by the Great Sun, they'll fall apart! They'll scatter!'

Menno Coehoorn was nervously chewing a fingernail, realised they were watching, and quickly took his finger out of his mouth.

'Let's strike,' repeated Kees van Lo calmly, now without emphasis. 'Nauzicaa's ready—'

'Nauzicaa is to stand by,' said Menno sharply. 'The Daerlanians, too. Mr Faoiltiarna!'

The commander of the Vrihedd Brigade, Isengrim Faoiltiarna, called the Iron Wolf, turned his awful face – disfigured by a scar running across his forehead, brow, bridge of the nose and cheek – towards the marshal.

'Strike,' Menno pointed with his baton. 'At the junction of Temeria and Redania. Over there.'

The elf saluted. His disfigured face didn't even twitch, his large eyes didn't change their expression.

Allies, thought Menno. *Confederates. We're fighting together. Against a common foe.*

But I don't understand them at all, those elves.

They're somehow alien.

Different.

*

'Interesting,' Rusty tried to rub his face with his elbow, but his elbow was also covered in blood. Iola hurried to help him.

'Curious,' repeated the surgeon, pointing at the patient. 'Stabbed by a pitchfork or some sort of two-pronged type of gisarme . . . One of the prongs punctured the heart, there, please look. The chamber undoubtedly perforated, the aorta almost severed. And he was still breathing for a while. Here, on the table. Gored right in the heart, he survived all the way to the table . . .'

'Do you wish to state,' a cavalryman from the light volunteer horse asked gloomily, 'that he's expired? We bore him from the battle in vain?'

'Nothing is in vain.' Rusty didn't lower his eyes. 'And for the sake of the truth, then yes, he's dead, sadly. *Exitus*. Take him away . . . Oh, bloody hell . . . Take a look, girls.'

Marti Sodergren, Shani and Iola bent over the body. Rusty pulled back the corpse's eyelid.

'Ever seen anything like that?'

All three of them shuddered.

'Yes,' they all said at the same time. They glanced at each other, as though slightly surprised.

'I have too,' said Rusty. 'It's a witcher. A mutant. That would explain why he lived so long . . . Was he your comrade-at-arms, men? Or did you bring him here by chance?'

'He was our comrade, Mr Medic,' confirmed another volunteer gloomily, a beanpole with a bandaged head. 'From our squadron, a volunteer like us. Eh, he was a master with a sword. They called him Coën.'

'And he was a witcher?'

'Aye. But he was a decent bloke otherwise.'

'Ha,' sighed Rusty, seeing four soldiers carrying another casualty on a blood-soaked cloak dripping with blood. He was very young, judging by how shrilly he was wailing.

'Ha, pity. I would have gladly taken that otherwise decent witcher for a post-mortem. I'm consumed with curiosity, and a paper could be written if one could just take a look inside him . . . But there's no time! Get the corpse off the table! Shani, water. Marti, disinfection. Iola, pass me . . . Hello, girl, are you shedding tears again? What's it this time?'

'Nothing, Mr Rusty. Nothing. Everything's all right now.'

*

'I feel,' repeated Triss Merigold, 'as though I've been robbed.'

Nenneke didn't answer for a long time, and looked from the terrace towards the temple garden, where the priestesses and novices were busily engaged in their springtime work.

'You made a choice,' she finally said. 'You chose your way, Triss. Your own destiny. Of your own free will. Now isn't the time for regrets.'

'Nenneke,' the sorceress lowered her eyes. 'I really can't say anything more than what I've said. Believe me and forgive me.'

'Who am I to forgive you? And what will you get from my forgiving you?'

'But I can see how you're glaring at me!' Triss exploded. 'You and your priestesses. I can see you asking me questions with your eyes. Like "What are you doing here, witch? Why aren't you where Iola, Eurneid, Katje and Myrrha are? And Jarre?"'

'You're exaggerating, Triss.'

The sorceress looked into the distance, at the forest, bluish beyond the temple wall, at the smoke of distant campfires.

Nenneke said nothing. She was also far away in her thoughts. Away where the fighting was raging and the blood was flowing. She thought about the girls she'd sent there.

313

'They talked me out of it all,' Triss said.

Nenneke said nothing.

'They talked me out of it all,' Triss repeated. 'So wise, so sensible, so logical . . . How not to believe them when they explained that there are more and less important matters, that one ought to give up the less important ones without a second thought, sacrifice them for the important ones without a trace of regret. That there's no point saving people you know and love, because they're individuals, and the fate of individuals is meaningless against the fate of the world. That there's no point fighting in the defence of virtue, honour and ideals, because they are empty notions. That the real battlefield for the fate of the world is somewhere else completely, that the fight will take place somewhere else. And I feel robbed. Robbed of the chance to commit acts of insanity. I can't insanely rush to help Ciri, I can't run and save Geralt and Yennefer like a madwoman. But that's not all, in the war being waged, in the war to which you sent your girls . . . In the war to which Jarre fled, I'm even refused the chance to stand on the Hill. To stand on the Hill once more. This time with the awareness of a truly conscious and correct decision.'

'Everybody has their own decision and their own Hill, Triss,' said the high priestess softly. 'Everybody. You can't run away from yours either.'

*

There was a commotion in the entrance to the tent. Another casualty was being carried in, accompanied by several knights. One, in full plate armour, was shouting, giving orders and urging the carriers on.

'Move, stretcher-bearers! Quicker! Put him here, here! Hey, you, medic!'

'I'm busy.' Rusty didn't even look up. 'Please put the wounded man on a stretcher. I'll see to him when I finish.'

'You'll see to him immediately, stupid leech! For it is none other than the Most Honourable Count of Garramone!'

'This hospital—' Rusty raised his voice, angry, because the broken arrowhead stuck in the casualty's guts had once again

314

slipped out of his forceps '—this hospital has very little in common with democracy. They mainly bring in knights and upward. Barons, counts, marquises, and various others of that ilk. Somehow few care about wounded men of humbler birth. But there is some kind of equality here, nonetheless. That is, on my table.'

'Eh? You what?'

'It doesn't matter—' Rusty once again stuck a cannula and pair of forceps into the wound '—if this one here, from whose guts I'm removing bits of iron, is a peasant, a member of the minor gentry, old nobility or aristocracy. He's lying on my table. And to me, as I hum to myself, a duke's worth a jester. Before God we are all equally wise – and equally foolish.'

'You what?'

'Your count will have to wait his turn.'

'You confounded halfling!'

'Help me, Shani. Take the other forceps. Look out for that artery! Marti, just a little more magic, if you would, we have serious haemorrhaging here.'

The knight took a step forward, teeth and armour grating.

'I'll have you hanged!' he roared. 'I'll order you hanged, you unhuman!'

'Silence, Papebrock,' the wounded count said with difficulty, biting his lips. 'Silence. Leave me and get back to the fighting—'

'No, my lord! Never!'

'That was an order.'

A thudding and clanging of iron, the snorting of horses and wild cries reached their ears from behind the tent flap. The wounded in the field hospital moaned in various keys.

'Please look.' Rusty raised his forceps, showing the splintered arrowhead he had finally extracted. 'A craftsman made this trinket, supporting a large family thanks to its manufacture, furthermore contributing to the growth of small craftwork, and thus also to general prosperity and universal happiness. And the way this ornament clings to human guts is surely protected by a patent. Long live progress.'

He casually threw the bloody blade into the bin, and glanced at the casualty, who had fainted during the operation.

'Sew him up and take him away,' he nodded. 'If he's lucky, he'll survive. Bring me the next in the queue. The one with the gashed head.'

'That one,' Marti Sodergren said calmly, 'just gave up his place. A moment ago.' Rusty sucked in and exhaled, moved away from the table without unnecessary comments and stood over the wounded count. Rusty's hands were bloody, and his apron splashed with blood like a butcher. Daniel Etcheverry, the Count of Garramone, paled even more.

'Well,' panted Rusty. 'It's your turn, Your Grace. Put him on the table. What do we have here? Ha, nothing remains of that joint that could be saved. It's porridge! It's pulp! What do you whack each other with, Count, that you smash each other's bones like that? Well, it'll hurt a bit, Your Grace. It'll hurt a bit. But please don't worry. It'll be just like it is in a battle. Tourniquet. Knife! We're going to amputate, Your Grace!'

Daniel Etcheverry, the Count of Garramone, who had put a brave face on it until then, howled like a wolf. Before he clenched his jaws from the pain, Shani quickly slipped a peg of linden wood between his teeth.

*

'Your Royal Highness! Lord Constable!'

'Talk, lad.'

'The Volunteer Regiment and the Free Company are holding the defile near Golden Pond . . . The dwarves and condottieri are holding fast, although they're awfully bloodied . . . They say Adieu Pangratt's dead, Frontino's dead, Julia Abatemarco's dead . . . All of them, all dead! The Dorian Company, which came to relieve them, is slaughtered . . .'

'Reserves, my lord constable,' Foltest said quietly, but clearly. 'If you want to know my opinion, it's time to send in the reserves. Have Bronibor throw his infantry at the Black Cloaks! Now! Forthwith! Otherwise they'll dismember our lines, and that means the end.'

Jan Natalis didn't answer, now observing the next liaison officer rushing towards them from a distance on a horse spraying flecks of foam.

316

'Get your breath back, lad. Get your breath back and speak concisely!'

'They've breached . . . the front . . . the elves of the Vrihedd Brigade. Graf de Ruyter informs Your Graces that . . .'

'What does he inform us? Talk!'

'That it's time to save your lives.'

Jan Natalis raised his eyes heavenwards.

'Blenckert,' he said hollowly. 'May Blenckert come now. Or may the night come.'

*

The ground around the tent trembled beneath hooves, and the tent walls, it seemed, billowed from the intensity of the cries and the neighing of horses. A soldier rushed into the tent, followed close behind by two orderlies.

'People, flee!' the soldier bellowed. 'Save yourselves! Nilfgaard is vanquishing our army! Destruction! Destruction! Defeat!'

'Clamp!' Rusty withdrew his face before the stream of blood, a potent and vivid fountain squirting from an artery. 'Clamp! And a compress! Clamp, Shani! Marti, do something, if you would, about that bleeding . . .'

Someone howled like an animal right beside the tent, briefly, stopping abruptly. A horse squealed, something hit the ground with a clank and a thud. A crossbow bolt punctured the canvas with a crack, hissed and flew out the other side, fortunately too high to threaten the wounded men lying on stretchers.

'Nilfgaaaaaard!' the soldier shouted again, in a high, trembling voice. 'Gentlemen medics! Can't you hear what I'm saying? Nilfgaard has breached the royal line, they're coming and murdering! Fleeeee!'

Rusty took a needle from Marti Sodergren, and put in the first suture. The man being operated on hadn't moved for a long time. But his heart was beating. Visibly.

'I don't want to diiiieee!' yelled one of the conscious wounded. The soldier cursed, dashed for the exit, suddenly yelled, crashed backwards, splashing blood, and tumbled onto the dirt floor. Iola, kneeling by the stretchers, leaped to her feet, and stepped back.

It suddenly went quiet.

Not good, thought Rusty, seeing who was entering the tent. Elves. Silver lightning bolts. The Vrihedd Brigade. The notorious Vrihedd Brigade.

'A field hospital,' the first of the elves stated. He was tall, with a pretty, oval, expressive face with large, cornflower blue eyes. 'Treating the wounded?'

No one said anything. Rusty felt his hands begin to tremble. He quickly handed the needle to Marti. He saw Shani's forehead and the bridge of her nose pale.

'So what's this about?' said the elf, drawling his words menacingly. 'Why do we wound our foes over there on the battlefield? Over there in the fighting we inflict wounds so men will die from them. And you treat them. I observe an absolute lack of logic here. And a conflict of interests.'

He stooped over and thrust his sword almost without a swing into the chest of the casualty on the stretcher nearest the entrance. Another elf pinned another wounded man with a half-pike. A third casualty, conscious, tried hard to stop a thrust with his left arm and the heavily bandaged stump of his right.

Shani screamed. Shrilly, piercingly. Drowning out the heavy, inhuman groaning of the mutilated man being murdered. Iola, throwing herself onto a stretcher, covered the next casualty with her body. Her face blanched like the linen of a bandage and her mouth began to twitch involuntarily. The elf squinted his eyes.

'*Va vort, beanna!*' he barked. 'Or I'll run you through along with this Dh'oine!'

'Get out of here!' Rusty was beside Iola in three bounds, shielding her. 'Get out of my tent, you murderer. Get back there to the battlefield. Your place is there. Among the other murderers. Murder each other there, if that is your will. But get out of here!'

The elf looked down at the pot-bellied halfling shaking with fear, the top of whose curly mop reached a little above his waist.

'*Bloede Pherian*,' he hissed. 'Toady to humans! Get out of my way!'

'Not a chance.' The halfling's teeth were chattering, but his words were distinct.

The second elf leaped forward and pushed the surgeon with the shaft of his half-pike. Rusty fell to his knees. The tall elf wrenched Iola away from the wounded man with a brutal tug and raised his sword.

And froze, seeing, on the rolled up cloak under the injured man's head, the silver flames of the Deithwen Division. And the insignia of a colonel.

'*Yaevinn!*' screamed an elf woman with dark hair woven into a plait, rushing into the tent. '*Caemm, veloe! Ess'evgyriad a'Dh'oine a'en va! Ess' tedd!*'

The tall elf looked at the wounded colonel for a moment, then at the eyes of the surgeon, which were watering in terror. Then he turned on his heel and left.

Once again the tramping of hooves, yelling and the clanging of iron could be heard from beyond the wall of the tent.

'Have at the Black Cloaks! Murder!' a thousand voices yelled. Someone howled like an animal, and the howling transformed into macabre wheezing.

Rusty tried to stand up, but his legs failed him. His arms weren't much use either.

Iola, trembling with powerful spasms of suppressed tears, curled up by the stretcher of the wounded Nilfgaardian. In a foetal position.

Shani was crying, not trying to hide her tears. But still holding the retractors. Marti was calmly putting in sutures, only her mouth moving in a kind of mute, silent monologue.

Rusty, still unable to stand up, sat back down. He met the gaze of the orderly, huddled and squeezed into a corner of the tent.

'Give me a swig of hooch,' said Rusty with effort. 'Just don't say you don't have any. I know you rascals. You always do.'

*

General Blenheim Blenckert stood up in his stirrups, stuck his neck out like a crane and listened to the sounds of the battle.

'Draw out the array,' he ordered his commanders. 'And we'll go at a trot at once behind that hill. From what the scouts say it appears that we'll come out straight on the Black Cloaks' right wing.'

'And we'll give them what for!' one of the lieutenants, a whippersnapper with a silky and very spare little moustache, shouted shrilly. Blenckert looked askance at him.

'A detachment with a standard at the head,' he ordered, drawing his sword. 'And in the charge cry "Redania!" Cry it at the top of your lungs! May Foltest and Natalis' boys know that the relief is coming.'

*

Graf Kobus de Ruyter had fought in various battles, for forty years, since he was sixteen. Furthermore, he was an eighth-generation soldier, without doubt he had something in his genes. Something that meant that the roar and hubbub of battle, for everyone else simply a horrifying hullabaloo that drowned out everything else, was like a symphony, like a concert for a full orchestra, to Kobus de Ruyter. De Ruyter at once heard other notes, chords and tones.

'Hurraaah, boys!' he roared, brandishing his baton. 'Redania! Redania is coming! The eagles! The eagles!'

From the north, from behind the hills, rolling towards the battle, came a mass of cavalry, over which an amaranth pennant and a great gonfalon with a silver Redanian eagle fluttered.

'Relief!' yelled de Ruyter. 'The relief's coming! Hurraaah! Death to the Black Cloaks!'

The eighth-generation soldier immediately noticed that the Nilfgaardian wing was wheeling around, trying to turn towards the charging relief with a disciplined, tight front. He knew he could not allow them to do that.

'Follow me!' he roared, wresting the standard from the standard-bearer's hands. 'Follow me! Tretogorians, follow me!'

They struck. They struck suicidally, dreadfully. But effectively. The Nilfgaardians of the Venendal Division fell into confusion and then the Redanian companies drove into them. A great shout rose into the sky.

Kobus de Ruyter didn't see or hear it. A stray bolt from a crossbow had struck him straight in the temple. The nobleman sagged in the saddle and fell from his horse, the standard covering him like a shroud.

Eight generations of de Ruyters who had fallen fighting and were following the battle from the beyond nodded in acknowledgement.

*

'It could be said, captain, that the Nordlings were saved by a miracle that day. Or a coincidence that no one could have predicted. Admittedly Restif de Montholon writes in his book that Marshal Coehoorn made a mistake in his assessment of the enemy's strength and plans. That he took too great a risk, splitting up the Centre Army Group and setting off with a cavalry troop. That he took on a risky battle, not having at least a threefold advantage. And that he neglected reconnaissance, he didn't uncover the Redanian Army arriving with reinforcements.'

'Cadet Puttkammer! Mr de Montholon's "work", which is of doubtful quality, is not included in this school's curriculum. And His Imperial Highness deigned to express himself extremely critically about the book. Thus you will not quote it here, Cadet. Indeed, it astonishes me. Until now your answers have been very good, positively excellent, and suddenly you begin to discourse about miracles and coincidences, while finally you take the liberty of criticising the leadership abilities of Menno Coehoorn, one of the greatest leaders the Empire has produced. Cadet Puttkammer – and all the rest of you cadets – if you're seriously thinking about passing the final exam, you'll listen and remember: at the Battle of Brenna no miracles or accidents were at work, but a conspiracy! Hostile saboteur forces, subversive elements, foul rabble-rousers, cosmopolites, political bankrupts, traitors and turncoats. A canker that was later burned out with white-hot iron. But before it came to that, those base traitors tangled up their own nation in spider webs and wove a snare of scheming! It was they who inveigled and betrayed Marshal Coehoorn then, deceived him and misled him! It was they; scoundrels without faith or honour . . .'

*

'Whoresons,' repeated Menno Coehoorn, without taking the telescope from his eye. 'Common whoresons. But I'll find you, just wait, I'll teach you what reconnaissance means. De Wyngalt! You will personally find the officer who was on the patrol beyond the hills to the north. Have all of them, the entire patrol, hanged.'

'Yes, sir.' Ouder de Wyngalt, the marshal's *aide-de-camp*, clicked his heels together. He could not know that right then Lamarr Flaut, the officer from the patrol, was dying, trampled by horses of the secret reserves of the Nordlings who were attacking the flanks, the reserves he hadn't uncovered. Neither could de Wyngalt know that he only had two hours of life left.

'How many of them are there, Mr Trahe?' Coehoorn still didn't take the telescope from his eye. 'In your opinion?

'At least ten thousand,' replied the commander of the 7th Daerlanian dryly. 'Mainly Redania, but I also see the chevron of Aedirn . . . The unicorn is also there, so we also have Kaedwen . . . With a detachment of at least a company . . .'

*

The company was galloping, sand and grit flew from beneath hooves.

'Forward, you Duns!' roared centurion Halfpot, drunk as usual. 'Attack, kill! Kaedweeen! Kaedweeeen!'

Dammit, but I'm dying for a piss, thought Zyvik. *I should have gone before the battle . . .*

Now there might not be a chance.

'Forward, you Duns!'

Always the Duns. Wherever things are going wrong, the Duns. Who did they send as an expeditionary force to Temeria? The Duns. Always the Dun Banner. I need a piss.

They arrived. Zyvik yelled, turned around in the saddle and slashed backhand, destroying the spaulder and shoulder of a horseman in a black cloak with an eight-pointed silver star.

'The Duns! Kaedweeen! Fight, kill!'

The Dun Banner Standard struck Nilfgaard with a thud, a clatter and a clank, amidst the roars of soldiers and the squeals of horses.

*

'De Mellis-Stoke and Braibant will cope with that relief,' said Elan Trahe, the commander of the 7th Daerlanian Brigade calmly. 'The forces are balanced, nothing has gone wrong yet. Tyrconnel's division is counterbalancing the left wing, Magne and Venendal are managing on the right. And we . . . We can tip the scale, sir—'

'By striking the line, going in after the elves,' Menno Coehoorn understood at once. 'By striking at the rear lines, sowing panic. That's it! That's what we shall do, by the Great Sun! To your companies, gentlemen! Nauzicaa and the 7th, your time has come!'

'Long live the Emperor!' yelled Kees van Lo.

'Lord de Wyngalt.' The marshal turned around. 'Please muster the adjutants and the guard troop. Enough inactivity! We're going to charge with the 7th Daerlanian.'

Ouder de Wyngalt paled slightly, but immediately regained control.

'Long live the Emperor!' he cried, and there was almost no tremor in his voice.

*

Rusty cut, and the wounded man wailed and scratched the table. Iola, bravely fighting giddiness, was taking care of the tourniquets and clamps. Shani's raised voice could be heard from the entrance to the tent.

'Where? Are you insane? The living are waiting to be saved here, and you're marching in with corpses?'

'But this is Baron Anzelm Aubry himself, Madam Medic! The company commander!'

'It *was* the company commander! Now it's a corpse. You only managed to bring him in one piece because his armour is watertight! Take him away. This is a field hospital, not a mortuary!'

'But Madam Medic—'

'Don't block the entrance! Look there, they're carrying one that's still breathing. Or at least he looks like he's still breathing. Because it might just be wind.'

Rusty snorted, but immediately afterwards raised an eyebrow.

'Shani! Come here at once!

'Remember, you chit,' he said through clenched teeth, bending over the mutilated leg, 'that a surgeon can only take the liberty of cynicism after ten years of experience. Will you remember that?'

'Yes, Mr Rusty.'

'Take the raspatory and strip off the periosteum ... Blast, it would be worth anaesthetising him a little more ... Where's Marti?'

'She's puking outside the tent,' said Shani without a trace of cynicism. 'Puking her guts out.'

'Sorcerers!' Rusty took hold of a saw. 'Instead of thinking up numerous awful and powerful spells they would be better thinking up one. One that would enable them to cast minor spells, for example anaesthetising ones, without difficulty. And without puking.'

The saw grated and crunched on bone. The wounded man moaned.

'Tighten the tourniquet, Iola!'

The bone finally gave way. Rusty tidied it up with a small chisel and wiped his forehead.

'Blood vessels and nerves,' he said mechanically and needlessly, because before he had finished the sentence the girls were already putting in the sutures. He removed the severed leg from the table and threw it down onto a pile of other severed limbs. The wounded man hadn't roared or moaned for some time.

'Fainted or dead?'

'Fainted, Mr Rusty.'

'Good. Sew up the stump, Shani. Bring on the next one! Iola, go and find out if Marti has puked everything up.'

'I wonder,' said Iola very quietly, without raising her head, 'how many years of experience you have, Mr Rusty. A hundred?'

*

After a quarter of an hour of strenuous marching and choking on dust, the yells of the centurions and decurions ceased and the Vizimian regiments spread out in a line. Jarre, gasping and gulping in air through his mouth like a fish, saw Voivode Bronibor strutting before the front on his beautiful armoured steed. The voivode himself was also in full plate armour. His armour was enamelled in blue stripes, making Bronibor look like a great steel-plated mackerel.

'How are you, you dolts?'

The rows of pikemen answered with a rumbling growl like distant thunder.

'You're issuing farting sounds,' the voivode noted, reining his armoured horse around and directing him to walk before the front. 'That means you're feeling good. When you're feeling bad, you don't fart in hushed tones, but you wail and howl like the damned. It's clear from your expressions that you're spoiling for a fight, that you're dreaming of battle, that you can't wait to get your hands on the Nilfgaardians! Right, you Vizimian brigands? Then I have good news for you! Your dream will come true in a short while. In a very short while.'

The pikemen muttered again. Bronibor, after riding to the end of the line, turned around, and spoke on, rapping his mace against the ornamented pommel of his saddle.

'You stuffed yourselves with dust, infantry, marching behind the armoured troops. Up until now, instead of glory and spoils, you've been sniffing horses' farts. And even today, when a great battle is upon us, you almost didn't make it to the field. But you managed it, so I congratulate you with all my heart. Here, outside this village, whose name I've forgotten, you will finally show how much worth you have as an army. That cloud you see on the battlefield is the Nilfgaardian horse, which means to crush our army with a flanking strike, shove us and drown us in the bogs of this little river, whose name I have also forgotten. The honour of defending the breach that has arisen in our ranks has fallen to you, celebrated Vizimian pikemen, by the grace of King Foltest and Constable Natalis. You will close that breach, so to speak, with your breasts, you will stop the Nilfgaardian charge. You're rejoicing, comrades, what? You're bursting with pride, eh?'

Jarre, squeezing his pikestaff, looked around. There was nothing to indicate that the soldiers were rejoicing at the prospect of the imminent battle, and if they were bursting with pride by virtue of the honour of closing the breach, they were skilfully disguising it. Melfi, standing on the boy's right, was mumbling a prayer under his breath. On his left, Deuslax, a hardened professional soldier, sniffed, swore and coughed nervously.

Bronibor reined his horse around and sat up straight in the saddle.

'I can't hear you!' he roared. 'I asked if you're bursting with fucking pride?'

This time the pikemen, seeing no alternative, roared with one, great voice that they were. Jarre also roared. If everyone was he might as well too.

'Good!' The voivode reined back his horse before the front. 'And now stand in an orderly array! Centurions, what are you waiting for, for fuck's sake? Form a square! The first rank kneels, the second stands! Ground your pikes! Not that end, ass! Yes, yes, I'm talking to you, you horrible little man! Higher, hold your pikestaffs higher, you wretches! Close ranks, close up, close ranks, shoulder to shoulder! Well, now you look impressive! Almost like an army!'

Jarre found himself in the second rank. He pushed the butt of his pike into the ground and gripped the pikestaff in his hands, sweaty from fear. Melfi was muttering indistinctly, repeating various words over and over, mainly concerning the private lives of the Nilfgaardians, dogs, bitches, kings, constables, voivodes and all their mothers.

The cloud in the battlefield grew.

'Don't fart there, don't chatter your teeth!' roared Bronibor. 'Thoughts of frightening the Nilfgaardian horses with those noises are misguided! Let no man deceive himself! What is heading for you are the Nauzicaa and 7th Daerlanian Brigades; splendid, valiant, superbly trained soldiers! They can't be scared! They can't be defeated! They have to be killed! Hold those pikes higher!'

From a distance the still soft but growing thud of hooves could now be heard. The ground began to shudder. Blades began to glint like sparks in the cloud of dust.

'It's your good fucking fortune, Vizimians,' the voivode roared once more. 'That the standard infantry pike of the new, modernised model is twenty-one feet long! And a Nilfgaardian sword is three-and-a-half feet long. Can you reckon? Know that they can too. But they are counting on your not holding out, that your true nature will emerge, that it will be confirmed and revealed that you are shitheads, cowards and mangy sheep shaggers. The Black

Cloaks are counting on you to throw down your poles and start running, and they will pursue you across the battlefield and hack you on the backs, heads and necks, hack you comfortably and with no difficulty. Remember, you little shits, that although fear lends the heels extraordinary speed, you won't outrun cavalrymen. Whoever wants to live, whoever wants glory and spoils, must stand! Stand firm! Stand like a wall! And close ranks!'

Jarre looked back. The crossbowmen standing behind the line of pikemen were already winding their cranks, and the interior of the square was bristling with the points of gisarmes, ranseurs, halberds, glaives, partizans, scythes and pitchforks. The ground trembled more and more distinctly and powerfully, and it was already possible to discern the shapes of horsemen in the black wall of cavalry hurtling towards them.

'Mamma, dear mother,' repeated Melfi through trembling lips. 'Mamma, dear mother—'

'—fucker,' mumbled Deuslax.

The hoof beats intensified. Jarre wanted to lick his lips, but he couldn't. His tongue had gone stiff. His tongue stopped behaving normally, it had stiffened strangely and was as dry as a bone. The hoof beats intensified.

'Close ranks!' roared Bronibor, drawing his sword. 'Feel your comrade's shoulder! Remember, none of you is fighting alone! And the only remedy for the fear you are feeling is the pike in your fist! Prepare to fight! Pikes aimed at the horses' chests! What are we going to do, Vizimian brigands? I'm asking!'

'Stand firm!' roared the pikemen with one voice. 'Stand like a wall! Close ranks!'

Jarre also roared. If everyone was he might as well too. Sand, grit and turf sprayed from beneath the hooves of the advancing wedge of cavalry. The charging horsemen yelled like demons, brandishing their weapons. Jarre leaned onto his pike, buried his head in his shoulders and shut his eyes.

*

Jarre shooed away a wasp circling above his inkwell with a violent movement of his stump, without interrupting his writing.

Marshal Coehoorn came to nothing. His flanking troop was stopped by the heroic Vizimian infantry under Voivode Bronibor, paying in blood for his heroism. And at the moment the Vizimians resisted, Nilfgaard fell into confusion on the left wing – some of them began to take flight, others to pull together and defend themselves in groups, surrounded on all sides. Soon after the same thing happened on the right wing, where the doggedness of the dwarves and condottieri finally overcame Nilfgaard's assault. A single great cry of triumph went up along the entire front, and a new spirit entered the royal knights. And the spirit fell in the Nilfgaardians, their hands weakened, and our men began to shell them like peas so loudly it echoed.

And Field Marshal Menno Coehoorn understood that the battle was lost, saw the brigades perishing and falling into confusion around him.

And then his officers and knights ran to him, giving him a fresh horse, calling for him to flee and save his own life. But a fearless heart beat in the breast of the Nilfgaardian field marshal. 'That will not do,' he called, pushing away the reins held out towards him. 'It will not do for me to flee like a coward from the field on which so many good men under my command have fallen for the emperor.' And the doughty Menno Coehoorn added . . .

*

'Besides, now there's nowhere to fuck off to,' Menno Coehoorn added calmly and soberly, looking around the battlefield. 'They're surrounding us on all sides.'

'Give me your cloak and helmet, sir.' Captain Sievers wiped blood and sweat from his face. 'Take mine, sir! Dismount your steed, and take mine . . . Don't protest! You must live, sir! You're indispensable to the empire, irreplaceable . . . We Daerlanians will strike the Nordlings, we'll draw them to us, you meanwhile try to break through down there, below the fishpond . . .'

'You won't get out of that alive,' muttered Coehoorn, taking the reins being offered to him.

'It's an honour.' Sievers straightened up in the saddle. 'I'm a soldier! Of the 7th Daerlanians! To me! Have faith! To me!'

'Good luck,' mumbled Coehoorn throwing over his back a

Daerlanian cloak with a black scorpion on the shoulder. 'Sievers?'

'Yes, sir, marshal, sir?'

'Nothing. Good luck, lad.'

'And may luck be on your side, sir. To horse, have faith!'

Coehoorn watched them ride off. For a long while. Until the moment Sievers' small group rode with a bang, a yell and a thud into the condottieri. Into a troop considerably outnumbering them, to whose aid, indeed, other troops hurried at once. The Daerlanians' black cloaks vanished among the greyness of the condottieri; all was lost in the dust.

The nervous coughing of de Wyngalt and the adjutants brought Coehoorn to his senses. The marshal adjusted the stirrup leathers and flaps. He brought the restless steed under control.

'To horse!' he commanded.

At first things went well for them. In the mouth of the valley leading to the riverlet a dwindling troop of survivors of the Nauzicaa Brigade was doggedly defending itself, forced into a circle bristling with blades, onto which the Nordlings had concentrated all their momentum and force, making a breach in the ring. Naturally, they didn't get away totally unscathed – they had to hack their way through a row of light volunteer horse, probably Bruggean, judging by their insignia. The skirmish was very short, but furiously fierce. Coehoorn had already lost and discarded all remains and appearances of lofty heroism and now just wanted to survive. Not even looking back at his escort trading vicious blows with the Bruggeans, he rushed towards the stream with his adjutants, pressing himself to and hugging the horse's neck.

The way was clear; beyond the little river, beyond the crooked willows, a barren plain spread out, on which no enemy troops could be seen. Ouder de Wyngalt, galloping beside Coehoorn, also saw it and yelled triumphantly.

Prematurely.

A meadow covered in bright-green knotgrass separated them from the sluggish, murky little river. When they charged into it at full gallop the horses suddenly plunged up to their bellies in the bog.

The marshal flew over his steed's head and fell headfirst into the bog. All around, horses were neighing and kicking, and men covered in mud and green duckweed were yelling. Menno suddenly heard another sound amidst this pandemonium. A sound that meant death.

The hiss of fletchings.

He dashed for the current of the small river, wading up to his hips in the thick marsh. An adjutant forcing his way through beside him suddenly tumbled face first into the mud, and the marshal saw a bolt stuck into his back up to the fletchings. At that same moment he felt a terrible blow to the head. He staggered but didn't fall, stuck in the mud and swamp. He wanted to scream, but only managed to splutter. *I'm alive*, he thought, trying to wriggle out of the clutch of the sticky slime. A horse struggling out of the marsh had kicked him in the helmet, and the deeply dented metal had shattered his cheek, knocked out some teeth and cut his tongue . . . *I'm bleeding . . . I'm swallowing blood . . . But I'm alive . . .*

Once again the slap of bowstrings, the hiss of fletchings, the thud and crack of arrowheads penetrating armour, yells, the neighing of horses, squelching, and blood splashing. The marshal looked back and saw bowmen on the bank; small, stocky, pot-bellied shapes in mail shirts, basinets and pointed chichaks. *Dwarves*, he thought.

The slap of bowstrings, the whistle of bolts. The squeal of horses threshing around. The yelling of men choking on water and mud.

Ouder de Wyngalt, turning towards the marksmen, cried in a high, squeaky voice that he was surrendering, asked for mercy and compassion, promised a ransom and begged for his life. Aware that no one understood his words, he raised his sword, held by the blade, above his head. He held the weapon out towards the dwarves in the international, outright cosmopolitan gesture of surrender. He wasn't understood, or was misunderstood, for two bolts slammed into his chest with such force that the impact hurled him up out of the bog.

Coehoorn tore the dented helmet from his head. He knew the Common Speech of the Nordlings quite well.

'I'm Marfal Coeoon . . .' he mumbled, spitting blood. 'Marfal Coeoon . . . I furrender . . . Merfy . . . Merfy . . .'

'What's he saying, Zoltan?' one of the crossbowmen asked in surprise.

'Bugger him and his chattering! Do you see the embroidery on

330

his cloak, Munro?'

'A silver scorpion! Haaaa! Wallop the whoreson, boys! For Caleb Stratton!'

'For Caleb Stratton!'

Bowstrings clanged. One bolt hit Coehoorn straight in the chest, the second in the hip and the third in the collar bone. The Nilfgaardian field marshal fell over backwards in the watery mush, the knotgrass and swamp yielding under his weight. *Who the bloody hell could Caleb Stratton be?* he managed to think, *I've never heard of any Caleb . . .*

The murky, viscous, muddied and bloodied water of the River Chotla closed over his head and gushed into his lungs.

*

She went outside the tent to get some fresh air. And then she saw him, sitting beside the blacksmith's bench.

'Jarre!'

He raised his eyes towards her. There was emptiness in those eyes.

'Iola?' he asked, moving his swollen lips with difficulty. 'How come you're—'

'What a question!' she interrupted him at once. 'You'd better tell me how you've ended up here!'

'We've brought our commander . . . Voivode Bronibor . . . He's wounded—'

'You're also wounded. Show me that hand. O goddess! But you'll bleed to death, lad!'

Jarre looked at her, and Iola suddenly began to doubt whether he could see her.

'It's a battle,' said the boy, teeth chattering slightly. 'You must stand like a wall . . . Steady in the line. The lightly wounded are to carry the heavily wounded to the field hospital. It's an order.'

'Show me your hand.'

Jarre howled briefly, his clenching teeth snapping in a wild staccato. Iola frowned.

'Oh my, it looks dreadful . . . Oh, dear, Jarre, Jarre . . . You'll see, Mother Nenneke will be angry . . . Come with me.'

She watched him blanch when he saw it. When he smelled the stench hanging beneath the roof of the tent. He staggered. She held him up. She saw him looking at the bloodied table. At the man lying there. At the surgeon, a small halfling, who suddenly leaped up, stamped his feet, cursed foully and threw a scalpel on the ground.

'Dammit! Fuck it! Why? Why is it like this? Why does it have to be like this?'

No one replied to the question.

'Who was it?'

'Voivode Bronibor,' explained Jarre in a feeble voice, looking straight ahead with his empty gaze. 'Our commander . . . We stood firm in the line. It was an order. Like a wall. And they killed Melfi . . .'

'Mr Rusty,' Iola asked. 'This boy's a friend of mine . . . He's wounded . . .'

'He's on his feet,' the surgeon assessed coldly. 'And here there's a dying man waiting for a trepanation. There's no room here for any sentimental connections . . .'

At that moment Jarre – with excellent timing – fainted dramatically and fell down on the dirt floor. The halfling snorted.

'Oh, very well, on the table with him,' he commanded. 'Oho, a nicely smashed arm. I wonder what's holding it on. His sleeve, I think? Tourniquet, Iola! Tightly! And don't you dare cry! Shani, give me a saw.'

The saw dug into the bone above the crushed elbow joint with a hideous crunching. Jarre came to and bellowed. Horribly, but briefly. For when the bone gave way he immediately fainted again.

*

And thus the might of Nilfgaard was reduced to dust on the Brenna battlefields, and an end was put to the march of the Empire northwards. Either by being killed or taken captive the Empire lost four and forty thousand men at the Battle of Brenna. The flower of the knighthood and the élite cavalry fell. Leaders of the stature of Menno Coehoorn, Braibant, de Mellis-Stoke, van Lo, Tyrconnel, Eggebracht and others whose names have not survived in our archives, fell, were taken prisoner or disappeared without trace.

Thus did Brenna become the beginning of the end. But it behoves me to write that that battle was but a small stone in the building, and superficial would have been its importance had the fruits of the victory not been wisely taken advantage of. It behoves us to recall that instead of resting on his laurels and bursting with pride, and awaiting honours and homage, Jan Natalis headed south almost without stopping. The cavalry troop under Adam Pangratt and Julia Abatemarco destroyed two divisions of the Third Army that had brought belated relief to Menno Coehoorn, routing them such that nec nuntius cladis. At news of this, the rest of the Centre Army Group took miserable flight and fled in haste to the far side of the Yaruga, and since Foltest and Natalis were on their heels, the imperial forces lost entire convoys and all their siege engines with which, in their hubris, they had meant to capture Vizima, Gors Velen and Novigrad.

And like an avalanche rolling down from the mountains, becoming covered in more and more snow and becoming greater, so also Brenna caused more and more severe results for Nilfgaard. Hard times came for the Verden Army under Duke de Wett, whom the corsairs from Skellige and King Ethain of Cidaris sorely vexed in a guerrilla war. When, meanwhile, de Wett learned about Brenna, when news reached him that King Foltest and Jan Natalis were marching briskly to him, he immediately ordered the trumpeting of the retreat and fled to Cintra, strewing the escape route with corpses, because at the news of the Nilfgaardian defeats an insurrection in Verden flared up anew. Only in the undefeated strongholds of Nastróg, Rozróg and Bodróg did powerful garrisons remain, for which reason only after the Peace of Cintra did they leave honourably and with their standards intact.

Whereas in Aedirn, the tidings about Brenna led to the feuding kings Demavend and Henselt shaking each other's right hands and taking arms against Nilfgaard together. The East Army Group, which under the command of Duke Ardal aep Dahy marched towards the Pontar valley, did not manage to challenge the two allied kings. Strengthened by reinforcements from Redania and Queen Meve's guerrillas, who had cruelly plundered Nilfgaard, Demavend and Henselt drove Ardal aep Dahy all the way to Aldersberg. Duke Ardal wanted to give battle, but by a strange twist of fate he suddenly fell ill, having eaten something. He came down with the colic and diarrhoea miserere, and

333

thus in two days he died in great pain. And Demavend and Henselt, without delay, attacked the Nilfgaardians, also there at Aldersberg, evidently for the sake of historical justice, and they routed them in a decisive battle, though Nilfgaard still had a significant numerical advantage. Thus do spirit and artistry usually triumph over dull and brutal force.

It behoves me to write about one more thing: what exactly happened to Menno Coehoorn himself at the Battle of Brenna no one knows. Some say: he fell and his body, unrecognised, was buried in a common grave. Others say: he escaped with his life, but fearing imperial wrath did not return to Nilfgaard, but hid in Brokilon among the dryads, and there became a hermit, letting his beard grow down to the ground. And there shortly after expired amidst his worries.

A story circulates among simple folk that the marshal returned at night to the Brenna battlefield and walked among the burial mounds, wailing 'Give me back my legions!', until finally he hanged himself on an aspen spike on the hill, called Gibbet Hill because of that. And at night one can happen upon the ghost of the celebrated marshal among other apparitions that commonly haunt the battlefield.

'Grandfather Jarre! Grandfather Jarre!'

Jarre raised his head from his papers and adjusted his spectacles, which were slipping down his sweaty nose.

'Grandfather Jarre!' his youngest granddaughter shouted in the upper register. She was a determined and bright six-year-old, who, thank the Gods, had taken more after her mother, Jarre's daughter, than his lethargic son-in-law.

'Grandfather Jarre! Grandmother Lucienne told me to tell you that that's enough for today of that layabout scribbling and that tea's on the table!'

Jarre meticulously assembled the written sheets and corked the inkwell. Pain throbbed in the stump of his arm. *The weather's changing*, he thought. *There'll be rain.*

'Grandfather Jaaaaarre!'

'I'm coming, Ciri. I'm coming.'

*

It was already well after midnight before they had dealt with the

334

last casualties. They carried out the final operations by artificial light – first from an ordinary lamp and later using magic. Marti Sodergren recovered after the crisis she had undergone and, although as pale as death, stiff and as unnatural in her movements as a golem, used her magic competently and effectively.

The night was black when they exited the tent, and all four of them sat down, leaning against the canvas.

The plain was full of fires. Various fires – the stationary fires of camps and the moving flames of torches. The night resounded with distant song, chanting, shouts and cheers.

The night around them was also alive with the intermittent cries and groans of the wounded. The pleading and sighs of the dying. They didn't hear it. They had become accustomed to the sounds of suffering and dying, and those sounds were ordinary, natural to them, as integrated into the night as the croaking of frogs in the marshes by the River Chotla or the singing of cicadas in the acacia trees by Golden Pond.

Marti Sodergren sat in lyrical silence resting on the halfling's shoulder. Iola and Shani, indifferent, cuddling one another, snorted from time to time with completely nonsensical laughter.

Before they sat down against the tent they had each drunk a cup of vodka, and Marti had treated all of them with her last spell: a cheering charm, typically used when extracting teeth. Rusty felt cheated by this treatment – the drink, combined with the magic, instead of relaxing him had stupefied him; instead of reducing his exhaustion had increased it. Instead of giving oblivion, brought back memories.

It looks, he thought, *as though the alcohol and magic have only acted as they were meant to on Iola and Shani.*

He turned around and in the moonlight saw sparkling, silvery tracks of tears on the girls' faces.

'I wonder,' he said, licking his numb, insensitive lips, 'who won this battle. Does anybody know?'

Marti turned her face towards him, but remained silent. The cicadas were singing among the acacias, willows and alders by Golden Pond, and the frogs croaked. The wounded moaned, begged and sighed. And died. Shani and Iola giggled through their tears.

Marti Sodergren died two weeks after the battle. She began meeting an officer of the Free Company of Condottieri. She treated the affair light-heartedly. Unlike the officer. When Marti, who liked change, began fraternising with a Temerian cavalry captain, the condottiero – mad with jealousy – stabbed her with a knife. He was hanged for it, but it was impossible to save the healer.

Rusty and Iola died a year after the battle, in Maribor, during the largest outbreak yet of an epidemic of viral haemorrhagic fever, a disease also called the Red Death or – from the name of the ship it was brought on – Catriona's Plague. All the physicians and most of the priests fled from Maribor then. Rusty and Iola remained, naturally. They treated the sick, because they were doctors. The fact that there was no cure for the Red Death was unimportant to them. They both became infected. He died in her arms, in the powerful, confidence-inspiring embrace of her large, ugly, peasant hands. She died four days later. Alone.

Shani died seventy-two years after the battle, as the celebrated and universally respected retired dean of the Department of Medicine at the University of Oxenfurt. Generations of future surgeons used to repeat her famous joke: 'Sew red to red, yellow to yellow, white to white. It's sure to be fine'.

Almost no one noticed how after delivering that witty anecdote the dean always wiped away a furtive tear.

Almost no one.

*

The frogs croaked and the cicadas sang among the willows by Golden Pond. Shani and Iola giggled through their tears.

'I wonder,' repeated Milo Vanderbeck, halfling, field surgeon, known as Rusty. 'I wonder who won?'

'Rusty,' Marti Sodergren said lyrically. 'Believe me, in your shoes it's the last thing I'd be worrying about.'

Some of the flames were tall and strong, burning brightly and vividly, while others were tiny, flickering and quavering, and their light diminished and died. At the very end was but one tiny flame, so weak it barely flickered and glimmered, now struggling to flare up, now almost going out entirely.

'Whose is the dying flame?' asked the Witcher.

'Yours,' Death replied.

Flourens Delannoy, *Fairy Tales and Stories*

CHAPTER NINE

The plateau, extending almost all the way to the distant mountain peaks, greyish-blue in the fog, was like an actual stone sea, here undulating in a hump or a ridge, there bristling with the sharp fangs of reefs. The impression was enhanced by shipwrecks. Dozens of wrecks. Of galleys, galeases, cogs, caravels, brigs, holks and longships. Some of them looked as though they had ended up there not long before, others were piles of barely recognisable planks and ribs, clearly having lain there for decades – if not centuries.

Some of the ships were lying keel up, others, turned over on their sides, looked as though they had been tossed up by devilish squalls and storms. Still others gave the impression they were sailing, making away, amidst that stone ocean. They stood even and straight, the chests of their figureheads proudly stuck out, their masts pointing to the zenith, the remains of sails, shrouds and stays fluttering. They even had their own ghostly crews – skeletons jammed between rotten planks and entangled in ropes, dead sailors, busy forever with endless navigation.

Flocks of black birds flew up, cawing, from the masts, yards, ropes and skeletons alarmed by the appearance of the rider, frightened by the clack of hooves. For a moment they flecked the sky, circled in a flock over the edge of the cliff, at the bottom of which lay a lake, as grey and smooth as quicksilver. On the edge could be seen a dark and gloomy stronghold, whose towers partly overlooked the graveyard of ships, and were partly suspended over the lake, with its bastions embedded in the vertical rock. Kelpie danced, snorted, and pricked up her ears, alarmed by the wrecks, the skeletons, at the whole landscape of death. At the cawing black birds, which had already returned, alighting again on the broken masts and crosstrees, on the shrouds and skulls. But if anyone ought to have been afraid there, it was the rider.

'Easy, Kelpie,' said Ciri in a changed voice. 'It's the end of the road. This is the right place and the right time.'

*

She found herself outside a gate, God knows how, and emerged like an apparition from between the wrecks. The guards at the foot of the gate noticed her first, alarmed by the cawing of rooks, and now shouted, gesticulating and pointing at her, calling others.

When she rode to the gatehouse, there was already a crush there. An excited hubbub. They were all staring at her. The few who knew her and had seen her before, like Boreas Mun and Dacre Silifant, and the considerably more numerous of them who had only heard about her: newly recruited soldiers from Skellen, mercenaries, and ordinary marauders from Ebbing and the surroundings, who were now looking in amazement at the ashen-haired girl with the scar on her face and the sword on her back. At the splendid black mare, holding her head high, and snorting, her horseshoes ringing on the flagstones of the courtyard.

The hubbub died down. It became very quiet. The mare trotted, lifting her legs like a ballerina, her horseshoes ringing like a hammer on an anvil. This went on for a long time before her way was finally barred by crossed gisarmes and ranseurs. Someone reached out a hesitant and frightened hand towards the bridle. The mare snorted.

'Take me to the lord of this castle,' the girl said confidently.

Boreas Mun, not knowing himself why he was doing it, held her stirrup steady and offered his hand. Others held the stamping and snorting mare.

'Do you recognise me, my lady?' Boreas asked softly. 'For we've already met.'

'Where?'

'On the ice.'

She looked him straight in the eye.

'I didn't look at your face then, sir,' she said unemotionally.

'You were the Lady of the Lake,' he nodded seriously. 'Why have you come here, girl? What for?'

'For Yennefer. And to claim my destiny.'

340

'Claim your death, more like,' he whispered. 'This is Stygga Castle. In your place I'd flee as far from here as you can.'

She looked again. And Boreas at once understood what she meant to say with that look.

Stefan Skellen appeared. He watched the girl for a long time, his arms crossed on his chest. Finally, he indicated with an energetic gesture that she was to follow him. She went without a word, escorted on all sides by armed men.

'A strange wench,' muttered Boreas. And shuddered.

'Fortunately, she isn't our concern now,' said Dacre Silifant. 'And I'm surprised at you for talking to her like that. It was she, the witch, who killed Vargas and Fripp, and later Ola Harsheim—'

'Tawny Owl killed Harsheim,' Boreas cut him off. 'Not she. She spared our lives, there on the pack ice, though she could have slaughtered and drowned us like pups. All of us. Tawny Owl too.'

'Very well.' Dacre spat on the flags of the courtyard. 'He'll reward her for that mercy, together with the sorcerer and Bonhart. You'll see, Mun, now they'll gut her ceremonially. They'll flay her in thin strips.'

'I'm inclined to believe they'll flay her,' snapped Boreas. 'Because they're butchers. And we ain't no better, since we serve under them.'

'And do we have a choice? We don't.'

One of Skellen's mercenaries suddenly cried softly, and another followed suit. One man swore, another gasped. Someone pointed silently.

As far as the eye could see black birds were sitting on the battlements, on the corbels, on the roofs of the towers, on the cornices, on the window sills and gables, on the gutters, and on the gargoyles and mascarons. They had flown from the ships' graveyard, noiselessly, without cawing, and now they were sitting in silence, waiting.

'They scent death,' mumbled one of the mercenaries.

'And carrion,' added a second.

'We don't have a choice,' Silifant repeated mechanically, looking at Boreas. Boreas Mun looked at the birds.

'Perhaps it's time we did?' he replied softly.

*

They climbed a great staircase with three landings, walked along a long corridor between an avenue of statues set in niches, and passed through a cloister surrounding a vestibule. Ciri walked boldly, feeling no anxiety; neither the weapons nor her escort's murderous visages caused her fear. She had lied saying she couldn't remember the faces of the men from the frozen lake. She did remember. She remembered seeing Stefan Skellen – the same man now leading her with a gloomy expression deeper into that huge, awful castle – as he shook, teeth chattering, on the ice.

Now, as he looked around and glared at her from time to time, she sensed he was still a little afraid of her. She breathed more deeply.

They entered a hall beneath a high star vault supported on columns, beneath great spidery chandeliers. Ciri saw who was waiting there for her. Fear dug its claw-like fingers into her guts, clenched its fist, tugged and twisted.

Bonhart was by her in three strides. He grabbed her by the front of her jerkin, lifted her up and pulled her towards him at the same time, bringing her face closer to his pale, fishy eyes.

'Hell must indeed be dreadful,' he roared, 'if you've chosen me.'

She didn't reply. She could smell alcohol on his breath.

'And maybe hell didn't want you, you little beast? Perhaps that devilish tower spat you out in disgust, after tasting your venom?'

He drew her closer. She turned aside and drew back her face.

'You're right,' he said softly. 'You're right to be afraid. It's the end of your road. You won't escape from here. Here, in this castle, I'll bleed you dry.'

'Have you finished, Mr Bonhart?'

She knew at once who had spoken. The sorcerer Vilgefortz, who first of all had been a prisoner in manacles, and afterwards pursued her in the Tower of the Gull. He had been very handsome then, on the island. Now something in his face had changed, something that made it ugly and fearful.

'Mr Bonhart—' the sorcerer didn't even move on his throne-like armchair '—let me assume the pleasant duty of welcoming to Stygga Castle our guest, Miss Cirilla of Cintra, the daughter

342

of Pavetta, the granddaughter of Calanthe, the descendant of the famous Lara Dorren aep Shiadhal. Greetings. Please come closer.'

The derision hidden beneath the mask of civility slipped out from the sorcerer's last words. There was nothing but a threat and an order in them. Ciri felt at once that she would be unable to resist that order. She felt fear. Ghastly fear.

'Closer,' hissed Vilgefortz. Now she noticed what was wrong with his face. His left eye, considerably smaller than his right, blinked, flickered and spun around like a mad thing in the wrinkled, grey-blue eye socket. The sight was gruesome.

'A brave pose, a trace of fear in the face,' said the sorcerer, tilting his head. 'My acknowledgements. Assuming your courage doesn't result from stupidity. I shall dispel any possible fantasies at once. You will not escape from here, as Mr Bonhart correctly observed. Neither by teleportation, nor with the help of your own special abilities.'

She knew he was right. Previously, she had persuaded herself that if it came to it she would always – even at the last moment – be able to flee and hide amidst times and places. Now she knew that was an illusory hope, a fantasy. The castle positively vibrated with strange, evil, hostile magic, and that magic was pervading, penetrating her. It crawled like a parasite over her innards, repulsively slithering over her brain. She could do nothing about it. She was in her enemy's power. Helpless.

Too bad, she thought, *I knew what I was doing. I knew what I was coming here for. The rest was really just fantasy. May what has to happen, happen.*

'Well done,' said Vilgefortz. 'An accurate assessment of the situation. What must happen, *will* happen. Or more precisely: what I decide will happen, will happen. I wonder if you're also guessing, my splendid one, what I shall decide?'

She was about to answer, but before she could overcome the resistance of her tight, dry throat, he anticipated her by reading her thoughts.

'Of course you know. Master of Worlds. Master of Times and Places. Yes, yes, my splendid one, your visit didn't surprise me. Quite simply, I know where you escaped to from the lake and how you did it. I know how you got here. The one thing I don't know is: was it a long way? And did it provide you with many thrills?

'Oh,' he smiled nastily, anticipating her once again. 'You don't have to reply. I know it was interesting and exciting. You see, I can't wait to try it myself. I'm very envious of your talent. You'll have to share it with me, my splendid one. Yes, "have to" are the right words. Until you share your talent with me I simply won't let you out of my hands. I won't let you out of my hands, neither by day nor by night.'

Ciri finally understood it wasn't only fear squeezing her throat. The sorcerer was gagging and choking her magically. He was mocking her. Humiliating her. In front of everyone.

'Let . . . Yennefer go.' She coughed so hard she arched her back with the effort. 'Let her go . . . And you can do what you want with me.'

Bonhart roared with laughter, and Stefan Skellen also laughed dryly. Vilgefortz poked the corner of his gruesome eye with his little finger.

'You can't be so slow-witted not to know that I can do what I want with you in any case. Your offer is pompous, and thus pathetic and ridiculous.'

'You need me . . .' She raised her head, although it cost her an enormous amount of strength. 'To have a child with me. Everybody wants that, you too. Yes, I'm in your power, I came here by myself . . . You didn't catch me, although you pursued me through half the world. I came here by myself and I'm giving myself up to you. For Yennefer. For her life. Is it so ridiculous to you? So try using violence and force with me . . . You'll see, you'll be over your desire to laugh in no time.'

Bonhart leaped at her and swung his scourge. Vilgefortz made an apparently careless gesture, just a slight movement of the hand, but even that was enough for the whip to fly from the hunter's hand, and he staggered as though hit by a coal wagon.

'I see Mr Bonhart still has difficulty understanding the responsibilities of a guest,' said Vilgefortz, massaging his fingers. 'Try to remember: when one is a guest, one doesn't destroy the furniture or works of art, nor steal small objects, nor does one soil the carpets or inaccessible places. One doesn't rape or beat other guests. The latter two not, at least, until the host has finished raping and beating, not until he gives the sign that one may now rape and beat. You too, Ciri, ought to be able to draw the appropriate conclusions from what I've said. You can't? I'll help you. You surrender yourself to me and humbly agree to everything, allow me to do anything I want with you. You think your offer highly generous. You're mistaken. For the matter is that I shall do with you what I have to do, not what I'd like to do. An example: I'd like to gouge out at least one of your eyes as revenge for Thanedd, but I can't, because I'm afraid you wouldn't survive it.'

Ciri knew it was now or never. She spun around in a half-turn, and jerked Swallow from the scabbard. The entire castle suddenly whirled and she felt herself falling, painfully banging her knees. She bent over, her forehead almost touching the floor, fighting the urge to vomit. The sword slipped from her numb fingers. Someone lifted her up.

'Yeees,' Vilgefortz drawled, resting his chin on hands held together as if in prayer. 'Where was I? Ah, yes, that's right, your offer. Yennefer's life and freedom in exchange . . . For what?' For your voluntary surrender, willingly, without violence or compulsion? I'm sorry, Ciri. Violence and compulsion are simply essential to what I shall do to you.

'Yes, yes,' he repeated, watching with interest as the girl wheezed, spat and tried to vomit. 'It simply won't happen without violence or compulsion. You would never agree voluntarily to what I shall do to you, I assure you. So, as you must see, your offer, still pathetic and ridiculous, is furthermore worthless. So I reject it. Go on, take her. To the laboratory! At once.'

*

The laboratory didn't differ much from the one Ciri knew from the Temple of Melitele in Ellander. It was also brightly lit, clean, with long metal-topped tables, laden with glass, large jars, retorts, flasks, test tubes, pipes, lenses, hissing and bubbling alembics and other strange apparatus. Here also, as in Ellander, it smelled strongly of ether, alcohol, formalin and something else, something that triggered fear. Even in the friendly temple, beside the friendly priestesses and a friendly Yennefer, Ciri had felt fear in the laboratory. And after all, in Ellander no one had dragged her to the laboratory by force, no one had brutally shoved her onto a bench, and no one had held her shoulders and arms in an iron grip. In Ellander there hadn't been a dreadful steel chair whose purpose was quite sadistically obvious. There had been no shaven-headed characters dressed in white in the middle of the laboratory, no Bonhart, and no Skellen, excited, flushed and licking his lips. And neither was there Vilgefortz, with one normal eye and the other tiny and twitching hideously.

Vilgefortz turned around from the table, where he had spent a long time arranging some sinister-looking instruments.

'Do you see, my splendid maiden,' he began, walking towards her, 'that you are the key to mastery and power? Not only over this world, a vanity of vanities, doomed in any case to early extinction, but over all worlds. Over the whole compass of places and times which have arisen since the Conjunction. You certainly understand me; you have already visited some of those places and times.

'I'm ashamed to admit it,' he continued a moment later, rolling up his sleeves, 'but I'm terribly attracted by power. It's crude, I know, but I want to be a ruler. A ruler before whom people will bow down, whom people will bless simply because I let them be, and whom they will worship as a god, if, let's say, I decide to save their world from a cataclysm. Even if I only save it on a whim. Oh, Ciri, my heart is gladdened by the thought of how magnanimously I shall reward the faithful, and how cruelly I shall punish the disobedient and arrogant. The prayers that shall be offered up by whole generations to me and for me; for my love and my mercy will be balm and honey to my soul. Whole generations, Ciri, whole worlds. Listen out. Do you hear? Deliver us from the plague, hunger, war and wrath of Vilgefortz . . .'

He moved his fingers just in front of her face, then violently seized her by the cheeks. Ciri screamed and struggled, but she was held firmly. Her lips began to tremble. Vilgefortz saw it and sniggered.

'The Child of Destiny,' he laughed nervously, and white flecks of foam appeared at the corners of his mouth. 'Aen Hen Ichaer, the sacred elven Elder Blood . . . Now all mine.'

He straightened up abruptly. And wiped his mouth.

'Various fools and mystics,' he now announced in his usually cold tone, 'have tried to adapt you to fairy tales, legends and prophecies; have tracked the genes you carry, your inheritance from your ancestors. Mistaking the sky for stars reflected in the surface of a pond, they mystically supposed that a gene determining great potential would continue to evolve, that it would achieve the height of power in your child or the child of your child. And a charming aura grew around you, incense smoke trailed behind you. But the truth is much more banal, much more mundane. Organically mundane, I'd say. Your blood, my splendid one, is important. But in the absolutely literal, quite unpoetic sense of the word.'

He picked up from the table a glass syringe measuring about six inches. The syringe ended in a thin, slightly curved capillary. Ciri felt her mouth go dry. The sorcerer examined the syringe under the light.

'In a moment,' he declared coldly, 'you will be undressed and placed on this chair, precisely this one, which you're contemplating with such curiosity. You'll spend some time in the chair, albeit in an uncomfortable position. With the help of this device, which also, as I see, is fascinating you, you will be impregnated. It won't be so awful, for almost the whole time you'll be befuddled by elixirs, which I shall give you intravenously, with the aim of implanting the foetal ovum properly and ruling out an ectopic pregnancy. You needn't be afraid, I'm skilled; I've done this hundreds of times. Never, admittedly, to a chosen one of fate and destiny, but I don't think the uteruses and ovaries of chosen ones differ so much from those of ordinary maids.

'And now the most important thing.' Vilgefortz savoured what he was saying. 'It may worry you, or it may gratify you, but know that you won't give birth to the infant. Who knows, perhaps it would also have been a great chosen one with extraordinary abilities, the saviour of the world and the king of nations? No one, however, is able to guarantee that, and I, furthermore, have no intention of waiting that long. I need blood. More precisely, placental blood. As soon as the placenta develops I shall remove it from you. The rest of my plans and intentions, my splendid one, will not, as you now comprehend, concern you, so there's no point informing you about them, it would only be an unnecessary frustration.'

He fell silent, leaving a masterly pause. Ciri couldn't control her trembling mouth.

'And now,' the sorcerer nodded theatrically, 'I invite you to the chair, Miss Cirilla.'

'It would be worth having that bitch Yennefer watching this.' Bonhart's teeth flashed beneath his grey moustaches. 'She deserves it!'

'Indeed she does.' Small white balls of froth appeared again in the corners of Vilgefortz's smiling mouth. 'Impregnation is, after all, a sacred thing, solemn and ceremonial, a mystery at which one's entire close family should assist. And Yennefer is, after all, your quasi-mother, and in primitive cultures the mother virtually takes an active part in her daughter's consummation ceremony. Go on, bring her here!'

'But regarding that impregnation . . .' Bonhart bent over Ciri, whom the sorcerer's shaven-headed acolytes had begun to undress. 'Couldn't one, Lord Vilgefortz, do it more normally? As nature intended?'

Skellen snorted, nodding his head. Vilgefortz frowned slightly.

'No,' he responded coolly. 'No, Mr Bonhart. One couldn't.'

Ciri, as though only now realising the gravity of the situation, uttered an ear-splitting scream. Once, and then a second time.

'Well, well.' The sorcerer grimaced. 'We entered the lion's den, bravely, with head and sword held high, and now we're afraid of a small glass tube? For shame, young lady.'

Ciri, not caring about shame, screamed so loudly the laboratory vessels jingled.

And the whole of Stygga Castle suddenly responded with yelling and commotion.

*

'There'll be trouble, boys,' repeated Zadarlik, scraping dried dung from between the stones of the courtyard with the metal-tipped butt of his ranseur. 'Oh, you'll see, there'll be trouble for us poor wretches.'

He looked at his comrades, but none of the guards commented. Neither did Boreas Mun speak. He had remained with the guards at the gate, from choice, not because of orders. He could have, like Silifant, followed Tawny Owl, could have seen with his own eyes what would happen to the Lady of the Lake, what fate she would suffer. But Boreas didn't want to watch it. He preferred to stay here, in the courtyard, beneath the open sky, far from the chambers and halls of the upper castle, where they had taken the girl. He was certain that not even her screams would reach here.

'Those black birds are a bad sign.' Zadarlik nodded at the rooks, still sitting on the walls and cornices. 'That young wench who came here on a black mare is an evil omen. We're serving Tawny Owl in an evil matter, I tell you. They're saying, in truth, that Tawny Owl himself isn't a coroner or important gentleman now, but an outlaw like us. That the emperor has it in cruelly for him. If he seizes us all, boys, there'll be trouble for us poor wretches.'

'Aye, aye!' added another guard, with long moustaches, wearing a hat decorated with black stork feathers. 'The noose is at hand! It's no good when the emperor's angry—'

'Blow that,' interjected a third, a new arrival to Stygga Castle with the last party of mercenaries recruited by Skellen. 'The emperor might not have enough time for us. They say he has other concerns. They say there was a decisive battle somewhere in the north. The Nordlings beat the imperial forces, thrashed them soundly.'

'In that case,' said a fourth, 'perhaps it isn't so bad that we're here with Tawny Owl? Always better to be with the victors.'

'Certainly it's better,' said the new one. 'Tawny Owl, it seems to me, will go far. And we'll go far with him too.'

'Oh, boys.' Zadarlik leaned on his ranseur. 'You're as thick as pig shit.'

The black birds took flight with a deafening flapping and cawing. They darkened the sky, wheeling in a flock around the bastion.

'What the fuck?' groaned one of the guards.

'Open the gate, please.'

Boreas Mun suddenly detected a powerful smell of herbs: sage, mint and thyme. He swallowed and shook his head. He closed and opened his eyes. It didn't help. The thin, grey-haired elderly man resembling a tax collector who had suddenly appeared beside

349

them had no intention of vanishing. He stood and smiled through pursed lips. Boreas's hair almost lifted his hat up.

'Open the gate, please,' repeated the smiling elderly gentleman. 'Without delay. It really will be better if you do.'

Zadarlik dropped his ranseur with a clank, stood stiffly and moved his mouth noiselessly. His eyes were empty. The remaining men went closer to the gate, striding stiffly and unnaturally, like automatons. They took down the bar. And opened the hasp and staple.

Four riders burst into the courtyard with a thudding of horseshoes.

One had hair as white as snow, and the sword in his hand flashed like lightning. Another was a fair-haired woman, bending a bow as she rode. The third rider, quite a young woman, carved open Zadarlik's temple with a sweeping blow of a curved sabre.

Boreas Mun picked up the ranseur and shielded himself with the shaft. The fourth rider suddenly towered over him. There were wings of a bird of prey attached to both sides of his helmet. His upraised sword shone.

'Leave him, Cahir,' said the white-haired man sharply. 'Let's save time and blood. Milva, Regis, that way . . .'

'No,' mumbled Boreas, not knowing himself why he was doing it. 'Not that way . . . That's only a dead end. Your way is there, up that staircase . . . To the upper castle. If you wish to rescue the Lady of the Lake . . . then you must hurry.'

'My thanks,' said the white-haired man. 'Thank you, stranger. Regis, did you hear? Lead on!'

A moment later only corpses remained in the courtyard. And Boreas Mun, still leaning on the pikestaff. Which he couldn't release, because his legs were shaking so much.

The rooks circled, cawing, over Stygga Castle, covering the towers and bastions in a shroud-like cloud.

*

Vilgefortz listened with stoical calm and an inscrutable expression to the breathless report of the mercenary who had come running. But his restless and blinking eye betrayed him.

'Last ditch reinforcements.' He ground his teeth. 'Unbelievable. Things like that don't happen. Or they do, but only in crummy, vulgar pageants, and it comes to the same thing. Do me the pleasure, good fellow, of telling me you've made it all up for, shall we say, a lark.'

'I'm not making it up!' the hireling said in indignation. 'I'm speaking the truth! Some horsemen have burst in . . . A whole *hassa* of them—'

'Very well, very well,' the sorcerer interrupted. 'I was joking. Skellen, deal with this matter personally. It will be a chance to demonstrate how much your army, hired with my gold, is worth.'

Tawny Owl leaped up, nervously waving his arms.

'Aren't you treating this too lightly, Vilgefortz?' he yelled. 'You, it seems, don't realise the gravity of the situation! If the castle is being attacked, it's by Emhyr's army! And that means—'

'It doesn't mean anything,' the sorcerer cut him off. 'But I know what you have in mind. Very well, if the fact that you have me behind you will improve your morale, have it as you will. Let's go. You too, Mr Bonhart.'

'As far as you're concerned—' he fixed his terrible eye on Ciri '—don't have any false hopes. I know who's turned up here with these pathetic reinforcements worthy of a cheap farce. And I assure you, I shall turn this cheap farce into a nightmare.

'Hey, you!' he nodded at the servants and acolytes. 'Shackle the girl in dimeritium, lock and bolt her in a cell, and don't move an inch from the door. You'll answer with your lives for her. Understood?'

'Yes, sire.'

*

They rushed into the corridor, and from the corridor into a large hall full of sculptures; a veritable glyptothek. No one barred their way. They only saw a few lackeys who immediately fled on seeing them.

They ran up some stairs. Cahir kicked a door open, Angoulême rushed inside with a battle cry and with a blow of her sabre knocked off the helmet of a suit of armour she took for a guard standing by the door. She realised her mistake and roared with laughter.

'Hee, hee, hee! Look at that . . .'

'Angoulême!' Geralt took her to task. 'Don't just stand there! Go on!'

A door opened in front of them. Shapes loomed in the doorway. Milva bent her bow and sent off an arrow without a second thought. Somebody screamed. The door was closed, Geralt heard a bolt thudding.

'Go on, go on!' he shouted. 'Don't just stand there!'

'Witcher,' said Regis. 'This running is senseless. I'll go off . . . I'll fly off and do some reconnaissance.'

'Fly.'

The vampire took off as though blown by the wind. Geralt had no time to be surprised.

Again they chanced upon some men, this time armed. Cahir and Angoulême jumped towards them with a yell, and the men bolted, mainly, it seemed, because of Cahir and his impressive winged helmet.

They dashed into the cloister, and the gallery surrounding the inner vestibule. Around twenty paces separated them from the portico leading into the castle when shapes appeared on the other side of the cloister. Loud shouts echoed out. And arrows whistled.

'Take cover!' the Witcher yelled.

Arrows rained down on them. Fletchings fluttered and arrowheads sent up sparks from the floor, chipping the mouldings from the walls and showering them in fine dust.

'Get down! Behind the balustrade!'

They dropped down, hiding pell-mell behind spiral columns carved with leaves. But they didn't get away with it entirely. The Witcher heard Angoulême cry out, and saw as she grabbed her arm, her sleeve, which immediately became blood-soaked.

'Angoulême!'

'It's nothing! It passed through muscle!' the girl shouted back in only a slightly trembling voice, confirming what he had seen. Had the arrowhead shattered the bone, Angoulême would have fainted from the shock.

The archers were shooting from the gallery without let-up and were shouting out, calling for reinforcements. Several of them ran off to the side, to fire at the pinned-down party from an acute angle. Geralt swore, assessing the distance separating them from the arcade. Things looked bad. But to stay where they were meant death.

'Let's make a run for it!' he yelled. 'Ready! Cahir, help Angoulême!'

'They'll slaughter us!'

'Run for it! We have to!'

'No!' screamed Milva, standing up with bow in hand.

She straightened up, assumed a shooting position; a veritable statue, a marble Amazon with a bow. The marksmen on the gallery yelled.

Milva lowered her head.

One of the archers flew backwards, slamming against the wall, and a bloody splash resembling a huge octopus bloomed on the stone. A cry resounded from the gallery, a roar of anger, fury and horror.

'By the Great Sun . . .' groaned Cahir. Geralt squeezed his shoulder.

'Let's make a run for it! Help Angoulême!'

The marksmen on the gallery directed all their fire at Milva. The archer didn't even twitch, although all around her it was dusty with plaster, chips of marble and splinters of shattering shafts. She calmly released the bowstring. Another yell, and another archer tumbled over like a ragdoll, splashing his companions with blood and brains.

'Now!' yelled Geralt, seeing the guards fleeing from the gallery, dropping to the floor, hiding from the deadly arrowheads. Only the three bravest were still shooting.

An arrowhead thudded against a pillar, showering Milva in a cloud of plaster dust. The archer blew on her hair, which was falling over her face, and bent her bow.

'Milva!' Geralt, Angoulême and Cahir had reached the arcade. 'Leave it! Run!'

'One more little shot,' said the archer with the fletching of an arrow in the corner of her mouth.

The bowstring slapped. One of the three brave men howled, leaned over the balustrade and plummeted downwards onto the flags of the courtyard. At the sight, courage immediately deserted the others. They fell to the floor and pressed themselves against it. Those who had arrived were in no hurry to come out onto the gallery and expose themselves to Milva's shooting.

With one exception.

Milva measured him up at once. Short, slim, swarthy. With a bracer on his left forearm rubbed to a shine and an archer's glove on his right hand. She saw him lift a shapely composite bow with a profiled, carved riser, saw him tauten it smoothly. She saw the bowstring – tightened to its full draw – cross his swarthy face, saw the red-feathered fletching touch his cheek. She saw him aim carefully.

She tossed her bow up, tightened it smoothly, already aiming as she did so. The bowstring touched her face, the feather of the fletching the corner of her mouth.

*

'Harder, harder, Marishka. All the way to your cheek. Twist the bowstring with your fingers, so the arrow doesn't fall from the rest. Hand tight against your cheek. Aim! Both eyes open! Now hold your breath. Shoot!'

The bowstring, in spite of the woollen bracer, stung her left forearm painfully.

Her father was about to speak when he was seized by a coughing fit. A heavy, dry, painful coughing fit. *He's coughing worse and worse*, thought Marishka Barring, lowering her bow. *More and more horribly, and more and more often. He started coughing yesterday as he was aiming at a buck. And for dinner there was only boiled pigweed. I can't stand boiled pigweed. I hate hunger. And poverty.*

Old Barring sucked in air, wheezing gratingly.

'Your arrow passed a span from the bull's eye, lass! A whole span! And I've told you, ain't I, not to twitch when you're letting the bowstring go? And you're hopping about like a slug's crawled into your arse crack. And you take too long aiming. You're shooting with a weary arm! That's how you waste arrows!'

'But I hit the target! And not a span at all, but half a span from the bull's eye.'

'Don't talk back! How the Gods punished me by sending me a clod of a lass instead of a son!'

'I ain't a clod!'

'We'll soon find out. Shoot one more time. And mark what I told you. You're to stand like you were sunk into the ground. Aim and shoot swiftly. Why are you making faces?'

'Because you're badmouthing me.'

'It's my fatherly right. Shoot.'

She drew back the bow, sullen and close to tears. He noticed.

'I love you, Marishka,' he said softly. 'Always mind that.'

She released the bowstring when the fletching had barely touched the corner of her mouth.

'Well done,' said her father. 'Well done, lass'

And coughed horribly, wheezingly.

*

The swarthy archer from the gallery died outright. Milva's arrow struck him below his left armpit and penetrated deep, more than halfway up the shaft, shattering his ribs, pulverising his lungs and heart.

The swarthy archer's red-feathered arrow, released a split second, earlier, struck Milva low in the belly and exited at the back, having shattered her pelvis and pulverised her intestines and arteries.

The archer fell to the floor as though rammed.

Geralt and Cahir shouted with one voice. Heedless that at the sight of Milva's collapse the marksmen from the gallery had once again picked up their bows, they jumped out from the portico protecting them, grabbed the archer and dragged her back, scornful of the hail of arrows. One of the arrowheads rang against Cahir's helmet. Another, Geralt would have sworn, parted his hair.

Milva left behind her a broad and glistening trail of blood. In the blink of an eye a huge pool had appeared in the place they laid her down. Cahir cursed, his hands shaking. Geralt felt despair overcoming him. And fury.

'Auntie,' howled Angoulême. 'Auntie, don't diiiiiieeeee!'

Maria Barring opened her mouth, coughed horrifyingly, spitting blood onto her chin.

'I love you too, Papa,' she said quite distinctly.

And died.

*

The shaven-headed acolytes couldn't cope with the struggling and yelling Ciri, and lackeys rushed to help them. One, kicked between the legs, leaped back, bent over double, and fell to his knees, grabbing his crotch and gasping spasmodically for air.

But that only infuriated the others. Ciri was punched in the neck and slapped in the face. They knocked her over, someone kicked her hard in the hip and someone else sat down on her shins. One of the bald acolytes, a young character with evil green and gold eyes, kneeled on her chest, dug his fingers into her hair and tugged it hard. Ciri howled.

The acolyte also howled. And goggled. Ciri saw streams of blood gushing from his shaven head, staining his white laboratory coat with a macabre design.

The next second, hell broke loose in the laboratory.

Overturned furniture banged. The high-pitched cracking and crunching of breaking glass merged with the hellish moaning of people. The decocts, philtres, elixirs, extracts and other magical substances spilling over the tables and floor mixed up and combined, some of them hissing on contact and belching clouds of yellow smoke. The room was instantly filled with a pungent stench.

Amidst the smoke, through tears brought on by the smell of burning, Ciri saw to her horror a black shape resembling an enormous bat dashing around the laboratory at an incredible speed. She saw the bat in flight slashing the men and saw them falling over screaming. In front of her eyes a lackey trying hard to flee was picked up from the floor and flung onto a table, where he thrashed around, splashed blood, and finally croaked among smashed retorts, alembics, test tubes and flasks.

The mixture of spilled liquids splashed onto a lamp. It hissed, stinking, and flames suddenly exploded in the laboratory. A wave

356

of heat dispersed the smoke. She clenched her teeth so as not to scream.

A slender, grey-haired man dressed elegantly in black was sitting on the steel chair meant for her. The man was calmly biting and sucking on the neck of the shaven-headed acolyte slumped over his knee. The acolyte squealed shrilly and twitched convulsively, his extended legs and arms jerking rhythmically.

Corpse-blue flames were dancing on the metal table-top. Retorts and flasks exploded with a thud, one after another.

The vampire tore his pointed fangs from his victim's neck and fixed his agate-black eyes on Ciri.

'There are occasions,' he said in an explanatory tone, licking blood from his lips, 'when it's simply impossible not to have a drink.

'Don't fear,' he smiled, seeing her expression. 'Don't fear, Ciri. I'm glad I found you. My name's Emiel Regis. I am, although it may seem strange to you, a comrade of the Witcher Geralt. I came here with him to rescue you.'

An armed mercenary rushed into the blazing laboratory. Geralt's comrade turned his head towards him, hissed and bared his fangs. The mercenary howled horrifyingly. The howling went on for a long time before it faded into the distance.

Emiel Regis threw the acolyte's body, motionless and soft as a rag, from his knee, stood up and stretched just like a cat.

'Who'd have thought it?' he said. 'Just some runt, and what good blood inside him! What hidden talents! Come with me, Cirilla, I'll take you to Geralt.'

'No,' mumbled Ciri.

'You don't have to be afraid of me.'

'I'm not,' she protested, bravely fighting with her teeth which insisted on chattering. 'That's not what it's about . . . But Yennefer is imprisoned here somewhere. I have to free her as quickly as possible. I'm afraid that Vilgefortz . . . Mr . . .'

'Emiel Regis.'

'Warn Geralt, good sir, that Vilgefortz is here. He's a sorcerer. A powerful sorcerer. Geralt has to be on his guard.'

*

357

'You're to be on your guard,' repeated Regis, looking at Milva's body. 'Because Vilgefortz is a powerful mage. Meanwhile, she's setting Yennefer free.'

Geralt swore.

'Come on!' he yelled, trying to revive the low spirits of his companions with a shout. 'Let's go!'

'Let's go.' Angoulême stood up and wipe away her tears. 'Let's go! It's time to kick a few fucking arses!'

'I feel such strength inside me I could probably lay waste to this entire castle,' hissed the vampire, smiling gruesomely.

The Witcher glanced at him suspiciously.

'Don't go that far,' he said, 'But force your way through to the upper floor and make a bit of a racket to draw their attention away from me. I'll try to find Ciri. It wasn't good, it wasn't good, vampire, that you left her alone.'

'She demanded it,' Regis explained calmly. 'Using a tone and attitude that ruled out any discussion. She astonished me, I admit.'

'I know. Go to the upper floor. Look after yourselves! I'll try to find her. Her, or Yennefer.'

*

He found her, and quite quickly.

He ran into them all of a sudden, completely unexpectedly coming around a bend in a corridor. He saw. And the sight made the adrenaline prick the veins on the backs of his hands.

Several lackeys were dragging Yennefer along the corridor. The sorceress was dishevelled and shackled in chains, which didn't stop her kicking and struggling and swearing like a trooper.

Geralt didn't let the lackeys get over their astonishment. He only struck once, with one short thrust from the elbow. The man howled like a dog, staggered, smashed his head with a clank and a thud against a suit of plate armour standing in an alcove, and slid down it, smearing blood over the steel plates.

The remaining ones – there were three of them – released Yennefer and leaped aside. Apart from the fourth, who seized the sorceress by the hair and held a knife to her throat, just above her dimeritium collar.

'Don't come any closer!' he howled. 'I'll slit her throat! I'm not joking!'

'Neither am I.' Geralt swung his sword around and looked the thug in the eyes. That was enough for him. He released Yennefer and joined his companions. All of them were now holding weapons. One of them wrenched an antique but menacing-looking halberd from a panoply on the wall. All of them, crouching, were vacillating between attack and defence.

'I knew you'd come,' said Yennefer straightening up proudly. 'Geralt, show these scoundrels what a witcher's sword can do.'

She raised her cuffed hands high, tautening the links of the chain.

Geralt grasped his sihill in both hands, tilted his head slightly and aimed. And smote. So swiftly no one saw the movement of the blade.

The links fell onto the floor with a clank. One of the servants gasped. Geralt grasped the hilt more tightly and moved his index finger under the cross guard.

'Stand still, Yen. Head slightly to one side, please.'

The sorceress didn't even flinch. The sound of metal being struck by the sword was very faint.

The dimeritium collar fell down beside the manacles. Only a single, tiny drop appeared on Yennefer's neck.

She laughed, massaging her wrists. And turned towards the lackeys. None of them could endure her gaze.

The one with the halberd placed the antique weapon gingerly on the floor, as though afraid it would clank.

'Let Tawny Owl,' he mumbled, 'fight someone like that himself. My life is dear to me.'

'They ordered us,' muttered another, withdrawing. 'They ordered us . . . We were captive . . .'

'After all, we weren't rude to you, madam . . . in your prison . . .' a third licked his lips. 'Testify to that . . .'

'Begone,' said Yennefer. Freed from the dimeritium manacles, erect, with her head proudly raised, she looked like a Titaness. Her unruly black mane seemed to reach up to the vault.

The lackeys fled. Furtively and without looking back. Having shrunk to her normal dimensions, Yennefer fell on Geralt's neck.

'I knew you'd come for me,' she murmured, searching for his mouth with hers. 'That you'd come, whatever might happen.'

'Let's go,' he said after a moment, gasping for air. 'Now for Ciri.'

'Ciri,' she said. And a second later a menacing violet glow lit up in her eyes.

'And Vilgefortz.'

*

A man with a crossbow came around the corner, yelled and shot, aiming at the sorceress. Geralt leaped as though propelled by a spring, brandished his sword and the deflected bolt flew right over the crossbowman's head, so close he had to crouch. He didn't manage to straighten up, though, for the Witcher leaped forward and filleted him like a carp. Two more were still standing in the corridor, also holding crossbows. They also fired, but their hands were shaking too much to find the target. The next moment the Witcher was upon them and they were both dead.

'Which way, Yen?'

The sorceress focused, closing her eyes.

'That way. Up those stairs.'

'Are you sure it's the right way?'

'Yes.'

They were attacked by thugs just around the bend in the corridor, not far from a portal decorated with an archivolt. There were more than ten of them, and they were armed with spears, partizans and corseques. They were even determined and fierce. In spite of that it didn't take long. Yennefer stabbed one of them in the centre of the chest at once with a fiery arrowhead shot from her hand. Geralt whirled in a pirouette and fell among the others, the dwarven sihill flashing and hissing like a snake. Once four had fallen the rest fled, the corridors echoing with their clanking and stamping.

'Everything in order, Yen?'

'Couldn't be better.'

Vilgefortz stood beneath the archivolt.

'I'm impressed,' he said calmly and resonantly. 'I really am impressed, Witcher. You're naive and hopelessly stupid, but your technique is impressive.'

'Your brigands,' Yennefer replied just as calmly, 'have just beaten a retreat, leaving you at our mercy. Hand Ciri over, and we'll spare your life.'

'Do you know, Yennefer, that that's the second such generous offer I've had today?' the sorcerer grinned. 'Thank you, thank you. And here's my answer.'

'Look out!' yelled Yennefer, jumping aside. Geralt also leaped aside. Just in time. The column of fire shooting from the sorcerer's outstretched hands transformed the place they had been standing a moment earlier into black and fizzing mud. The Witcher wiped soot and the remains of his eyebrows off his face. He saw Vilgefortz extend a hand. He dived aside and flattened himself against the floor behind the base of a column. There was a boom so loud it hurt their ears, and the whole castle was shaken to its foundations.

*

Booming echoed through the castle, the walls trembled and the chandeliers jingled. A large oil portrait in a gilded frame fell with a great clatter.

The mercenaries who ran up from the vestibule had abject fear in their eyes. Stefan Skellen calmed them with a menacing look, and took them to task with his grim expression and voice.

'What's going on there? Talk!'

My Lord Coroner . . .' wheezed one of them. 'There's horror there! There's demons and devils there . . . They're shooting unerringly. . . It's a massacre . . . Death is there . . . It's red with gore everywhere!'

'Some ten men have fallen . . . Perhaps more . . . Over yonder . . . Do you hear, sir?'

There was another boom and the castle shook.

'Magic,' muttered Skellen. 'Vilgefortz . . . Well, we shall see. We'll find out who's beating whom.'

Another hireling came running. He was pale and covered in plaster. For a long time he couldn't utter a word, and when he finally spoke his hands trembled and his voice shook.

'There's . . . There's . . . A monster . . . Lord Coroner . . . Like a great, black flittermouse . . . It was tearing people's heads off before my very eyes . . . Blood was gushing everywhere! And it was darting around and laughing . . . It had teeth like this!'

'We won't escape with our lives . . .' whispered a voice behind Tawny Owl's back.

'Lord Coroner.' Boreas Mun decided to speak. 'They are spectres. I saw . . . the young Graf Cahir aep Ceallach. But he's dead.'

Skellen looked at him, but didn't say anything.

'Lord Stefan . . .' mumbled Dacre Silifant. 'Who are we to fight here?'

'They aren't men,' groaned one of the mercenaries. 'They are sorcerers and hellish devils! Human strength cannot cope against such as them . . .'

Tawny Owl crossed his arms on his chest and swept a bold and imperious gaze over the mercenaries.

'So we shall not get involved in this conflict of hellish forces!' he announced thunderously and emphatically. 'Let demons fight with demons, witches with witches, and ghosts with corpses risen from the grave. We won't interfere with them! We shall wait here calmly for the outcome of the battle.'

The mercenaries' faces brightened up. Their morale rose perceptibly.

'That staircase is the only way out,' Skellen continued in a powerful voice. 'We'll wait here. We shall see who tries coming down it.'

A terrible boom resounded from above and mouldings fell from the vault with an audible rustle. There was a stench of sulphur and burning.

'It's too dark here!' called Tawny Owl, thunderously and boldly, to raise his troops' spirits. 'Briskly, light whatever you can! Torches, brands! We have to see well whoever appears on those stairs! Fill those iron cressets with some fuel or other!'

'What kind of fuel, sir?'

Skellen indicated wordlessly what kind.

'Pictures?' a mercenary asked in disbelief. 'Paintings?'

'Yes, indeed,' snorted Tawny Owl. 'Why are you looking like that? Art is dead!'

Frames were splintered and paintings shredded. The well-dried wood and canvas, saturated with linseed oil, caught fire immediately and flared up with a bright flame.

Boreas Mun watched. His mind completely made up.

*

There was a boom and a flash, and the column they had managed to jump away from at almost the last moment disintegrated. The shaft broke, the capital decorated with acanthus-leaves crashed to the floor, destroying a terracotta mosaic. A ball of lightning hurtled towards them with a hiss. Yennefer deflected it, screaming out a spell and gesticulating.

Vilgefortz walked towards them, his cloak fluttering like a dragon's wings.

'I'm not surprised at Yennefer,' he said as he walked. 'She is a woman and thus an evolutionary inferior creature, governed by hormonal chaos. But you, Geralt, are not only a man who is sensible by nature, but also a mutant, invulnerable to emotions.'

He waved a hand. There was a boom and a flash. A lightning bolt bounced off the shield Yennefer had conjured up.

'In spite of your good sense—' Vilgefortz continued to talk, pouring fire from hand to hand '—in one matter you demonstrate astounding and foolish perseverance: you invariably desire to row upstream and piss into the wind. It had to end badly. Know that today, here, in Stygga Castle, you have pissed into a hurricane.'

*

A battle was raging somewhere on the lower storeys. Someone screamed horribly, moaned, and wailed in pain. Something was burning. Ciri could smell smoke and burning, and felt a waft of hot air.

Something boomed with such force that the columns holding up the vault trembled and stuccoes fell off the walls.

Ciri cautiously looked around the corner. The corridor was empty. She walked along it quickly and silently, with rows of statues standing in alcoves on her right and left. She had seen those statues once.

In her dreams.

She exited the corridor. And ran straight into a man with a spear. She sprang aside, ready to dodge and somersault. And then she realised it wasn't a man but a thin, grey-haired, stooped woman. And that it wasn't a spear, but a broom.

'A sorceress with black hair is imprisoned somewhere around here.' Ciri cleared her throat. 'Where?'

The woman with the broom was silent for a long time, moving her mouth as though chewing something.

'And how should I know, treasure?' she finally mumbled. 'For I only clean here. Nothing else, just clean up after them,' she repeated, not looking at Ciri at all. 'And all they do is keep dirtying the place. Look for yourself, treasure.'

Ciri looked. There was a smudged zigzag streak of blood on the floor. The streak extended for a few paces and ended beside a corpse huddled up by the wall. Two more corpses lay further on, one curled up in a ball, the other positively indecently spread-eagled. Beside them lay crossbows.

'They keep making a mess.' The woman took a pail and rag, kneeled down and set about cleaning. 'Dirt, nothing but dirt, all the time dirt. And I must clean and clean. Will there ever be an end to it?'

'No,' Ciri said softly. 'Never. That's what this world's come to.'

The woman stopped cleaning. But didn't raise her head.

'I clean,' she said. 'Nothing more. But I'll tell you, treasure, that you must go straight, and then left.'

'Thank you.'

The woman bowed her head even lower and resumed her cleaning.

*

She was alone. Alone and lost in the maze of corridors.

'Madam Yenneeefeeer!'

Up until then she had kept quiet, afraid of saddling herself with Vilgefortz's men. But now . . .

'Yeeneeeefeeer!'

She thought she'd heard something. Yes, for sure!

She ran into a gallery, and from there into a large hall, between slender pillars. The stench of burning reached her nostrils again.

Bonhart emerged like a ghost from a niche and punched her in the face. She staggered, and he leaped on her like a hawk, seized her by the throat, pinning her to the wall with his forearm. Ciri looked into his fishlike eyes and felt her heart drop downwards to her belly.

'I wouldn't have found you if you hadn't called,' he wheezed out. 'But you called, and longingly, to cap it all off! Have you missed me so? My little darling?'

Still pinning her to the wall, he slipped his hand into the hair on her nape. Ciri jerked her head. The bounty hunter grinned. He ran his hand over her arm, squeezed her breast, and grabbed her roughly by the crotch. Then he released her and pushed her so that she slid down the wall.

And tossed a sword at her feet. Her Swallow. And she knew at once what he wanted.

'I'd have preferred it in the ring,' he drawled. 'As the crowning achievement, as the grand finale of many beautiful performances. The witcher girl against Leo Bonhart! Eh, people would pay to see something like that! Go on! Pick up the weapon and draw it from the scabbard.'

She did as he said. But she didn't draw the blade, just slung it across her back so the hilt would be within reach.

Bonhart took a step back.

'I thought it would suffice me to gladden my eyes with the sight of that surgery Vilgefortz is preparing for you,' he said. 'I was mistaken. I must feel your life flowing down my blade. I defy witchcraft and sorcerers, destiny, prophecies, the fate of the world, I defy the Elder and Younger Blood. What do all these predictions and spells mean to me? What do I gain from them? Nothing! Nothing can compare with the pleasure—'

He broke off. She saw him purse his lips, saw his eyes flash ominously.

'I'll bleed you to death, witcher girl,' he hissed. 'And afterwards, before you cool off, we'll celebrate our nuptials. You are mine. And you'll die mine. Draw your weapon.'

A distant thud resounded and the castle shuddered.

'Vilgefortz,' Bonhart explained with an inscrutable expression, 'is reducing your witcher rescuers to pulp. Go on, girl, draw your sword.'

Shall I run away, she thought, frozen in terror, *flee to other places, to other times? If only I could get far from him, if only.* She felt shame: *how can I run away? Leave Yennefer and Geralt at their mercy?* But good sense told her: *I'm not much use to them dead . . .*

She focused, pressing her fists to her temples. Bonhart knew immediately what she was planning and lunged for her. But it was too late. There was a buzzing in Ciri's ears, something flashed. *I've done it*, she thought triumphantly.

And at once realised her triumph was premature. She realised it on hearing furious yelling and curses. The evil, hostile and paralysing aura of the place was probably to blame for the fiasco. She hadn't travelled far. Not even out of eyeshot – only to the opposite end of the gallery. Not far from Bonhart. But beyond the range of his hands and his sword. Temporarily, at least.

Pursued by his roar, Ciri turned and ran.

*

She ran down a long, wide corridor, followed by the dead glances of the alabaster caryatids holding up the arcades. She turned once and then again. She wanted to lose and confuse Bonhart, and furthermore she was heading towards the noises of the battle. Her friends would be where the fighting was raging, she was sure.

She rushed into a large, round room, in the centre of which a sculpture portraying a woman with her face covered, most probably a goddess, stood on a marble plinth. Two corridors led away from the room, both quite narrow. She chose at random. Naturally she chose wrongly.

'The wench!' roared one of the thugs. 'We have her!'

There were too many of them to be able to risk fighting, even in a narrow corridor. And Bonhart was surely nearby. Ciri turned back and bolted. She burst into the room with the marble goddess. And froze.

Before her stood a knight with a great sword, in a black cloak and helmet decorated with the wings of a bird of prey.

The town was burning. She heard the roar of fire, saw flames flickering and felt the heat of the conflagration. The neighing of horses and the screaming of the murdered were in her ears. The black bird's wings suddenly flapped, covering everything . . . *Help!*

Cintra, she thought, coming to her senses. *The Isle of Thanedd. He's followed me all the way here. He's a demon. I'm surrounded by demons, by nightmares from my dreams. Bonhart behind me, him in front of me.*

The shouting and stamping of enemies coming running could be heard behind her.

The knight in the plumed helmet suddenly took a step forward. Ciri overcame her fear. She yanked Swallow from its scabbard.

'You will not touch me!'

The knight moved forward and Ciri noticed in amazement that a fair-haired girl armed with a curved sabre was hiding behind his cloak. The girl flashed past Ciri like a lynx, sending one of the approaching lackeys sprawling with a slash of her sabre. And the black knight, astonishingly, rather than attacking Ciri, slit open another thug with a powerful blow. The remaining ones retreated into the corridor.

The fair-haired girl rushed for the door, but didn't manage to close it. Although she was whirling her sabre menacingly and yelling, the lackeys shoved her back from the portal. Ciri saw one of them stab her with a pilum, saw the girl fall to her knees. Ciri leaped and slashed backhand with Swallow, while the Black Knight ran up on the other side, hacking terribly with his long sword. The fair-haired girl, still on her knees, drew an axe from her belt and hurled it, hitting one of the bruisers right in the face. Then she lunged for the door, slammed it and the knight bolted it.

'Phew,' said the girl. 'Oak and iron! It'll take them some time to chop their way through that!'

'They won't waste time, they'll search for another way,' commented the Black Knight soberly, after which his face suddenly darkened on seeing the girl's blood-soaked trouser leg. The girl waved a hand dismissively.

'Let's be away.' The knight removed his helmet and looked at Ciri. 'I'm Cahir Mawr Dyffryn, son of Ceallach. I came here with Geralt. To rescue you, Ciri. I know it's unbelievable.'

'I've seen more unbelievable things,' Ciri growled. 'You've come a long way . . . Cahir . . . Where's Geralt?'

He looked at her. She remembered his eyes from Thanedd. Dark blue and as soft as silk. Pretty.

'He's rescuing the sorceress,' he answered. 'That—'

'Yennefer. Let's go.'

'Yes!' said the fair-haired girl, putting a makeshift dressing on her thigh. 'We still have to kick a few arses! For auntie!'

'Let's go,' repeated the knight.

But it was too late.

'Run away,' whispered Ciri, seeing who was approaching along the corridor. 'He's the devil incarnate. But he only wants me. He won't come after you . . . Run . . . Help Geralt . . .'

Cahir shook his head.

'Ciri,' he said kindly. 'I'm surprised by what you're saying. I came here from the end of the world to find you, rescue you and defend you. And now you want me to run away?'

'You don't know who you're up against.'

Cahir pulled up his sleeve, tore off his cloak and wrapped it around his left arm. He brandished his sword and whirled it so fast it hummed.

'I'll soon find out.'

Bonhart, seeing the three of them, stopped. But only for a moment.

'Aha!' he said. 'Have the reinforcements arrived? Your companions, witcher girl? Very well. Two less, two more. Makes no difference.'

Ciri had a sudden flash of inspiration.

'Say farewell to your life, Bonhart!' she yelled. 'It's the end of you! You've met your match!'

She must have overdone it and he caught the lie in her voice. He stopped and looked suspiciously.

'The Witcher? Really?'

Cahir whirled his sword, standing in position. Bonhart didn't budge.

'This witch has more of a liking for younger men than I expected,' he hissed. 'Just look here, my young blade.'

He pulled his shirt open. Silver medallions flashed in his fist. A cat, a gryphon and a wolf.

'If you are truly a witcher—' he ground his teeth '—know that your own quack amulet will soon embellish my collection. If you're not a witcher, you'll be a corpse before you manage to blink. It would be wise, therefore, to get out of my way and take to your heels. I want this wench; I don't bear a grudge against you.'

'You talk big,' Cahir said calmly, twirling the blade. 'Let's see if your bite's worse than your bark. Angoulême, Ciri. Flee!'

'Cahir—'

'Run,' he corrected himself, 'and help Geralt.'

They ran. Ciri was holding up the limping Angoulême.

'You asked for it.' Bonhart squinted his pale eyes and moved forward, whirling his sword.

'I asked for it?' Cahir Mawr Dyffryn aep Ceallach repeated dully. 'No. It's what destiny wants!'

They leaped at each other, quickly engaged, surrounding each other with a frantic kaleidoscope of blades. The corridor filled with the clang of iron, seemingly making the marble sculpture tremble and rock.

'You aren't bad,' rasped Bonhart when they came apart. 'You aren't bad, my young blade. But you're no witcher. The little viper deceived me. You're done for. Prepare for death.'

'You talk big.'

Cahir took a deep breath. The clash had convinced him he had faint chance with the fishy-eyed man. This man was too fast and too strong for him. The only chance was that Bonhart was in a hurry to get after Ciri. And he was clearly irritated.

Bonhart attacked again. Cahir parried a cut, stooped, jumped, seized his opponent by the belt, shoved him against the wall and kneed him hard in the crotch. Bonhart caught him by the face, battered him powerfully on the side of the head with his sword pommel; once, twice, thrice. The third blow shoved Cahir back. He saw the flash of the blade. He parried instinctively.

Too slowly.

*

It was a strictly observed tradition in the Dyffryn family that all male members would hold a silent vigil lasting a whole day and night over the body of a fallen kinsman once he was inhumed in the castle armoury. The women – gathered in a remote wing of the castle so as not to disturb the men, not to distract them or disrupt their reflections – would sob, keen and faint. When brought round they sobbed and keened again. And *da capo*.

Sobbing and weeping, even among women, Vicovarian noblewomen, was an unwelcome faux pas and a great dishonour. But among the Dyffryns that and no other was the tradition and no one ever changed it. Or meant to change it.

The ten-year-old Cahir, the youngest brother of Aillil, who had fallen in Nazair and was then lying in the castle armoury, was not yet a man in terms of customs and traditions. He was not allowed to join the group of men gathered around the open coffin, and he was not permitted to sit in silence with his grandfather Gruffyd, his father Ceallach, his brother Dheran or the whole collection of uncles and cousins. Neither was he permitted, naturally, to sob and faint along with his grandmother, mother, three sisters and the whole collection of aunts and cousins. Cahir clowned about and made mischief on the castle walls along with the rest of his young relatives who had come to Darn Dyffra for the obsequies, funeral and wake. And he pummelled any boys who considered that the bravest of the brave in the fighting for Nazair were their own fathers and older brothers, but not Aillil aep Ceallach.

'Cahir! Come here, my son!'

In the cloister stood Mawr, Cahir's mother, and her sister, his aunt Cinead var Anahid. His mother's face was red and so swollen from weeping that Cahir was terrified. It shocked him that weeping could make such a monster out of such a comely woman as his mother. He made a firm resolution never, ever, to cry.

'Remember, son,' Mawr sobbed, pressing the boy so hard to her breast he couldn't catch his breath. 'Remember this day. Remember who took the life from your dear brother Aillil. The damned Nordlings did it. Your foes, my son. You are ever to hate them. You are to hate that damned, murderous nation!'

'I shall hate them, mother of mine,' Cahir promised, somewhat surprised. Firstly, his brother Aillil had died the praiseworthy and enviable death of a warrior, in battle, with honour. What was one to shed tears over? Secondly, it was no secret that his grandmother Eviva – Mawr's mother – was descended from Nordlings. Papa had more than once called his grandmother in anger 'She-Wolf from the North'. Behind her back, naturally.

Well, but if mother is now ordering me . . .

'I shall hate them,' he pledged eagerly. 'I already hate them! And when I'm big and have a real sword I'll go to war and chop off their heads! You'll see, ma'am!'

His mother took a breath and began sobbing. Aunt Cinead held her up. Cahir clenched his little fists and trembled with hatred. With hatred for those who had wronged his mamma, making her so ugly.

*

Bonhart's blow clove his temple, cheek and mouth. Cahir dropped his sword and staggered, and the bounty hunter cut him between his neck and collar bone using the force of a half-turn. Cahir tumbled at the feet of the marble goddess, and his blood splashed the statue's plinth, like a pagan sacrifice.

*

There was a boom, the floor trembled beneath feet and a shield fell with a thud from a wall panoply. Acrid smoke trailed and crept along the corridor. Ciri wiped her face. The fair-haired girl she was supporting weighed her down like a millstone.

'Quick . . . We must run quicker . . .'

'I can't run any quicker,' said the girl. And suddenly sat down heavily on the floor. Ciri saw with horror a red puddle begin to

371

spill out and collect beneath the seated girl, beneath her blood-soaked trouser leg.

The girl was as white as a sheet.

Ciri threw herself on her knees beside her, pulled off her scarf and then her belt, trying to apply tourniquets. But the wound was too severe. And too near her groin. The blood kept dripping.

The girl grasped her by the hand, her fingers as cold as ice.

'Ciri . . .'

'Yes.'

'I'm Angoulême. I didn't believe . . . I didn't believe we'd find you. But I followed Geralt . . . Because it's impossible not to follow him. Isn't it?'

'It is. That's how he is.'

'We found you. And rescued you. And Fringilla mocked us . . . Tell me . . .'

'Don't say anything. Please.'

'Tell me . . .' Angoulême was moving her lips slower and slower, and with greater difficulty. 'Tell me. You're a queen, aren't you . . . In Cintra . . . We'll be in your good graces, won't we? Will you make me a . . . countess? Tell me. But don't lie . . . Can you? Tell me!'

'Don't say anything. Save your strength.'

Angoulême sighed, suddenly leaned over forward and rested her brow against Ciri's shoulder.

'I knew . . .' she said quite clearly. 'I knew that a brothel in Toussaint would be a better fucking way of making a living.'

A long, long time passed before Ciri realised she was holding a dead girl in her arms.

*

She saw him as he approached, being led by the lifeless looks of the alabaster caryatids holding up the arcades. And suddenly understood that flight was impossible, that it was impossible to escape from him. That she would have to face him. She knew it.

But was still too afraid of him.

He drew his weapon. Swallow's blade sang softly. She knew that song.

372

She retreated down the wide corridor, and he followed her, holding his sword in both hands. Blood trickled down the blade, heavy drops dripping from the cross guard.

'Dead,' he judged, stepping over Angoulême's body. 'Well and good. Your young blade has also fallen.'

Ciri felt desperation seizing her. Felt her fingers gripping the hilt so tightly it hurt.

She retreated.

'You deceived me,' drawled Bonhart, following her. 'The young blade didn't have a medallion. But something tells me somebody *will* be found in this castle who wears one. Someone like that will be found, old Leo Bonhart stakes his life on it, somewhere near the witch Yennefer. But first things first, viper. First of all, us. You and me. And our nuptials.'

Ciri got her bearings. Describing a short arc with Swallow she took up her position. She began to circle him, quicker and quicker, forcing the bounty hunter to move around on the spot.

'Last time,' he muttered, 'that trick wasn't much use to you. Well? Can't you learn from your mistakes?'

Ciri speeded up. She deceived and beguiled, tantalised and hypnotised with flowing, soft movements of her blade.

Bonhart whirled his sword in a hissing moulinet.

'That doesn't work on me,' he snarled. 'And it bores me!'

He shortened the distance with two rapid strides.

'Play, music!'

He leaped, cut hard. Ciri spun around in a pirouette, jumped, landed confidently on her left foot, and struck at once, without assuming a position. Before the blade had clanged on Bonhart's parry she had spun past, smoothly moving in under the whistling blow. She struck again, without a back swing, using an unnatural, unorthodox bend of the elbow. Bonhart blocked, using the momentum of the parry to immediately slash from the left. She was expecting that, and all she needed was a slight bend of the knees and a sway of her trunk to move her whole body aside from under the blade. She countered and thrust at once. But this time he was waiting for her, and deceived her with a feint. Not meeting a parry, she almost lost her balance, saving herself with a lightning-fast leap, but his sword caught her arm anyway. At first she thought the blade had only cut through her padded sleeve, but a moment later she felt the warm liquid in her armpit and on her arm.

The alabaster caryatids observed them with indifferent eyes.

She drew back and he followed her, hunched, making wide, sweeping movements with his sword. Like the bony Death Ciri had seen on paintings in the temple. *The dance of the skeletons*, she thought. *The Grim Reaper is coming.*

She drew back. The warm liquid was now dripping down her forearm and hand.

'First blood to me,' he said at the sight of the drops splattering star-like on the floor. 'Who'll draw the second blood? My betrothed?'

She retreated.

'Look around. It's the end.'

He was right. The corridor ended in nothingness, in an abyss, at the bottom of which could be seen the dust-covered, dirty and smashed up floorboards of the lower storey. This part of the castle was destroyed, there was no floor at all. There was only a framework of load-bearing timbers: posts, ridges and a lattice of beams.

She didn't hesitate for long. She stepped onto a beam and moved backwards along it, without taking her eyes off Bonhart, watching his every move. That saved her. For he suddenly charged her, running along the beam, slashing with rapid, diagonal blows, whirling his sword in lightning-fast feints. She knew what he was counting on. A wrong parry or mistake with a feint would have upset her balance, and then she would have fallen off the beam, onto the smashed up woodblocks of the lower floor.

This time Ciri didn't let the feints deceive her. Quite the opposite. She spun around nimbly and feinted a blow from the right, and when for a split second he hesitated, cut with a right seconde, so quickly and powerfully that Bonhart rocked after parrying. And would have fallen if not for his height. He managed to hold on to a ridge by reaching up with his left hand, keeping his balance. But he lost concentration for a split second. And that was enough for Ciri. She lunged, hard, fully extending her arm and blade.

He didn't even flinch as Swallow's blade passed with a hiss across his chest and left arm. He immediately countered so viciously that had Ciri not turned a back somersault the blow would probably

374

have cut her in half. She hopped onto the adjacent beam, dropping onto one knee with her sword held horizontally over her head.

Bonhart glanced at his shoulder and raised his left arm, already marked by a pattern of wavy crimson lines. He looked at the thick drops dripping downwards into the abyss.

'Well, well,' he said. 'You do know how to learn from your mistakes.'

His voice trembled with fury. But Ciri knew him too well. He was calm, composed and ready to kill.

He leaped onto her beam, whirling his sword, went for her like a hurricane, treading surely, without wobbling, or even looking at his feet. The beam creaked, raining down dust and rotten wood.

He pushed on, slashing diagonally. He forced her backwards. He attacked so quickly she couldn't risk a leap or a somersault, so she had to keep parrying and dodging.

She saw a flash in his fishy eyes. She knew what was afoot. He was driving her against a post, to the truss beneath the ridge. He was pushing her back to a place from where there was no escape.

She had to do something. And she suddenly knew what.

Kaer Morhen. The pendulum.

You push off from the pendulum, you take its momentum, its energy. You take its momentum by pushing off. Do you understand?

Yes, Geralt.

All of a sudden, with the speed of a striking viper, she went from a parry to a cut. Swallow's blade groaned, striking against Bonhart's edge. Simultaneously Ciri pushed off and jumped onto the adjacent beam. She landed, miraculously keeping her balance. She took a few quick, light steps and leaped again, back onto Bonhart's beam, landing behind his back. He spun around in time, made a sweeping cut, almost blindly, to where her leap should have carried her. He missed by a hair's breadth, and the force of the blow made him stagger. Ciri attacked like a lightning strike. She lunged, dropping onto one knee. She struck powerfully and surely.

And she froze with her sword held out to the side. Watching calmly as the long, slanting, perfectly straight slit in his jacket began to well up and brim a dense red.

'You . . .' Bonhart staggered. 'You . . .'

He came for her. He was already slow and sluggish. She eluded him by leaping backwards, and he lost his balance. He fell onto one knee but did not plant his other on the beam. And the wood was now wet and slippery. He looked at Ciri for a second. Then he fell.

She saw him tumble onto the parquet floor in a geyser of dust, plaster and blood, saw his sword fly several yards to one side. He lay motionless, spread out, huge and gaunt. Wounded and utterly defenceless. But still terrible.

It took some time but he finally twitched. Groaned. Tried to raise his head. He moved his arms. He moved his legs. He crept to a post and propped his back up against it. He groaned again, feeling his bloodied chest and belly with both hands.

Ciri leaped down. And fell beside him onto one knee. As softly as a cat. She saw his fishy eyes widen in fear.

'You won . . .' he wheezed, looking at Swallow's blade. 'You won, witcher girl. Pity it wasn't in the arena . . . It would have been some spectacle . . .'

She didn't reply.

'It was I who gave you that sword, do you remember?'

'I remember everything.'

'Surely you won't . . .' he grunted. 'Surely you won't finish me off, will you? You won't do it . . . You won't finish off a beaten and defenceless man . . . I know you, after all, Ciri. You're too . . . noble . . . for that.'

He looked long at her. Very long. Then she bent over. Bonhart's eyes widened even more. But she just tore from his neck the medallions: the wolf, the cat and the gryphon. Then she turned around and walked towards the exit.

He lunged at her with a knife, sprang at her dishonourably and treacherously. And as silent as a bat. Only at the last moment, when the dagger was about to plunge up to the guard in her back, did he roar, putting all his hatred into the bellow.

She dodged the treacherous thrust with a swift half-turn and leap, swung her arm and struck quickly and widely, powerfully, with a full swing, increasing the power with a twist of the hips.

Swallow swished and cut, cut with the very tip of the blade. There was a hiss and a squelch and Bonhart grabbed his throat. His fishy eyes were popping out of his head.

'Didn't I tell you,' Ciri said coldly, 'that I remember everything?'

Bonhart goggled even more. And then fell. He overbalanced and tumbled over backwards, raising dust. And he lay like that, huge, as bony as the Grim Reaper, on the dirty floor, among broken woodblocks. He was still clutching his throat, tightly, with all his might. But although he squeezed hard, his life was draining away fast between his fingers, spreading out around his head in a great, black halo.

Ciri stood over him. Without a word. But allowing him to see her clearly. So as to take her image, her image alone, with him where he was going.

Bonhart glanced at her, his gaze growing dull and blurred. He was shivering convulsively, scraping his heels over the floorboards. Then he uttered a gurgle of the kind a funnel gives just before it empties.

And it was the last sound he made.

*

There was a bang, and the stained-glass windows exploded with a thud and a clink.

'Look out, Geralt!'

They jumped aside just in time. A blinding flash of lightning ploughed up the floor, chips of terracotta and sharp shards of mosaic wailed in the air. Another flash of lightning hit the column the Witcher was hiding behind. The column broke into three parts. Half the arcade broke off the vault and crashed onto the floor with a deafening boom. Geralt, lying flat on the floor, shielded his head with his hands, aware of what poor protection they were against more than ten tons of rubble. He had prepared himself for the worst, but things were not too bad. He got up quickly, managed to see the glow of a magical shield above him and realised that Yennefer's magic had saved him.

Vilgefortz turned towards the sorceress and pulverised the pillar she was sheltering behind. He roared furiously, sewing together a cloud of smoke and dust with threads of fire. Yennefer managed to jump clear, and retaliated, firing at the sorcerer her own flash of lightning, which, nonetheless, Vilgefortz deflected effortlessly and with sheer contempt. He replied with a blow that hurled Yennefer to the floor.

Geralt rushed at him, wiping plaster from his face. Vilgefortz turned his eyes towards him and a hand from which flames exploded with a roar. The Witcher instinctively shielded himself with his sword. The rune-covered dwarven blade protected him, astonishingly, cutting the stream of fire in half.

'Ha!' roared Vilgefortz. 'Impressive, Witcher! And what say you to this?'

The Witcher said nothing. He flew as if he'd been rammed, fell onto the floor and shot across it, only stopping at the base of the column. The column broke up and fell to pieces, again taking a considerable part of the vault with it. This time Yennefer wasn't quick enough to give him magical protection. A huge lump broken off from the arcade hit him in the shoulder. The pain paralysed him for a moment.

Yennefer, chanting spells, sent flash after flash of lightning towards Vilgefortz. None of them hit the target, all harmlessly bouncing off the magical sphere protecting the sorcerer. Vilgefortz stretched out his arms and suddenly spread them. Yennefer cried out in pain and soared up into the air, levitating. Vilgefortz twisted his hands, exactly as though he were wringing out a wet rag. The sorceress howled piercingly. And began to spin.

Geralt sprang up, overcoming the pain. But Regis was quieter.

The vampire appeared out of nowhere in the form of an enormous bat and fell on Vilgefortz with a noiseless glide. Before the sorcerer could protect himself with a spell, Regis had slashed him across the face with his claws, only missing his eye because of its tiny size. Vilgefortz bellowed and waved his arms. Yennefer, now released, tumbled down onto a heap of rubble with an ear-splitting groan, blood bursting from her nose onto her face and chest.

Geralt was now close, was already raising the sihill to strike. But Vilgefortz was not yet defeated and did not mean to surrender. He threw off the Witcher with a great surge of power and shot a blinding white flame at the attacking vampire, which sliced through a column like a hot knife through butter. Regis nimbly avoided the flame and materialised in his normal shape alongside Geralt.

'Beware,' grunted the Witcher, trying to see how Yennefer was. 'Beware, Regis—'

'Beware?' yelled the vampire. 'Me? I didn't come here to beware!'

With an incredible, lightning-fast, tiger-like bound he fell on the sorcerer and grabbed him by the throat. His fangs flashed.

Vilgefortz howled in horror and rage. For a moment it seemed as though it would be the end of him. But that was an illusion. The sorcerer had a weapon in his arsenal for every occasion. And for every opponent. Even a vampire. The hands that seized Regis glowed like red-hot iron. The vampire screamed. Geralt also screamed, seeing the sorcerer literally tearing Regis apart. He leaped to his aid, but wasn't fast enough. Vilgefortz pushed the mutilated vampire against a column and shot white fire at him from close up out of both hands. Regis screamed, screamed so horribly that the Witcher covered his ears with his hands. The rest of the stained-glass windows exploded with a roar and a smash. And the column simply melted. The vampire melted along with it, fusing into an amorphous lump.

Geralt swore, putting all his rage and despair into the curse. He leaped at Vilgefortz, raising his sihill to strike. But failed. Vilgefortz turned around and struck him with magical energy. The Witcher flew the whole length of the hall and slammed into the wall, sliding down it. He lay like a fish gasping for air, not wondering what was broken, but what was intact. Vilgefortz walked towards him. A six-foot iron bar materialised in his hand.

'I could have reduced you to ashes with a spell,' he said. 'I could have melted you into clinker like I did to that monster a moment ago. But you, Witcher, ought to die differently. In a fight. Not a very honest one, perhaps, but still.'

Geralt didn't believe he'd be able to stand. But he did. He spat blood from his cut lip. He gripped his sword more tightly.

'On Thanedd—' Vilgefortz came closer, whirled the bar in a moulinet '—I only broke you a little bit, sparingly, for it was meant to be a lesson. Since it wasn't learned, this time I'll break you thoroughly, into tiny little bones. So that no one will ever be able to stick you back together again.'

He attacked. Geralt didn't run away. He took on the fight.

The bar flickered and whistled, the sorcerer circled around the dancing Witcher. Geralt avoided the blows and delivered his own, but Vilgefortz deftly parried, and then steel groaned mournfully as it struck steel.

The sorcerer was as quick and agile as a demon.

He tricked Geralt with a twist of his trunk and a feigned blow from the left, and slammed him in the ribs from below. Before the Witcher could get his balance and his breath back he was hit in the shoulder so hard he fell to his knees. He dodged aside, saving his skull from a blow from above, but could not avoid a reverse thrust from below, above the hip. He staggered and struck his back against the wall. He still had enough wits about him to fall to the floor. Just in time, because the iron bar grazed his hair and slammed into the wall, sending sparks flying.

Geralt rolled over, and the bar struck sparks on the floor right beside his head. The second blow hit him in the shoulder blade. There was shock, and paralysing pain; weakness flowed down to his legs. The sorcerer raised the bar. Triumph burned in his eyes.

Geralt clenched Fringilla's medallion in his fist.

The bar fell with a clang, striking the floor a foot from the Witcher's head. Geralt rolled away and quickly got up on one knee. Vilgefortz leaped forward and struck. The bar missed the target again by a few inches. The sorcerer shook his head in disbelief and hesitated for a second.

He sighed, suddenly understanding. His eyes lit up. He leaped, taking a swing. Too late.

Geralt slashed him hard across the belly. Vilgefortz screamed, dropped the bar, and staggered back, bent over. The Witcher was already upon him. He pushed him with his boot onto the stump of the broken column and cut vigorously, diagonally, from collarbone to hip. Blood gushed on the floor, painting an undulating pattern. The sorcerer screamed and fell to his knees. He lowered his head and looked down at his belly and chest. For a long time he could not tear his eyes away from what he saw.

Geralt waited calmly, in position, with the sihill ready to strike.

Vilgefortz groaned piercingly and raised his head.

'Geraaalt . . .'

The Witcher didn't let him finish.

It was very quiet for a long time.

'I didn't know . . .' Yennefer said at last, scrambling out of a pile of rubble. She looked terrible. The blood trickling from her nose had poured all over her chin and cleavage. 'I didn't know you could cast illusory spells,' she repeated, seeing Geralt's uncomprehending gaze, 'capable even of deceiving Vilgefortz.'

'It's my medallion.'

'Aha.' She looked suspicious. 'A curious thing. But anyway, we're only alive thanks to Ciri.'

'I beg your pardon?'

'His eye. He never regained full coordination. He didn't always land his blow. But I mainly owe my life to . . .'

She fell silent, glanced at the remains of the melted column, in which the outline of a shape could be discerned.

'Who was that, Geralt?'

'A friend. I'm going to miss him.'

'Was he a human?'

'The epitome of humanity. How are you, Yen?'

'A few broken ribs, concussion, twisted hip joint, bruised spine. Besides that, excellent. And yourself?'

'More or less the same.'

She looked impassively at Vilgefortz's head lying exactly in the centre of the floor mosaic. The sorcerer's small eye, already glazed, looked at them with mute reproach.

'That's a nice sight,' she said.

'It is,' he admitted a moment later. 'But I've already seen enough. Will you be able to walk?'

'With your help, yes.'

*

And they met, all three of them, in a place where the corridors came together, under the arcades. They met beneath the dead gazes of the alabaster caryatids.

'Ciri,' said the Witcher. And rubbed his eyes.

'Ciri,' said Yennefer, being held up by the Witcher.

'Geralt,' said Ciri.

'Ciri,' he replied, overcoming a sudden tightening of the throat. 'Good to see you again.'

'Madam Yennefer.'

The sorceress freed herself from the Witcher's arm and straightened up with the greatest of effort.

'What *do* you look like, girl?' she said severely. 'Just look at you! Tidy up your hair! Don't stoop. Come here please.'

Ciri approached, as stiff as an automaton. Yennefer straightened and smoothed her collar, and tried to wipe the now dried blood from Ciri's sleeve. She touched her hair. And uncovered the scar on her cheek. She hugged her tightly. Very tightly. Geralt saw her hands on Ciri's back. Saw the deformed fingers. He didn't feel anger, resentment or hatred. He felt only weariness. And a huge desire to be done with all of it.

'Mamma.'

'Daughter.'

'Let's go.' He decided to interrupt them. But only after a long while.

Ciri sniffed noisily and wiped her nose with the back of her hand. Yennefer shot an angry look at her, and wiped her eye, which something had probably got into. The Witcher looked down the corridor from where Ciri had exited, as though expecting somebody else to come out of it. Ciri shook her head. He understood.

'Let's get out of here,' he repeated.

'Yes,' said Yennefer. 'I want see the sky.'

'I'll never leave you both,' Ciri said softly. 'Never.'

'Let's get out of here,' he repeated. 'Ciri, hold Yen up.'

'I don't need holding up!'

'Let me, Mamma.'

In front of them was a stairway, a great stairway drowning in smoke, in the twinkling glow of torches and fire in iron cressets. Ciri shuddered. She had seen that stairway before. In dreams and visions.

Down below, far away, armed men were waiting.

'I'm tired,' she whispered.

'Me too,' admitted Geralt, drawing the sihill.

'I've had enough of killing.'

'Me too.'

'Is there no other way out?'

'No. There isn't. Only this stairway. We must, girl. Yen wants to see the sky. And I want to see the sky, Yen and you.'

Ciri looked back, and glanced at Yennefer, who was resting on the balustrade in order not to fall down. She took out the medallions taken from Bonhart. She put the cat around her neck and gave Geralt the wolf.

'I hope you know it's just a symbol?' he said.

'Everything's just a symbol.'

She removed Swallow from its scabbard.

'Let's go, Geralt.'

'Let's go. Keep close beside me.'

Skellen's mercenaries were waiting at the bottom of the stairway, gripping their weapons in sweaty fists. Tawny Owl sent the first wave up the stairs. The mercenaries' iron-shod boots thudded on the steps.

'Slowly, Ciri. Don't rush. Close to me.'

'Yes, Geralt.'

'And calmly, girl, calmly. Remember, without anger, without hatred. We have to get out and see the sky. And the men that are standing in our way must die. Don't hesitate.'

'I won't hesitate. I want to see the sky.'

They got to the first landing without mishap. The mercenaries retreated before them, astonished and surprised by their calm. But after a moment three of them leaped towards them, yelling and whirling their swords. They died at once.

'Swarm them!' Tawny Owl bellowed from below. 'Kill them!'

The next three leaped forward. Geralt quickly sprang out to meet them, deceived them with a feint, and cut one of them from below in the throat. He turned around, made way for Ciri under his right arm, and Ciri smoothly slashed the next soldier in the armpit. The third one tried to save his life by leaping over the balustrade. He was too slow.

Geralt wiped splashes of blood from his face.

'Calmly, Ciri.'

'I am calm.'

The next three. A flash of blades, screams, death.

Thick blood crawled downwards, dribbling down the steps.

A soldier in a brass-studded brigantine leaped towards them with a long pike. His eyes were wild from narcotics. Ciri shoved the shaft aside with a diagonal parry and Geralt slashed. He wiped his face. They walked on, not looking back.

The second landing was now close.

'Kill them!' yelled Skellen. 'Have at them! Kiiiilll theeeem!'

Stamping and yelling on the stairs. The flash of blades, screams. Death.

'Good, Ciri. But more calmly. Without euphoria. And close to me.'

'I'll always be close to you.'

'Don't cut from the shoulder if you can from the elbow. Take heed.'

'I am.'

The flash of a blade. Screams, blood. Death.

'Good, Ciri.'

'I want to see the sky.'

'I love you very much.'

'I love you too.'

'Take heed. It's getting slippery.'

The flash of blades, moaning. They walked on, catching up with the blood pouring down the steps. They walked down, always down, down the steps of Stygga Castle.

A soldier attacking them slipped on a bloody step, fell flat on the ground right at their feet and howled for mercy, covering his head with both hands. The passed him without looking.

No one dared to bar their way until the third landing.

'Bows,' Stefan Skellen bellowed from below. 'Fire the crossbows! Boreas Mun was meant to bring the crossbows! Where is he?'

Boreas Mun – which Tawny Owl couldn't have known – was already quite far away. He was riding eastwards, with his forehead against his horse's mane, squeezing as much gallop out of his steed as he could.

Only one of the men sent for the bows had returned.

The man who had decided to shoot had slightly shaking hands and eyes watering from fisstech. The first bolt barely grazed the balustrade. The second didn't even hit the stairs.

'Higher!' yelled Tawny Owl. 'Go higher, you fool! Shoot from up close.'

The crossbowmen pretended he hadn't heard. Skellen cursed

at great length, snatched the crossbow from him, leaped onto the stairway, kneeled down and took aim. Geralt quickly covered Ciri with his body. But the girl slipped out from behind him like lightning, so when the bowstring clanged she was already in position. She twisted her sword to the upper quarter and hit the bolt back so hard it somersaulted many times before it fell.

'Very good,' muttered Geralt. 'Very good, Ciri. But if you ever do that again, I'll tan your hide.'

Skellen dropped the crossbow. And suddenly realised he was alone.

All of his men were at the very bottom in a tight little group. None of them were too keen to go up the stairs. There seemed to be fewer than there were before. Once more several ran off somewhere. Probably to fetch crossbows.

And the Witcher and the witcher girl – not hurrying, but not slowing either – walked down, down the blood-covered stairway of Stygga Castle. Close to each other, shoulder to shoulder, tantalising and bamboozling their foes with fast movements of their blades.

Skellen walked backwards. And didn't stop. Right down to the very bottom. When he found himself in the group of his own men he noticed that the retreat was continuing. He swore impotently.

'Lads!' he yelled, and his voice broke discordantly. 'On you go! Have at them! En masse! Go on, have at them! Follow me!'

'Go yourself, sir,' mumbled one of them, raising a hand with fisstech to his nose. Tawny Owl punched him, covering the man's face, sleeve and the front of his jacket in white powder.

The Witcher and the witcher girl passed another landing.

'When they get to the very bottom we'll be able to surround them!' roared Skellen. 'Go on, lads! Have at them! To arms!'

Geralt glanced at Ciri. And almost howled with fury, seeing streaks shining white as silver in her ashen hair. He controlled himself. It wasn't the time for anger.

'Be careful,' he said softly. 'Stay close to me.'

'I'm always going to be close to you.'

'It'll be hot down there.'

'I know. But we're together.'

'We're together.'

385

'I'm with you,' said Yennefer, following them down the stairs, red and slippery with blood.

'Form up! Form up!' roared Tawny Owl.

Several of the men who had run to get crossbows returned. Without them. Very terrified.

The rumble of doors being forced by battle-axes, thudding, the clanking of iron and the sound of heavy steps resounded from all three corridors leading to the stairway. And suddenly soldiers in black helmets, armour and cloaks with the sign of a silver sala-mander marched out of all three corridors. On being shouted at thunderously and menacingly Skellen's mercenaries threw their weapons on the floor, one after the other. Crossbows and the blades of glaives and bear spears were aimed at the more hesitant, and they were urged on by even more menacing shouts. Now all of them obeyed, for it was evident that the black-cloaked soldiers were extremely keen to kill somebody and were only waiting for a pretext. Tawny Owl stood at the foot of a column, arms crossed on his chest.

'Miraculous relief?' muttered Ciri. Geralt shook his head.

Crossbows and spear blades were also being aimed at them.

'*Glaeddyvan vort!*'

There was no sense in resisting. Black-cloaked soldiers were swarming like ants at the bottom of the stairs, and the witchers were very, very weary. But they didn't drop their swords. They placed them carefully on the steps. And then sat down. Geralt felt Ciri's warm shoulder and heard her breath.

Yennefer descended, walking past corpses and pools of blood, showing the black-cloaked soldiers her unarmed hands. She sat down heavily beside them on a step. Geralt also felt the warmth against his other shoulder. *It's a pity it can't always be like this*, he thought. And he knew it couldn't.

Tawny Owl's men were tied up and escorted away one after the other. There were more and more soldiers in black cloaks bearing the salamander. Suddenly, high-ranking officers appeared among them, recognisable by the white plumes and silver edging on their suits of armour. And by the respect which the others showed in parting to let them pass.

The soldiers stood back with even greater respect before one of the officers, whose helmet was particularly sumptuously decorated with silver, bowing before him.

The man stopped in front of Skellen, who was standing at the foot of the column. Tawny Owl – it was very obvious even in the flickering light of the torches and the paintings burning out in the cressets – paled, becoming as white as a sheet.

'Stefan Skellen,' said the officer, in a resonant voice, a voice which sounded right up to the vault of the hall. 'You will be tried in court. And punished for treason.'

Tawny Owl was led away, but his hands weren't tied like the ordinary soldiers' had been.

The officer turned around. A burning rag broke off from a tapestry up above. It fell, swirling like a huge fiery bird. The brightness shone on the silver-edged armour, on the visor extending halfway down the cheeks which was – like all the black-cloaked soldiers' – shaped like horrendous toothed jaws.

Now our turn, thought Geralt. He wasn't mistaken.

The officer looked at Ciri, and his eyes burned in the slits of the helmet, noticing and registering everything. The paleness. The scar on her cheek. The blood on her sleeve and hand. The white streaks in her hair.

Then the Nilfgaardian turned his gaze onto the Witcher.

'Vilgefortz?' he asked in his resonant voice. Geralt shook his head.

'Cahir aep Ceallach?'

Another shake of the head.

'A slaughter,' said the officer, looking at the stairs. 'A bloodbath. Well, he who lives by the sword . . . Furthermore, you've saved the hangmen work. You've travelled a long way, Witcher.'

Geralt didn't comment. Ciri sniffed loudly and wiped her nose with her wrist. Yennefer gave her a scolding look. The Nilfgaardian also noticed that and smiled.

'You've travelled a long way,' he repeated. 'You've come here from the end of the world. Following her and for her sake. Even if only for that reason you deserve something. Lord de Rideaux!'

'Yes sir, Your Imperial Highness!'

The Witcher wasn't surprised.

'Please find a discreet chamber in which I shall be able to

converse, completely undisturbed, with Sir Geralt of Rivia. During that time please offer all possible comforts and services to the two ladies. Under vigilant and unremitting guard.'

'Yes, sir, Your Imperial Majesty.'

'Sir Geralt, please follow me.'

The Witcher stood up. He glanced at Yennefer and Ciri, wanting to calm them and warn them not to do anything foolish. But it wasn't necessary. They were both terribly tired. And resigned.

*

'You've travelled a long way,' repeated Emhyr var Emreis, Deithwen Addan yn Carn aep Morvudd, the White Flame Dancing on the Barrows of his Enemies, removing his helmet.

'I'm not sure,' Geralt calmly replied, 'if you haven't travelled further, Duny.'

'You've recognised me, well, well.' The emperor smiled. 'And they say the lack of a beard and my way of holding myself have changed me utterly. Many of the people who used to see me earlier in Cintra came to Nilfgaard later and saw me during audiences. And no one recognised me. But you only saw me once, and that was sixteen years ago. Did I become so embedded in your memory?'

'I wouldn't have recognised you, you have indeed changed greatly. I simply worked out who you were. Some time ago. I guessed – not without help and a hint from someone else – what role incest played in Ciri's family. In her blood. I even dreamed about the most awful, the most hideous incest imaginable in a gruesome nightmare. And well, here you are, in person.'

'You can barely stand,' said Emhyr coldly. 'And deliberate impertinence is making you even more unsteady. You may sit in the presence of the emperor. I grant you that privilege . . . until the end of your days.'

Geralt sat down with relief. Emhyr continued to stand, leaning against a carved wardrobe.

'You saved my daughter's life,' he said. 'Several times. I thank you for that. On behalf of myself and posterity.'

'You disarm me.'

'Cirilla will go to Nilfgaard.' Emhyr was not bothered by the mockery. 'She will become empress at a suitable moment. In precisely the same way that dozens of girls have become and do become queens. Meaning almost not knowing their spouses. Often not having a good opinion of them on the basis of their first encounter. Often disappointed by the first days and . . . first nights . . . of marriage. Cirilla won't be the first.'

Geralt refrained from comment.

'Cirilla,' continued the emperor, 'will be happy, like most of the queens I was talking about. It will come with time. Cirilla will transfer the love that I do not demand at all onto the son I will beget with her. An archduke, and later an emperor. An emperor who will beget a son. A son, who will be the ruler of the world and will save the world from destruction. Thus speaks the prophecy whose exact contents only I know.

'Naturally,' the White Flame continued, 'Cirilla will never find out who I am. The secret will die. Along with those who know it.'

'That's clear,' Geralt nodded. 'It can't be clearer.'

'You cannot fail to detect the hand of destiny in all of this,' Emhyr said after a long time, 'All of this. Including your activities. From the very beginning.'

'I see rather the hand of Vilgefortz. For it was he who directed you to Cintra, wasn't it? When you were the Enchanted Urcheon? He made Pavetta—'

'You're stumbling in the dark,' Emhyr interrupted brutally, tossing his salamander-decorated cloak over his shoulder. 'You don't know anything. And you don't have to know. I didn't ask you here to tell you my life story. Or to excuse myself before you. The only thing you have earned is the assurance that the girl will not be harmed. I have no debts towards you, Witcher. None—'

'Yes you do!' Geralt interrupted brutally. 'You broke the contract. You went back on your word. They are debts, Duny. You broke a promise as a princeling, and you have a debt as an emperor. With imperial interest. Ten years worth!'

'Is that all?'

'That is all. For only that is owed to me, nothing more. But nothing less, either. I was to collect the child when it turned six. You didn't wait for the promised date. You planned to steal it from me before it passed. The destiny you keep talking about sneered

389

at you, however. You tried to fight that destiny for the following ten years. Now you have her, you have Ciri, your own daughter, whom you once basely deprived of parents, and with whom you now mean to vilely beget incestuous children. Without demanding love. Rightly, as a matter of fact. You do not deserve her love. Just between us, Duny, I don't know how you will manage to look her in the eyes.'

'The end justifies the means,' Emhyr said dully. 'What I'm doing, I'm doing for posterity. To save the world.'

'If the world is to be saved like that—' the Witcher lifted his head '—it would be better for it to perish. Believe me, Duny, it'd be better if it perished.'

'You're pale,' Emhyr var Emreis said, almost gently. 'Don't get so excited, for you are liable to faint.'

He moved away from the wardrobe, selected a chair and sat down. The Witcher's head was indeed spinning.

'The Iron Urcheon,' the emperor began calmly and quietly, 'was to be a way of forcing my father to collaborate with the usurper. It was after the coup. My father, the overthrown emperor, was in prison and being tortured. He couldn't be broken, so another way was tried. A sorcerer hired by the usurper changed me into a monster in front of my father's eyes. The sorcerer added a little something on his own initiative. Namely humour. Eimyr in our language means an "urcheon", an old name for a hedgehog.

'My father didn't allow himself to be broken and so they murdered him. I, meanwhile, was released into a forest amidst mockery and scorn, and dogs were set on me. I survived. I wasn't hunted too seriously, for it wasn't known that the sorcerer had botched his work, and that my human form returned at night. Fortunately, I knew several people of whose loyalty I could be certain. And at that time I was, for your information, thirteen.

'I had to flee the country. And the fact that I ought to search for a cure to the spell in the North, beyond the Marnadal Stairs, was read in the stars by a slightly crazy astrologer by the name of Xarthisius. Later, when I was emperor, I gave him a tower and apparatus for that. At that time, he had to work on borrowed equipment.

'You know, it's a waste of time getting bogged down in what

happened in Cintra. I deny, however, that it supposedly had anything to do with Vilgefortz. Firstly, I didn't know him then, and secondly I had a strong aversion to mages. Even today I don't like them, actually. Ah, while I remember: when I regained the throne I caught up with the sorcerer who had served the usurper and tortured me in front of my father's eyes. I also displayed a sense of humour. The mage's name was Braathens, and in our language that sounds almost the same as "fried".

'Enough digressions, though, let's get back to the matter at hand. Vilgefortz visited me secretly in Cintra, shortly after Ciri's birth. He passed himself off as a trusted friend of people in Nilfgaard who were still loyal to me and had conspired against the usurper. He offered help and soon proved to be capable of helping. When, still mistrustful, I asked about his motives, he bluntly declared he was counting on gratitude. For the favours, privileges and power he would be given by the great Emperor of Nilfgaard. Meaning me. A powerful ruler who would govern half the world. Who would beget an heir who would govern half the world. He intended to rise high himself – or so he declared, without inhibition – at the side of those great rulers. Here he took out some scrolls bound with snake skin and commended the contents to my attention.

'Thus I learned of the prophecy. I learned about the fate of the world and the universe. I found out what I had to do. And came to the conclusion that the end justifies the means.'

'Of course.'

'My affairs were prospering in Nilfgaard, meanwhile.' Emhyr ignored the sarcasm. 'My partisans were gaining more and more influence. Finally, having a group of front line officers and a corps of cadets, they decided to launch a coup d'état. I was needed for that, nonetheless. Me myself. The rightful heir to the throne and crown of the empire, a rightful Emreis with the blood of the Emreises. I was to be something akin to the standard of the revolution. Just between us, plenty of the revolutionaries cherished the hope that I would be nothing more than that. Those among them who are still alive cannot get over it to this day.

'But, as has been said before, let us leave the digressions. I had to return to home. The time came for Duny, the false prince of Maecht and the phoney duke of Cintra, to demand his inheritance.

I hadn't forgotten about the prophecy, however. I had to return with Ciri. And Calanthe was keeping a weather eye on me.'

'She never trusted you.'

'I know. I think she knew something about that prediction. And would have done anything to hamper me, and in Cintra I was in her power. It was clear: I had to return to Nilfgaard, but in a way that no one could guess that I was Duny and Ciri was my daughter. Vilgefortz suggested a way. Duny, Pavetta and their child had to die. Vanish without trace.'

'In a staged shipwreck.'

'That's right. During the voyage from Skellige to Cintra, Vilgefortz was to pull the ship into a magical whirlpool over the Sedna Abyss. Pavetta, Ciri and I were supposed to have previously locked ourselves in a specially secured lifeboat and survive. And the crew—'

'Were meant not to survive,' finished the Witcher. 'And that's how your ruthless path began.'

Emhyr var Emreis said nothing for some time.

'It began earlier,' he finally said, and his voice was soft. 'Regrettably. At the moment it turned out Ciri wasn't on board.'

Geralt raised his eyebrows.

'Unfortunately, I hadn't appreciated Pavetta in my planning.' The emperor's face didn't express anything. 'That melancholy wench with her permanently lowered eyes had seen through me and my plans. She had sent the child ashore in secret before the anchor was weighed. I fell into a fury. As she did. She had an attack of hysteria. During the struggle . . . she fell overboard. Before I could dive after her, Vilgefortz had drawn the ship into his maelstrom. I hit my head against something and lost consciousness. I survived by a miracle, entangled in the ropes. I came to, covered in bandages. I had a broken arm.'

'I wonder how a man feels after murdering his wife,' the Witcher said coldly.

'Lousy,' replied Emhyr without delay. 'I felt and I feel lousy and bloody shabby. Even the fact that I never loved her doesn't change that. The end justifies the means, yet I sincerely do regret her death. I didn't want it or plan it. Pavetta died by accident.'

'You're lying,' Geralt said dryly, 'and that doesn't befit an emperor. Pavetta could not live. She had unmasked you. And would never have let you do what you wanted to do to Ciri.'

'She would have lived,' Emhyr retorted. 'Somewhere . . . far away. There are enough castles . . . Darn Rowan, for instance. I couldn't have killed her.'

'Even for an end that was justified by the means?'

'One can always find a less drastic means.' The emperor wiped his face. 'There are always plenty of them.'

'Not always,' said the Witcher, looking him in the eyes. Emhyr avoided his gaze.

'That's exactly what I thought,' Geralt said, nodding. 'Finish your story. Time's passing.'

'Calanthe guarded little Ciri like the apple of her eye. I couldn't even have dreamed of kidnapping her. My relations with Vilgefortz had cooled considerably, and I still had a dislike of other mages . . . But my military men and aristocracy were urging me hard towards war, towards an attack on Cintra. They vouched that the people were demanding it, that the people wanted living space, that listening to the *vox populi* would be a kind of imperial test. I decided to kill two birds with one stone. By capturing both Cintra and Ciri in one go. You know the rest.'

'I do,' Geralt nodded. 'Thank you for the conversation, Duny. I'm grateful that you were willing to devote your time to me. But I cannot delay any longer. I am very tired. I watched the death of my friends who followed me here to the end of the world. They came to rescue your daughter. Not even knowing her. Apart from Cahir, none of them even knew Ciri. But they came here to rescue her. For there was something in her that was decent and noble. And what happened? They found death. I consider that unjust. And if anyone wants to know, I don't agree with it. Because a story where the decent ones die and the scoundrels live and carry on doing what they want is full of shit. I don't have any more strength, Emperor. Summon your men.'

'Witcher—'

'The secret has to die with those who know it. You said it yourself. You don't have a choice. It's not true that you have plenty of them. I'll escape from any prison. I'll take Ciri from you. There's no price I wouldn't pay to take her away. As you well know.'

'I do.'

'You can let Yennefer live. She doesn't know the secret.'

'She would pay any price to rescue Ciri,' Emhyr said gravely. 'And avenge your death.'

'True,' the Witcher nodded. 'Indeed, I'd forgotten how much she loves Ciri. You're right, Duny. Well, you can't run from destiny. I have a request.'

'Yes.'

'Let me say goodbye to them both. Then I'll be at your disposal.'

Emhyr stood by the window, staring at the mountain peaks.

'I cannot decline you. But—'

'Don't worry. I won't tell Ciri anything. I'd be harming her by telling her who you are. And I couldn't harm her.'

Emhyr said nothing for a long time, still turned towards the window.

'Perhaps I do have a debt to you.' He turned on his heel. 'So hear what I will offer you in payment. Long, long ago, in former times, when people still had honour, pride and dignity, when they valued their word, and were only afraid of shame, it happened that persons of honour, when sentenced to death, and to escape the shameful hand of the executioner, would enter a bath of hot water and open their veins. Is it possible—?'

'Order the bath filled.'

'Is it possible,' the emperor calmly continued, 'that Yennefer might wish to accompany you in that bath?'

'I'm almost certain of it. But you must ask. She has quite a rebellious nature.'

'I know.'

*

Yennefer agreed at once.

'The circle is closed,' she added, looking down at her wrists. 'The serpent Ouroboros has sunk its teeth into its own tail.'

*

394

'I don't understand!' Ciri hissed like an infuriated cat. 'I don't understand why I have to go with him. Where to? What for?'

'Daughter,' Yennefer said softly. 'This, and no other, is your destiny. Understand that it simply can't be otherwise.'

'And you?'

'Our destiny awaits us.' Yennefer looked at Geralt. 'This is the way it has to be. Come here, my daughter. Hug me tightly.'

'They want to murder you, don't they? I don't agree! I've only just got you back! It's not fair!'

'He who lives by the sword,' Emhyr var Emreis said softly, 'dies by the sword. They fought against me and lost. But they lost with dignity.'

Ciri was standing before him in three strides, and Geralt silently sucked in air. He heard Yennefer's gasp. *Dammit*, he thought, *everybody can see it! All his black-uniformed army can see what can't be hidden! The same posture, the same sparkling eyes, the same grimace. Arms crossed on the chest identically. Fortunately, extremely fortunately, she inherited her ashen hair from her mother. But anyhow, when you scrutinise them, it's clear whose blood . . .*

'But you won,' said Ciri, glaring at him passionately. 'You won. And do you think it was with dignity?'

Emhyr var Emreis didn't reply. He just smiled, eyeing the girl with a clearly contented gaze. Ciri clenched her teeth.

'So many have died. So many people have died because of all this. Did they lose with dignity? Is death dignified? Only a beast could think like that. Though I looked on death from close up it wasn't possible to turn me into a beast. And it won't be possible.'

He didn't answer. He looked at her, and it seemed he was drinking her in with his gaze.

'I know what you're plotting,' she hissed, 'Know what you want to do with me. And I'll tell you right now: I won't let you touch me. And if you . . . If you . . . I'll kill you. Even tied up. When you fall asleep I'll tear your throat out with my teeth.'

With a rapid gesture, the imperator quietened the rumble gathering among the officers surrounding them.

'What is destined, shall be,' he drawled, not taking his eyes off Ciri. 'Say goodbye to your friends, Cirilla Fiona Elen Riannon.'

Ciri looked at the Witcher. Geralt shook his head. The girl sighed.

She and Yennefer hugged and whispered for a long time. Then Ciri went closer to Geralt.

'Pity,' she said quietly. 'Things were looking more promising.'

'Much more.'

They hugged each other.

'Be brave.'

'He won't have me,' she whispered. 'Don't worry. I'll escape from him. I have a way—'

'You may not kill him. Remember, Ciri. You may not.'

'Don't worry. I wasn't thinking about killing at all. You know, Geralt, I've had enough of killing. There's been too much of it.'

'Too much. Farewell, Witcher Girl.'

'Farewell, Witcher.'

'Just don't cry.'

'Easier said than done.'

*

Emhyr var Emreis, Imperator of Nilfgaard, accompanied Yennefer and Geralt all the way to the bathroom. Almost to the edge of a large, marble pool, full of steaming, fragrant water.

'Farewell,' he said. 'You don't have to hurry. I'm going, but I'm leaving people here who I shall instruct and to whom I shall issue orders. When you're ready, just call, and a lieutenant will give you a knife. But I repeat: you don't have to hurry.'

'We appreciate your favour,' Yennefer nodded gravely. 'Your Imperial Majesty?'

'Yes?'

'Please, as far as possible, don't harm my daughter. I wouldn't want to die with the thought that she's crying.'

Emhyr was silent for a long time. A very long time. Leaning against a window. With his head turned away.

'Madam Yennefer,' he finally answered, and his face was very strange. 'You may be certain I shall not harm your and Witcher Geralt's daughter. I've trampled human bodies and danced on the barrows of my foes. And I thought I was capable of anything. But what you suspect me of, I simply wouldn't be capable of doing. I know it now. So I thank you both. Farewell.'

He went out, quietly closing the door behind him. Geralt sighed.

'Shall we undress?' He glanced at the steaming pool. 'The thought that they'll haul me out of here as a naked corpse doesn't especially delight me.'

'And, can you believe it, to me it's all the same.' Yennefer threw off her slippers and unfastened her dress with swift movements. 'Even if it's my last bath, I'm not going to bathe in my clothes.'

She pulled her blouse over her head and entered the pool, energetically splashing water around.

'Well, Geralt? Why are you standing there like a statue?'

'I'd forgotten how beautiful you are.'

'You forget easily. Come on, into the water.'

When he sat down beside her she immediately threw her arms around his neck. He kissed her, stroking her waist, above and below the water.

'Is it,' he asked for form's sake, 'an appropriate time?'

'Any time,' she muttered, putting a hand under the water and touching him, 'is the right time for this. Emhyr repeated twice that we don't have to hurry. What would you prefer to spend doing during the last minutes given to you? Weeping and wailing? That's undignified, isn't it? Examining your conscience? That's banal and stupid, isn't it?'

'That's not what I meant.'

'So what did you mean?'

'The cuts will be painful if the water cools down,' he murmured, caressing her breasts.

'It's worth paying in pain—' Yennefer put her other hand in the water '—for pleasure. Are you afraid of pain?'

'No.'

'Neither am I. Sit on the edge of the pool. I love you, but I'm not bloody going to do it underwater.'

*

397

'Oh my, oh my,' said Yennefer, tilting her head back so that her hair, damp from the steam, spread over the edge like little black vipers. 'Oh my . . . oh.'

*

'I love you, Yen.'

'I love you, Geralt.'

'It's time. We'll call them.'

'We'll call them.'

They called. First the Witcher called, and then Yennefer called. Then, not having heard any reaction, they yelled in unison.

'Now! We're ready! Give us that knife! Heeey! Dammit! The water's cooling down!'

'Get out of there,' said Ciri, peeping into the bathroom. 'They've all gone.'

'What?'

'I'm telling you. They've gone. Apart from us three there isn't a living soul here. Get dressed. You look awfully funny in the nude.'

*

As they were dressing, their hands began to tremble. Both Geralt's and Yennefer's. They had great difficulty coping with the hooks and eyes, clasps and buttons. Ciri was jabbering away.

'They rode away. Just like that. All of them, as many as there were of them. They took everyone from here, mounted their horses and rode away. As fast as they could.'

'Didn't they leave anybody?'

'Nobody at all.'

'That's staggering,' whispered Geralt. 'It's staggering.'

'Has anything happened—' Yennefer cleared her throat '—to explain it?'

'No,' Ciri quickly replied. 'Nothing.'

She was lying.

*

At first she put on a brave front. Erect, with head haughtily raised and stony-faced, she pushed away the gloved hands of the black-cloaked knights, looking boldly and defiantly at the menacing nose-guards and visors of their helmets. They didn't touch her any longer, particularly since they were stopped from doing so by the growl of an officer, a broad-shouldered soldier with silver braid and a white heron-feather plume.

She walked towards the exit, escorted on both sides. With her head proudly raised. Heavy boots thudded, mail shirts clanked and weapons jingled.

After a dozen paces she looked back for the first time. After the next few the second time. *Why, I'll never, ever see them again.* The thought flashed with terrifying and cool clarity beneath her crown. *Neither Geralt nor Yennefer. Never.*

That awareness immediately, all at once, wiped away the mask of feigned courage. Ciri's face contorted and grimaced, her eyes filled with tears and her nose ran. The girl fought with all her strength, but in vain. A wave of tears breached the dam of pretence.

The Nilfgaardians with salamanders on their cloaks looked at her in silence and amazement. Some of them had seen her on the bloody staircase, all of them had seen her in conversation with the emperor. The witcher girl with a sword, the unvanquished witcher girl, arrogantly challenging the imperator to his face. And now they were surprised to see a snivelling, sobbing child.

She was aware of it. Their eyes burned her like fire, pricked her like pins. She fought, but ineffectively. The more powerfully she held back her tears, the more powerfully they exploded.

She slowed down and then stopped. The escort also stopped. But only for a moment. On the growling command of an officer iron hands grasped her by the upper arms and wrists. Ciri, sobbing and swallowing back tears, looked back for the last time. Then they dragged her. She didn't resist, but sobbed louder and louder and more and more despairingly.

They were stopped by Emperor Emhyr var Emreis, that dark-haired man with a face which awoke strange, vague memories in her. They released her when he gave a curt order. Ciri sniffed and wiped her eyes with her sleeve. Seeing him approaching, she stopped sobbing and raised her head haughtily. But now – she was aware of it – it just looked ridiculous.

Emhyr looked at her for a long while. Without a word. Then he approached her. And held out a hand. Ciri, who always reacted to gestures like that by pulling away involuntarily, now, to her great amazement, didn't react. To her even greater amazement she found his touch wasn't unpleasant at all.

He touched her hair, as though counting the snow-white streaks. He touched her cheek, disfigured by the scar. Then he hugged her and stroked her head and back. And she, overwhelmed by weeping, let him, although she held her arms as stiffly as a scarecrow.

'It's a strange thing, destiny,' she heard him whisper. 'Farewell, my daughter.'

*

'What did he say?'

Ciri's face grimaced slightly.

'He said: *va faill, luned.* In the Elder Speech: farewell, girl.'

'I know,' Yennefer nodded. 'What then?'

'Then . . . Then he let me go, turned around and walked away. He shouted some orders. And everybody went. They passed me, utterly indifferently, with stamping, thudding and the clanking of armour echoing down the corridor. They mounted their horses and rode away, I heard the neighing and tramping of hooves. I'll never understand that. For if I were to wonder—'

'Ciri.'

'What?'

'Don't wonder about it.'

*

'Stygga Castle,' repeated Philippa Eilhart, looking at Fringilla Vigo from under her eyelashes. Fringilla didn't blush. During the past three months she had managed to manufacture a magical cream which made the blood vessels contract. Thanks to the cream she didn't blush, no matter how embarrassed she was.

'Vilgefortz's hide-out was in Stygga Castle,' confirmed Assire var Anahid. 'In Ebbing, above a mountain lake, whose name my informer, a simple soldier, was unable to recall.'

'You said: "was"—' Francesca Findabair observed.

'Was,' Philippa interrupted in mid-sentence. 'Because Vilgefortz is dead, my dear ladies. He and his accomplices, the entire gang, are no more. That favour was done for us by no other than our good friend the Witcher, Geralt of Rivia. Whom we didn't appreciate. None of us. About whom we were mistaken. All of us. Some of us less seriously, others more.'

All the sorceresses looked at Fringilla in unison, but the cream really did act effectively. Assire var Anahid sighed. Philippa tapped her hand on the table.

'Although the multitude of activities connected to the war and the preparations for the peace negotiations excuse us,' she said dryly, 'we ought to admit that the fact of being thoroughly out-manoeuvred in the case of Vilgefortz is a defeat for the lodge. That must never happen to us again, my dear ladies.'

The lodge – with the exception of the ashen-pale Fringilla Vigo – nodded.

'Right now,' continued Philippa, 'the Witcher Geralt is somewhere in Ebbing. Along with Yennefer and Ciri, whom he freed. We ought to ponder over how to find them—'

'And that castle?' Sabrina Glevissig interrupted. 'Haven't you forgotten something, Philippa?'

'No, no I haven't. The legend, if it should arise, ought to have a single, faithful version. Thus I'd like to ask you to do it, Sabrina. Take Keira and Triss with you. Sort out the matter. So that no trace remains.'

*

The roar of the explosion was heard as far away as in Maecht, and the flash – since it took place at night – was visible even in Metinna and Geso. The series of further tectonic shocks were perceptible even further away. At the remotest ends of the world.

Congreve, *Estella or Stella, the daughter of Baron Otto de Congreve, espoused to the Count of Liddertal, managed his estates extremely judiciously following his early death, owing to which she amassed a considerable fortune. Enjoying the great estimation of Emperor Emhyr var Emreis (q.v.), she was a greatly important personage at his court. Although she held no position, it was known that the emperor was always in the habit of gracing her voice and opinion with his attention and consideration. Owing to her great affection for the young Empress Cirilla Fiona (see also), whom she loved like her own daughter, she was jokingly called the 'empress mother'. Having survived both the emperor and the empress, she died in 1331, and her immense estate was left in her will to distant relatives, a side branch of the Liddertals called the White Liddertals. They, however, being careless and giddy-headed people, utterly squandered it.*

Effenberg and Talbot,
Encyclopaedia Maxima Mundi, vol. III

CHAPTER TEN

The man stealing up to the camp, to give him his due, was as spry and cunning as a fox. He changed his position so swiftly, and moved so agilely and quietly, that he could have sneaked up on anyone. Anyone. But not Boreas Mun. Boreas Mun had too much experience in the matter of stalking.

'Come out, fellow!' he called, trying hard to colour his voice with self-assured and confident arrogance. 'Those tricks of yours are in vain. I see you. You're over there.'

One of the megaliths, a ridge of which bristled on the hillside, twitched against the deep blue, starry sky. It moved. And assumed human form.

Boreas turned some meat roasting on a spit, for he could smell burning. He laid his hand on his bow's riser, pretending to be leaning carelessly.

'My belongings are meagre.' He wove a gruff, metallic thread of warning into his apparently calm tone. 'There are a few of them. But I'm attached to them. I shall defend them to the death.'

'I'm no bandit,' said the man, who had pretended to be a menhir, in a deep voice. 'I'm a pilgrim.'

The pilgrim was tall and powerfully built, easily measuring seven feet, and in order to balance him on a weighing scales Boreas would have bet anything that a weight of at least five-and-twenty stone would have been required. His pilgrim's staff, a pole as thick as a cart shaft, looked like a walking cane in his hand. Boreas Mun was indeed amazed how such a huge clodhopper was able to steal up so agilely. He was also somewhat alarmed. His bow, a composite seventy-pounder, with which he could down an elk at four dozen paces, suddenly seemed a small, fragile child's toy.

'I'm a pilgrim,' repeated the powerful man. 'I mean no—'

'And the other man,' Boreas interrupted sharply. 'Let him come out too.'

'What oth—?' stammered the pilgrim and broke off, seeing a slender silhouette, noiseless as a shadow, emerging from the gloom on the other side. This time Boreas Mun wasn't at all amazed. The other man – his way of moving immediately betrayed it to the tracker's trained eye – was an elf. And it is no disgrace to be sneaked up on by an elf.

'I ask for forgiveness,' said the elf in a strangely un-elven, slightly husky voice. 'I hid from both of you gentlemen not from evil intentions, but from fear. I'd turn that spit over.'

'Indeed,' said the pilgrim, leaning on his staff and sniffing audibly. 'The meat's cooked more than enough on that side.'

Boreas turned the spit, sighed and cleared his throat. And sighed again.

'Sit you down, gentlemen,' he decided. 'And wait. The animal will be done any minute. Ha, verily, he's a fool who denies meat to travellers on the road.'

The fat dribbled onto the fire with a hiss, the fire flared up. It became brighter.

The pilgrim was wearing a felt hat with a broad brim, whose shadow quite effectively covered his face. A turban made from colourful cloth, not covering his face, served as headgear for the elf. When they saw his face in the glare of the campfire, both men – Boreas and the pilgrim – shuddered. But didn't utter so much as a gasp, not even a soft one, at the sight of the face, once no doubt elfinly beautiful, now disfigured by a hideous scar running diagonally across his forehead, brow, nose and cheek to his chin.

Boreas Mun cleared his throat and turned the spit again.

'This sweet fragrance lured you to my campfire,' he stated rather than asked. 'Didn't it, gentlemen?'

'Indeed.' The pilgrim tipped the brim of his hat and his voice changed a little. 'I smelled out the roast from far away, with all due modesty. But I remained cautious. They were roasting a woman on a campfire I approached two days ago.'

'That's true,' confirmed the elf. 'I was there the next morning, I saw human bones in the ashes.'

'The next morning,' the pilgrim repeated in a slow, drawling voice, and Boreas would have bet anything that a nasty smile had appeared on the face concealed by the shadow of the hat.

'Have you been tracking me in secret for long, Master Elf?'

'Aye.'

'And what stopped you revealing yourself?'

'Good sense.'

'The Elskerdeg pass—' Boreas Mun turned the spit and interrupted the awkward silence '—is a place that doesn't enjoy the best of reputations. I've also seen bones on campfires, skeletons on stakes. Men hanged from trees. This place is full of the savage followers of cruel cults. And creatures just waiting to eat you. According to hearsay.'

'It's not hearsay,' the elf corrected him. 'It's the truth. And the further into the mountains towards the east, the worse it'll be.'

'Are you gentlemen also travelling eastwards? Beyond Elskerdeg? To Zerrikania? Or perhaps even further, to Hakland?'

Neither the pilgrim nor the elf replied. Boreas hadn't really expected an answer. Firstly, the question had been indiscreet. Secondly, it had been stupid. From where they were it was only possible to go back or eastwards. Through Elskerdeg. Where he too was headed.

'Roast's ready.' Boreas opened a butterfly knife with a deft flourish, meant to impress. 'Go ahead, gentlemen. Help yourselves.'

The pilgrim had a cutlass, and the elf a dagger, which also didn't resemble a kitchen knife at all. But all three blades, sharpened for more menacing purposes, served to carve meat that day. For some time all that could be heard was crunching and munching. And the sizzling of chewed bones thrown into the embers.

The pilgrim belched in a dignified manner.

'Strange little creature,' he said, examining the shoulder blade which he had gnawed clean and licked until it looked as though it had been kept for three days in an anthill. 'It tasted a bit like goat, and it was as tender as coney . . . I don't recall eating anything like that.'

'It was a skrekk,' said the elf, crunching the gristle with a crack. 'Neither do I recall eating it at any time.'

Boreas cleared his throat quietly. The barely audible note of sarcastic merriment in the elf's voice proved he knew that the roast came from an enormous rat with bloodshot eyes and huge teeth, only the tail of which measured three ells. The tracker had by no

407

means hunted the gigantic rodent. He had shot it in self-defence, but had decided to roast it. He was a sensible and clear-headed man. He wouldn't have eaten a rat scavenging on rubbish heaps and eating scraps. But it was a good three hundred miles from the narrow passage of the Elskerdeg pass to the nearest community capable of generating waste. The rat – or, as the elf had said, skrekk – must have been clean and healthy. It hadn't had any contact with civilisation. So there was nothing it could have been soiled by or infected with.

Soon the last, smallest bone, chewed and sucked clean, landed in the embers. The moon rose over the jagged range of the Fiery Mountains. The wind fed the fire and sparks shot up, dying out and fading amidst the countless twinkling stars.

'Long on the road, gentlemen?' Boreas Mun risked another none-too-discreet question, 'Here, in the Wildernesses? Left the Solveiga Gate behind you long since, if you'll pardon my asking?'

'Long since, long since,' said the pilgrim, 'is a relative thing. I passed through Solveiga the second day after the September full moon.'

'Me on the sixth day,' said the elf.

'Ha,' continued Boreas Mun, encouraged by the reaction. 'It's a wonder we've only met up now, because I also walked that way, or actually rode, for I still had a horse then.'

He fell silent, driving away the unpleasant thoughts and recollections linked to the horse and its loss. He was sure his accidental companions must also have had similar adventures. If they'd been walking the whole time they never would have caught up with him here, near Elskerdeg.

'I venture, thus,' he continued, 'that you set off right after the war, after the Peace of Cintra was concluded, gentlemen. It's none of my business, naturally, but I dare suppose that you were not pleased by the order and vision of the world created and established in Cintra.'

The lengthy silence that fell by the campfire was interrupted by distant howling. A wolf, probably. Although in the vicinity of the Elskerdeg pass you could never be certain.

'If I'm to be frank,' the elf spoke up unexpectedly, 'I didn't have the grounds to be pleased with the world and its image following the Peace of Cintra. Not to mention the new order.'

'In my case it was similar,' said the pilgrim, crossing his powerful forearms on his chest. 'Though I came to realise it, as a friend said, *post factum*.'

Silence reigned for a long time. Even whatever had been howling on the pass was silent.

'At first,' continued the pilgrim – although Boreas and the elf had been ready to bet he would not – 'At first, everything indicated that the Peace of Cintra would bring favourable changes, would create quite a tolerable world order. If not for everyone, then at least for me . . .'

'If my memory serves me—' Boreas cleared his throat '—the kings arrived in Cintra in April?'

'The second of April, to be precise,' the pilgrim corrected him. 'It was, I recall, a full moon.'

*

Along the walls, positioned below the dark beams supporting a small gallery, hung rows of shields with colourful representations of the heraldic emblems and coats of arms of the Cintran nobility. A first glance revealed the differences between the now somewhat faded arms of the ancient families and those of families ennobled more recently during the reigns of Dagorad and Calanthe. The newer ones had vivid and not yet cracked paint, and no peppering of woodworm holes was visible on them.

Whereas the escutcheons of the more recently ennobled Nilfgaardian families, rewarded during the capture of the castle and the five-year imperial administration, had the most vivid colours.

When we regain Cintra, thought King Foltest, *it will be necessary to make sure the Cintrans don't destroy those shields in a fervour of revival. Politics is one thing, the hall's decor another. Changes in regimes cannot be a justification for vandalism.*

So everything began here, thought Dijkstra, looking around the great hall. *The celebrated betrothal banquet, during which the Steel Urcheon appeared and demanded the hand of Princess Pavetta . . . And Queen Calanthe engaged the Witcher . . .*

How bizarre are the twists of human fate, thought the spy, surprising himself at the banality of his own musings.

Five years ago, thought Queen Meve, *five years ago, the brain of Calanthe, the Lioness of the blood of the Cerbins, splashed onto the floor of the courtyard, this very courtyard I can see from the windows. Calanthe, whose proud portrait we saw in the corridor, was the penultimate living carrier of the royal blood. After her daughter, Pavetta, drowned, the only one left was her granddaughter. Cirilla. Unless the news that Cirilla is also dead is true.*

'Please.' Cyrus Engelkind Hemmelfart, the Hierarch of Novigrad, accepted on grounds of age, position and universal respect *per acclamationem* as the chairman of the meeting, beckoned with a trembling hand. 'Please take your seats.'

They found their chairs, which were marked by mahogany plaques, and sat down at the round table. Meve, Queen of Rivia and Lyria. Foltest, King of Temeria, and his vassal, King Venzlav of Brugge. Demavend, King of Aedirn. Henselt, King of Kaedwen. King Ethain of Cidaris. Young King Kistrin of Verden. Duke Nitert, head of the Redanian Regency Council. And Count Dijkstra.

We must rid ourselves of that spy, remove him from the conference table, thought the hierarch. *King Henselt and King Foltest, why, even young Kistrin, have taken the liberty of making sour remarks, so at any moment there'll be a* démarche *from the Nilfgaardian representatives. Sigismund Dijkstra is a man of unseemly breeding, and furthermore a person with a dirty past and bad reputation, a* persona turpis. *One cannot let the presence of a* persona turpis *infect the atmosphere of the negotiations.*

The head of the Nilfgaardian delegation, Baron Shilard Fitz-Oesterlen, who had been allotted a place at the round table immediately opposite Dijkstra, greeted the spy with a polite diplomatic bow.

Seeing that everybody was now seated, the Hierarch of Novigrad also sat down. Not without the help of pages supporting him by his trembling arms. The hierarch sat down on a chair made for Queen Calanthe many years before. The chair had an impressively high and richly decorated backrest, making it stand out among the other ones.

So it was here, thought Triss Merigold, looking around the chamber, staring at the tapestries, paintings and numerous hunting trophies, and the antlers of a horned animal totally unfamiliar to her. *It was here, after the infamous shambles in the throne room, where the famous private conversation between Calanthe, the Witcher, Pavetta and the Enchanted Urcheon occurred. When Calanthe gave her agreement to that bizarre marriage. And Pavetta was already pregnant. Ciri was born almost eight months later . . . Ciri, the heir to the throne . . . The Lion Cub from the Lioness' blood . . . Ciri, my little sister. Who's still somewhere far away in the South. Fortunately, she's no longer alone. She's with Geralt and Yennefer. She's safe.*

Unless they've lied to me again.

'Sit down, dear ladies,' urged Philippa Eilhart, who had been scrutinising Triss closely for some time. 'In a short while the rulers of the world will begin making their inaugural speeches one after another; I wouldn't want to miss a word.'

The sorceresses, interrupting their furtive gossiping, quickly took their seats. Sheala de Tancarville, in a boa of silver fox, which gave a feminine accent to her severe male outfit. Assire var Anahid, in a dress of mauve silk, which extremely gracefully combined modest simplicity with chic elegance. Francesca Findabair, regal, as usual. Ida Emean aep Sivney, mysterious, as usual. Margarita Laux-Antille, distinguished and serious. Sabrina Glevissig in turquoise. Keira Metz in green and daffodil yellow. And Fringilla Vigo. Dejected. Sad. And pale with a truly deathly, morbid, utterly ghastly paleness.

Triss Merigold was sitting beside Keira, opposite Fringilla. A painting depicting a horseman galloping headlong down a road between an avenue of alders hung above the head of the Nilfgaardian sorceress. The alders were holding out their monstrous arm-like boughs towards the rider, sneeringly smiling with the ghastly maws of their hollows. Triss shuddered involuntarily.

The three-dimensional telecommunicator standing in the middle of the table was active. Philippa Eilhart used a spell to focus the image and sound.

'Ladies, as you can see and hear,' she said, not without a sneer, 'the rulers of the world are, at this very moment, getting down to deciding the fate of it in the throne room of Cintra, plumb beneath us, one floor lower. And we, here, one floor above them, will be watching over so that the boys don't go too wild.'

*

Other howlers joined the howler howling in Elskerdeg. Boreas had no doubt. They weren't wolves.

'I hadn't expected much from those Cintran talks either,' he said, in order to revive the dead conversation. 'Why, no one I know expected any good to come of them.'

'The simple fact that the negotiations began was important,' calmly protested the pilgrim. 'A simple fellow, and I indeed am just such a fellow, if I may say so, thinks simply. A simple fellow knows that the warring kings and emperors aren't that furious with each other. If they could have, if they'd had the strength, they'd have killed each other. That they've stopped trying to kill each other, and instead of that have sat down to a round table? That means they have no more power. They are, to put it simply, powerless. And the result of that powerlessness is that no armed men are attacking a simple fellow's homestead; they aren't killing, aren't mutilating, aren't burning down buildings, they aren't cutting children's throats, aren't raping wives, or driving people into captivity. No. Instead of that they've gathered in Cintra and are negotiating. Let's rejoice!'

The elf finished poking with his stick a log in the fire that was shooting sparks and looked askance at the pilgrim.

'Even a simple fellow,' he said, not concealing the sarcasm, 'even if he's joyful, why, even euphoric, ought to understand that politics is also a war, just conducted a little differently. He ought to understand that negotiations are like trade. They have the same self-propelling mechanism. Negotiated successes are bought with concessions. You win some, you lose some. In other words, in order for some people to be bought, others have to be sold.'

'Indeed,' the pilgrim said after a while. 'It's so simple and obvious that every man understands it. Even a simple one.'

'No, no and once more, no!' yelled King Henselt, banging both fists on the table so hard he knocked over a goblet and made the inkwells jump. 'No discussions on that subject! No horse-trading in this matter! That's the end, that's that, *deireadh*!'

'Henselt.' Foltest spoke calmly, soberly and very placatingly. 'Don't make things difficult. And don't embarrass us in front of His Excellency with your yelling.'

Shilard Fitz-Oesterlen, negotiator for the Empire of Nilfgaard, bowed with a false smile which was meant to imply that the King of Kaedwen's antics were neither shocking nor bothering him.

'We are negotiating with the Empire,' continued Foltest, 'and amongst ourselves we've suddenly begun to bite each other like dogs? It's a disgrace, Henselt.'

'We've reached agreement with Nilfgaard in matters as difficult as Dol Angra and Riverdell,' said Dijkstra apparently casually. 'It would be stupid—'

'I won't have such remarks!' roared Henselt, this time so loudly that not even a buffalo would have matched him. 'I won't put up with such remarks, particularly from spies, of all people! I'm the king, for fuck's sake!'

'That's quite plain,' snorted Meve. Demavend, his back to them, was looking at the escutcheons on the wall, smiling contemptuously, quite as if the game was not about his kingdom.

'Enough,' panted Henselt, eyes roving around. 'Enough, enough by the Gods, or my blood will boil. I said: not a span of land. No, but no, repossession! I won't agree to my kingdom being reduced by so much as a span, even half a span of land! The Gods entrusted me with the honour of Kaedwen and only to the Gods will I give it up! The Lower Marches is our land . . . Our . . . eth . . . ethic . . . ethnic land. The Lower Marches have belonged to Kaedwen for centuries . . .'

'Upper Aedirn,' Dijkstra spoke again, 'has belonged to Kaedwen since last year. To be precise, since the twenty-fourth of July last year. From the moment a Kaedwenian occupying force invaded it.'

'I request,' Shilard Fitz-Oesterlen said without being asked, 'for it to be minuted *ad futuram rei memoriam* that the Empire of Nilfgaard had nothing to do with that annexation.'

'Apart from the fact that it was pillaging Vengerberg at the time.'

'*Nihil ad rem!*'

'Indeed?'

'Gentlemen!' Foltest admonished.

'The Kaedwenian Army,' rasped Henselt, 'entered the Lower Marches as liberators! My soldiers were welcomed there with flowers! My soldiers—'

'Your *bandits*.' King Demavend's voice was calm, but it was apparent from his face how much effort it was costing him. 'Your brigands, who invaded my kingdom with a murderous *hassa*, murdered, raped and looted. Gentlemen! We have gathered here and have been debating for a week, we're debating about what the future face of the world should be. By the Gods, is it to be a face of crime and pillage? Is the murderous *status quo* to be maintained? Are plundered goods to remain in the hands of the thug and the marauder?'

Henselt seized a map from the table, tore it up with a violent movement and hurled it towards Demavend. The King of Aedirn didn't even move.

'My army,' wheezed Henselt, and his face took on the colour of good, old wine, 'captured the Marches from the Nilfgaardians. Your woeful kingdom didn't even exist then, Demavend. I shall say more: had it not been for my army you wouldn't even have a kingdom today. I'd like to see you driving the Black Cloaks over the Yaruga and beyond Dol Angra without my help. Thus the statement that you're king by my grace wouldn't be much of an exaggeration. But here my generosity ends! I said I won't give up even a span of my land. I won't let my kingdom be diminished.'

'Nor I!' Demavend stood up. 'We shall not reach agreement, then!'

'Gentlemen.' Cyrus Hemmelfart, the Hierarch of Novigrad, who had been slumbering until then, suddenly spoke in a placatory manner. 'Some kind of compromise is surely possible—'

'The Empire of Nilfgaard,' began again Shilard Fitz-Oesterlen, who liked to butt in out of the blue, 'will not accept any deal that

414

would be damaging to the Land of Elves in Dol Blathanna. If necessary, I shall read you once again the contents of the memorandum . . .'

Henselt, Foltest and Dijkstra snorted, but Demavend looked at the imperial ambassador calmly and almost benignly.

'For the general good and for peace,' he declared, 'I recognise the autonomy of Dol Blathanna. Not as a kingdom, but as a duchy. The condition is that Duchess Enid an Gleanna pays liege homage to me and obligates herself to grant equal rights and privileges to humans and elves. I'm prepared to do that, as I have said, *pro publico bono.*'

'Spoken like a true king,' said Meve.

'*Salus publica lex suprema est,*' said Hierarch Hemmelfart, who had also been searching for some time for the chance to show off his knowledge of diplomatic jargon.

'I shall add, nonetheless,' continued Demavend, looking at the pompous Henselt, 'that the concession regarding Dol Blathanna is not a precedent. It is the only encroachment on the integrity of my lands to which I shall agree. I shall not recognise any other partition. The Kaedwenian Army that invaded my borders as an aggressor and invader has one week to abandon the illegally occupied fortalices and castles of Upper Aedirn. That is the condition of my further participation in this conference. And because *verba volant*, my secretary shall submit to the minutes an official *démarche* in the case.'

'Henselt?' Foltest looked hesitantly at the bearded king.

'Never!' roared the King of Kaedwen, knocking over a chair and hopping like a chimpanzee stung by a hornet. 'I'll never give up the Marches! Over my dead body! Never! Nothing will make me! No force! No fucking force!'

And in order to prove he was also well-born and educated he howled: '*Non possumus!*'

*

'I'll give him *non possumus*, the old fool!' snorted Sabrina Glevissig in the upstairs chamber. 'You need not worry, ladies, I'll force that blockhead to recognise the repossession demands in the case of

Upper Aedirn. The Kaedwenian Army will leave before ten days are up. The matter is clear. No two ways about it. If any of you doubted it I have the right to feel piqued, indeed.'

Philippa Eilhart and Sheala de Tancarville expressed their acknowledgement by bowing. Assire var Anahid gave her thanks with a smile.

'All that remains today,' said Sabrina, 'is to settle the matter of Dol Blathanna. We know the contents of Emperor Emhyr's memorandum. The kings down below still haven't had the chance to discuss that matter, but have signalled their preferences. And the most – I would say – interested party has taken a stance. That's King Demavend.'

'Demavend's stance,' said Sheala de Tancarville, wrapping the silver fox boa around her neck, 'bears the features of a far-reaching compromise. It's a positive, considered and balanced stance. Shilard Fitz-Oesterlen will have considerable difficulty trying to argue in the direction of greater concessions. I don't know if he'll want to.'

'He will,' Assire var Anahid stated calmly. 'Because those are the instructions he has from Nilfgaard. He will invoke *ad referendum* and submit notes. He'll argue for at least a day. After that time has passed he'll begin to make concessions—'

'That's normal,' Sabrina Glevissig cut her off. 'It's normal that they'll finally find some common ground and agree on something. We won't wait for that, we'll decide right away what they'll ultimately be permitted to do. Francesca! Say something! It's about your country, after all.'

'Just for that reason—' the Daisy of the Valleys smiled very beautifully '—just for that reason I'm keeping quiet, Sabrina.'

'Get over your pride,' Margarita Laux-Antille said gravely. 'We have to know what we can allow the kings.'

Francesca Findabair smiled even more beautifully.

'For the sake of peace and *pro bono publico*,' she said, 'I agree to King Demavend's offer. From this moment you may stop addressing me as Your Royal Highness, my dear girls; an ordinary "Your Enlightenment" will suffice.'

'Elven jokes,' Sabrina grimaced, 'don't amuse me at all, probably because I don't understand them. What about Demavend's other conditions?'

Francesca fluttered her eyelashes.

'I agree to the re-immigration of human settlers and the return of their estates,' she said gravely. 'I guarantee equality to all races . . .'

'For the love of the Gods, Enid,' laughed Philippa Eilhart. 'Don't agree to everything! Set some conditions!'

'I shall.' The elf suddenly grew more serious. 'I don't agree to liege homage. I want Dol Blathanna as a freehold. No vassal duties apart from an oath of loyalty and no actions to the detriment of the suzerain.'

'Demavend won't agree,' Philippa commented curtly. 'He won't waive the income and rent that the Valley of Flowers gave him.'

'In that matter—' Francesca raised her eyebrows '—I'm prepared to negotiate bilaterally; I'm sure we can achieve consensus. The freehold doesn't demand payment, but it doesn't forbid nor exclude it either.'

'And what about familial inheritance?' Philippa Eilhart kept digging. 'What about primogeniture? By agreeing to a freehold, Foltest will want a guarantee of the duchy's indivisibility.'

'My complexion and figure may indeed beguile Foltest,' Francesca smiled again, 'but I'm surprised at you, Philippa. The age when falling pregnant was a possibility is far, far behind me. Regarding primogeniture and fideicommissum Demavend ought not to be afraid. For I shall be the *ultimus familiae* of the dynasty of Dol Blathanna's monarchs. But in spite of the age difference Demavend sees as advantageous, we will be resolving the issue of inheritance not with him, but rather his grandchildren. I assure you, ladies, there will be no moot points in this matter.'

'Not in this one,' agreed Assire var Anahid, looking into the sorceress's elven eyes. 'And what about the matter of the Squirrel commando units? What about the elves who fought for the Empire? If I'm not mistaken, this mainly concerns your subjects, Madam Francesca?'

The Daisy of the Valleys stopped smiling. She glanced at Ida Emean, but the silent elf from the Blue Mountains avoided her gaze.

'*Pro publico bono*—' she began and broke off. Assire, also very serious, nodded her understanding.

417

'What to do?' she said slowly. 'Everything has its price. War demands casualties. Peace, it turns out, does too.'

*

'Aye, true in every respect,' the pilgrim repeated pensively, looking at the elf sitting with head lowered. 'Peace talks are a market. A country fair. So that some people can be bought, others must be sold. Thus the world runs its course. The point is not to pay too high a price . . .'

'And not to sell oneself too cheaply,' finished the elf, without raising his head.

*

'Traitors! Despicable good-for-nothings!'

'Whoresons!'

'An'badraigh aen cuach!'

'Nilfgaardian dogs!'

'Silence!' roared Hamilcar Danza, slamming an armoured fist onto the balustrade of the cloister. The archers on the gallery pointed their crossbows at the elves crowded into the cul-de-sac.

'Calm down!' Danza roared even more loudly. 'Enough! Quieten down, gentlemen officers! A little more dignity!'

'Do you have the audacity to talk of dignity, blackguard?' yelled Coinneach Dá Reo. 'We spilled blood for you, accursed Dh'oine! For you and your emperor, who received an oath of fealty from us! And this is how you repay it? You hand us over to those murderers from the North? As felons! As criminals!'

'Enough, I said!' Danza slammed his fist hard onto the balustrade again. 'Acknowledge this *fait accompli*, gentle-elves! The agreements reached in Cintra, as conditions of the peace treaty being concluded, impose on the Empire the duty to turn over war criminals to the Nordlings—'

'Criminals?' shouted Riordain. 'Criminals? You wretched Dh'oine!'

'War criminals,' repeated Danza, paying no attention whatsoever to the unrest below him. 'Any officers who stand accused

418

of proven charges of terrorism, murdering civilians, killing and torturing captives, massacring the wounded in field hospitals—'

'You whoresons!' yelled Angus Bri Cri. 'We killed, because we were at war!'

'We killed on your orders!'

'Cuach'te aep arse, bloede Dh'oine!'

'It has been ruled!' repeated Danza. 'Your insults and shouts won't change anything. Please go to the guardhouse one at a time and put up no resistance while being manacled.'

'We should have stayed when they were fleeing across the Yaruga.' Riordain ground his teeth. 'We should have stayed and fought on in the commando units. But we, idiots, fools, dolts, kept our soldierly oath! Serves us right!'

Isengrim Faoiltiarna, the Iron Wolf, the most celebrated, now almost legendary commander of the Squirrels, presently an imperial colonel, tore the silver lightning bolts of the Vrihedd Brigade from his sleeve and spaulder, stony-faced, and threw them down in the courtyard. The other officers followed his example. Hamilcar Danza frowned from the gallery as he watched this.

'An irresponsible demonstration,' he said. 'Furthermore, in your place I wouldn't rid myself so lightly of imperial insignia. I feel the duty to inform you that as imperial officers, during the negotiations of the conditions of the peace treaty, you were guaranteed fair trials, lenient sentences and a swift amnesty . . .'

The elves crowded into the cul-de-sac roared in unison with laughter that thundered and boomed amidst the walls.

'I also draw your attention to the fact,' Hamilcar Danza added calmly, 'that it's only you we are handing over to the Nordlings. Thirty-two officers. And not one of the soldiers you commanded. Not one.'

The laughter in the cul-de-sac ceased in an instant.

*

The wind blew on the campfire, stirring up a shower of sparks and blowing smoke into their eyes. Again, howling could be heard from the pass.

'They prostituted everything.' The elf broke the silence. 'Everything was for sale. Honour, loyalty, our bonds, vows, everyday decency . . . They were simply chattels, having a value as long as there was a trade in them and a demand. And once there wasn't, they weren't worth a straw and were discarded. Onto the dust heap.'

'Onto the dust heap of history,' the pilgrim nodded. 'You're right, master elf. That's how it was back then in Cintra. Everything had its price. And was worth as much as it could be traded for. The market opened every morning. And like a real market, now and again there'd be unexpected booms and crashes. And just like a real market, one couldn't help but get the impression somebody was pulling the strings.'

*

'Am I hearing right?' Shilard Fitz-Oesterlen asked in a slow, drawling voice, expressing disbelief in his tone and facial expression. 'Do my ears deceive me?'

Berengar Leuvaarden, special imperial envoy, didn't deign to reply. Sprawled in an armchair, he continued to contemplate the ripples of wine as he rocked his goblet.

Shilard puffed himself up, then assumed a mask of contempt and superiority. Which said, *either you're lying, blackguard, or you wish to trick me, test me out. In both cases I've seen through you.*

'So am I to understand,' he said, sticking his chest out, 'that after far-reaching concessions in the matter of borders, in the matter of prisoners of war and the repayment of spoils, in the matter of the officers of the Vrihedd Brigade and the Scoia'tael commando units, the emperor orders me to compromise and accept the Nordlings' impossible claims regarding the repatriation of settlers?'

'You understood perfectly, Baron,' replied Berengar Leuvaarden, drawing out his syllables characteristically. 'Indeed, I'm full of admiration for your perspicacity.'

'By the Great Sun, Lord Leuvaarden, do you in the capital ever consider the consequences of your decisions? The Nordlings are already whispering that our empire is a giant with feet of clay! Now they're crying that they've defeated us, beaten us, driven us away! Does the emperor understand that to make further concessions means to accept their arrogant and excessive ultimatums? Does the Emperor understand that if they treat this as a sign of weakness it may have lamentable results in the future? Does the Emperor understand, finally, what fate awaits those several thousand settlers of ours in Brugge and Lyria?'

Berengar Leuvaarden stopped rocking his goblet and fixed his coal-black eyes on Shilard.

'I have given you an imperial order, Baron,' he muttered through his teeth. 'When you've carried it out and returned to Nilfgaard you may ask the emperor yourself why he's so unwise. Perhaps you mean to reprimand the emperor. Scold him. Chide him. Why not? But alone. Without my mediation.'

Aha, thought Shilard. *Now I know. The new Stefan Skellen is sitting before me. And I must behave with him as with Skellen.*

But it's obvious he didn't come here without a goal. An ordinary courier could have brought the order.

'Well,' he began, apparently freely, in a positively familiar tone. 'Woe to the vanquished! But the imperial order is clear and precise, and it shall be carried out thus. I shall also try hard to make it look like the result of negotiations and not abject submissiveness. I know something about that. I've been a diplomat for thirty years. With four generations before me. My family is one of the wealthiest, most prominent. . . and influential—'

'I know, I know, to be sure.' Leuvaarden interrupted him with a slight smirk. 'That's why I'm here.'

Shilard bowed slightly. And waited patiently.

'The difficulties in understanding,' began the envoy, rocking his goblet, 'occurred because you, dear Baron, chose to think that victory and conquest are based on senseless genocide. On thrusting a standard somewhere in the blood-soaked ground and crying: "All this is mine, I have captured it!" A similar opinion is, regrettably, quite widespread. For me though, sir, as also for the people who gave me my powers, victory and conquest depend on diametrically different things. Victory should look thus: the defeated are compelled to buy goods manufactured by the victors. Why, they do it willingly, because the victors' goods are better and cheaper. The victors' currency is stronger than the currency of the defeated, and the vanquished trust it much more than their own. Do you understand me, Baron Fitz-Oesterlen? Are you beginning slowly to differentiate the victors from the vanquished? Do you comprehend whom woe actually betides?'

The ambassador nodded to confirm he did.

'But in order to consolidate the victory and render it binding,' Leuvaarden continued a moment later, drawing out his syllables, 'peace must be concluded. Quickly and at any cost. Not some truce or armistice, but peace. A creative compromise. A constructive accord. And without the imposition of trade embargoes, retorsions of customs duty and protectionism.'

Shilard nodded again to confirm he knew what it was about.

'Not without reason have we destroyed their agriculture and ruined their industry,' Leuvaarden continued in a calm, drawling, unemotional voice. 'We did it in order for them to have to buy our goods owing to a scarcity of theirs. But our merchants and goods won't get through hostile and closed borders. And what will happen then? I shall tell you what will happen then, my dear Baron. A crisis of over-production will occur, because our manufactories are working at full tilt. The maritime trading companies who entered into collaboration with Novigrad and Kovir would also suffer great losses. Your influential family, my dear baron, has considerable shares in those companies. And the family, as you are no doubt aware, is the basic unit of society. Are you aware of that?'

'I am.' Shilard Fitz-Oesterlen lowered his voice, although the chamber was tightly sealed against eavesdropping. 'I understand, I comprehend. Though I'd like to be certain I'm carrying out the emperor's order . . . Not that of some . . . corporation . . .'

'Emperors pass,' drawled Leuvaarden. 'And corporations survive. And will survive. But that's a truism. I understand your anxieties, Baron. You can be certain, sir, that I'm carrying out an order issued by the emperor. Aimed at the empire's good and in its interest. Issued, I don't deny it, as a result of advice given to the emperor by a certain corporation.'

The envoy opened his collar and shirt, demonstrating a golden medallion on which was depicted a star set in a triangle surrounded by flames.

'A pretty ornament,' Shilard confirmed with a smile and a slight bow that he understood. 'I'm aware it is very expensive . . . and exclusive . . . Can they be had anywhere?'

'No,' stated Berengar Leuvaarden with emphasis. 'You have to earn them.'

*

'If you permit, m'lady and gentlemen.' The voice of Shilard Fitz-Oesterlen assumed a special tone, already familiar to the debaters, that signified that what the ambassador was about to say was considered by him to be of the utmost importance. 'If you permit, m'lady and gentlemen, I shall read the *aide memoire* sent to me by His Imperial Highness Emhyr var Emreis, by grace of the Great Sun, the Emperor of Nilfgaard . . .'

'Oh no. Not again.' Demavend ground his teeth, and Dijkstra just groaned. This did not escape Shilard's attention, because it couldn't have.

'The note is long,' he admitted. 'So I shall precis it, rather than read it. His Imperial Highness expresses his great gladness concerning the course of the negotiations, and as a peace-loving man joyfully receives the compromises and reconciliations achieved. His Imperial Highness wishes further progress in the negotiations and a resolution to them to the mutual benefit of—'

'Let us get down to business then,' Foltest interrupted in mid-sentence. 'And briskly!' Let's finish it to our mutual benefit and return home.'

'That's right,' said Henselt, who had the furthest to go. 'Let's finish, for if we dally we're liable to be caught by the winter!'

'One more compromise awaits us,' reminded Meve. 'A matter which we have barely touched on several times. Probably for fear that we're liable to fall out over it. It's time to overcome that fear. The problem won't vanish just because we're afraid of it.'

'Indeed,' confirmed Foltest. 'So let's get to work. Let's settle the status of Cintra, the problem of succession to the throne, of Calanthe's heir. It's a difficult problem, but I don't doubt we'll cope with it. Shall we not, Your Excellency?'

'Oh.' Fitz-Oesterlen smiled diplomatically and mysteriously.

'I'm certain that the matter of the succession to the throne of Cintra will go like clockwork. It's an easier matter than you all suppose, m'lady and gentlemen.'

*

'I submit for consideration,' announced Philippa Eilhart in quite an indisputable tone, 'the following project: we shall turn Cintra into a trust territory. We'll grant Foltest of Temeria a mandate.'

'That Foltest is getting too big for his boots,' Sabrina Glevissig grimaced. 'He has too large an appetite. Brugge, Sodden, Angren—'

'We need—' Philippa cut her off '—a strong state at the mouth of the Yaruga. And on the Marnadal Stairs.'

'I don't deny it.' Sheala de Tancarville nodded. 'It's of necessity to us. But not to Emhyr var Emreis. And compromise – not conflict – is our aim.'

'A few days ago,' reminded Francesca Findabair, 'Shilard suggested building a demarcation line, dividing Cintra into spheres of influence; into northern and southern zones—'

'Nonsense and childishness,' snorted Margarita Laux-Antille. 'Such divisions are senseless, are only the seeds of conflicts.'

'I think Cintra ought to be turned into a jointly governed principality,' said Sheala. 'With power exercised by appointed representatives of the northern kingdoms and the Empire of Nilfgaard. The city and port of Cintra will receive the status of a free city . . . Would you like to say something, my dear Madam Assire? Please do. I admit I usually prefer discourses consisting of full, complete utterances, but please proceed. We're listening.'

All of the sorceresses, including Fringilla Vigo, who was as white as a sheet, fixed their eyes on Assire var Anahid. The Nilfgaardian sorceress wasn't disconcerted.

'I suggest we concentrate on other problems,' she declared in her soft, pleasant voice, 'Let's leave Cintra in peace. I have so far been unable to inform you all of certain matters about which I've received reports. The matter of Cintra, distinguished sisters, has already been solved and taken care of.'

'I beg your pardon?' Philippa's eyes narrowed. 'What do you mean by that, if one may ask?'

Triss Merigold gasped loudly. She had already guessed, already knew what was meant by it.

*

Vattier de Rideaux was downhearted and morose. His charming and wonderful lover, the golden-haired Cantarella, had dropped him, suddenly and unexpectedly, without giving any arguments or explanations. For Vattier it was a blow, an awful blow, following which he moped about dejectedly, and was agitated, distracted and stupefied. He had to be very attentive, be very guarded, so as not to blot his copybook, nor make a faux pas in conversation with the emperor. Times of great changes did not favour the agitated and incompetent.

'We have already repaid the Guild of Merchants for their invaluable help,' said Emhyr var Emreis, frowning. 'We've given them enough privileges, more than they received from the previous three emperors combined. As regards Berengar Leuvaarden, we're also indebted to him for his help in uncovering the conspiracy. He has received a senior and remunerative position. But if it turns out he is incompetent he'll be kicked out, in spite of his services. It would be well if he knew that.'

'I'll do my utmost, Your Highness. And what about Dijkstra? And that mysterious informer of his?'

'Dijkstra would rather die than reveal who his informer is. It would indeed be worth repaying him for that invaluable news . . . But how? Dijkstra won't accept anything from me.'

'If I may, Your Imperial Majesty—'

'Speak.'

'Dijkstra will accept information. Something he doesn't know and would like to. Your Highness can repay him with information.'

'Well done, Vattier.'

Vattier de Rideaux sighed with relief. He turned his head away and took a deep breath. For which reason he was first to notice the ladies approaching. Stella Congreve, the Countess of Liddertal, and the fair-haired girl entrusted into her care.

425

'They're coming.' He gestured with a movement of his eyebrows. 'Your Imperial Majesty, may I take the liberty of reminding . . . Reasons of state . . . The empire's interests—'

'Stop.' Emhyr var Emreis cut him off truculently. 'I said I'd ponder it. I'll think the matter over and make a decision. And after taking it I'll inform you what the decision is.'

'Yes, Your Imperial Majesty.'

'What else?' The White Flame of Nilfgaard impatiently slapped a glove against the hip of a marble nereid adorning the fountain's pedestal. 'Why are you still here, Vattier?'

'The matter of Stefan Skellen—'

'I shall not show mercy. Death to the traitor. But after an honest and thorough trial.'

'Yes, Your Imperial Majesty.'

Emhyr didn't even glance at him as he bowed and walked away. He was looking at Stella Congreve. And the fair-haired girl.

Here comes the interest of the empire, he thought. *The bogus princess, the bogus queen of Cintra. The bogus ruler of the mouth of the River Yarra, which means so much to the empire. Here she approaches, eyes lowered, terrified, in a white, silk dress and green gloves with a peridot necklace on her slight décolletage. Back then in Darn Rowan, I complimented her on that dress, praised the choice of jewellery. Stella knows my taste. But what am I to do with the young thing? Put her on a pedestal?*

'Noble ladies.' He bowed first. In Nilfgaard – apart from in the throne room – courtly respect and courtesy regarding women even applied to the emperor.

They responded with deep curtseys and lowered heads. They were standing before a courteous emperor, but still an emperor.

Emhyr had had enough of etiquette.

'Stay here, Stella,' he ordered dryly. 'And you, girl, will accompany me on a stroll. Take my arm. Head up. Enough, I've had enough of those curtseys. It's just a walk.'

They walked down an avenue, amidst shrubs and hedges barely in leaf. The imperial bodyguard, soldiers from the elite Impera Brigade, the famous Salamanders, stayed on the sidelines, but always on the alert. They knew when not to disturb the emperor.

They passed a pond, empty and melancholy. The ancient carp

released by Emperor Torres had died two days earlier. *I'll release a new, young, strong, beautiful specimen*, thought Emhyr var Emreis, *I'll order a medal with my likeness and the date to be attached to it*. Vaesse deireadh aep eigean. *Something has ended, something is beginning. It's a new era. New times. A new life. So let there be a new carp too, dammit.*

Deep in thought, he almost forgot about the girl on his arm. About her warmth, her lily-of-the-valley fragrance and the interest of the empire. In that order, and no other.

They stood by the pond, in the middle of which an artificial island rose out of the water, and on it a rock garden, a fountain and a marble sculpture.

'Do you know what that figure depicts?'

She didn't reply right away. 'Yes, Your Imperial Majesty. It's a pelican, which pecks its own breast open to feed its young on its blood. It is an allegory of noble sacrifice. And also—'

'I'm listening to you attentively.'

'—and also of great love.'

'Do you think—' he turned her to face him and pursed his lips '—that a torn-open breast hurts less because of that?'

'I don't know . . .' she stammered. 'Your Imperial Majesty . . . I . . .'

He took hold of her hand. He felt her shudder; the shudder ran along his hand, arm and shoulder.

'My father,' he said, 'was a great ruler, but never had a head for legends or myths, never had time for them. And always mixed them up. Whenever he brought me here, to the park, I remember it like yesterday, he always said that the sculpture shows a pelican rising from its ashes. Well, girl, at least smile when the emperor tells a funny story. Thank you. That's much better. The thought that you aren't glad to be walking here with me would be unpleasant to me. Look me in the eyes.'

'I'm glad . . . to be able to be here . . . with Your Imperial Majesty. It's an honour for me, I know . . . But also a great joy. I'm enjoying—'

'Really? Or is it perhaps just courtly flattery? Etiquette, the good school of Stella Congreve? A line that Stella has ordered you to learn by heart? Admit it, girl.'

She was silent, and lowered her eyes.

'Your emperor has asked you a question,' repeated Emhyr var Emreis. 'And when the emperor asks no one can dare be silent. No one can dare to lie either, of course.'

'Truly,' she said melodiously. 'I'm truly glad, Your Imperial Majesty.'

'I believe you,' Emhyr said a moment later. 'I believe you. Although I'm surprised.'

'I also . . .' she whispered back. 'I'm also surprised.'

'I beg your pardon? Don't be shy, please.'

'I'd like to be able . . . to go for walks more often. And talk. But I understand . . . I understand that it's not possible.'

'You understand well.' He bit his lip. 'Emperors rule their empires, but two things they cannot rule: their hearts and their time. Those two things belong to the empire.'

'I know that only too well,' she whispered.

'I shall not be staying here long,' he said after a moment of oppressive silence. 'I must ride to Cintra and grace with my person the ceremony of the peace treaty being signed. You will return to Darn Rowan . . . Raise your head, girl. Oh no. That's the second time you've sniffed in my presence. And what's that in your eyes? Tears? Oh, those are serious breaches of etiquette. I will have to express my most serious discontent to the Countess of Liddertal. Raise your head, I said . . .'

'Please . . . forgive Madam Stella . . . Your Imperial Majesty. It's my fault. Only mine. Madam Stella has taught me . . . And prepared me well.'

'I've noticed and appreciate that. Don't worry, Stella Congreve isn't in danger of my disfavour. And never has been. I was making fun of you. Reprehensibly.'

'I noticed,' whispered the girl, paling, horrified by her own audacity. But Emhyr just laughed. Somewhat stiffly.

'I prefer you like that,' he stated. 'Believe me. Bold. Just like—'

He broke off. Like my daughter, he thought. A sense of guilt tormented him like a dog worrying at him.

The girl didn't take her eyes off him. *It's not just Stella's work*, thought Emhyr. *It really is her nature. In spite of appearances she's a diamond that's hard to scratch. No. I won't let Vattier murder this child. Cintra is Cintra, and the interest of the empire is the interest of the empire, but this matter seems only to have one sensible and honourable solution.*

'Give me your hand.'

It was an order delivered in a stern voice and tone. But in spite of that he couldn't help but get the impression it was carried out willingly. Without compulsion.

Her hand was small and cool. But wasn't trembling now.

'What's your name? Just please don't say it's Cirilla Fiona.'

'Cirilla Fiona.'

'I feel like punishing you, girl. Severely.'

'I know, Your Imperial Majesty. I deserve it. But I . . . I have to be Cirilla Fiona.'

'One might suppose you regret you are not she,' he said, not letting go of her hand.

'I do,' she whispered. 'I do regret I am not she.'

'Indeed?'

'If I were . . . the real Cirilla . . . the emperor would look more favourably on me. But I'm only a counterfeit. A poor imitation. A double, not worthy of anything. Nothing . . .'

He turned around suddenly and grabbed her by the arms. And released her at once. He took a step back.

'Yearning for a crown? Power?' he was speaking softly, but quickly, pretending not to see as she denied it with abrupt movements of her head. 'Honours? Accolades? Luxuries—'

He broke off, breathing heavily. Pretending he couldn't see the girl still shaking her lowered head, still denying further hurtful accusations, perhaps all the more hurtful because of being unexpressed.

He breathed out deeply and loudly.

'Do you know, little moth, that what you see before you is a flame?'

'I do, Your Imperial Majesty.'

They were silent for a long time. The scent of spring suddenly made them feel light-headed. Both of them.

'In spite of appearances,' Emhyr finally said dully, 'being empress is not an easy job. I don't know if I'll be able to love you.'

She nodded to show she also knew. He saw a tear on her cheek. Just like in Stygga Castle, he felt the tiny shard of cold glass lodged in his heart shift.

He hugged her, pressed her hard to his chest, stroked her hair, which smelled of lilies-of-the-valleys.

'My poor little one . . .' he said in an unfamiliar voice. 'My little one, my poor raison d'état.'

*

Bells rang throughout Cintra. In a stately manner, deeply, solemnly. But somehow strangely mournfully.

Unusual looks, thought Hierarch Hemmelfart, looking, like everybody else, at the hanging portrait which measured, like all the others, at least one yard by two. *Strange looks. I'm absolutely certain she's some kind of half-breed. I'd swear she has the blood of the accursed elves in her veins.*

Pretty, thought Foltest, *prettier than the miniature the people from the intelligence service showed me. Ah well, portraits usually flatter.*

Utterly unlike Calanthe, thought Meve. *Utterly unlike Roegner. Utterly unlike Pavetta . . . Hmmm . . . There've been rumours . . . But no, that's impossible. She must have royal blood, must be the rightful ruler of Cintra. She must. It is demanded by raison d'état. And history.*

She's not the one I saw in my dreams, thought Esterad Thyssen, King of Kovir, who had recently arrived in Cintra. *She's certainly not that one. But I shan't tell that to anyone. I'll keep it to myself and my Zuleyka. Zuleyka and I shall decide how we shall use the knowledge those dreams gave us.*

She was almost my wife, that Ciri, thought Kistrin of Verden. *I'd have been Duke of Cintra then, according to custom the heir to the throne . . . And I'd probably have perished like Calanthe. It was fortunate, oh, it was fortunate that she ran away from me then.*

Not even for a moment did I believe in the tale of great love at first sight, thought Shilard Fitz-Oesterlen. *Not even for a moment. And yet Emhyr is marrying that girl. He's rejecting the chance for reconciliation with the dukes. Instead of the daughter of one of the Nilfgaardian dukes he's taking Cirilla of Cintra for his wife. Why? In order to seize that miserable little country, half of which, if not more,*

430

I would anyway have gained for the empire in negotiations. To seize the mouth of the Yaruga, which is in any case under the dominion of a Nilfgaardian-Novigradian-Koviran maritime trading company.

I don't understand anything of this raison d'état.

I suspect they aren't telling me everything.

Sorceresses, thought Dijkstra. *It's the sorceresses' handiwork. But let it be. It was clearly written that Ciri would become the Queen of Cintra, the wife of Emhyr and the Empress of Nilfgaard. Destiny clearly wanted that. Fate.*

Let it be, thought Triss Merigold. *May it remain like that. Well and good. Ciri will be safe now. They'll forget about her. They'll let her live.*

The portrait finally ended up in its place, and the servants who had hung it stood back and removed the ladders.

In the long row of darkened and somewhat dusty paintings of the rulers of Cintra, beyond the collection of Cerbins and Corams, beyond Corbett, Dagorad and Roegner, beyond the proud Calanthe and the melancholy Pavetta, hung the last portrait. Depicting the currently reigning gracious monarch. The successor to the throne and to the royal blood.

The portrait of a slim girl with fair hair and a sad gaze. Wearing a white dress with green gloves.

Cirilla Fiona Elen Riannon.

The Queen of Cintra and the Empress of Nilfgaard.

Destiny, thought Philippa Eilhart, feeling Dijkstra's eyes on her.

Poor child, thought Dijkstra, looking at the portrait. *She probably thinks it's the end of her worries and misfortunes. Poor child.*

The bells of Cintra rang, frightening the seagulls.

*

'Shortly after the end of the negotiations and the signing of the Peace of Cintra—' the pilgrim picked up the story '—a grand holiday, a celebration lasting several days, was held in Novigrad, the crowning moment of which was a great and ceremonial military parade. The day, as befitted the first day of a new era, was truly beautiful . . .'

'Are we to understand,' the elf asked sarcastically, 'that you were present there, sir? At that parade?'

'In truth, I was a little late.' The pilgrim clearly wasn't the type to be disconcerted by sarcasm. 'The day, as I said, was beautiful. It promised thus from the very dawn.'

*

Vascoigne, the commandant of Drakenborg – until recently deputy to the chief of political affairs – impatiently struck his whip against the side of his boot.

'Faster over there, faster,' he urged. 'The next ones are waiting! After that peace treaty signed in Cintra we're snowed under here.'

The hangmen, having put the nooses around the condemned men's necks, stepped back. Vascoigne whacked his whip against his boot.

'If any of you has anything to say,' he said dryly, 'now is your last chance.'

'Long live freedom,' said Cairbre aep Diared.

'The trial was fixed,' said Orestes Kopps, marauder, robber and killer.

'Kiss my arse,' said Robert Pilch, deserter.

'Tell Lord Dijkstra I'm sorry,' said Jan Lennep, secret agent, condemned for bribery and thievery.

'I didn't mean to . . . I really didn't mean to,' sobbed Istvan Igalffy, the fort's former commandant, removed from his position and arraigned before the tribunal for acts committed against female prisoners, as he tottered on a birch stump.

The sun, as blinding as liquid gold, exploded above the fort's palisade. The gallows poles cast long shadows. A beautiful, new sunny day rose over Drakenborg.

The first day of a new era.

Vascoigne hit his whip against his boot. He raised and lowered his hand.

Stumps were kicked out from under feet.

*

All the bells of Novigrad tolled, their deep and plaintive sounds echoing against the roofs and mansards of merchants' residences, the echoes fading amongst the narrow streets. Rockets and fireworks shot up high. The crowd roared, cheered, threw flowers, tossed up their hats, waved handkerchiefs, favours, flags, why, even trousers.

'Long live the Free Company!'

'Hurraaaah!'

'Long live the condottieri!'

Lorenzo Molla saluted the crowd, blowing kisses to beautiful townswomen.

'If they're going to pay bonuses as effusively as they cheer,' he shouted over the tumult, 'then we'll be rich!'

'Pity,' said Julia Abatemarco, with a lump in her throat. 'Pity Frontino didn't live to see this . . .'

They walked their horses through the town's main street, Julia, Adam 'Adieu' Pangratt and Lorenzo Molla, at the head of the Company, dressed in their best regalia, formed up into fours so even that none of the groomed and gleaming horses stuck their muzzles even an inch out of line. The condottieri's horses were, like their riders, calm and proud; they weren't frightened by the crowd's cheers and shouts, reacting with slight, faint, almost imperceptible jerks of their heads at the wreaths and flowers flying at them.

'Long live the condottieri!'

'Long live Adieu Pangratt! Long live Pretty Kitty!'

Julia furtively wiped away a tear, catching a carnation thrown from the crowd.

'I never dreamed . . .' she said. 'Such a triumph . . . Pity Frontino . . .'

'You're a romantic,' smiled Lorenzo Molla. 'You're getting emotional, Julia.'

'I am. Attention, by my troth! Eyes leeeft! Look!'

They sat up straight in the saddle, turning their heads towards the review stand and the thrones and seats arranged there. *I see Foltest*, thought Julia. *That bearded one is probably Henselt of Kaedwen, and that handsome one Demavend of Aedirn. That matron must be Queen Hedwig . . . And that pup beside her is Prince Radovid, son of the murdered king . . . Poor boy . . .*

'Long live the condottieri! Long live Julia Abatemarco! Hurrah for Adieu Pangratt! Hurrah for Lorenzo Molla!'

'Long live Constable Natalis!'

'Long live the kings! Long live Foltest, Demavend and Henselt!'

'Long live Dijkstra!' roared some toady.

'Long live His Holiness!' yelled several voices paid to do so. Cyrus Engelkind Hemmelfart, the Hierarch of Novigrad, stood up and greeted the crowd and the marching army with arms raised, rather inelegantly turning his rear towards Queen Hedwig and the minor Radovid, obscuring them with the tails of his voluminous robes.

No one's going to shout 'Long live Radovid', thought the prince, blocked by the hierarch's fat backside. *No one's even going to look at me. No one will raise a cry in honour of my mother. Nor mention my father; they won't shout his glory. Today, on the day of triumph, on the day of reconciliation, of the alliance to which my father, after all, contributed. Which was why he was murdered.*

He felt someone's eyes on the nape of his neck. As delicate as something he didn't know – or did, but only from his dreams. Something like the soft, hot caress of a woman's lips. He turned his head. He saw the dark, bottomless eyes of Philippa Eilhart fixed on him.

Just you wait, thought the prince, looking away. *Just you wait.*

No one could have predicted then or guessed that this thirteen-year-old boy – now a person without any significance in a country ruled by the Regency Council and Dijkstra – would grow into a king. A king, who – after paying back all the insults borne by himself and his mother – would pass into history as Radovid V the Stern.

The crowd cheered. Flowers rained down under the hooves of the parading horses of the condottieri.

*

'Julia?'

'Yes, Adieu.'

'Marry me. Be my wife.'

Pretty Kitty delayed her answer a long time, as she recovered from her astonishment. The crowd cheered. The Hierarch of Novigrad, sweaty, gasping for air, like a large, fat catfish, blessed the townspeople and the procession, town and world from the viewing stand.

'But you *are* married, Adam Pangratt!'

'I'm separated. I'll get a divorce.'

Julia Abatemarco didn't answer. She turned her head away. Astonished. Disconcerted. And very happy. God knows why.

The crowd cheered and threw flowers. Rockets and fireworks exploded with a crack over the rooftops.

The bells of Novigrad moaned plaintively.

*

A woman, thought Nenneke. *When I sent her away to war she was a girl. She's returned a woman. She's confident. Self-aware. Serene. Composed. Feminine.*

She won that war. By not allowing the war to destroy her.

'Debora,' Eurneid continued her litany in a soft, but sure voice, 'died of typhus in a camp at Mayena. Prine drowned in the Yaruga when a boat full of casualties capsized. Myrrha was killed by Squirrel elves, during an attack on a field hospital at Armeria . . . Katje—'

'Go on, my child,' Nenneke urged her on gently.

'Katje—' Eurneid cleared her throat '—met a wounded Nilfgaardian in hospital. She went back to Nilfgaard with him after the peace was concluded, when prisoners of war were exchanged.'

'I always say,' sighed the stout priestess, 'that love knows no borders or cordons. What about Iola the Second?'

'She's alive,' Eurneid hurried to assure her. 'She's in Maribor.'

'Why doesn't she come back?'

The novice bowed her head.

'She won't return to the temple, Mother,' she said softly. 'She's in the hospital of Mr Milo Vanderbeck, the surgeon, the halfling. She said she wants to tend the sick. That she'll only devote herself to that. Forgive her, Mother Nenneke.'

'Forgive her?' the priestess snorted. 'I'm proud of her.'

'You're late,' Philippa Eilhart hissed. 'You're late for a ceremony graced by kings. By a thousand devils, Sigismund, your arrogance regarding etiquette is well known enough for you not to have to flaunt it so blatantly. Particularly today, on a day like this . . .'

'I had my reasons.' Dijkstra responded to the look of Queen Hedwig and the raised eyebrows of the Hierarch of Novigrad with a bow. He noticed the grimace on the face of priest Willemer and the expression of contempt on the impossibly handsome countenance of King Foltest.

'I have to talk to you, Phil.'

Philippa frowned.

'In private, most probably?'

'That would be best.' Dijkstra smiled faintly. 'If, however, you consider it appropriate, I'll agree to a few additional pairs of eyes. Let's say those of the beautiful ladies of Montecalvo.'

'Hush,' hissed the sorceress from behind her smiling lips.

'When can I expect an audience?'

'I'll think about it and let you know. Now leave me in peace. This is a stately ceremony. It's a great celebration. Let me remind you of that, if you hadn't noticed yourself.'

'A great celebration?'

'We're on the threshold of a new era, Dijkstra.'

The spy shrugged.

The crowd cheered. Fireworks shot into the sky. The bells of Novigrad tolled, tolled for the triumph, for the glory. But somehow they sounded strangely mournful.

*

'Hold the reins, Jarre,' said Lucienne. 'I've grown hungry, I'd like a bite of something. Here, I'll wrap the strap over your arm. I know one's not much use.'

Jarre felt a blush of shame and humiliation burning on his face. He still hadn't got used to it. He still had the impression that the whole world didn't have anything better to do than stare at his stump, at the sleeve sewn up over it. That the whole world

436

didn't think of anything else but to look at his disability, to falsely sympathise with the cripple and falsely pity him, and secretly disdain him and treat him as something that unpleasantly disturbs the nice order by repulsively and blatantly existing. By daring to exist.

Lucienne, he had to hand it to her, differed a little from the whole world in this respect. She neither pretended she couldn't see it, nor adopted an affected style of humiliating help and even more humiliating pity. Jarre was close to thinking that the fair-haired young wagoner treated him naturally and normally. But he drove that thought away. He didn't accept it.

For he still hadn't managed to treat himself normally.

The wagon carrying military invalids creaked and rattled. Hot weather had come after a short period of rain, and the ruts created by military convoys had dried out and hardened into ridges and humps of fantastic shapes, over which the vehicle being pulled by four horses had to trundle. The wagon positively jumped over the bigger ruts, creaking, the coach body rocking like a ship in a storm. The swearing of the crippled soldiers – mainly lacking legs – was as exquisite as it was filthy, and in order not to fall Lucienne hung on to Jarre and hugged him, generously giving the boy her magical warmth, extraordinary softness and the exciting mixture of the smell of horses, leather straps, hay, oats and young, intense, girlish sweat.

The wagon lurched out of another pothole and Jarre took in the slack from the reins wound around his wrist. Lucienne, taking bites in turn from a hunk of bread and a sausage, cuddled up to his side.

'Well, well.' She noticed his brass medallion and disgracefully exploited the fact that his hand was taken up by the reins. 'Did they take you in too? A forget-me-not amulet? Oh, whoever invented that trinket was a real trickster. There was great demand for them during the war, probably second only to vodka. And what girl's name is inside it? Let's take a gander—'

'Lucienne.' Jarre blushed like a beetroot and felt as though the blood would gush from his cheeks at any moment. 'I must ask you . . . not to open it . . . Forgive me, but it's personal. I don't want to offend you, but . . .'

The wagon bounced, Lucienne cuddled up to him, and Jarre shut up.

'Ci . . . ri . . . lla,' the wagoner spelled it out with difficulty, but it surprised Jarre, who hadn't suspected the peasant girl of such far-reaching talents.

'She won't forget you.' She slammed the medallion shut, let go of the chain and looked at the boy. 'That Cirilla, I mean. If she really loved you. Foolish spells and amulets. If she really loved you, she won't forget, she'll be faithful. She'll wait.'

'What for?' Jarre lifted his stump.

The girl squinted her cornflower-blue eyes slightly.

'If she really loved you,' she repeated firmly, 'she's waiting, and the rest's codswallop. I know it.'

'Do you have such great experience in this regard?'

'None of your business—' now it was Lucienne's turn to blush slightly '—what I've had and with whom. And don't think I'm one of those what you only have to nod at and she's ready to have some exspermience in the hay. But I know what I know. If you love a fellow, you love all of him and not just bits. Then it's a hill of beans even if he's lost one of those bits.'

The wagon jumped.

'You're simplifying it a bit,' Jarre said through clenched teeth, greedily sniffing up the girl's fragrance. 'You're simplifying it a lot and you're idealising it a lot, Lucienne. You deign not to notice even a detail so slight that a man's ability to support a wife and family depends on whether he's in one piece. A cripple isn't capable—'

'Hey, hey, hey!' she bluntly interrupted him. 'Don't be blubbering on me frock. The Black Cloaks didn't tear your head off, and you're a brainbox, you toil with your noggin. What you staring at? I'm from the country, but I have ears and eyes. Quick enough to notice a detail so slight as someone's manner of speech, that's truly lordly and learned. And what's more . . .'

She bent her head and coughed. Jarre also coughed. The wagon jumped.

'And what's more,' the girl finished, 'I've heard what the others said. That you're a scribe. And the priest at a temple. Then see for yourself that that hand's . . . A trifle. And that's that.'

The wagon hadn't bounced for some time, but Jarre and Lucienne seemed not to notice it at all. And it didn't bother them at all.

'I seem to attract scholars,' the girl said after a longer pause, 'There was one . . . Once . . . Made advances towards me . . . He was book-learned and schooled in academies. You could tell it from his name alone.'

'And what was it?'

'Semester.'

'Hey there, miss,' Gefreiter Corncrake called from behind their backs. He was a nasty, gloomy man, wounded during the fighting for Mayena. 'Crack the whip above the geldings' rumps, miss, your cart's crawling along like snot down a wall!'

'I swear,' added another cripple, scratching himself on a stump covered in shiny scar tissue visible under a rolled up trouser leg, 'this wilderness is getting me down! I'm really missing a tavern, since, I tell you, I'd verily love a beer. Can't we go any brisker?'

'We can.' Lucienne turned around on the box. 'But if the shaft or a hub breaks on a clod, then for a Sunday or two you'll not be drinking beer but rainwater or birch juice, waiting for a lift. You can't walk, and I'm not going to take you on my back, am I?'

'That's a great pity,' Corncrake grinned. 'For I dream at night of you taking me. On your back, I mean from behind. I like it like that. And you, miss?'

'You arsehole of a cripple!' Lucienne yelled. 'You stinking old goat! You—'

She broke off, seeing the faces of all the invalids sitting on the wagon suddenly covered in a deathlike pallor.

'Damn,' sobbed one of them. 'And we were so close to home . . .'

'We're done for,' said Corncrake quietly and utterly without emotion. Simply stating the fact.

And they said – the thought flashed through Jarre's head – *that there weren't any more Squirrels. That they'd all been killed. That the elven question, as they said, had been solved.*

There were six horsemen. But after a closer look it turned out there were six horses, but eight riders. Two of the steeds were carrying a pair of riders. All the horses were treading stiffly and out of rhythm, their heads drooping. They looked miserable.

Lucienne gasped loudly.

The elves came closer. They looked even worse than the horses.

Nothing remained of their pride, of their hard-earned, supercilious, charismatic otherness. Their clothing – usually even on guerrillas from the commando units smart and beautiful – was dirty, torn and stained. Their hair – their pride and joy – was dishevelled, matted with sticky filth and clotted blood. Their large eyes, usually vain and lacking in any expression, were now abysses of panic and despair.

Nothing remained of their otherness. Death, terror, hunger and homelessness had made them become ordinary. Very ordinary.

They had even stopped being frightening.

For a moment Jarre thought they would pass them, would simply cross the road and disappear into the forest on the other side, not gracing the wagon or its passengers with even a glance. That all that would remain of them would be that utterly non-elven, unpleasant, foul smell, a smell that Jarre knew only too well from the field hospitals – the smell of misery, urine, dirt and festering wounds.

They passed them without looking.

But not all of them.

An elf woman with long, dark hair caked together with congealed blood stopped her horse right beside the wagon. She sat in the saddle leaning over awkwardly, protecting an arm in a bloodsoaked sling around which flies buzzed and swarmed.

'Toruviel,' said one of the elves, turning around. '*En'ca digne, luned.*'

Lucienne instantly realised, understood, what it was about. She understood what the elf woman was looking at. The peasant girl had been familiar from childhood with the blue-grey, swollen spectre, the apparition of famine, lurking around the corner of her cottage. So she reacted instinctively and unerringly. She held out the bread towards the elf woman.

'*En'ca digne*, Toruviel,' repeated the elf. He was the only one of the entire commando unit to have the silver lightning bolts of the Vrihedd Brigade on the torn sleeve of his dust-covered jacket.

The invalids on the wagon, until then petrified and frozen in their tracks, suddenly twitched, as though animated by a magic spell. Quarter loaves of bread, rounds of cheese, pieces of fatback and sausage appeared – as if by magic – in the hands that they held out towards the elves.

And for the first time in a thousand years elves were holding their hands out towards humans.

And Lucienne and Jarre were the first people to see elves crying. To see them choking on their sobs, not even trying to wipe away the tears flowing down their dirty faces. Giving the lie to the claim that elves supposedly had no lachrymal glands at all.

'*En'ca . . . digne,*' repeated the elf with the lightning bolts on his sleeve, in a faltering voice.

And then he held out a hand and took the bread from Corncrake. 'Thank you,' he said hoarsely, struggling to adapt his lips and tongue to the foreign language. 'Thank you, human.'

After some time, noticing that it had all gone, Lucienne clicked her tongue at the horses and flicked the reins. The wagon creaked and rattled. No one spoke.

It was well on towards evening when the highway began to teem with armoured horsemen. They were commanded by a woman with completely white, close-cropped hair, with an evil, fierce face disfigured by scars, one of which crossed her cheek from her temple to the corner of her mouth, and another of which, describing a horseshoe, encircled her eye socket. The woman also lacked a large part of her right ear, and her left arm below the elbow ended in a leather sleeve and a brass hook to which her reins were attached.

The woman, staring malevolently at them with a glare full of vindictiveness, asked about the elves. About the Scoia'tael. About terrorists. About fugitives, survivors of a commando unit destroyed two days back.

Jarre, Lucienne and the invalids, avoiding the gaze of the white-haired, one-armed woman, spoke, mumbling indistinctly that no, they hadn't encountered anyone or seen anyone.

You're lying, thought White Rayla, once Black Rayla. *You're lying, I know you are. You're lying out of pity.*

But it doesn't matter anyway.

For I, White Rayla, have no pity.

*

441

'Hurraaaah, up with the dwarves! Long live Barclay Els!'

'Long liiiive the dwaaarves!'

The Novigrad streets thudded beneath the heavy, iron-shod boots of the old campaigners of the Volunteer Regiment. The dwarves marched in a formation typical for them, in fives, and the hammers on their standard fluttered over the column.

'Long live Mahakam! *Vivant* the dwarves!'

'Glory to them! And fame!'

Suddenly someone in the crowd laughed. Several others joined in. And a moment later everybody was roaring with laughter.

'It's an insult . . .' Hierarch Hemmelfart gasped for air. 'It's a scandal . . . It's unpardonable . . .'

'Vile people,' hissed priest Willemer.

'Pretend you can't see it,' Foltest advised calmly.

'We shouldn't have economised on their pay,' Meve said sourly. 'Or refused them rations.'

The dwarven officers kept their countenance and form, standing erect and saluting in front of the review stand. Whereas the non-commissioned officers and soldiers of the Volunteer Regiment expressed their disapproval of the budget cuts applied by the kings and the hierarch. Some crooked their elbows as they passed the stand, while others demonstrated their other favourite gesture: a fist with the middle finger stuck stiffly upwards. In academic circles that gesture bore the name *digitus infamis*. The plebs had a cruder name for it.

The blushes on the faces of the kings and the hierarch demonstrated that they knew both names.

'We ought not to have insulted them by our miserliness,' Meve repeated. 'They're an ambitious nation.'

*

The howler in Elskerdeg howled; the howling turned into a horrifying wailing call. None of the men sitting by the campfire turned his head around.

Boreas Mun was the first to speak after a long silence.

'The world has changed. Justice has been done.'

'Well, you might be exaggerating with that justice.' The pilgrim smiled slightly. 'I would agree, though, that the world has in some way adapted itself to the basic law of physics.'

'I wonder if we have the same law in mind,' the elf said in a slow, drawling voice.

'Every action causes a reaction,' said the pilgrim.

The elf snorted, but it was quite a friendly snort.

'That's a point for you, human.'

*

'Stefan Skellen, son of Bertram Skellen, you, who were Imperial Coroner, be upstanding. The High Tribunal of the Eternal Empire by grace of the Great Sun has found you guilty of the crimes and illegitimate acts of which you have been charged, namely: treason and participation in a conspiracy intended to bring about a murderous assault on the statutory order of the Empire, and also on the person of the Imperial Majesty. Your guilt, Stefan Skellen, has been confirmed and proven, and the Tribunal has not found extenuating circumstances. His Royal Imperial Majesty has thus not granted you an imperial pardon.

'Stefan Skellen, son of Bertram Skellen. You will be taken from the courtroom to the Citadel, from where, when the apposite time comes, you will be led out. As a traitor, unworthy of treading the soil of the Empire, you will be placed on a wooden cart and horses will pull you to Millennium Square on that cart. As a traitor, unworthy of breathing the air of the Empire, you will be hanged by the neck on a gallows by the hand of an executioner, between heaven and earth. And you will hang until you are dead. Your corse will be cremated and the ashes tossed to the four winds.

'O Stefan Skellen, son of Bertram, traitor. I, the head of the Highest Tribunal of the Empire, sentencing you, utter your name for the last time. May it henceforth be forgotten.'

*

'It works! It works!' shouted Professor Oppenhauser, rushing into the dean's office. 'It works, gentlemen! Finally! Finally! It functions. It rotates. It works! It works!'

'Really?' Jean La Voisier, Professor of Chemistry, called Rotten Eggs by his students, asked bluntly and quite sceptically. 'It can't be! And what, out of interest, works?'

'My perpetual motion machine!'

'A *perpetum mobile*?' Edmund Bumbler, venerable Zoology lecturer, asked curiously. 'Indeed? You aren't exaggerating, my dear colleague?'

'Not in the slightest!' yelled Oppenhauser, and leaped like a goat. 'Not a bit! It works! The machine works. I set it in motion and it works. It runs continuously. Without stopping. Permanently. Forever and ever. It can't be described, colleagues, you must see it! Come to my lab, quickly!'

'I'm having my breakfast,' protested Rotten Eggs, but his protest was lost in the hubbub and general excited commotion. Professors, magisters and bachelors threw coats and fur coats over their gowns and ran for the exit, led by Oppenhauser, still shouting and gesticulating. Rotten Eggs pointed his *digitus infamis* at them and returned to his roll and forcemeat.

The small group of scholars, constantly being joined by more scholars greedy to see the fruits of Oppenhauser's thirty years of labours, briskly covered the distance separating them from the laboratory of the famous physicist. They were just about to open the door when the ground suddenly shook. Perceptibly. Powerfully, actually. Very powerfully, actually.

It was a seismic wave, one of the series of earthquakes caused by the destruction of Stygga Castle, Vilgefortz's hide-out, by the sorceresses. The seismic wave had come all the way to Oxenfurt from distant Ebbing.

Dozens of pieces of glass exploded with a crash from the stained-glass window on the frontage of the Department of Fine Arts. The bust of Nicodemus de Boot, the academy's first rector, scrawled over with rude words, fell from its plinth. The cup of herb tea with which Rotten Eggs was washing down his roll and forcemeat fell from the table. A first-year physics student, Albert Solpietra, fell from a plantain tree in the academy grounds that he had climbed to impress some female medical students.

And Professor Oppenhauser's perpetum mobile, his legendary

perpetual motion engine, turned over once more and stopped. Forever.

And it was never possible to start it again.

*

'Long live the dwarves! Long live Mahakam!'

What kind of mixed bunch is this, what gang of ruffians? thought Hierarch Hemmelfart, blessing the parade with a trembling hand. *Who's being cheered here? Venal condottieri, obscene dwarves; what a bizarre bunch! Who won this war, after all, them or us? By the Gods, I must draw the kings' attention to this. When historians and writers get down to their work, their scribblings ought to be censored. Mercenaries, witchers, hired brigands, non-humans and all other suspicious elements are to vanish from the chronicles of humanity. Are to be deleted, expunged. Not a word about them. Not a word.*

And not a word about him either, he thought, pursing his lips and looking at Dijkstra, who was observing the parade with a distinctly bored expression.

It will be necessary, thought the hierarch, *to issue the kings with instructions regarding Dijkstra. His presence is an insult to decent people.*

He's a heathen and a scoundrel. May he disappear without trace. And may he be forgotten.

*

Over my dead body, you sanctimonious purple hog, thought Philippa Eilhart, effortlessly reading the hierarch's feverish thoughts. *You'd like to rule, you'd like to dictate and influence? You'd like to decide things? Over my dead body.*

All you can make judgements about are your piles, which don't count for much beyond your own arse.

And Dijkstra will remain. As long as I need him.

*

445

You'll make a mistake one day, thought priest Willemer, looking at Philippa's shining, crimson lips. *One day, one of you will make a mistake. Your vainglory, arrogance and hubris will be your undoing. And your scheming. Your immorality. The baseness and perversion you give yourselves unto, in which you live. It will come to light. The stench of your sins will spread when you make a mistake. Such a moment has to come.*

And even if you don't make a mistake, an opportunity will arise to blame you for something. Some misfortune, some disaster, some pestilence, perhaps a plague or an epidemic, will fall on humanity . . . Then your guilt will descend on you. You will not be blamed for having been unable to prevent the plague, but for being unable to remove its effects.

You shall be to blame for everything.

And then fires will be lit under stakes.

*

The stripy old tomcat, called Ginger because of its colouring, was dying. Dying hideously. He was rolling around, writhing, scratching the ground, vomiting blood and mucus, racked by convulsions. On top of that he had bloody diarrhoea. He was meowing, although it was beneath his dignity. Meowing mournfully, softly. He was weakening fast.

Ginger knew why he was dying. Or at least guessed what was killing him.

Several days before, a strange freighter, an old and very dirty hulk, a neglected tub, almost a wreck, had called at the port of Cintra. '*Catriona*' announced the barely visible letters on the hulk's prow. Ginger – naturally – couldn't read the letters. A rat climbed down the mooring line to alight on the quay from the strange old tub. A single rat. The rat was hairless, lousy and sluggish. And only had one ear.

Ginger killed the rat. He was hungry, but instinct prevented him from eating the hideous creature. However, several fleas, big, shiny fleas, teeming in the rodent's fur, managed to crawl onto Ginger and settle in his coat.

'What's up with that sodding cat?'

'Someone probably poisoned it. Or put a spell on it!'

'Ugh, abomination! He doesn't half stink, the scoundrel. Get him off those steps, woman!'

Ginger stiffened and silently opened his bloody maw. He no longer felt the kicks or pokes of the broom with which the housewife was now thanking him for eleven years of catching mice. Kicked out of the yard, he was dying in a gutter frothing with soap suds and urine. He died, wishing that those ungrateful people would also fall ill. And suffer like him.

His wishes were about to come true. And on a great scale. A great scale indeed.

The woman who had kicked and swept Ginger from the yard stopped, lifted her frock and scratched her calf below the knee. It was itchy.

A flea had bitten her.

*

The stars over Elskerdeg twinkled intensively. They formed the backdrop against which the sparks from the campfire were dying out.

'Neither can the Peace of Cintra,' said the elf, 'nor yet the bombastic Novigradian parade, be considered a watershed or a milestone. What kind of notions are they? Political authority cannot create history with the help of acts or decrees. Neither can political authority assess history, give grades or characterise it, although in its pride no authority would ever acknowledge that truth. One of the more extreme signs of your human arrogance is so-called historiography, the attempts to give opinions and pass sentences about what you call "ancient history". It's typical for you people, and results from the fact that nature gave you an ephemeral, insectile, ant-like life, and an average lifespan of less than a hundred years. You, however, try to adapt the world to that insectile existence. And meanwhile history is a process that occurs ceaselessly and never ends. It's impossible to separate history into episodes, from here to there, from here to there, from date to date. You can't define history, nor change it with a royal address. Even if you've won a war.'

'I won't enter into a philosophical dispute,' said the pilgrim. 'As it's been said before, I'm a simple and not very eloquent fellow. But I dare observe two things. Firstly, a lifespan as short as insects protects us, people, from decadence, and inclines us to respect life, live intensively and creatively in order to make the most of every moment of life and enjoy it. I speak and think like a man, but after all, the long-lived elves thought likewise, going to fight and die in the Scoia'tael commando units. If I'm wrong, please correct me.'

The pilgrim waited a suitable length of time, but no one corrected him.

'Secondly,' he continued, 'it seems to me that political authority, although unable to change history, may by its actions produce quite a fair illusion and appearance of such an ability. Political power has methods and instruments to do so.'

'Oh, yes,' replied the elf, turning his face away. 'Here you've hit the nail on the head, master pilgrim. Power has methods and instruments. Which are in no way open to discussion.'

*

The galley's side struck the seaweed- and shell-covered piles. Mooring ropes were thrown. Shouts, curses and commands resounded.

Seagulls shrieked as they scavenged for the refuse floating in the port's dirty green water. The quayside was teeming with people. Mainly uniformed.

'End of the voyage, gentlemen elves,' said the Nilfgaardian commander of the convoy. 'We're in Dillingen. Everybody off! You're being waited for here.'

It was a fact. They were being waited for.

None of the elves – and certainly not Faoiltiarna – had any faith in the assurances of fair trials or amnesties. The Scoia'tael and officers of the Vrihedd Brigade had no illusory hopes about the fate awaiting them on the far side of the Yaruga. In the majority of cases they had become accustomed to it, accepted it stoically, with resignation even. Nothing, they thought, could astonish them now.

They were mistaken.

They were chased from the galley, jingling and clanking their

448

manacles, driven onto the jetty and then onto the quay, between a double line of armed mercenaries. There were also civilians there, whose sharp eyes flashed quickly, flitting from face to face, from figure to figure.

Selectors, thought Faoiltiarna. He wasn't mistaken.

He couldn't expect, naturally, his disfigured face to be overlooked. And he wasn't.

'Mr Isengrim Faoiltiarna? The Iron Wolf? What a pleasant surprise! Come this way, come this way!'

The mercenaries dragged him out of the ranks.

'*Va fail!*' Coinneach Dá Reo shouted to him. He had been recognised and hauled out by other soldiers wearing gorgets with the Redanian eagle. '*Se'ved, se caerme dea!*'

'You'll be seeing each other,' hissed the civilian who had selected Faoiltiarna, 'but probably in hell. They're already waiting for him in Drakenborg. Hullo, stop! Isn't that by chance Mr Riordain? Seize him!'

In all, they pulled out three of them. Just three. Faoiltiarna understood and suddenly – to his surprise – began to be afraid.

'*Va fail!*' Angus Bri Cri, shouted to his comrades as he was pulled out of the rank, manacles jingling. '*Va fail, fraeren!*'

A mercenary shoved him roughly.

They weren't taken far. They only got to one of the sheds close to the harbour. Right next to the dock, over which a forest of masts swayed.

The civilian gave a sign. Faoiltiarna was pushed against a post, under a beam over which a rope was slung. An iron hook was attached to the rope. Riordain and Angus were sat down on two stools on the dirt floor.

'Mr Riordain, Mr Bri Cri,' said the civilian coldly. 'You have been given an amnesty. The court decided to show mercy.

'But justice must be done,' he added, not waiting for a reaction. 'And the families of those whom you murdered have paid for it to happen, gentlemen. The verdict has been reached.'

Riordain and Angus didn't even manage to cry out. Nooses were thrown over their necks, they were throttled, knocked down along with the stools and dragged across the floor. As they vainly tried with their manacled hands to tear off the nooses biting into their necks, the executioners kneeled on their chests. Knives flashed and fell, blood spurted. Now even the nooses were unable to stifle their screams, their hair-raising shrieks.

It lasted a long time. As always.

'Your sentence, Mr Faoiltiarna, was equipped with an additional clause,' said the civilian, turning his head slowly, 'Something extra—'

Faoiltiarna had no intention of waiting for that something extra. The manacle's clasp, which the elf had been working on for two days and nights, now fell from his wrist as though tapped by a magic wand. With a terrible blow of the heavy chain he knocked down both mercenaries guarding him. Faoiltiarna – in full flight – kicked the next one in the face, lashed the civilian with the manacles, hurled himself straight at the cobweb-covered window of the shed and flew through it taking the frame and casing with him, leaving blood and shreds of clothing on the nails. He landed on the planks of the jetty with a thud. He turned, tumbled forward, rolled over and dived into the water, between the fishing boats and launches. The heavy chain, still attached to his right wrist, was dragging him down to the bottom. Faoiltiarna fought. He fought with all his strength for his life, which not so long before he hadn't thought he cared about.

'Catch him!' yelled the mercenaries, rushing from the shed. 'Catch him! Kill him!'

'Over there!' yelled others, running up along the jetty. 'There, he came up there!'

'To the boats!'

'Shoot!' roared the civilian, trying with both hands to stop the blood gushing from his eye socket. 'Kill him!'

The strings of crossbows twanged. Seagulls flew up shrieking. The dirty green water between the launches seethed with crossbow bolts.

*

'*Vivant!*' The parade stretched out and the crowd of Novigradians were now displaying signs of fatigue and hoarseness. '*Vivant!* Long live the army!'

'Hurrah!'

'Glory to the kings! Glory!'

Philippa Eilhart looked around to see that no one was listening, then leaned over towards Dijkstra.

'What do you want to talk to me about?'

The spy also looked around.

'About the assassination of King Vizimir carried out last July.'

'I beg your pardon?

'The half-elf who committed that murder—' Dijkstra lowered his voice even more '—was by no means a madman, Phil. And wasn't acting alone.'

'What are you saying?'

'Hush.' Dijkstra smiled. 'Hush, Phil.'

'Don't call me Phil. Do you have any proof? What kind? Where did you get it?'

'You'd be surprised, Phil, if I told you where. When can I expect an audience, Honourable Lady?'

Philippa Eilhart's eyes were like two black, bottomless lakes.

'Soon, Dijkstra.'

The bells tolled. The crowd cheered hoarsely. The army paraded. Petals covered the Novigradian cobbles like snow.

*

'Are you still writing?'

Ori Reuven started and made a blot. He had served Dijkstra for nineteen years but was still not accustomed to the noiseless movements of his boss, appearing from God knows where and God knows how.

'Good evening, hem, hem, Your Hon—'

'*Men from the Shadows.*' Dijkstra read the title page of the manuscript, which he had picked up unceremoniously from the table. '*The History of the Royal Secret Services, written by Oribasius Gianfranco Paolo Reuven, magister* . . . Oh, Ori, Ori. An old fellow, and such foolishness—'

'Hem, hem . . .'

'I came to say goodbye, Ori.'

Reuven looked at him in surprise.

451

'You see, my loyal comrade,' continued the spy, without waiting for his secretary to cough anything up, 'I'm also old, and it turns out I'm also foolish. I said one word to one person. Just one person. And just one word. It was one word too many and one person too many. Listen carefully, Ori. Can you hear them?'

Ori Reuven shook his head, his eyes wide open in amazement. Dijkstra said nothing for a time.

'You can't hear,' he said after a moment. 'But I can hear them. In all the corridors. Rats are running through the city of Tretogor. They're coming here. They're coming on soft little rat's paws.'

*

They came out of the shadows, out of the darkness. Dressed in black, masked, as nimble as rats. The sentries and bodyguards from the antechambers dropped without moaning under the quick thrusts of daggers with narrow, angular blades. Blood flowed over the floors of Tretogor Castle, spilled over the tiles, stained the woodblocks, soaked into the Vengerbergian carpets.

They approached along all the corridors and left corpses behind them.

'He's there,' said one of them, pointing. The scarf shrouding his face up to his eyes muffled his voice. 'He went in there. Through the chancery where Reuven, that coughing old coot, works.'

'There's no way out of there.' The eyes of the other one, the commander, shone in the slits of his black, velvet mask. 'The chamber behind the chancery is windowless. There's no way out.'

'All of the other corridors are covered. All the doors and windows. He can't escape. He's trapped.'

'Forward!'

The door gave away to kicks. Daggers flashed.

'Death! Death to the bloody killer!'

'Hem, hem?' Ori Reuven raised his myopic, watery eyes above the papers. 'Yes? How can I, hem, hem, help you gentlemen?'

The murderers smashed open the door to Dijkstra's private chambers, scurried around them like rats, searching through all the nooks and crannies. Tapestries, paintings and panels were torn from the walls, fell onto the floor. Daggers slashed curtains and upholsteries.

'He's not here!' yelled one of them, rushing into the chancery. 'He's not here!'

'Where is he?' rasped the gang leader, leaning over Ori, staring at him through the slits in his black mask. 'Where is that blood-thirsty dog?'

'He's not here,' Ori Reuven replied calmly. 'You can see for yourself.'

'Where is he? Talk! Where's Dijkstra?'

'Am I,' coughed Ori, 'hem, hem, my brother's keeper?'

'Die, old man!'

'I'm old. Sick. And very weary. Hem, hem. I fear neither you nor your knives.'

The murderers ran from the chamber. They vanished as quickly as they had appeared.

They didn't kill Ori Reuven. They were paid killers. And there hadn't been the slightest mention of Ori Reuven in their orders.

Oribasius Gianfranco Paolo Reuven, master at law, spent six years in various prisons, constantly interrogated by various investigators, asked about all sorts of apparently senseless things and matters.

He was released after six years. He was very ill by then. Scurvy had taken away all his teeth, anaemia his hair, glaucoma his eyesight, and asthma his breath. The fingers of both hands had been broken during the interrogations.

He lived for less than a year after being freed. He died in a temple poorhouse. In misery. Forgotten.

The manuscript of the book *Men from the Shadows, the History of the Royal Secret Services* vanished without trace.

*

The sky in the east brightened. A pale glow appeared above the hills, the harbinger of the dawn.

Silence had reigned by the campfire for a long time. The pilgrim, the elf and the tracker looked into the dying fire in silence.

Silence reigned in Elskerdeg. The howling phantom had gone

away, bored by its vain howling. The phantom must have finally understood that the three men sitting by the campfire had seen too many atrocities lately to worry about any old spectre.

'If we are to travel together we must abandon mistrust,' Boreas Mun said suddenly, looking into the campfire's ruby glow. 'Let's leave behind us what was. The world has changed. There's a new life in front of us. Something has ended, something is beginning. Ahead of us—'

He broke off and coughed. He was not accustomed to speeches like that, was afraid of looking ridiculous. But his accidental companions weren't laughing. Why, Boreas positively sensed friendliness emanating from them.

'The pass of Elskerdeg is ahead of us,' he ended in a more confident voice, 'and beyond the pass Zerrikania and Hakland. There's a long and dangerous road ahead of us. If we are to travel together . . . Let's abandon mistrust. I am Boreas Mun.'

The pilgrim in the wide-brimmed hat stood up, straightening his great frame, and shook the hand being held out towards him. The elf also stood up. His horrifyingly disfigured face contorted strangely.

After shaking the tracker's hand the pilgrim and the elf held out their right hands towards each other.

'The world has changed,' said the pilgrim. 'Something has ended. I am . . . Sigi Reuven.'

'Something is beginning.' The elf twisted his ravaged face into something that according to all evidence was a smile. 'I am . . . Wolf Isengrim.'

They shook hands, quickly, firmly, downright violently. For a moment it looked more like the preliminaries to a fight than a gesture of reconciliation. But only for a moment.

The log in the campfire shot out sparks, celebrating the event with a joyful firework.

'God strike me down—' Boreas Mun smiled broadly '—if this isn't the start of a beautiful friendship.'

... along with the other Martyr Sisters, St Philipa was also calumniated for betraying the kingdom, for fomenting tumults and sedition, for inciting the people and plotting an insurrection. Wilmerius, a heretic and cultist, and self-appointed high priest, ordered the Saint to be seized, thrown into a dark and foul prison beset with cold and stench, calling on her to confess her sins and declare those that she had committed. And Wilmerius showed St Philipa divers instruments of torture and menaced her greatly, but the Saint merely spat in his countenance and accused him of sodomy.

The heretic ordered her stripped of her raiment and thrashed mercilessly with leather straps and for splinters to be driven under her fingernails. And then he asked and called on her to disavow her faith and the Goddess. But the Saint merely laughed and advised him to distance himself.

Then he ordered her dragged to the torture chamber and her whole body to be harrowed with iron gaffs and hooks and her sides scorched with candles. And although thus tormented, the Saint in her mortal corps showed immortal forbearance. Until the torturers were enfeebled and withdrew in great horror, but Wilmerius fiercely admonished them and ordered them further to torture her and soundly belabour her. They then began to scorch St Philipa with red hot irons, dislocate her members from the joints and rend the woman's breast with pincers. And in this suffering she, having confessed nothing, expired.

And the godless, shameless Wilmerius, about whom you may read in the works of the Holy Fathers, met such a punishment that lice and wyrms spread over him and overcame him until he was decayed all over and expired. And he reeked like a cur such that he needs must be cast into a river without burial.

For which praise and a martyr's crown are due to St Philipa, and glory forever to the Great Mother Goddess, and to us a lesson and a warning, Amen.

The Life of St Philipa the Martyr of Mons Calvus, copied from the martyr scribes, in the Tretorian Breviary summarised, drawn from many Holy Fathers who praise her in their writings.

CHAPTER ELEVEN

They rushed like the wind, like mad things, at breakneck speed. They rode through the days, now burgeoning with spring. The horses carried them in a light-footed gallop, and the people, straightening their necks and backs from toiling on the soil, watched them as they went, uncertain of what they had seen: riders or apparitions?

They rode through the nights, dark and wet from the warm rain, and the people, woken and sitting up on their pallets, looked around, terrified, fighting the choking pain that rose in their throats and chests. People sprang up, listening to the thud of shutters, to the crying of those wrested from sleep, to the howling of dogs. They pressed their faces to the parchment in their windows, uncertain of what they had seen: riders, or apparitions?

After Ebbing, tales of the three demons began to circulate.

*

The three riders appeared from God knows where and God knows how, completely astonishing Peg Leg and giving him no chance to flee. Neither was there any help to call for. A good five hundred paces separated the cripple from the outermost buildings of the small town. And even had it been closer, there was a slender chance that any of Jealousy's inhabitants would bother about someone calling for help. It was siesta time, which in Jealousy usually lasted from late morning until early evening. Aristoteles Bobeck, nicknamed Peg Leg, the local beggar and philosopher, knew only too well that Jealousy residents didn't react to anything during siesta time.

There were three riders. Two women and a man. The man had white hair and wore a sword slung across his back. One of the women, more mature and dressed in black and white, had raven-black hair, curled in locks. The younger one, whose straight hair was the colour of ash, had a hideous scar on her left cheek. She was sitting on a splendid black mare. Peg Leg felt he'd seen a mare like that before.

It was the younger one that spoke first.

'Are you from around here?'

'It wasn't me!' Peg Leg said, teeth chattering. 'I'm nobbut gathering mushrooms! Forgive me, don't harm a cripple—'

'Are you from round here?' she repeated, and her green eyes flashed menacingly. Peg Leg cowered.

'Aye, noble lady,' he mumbled. 'I'm a local, right enough. I was born here, in Birka, I mean in Jealousy. And I shall no doubt die here—'

'Last year, in the summer and autumn, were you here?'

'Where should I have bin?'

'Answer when I ask you.'

'I was, good lady.'

The black mare shook its head and pricked up its ears. Peg Leg felt the eyes of the other two – the black-haired woman and the white-haired man – pricking him like hedgehog's spines. The white-haired man scared him the most.

'A year ago,' continued the girl with the scar, 'in the month of September, the ninth of September to be precise, in the first quarter of the moon, six young people were murdered here. Four lads . . . and two girls. Do you recall?'

Peg Leg swallowed. For some time he had suspected, and now he knew, now he was certain.

The girl had changed. And it wasn't just that scar on her face. She was completely different to how she had been when she was screaming, tied to a hitching post, watching as Bonhart cut off the heads of the murdered Rats. Quite different to how she had been in the Chimera's Head when Bonhart undressed and beat her. Only the eyes . . . The eyes hadn't changed.

'Talk,' the other – black-haired – woman urged him. 'You were asked a question.'

'I remember, my lord and ladies,' confirmed Peg Leg. 'How could I not remember? Six youngsters were killed. By truth, it was last year. In September.'

The girl said nothing for a long time, looking not at him, but somewhere in the distance, over his shoulder.

'So you must know . . .' she finally said with effort. 'You must know where those boys and those girls were buried. By which fence . . . On what rubbish tip or muck heap . . . Or if their bodies were cremated . . . If they were taken to the forest and left for the foxes and wolves . . . You'll show me that place. You'll take me there. Understand?'

'I understand, noble lady. Come with me. For it's not far at all.'

He hobbled, feeling on his neck the hot breath of their horses. He didn't look back. Something told him he shouldn't.

'Here it is,' he finally pointed. 'This is our Jealousy boneyard, here in this grove. And the ones you was asking about, Miss Falka, they lie over there.'

The girl gasped audibly. Peg Leg glanced furtively, and saw her face changing. The white-haired man and the black-haired woman were silent and their faces inscrutable.

The girl looked long at the small barrow. It was orderly, level, tidy, edged by blocks of sandstone and slabs of spar and slate. The fir branches that the burial mound had been decorated with had turned brown. The flowers that had once been laid there were dry and yellowed.

The girl dismounted.

'Who?' she asked dully, still looking, not turning her head away.

'Well, many Jealousy people helped.' Peg Leg cleared his throat. 'But chiefly the widow Goulue. And young Nycklar. The widow was always a good and sincere dame . . . And Nycklar . . . His dreams tormented him terribly. They wouldn't give him rest. Until 'e'd given the murdered ones a decent burial—'

'Where shall I find them? The widow and Nycklar?'

Peg Leg said nothing for a long time.

'The widow is buried there, beyond that crooked little birch,' he said at last, looking without fear into the girl's green eyes. 'She died of pneumonia in the winter of the year. And Nycklar joined the army somewhere in foreign parts . . . Folks say he fell in the war.'

'I forgot,' she whispered. 'I forgot that destiny tied both of them to me.'

459

She approached the small burial mound and knelt down, or rather fell onto one knee. She bent over low, very low, her forehead almost touching the stones around the base. Peg Leg saw the white-haired man make a movement, as though meaning to dismount, but the black-haired woman caught him by the arm, stopping him with a gesture and a look.

The horses snorted, shook their heads, the rings of their bits jingling.

The girl knelt for a long, long time at the foot of the burial mound, bent over, and her mouth moved in some silent litany.

She staggered as she stood up. Peg Leg held her up instinctively. She flinched hard, jerked her elbow away, and looked at him malevolently through her tears. But she didn't say a word. She even thanked him with a nod when he held her stirrup for her.

'Yes, noble Miss Falka,' he dared to say. 'Fate ran a strange course. You were in grievous strife then, in bitter times . . . Few of us here in Jealousy thought you'd get out of it alive . . . And finally you're healthy today, my lady, and Goulue and Nycklar are in the beyond. There's not even anyone to thank, eh? To repay for the burial mound—'

'My name's not Falka,' she said harshly. 'My name's Ciri. And as far as thanks are concerned—'

'Feel honoured by her,' the black-haired woman interjected coldly, and there was something in her voice that made Peg Leg tremble.

'Grace, gratitude and reward have befallen you, you and your entire settlement. You know not even how great,' said the black-haired woman, slowly enunciating her words. 'For the burial mound. For your humanity, and for your human dignity and decency.'

*

On the ninth of April, soon after midnight, the first residents of Claremont were awoken by a flickering brightness, a red blaze, that struck and flooded into the windows of their homesteads. The rest of the town's residents were roused from their beds by screams, commotion and the insistent sounds of the bell tolling the alarm.

460

Only one building was burning. It was huge and wooden, formerly a temple, once consecrated to a deity whose name even the oldest grandmothers couldn't remember. A temple, now converted into an amphitheatre, where animal-baiting, fights and other entertainment was held, capable of hauling the small town of Claremont out of its boredom, depression and drowsy torpor.

It was the amphitheatre that was now burning in a sea of roaring fire, shaking from explosions. Ragged tongues of flame, several yards long, shot from all the windows.

'Fiiiire!' roared the merchant Houvenaghel, the owner of the amphitheatre, running and waving his arms around, his great paunch wobbling. He was wearing a nightcap and a heavy, karakul coat he had thrown over his nightshirt. He was kneading the dung and mud of the street with his bare feet.

'Fiiiire! Heeeelp! Waaaaaateeer!'

'It's a divine punishment,' pronounced one of the oldest grandmothers authoritatively. 'For those rumpuses they held in the house of worship . . .'

'Yes, yes, madam. No doubt about it!'

A glow emanated from the roaring theatre, horse urine steamed and stank, and sparks hissed in puddles. A wind had got up from God knows where.

'Put out the fiiiire!' Houvenaghel howled desperately, seeing it spreading to the brewery and granary. 'Heeeelp! Fetch buckets! Fetch buuuuckets!'

There was no shortage of volunteers. Why, Claremont even had its own fire brigade, equipped and maintained by Houvenaghel. They tried to put the fire out doggedly and with dedication. But in vain.

'We can't cope . . .' groaned the chief of the fire brigade, wiping his blistered face. 'That's no ordinary fire . . . It's the devil's work!'

'Black magic . . .' another fireman choked on the smoke.

From inside the amphitheatre could be heard the terrible cracking of rafters, ridges and posts breaking. There was a roar, a bang and a crash, a great column of fire and sparks exploded into the sky, and the roof caved in and fell onto the arena. Meanwhile, the whole building listed over — you could say it was bowing

461

to the audience, which it was entertaining and diverting for the last time, pleasing it with a stunning, truly fiery spectacle.

And then the walls collapsed.

The efforts of the fire fighters and rescuers meant half of the granary and about a quarter of the brewery were saved.

A foul-smelling dawn arose.

Houvenaghel sat in the mud and ash, in his soot-covered night-cap and karakul coat. He sat and wept woefully, whimpering like a child.

The theatre, brewery and granary he owned were insured, naturally. The problem was that the insurance company was also owned by Houvenaghel. Nothing, not even a tax swindle, could have made good even a fraction of the losses.

*

'Where to now?' asked Geralt, looking at the column of smoke, a smudged streak discolouring the sky glowing pink in the dawn. 'Who do you still have to pay back, Ciri?'

She glanced at him and he immediately regretted his question. He suddenly desired to hug her, dreamed of embracing her, cuddling her, stroking her hair. Protecting her. Never allowing her to be alone again. To encounter evil. To encounter anything that would make her desire revenge.

Yennefer remained silent. Yennefer had spent a lot of time silent lately.

'Now,' Ciri said calmly, 'we're going to ride to a settlement called Unicorn. The name comes from a straw unicorn: the poor, ridiculous, miserable effigy that looks after the village. I want the residents to have, as a souvenir of what happened, a . . . Well, if not a more valuable, then at least a more tasteful totem. I'm counting on your help, Yennefer, for without magic . . .'

'I know, Ciri. And after that?'

'The swamps of Pereplut. I hope I can find my way . . . To a cottage amidst the swamps. We'll find the remains of a man in a cottage. I want those remains to be buried in a decent grave.'

Geralt still said nothing. And didn't lower his gaze.

'After that,' Ciri continued, holding his stare without the

slightest difficulty, 'we'll stop by the settlement of Dun Dare. The inn there was probably burned down, and the innkeeper may have been murdered. Because of me. Hatred and vengeance blinded me. I shall try somehow to make it up to his family.'

'There's no way of doing that,' he said, still looking.

'I know,' she replied at once, hard, almost angrily. 'But I shall stand before them in humility. I shall remember the expression in their eyes. I hope the memory of those eyes will stop me making a similar mistake. Do you understand that, Geralt?'

'He understands, Ciri,' said Yennefer. 'Both of us, believe us, understand you very well, daughter. Let's go.'

*

The horses bore them like the wind. Like a magical gale. Alarmed by the three riders flashing by, a traveller on the road raised his head. A merchant on a cart with his wares, a villain fleeing from the law, and a wandering settler driven by politicians from the land he had settled, having believed other politicians, all raised their heads. A vagabond, a deserter and a pilgrim with a staff raised their heads. They raised their heads, amazed, alarmed. Uncertain of what they had seen.

Tales began to circulate around Ebbing and Geso. About the Wild Hunt. About the Three Spectral Riders. Stories were made up and spun in the evenings in rooms smelling of melting lard and fried onions, village halls, smoky taverns, roadhouses, crofts, tar kilns, forest homesteads and border watchtowers. Tales were spun and told. About war. About heroism and chivalry. About friendship and hatred. About wickedness and betrayal. About faithful and genuine love, about the love that always triumphs. About the crimes and punishments that always befall criminals. About justice that is always just.

About truth, which always rises to the surface like oil.

Tales were told; people rejoiced in them. Enjoyed the fairy-tale fictions. Because, indeed, all around, in real life, things happened entirely back to front.

The legend grew. The listeners – in a veritable trance – drank in the carefully measured words of the storyteller telling of the

Witcher and the sorceress. Of the Tower of the Swallow. Of Ciri, the witcher girl with the scar on her face. Of Kelpie, the enchanted black mare.

Of the Lady of the Lake.

That came later, years later. Many, many years later.

But right now, like a seed swollen after warm rain, the legend was sprouting and growing inside people.

*

May came, suddenly. First at night, which flared up and sparkled with the distant fires of Beltane. When Ciri, strangely excited, leaped onto Kelpie and galloped towards the campfires, Geralt and Yennefer took advantage of the opportunity for a moment of intimacy. Undressing only as much as was absolutely necessary, they made love on a sheepskin coat flung onto the ground. They made love hurriedly and with abandon, in silence, without a word. They made love quickly and haphazardly. Just to have more of it.

And when they had both calmed down, trembling and kissing away each other's tears, they were greatly surprised how much happiness such hurried lovemaking had brought them.

*

'Geralt?'

'Yes, Yen.'

'When I . . . When we weren't together, did you go with any other women?'

'No.'

'Not once?'

'Not once.'

'Your voice didn't even waver. So I don't know why I don't believe you.'

'I only ever thought about you, Yen.'

'Now I believe you.'

*

464

May came unexpectedly. During the daytime, too. Dandelions spattered and dotted the meadows yellow, and the trees in the orchards became fluffy and heavy with blossom. The oak woods, too distinguished to hurry, remained dark and bare, but were already being covered in a green haze and at the edges grew bright with green splashes of birch.

*

One night, when they were camping in a valley covered in willows, the Witcher was woken by a dream. A nightmare, where he was paralysed and defenceless, and a huge grey owl raked his face with its talons and searched for his eyes with its curved beak. He awoke. And wasn't sure if he hadn't been transported from one nightmare into another.

There was a brightness billowing over their camp that the snorting horses took fright at. There was something inside the brightness, something like a dark interior, something shaped like a castle hall with a black colonnade. Geralt could see a large table around which sat ten shapes. Ten women.

He could hear words. Snatches of words.

. . . bring her to us, Yennefer. We order you.

You may not order me. You may not order her! You have no power over her!

I'm not afraid of them, Mamma. They can't do anything to me. If they want, I'll stand before them.

. . . is meeting the first of June, at the new moon. We order you both to appear. We warn you that we shall punish disobedience.

I shall come right away, Philippa. Let her stay with him a little longer. Let him not be alone. Just a few days. I shall come immediately. As a hostage of goodwill.

Comply with my request, Philippa. Please.

The brightness pulsated. The horses snorted wildly, banging their hooves.

The Witcher awoke. This time for real.

*

465

The following day Yennefer confirmed his fears. After a long conversation conducted with Ciri in private.

'I'm going away,' she said dryly and without any preliminaries. 'I must. Ciri's staying with you. For some time at least. Then I'll summon her and she'll also go away. And then we'll all meet again.'

He nodded. Reluctantly. He'd had enough of silent assent. Of agreeing to everything she communicated to him, with everything she decided. But he nodded. He loved her, when all was said and done.

'It's an imperative that cannot be opposed,' she said more gently. 'Neither can it be postponed. It simply has to be taken care of. I'm doing it for you, in any case. For your good. And especially for Ciri's good.'

He nodded.

'When we meet again,' she said even more gently, 'I'll make up for everything, Geralt. The silence, too. There's been too much silence, too much silence between us. And now, instead of nodding, hug me and kiss me.'

He did as he was asked. He loved her, when all was said and done.

*

'Where to now?' Ciri asked dryly, a short while after Yennefer had vanished in the flash of the oval teleporter.

'The river . . .' Geralt cleared his throat, fighting the pain behind his breastbone that was taking his breath away. 'The river we're riding up is the Sansretour. It leads to a country I must show you. For it's a fairy-tale country.'

Ciri turned gloomy. He saw her clench her fists.

'Every fairy tale ends badly,' she drawled. 'And there aren't any fairy-tale lands.'

'Yes there are. You'll see.'

*

It was the day after the full moon when they saw Toussaint bathed in greenery and sunshine. When they saw the hills, the slopes and the vineyards. The roofs of the castles' towers glistening after a morning shower.

The view didn't disappoint. It was stunning. It always was.

'How beautiful it is,' said Ciri, enraptured. 'Oh my! Those castles are like children's toys . . . Like icing decorations on a birthday cake. It makes me want to lick them!'

'Architecture by Faramond himself,' Geralt informed her knowledgeably. 'Wait till you see the palace and grounds of Beauclair close up.'

'Palace? We're going to a palace? Do you know the king here?'

'Duchess.'

'Does the duchess,' she asked sourly, observing him intently under her fringe, 'have green eyes, perhaps? And short, black hair—?'

'No.' He cut her off, looking away. 'She looks completely different. I don't know where you got that from—'

'Leave it, Geralt, will you? What is it about this duchess, then?'

'As I said, I know her. A little. Not too well and . . . not too close, if you want to know. But I *do* know the duchess's consort, or rather a candidate for the duchess's consort. You do too, Ciri.'

Ciri jabbed Kelpie with a spur, making her dance around the highway.

'Don't torment me any longer!'

'Dandelion.'

'Dandelion? And the duchess? How come?'

'It's a long story. We left him here, at the side of his beloved. We promised to visit him, returning after—'

He fell silent and turned gloomy.

'You can't do anything about it,' Ciri said softly. 'Don't torment yourself, Geralt. It's not your fault.'

Yes it is, he thought. *It's mine. Dandelion's going to ask. And I'll have to answer.*

Milva. Cahir. Regis. Angoulême.

A sword is a double-edged weapon.

Oh, by the Gods, I've had enough of this. Enough. Time I was done with this!

'Let's go, Ciri.'

'In these clothes?' she croaked. 'To a palace—?'

467

'I don't see anything wrong with our clothes,' he cut her off. 'We aren't going there to present our credentials. Or to a ball. We can even meet Dandelion in the stables.

'Anyhow,' he added, seeing her looking sulky, 'I'm going to the bank in the town first. I'll take a little cash out, and there are countless tailors and milliners in the cloth halls in the town square. You can buy what you want and dress as you wish.'

'Have you got so much cash?' she tilted her head mischievously.

'You can buy what you want,' he repeated. 'Even ermine. And basilisk-leather slippers. I know a shoemaker who ought to have some of it left in stock.'

'How did you make so much money?'

'By killing. Let's ride, Ciri, and not waste time.'

*

Geralt made a transfer and prepared a letter of credit, received a cheque and some cash in the branch of the Cianfanellis' bank. He wrote some letters that were to be taken by the express courier service heading over the Yaruga. He politely excused himself from the luncheon the attentive and hospitable banker wanted to entertain him with.

Ciri was waiting in the street, watching the horses. The street, empty a moment earlier, now teemed with people.

'We must have happened on some feast or other.' Ciri gestured with her head towards a crowd heading for the town square. 'A fair, perhaps . . .'

Geralt looked keenly ahead.

'It's not a fair.'

'Ah . . .' she also looked, standing up in the stirrups. 'It's not another—'

'Execution,' he confirmed. 'The most popular amusement since the war. What have we seen so far, Ciri?'

'Desertion, treason, cowardice in the face of the enemy,' she quickly recited. 'And financial cases.'

'For supplying mouldy hardtack to the army.' The Witcher nodded. 'The life of an enterprising merchant is tough in wartime.'

'They aren't going to execute a tradesman here.' Ciri reined back Kelpie, who was already submerged in the crowd as though in a rippling field of corn. 'Just look, the scaffold's covered in a cloth, and the executioner has a fresh new hood on. They'll be executing somebody important, at least a baron. So it probably *is* cowardice in the face of the enemy.'

'Toussaint didn't have an army in the face of any foe.' Geralt shook his head, 'No, Ciri, I think it's economics again. They're executing somebody for swindles in the trade of their famous wine, the basis of the economy here. Let's ride on, Ciri. We won't watch.'

'Ride on? How exactly?'

Indeed, riding on was impossible. In no time at all they had become stuck in the crowd gathered in the square, and were mired in the throng. There was no chance of their getting to the other side of the square. Geralt swore foully and looked back. Unfortunately, retreat was also impossible, for the wave of people pouring into the square had totally clogged up the street behind them. For a moment the crowd carried them like a river, but the movement stopped when the common folk came up against the serried wall of halberdiers surrounding the scaffold.

'They're coming!' somebody shouted, and the crowd buzzed, swayed and took up the cry. 'They're coming!'

The clatter of hooves and the rattle of a wagon faded and was lost amidst the throng's beelike humming. So they were astonished when a rack wagon pulled by two horses trundled out of a side street. And on it, having difficulty keeping his balance, stood . . .

'Dandelion . . .' groaned Ciri.

Geralt suddenly felt bad. Very bad.

'That's Dandelion,' Ciri repeated in an unfamiliar voice. 'Yes, it's him.'

It's unfair, thought the Witcher. *It's one big, bloody injustice. It can't be like this. It shouldn't be like this. I know it was stupid and naive to think that anything ever depended on me, that I somehow influenced the fate of this world, or that this world owes me something. I know it was a naive, arrogant opinion . . . But I know it! There's no need to convince me about it! It doesn't have to be proved to me! Particularly like this . . .*

It's unfair!

'It can't be Dandelion,' he said hollowly, looking down at Roach's mane.

'It *is* Dandelion,' Ciri said again. 'Geralt, we have to do something.'

'What?' he asked bitterly. 'Tell me what.'

Some soldiers pulled Dandelion from the wagon, treating him, however, with astonishing courtesy, without brutality, with positive reverence, the most they were capable of. They untied his hands before the steps leading to the scaffold. Then he nonchalantly scratched his behind and climbed the steps without being urged.

One of the steps suddenly creaked and the railing, made of a rough pole, cracked. Dandelion almost lost his balance.

'That needs fixing, dammit!' he yelled. 'You'll see, one day somebody will kill themselves on these steps. And that wouldn't be funny.'

Dandelion was intercepted on the scaffolding by two hangman's assistants in sleeveless leather jerkins. The executioner, as broad in the shoulders as a castle keep, looked at the condemned man through slits in his hood. Beside him stood a character in a sumptuous, though funereally black outfit. He also wore a funereal expression.

'Good gentlemen and burghers of Beauclair and the surroundings!' he read thunderously and funereally from an unrolled parchment. 'It is known that Julian Alfred Pankratz, Viscount de Lettenhove, alias Dandelion—'

'Pancratts what?' Ciri whispered a question.

'—by sentence of the Ducal High Court has been found guilty of all the crimes, misdeeds and offences of which he is accused, namely: lèse-majesté, treason, and furthermore sullying the dignity of the noble estate through perjury, lampooning, calumny and slander, also roistering and indecency as well as debauchery, in other words harlotry. Thus the tribunal has adjudged to punish Viscount Julian *et cetera*, primo: by defacing his coat of arms, by painting diagonal black lines on his escutcheon. Secundo: by the confiscation of his property, lands, estates, copses, forests and castles . . .'

'Castles,' groaned the Witcher. 'What castles?'

Dandelion snorted insolently. The expression on his face demonstrated emphatically that he was heartily amused by the confiscation announced by the tribunal.

'Tertio: the chief penalty. Anna Henrietta, reigning over us as Her Enlightenment the Duchess of Toussaint and Lady of Beauclair, has deigned to commute the punishment provided for the above-mentioned crimes of being dragged behind horses, broken on the wheel and quartered, to beheading by axe. May justice be done!'

The crowd raised several incoherent shouts. The women standing in the front row began to hypocritically wail and falsely lament. Children were lifted up or carried on shoulders so as not to miss any of the spectacle. The executioner's assistants rolled a stump into the centre of the scaffold and covered it with a napkin. There was something of a commotion, since it turned out someone had swiped the wicker basket for the severed head, but another one was quickly found.

Four ragged street urchins had spread out a kerchief beneath the scaffold to catch blood on it. There was great demand for that kind of souvenir, you could earn good money from them.

'Geralt.' Ciri didn't raise her lowered head. 'We have to do something . . .'

He didn't answer.

'I wish to address the townspeople,' Dandelion proudly declared.

'Make it short, Viscount.'

The poet stood on the edge of the scaffold and raised his hands. The crowd murmured and fell silent.

'Hey, people,' called Dandelion. 'What cheer? How go you?'

'Ah, muddling along,' muttered someone, after a long silence, in a row towards the back.

'That's good,' the poet nodded. 'I'm greatly content. Well, now we may begin.'

'Master executioner,' the funereal one said with artificial emphasis. 'Do your duty!'

The executioner went closer, knelt down before the condemned man in keeping with the ancient custom, and lowered his hooded head.

'Forgive me, good fellow,' he requested gravely.

471

'Me?' asked Dandelion in astonishment. 'Forgive you?'

'Uh-huh.'

'Not a chance.'

'Eh?'

'I'll never forgive you. Why should I? Have you heard him, the prankster! He's about to cut my head off, and I'm supposed to forgive him? Are you mocking me or what? At a time like this?'

'How can you, sir?' asked the executioner, saddened. 'For there's a law . . . And a custom . . . The condemned man must forgive the executioner in advance. Good sir! Expunge my guilt, absolve my sin . . .'

'No.'

'No?'

'No!'

'I won't behead him,' the executioner declared gloomily, getting up from his knees. 'He must forgive me, otherwise there's nothing doing.'

'Lord Viscount.' The funereal clerk caught Dandelion by the elbow. 'Don't make things difficult. People have gathered, they're waiting . . . Forgive him. He's asking politely, isn't he?'

'I won't forgive him, and that's that!'

'Master executioner!' The funereal man approached the executioner. 'Chop off his head without being forgiven, eh? I'll see you right . . .'

Without a word, the executioner held out a hand a large as a frying pan. The funereal man sighed, reached into a pouch and tipped some coins out into his hand. The executioner looked at them for a while, then clenched his fist. The eyes in the slits of his hood flashed malevolently.

'Very well,' he said, putting the money away and turning towards the poet. 'Kneel down then, Mr Stubborn. Put your head on the block, Mr Spiteful. I can also be spiteful, if I want to. I'll take two blows to behead you. Three, if I'm lucky.'

'I absolve you!' howled Dandelion. 'I forgive you!'

'Thank you.'

'Since he's forgiven you,' said the funereal clerk gloomily, 'give me back my money.'

The executioner turned around and raised the axe.

'Step aside, noble sir,' he said forebodingly in a dull voice. 'Don't get in the way of the tool. For where heads are being chopped off, if you get too close you might lose an ear.'

The clerk stepped back suddenly and almost fell off the scaffold.

'Like this?' Dandelion kneeled down and stretched his neck on the block. 'Master? Hey, master?'

'What?'

'You were joking, weren't you? You'll behead me with one blow? With one swing? Well?'

The executioner's eyes flashed.

'Let it be a surprise,' he snapped portentously.

The crowd suddenly swayed, yielding before a rider bursting into the square on a foaming horse.

'Stop!' yelled the rider, waving a large roll of parchment hung with red seals. 'Stop the execution! By ducal order! Out of my way! Stop the execution! I bear a pardon for the condemned man.'

'Not again?' the executioner snarled, lowering the already raised axe. 'Another reprieve? It's starting to get boring.'

'Mercy! Mercy!' bellowed the crowd. The matrons in the front row began to lament even louder. A lot of people, mainly youngsters, whistled and moaned in disapproval.

'Quieten down, good gentlemen and burghers!' yelled the funereal man, unrolling the parchment. 'This is the will of Her Grace Anna Henrietta! In her boundless goodness, in celebration of the peace treaty, which, as rumour has it, was signed in the city of Cintra, Her Grace pardons Viscount Julian Alfred Pankratz de Lettenhove, alias Dandelion, and his misdeeds, and waives his execution—'

'Darling Little Weasel,' said Dandelion, smiling broadly.

'—ordering at the same time that the above-mentioned Viscount Julian Pankratz *et cetera* without delay doth leave the capital and borders of the Duchy of Toussaint and never return, since he offends Her Grace, and Her Grace can no longer countenance him! You are free to go, Viscount.'

'And my property?' yelled Dandelion. 'Eh? You can keep my chattels, copses, forests and castles, but give me back, sod the lot of you, my lute, my horse Pegasus, a hundred and forty talars and eighty halers, my raccoon-lined cloak, my ring—'

'Shut up!' shouted Geralt, jostling the fulminating and reluctantly parting crowd with his horse. 'Shut up, get down and come here, you blockhead! Ciri, clear the way! Dandelion! Do you hear me?'

'Geralt? Is that you?'

'Don't ask, just get down! Over here! Leap onto my horse!'

They forced their way through the throng and galloped down the narrow street. Ciri first and Geralt and Dandelion on Roach behind her.

'Why the hurry?' said the bard behind the Witcher's back. 'No one's following us.'

'For now. Your duchess likes to change her mind and suddenly cancel what she's already decided. Come clean; did you know about the pardon?'

'No, no I didn't,' murmured Dandelion. 'But, I confess I was counting on it. Little Weasel is a darling and has a very kind heart.'

'Enough of that bloody "Little Weasel", dammit. You've only just wriggled out of lèse-majesté, do you want to fall back into recidivism?'

The troubadour fell silent. Ciri reined back Kelpie and waited for them. When they caught up she looked at Dandelion and wiped away a tear.

'Oh, you . . .' she said. 'You . . . Pancratts . . .'

'Let's go,' urged the Witcher. 'Let's leave this town and the borders of this enchanting duchy. While we still can.'

*

A ducal messenger caught up with them almost at the very border of Toussaint, from where one could already see Gorgon Mountain. He was pulling behind him a saddled Pegasus and was carrying Dandelion's lute, cloak and ring. He ignored the question about the one hundred and forty talars and eighty halers. He listened stony-faced to the bard's request to give the duchess a kiss.

They rode up the Sansretour, which was now a tiny, fast-flowing stream. They bypassed Belhaven and camped in the Newi valley. In a place the Witcher and the bard remembered.

Dandelion held out for a very long time. He didn't ask any questions.

But he finally had to be told everything.

And be accompanied in his silence. In the dreadful, pregnant silence that fell after the telling, and festered like a sore.

＊

At noon the next day they were at the Slopes, outside Riedbrune. Peace and order reigned all around. The people were sanguine and helpful. It felt safe.

Gibbets, heavy with hanging corpses, stood everywhere.

They steered clear of the town, heading towards Dol Angra.

'Dandelion!' Geralt had only just noticed what he should have noticed much earlier. 'Your priceless tube! Your centuries of poetry! The messenger didn't have them. They were left in Toussaint!'

'They were.' The bard nodded indifferently. 'In Little Weasel's wardrobe, under a pile of dresses, knickers and corsets. And may they lie there forever.'

'Would you like to explain?'

'What's there to explain? I had enough time in Toussaint to read closely what I'd written.'

'And?'

'I'm going to write it again. Anew.'

'I understand.' Geralt nodded. 'In short, you turned out to be as poor a writer as you were a favourite. Or to put it more bluntly: you make a fucking mess of whatever you touch. Well, but even if you have the chance to improve and rewrite your *Half a Century*, you haven't got a fucking prayer with Duchess Anarietta. Ugh, the lover driven away in disgrace. Yes, yes, no point making faces! You weren't meant to be ducal consort in Toussaint, Dandelion.'

'We shall see about that.'

'Don't count on me. I don't mean to be there to see it.'

'And no one's asking you to. I tell you though, Little Weasel has a good and understanding little heart. In truth, she got somewhat carried away when she caught me with young Nique, the baron's daughter . . . But now she's sure to have cooled off. Understood that a man isn't created for monogamy. She's forgiven me and is no doubt waiting—'

'You're hopelessly stupid,' stated Geralt, and Ciri confirmed she thought the same with an energetic nod of her head.

'I'm not going to discuss it with you,' Dandelion sulked. 'Particularly since it's an intimate matter. I tell you one more time: Little Weasel will forgive me. I'll write a suitable ballad or sonnet, send it to her, and she'll . . .'

'Have mercy, Dandelion.'

'Oh, there's really no point talking to you. Let's ride on! Gallop, Pegasus! Gallop, you white-legged flyer!'

They rode on.

It was May.

*

'Because of you,' the Witcher said reproachfully, 'because of you, O my banished lover, I also had to flee from Toussaint like some outlaw or exile. I didn't even manage to meet up with . . .'

'Fringilla Vigo? You wouldn't have seen her. She left soon after you set off in January. She simply vanished.'

'I wasn't thinking about her.' Geralt cleared his throat, seeing Ciri prick up her ears in interest. 'I wanted to meet Reynart. And introduce him to Ciri . . .'

Dandelion fixed his eyes on Pegasus's mane.

'Reynart de Bois-Fresnes,' he mumbled, 'fell in a skirmish with marauders on the Cervantes pass sometime at the end of February, in the vicinity of the Vedette watchtower. Anarietta honoured him with a posthumous medal—'

'Shut up, Dandelion.'

Dandelion shut up, admirably obedient.

*

May marched on and matured. The vivid yellow of dandelions disappeared from the meadows, replaced by the downy, grubby, fleeting white of their parachutes.

It was green and very warm. The air, if it wasn't freshened by brief storms, was thick, hot and as sticky as mead.

*

They crossed the Yaruga on the twenty-sixth of May over a very new, very white bridge smelling of resin. The remains of the old bridge – black, scorched, charred timbers – could be seen in the water and on the bank.

Ciri became anxious.

Geralt knew. He knew her intentions, knew about her plans, about the agreement with Yennefer. He was ready. But in spite of that the thought of parting stung him painfully. As though a nasty little scorpion had been sleeping in his chest, within him, behind his ribcage and had now suddenly come awake.

*

A spreading oak tree stood – as it had for at least a hundred years, actually – at the crossroads outside the village of Koprzywnica, beyond the ruins of the burnt-down inn. Now, in the spring, it was laden with tiny buds of blossom. People from the whole region, even the remote Spalla, were accustomed to using the huge and quite low boughs of the oak to hang up slats and boards bearing all sorts of information. For that reason, the oak tree that served for communication between people was called the Tree of Tidings of Good and Evil.

'Ciri, start on that side,' ordered Geralt, dismounting. 'Dandelion, have a look on this side.'

The planks on the boughs swayed in the wind, clattering against each other.

Searches for missing and separated families usually dominated after a war. There were plenty of declarations of the following kind: COME BACK, I FORGIVE YOU, plenty of offers of erotic massage and similar services in the neighbouring towns and villages, and plenty of announcements and advertisements. There were love letters, there were denunciations signed by well-meaning people, and poison pen letters. There were also boards expressing

477

the philosophical views of their authors – the vast majority of them moronically nonsensical or repulsively obscene.

'Ha!' called Dandelion. 'A witcher is urgently sought in Rastburg Castle. They write that good pay, luxurious accommodation and extraordinarily tasty board are guaranteed. Will you avail yourself of it, Geralt?'

'Absolutely not.'

Ciri found the information they were looking for.

And then announced to the Witcher what he had been expecting for a long time.

*

'I'm going to Vengerberg, Geralt,' she repeated. 'Don't make faces like that. You know I have to, don't you? Yennefer's summoned me. She's waiting for me there.'

'I know.'

'You're going to Rivia, to that rendezvous you're still keeping a secret—'

'A surprise,' he interrupted. 'It's a surprise, not a secret.'

'Very well, a surprise. I, meanwhile, will sort out what I need to in Vengerberg, pick up Yennefer and we'll both be in Rivia in six days. Don't make faces, please. And let's not part like it was forever. It's just six days! Goodbye.'

'Goodbye, Ciri.'

'Rivia, in six days,' she repeated once more, reining Kelpie around.

She galloped away at once. She was out of sight very quickly, and Geralt felt as though a cold, awful clawed hand was squeezing his stomach.

'Six days,' Dandelion repeated pensively. 'From here to Vengerberg and back to Rivia . . . All together it'll be close to two hundred and fifty miles . . . It's impossible, Geralt. Indeed, on that devilish mare, on which the girl can travel at the speed of a courier, three times quicker than us, theoretically, very theoretically, she could cover such a distance in six days. But even the devilish mare has to rest. And that mysterious matter that Ciri has to take care of will also take some time. And thus it's impossible . . .'

'Nothing is impossible—' the Witcher pursed his lips '—for Ciri.'

'Can it be—?'

'She's not the girl you knew,' Geralt interrupted him harshly. 'Not any longer.'

Dandelion was silent for a long time.

'I have a strange feeling . . .'

'Be quiet. Don't say anything. I beg you.'

*

May was over. The new moon was coming, the old moon was waning. It was very thin. They rode towards the mountains, barely visible on the horizon.

*

It was a typical landscape after a war. All of a sudden, graves and burial mounds had sprung up among the fields; skulls and skeletons lay white amidst the lush, spring grass. Corpses hung on roadside trees, and wolves sat beside the roads, waiting for the miserable travellers to weaken.

Grass no longer grew on the black patches of land where fires had passed through.

The villages and settlements, of which only charred chimneys remained, resounded with the banging of hammers and the rasping of saws. Near the ruins, peasant women dug holes in the scorched earth with hoes. Some of them, stumbling, were pulling harrows and ploughs and the webbing harnesses bit into their gaunt shoulders. Children hunted for grubs and worms in the newly ploughed furrows.

'I have a vague feeling that something's not as it should be here,' said Dandelion, 'Something's missing . . . Do you have that impression, Geralt?'

'Eh?'

'Something's not normal here.'

'Nothing's normal here, Dandelion. Nothing.'

During the warm, black and windless night, lit up by distant flashes of lightning and restless growls of thunder, Geralt and Dandelion saw from their camp the horizon in the west blooming with the red glow of fire. It wasn't far and the wind that blew up brought the smell of smoke. The wind also brought snatches of sound. They heard – like it or not – the howling of people being murdered, the wailing of women, and the brash and triumphant yelling of bandits.

Dandelion said nothing, glancing fearfully at the Witcher every now and then.

But the Witcher didn't even twitch, didn't even turn his head around. And his face seemed to be cast in bronze.

They continued on their journey the next morning. They didn't even look at the thin trail of smoke rising above some trees.

And later they chanced upon a column of settlers.

*

They were walking in a long line. Slowly. Carrying small bundles. They walked in complete silence. Men, boys, women and children. They walked without grumbling, without tears, without a word of complaint. Without screams, without any desperate wailing.

But there were screams and despair in their eyes. In the empty eyes of people who had been damaged. Robbed, beaten, driven away.

'Who are they?' Dandelion ignored the hostility visible in the eyes of the officer supervising the march. 'Who are you driving like this?'

'They're Nilfgaardians,' snapped a sub-lieutenant from the height of his saddle. He was a ruddy-faced stripling, of no more than eighteen summers. 'Nilfgaardian settlers. They appeared in our lands like cockroaches! And we'll sweep them away like cockroaches. So was it decided in Cintra and so was it written in the peace treaty.'

He leaned over and spat.

'And if it was up to me,' he continued, looking defiantly at

Dandelion and the Witcher, 'I wouldn't let them get out of here alive, the rats.'

'And if it depended on me,' said a non-commissioned officer with a grey moustache in a slow, drawling voice, looking at his commander with a gaze strangely devoid of respect, 'I'd leave them in peace on their farms. I wouldn't drive good farmers from the land. I'd be glad that agriculture was prospering. That there's something to eat.'

'You're as thick as pig shit, Sergeant,' snapped the sub-lieutenant. 'It's Nilfgaard! It's not our language, not our culture, not our blood. We'd be glad of the agriculture and nursing a viper in our bosom. Traitors, ready to stab us in the back. Perhaps you think there'll be harmony with the Black Cloaks forever. No, they can go back where they came from . . . Hey, soldiers! That one has a cart! Get it off him, at the double!'

The order was carried out extremely zealously. With the use not only of heels and fists, but truncheons too.

Dandelion gave a slight cough.

'What, something not to your liking, perhaps?' The youthful sub-lieutenant glared at him. 'Perhaps you're a Nilfgaard-lover?'

'Heaven forbid,' Dandelion swallowed.

Many of the empty-eyed women and girls walking like automatons had torn garments, swollen and bruised faces, and thighs and calves marked by trickles of dried blood. Many of them had to be supported as they walked. Dandelion looked at Geralt's face and began to be afraid.

'Time we were going,' he mumbled. 'Farewell, gentlemen.'

The sub-lieutenant didn't even turn his head around, preoccupied with checking that none of the settlers were carrying luggage larger than the Peace of Cintra had determined.

The column of settlers walked on.

They heard the high-pitched, desperate screams of a woman in great pain.

'Geralt, no,' groaned Dandelion. 'Don't do anything, I beg you . . . Don't get involved . . .'

The Witcher turned his face towards him, and Dandelion didn't recognise it.

'Get involved?' he repeated. 'Intervene? Rescue somebody?

481

Risk my neck for some noble principles or ideas? Oh, no, Dandelion. Not any longer.'

*

One night, a restless night lit up by distant flashes of lightning, a dream woke the Witcher again. He wasn't certain this time, either, if he hadn't gone straight from one nightmare to another.

Once again, a pulsating brightness that frightened the horses rose above the remains of the campfire. Once again, there was a great castle, black colonnades, and a table with women sitting around it in the brightness.

Two of the women weren't sitting but standing. One in black and white and the other in black and grey.

It was Yennefer and Ciri.

The Witcher groaned in his sleep.

*

Yennefer was right to quite categorically advise Ciri against wearing male clothing. Dressed like a boy, Ciri would have felt foolish, here, now, in the hall among these elegant women sparkling with jewellery. She was pleased she'd agreed to dress in a combination of black and grey. It flattered her when she felt approving looks on her puffed, paned sleeves and high waist, on the velvet ribbon bearing the small rose-shaped diamond brooch.

'Please come closer.'

Ciri shuddered a little. Not just at the sound of that voice. Yennefer, it turned out, had been right in one more thing – she had advised against a plunging neckline. Ciri, however, had insisted and now had the impression the draught was literally raging over her chest, and her whole front, almost to her navel, was covered in gooseflesh.

'Come closer,' repeated the dark-haired, dark-eyed woman whom Ciri knew and remembered from the Isle of Thanedd. And although Yennefer had told her whom she would meet in Montecalvo, had described them all and taught her all of their names, Ciri at once began to entitle her 'Madam Owl' in her thoughts.

'Welcome to the Montecalvo Lodge,' said Madam Owl. 'Miss Ciri.'

Ciri bowed as Yennefer had instructed, politely, but more in the male fashion, without a ladylike curtsey, without a modest and submissive lowering of her eyes. She responded with a smile to Triss Merigold's sincere and pleasant smile, and with a somewhat lower nod of the head to Margarita Laux-Antille's friendly look. She endured the remaining eight pairs of eyes, although they pierced like gimlets. Stabbed like spear blades.

'Please be seated,' beckoned Madam Owl with a truly regal gesture. 'No, not you, Yennefer! Just her. You, Yennefer, are not an invited guest, but a felon, summoned to be judged and punished. You will stand until the Lodge decides on your fate.'

Protocol was over for Ciri in a flash.

'In that case I shall also stand,' she said, not at all quietly. 'I'm no guest either. I was also summoned to be informed about my fate. That's the first thing. And the second is that Yennefer's fate is my fate. What applies to her applies to me. We cannot be rent asunder. With all due respect.'

Margarita Laux-Antille smiled, looking her in the eyes. The modest, elegant woman with the slightly aquiline nose, who could only be the Nilfgaardian, Assire var Anahid, nodded, and tapped her fingers lightly on the table.

'Philippa,' said a woman with her neck wrapped in a silver fox-fur boa. 'We don't have to be so uncompromising, it seems to me. At least not today, not right now. This is the Lodge's round table. We sit at it as equals. Even if we are to be judged. I think we can all agree about what we should—'

She didn't finish, but swept her eyes over the remaining sorceresses. They, meanwhile, expressed their agreement by nodding: Margarita, Assire, Triss, Sabrina Glevissig, Keira Metz, and the two beautiful elf women. Only the other Nilfgaardian, the raven-haired Fringilla Vigo, sat motionless, very pale, not wresting her eyes from Yennefer.

'Let it be so.' Philippa Eilhart waved a ringed hand. 'Sit down, both of you. Despite my opposition. But the Lodge's unity comes before everything. The Lodge's interests before everything. And above everything. The Lodge is everything, the rest nothing. I hope you understand, Ciri?'

'Very well.' Ciri had no intention of lowering her gaze. 'Particularly since I am that nothing.'

Francesca Findabair, the stunning elf woman, gave a peal of resonant laughter.

'Congratulations, Yennefer,' she said in her hypnotically melodic voice. 'I recognise an outstanding hallmark, the purity of the gold. I recognise the school.'

'It isn't difficult to recognise.' Yennefer swept a passionate look around her. 'For it's the school of Tissaia de Vries.'

'Tissaia de Vries is dead,' Madam Owl said calmly. 'She's not present at this table. Tissaia de Vries died, and the matter has been grieved and mourned. It was simultaneously a landmark and a turning point. For a new time has dawned, a new era has come, and great changes are coming. And fate has assigned you an important role in these transformations, Ciri; you who once were Cirilla of Cintra. You probably already know what role.'

'I know,' she snapped, not reacting to Yennefer's restraining hiss. 'Vilgefortz explained it to me! While preparing to stick a glass syringe between my legs. If that's supposed to be my destiny, then I – respectfully – decline.'

Philippa's dark eyes flashed with a cold anger. But it was Sheala de Tancarville who spoke.

'You still have much to learn, child,' she said, wrapping the silver fox-fur boa around her neck. 'You will have to unlearn many things, I see and hear, by your own efforts or with someone's help. You have lately come into possession, it can be gathered, of much evil knowledge. You have also certainly endured evil, experienced evil. Now, in your childish rage, you refuse to notice the good, you deny the good and good intentions. You bristle like a hedgehog, unable to recognise precisely those who are concerned with your good. You snort and bare your claws like a wild kitten, without leaving us a choice: you need to be grabbed by the scruff of the neck. And we shall do that, child, without a second thought. For we are older than you, we're wiser, we know everything about what has been and what is, and we know much about what will be. We shall take you by the scruff of the neck, kitty, so you may one day soon, sit here among us at this table, as an experienced and wise she-cat. As one of us. No! Not a word! Don't you dare open your mouth when Sheala de Tancarville is speaking!'

The voice of the Koviran sorceress, sharp and piercing like a knife scraping against iron, suddenly hung in mid-air over the table. Not only Ciri cowered; the other witches of the Lodge shuddered slightly and drew their heads into their shoulders. Well, perhaps with the exception of Philippa, Francesca and Assire. And Yennefer.

'You were right,' continued Sheala, wrapping the boa around her neck, 'in thinking that you were summoned to Montecalvo to be informed about your fate. You weren't right to think you are nothing. For you are everything, you are the future of the world. At this moment, naturally, you don't know that, can't know that, at this moment you're a puffed up and spitting kitten, a traumatised child, who sees in everybody Emhyr var Emreis or Vilgefortz holding his inseminator. And there's no point now, at this moment, explaining to you that you are mistaken, that it concerns your good and the good of the world. The time will come for such explanations. One day. Now, hot under the collar, you don't want to listen to the voice of reason. Now, for every argument you will have a riposte in the form of childish stubbornness and noisy indignation. Now you will simply be grabbed by the scruff of the neck. I have finished. Inform the girl of her fate, Philippa.'

Ciri sat stiff, stroking the heads of the sphinxes carved into the armrests of the chair.

'You will go to Kovir with Sheala and I.' Madam Owl broke the heavy and dead silence. 'To Point Vanis, the royal summer capital. Because you are no longer Cirilla of Cintra, you will be presented at the audience as a novice in magic, our pupil. At the audience you will meet a very wise king, Esterad Thyssen, of genuine royal blood. You will meet his wife, Queen Zuleyka, a person of extraordinary nobility and goodness. You will also meet the royal couple's son, Prince Tankred.

Ciri, beginning to understand, opened her eyes widely. Madam Owl noticed it.

'Yes,' she confirmed. 'You must make an impression on Prince

Tankred, above all. For you will become his lover and bear his child.'

'Were you still Cirilla of Cintra—' Philippa took the conversation up after a long pause '—were you still the daughter of Pavetta and the granddaughter of Calanthe, we would make you Tankred's wedded wife. Princess, and later Queen of Kovir and Poviss. Sadly, and I say this with real sorrow, fate has deprived you of everything. Including the future. You will only be a lover. A favourite—'

'By name and formally,' interjected Sheala, 'for in practice we shall try hard for you to gain the status of princess by Tankred's side, and afterwards even of queen. Your help will be necessary, naturally. Tankred must desire you to be at his side. Day and night. We'll teach you how to fuel such a desire. But whether the lesson is learned will depend on you.'

'Those titles are essentially trifles,' said Madam Owl. 'It's important that Tankred impregnates you as quickly as possible.'

'Well, that's obvious,' Ciri muttered.

'The Lodge will provide for the future and position of your child.' Philippa didn't take her eyes off Ciri. 'You deserve to know we're thinking here about matters of great note. You will be participating in it, in any case, since right after the birth of the child you will begin to take part in our gatherings. You will learn. Since you are, although it may be incomprehensible to you today, one of us.'

'You called me a monster on the Isle of Thanedd, Madam Owl.' Ciri overcame the constriction in her throat. 'And today you tell me I'm one of you.'

'There's no contradiction in that,' resounded the voice of Enid an Gleanna, the Daisy of the Valleys, as melodic as the burbling of a stream. 'We, *me luned*, are all monsters. Each in our own way. Isn't that right, Madam Owl?'

Philippa shrugged.

'We shall disguise that hideous scar on your face with an illusion,' Sheala spoke again, tugging at her boa apparently indifferently. 'You will be beautiful and mysterious, and Tankred Thyssen, I assure you, will lose his head for you. We'll have to invent some personal details for you. Cirilla is a nice name and is by no means so rare that you would have to give it up to remain incognito. But we have to give you a surname. I wouldn't protest if you chose mine.'

'Or mine,' said Madam Owl, smiling with the corners of her mouth. 'Cirilla Eilhart also sounds nice.'

'That name—' the silver bells of the Daisy of the Valleys jingled in the hall again '—sounds nice in every combination. And each of us, sitting here, would like to have a daughter like you, Zireael, O Swallow with the eyes of a falcon, you, who bear the blood and bones of Lara Dorren's blood and bones. Each of us would give up everything, even the Lodge, even the fate of the kingdoms and the whole world, to have a daughter like you. But it's impossible. We know that it's impossible. Which is why we envy Yennefer.'

'Thank you, Madam Philippa,' Ciri said a moment later, clenching her hands on the sphinxes' heads. 'I'm also honoured at the offer of bearing the name Tancarville. However, because a surname is the only thing in this whole matter that depends on me and my choice, the only thing that isn't being imposed on me, I have to gratefully decline and choose for myself. I want to be called Ciri of Vengerberg, daughter of Yennefer.'

'Ha!' A black-haired sorceress, whom Ciri guessed was Sabrina Glevissig of Kaedwen, flashed her teeth. 'Tankred Thyssen will prove to be an ass if he doesn't wed her morganatically. If instead of her he lets some drippy princess be foisted upon him, he'll turn out to be an ass and a blind man, unable to recognise a diamond among pieces of glass. Congratulations, Yenna. I envy you. And you know how sincerely I can envy.'

Yennefer thanked her with a nod of her head. Without even the ghost of a smile.

'And thus,' said Philippa, 'everything is settled.'

'No,' said Ciri.

Francesca Findabair snorted softly. Sheala de Tancarville raised her head and her facial features hardened unpleasantly.

'I have to think the matter over,' Ciri declared. 'Ponder it. Sort everything out in my mind. Calmly. Once I've done that I'll return here, to Montecalvo. I'll appear before you, ladies. I'll tell you what I've decided.'

Sheala moved her lips, as though she'd found something in her mouth she ought to spit out at once. But she didn't speak.

'I have arranged to meet the Witcher Geralt in the city of Rivia.' Ciri lifted her head up. 'I promised him I'd meet him there, that I'd ride there with Yennefer. I'll keep that promise, with your permission or without it. Madam Rita, who is here, knows that I always find a crack in the wall if I'm going to Geralt.'

Margarita Laux-Antille nodded with a smile.

'I must talk to Geralt. Say goodbye to him. And admit he's right. Because you ought to know one thing, ladies. When we were riding away from Stygga Castle, leaving corpses in our wake, I asked Geralt if it was the end, if we were victorious, if evil had been overcome, and if good had triumphed. And he just smiled somehow strangely and sadly. I thought it was from tiredness, because we had buried all of his friends at the foot of Stygga. But now I know what that smile meant. It was a smile of pity at the naivety of a child who thought that the slit throats of Vilgefortz and Bonhart meant the triumph of good over evil. I really must tell him I've grown wiser, that I've understood. I really must tell him.

'I must also try to convince him that what you want to do with me fundamentally differs from what Vilgefortz wanted to do to me with a glass syringe. I have to explain to him that there is a difference between Montecalvo Castle and Stygga Castle, even though Vilgefortz was concerned with the good of the world and you are also concerned with the good of the world.

'I know it won't be easy to convince an old wolf like Geralt. Geralt will say I'm a chit, that it's easy to beguile me with appearances of nobility, that all this bloody *destiny* and *good of the world* are stupid platitudes. But I must try. It's important that he understands and accepts it. It's very important. For you too, ladies.'

'You haven't understood anything,' said Sheala de Tancarville harshly. 'You're still a child passing from the stage of callow howling and foot-stamping to callow arrogance. The only thing that raises hope is your sharpness of mind. You'll learn quickly. Soon, believe me, you'll laugh, recalling the nonsense you talked here. As regards your trip to Rivia, I pray you, let the Lodge express its opinion. I'm expressing my firm opposition. For fundamental reasons. To prove to you that I, Sheala de Tancarville, never waste words. And am capable of making you bend your proud neck. You need to be taught discipline, for your own good.'

488

'Let's settle this matter then.' Philippa Eilhart placed her palms on the table. 'Ladies, please express your opinions. Are we to permit the haughty maid Ciri to ride to Rivia? For a meeting with some witcher for whom there soon won't be a place in her life? Are we to let sentimentalism grow in her, sentimentality that she will soon have to utterly get rid of? Sheala is opposed. And the rest of you ladies?'

'I'm against,' declared Sabrina Glevissig. 'Also for fundamental reasons. I like the girl, I like what she says, her insolence and hot-tempered impudence. I prefer it to spineless acquiescence. I wouldn't have anything against her request, particularly since she would certainly return; people such as she don't break their word. But the little madam has threatened us. She must know we disregard such threats!'

'I'm opposed,' said Keira Metz. 'For practical reasons. I like the girl too, and Geralt carried me in his arms on Thanedd. There isn't a scrap of sentimentality in me, but it was awfully pleasant. It would be a way of repaying him. But no! For you are mistaken, Sabrina. The girl is a witcher and is trying to outwit us. In short, make a run for it.'

'Does anyone here,' Yennefer drawled malevolently, 'dare to doubt the words of my daughter?'

'You, Yennefer, be quiet,' hissed Philippa. 'Don't speak, or I'll lose my patience. There are three votes against. Let's hear the rest.'

'I vote to allow her to go,' said Triss Merigold. 'I know her and vouch for her. I'd also like to accompany her on her journey, if she agrees. Help her in her deliberations and reflections, if she agrees. And in her conversation with Geralt, if she agrees.'

'I'm also in favour,' smiled Margarita Laux-Antille. 'What I say will astonish you, ladies, but I'm doing it for Tissaia de Vries. Were Tissaia here, she would be outraged at the suggestion that compulsion and the restriction of personal freedom are necessary to maintain the unity of the Lodge.'

'I vote in favour,' said Francesca Findabair, straightening the lace on her neckline. 'There are many reasons, but I don't have to reveal them nor do I intend to.'

'I vote in favour,' said Ida Emean aep Sivney, just as laconically. 'Because my heart compels me thus.'

'And I'm opposed,' declared Assire var Anahid dryly. 'I'm not driven by any sympathy, antipathy or fundamental issues. I fear for Ciri's life. She is safe in the Lodge's care, but an easy target on the roads leading to Rivia. And I worry that there are people who, even having taken away her name and identity, will still think that's not enough.'

'It remains for us to learn the position of Madam Fringilla Vigo,' said Sabrina Glevissig quite scathingly. 'Although it should be obvious. For I take the liberty of reminding you all of Rhys-Rhun Castle.'

'Although I am grateful for the reminder—' Fringilla Vigo lifted her head proudly '—I vote for Ciri. To show the respect and affection I have for the girl. And more than anything I'm doing it for Geralt of Rivia, the Witcher, without whom that girl wouldn't be here today. Who, in order to rescue Ciri, went to the end of the world, fighting everything that stood in his way, even himself. It would be a wickedness to deny him a meeting with her.'

'Yet there was too little wickedness,' Sabrina said cynically, 'and too much naive sentimentality; the same sentimentality we mean to eradicate from this maiden. Why, there was even talk about hearts. And the result is that the scales are in the balance. In deadlock. We haven't decided anything. We'll have to vote again. I suggest by secret ballot.'

'What for?'

They all looked at the person who had spoken. Yennefer.

'I am still a member of this Lodge,' said Yennefer. 'No one has taken my membership away from me. No one has taken my place. I have the formal right to vote. I think it's clear who I'm voting for. The votes in favour prevail, so the matter is settled.'

'Your insolence,' said Sabrina, locking her fingers, armed with onyx rings, 'borders on bad taste, Yennefer.'

'In your place, madam, I would sit in humble silence,' added Sheala grimly. 'Bearing in mind the voting of which you will soon be the subject.'

'I backed Ciri,' said Francesca, 'but I must take you to task, Yennefer. You left the Lodge, fleeing from it and refusing to cooperate. You don't have any rights. You do, though, have obligations, debts to pay, a sentence to hear. Were it not for that, you wouldn't have been allowed to cross Montecalvo's threshold.'

Yennefer restrained Ciri, who was itching to stand up and shout. Without resisting and in silence, Ciri sank into the chair with the armrests carved into sphinxes, watching Madam Owl – Philippa Eilhart – getting up from her chair and suddenly towering over the table.

'Yennefer doesn't have the right to vote, that is clear,' she announced in a ringing voice. 'But I do. I've listened to the votes of all the women present here, so I can finally vote myself, I believe.'

'What do you mean by that, Philippa?' Sabrina frowned.

Philippa Eilhart looked across the table. She met Ciri's eyes and looked into them.

*

The bottom of the pool is made of a many-coloured mosaic, the tiles shimmering and seeming to move. The entire surface trembles, glimmering with light and shade. Carp and orfe flash by under lily leaves as large as plates, amidst green pond weed. The young girl's large dark eyes reflect in the water, her long hair reaches down to the surface, floating on it.

The girl, forgetting about the whole world, runs her little hands among the stems of water lilies, and hangs over the edge of the pool surrounding the fountain. She would love to touch one of the small gold and red fishes. The fish swim up to the girl's hands, they circle around her curiously, but they won't let themselves be seized; they're as elusive as apparitions, like the water itself. The dark-eyed girl's fingers close on nothingness.

'Philippa!'

It's her most favourite voice. In spite of that the little girl doesn't react right away. She continues to look at the water, at the little fish, at the water lilies and at her own reflection.

'Philippa!'

*

'Philippa.' Sheala de Tancarville's harsh voice shook her out of her reverie. 'We're waiting.'

A cold, spring wind blew in through the open window. Philippa Eilhart shuddered. *Death*, she thought. *Death passed beside me.*

'This Lodge,' she finally said confidently, loudly and emphatically, 'will decide the fates of the world. Because this Lodge is like the world, is its mirror. Good sense, which doesn't always mean cold wickedness and calculation, is balancing out sentimentality, which is not always naive. Responsibility, iron discipline – even if imposed by force – and aversion to violence; gentleness and trust. The matter-of-fact coolness of omnipotence . . . and heart.

'I, casting my vote last, take one more thing into consideration,' she continued in the silence that had descended on the colonnaded hall in Montecalvo. 'One that, though it doesn't balance out anything, counterbalances everything.'

Following her gaze, all the women looked at the wall, at the mosaic constructed from tiny coloured tiles, depicting the snake Ouroboros grasping its tail in its teeth.

'That thing is destiny,' she continued, fixing her dark eyes on Ciri. 'Which I, Philippa Eilhart, have only recently begun to believe in. Which I, Philippa Eilhart, have only recently begun to understand. Destiny isn't the judgements of providence, isn't scrolls written by the hand of a demiurge, isn't fatalism. Destiny is hope. Being full of hope, believing that what is meant to happen will happen, I cast my vote. I vote for Ciri. The Child of Destiny. The Child of Hope.'

The silence in the colonnaded hall of Montecalvo Castle, plunged in subtle chiaroscuro, lasted a long time. The cry of an osprey circling over the lake reached them from outside the window.

'Madam Yennefer,' Ciri whispered. 'Does that mean . . .'

'Let's go, daughter,' answered Yennefer in a soft voice. 'Geralt's waiting for us and there's a long road ahead.'

*

Geralt awoke and leaped to his feet with the cry of a night bird in his ears.

Then the sorceress and the witcher were married and held a grand wedding party. I too was there, I drank mead and wine. And then they lived happily ever after, but for a very short time. He died ordinarily, of a heart attack. She died soon after him, but of what the tale does not say. They say of sorrow and longing, but who would lend credence to fairy tales?

Flourens Delannoy, *Fairy Tales and Stories*

CHAPTER TWELVE

It was the sixth day after the June new moon when they arrived in Rivia.

They rode out of the forests onto the hillsides and then, beneath them, down below, suddenly and without warning, twinkled and glittered the surface of Loch Eskalott, which filled the valley in the shape of the rune from which it took its name. The hillsides of Craag Ros, the protruding end of the Mahakam massif, covered in fir and larch, gazed at their own reflections in the lake surface. As did the red tiles of the towers of the stout Rivia Castle, the winter seat of the kings of Lyria, standing on a headland extending into the lake. And by a bay at the southern end of Loch Eskalott lay the town of Rivia, with the bright thatch of the cottages around the castle and dark houses growing by the lake shore like mushrooms.

'Well, we seem to have arrived,' Dandelion stated, shielding his eyes with his hand. 'Now we've come full circle, we're in Rivia. Strange, how strange are the twists of fate . . . I don't see blue and white pennants on any of the castle towers, and thus Queen Meve is not residing at the castle. I don't suppose, in any case, that she still remembers our desertion—'

'Believe me, Dandelion,' Geralt interrupted, steering his horse down the hillside. 'I don't give a damn who remembers what.'

A colourful tent resembling a cake stood outside the city, not far from the turnpike. A white shield with a red chevron hung on a pole in front of it. A knight in full armour and a white surcoat decorated with the same arms as the shield was standing under the raised flap of the tent. The knight was scrutinising women in headscarves, tar and pitch makers with kegs containing their wares, herdsmen, pedlars and beggars. His eyes lit up in hope at the sight of Geralt and Dandelion riding slowly along.

'The lady of your heart—' Geralt dispelled the knight's hope in an icy voice '—whoever she is, is the most beautiful and most virtuous virgin from the Yaruga to the Buina.'

'By my troth,' the knight snapped back. 'You speak the truth, sir.'

*

A fair-haired girl in a densely studded leather jacket vomited in the middle of the street, bent in two, holding on to the stirrup of a flea-bitten grey mare. The girl's two male companions, identically attired, carrying swords on their backs and wearing bands on their foreheads, cursed the passers-by filthily, in somewhat incoherent voices. Both were more than tipsy, unsteady on their feet, bumping into horses' sides and the bar of the hitching post situated outside the inn.

'Must we really go in there?' asked Dandelion. 'There may be more nice lads like that inside.'

'I'm meeting someone here. Have you forgotten? This is The Rooster and Mother Hen mentioned in a notice on the oak tree.'

The fair-haired girl bent over again, puked spasmodically and extremely profusely. The mare snorted loudly and jerked, knocking the girl over and dragging her through the vomit.

'What are you gawking at, you fool?' mumbled one of the youngsters. 'You grey-haired old bum?'

'Geralt,' muttered Dandelion, dismounting. 'Don't do anything foolish, please.'

'Fear not. I won't.'

They tied their horses to the hitching post on the other side of the steps. The young men stopped paying attention to them and began insulting and spitting at a townswoman crossing the street with a child. Dandelion glanced at the Witcher's face. He didn't like what he saw.

The first thing that stuck out after entering the inn was a sign: WANTED: COOK. The next was a large picture on a signboard made of planks of wood, portraying a bearded monster holding a battle axe dripping blood. The caption announced: THE DWARF – A WRETCHED, TREACHEROUS RUNT.

Dandelion was right to be worried. In practice, the only guests in the inn – apart from a few seriously drunk drunks and two skinny prostitutes with dark circles around their eyes – were more 'lads' dressed up in leather sparkling with studs, with swords on their backs. There were eight of them of both sexes, but they were making enough of a commotion for eighteen, shouting over each other and swearing.

'I recognise you and know who you are, gentlemen.' The inn-keeper surprised them as soon as he saw them. 'And I have news for you. You're to go to a tavern called Wirsing's in Elm.'

'Oooh.' Dandelion cheered up. 'That's good . . .'

'I wouldn't know about that.' The innkeeper went back to drying a mug on his apron. 'If you disdain my establishment, that's your choice. But I'll tell you that Elm's a dwarven district, where non-humans reside.'

'And what of it?' Geralt squinted his eyes.

'Aye, I'm sure it doesn't bother you.' The innkeeper shrugged. 'Why, the one who left the news was a dwarf. Since you associate with such as he . . . that's your affair. It's your affair whose company you find more agreeable.'

'We aren't particularly fussy as regards company,' announced Dandelion, nodding towards the youths in black jackets with bands around their pimply foreheads yelling and wrestling at a table. 'But I swear we aren't fond of that kind.'

The innkeeper put down the dry mug and glared at them unpleasantly.

'You should be more understanding,' he instructed with emphasis. 'Youngsters have to let off steam. There's a certain saying, youngsters have to let off steam. The war damaged them. Their fathers perished . . .'

'And their mothers screwed around,' finished Geralt with a voice as icy as a mountain lake. 'I understand and I'm full of un-derstanding. At least, I'm trying hard to be. Let's go, Dandelion.'

'Be off with you – with respect,' said the innkeeper without respect. 'But don't be a-complaining about what I warned you of. These days it's easy to get a sore head in the dwarven district. If anything were to happen.'

'If what were to happen?'

'How would I know? Is it any business of mine?'

'Let's go, Geralt,' urged Dandelion, seeing out of the corner of one eye that the war-damaged youngsters, those who were still reasonably conscious, were observing them with eyes shining with fisstech.

'Goodbye, master innkeeper. Who knows, perhaps we'll visit your establishment one day, in a while. Once those signs have gone from the entrance.'

'And which one don't you gentlemen like?' The innkeeper frowned and stood with legs aggressively apart. 'Eh? The one about the dwarf, perhaps?'

'No. The one about the cook.'

Three youngsters got up from the table, slightly unsteady on their feet, clearly intending to bar their way. A girl and two boys in black jackets. With swords on their backs.

Geralt didn't slow his stride, he walked on and his face and eyes were cold and totally indifferent.

Almost at the last moment the striplings parted, stepping back. Dandelion smelled the beer on their breath. And sweat. And fear.

'You have to get used to it,' said the Witcher, when they were outside. 'You have to adapt.'

'It's hard sometimes.'

'That's no argument. That's no argument, Dandelion.'

The air was hot, dense and sticky. Like soup.

*

Outside, in front of the inn, the two boys in black jackets were helping the fair-haired girl wash in a horse trough. The girl snorted, incoherently indicating that she was feeling better and announced that she needed a drink. And of course she'd go to the bazaar to overturn some stalls for a lark, but first she needed a drink.

The girl's name was Nadia Esposito. That name became etched in the annals. It passed into history.

But Geralt and Dandelion couldn't have known that then. Neither could the girl.

*

498

The narrow streets of the city of Rivia bustled with life, and what seemed to wholly occupy the residents and visitors was trade. It seemed as though everybody was trading in everything there and trying to exchange anything for something more. A cacophony of shouts resounded from all sides – goods were being advertised, people were bargaining heatedly, insulting each other, thunderously accusing each other of cheating, thievery and swindles, as well as other peccadilloes absolutely unconnected to commerce.

Before Geralt and Dandelion had reached Elm they were presented with a great deal of attractive offers. They were offered, among other things, an astrolabe, a brass trumpet, a set of cutlery decorated with the coat of arms of the Frangipani family, stocks in a copper mine, a large jar of leeches, a tattered book entitled *An Alleged Miracle or the Medusa's Head*, a pair of ferrets, an elixir to increase potency and – as part of a package deal – a none too young, none too slim and none too fresh woman.

A black-bearded dwarf tried to convince them extremely aggressively to buy a shoddy little mirror in a pinchbeck frame, attempting to prove it was the magical looking glass of Cambuscan, when soon after somebody threw a stone and knocked the ware out of his hand.

'Lousy kobold!' bellowed a barefoot and dirty street urchin. 'Unhuman! Bearded old goat!'

'And may your guts rot, you human shithead!' roared the dwarf. 'May they rot and leak out of your arse.'

People looked on in gloomy silence.

*

The district of Elm lay right beside the lake, in a bay among alders, weeping willows and – naturally – elms. It was much more quiet and peaceful, no one bought anything or wanted to sell anything here. A light breeze was blowing from the lake, especially pleasant after getting out of the stuffy, flyblown stink of the city.

They didn't have to search long to find Wirsing's tavern. The first passer-by they encountered pointed it out to them without hesitation.

Two bearded dwarves, sipping beer from mugs hugged against their bellies, were sitting beneath a roof covered in bright green moss and swallows' nests on the steps of a porch enveloped in climbing peas and wild roses.

'Geralt and Dandelion,' said one of the dwarves and belched daintily. 'What took you so long, you rogues?'

Geralt dismounted.

'Greetings, Yarpen Zigrin. Glad to see you, Zoltan Chivay.'

*

They were the only guests of the tavern, which smelled strongly of roast meat, garlic, herbs and something else, something elusive, but very pleasant. They sat at a heavy table with a view of the lake, which looked mysterious, charming and romantic through tinted panes in lead frames.

'Where's Ciri?' Yarpen Zigrin asked bluntly. 'She can't be—'

'No,' Geralt quickly interrupted. 'She's coming here. She'll be here any moment. Well, beardies, tell us how things are going.'

'Didn't I say?' Yarpen said with a sneer. 'Didn't I say, Zoltan? Comes back from the end of the world, where, if rumours can be believed, he waded in blood, killed dragons and overthrew empires. And he asks *us* how things are going. That's the Witcher all over—'

'What smells so appetising here?' Dandelion interjected.

'Dinner,' said Yarpen Zigrin. 'Meat. Dandelion, ask me where we got the meat.'

'I won't, because I know that joke.'

'Don't be a swine.'

'Where did you get the meat?'

'Crawled here itself.'

'And now more seriously—' Yarpen wiped away tears, although the joke, to tell the truth, was pretty hoary '—the situation with vittles is quite critical, as usual after a war. You won't find meat, not even poultry, it's also hard to get fish . . . Things are bad with flour and spuds, peas and beans . . Farms have been burned down, stores plundered, fishponds emptied and fields lie fallow . . .'

'There's no turnover,' added Zoltan. 'There's no transport.

Only usury and barter are functioning. Did you see the bazaar? Profiteers are making fortunes beside beggars selling and exchanging the remains of their possessions . . .'

'If the crops fail on top of that, people will begin to die of hunger in the winter.'

'Is it really that bad?'

'Riding from the South you must have passed villages and settlements. Think back to how often you heard dogs barking.'

'Bloody hell.' Dandelion slapped himself on the forehead. 'I knew it . . . I told you, Geralt, that it wasn't normal! That something was missing! Ha! Now I get it! We didn't hear any dogs! There weren't any around—'

He suddenly broke off and glanced towards the kitchen and the smell of garlic and herbs with terror in his eyes.

'Fear not,' snorted Yarpen. 'Our meat doesn't come from anything that barks, meows or calls out "Mercy!". Our meat is totally different. It's fit for kings!'

'Let us in on it, dwarf!'

'When we received your letter and it was clear we'd meet in Rivia, Zoltan and I pondered over what to serve you. We racked our brains till all that racking made us want to piss, and then we went down to a little lakeside alder. We looked, and there were positively tons of snails. So we took a sack and caught a load of the dear molluscs, as many as we could stuff in it . . .'

'A lot of them escaped,' Zoltan Chivay nodded, 'We were a tad drunk and they're devilish fast.'

Again, both dwarves wept with laughter at another old chestnut.

'Wirsing—' Yarpen pointed at the innkeeper bustling around by the stove '—knows how to cook snails, and that, you ought to know, demands considerable arcane knowledge. He nonetheless is a born chef de cuisine. Before he became a widower he and his wife ran the roadhouse in Maribor with such a table that the king himself entertained guests there. We'll soon be tucking in, I tell you!'

'And before that,' nodded Zoltan, 'we'll have a starter of freshly smoked whitefish caught on a gaff in the bottomless depths of this lake. And we'll wash it down with hooch from the depths of the cellar.'

'And the story, gentlemen,' reminded Yarpen, pouring. 'The story!'

*

The whitefish was still hot, oily and smelled of smoke from alder chips. The vodka was so cold it stung the teeth.

Dandelion spoke first; elaborately, fluently, colourfully and volubly, embellishing his tale with ornaments so beautiful and fanciful they almost obscured the fibs and confabulations.

Then the Witcher spoke. He spoke the same truth, and spoke so dryly, boringly and flatly that Dandelion couldn't bear it and kept butting in, for which the dwarves reprimanded him.

And then the story was over and a lengthy silence fell.

'To the archer Milva!' Zoltan Chivay cleared his throat, saluting with his cup. 'To the Nilfgaardian. To Regis the herbalist who entertained the travellers in his cottage with moonshine and mandrake. And to Angoulême, whom I never knew. May the earth lie lightly on them all. May they have in the beyond plenty of whatever they were short of on earth. And may their names live forever in songs and tales. Let's drink to them.'

*

Wirsing, a grey-haired fellow, pale and as thin as a rake, the sheer opposite of the stereotype of an innkeeper and master of culinary secrets, brought to the table a basket of snow-white, aromatic bread, and after that a huge, wooden dish of snails on a bed of horseradish leaves, sizzling and spitting garlic butter. Dandelion, Geralt and the dwarves set about eating with a will. The meal was exquisitely tasty and at the same time extremely comical, considering the need to fiddle with bizarre tongs and little forks.

They ate, smacked their lips and caught the dripping butter on bread. They swore cheerfully as one snail after another slipped from the tongs. Two young kittens had great fun rolling and chasing the empty shells across the floor.

The smell coming from the kitchen indicated that Wirsing was cooking another batch.

*

Yarpen Zigrin reluctantly waved a hand, but realised that the Witcher wouldn't give up.

'Nothing new with me, by and large,' he said, sucking out a shell. 'A bit of soldiering . . . A bit of politicking, because I was elected vice-starosta. I'm going to make a career in politics. There's great competition in every other trade. And there are no end of fools, bribe-takers and thieves in politics. It's easy to make a name for yourself.'

'While I don't have a flair for politics,' said Zoltan Chivay, gesticulating with a snail held in his tongs, 'I'm setting up a steam and water hammer works, in partnership with Figgs Merluzzo and Munro Bruys. Remember them, Witcher, Figgs and Bruys?'

'Not just them.'

'Yazon Varda fell at the Battle of the Yaruga,' Zoltan informed them dryly. 'Pretty stupidly, in one of the last skirmishes.'

'Shame. And Percival Schuttenbach?'

'The gnome? Oh, he's doing well. The crafty thing, he got out of the draft using some ancient gnomish laws as an excuse, claiming his religion forbad him from soldiering. And he managed it, even though everybody knows he'd give the whole pantheon of gods and goddesses for a marinated herring. He has a jeweller's workshop in Novigrad. Do you know, he bought that parrot Field Marshal Duda and turned the bird into a living advertisement, after teaching it to call: "Diiiamonds, diiiamonds". And just imagine, it works. The gnome has lots of custom, hands full of work and a well-stuffed safe. Yes, yes, that's Novigrad! Money lies in the streets there. That's also why we want to start our hammer works in Novigrad.'

'People will be smearing shit on your door,' said Yarpen. 'And throwing stones at the windows. And calling you a filthy short-arse. It won't help you at all that you're a war veteran, that you fought for them. You'll be a pariah in that Novigrad of yours.'

'Be all right,' said Zoltan cheerfully. 'There's too much competition in Mahakam. And too many politicians. Let's drink a toast, lads. To Caleb Stratton. And Yazon Varda.'

503

'To Regan Dahlberg,' added Yarpen, growing gloomy. Gerald shook his head.

'Regan too . . .'

'Aye. At Mayena. Old Mrs Dahlberg was left a widow. Ah, by the devil, enough, enough of that, let's drink. And hurry with those snails, I see Wirsing's bringing another bowl!'

*

The dwarves, belts loosened, listened to Geralt's story about how Dandelion's ducal romance finished up on the scaffold. The poet pretended to be piqued and didn't comment. Yarpen and Zoltan roared with laughter.

'Yes, yes,' said Yarpen Zigrin at the end, grinning. 'As the old song goes: *Though man can bend rods of steel, women will always bring him to heel*. Several wonderful examples of the aptness of that adage are gathered around one table today. Zoltan Chivay springs to mind. When I told you what's new with him, I forgot to add he's taking a wife. And soon, in September. The lucky girl is called Eudora Brekekeks.'

'Breckenriggs!' Zoltan corrected emphatically, frowning. 'I'm beginning to have enough of correcting your pronunciation, Zigrin. Take heed, for I'm liable to start cracking heads when I've had enough of something—!'

'Where's the wedding? And when exactly?' Dandelion interrupted in mid-sentence placatingly. 'I'm asking, because we might look in. If you invite us, naturally.'

'It hasn't been decided what, where or how, or even if it's happening,' Zoltan mumbled, clearly disconcerted. 'Yarpen's getting ahead of himself. Eudora and I are engaged, right enough, but who knows what might happen? In these fuck-awful times?'

'The second example of woman's omnipotence,' continued Yarpen Zigrin, 'is Geralt of Rivia, the Witcher.'

Geralt pretended to be occupied with a snail. Yarpen snorted.

'Having miraculously regained Ciri,' he continued, 'he lets her ride off, agreeing to another farewell. He leaves her on her own again, although, as somebody here rightly observed, the times are not too peaceful, for fuck's sake. And said witcher does all that

504

because that's what a certain woman wants. The Witcher always does everything that that woman – known to society as Yennefer of Vengerberg – wants. And if only said Witcher got any benefit from it. But he doesn't. Indeed, as King Dezmod used to say when looking into his chamber pot after completing a motion, "The mind is unable to grasp it".'

'I suggest—' Geralt raised his cup with a charming smile '—we drink up and change the subject.'

'Well said,' said Dandelion and Zoltan in unison.

*

Wirsing brought to the table a third, and then a fourth great bowl of snails. Neither did he forget, naturally, about the bread and vodka. The diners had now eaten their fill, so it was no surprise that toasts were being drunk somewhat more frequently. Neither was it a surprise that philosophy crept into the discourse more and more often.

*

'The evil I fought against,' repeated the Witcher, 'was a sign of the activities of Chaos, activities calculated to disturb Order. Since wherever Evil is at large, Order may not reign, and everything Order builds collapses, cannot endure. The little light of wisdom and the flame of hope, the glow of warmth, instead of flaring up, go out. It'll be dark. And in the darkness will be fangs, claws and blood.'

Yarpen Zigrin stroked his beard, greasy from the herb and garlic butter that had dripped from the snails.

'Very prettily said, Witcher,' he admitted. 'But, as the young Cerro said to King Vridanek during their first tryst: "It's not a bad-looking thing, but does it have any practical use?"'

'The reason for existence—' the Witcher didn't smile '—and the raison d'être of witchers has been undermined, since the fight between Good and Evil is now being waged on a different battle-field and is being fought completely differently. Evil has stopped being chaotic. It has stopped being a blind and impetuous force,

505

against which a witcher, a mutant as murderous and chaotic as Evil itself, had to act. Today Evil acts according to rights – because it is entitled to. It acts according to peace treaties, because it was taken into consideration when the treaties were being written . . .'

'He's seen the settlers being driven south,' guessed Zoltan Chivay.

'Not only that,' Dandelion added grimly. 'Not only that.'

'So what?' Yarpen Zigrin sat more comfortably, locking his hands on his belly. 'Everyone's seen things. Everybody's been pissed off, everybody has lost his appetite for a shorter or a longer time. Or lost sleep. That's how it is. That's how it was. And how it's going to be. Like these shells here, I swear you won't squeeze any more philosophy out of it. Because there isn't any more. What's not to your liking, Witcher, what doesn't suit you? The changes the world's undergoing? Development? Progress?'

'Perhaps.'

Yarpen said nothing for a long time, looking at the Witcher from under his bushy eyebrows.

'Progress,' he said finally, 'is like a herd of pigs. That's how you should look at progress, that's how you should judge it. Like a herd of pigs trotting around a farmyard. Numerous benefits derive from the fact of that herd's existence. There's pork knuckle. There's sausage, there's fatback, there are trotters in aspic. In a word, there are benefits! There's no point turning your nose up at the shit everywhere.'

They were all silent for some time, weighing up in their minds and consciences the various important issues and matters.

'Let's have a drink,' said Dandelion finally.

No one protested.

*

'Progress,' said Yarpen Zigrin amidst the silence, 'will eventually light up the darkness. The darkness will yield before the light. But not right away. And definitely not without a fight.'

Geralt, staring at the window, smiled at his own thoughts and dreams.

'The darkness you're talking about,' he said, 'is a state of mind,

506

not matter. Quite different witchers will have to be trained to fight something like that. It's high time to start.'

'Start retraining? Is that what you had in mind?'

'Not entirely. Being a witcher doesn't interest me any longer. I'm retiring.'

'Like hell!'

'I'm totally serious. I'm done with being a witcher.'

A long silence fell, broken only by the furious meowing of the kittens which were scratching and biting one another under the table, faithful to the custom of that species, for whom there's no sport without pain.

'He's done with being a witcher,' Yarpen Zigrin finally repeated in a drawling voice. 'Ha! I don't know what to think about it, as King Dezmod said when he was caught cheating at cards. But one may suspect the worse. Dandelion, you travel with him, spend a lot of time with him. Is he showing any other signs of paranoia?'

'Yes, yes.' Geralt was stony-faced. 'Joking aside, as King Dezmod said when the guests at the banquet suddenly began to go blue and die. I've said what I intended to say. And now to action.'

He picked up his sword from the back of the chair.

'This is your sihill, Zoltan Chivay. I return it to you with thanks and a low bow. It has served. It has helped. Saved lives. And taken lives.'

'Witcher . . .' The dwarf raised his hands in a defensive gesture. 'The sword is yours. I didn't lend it to you, I gave it. Gifts—'

'Quiet, Chivay. I'm returning your sword. I won't need it any longer.'

'Like hell,' repeated Yarpen. 'Pour him some vodka, Dandelion, because he sounds like old Schrader when a pickaxe fell on his head down a mine shaft. Geralt, I know you have a profound nature and a lofty soul, but don't talk such crap, please, because, as it's easy to see, neither Yennefer nor any other of your magical concubines are in the audience; just us old buggers. You can't tell old buggers like us that your sword's not needed, that witchers aren't needed, that the world's rotten, that this, that and the other. You're a witcher and always will be—'

'No, I won't,' Geralt responded mildly. 'It may surprise you old

507

buggers, but I've come to the conclusion that pissing into the wind is stupid. That risking your neck for anybody is stupid. Even if they're paying. And existential philosophy has nothing to do with it. You won't believe it, but my own skin has suddenly become extremely dear to me. I've come to the conclusion it would be foolish to risk it in someone else's defence.'

'I've noticed.' Dandelion nodded. 'On one hand that's wise. On the other—'

'There is no other.'

'Do Yennefer and Ciri,' Yarpen asked after a short pause, 'have anything to do with your decision?'

'A great deal.'

'Then everything's clear,' sighed the dwarf. 'Admittedly, I don't exactly know how you, a professional swordsman, intend to sustain yourself and intend to organise your worldly existence. Even though, however you slice it, I can't see you in the role of, let's say, a cabbage planter, nonetheless one must respect your choice. Innkeeper, if you'd be so kind! This is a Mahakam sihill sword from the very forge of Rhundurin. It was a gift. The receiver doesn't want it, the giver may not take it back. So you take it, fasten it above the fireplace. Change the name of the tavern to The Witcher's Sword. May tales of treasure and monsters, of bloody wars and fierce battles, of death, be told here on winter evenings. Of great love and unfailing friendship. Of courage and honour. May this sword cheer up the listeners and inspire the storytellers. And now pour me vodka, gentlemen, for I shall continue talking, shall present profound truths and diverse philosophies, including existential ones.'

The cups were filled with vodka silently and solemnly. They looked into each other's eyes and drank. No less solemnly. Yarpen Zigrin cleared his throat, swept his eyes over his audience and made certain they were sufficiently rapt and solemn.

'Progress,' he said with reverence. 'will lighten up the gloom, for that is what progress is for, as – if you'll pardon me – the arsehole is for shitting. It will be brighter and brighter, and we shall fear less and less the darkness and the Evil hidden in it. And a day will come, perhaps, when we shall stop believing at all that something is lurking in the darkness. We shall laugh at such fears. Call them childish. Be ashamed of them! But darkness will always, always exist. And there will always be Evil in the darkness, always be fangs and claws, death and blood in the darkness. And witchers will always be needed.'

*

They sat in reflection and silence, so deeply plunged in their thoughts that the suddenly increasing murmur and noise of the town – angry, baleful, intensifying like the buzzing of annoyed wasps – escaped their attention.

They barely noticed as a first, a second and a third shape stole along the silent and empty lakeside boulevard.

Just as a roar exploded over the town, the door to Wirsing's inn slammed wide open and a small dwarf rushed in, red from effort and panting heavily.

'What is it?' Yarpen Zigrin lifted his head.

The dwarf, still unable to catch his breath, pointed towards the town centre. His eyes were frantic.

'Take a deep breath,' advised Zoltan Chivay, 'and tell us what's going on.'

*

It was later said that the tragic events in Rivia were an absolutely chance occurrence, that it was a spontaneous reaction, a sudden and unpredictable explosion of justified anger, springing from the mutual hostility and dislike between humans, dwarves and elves. It was said that it wasn't the humans, but the dwarves who attacked first, that the aggression came from them. That a dwarven market trader had insulted a young noblewoman, Nadia Esposito, a war orphan, that he had used violence against her. When, then, her friends came to her defence, the dwarf mustered his fellows. A scuffle broke out and then a fight, which took over the whole bazaar in an instant. The fight turned into a massacre, into a massed attack by humans on the part of the suburbs occupied by non-humans and the district of Elm. In less than an hour, from the time of the incident at the bazaar to the intervention by sorcerers, a hundred and eighty-four individuals had been killed, and almost half of the victims were women and children.

Professor Emmerich Gottschalk of Oxenfurt gives the same version of events in his dissertation.

But there were also those who said something different. How could it have been spontaneous, how could it have been a sudden and unforeseeable explosion, they asked, if in the course of a few minutes from the altercation at the bazaar, wagons had appeared in the streets from which people began to hand out weapons? How could it have been sudden and justified anger if the ringleaders of the mob – who were the most visible and active during the massacre – were people no one knew, and who had arrived in Rivia several days before the riots, from God knows where? And afterwards vanished without trace? Why did the army intervene so late? And so tentatively at first?

Still other scholars tried to identify Nilfgaardian provocation in the Rivian riots, and there were those who claimed it was all concocted by the dwarves and elves together. That they had killed each other to blacken the name of the humans.

Utterly lost among the serious academic voices was the extremely bold theory of a certain young and eccentric graduate, who – until he was silenced – claimed that it was not conspiracies or secret plots that had manifested themselves in Rivia, but the simple and indeed universal traits of the local people: ignorance, xenophobia, callous boorishness and thorough brutishness.

And then everybody lost interest in the matter and stopped talking about it at all.

*

'Into the cellar!' repeated the Witcher, anxiously listening to the quickly growing roar and yelling of the mob. 'Dwarves into the cellar! Without any stupid heroics!'

'Witcher,' Zoltan grunted, clenching the haft of his battle axe. 'I can't . . . My brothers are dying out there . . .'

'Into the cellar. Think about Eudora Brekekeks. Do you want her to be a widow before her wedding?'

The argument worked. The dwarves went down into the cellar.

Geralt and Dandelion covered the entrance with straw mats. Wirsing, who was usually pale, was now white as cottage cheese.

'I saw a pogrom in Maribor,' he stammered out, looking at the entrance to the cellar. 'If they find them there . . .'

'Go to the kitchen.'

Dandelion was also pale. Geralt wasn't especially surprised. Individual accents were sounding in the hitherto indistinct and monotonous roar that reached their ears. Notes that made the hair stand up on their heads.

'Geralt,' groaned the poet. 'I'm somewhat similar to an elf . . .'

'Don't be stupid.'

Clouds of smoke billowed above the rooftops. And fugitives dashed out of a narrow street. Dwarves. Of both sexes.

Two dwarves dived into the lake without thinking and began to swim, churning up the water, straight ahead towards the middle. The others dispersed. Some of them turned towards the tavern.

The mob rushed out of the narrow street. They were quicker than the dwarves. Lust for slaughter was winning out in this race.

The screaming of people being killed pierced the ears and made the coloured glass in the tavern's windows jingle. Geralt felt his hands begin to shake.

One dwarf was literally torn apart, rent into pieces. Another, thrown onto the ground, was turned into a shapeless, bloody mass in a few moments. A woman was stabbed with pitchforks and pikes, and the child she had defended until the end was trampled, crushed under the blows of boot heels.

Three of them – a dwarf and two dwarf women – fled straight towards the tavern. The crowd raced after them, yelling.

Geralt took a deep breath. He stood up. Feeling on him the terrified eyes of Dandelion and Wirsing, he took the sihill, the sword wrought in Mahakam, in the very forge of Rhundurin, down from the shelf over the fireplace.

'Geralt . . .' the poet groaned pathetically.

'Very well,' said the Witcher, walking towards the exit. 'But this is the last time! Dammit, it really is the last time!'

He went out onto the porch and jumped straight down from it, filleting with a rapid slash a roughneck in bricklayer's overalls who was aiming a blow with a trowel at a woman. He cut off the hand of the next one, who was grasping the hair of another woman. He hacked down two men kicking a dwarf on the ground with two swift, diagonal slashes.

And he entered the crowd quickly, spinning around in half-turns. He cut with wide blows, apparently chaotically – knowing that such strokes are bloodier and more spectacular. He didn't mean to kill them. He just wanted to wound them.

'He's an elf! He's an elf!' yelled someone in the mob savagely. 'Kill the elf!'

That's going too far, he thought. *Dandelion perhaps, but I don't resemble an elf in any way.*

He spotted the one who had shouted, probably a soldier, because he was wearing a brigantine and high boots. The Witcher wormed his way into the crowd like an eel. The soldier shielded himself with a javelin held in both hands. Geralt cut along the shaft, chopping off the soldier's fingers. The Witcher whirled, bringing forth shrieks of pain and fountains of blood with the next broad stroke.

'Mercy!' an unkempt young man with crazy eyes fell on his knees in front of him. 'Spare me!'

Geralt spared him, stopped the movement of his arm and sword, using the momentum intended for the blow to spin away. Out of the corner of his eye he saw the unkempt youth spring to his feet and saw what he was holding. Geralt interrupted the turn to spin back the other way. But he was stuck in the crowd. He was stuck in the crowd for a split second.

All he could do was watch as the three-fanged fork flew towards him.

*

The fire in the grate of the huge hearth went out, and it grew dark in the hall. The strong wind gusting from the mountains whistled in the cracks in the walls, wailed, blowing in through the draughty shutters of Kaer Morhen, the Seat of the Witchers.

'Dammit!' Eskel blurted out, stood up and opened the side-board. '"Seagull" or vodka?'

'Vodka,' said Coën and Geralt as one.

'Of course,' said Vesemir, hidden in the shadows. 'Of course, naturally! Drown your stupidity in booze. Sodding fools!'

'It was an accident . . .' muttered Lambert. 'She was managing well on the comb.'

'Shut your trap, you ass! I don't want to hear your voice! I tell you, if anything's the matter with the girl—'

'She's good now,' Coën interrupted gently. 'She's sleeping peacefully. Deeply and soundly. She'll wake up a bit sore, and that's all. She won't remember at all about the trance or what happened.'

'As long as *you* remember!' panted Vesemir. 'Blockheads! Pour me one too, Eskel.'

They were silent for a long time, engrossed in the howling of the wind.

'We'll have to summon someone,' said Eskel finally. 'We'll have to get some witch to come. It's not normal what's happening to that girl.'

'That's the third trance already.'

'But it's the first time she's used articulated speech . . .'

'Tell me again what she said,' ordered Vesemir, emptying the goblet in one draught. 'Word for word.'

'I can't tell you word for word,' said Geralt, staring into the embers. 'And the meaning, if there's any point looking for meaning in it was: me and Coën are going to die. Teeth will be our undoing. We'll both be killed by teeth. In his case two. In mine three.'

'It's quite likely we'll be bitten to death,' snorted Lambert, 'Teeth could be the downfall of any of us at any moment. Although if that prediction is a real prophecy you two will be finished off by some extremely gap-toothed monsters.'

'Or by purulent gangrene from rotten teeth,' Eskel nodded, apparently serious. 'Except our teeth aren't rotting.'

'I wouldn't make fun of the matter,' said Vesemir.

The witchers said nothing.

The wind howled and whistled in the walls of Kaer Morhen.

*

The unkempt young man, as though horrified by what he'd done, dropped the shaft. The Witcher cried out in pain in spite of himself and bent over. The trident sticking into his stomach overbalanced him and when he fell onto his knees, it slid out of his body and fell onto the cobbles. Blood poured out with a swoosh and a splash worthy of a waterfall.

Geralt tried to rise from his knees. Instead, he fell over on his side.

The sounds around him resonated and echoed. He heard them as though his head was under water. His vision was also blurred, with distorted perspective and totally false geometry.

But he saw the crowd take flight. Saw them run from the relief. From Zoltan and Yarpen holding battle axes, Wirsing holding a meat cleaver and Dandelion armed with a broom.

Stop, he wanted to cry, *where are you going? It's enough that I always piss into the wind.*

But he couldn't cry out. His voice was choked by a gush of blood.

*

It was getting towards noon when the sorceresses reached Rivia. Down below, viewed from the perspective of the highway, the surface of Loch Eskalott glittered with the sparkling reflections of the castle's red tiles and the town's roofs.

'Well, we've arrived,' stated Yennefer. 'Rivia! Ha, how strange are the twists of fate.'

Ciri, who had been excited for a long time, made Kelpie dance and take short steps. Triss Merigold sighed imperceptibly. At least she thought it was imperceptible.

'Well, well.' Yennefer glared at her. 'What strange sounds are lifting your virgin breast, Triss. Ciri, ride on ahead and see if you're already there.'

Triss turned her face away, determined not to provoke or give any pretext. She wasn't counting on a result. For a long time she had sensed the anger and aggression in Yennefer getting stronger the closer they got to Rivia.

'You, Triss,' Yennefer repeated scathingly. 'Don't blush, don't sigh, don't slaver and don't wiggle your bum in the saddle. Do you think that's why I yielded to your request, agreed to you coming with us? For a languorously blissful meeting with your erstwhile sweetheart? Ciri, I asked you to ride on ahead a little! Let us have a talk!'

'It's a monologue, not a talk,' said Ciri impertinently, but she yielded at once under the menacing violet glare, whistled at Kelpie and galloped down the highway.

'You aren't riding to a rendezvous with your lover, Triss,' Yennefer continued. 'I'm neither so noble, nor so stupid as to give you the chance and him the temptation. Just this once, today, and then I'll make sure that neither of you has any temptations or opportunities. But today I won't deny myself that sweet and perverted pleasure. He knows about the role you played. And will thank you for it with his eyes. And I shall look at your trembling lips and shaking hands, listen to your lame apologies and excuses. And do you know what, Triss? I'll be swooning with delight.'

'I knew you wouldn't forget what I did, that you would take your revenge,' muttered Triss. 'I accept that, because I was indeed to blame. But I have to tell you one thing, Yennefer. Don't count too much on my swooning. He knows how to forgive.'

'For what was done to him, indeed.' Yennefer squinted her eyes. 'But he'll never forgive you for what was done to Ciri. And to me.'

'Maybe,' Triss swallowed. 'Maybe he won't. Particularly if you do your utmost to stop him. But he definitely won't bully me. He won't stoop to that.'

Yennefer swiped her horse with her whip. The horse whinnied, jumped and cavorted so suddenly that the sorceress swayed in the saddle.

'That's enough of this discussion!' she snapped. 'A little more humility, you arrogant slut! He's my man, mine and only mine! Do you understand? You're to stop talking about him, you're to stop thinking about him, you're to stop delighting in his noble character . . . Right away, at once! Oh, I feel like grabbing you by that ginger mop of hair—'

'Just you try!' yelled Triss. 'Just try, you bitch, and I'll scratch your eyes out! I—'

They fell silent, seeing Ciri hurtling towards them in a cloud of dust. They knew right away that something was afoot. And saw at once what it was. Before Ciri even reached them.

Tongues of flame suddenly shot up over the thatched roofs of the now nearby suburbs and over the tiles and chimneys of the city, and smoke belched in billows. Screaming, like the distant buzzing of annoying flies, like the droning of angry bumblebees, reached the sorceresses' ears. The screaming grew, it increased, counterpointed by single high-pitched cries.

'What the bloody hell is going on there?' Yennefer stood up in the stirrups. 'A raid? A fire?'

'Geralt . . .' Ciri suddenly groaned, becoming as white as vellum. 'Geralt!'

'Ciri? What's the matter with you?'

Ciri raised her hand, and the sorceresses saw blood dribbling over it. Along the life-line.

'The circle has closed,' said the girl, closing her eyes. 'A thorn from Shaerrawedd pricked me, and the snake Ouroboros has sunk its teeth into its own tail. I'm coming, Geralt! I'm coming to you! I won't leave you alone!'

Before either of the sorceresses had time to protest, the girl had turned Kelpie around and galloped off at once.

They had enough presence of mind to immediately urge their own horses into a gallop. But their steeds were no match for Kelpie.

'What is it?' screamed Yennefer, gulping the wind. 'What's happening?'

'But you know!' sobbed Triss, galloping beside her. 'Fly, Yennefer!'

Before they had dashed among the shacks of the suburbs, before they were passed by the first fugitives fleeing the town, Yennefer already had a clear enough picture of the situation to know that what was happening in Rivia wasn't a fire, or a raid by enemy troops, but a pogrom. She also knew what Ciri had felt, where – and to whom – she was rushing so quickly. She also knew she couldn't catch up with her. There was no chance. Kelpie had simply jumped over the panicked people crushed together into a crowd knocking off several hats and caps with her hooves. She and Triss had had to rein in their steeds so abruptly they almost tumbled over their horses' heads.

'Ciri! Stop!'

They suddenly found themselves amidst narrow streets full of the running and wailing mob. As she passed, Yennefer noticed bodies lying in the gutters, saw corpses hanging by their legs from posts and beams. She saw a dwarf lying on the ground being kicked and beaten with sticks, saw another being battered with the necks of broken bottles. She heard the shouts of the assailants, the screaming and howling of the beaten. She saw a throng clustering around a woman who had been thrown from a window and the glint of metal bars rising and falling.

The crowd closed in, the roar intensified. It seemed to the sorceresses that the distance between them and Ciri had shortened. The next obstacle in Kelpie's way was a small group of disorientated halberdiers, whom the black mare treated like a fence and jumped over, knocking a flat kettle hat off one of them. The others simply squatted down in fear.

They burst into a square at full gallop. It was black with people. And smoke. Yennefer realised that Ciri, unerringly led by her prophetic vision, was heading for the very heart, the very centre of events. To the very core of the conflagrations, where murder was rampaging.

For a battle was raging in the street she had turned towards. Dwarves and elves were fiercely defending a makeshift barricade, defending a lost position, falling and dying under the pressure of the howling rabble attacking them. Ciri screamed and pressed herself to her horse's neck. Kelpie took off and flew over the barricade, not like a horse, but like a huge black bird.

Yennefer rode into the crowd and reined her horse in sharply, knocking a few people over. She was dragged from the saddle before she managed to yell. She was hit on the shoulders, on the back, and on the back of her head. She fell onto her knees and saw an unshaven character in a shoemaker's apron preparing to kick her.

Yennefer had had enough of people kicking her.

From her spread fingers shot pale blue, hissing fire, cutting like a horsewhip the faces, torsos and arms of the people surrounding her. There was a stench of burning flesh and for a moment howling and squealing rose above the general commotion and hullabaloo.

'Witch! Elven witch! Enchantress!'

The next character leaped at her with a raised axe. Yennefer shot fire straight in his face. His eyeballs burst, seethed and spilled out onto his cheeks with a hiss.

The crowd thinned out. Someone grabbed her by the arm, and she recoiled, ready to fire, but it was Triss.

'Let's flee from here . . . Yenna . . . Flee . . . from here . . .'

I've heard her talking in a voice like that before, flashed a thought through Yennefer's head. *With lips like wood that not even a droplet of saliva can moisten. Lips that fear paralyses, that panic makes tremble.*

I heard her talking in a voice like that. On Sodden Hill.

When she was dying of fear.

Now she's dying of fear too. She's going to die of fear her whole life. For whoever doesn't overcome the cowardice inside themselves will die of fear to the end of their days.

The fingers that Triss dug into her arm seemed to be made of steel, and Yennefer only freed herself from their grasp with the greatest of effort.

'Flee if you want to!' she cried. 'Hide behind the skirts of your Lodge! I have something to defend! I shan't leave Ciri alone. Or Geralt! Get away, you rabble! Out of the way if you value your lives!'

The crowd separating her from her horse retreated before the lightning bolts shooting from the sorceress's eyes and hands. Yennefer tossed her head, ruffling up her black locks. She looked like fury incarnate, like an angel of destruction, a punishing angel of destruction with a flaming sword.

'Begone, get you home, you swine!' she yelled, lashing the rabble with a flaming whip. 'Begone! Or I'll brand you with fire like cattle.'

'It's only one witch, people!' a resonant and metallic voice sounded from the crowd. 'A single bloody elven spell-caster!'

'She's alone! The other bolted! Hey, children, take up stones!'

'Death to the non-humans! Woe betide the witch!'

'To her confusion!'

The first stone whistled past her ear. The second thudded into her arm, making her stagger. The third hit her directly in the face. First the pain exploded intensely in her eyes, then wrapped everything in black velvet.

518

She came to, groaning in pain. Pain shot through both her fore-arms and wrists. She groped involuntarily, felt the thick layers of bandage. She groaned again, dully, despairingly. Sorry that it wasn't a dream. And sorry that she'd failed.

'You didn't succeed,' said Tissaia de Vries, sitting beside the bed.

Yennefer was thirsty. She wanted somebody to at least moisten her lips, which were covered in a sticky coating. But she didn't ask. Her pride wouldn't let her.

'You didn't succeed,' repeated Tissaia de Vries. 'But not because you didn't try hard. You cut well and deep. That's why I am here with you. Had it only been silly games, had it been a foolish, irresponsible demonstration, I would have nothing but contempt for you. But you cut deeply. Purposefully.'

Yennefer looked at the ceiling vacantly.

'I shall take care of you, girl. Because I believe it's worth it. And it'll require a good deal of work, oh, but it will. I'll not only have to straighten your spine and shoulder blade, but also heal your hands. When you slit your wrists you severed the tendons. And a sorceress's hands are important instruments, Yennefer.'

Moisture on her mouth. Water.

'You shall live,' Tissaia's voice was matter-of-fact, grave, stern even. 'Your time has not yet come. When it does, you will recall this day.'

Yennefer greedily sucked the moisture from a stick wrapped in a wet bandage.

'I shall take care of you,' Tissaia de Vries repeated, gently touching her hair. 'And now . . . We are alone here. Without witnesses. No one will see and I shan't tell anyone. Weep, girl. Have a good cry. Weep your heart out for the last time. For later you won't be able to. There isn't a more hideous sight than a sorceress weeping.'

*

She came to, hawked and coughed up blood. Someone was dragging her across the ground. It was Triss, she recognised her by the scent of her perfume. Not far from them iron-shod hooves rang on the cobbles and yelling resounded. Yennefer saw a rider in full armour, in a white surcoat with a red chevron, pummelling the crowd with a bullwhip from a high lancer's saddle. The stones being hurled by the mob bounced harmlessly off his armour and visor. The horse neighed, thrashed around and kicked.

Yennefer felt she had a great potato instead of her upper lip. At least one front tooth had been broken or knocked out and was cutting her tongue painfully.

'Triss . . .' she gibbered. 'Teleport us out of here!'

'No, Yennefer,' Triss's voice was very calm. And very cold.

'They'll kill us . . .'

'No, Yennefer. I shan't run away. I shan't hide behind the Lodge's skirts. And don't worry, I shan't faint from fear like I did at Sodden. I shall vanquish it inside me. I've already vanquished it!'

A great pile of compost, dung and waste in a recess of moss-covered walls rose up near the exit of the narrow street. It was a magnificent pile. A hill, one could say.

The crowd had finally succeeded in seizing and immobilising the knight and his horse. He was knocked to the ground with a terrible thud and the mob crawled over him like lice, covering him in a moving layer.

After hauling Yennefer up, Triss stood on the top of the pile of garbage and raised her arms in the air. She screamed out a spell; screamed it out with true fury. So piercingly that the crowd fell silent for a split second.

'They'll kill us,' Yennefer spat blood. 'As sure as anything . . .'

'Help me.' Triss interrupted the incantation for a moment. 'Help me, Yennefer. We'll cast Alzur's Thunder at them.'

And we'll kill about five of them, thought Yennefer. *Then the rest will tear us to pieces. But very well, Triss, as you wish. If you don't run away, you won't see me running away.*

She joined in the incantation. The two of them screamed.

The crowd stared at them for a second, but quickly came to their senses. Stones whistled around the sorceresses again. A javelin flew just beside Triss's temple. Triss didn't even flinch.

It isn't working at all, thought Yennefer, *our spell isn't working at all. We don't have a chance of casting anything as complicated as Alzur's Thunder. Alzur, it is claimed, had a voice like a bell and the diction of an orator. And we're squeaking and mumbling, mixing up the words and the intonation pattern.*

She was ready to interrupt the chant and concentrate the rest of her strength on some other spell, capable either of teleporting them both away, or treating the charging rabble – for a split second at least – to something unpleasant. But it turned out there was no need.

The sky suddenly darkened and clouds teemed above the town. It became devilishly sombre. And there was a cold wind.

'Oh my,' Yennefer groaned. 'I think we've stirred something up.'

*

'Merigold's Destructive Hailstorm,' repeated Nimue. 'Actually that name is used illegally. The spell was never registered, because no one ever managed to repeat it after Triss Merigold. For mundane reasons. Triss's mouth was cut and she was speaking indistinctly. Malicious people claim, furthermore, that her tongue was faltering from fear.'

'It's hard to believe that.' Condwiramurs pouted her lips. 'There's no shortage of examples of the Venerable Triss's valour and courage; some chronicles even call her "the Fearless". But I want to ask about something else. One of the legend's versions says that Triss wasn't alone on the Rivian Hill. That Yennefer was there with her.'

Nimue looked at the watercolour portraying the steep, black, razor-sharp hill against a background of deep blue clouds lit from below. The slender figure of a woman with arms outstretched and hair streaming around was visible on the hill's summit.

The rhythmic rattle of the Fisher King's oars reached them from the fog covering the surface of the water.

'If anyone was there with Triss, they didn't endure in the artist's vision,' said the Lady of the Lake.

*

'Oh, what a mess,' Yennefer repeated. 'Look out, Triss!'

In a moment, hailstones, angular balls of ice the size of hen's eggs, plummeted onto the town from the black cloud billowing above Rivia. They fell so heavily that the entire square was immediately covered in a thick layer. There was a sudden surge in the throng, people fell, covering their heads, they crawled one under the other, ran away, falling over, crowding into doorways and under arcades, and cowering by walls. Not all of them were successful. Some remained, lying like fish on the ice, which was copiously stained with blood.

The hailstones pelted down so hard that the magical shield Yennefer had managed to conjure up over their heads almost at the last moment trembled and threatened to break. She didn't even try any other spells. She knew that what they had triggered could not be halted, that they had unleashed by accident an element that had to run riot, that they had freed a force that had to reach a climax. And would soon reach that climax.

At least so she hoped.

Lightning flashed. There was a sudden peal of thunder, which rumbled on, and then gave a crack. Making the ground tremble. The hail lashed the roofs and cobblestones; fragments of shattering hailstones flew all around.

The sky brightened up a little. The sun shone. A ray breaking through the clouds lashed the town like a horsewhip. Something escaped Triss's lips; neither a groan nor a sob.

The hail was still falling, hammering down, covering the square in a thick layer of icy balls gleaming like diamonds. But now the hail was lighter and more patchy, Yennefer could tell from the change in the thudding on the magical shield. And then it stopped. All at once. All of a sudden. Armed men rushed into the square, iron-shod hooves crunched on the ice. The mob roared and fled, whipped by knouts, struck by spear shafts and the flats of swords.

'Bravo, Triss,' Yennefer croaked. 'I don't know what that was . . . But you did a nice job.'

'There was something worth defending,' croaked Triss Merigold. The heroine of the hill.

'There always is. Let's run, Triss. Because it probably isn't over yet.'

It *was* over. The hail that the sorceresses had unleashed on the town cooled down hot heads. Enough for the army to dare to strike and bring order. The soldiers had been afraid before. They knew what they were risking with an attack on the enraged mob, on a rabble drunk on blood and killing that feared nothing and would retreat before nothing. But the explosion of the elements had brought the cruel, many-headed beast under control and a charge by the army accomplished the rest.

The hailstones had caused awful havoc in the town. And a man who a moment earlier had beaten a dwarf woman to death with a swingletree and shattered her child's head against a wall was now sobbing, was now weeping, was now swallowing back tears and snot, looking at what was left of the roof of his house.

Peace reigned in Rivia. Were it not for the almost two hundred mutilated corpses and a dozen burned down homesteads, one might think nothing had happened. In the district of Elm, on Loch Eskalott, over which the gorgeous arc of a rainbow was shining, weeping willows were reflected beautifully in the smooth, mirror-like water, birds had resumed their singing and it smelt of wet foliage. Everything looked pastoral. Even the Witcher, lying in a pool of blood with Ciri kneeling over him.

*

Geralt was unconscious and as white as a sheet. He lay motionless, but when they stood over him he began to cough, wheeze and spit blood. He began to shake and tremble so hard Ciri couldn't stop him. Yennefer kneeled down beside her. Triss saw that her hands were shaking. She herself suddenly felt as weak as a kitten, and everything went black. Someone held her up, stopped her from falling. She recognised Dandelion.

'It's not working at all.' She heard Ciri's voice emanating despair. 'Your magic isn't healing him at all, Yennefer.'

'We arrived . . .' Yennefer had difficulty moving her lips. 'We arrived too late.'

'Your magic's not working,' Ciri repeated, as though she hadn't heard her. 'What's it worth then, your confounded magic?'

You're right, Ciri, thought Triss, feeling a lump in her throat. *We know how to cause a hailstorm, but we can't drive death away. Although the latter would seem to be easier.*

'We've sent for a physician,' said the dwarf standing beside Dandelion hoarsely. 'But he's taking his time . . .'

'It's too late for a physician,' said Triss, surprising herself by the calm in her voice. 'He's dying.'

Geralt trembled once more, coughed up blood, tensed and went still. Dandelion, supporting Triss, sighed in despair and the dwarf swore. Yennefer groaned. Her face suddenly changed, contorted and grew ugly.

'There's nothing more pathetic,' Ciri said sharply, 'than a weeping sorceress. You taught me that yourself. But now you're pathetic, really pathetic, Yennefer. You and your magic, which isn't fit for anything.'

Yennefer didn't respond. She was holding Geralt's limp, paralysed head in both hands and repeating spells, her voice quavering. Pale blue sparks and crackling glimmers danced over her hands and the Witcher's cheeks and forehead. Triss knew how much energy spells like that used up. She also knew the spells wouldn't help in any way. She was more than certain that even the spells of expert healers would have been powerless. It was too late. Yennefer's spells were only exhausting her. Triss was amazed that the black-haired sorceress was holding out so long.

She stopped being amazed, when Yennefer fell silent halfway through the next magical formula and slumped down onto the cobbles beside the Witcher.

One of the dwarves swore again. The other stood with head lowered. Dandelion, still holding Triss up, sniffed.

It suddenly became very cold. The surface of the lake filled with fog like a sorceress's cauldron, became enveloped in mist. The fog rose swiftly, billowed over the water and rolled onto the land in waves, enveloping everything in a thick, white milk in which sounds grew quieter and died away, in which shapes vanished and forms blurred.

'And I once renounced my power,' said Ciri slowly, still kneeling on the blood-soaked cobbles. 'Had I not renounced it I would have saved him now. I would have healed him, I know it. But it's too late. I renounced it and now I can't do anything. It's as though I've killed him.'

The silence was first interrupted by Kelpie's loud neighing. Then by Dandelion's muffled cry.

Then they were all struck dumb.

*

A white unicorn emerged from the fog, running very lightly, ethereally and noiselessly, gracefully raising its shapely head. There actually wasn't anything unusual in that – everybody knew the legends, and they were unanimous about unicorns running very lightly, ethereally and noiselessly and raising their heads with characteristic grace. If anything was strange it was that the unicorn was running over the surface of the water and the water wasn't even rippling.

Dandelion groaned, but this time in awe. Triss felt herself being seized by a thrill. By euphoria.

The unicorn clattered its hooves on the stone boulevard. It shook its mane. And neighed lengthily and melodically.

'Ihuarraquax,' said Ciri. 'I'd hoped you'd come.'

The unicorn came closer, neighed again, tapped with a hoof and then struck the cobbles hard. He bent his head. The horn sticking out of his domed forehead suddenly lit up with a bright glare, a brilliance that dispersed the fog for a moment.

Ciri touched the horn.

Triss cried out softly, seeing the girl's eyes suddenly lighting up with a milky glow, saw her surrounded by a fiery halo. Ciri couldn't hear her, couldn't hear anyone. She was still holding the unicorn's horn in one hand, and pointed the other towards the motionless Witcher. A ribbon of flickering brightness that glowed like lava flowed from her fingers.

*

No one could tell how long it lasted. Because it was unreal.

Like a dream.

The unicorn, almost blurring in the thickening fog, neighed, struck its hoof, and shook its head and horn, as though pointing at something. Triss looked. She saw a dark shape on the water under the canopy of willow branches hanging over the lake. It was a boat.

The unicorn pointed again with its horn. And quickly began to vanish into the mist.

'Kelpie,' said Ciri. 'Follow him.'

Kelpie snorted. And tossed her head. She followed the unicorn obediently. Her horseshoes rang on the cobbles for a while. Then the sound suddenly broke off. As though the mare had taken wing, disappeared, dematerialised.

The boat was beside the very bank, and in the moments when the fog dispersed Triss could see it clearly. It was a primitively constructed barge, as clumsy and angular as a large pig trough.

'Help me,' said Ciri. Her voice was confident and determined.

No one knew at the beginning what the girl meant, what help she was expecting. Dandelion was the first to understand. Perhaps because he knew the legend, had once read one of its poeticized versions. He picked up the still unconscious Yennefer. He was astonished at how dainty and light she was. He could have sworn somebody was helping him carry her. He could have sworn he could feel Cahir's shoulder beside his arm. Out of the corner of one eye he caught sight of a flash of Milva's flaxen plait. When he placed the sorceress in the boat he could have sworn he saw Angoulême's hands steadying the side.

The dwarves carried the Witcher, helped by Triss, who was supporting his head. Yarpen Zigrin positively blinked on seeing both Dahlberg brothers for a second. Zoltan Chivay could have sworn that Caleb Stratton had helped him lay the Witcher in the boat. Triss Merigold was absolutely certain she could smell the perfume of Lytta Neyd, also called Coral. And for a moment she saw amidst the haze the bright, yellow-green eyes of Coën from Kaer Morhen.

That was the kind of tricks played on the senses by the fog, the thick fog over Loch Eskalott.

'It's ready, Ciri,' the sorceress said dully. 'Your boat is waiting.'

Ciri brushed her hair back from her forehead and sniffed.

'Apologise to the ladies of Montecalvo, Triss,' she said. 'But it can't be otherwise. I cannot stay when Geralt and Yennefer are departing. I simply cannot. They ought to understand.'

'They ought to.'

'Farewell then, Triss Merigold. Farewell, Dandelion. Farewell all of you.'

'Ciri,' whispered Triss. 'Little sister . . . Let me sail away with you . . .'

'You don't know what you're asking, Triss.'

'Will you ever—?'

'For certain,' she interrupted firmly.

She boarded the boat, which rocked and immediately began to sail away. To fade into the fog. Those that were standing on the bank didn't hear even the merest splash, didn't see any ripples or movements of the water. As though it wasn't a boat but an apparition.

For a very short time they could still see Ciri's slight and ethereal silhouette, saw her push off from the bottom with a long pole, saw her urge on the already quickly gliding barge.

And then there was only the fog.

She lied to me, thought Triss. *I'll never see her again. I'll never see her, because . . . Vaesse deireadh aep eigean. Something ends . . .*

'Something has ended,' said Dandelion in an altered voice.

'Something is beginning,' Yarpen Zigrin chimed in.

A rooster crowed loudly somewhere in the direction of the town. The fog quickly began to rise.

*

Geralt opened his eyes, irritated by the play of light and shadow through his eyelids. He saw leaves above him, a kaleidoscope of leaves flickering in the sun. He saw branches heavy with apples.

He felt the soft touch of fingers on his temple and cheek. Fingers he knew. Fingers he loved so much it hurt.

His belly and chest hurt, his ribs hurt and the tight corset of bandages left him in no doubt that the town of Rivia and the three-fanged trident hadn't been a nightmare.

'Lie still, my darling,' Yennefer said gently. 'Lie still. Don't move.'

'Where are we, Yen?'

'Is it important? We're together. You and me.'

Birds – either greenfinches or thrushes – were singing. It smelled of grass, herbs and flowers. And apples.

'Where's Ciri?'

'She's gone away.'

She changed her position, gently freeing her arm from under his head and lay down beside him on the grass so that she could look in his eyes. She looked at him voraciously, as though she wanted to feast her eyes on the sight, as though she wanted to eat him up with her eyes to store it away, for the whole of eternity. He looked at her too, and longing choked him.

'We were with Ciri in a boat,' he recalled. 'On a lake. Then on a river. On a river with a strong current. In the fog.'

Her fingers found his hand and squeezed it strongly.

'Lie still, my darling. Lie still. I'm beside you. It doesn't matter what happened, doesn't matter where we were. Now I'm beside you. And I'll never leave you. Never.'

'I love you, Yen.'

'I know.'

'All the same,' he sighed, 'I'd like to know where we are.'

'Me too,' said Yennefer, quietly and not right away.

*

'And is that the end of the story?' Galahad asked a moment later.

'Not at all,' protested Ciri, rubbing one foot against the other, wiping off the dried sand that had stuck to her toes and the sole of her foot. 'Would you like the story to end like that? Like hell! I wouldn't!'

'So what happened then?'

'Nothing special,' she snorted. 'They got married.'

'Tell me.'

'Aaah, what is there to tell? There was a great big wedding. They all came: Dandelion, Mother Nenneke, Iola and Eurneid, Yarpen Zigrin, Vesemir, Eskel . . . Coën, Milva, Angoulême . . .

And my Mistle . . . And I was there, I drank mead and wine. And they, I mean Geralt and Yennefer, had their own house afterwards and were happy, very, very happy. Like in a fairy tale. Do you understand?'

'Why are you weeping like that, O Lady of the Lake?'

'I'm not weeping at all. My eyes are watering from the wind. And that's that!'

They were silent for a long time, and looked as the red-hot glowing ball of the sun touched the mountain peaks.

'Indeed—' Galahad finally interrupted the silence '—it was a very strange story, oh, very strange. Truly, Miss Ciri, the world you came from is incredible.'

Ciri sniffed loudly.

'Yeees,' continued Galahad, clearing his throat several times, feeling a little uncomfortable by her silence. 'But astounding adventures also occur here, in our world. Let's take, for instance, what happened to Sir Gawain and the Green Knight . . . Or to my uncle, Sir Bors, and Sir Tristan . . . Just consider, Lady Ciri, Sir Bors and Sir Tristan set off one day for the West, towards Tintagel. The road led them through forests untamed and perilous. They rode and rode, and looked, and there stood a white hind, and beside it a lady, dressed in black. Truly a blacker black you couldn't even see in nightmares. And that comely lady, so comely you couldn't see a comelier one in the whole world, well, apart from Queen Guinevere . . . That lady standing by the hind saw the knights, beckoned and spake thus to them . . .'

'Galahad.'

'Yes?'

'Be quiet.'

He coughed, cleared his throat and fell silent. They were both silent, looking at the sun. They were silent for a long time.

'Lady of the Lake?'

'I've asked you not to call me that.'

'Lady Ciri?'

'Yes.'

'Ride with me to Camelot, O Lady Ciri. King Arthur, you'll see, will show you honour and respect . . . While I . . . I shall always love you and revere you—'

'Get up from your knee, at once! Or maybe not. If you're there, rub my feet. They're really frozen. Thank you. You're sweet. I said my feet! My feet finish at the ankles!'

'Lady Ciri?'

'I haven't gone anywhere.'

'The day is drawing to a close . . .'

'Indeed.' Ciri fastened her boot buckles and stood up. 'Let's saddle up, Galahad. Is there somewhere around here we can spend the night? Ha, I see from your expression that you know this place as well as I do. But never mind, let's set off, even if we have to sleep under an open sky, let's go a bit further, into a forest. There's a breeze coming off the lake . . . Why are you looking like that?

'Aha,' she guessed, seeing him blush. 'Are you imagining a night under a filbert bush, on a carpet of moss? In the arms of a fairy? Listen, young man, I don't have the slightest desire—'

She broke off, looking at his blushing cheeks and shining eyes. At his actually not bad-looking face. Something squeezed her belly and it wasn't hunger.

What's happening to me? she thought. *What's happening to me?*

'Don't dilly-dally!' she almost shouted. 'Saddle your stallion!'

When they mounted she looked at him and laughed out loud. He glanced at her, and his gaze was one of amazement and questioning.

'Nothing, nothing,' she said freely. 'I just thought of something. On we go, Galahad.'

A carpet of moss, she thought, suppressing a giggle. *Under a filbert bush. With me playing the fairy. Well, well.*

'Lady Ciri . . .'

'Yes?'

'Will you ride with me to Camelot?'

She held out her hand. And he held out his. They joined hands, riding side by side.

By the devil, she thought, *why not? I'd bet any money that in this world a job could be found for a witcher girl.*

Because there isn't a world where there wouldn't be work for a witcher.

'Lady Ciri . . .'

'Let's not talk about it now. Let's go.'

They rode straight into the setting sun. Leaving behind them the darkening valley. Behind them was the lake, the enchanted lake, the blue lake as smooth as a polished sapphire. They left behind them the boulders on the lakeside. The pines on the hillsides.

That was all behind them.

And before them was everything.

Turn the page for a glimpse into
The Witcher's past . . .
An extract from the next tale of Geralt of Rivia:

SEASON OF STORMS*

CHAPTER ONE

It only lived to kill.

It was lying on the sun-warmed sand.

It could sense the vibrations being transmitted through its hair-like feelers and bristles. Though the vibrations were still far off, the idr could feel them distinctly and precisely; it was thus able to determine not only its quarry's direction and speed of movement, but also its weight. As with most similar predators, the weight of the prey was of cardinal importance. Stalking, attacking and giving chase meant a loss of energy that had to be compensated by the calorific value of its food. Most predators similar to the idr would quit their attack if their prey was too small. But not the idr. The idr didn't exist to eat and sustain the species. It hadn't been created for that.

It lived to kill.

Moving its limbs cautiously, it exited the hollow, crawled over a rotten tree trunk, covered the clearing in three bounds, plunged into the fern-covered undergrowth and melted into the thicket. It moved swiftly and noiselessly, now running, now leaping like a huge grasshopper.

It sank into the thicket and pressed the segmented carapace of its abdomen to the ground. The vibrations in the ground became more and more distinct. The impulses from the idr's feelers and bristles formed themselves into an image. Into a plan. The idr now knew where to approach its victim from, where to cross its path, how to force it to flee, how to swoop on it from behind with a great leap, from what height to strike and lacerate with its razor-sharp mandibles. Within in it the vibrations and impulses were already arousing the joy it would experience when its victim started struggling under its weight, arousing the euphoria that the taste of hot blood would induce in it. The ecstasy it would feel when the air was rent by a scream of pain. It trembled slightly, opening and closing its pincers and pedipalps.

The vibrations in the ground were very distinct and had also diversified. The idr now knew there was more than one victim – probably three or, perhaps, four. Two of them were shaking the ground in a normal way; the vibrations of the third suggested a small mass and weight. The fourth, meanwhile – provided there really was another – was causing irregular, weak and hesitant vibrations. The idr stopped moving, tensed and extended its antennae above the grass, scrutinising the movements of the air.

The vibrations in the ground finally signalled what the idr had been waiting for. Its quarry had separated. One of them, the smallest, had fallen behind. And the fourth – the vague one – had disappeared. It had been a fake signal, a false echo. The idr ignored it.

The smallest target moved even further away from the others. The trembling in the ground was more intense. And closer. The idr braced its rear limbs, pushed off and leaped.

*

The little girl gave an ear-splitting scream. Rather than running away, she had frozen to the spot. And was screaming unremittingly.

*

The Witcher darted towards her, drawing his sword mid-leap. And realised at once that something was wrong. That he'd been tricked.

The man pulling a handcart loaded with faggots screamed and shot six feet up into the air in front of Geralt's eyes, blood spraying copiously from him. He fell, only to immediately fly up again, this time in two pieces, each spurting blood. He'd stopped screaming. Now the woman was screaming piercingly and, like her daughter, was petrified and paralysed by fear.

Although he didn't believe he would, the Witcher managed to save her. He leaped and pushed hard, throwing the blood-spattered woman from the path into the forest, among the ferns. And realised at once that this time, too, it had been a trick. A ruse. For the flat, grey, many-limbed and incredibly quick shape was

535

now moving away from the handcart and its first victim. It was gliding towards the next one. Towards the still shrieking little girl. Geralt sped after the idr.

Had she remained where she was, he would have been too late. But the girl demonstrated presence of mind and bolted frantically. The grey monster, however, would easily have caught up with her, killed her and turned back to dispatch the woman, too. That's what would have happened had it not been for the Witcher.

He caught up with the monster and jumped, pinning down one of its rear limbs with his heel. If he hadn't jumped aside immediately he would have lost a leg – the grey creature twisted around with extraordinary agility, and its curved pincers snapped shut, missing him by a hair's breadth. Before the Witcher could regain his balance the monster sprang from the ground and attacked. Geralt defended himself instinctively with a broad and rather haphazard swing of his sword that pushed the monster away. He hadn't wounded it, but now he had the upper hand.

He sprang up and fell on the monster, slashing backhand, cleaving the carapace of the flat cephalothorax. Before the dazed creature came to its senses, a second blow hacked off its left mandible. The monster attacked, brandishing/flailing its limbs and trying to gore him with its remaining mandible like an aurochs. The Witcher hacked that one off too. He slashed one of the idr's pedipalps with a swift reverse cut. Then hacked at the cephalothorax again.

*

It finally dawned on the idr that it was in danger. That it must flee. Flee far from there, take cover, find a hiding place. It only lived to kill. In order to kill it must regenerate. It must flee . . . Flee . . .

*

The Witcher didn't let it. He caught up with it, stepped on the rear segment of the thorax and cut from above with a fierce blow. This time, the carapace gave way, and viscous, greenish fluid gushed and poured from the wound. The monster flailed around, its limbs thrashing the ground chaotically.

536

Geralt cut again with his sword, this time completely severing the flat head from the body.

He was breathing heavily.

It thundered in the distance. The growing wind and darkening sky heralded an approaching storm.

*

Right from their very first encounter, Albert Smulka, the newly appointed district reeve, reminded Geralt of a swede – he was stout, unwashed, thick-skinned and generally pretty dull. In other words, he didn't differ much from all the other district clerks Geralt had come into contact with.

'Would seem to be true,' said the reeve. 'Nought like a witcher for dealing with troubles. 'Jonas, my predecessor, couldn't speak highly enough of you,' he continued a moment later, not waiting for any reaction from Geralt. 'To think, I considered him a liar. I mean that I didn't completely lend credence to him. I know how things can grow into fairy tales. Particularly among the common folk, with them there's always either a miracle or a marvel, or some witcher with superhuman powers. And here we are, turns out it's the honest truth. Uncounted people have died in that forest beyond the little river. And because it's a shortcut to the town the fools went that way . . . to their own doom. Heedless of warnings. These days it's better not to loiter in badlands or wander through forests. Monsters and man-eaters everywhere. A dreadful thing has just happened in the Tukaj Hills of Temeria – a sylvan ghoul killed fifteen people in a charcoal-burners' settlement. It's called Rogovizna. You must have heard. Haven't you? But it's the truth, cross my heart and hope to die. It's said even the wizardry have started an investigation in that there Rogovizna. Well, enough of stories. We're safe here in Ansegis now. Thanks to you.'

He took a coffer from a chest of drawers, spread out a sheet of paper on the table and dipped a quill in an inkwell.

'You promised you'd kill the monster,' he said, without raising his head. 'Seems you weren't having me on. You're a man of your word, for a vagabond . . . And you saved those people's lives.

537

That woman and the lass. Did they even thank you? Express their gratitude?'

No, they didn't. The Witcher clenched his jaw. *Because they haven't yet fully regained consciousness. And I'll be gone before they do. Before they realise I used them as bait, convinced in my conceited arrogance that I was capable of saving all three of them. I'll be gone before it dawns on the girl, before she understands I'm to blame for her becoming a half-orphan.*

He felt bad. No doubt because of the elixirs he'd taken before the fight. No doubt.

'That monster is a right abomination.' The reeve sprinkled some sand over the paper, and then shook it off onto the floor. 'I had a look at the carcass when they brought it here . . . What on earth was it?'

Geralt wasn't certain in that regard, but didn't intend to reveal his ignorance.

'An arachnomorph.'

Albert Smulka moved his lips, vainly trying to repeat the word.

'Ugh, makes no difference, when all's said and done. Did you dispatch it with that sword? With that blade? Can I take a look?'

'No, you can't.'

'Ha, because it's no doubt enchanted. And it must be dear . . . Quite something . . . Well, here we are jawing away and time's passing. The task's been executed, time for payment. But first the formalities. Make your mark on the bill. I mean, put a cross or some such.'

The Witcher took the bill from Smulka and held it up to the light.

'Look at 'im.' The reeve shook his head, grimacing. 'What's this, can he read?'

Geralt put the paper on the table and pushed it towards the official.

'A slight error has crept into the document,' he said, calmly and softly. 'We agreed on fifty crowns. This bill has been made out for eighty.'

Albert Smulka clasped his hands together and rested his chin on them.

'It isn't an error.' He also lowered his voice. 'Rather, a token of

538

gratitude. You killed the monster and I'm sure it was an exacting job . . . So the sum won't astonish anyone . . .'

'I don't understand.'

'Pull the other one. Don't play the innocent. Trying to tell me that when Jonas was in charge he never made out bills like this? I swear I—'

'What do you swear?' Geralt interrupted. 'That he inflated bills? And went halves with me on the sum the royal purse was deprived of?'

'Went halves?' the reeve sneered. 'Don't be soft, witcher, don't be soft. Think you're that important? You'll get a third of the difference. Ten crowns. It's a decent bonus for you anyway. For I deserve more, if only owing to my function. State officials ought to be wealthy. The wealthier the official, the greater the prestige to the state. Besides, what would you know about it? This conversation's beginning to weary me. You signing it or what?'

The rain hammered on the roof. It was pouring down outside. But the thunder had stopped; the storm had moved away.

THE KIDNAPPING OF CHRISTINA LATTIMORE

THE KIDNAPPING OF

JOAN LOWERY NIXON

CHRISTINA LATTIMORE

 Harcourt Brace Jovanovich, New York and London

F
Ni

Requests for permission to make copies of any part
of the work should be mailed to:
Permissions, Harcourt Brace Jovanovich, Inc.,
757 Third Avenue, New York, N.Y. 10017

Printed in the United States of America

Library of Congress Cataloging in Publication Data

Nixon, Joan Lowery.
The kidnapping of Christina Lattimore.

SUMMARY: A teenage girl is kidnapped, but when
freed, is accused of masterminding the scheme to
extort money from her wealthy grandmother.
[1. Kidnapping—Fiction. 2. Mystery and
detective stories] I. Title.
PZ7.N65Ki   [Fic]   78-20570
ISBN 0-15-242657-4

First edition

B C D E F G H I J K

To Kathleen Nixon Brush,
with love and appreciation

THE KIDNAPPING OF
CHRISTINA LATTIMORE

1
***

I don't like the way he's looking at me.

It's a kind of creepy look as though the two of us shared some kind of secret, and it's making me uncomfortable.

He's the counterman here at this hamburger place—a tall, stoop-shouldered, skinny guy with dull blond hair that always looks dirty. His beery friends in their sweat-stained shirts, who hunch over the counter talking and laughing in short burps, call him Zack. I don't like the way Zack is staring at me.

He's never done that before, and Lorna and I have been in here countless times. We come in every Friday after class lets out at Madame DeJon's school for girls. It's our way of celebrating our freedom for another weekend.

I guess it's my idea that we come here. Lorna's a good friend in spite of the fact that she always follows Madame DeJon's rules and looks ready to enter the portals of the River Oaks Country Club at any given moment. She'd be happy to stop for something to eat in Sakowitz's garden tearoom, except that I like to come to this greasy hamburger place, which is really the pits. It's all done in a faded red and white, with the pattern on the floor nearly rubbed out, and it faces the frantic Katy freeway, which leads from Houston toward San Antonio.

I like to eat these big, sloppy hamburgers with the mustard dripping on the scratched Formica tabletop, while I look out

3

the window and watch all the maniacs in automobiles racing down the Katy, trying not to sideswipe each other.

Sometimes I wish I were like Lorna. It would certainly please my proper parents and my ultra-proper grandmother. Lorna is what they call "outgoing" and always seems to know the right things to say. I've never seen Lorna fall over a chair, or trip over her own feet.

I tend to keep things all bottled up inside me, things that bother me a lot. Maybe too many things bother me, because they get into a muddle, and I don't really know what I want or where I'm going. Lorna and I haven't got a thing in common except that we seem to need each other and have since we met in the first grade and I was afraid to answer when the teacher called my name; and Lorna answered for me, because she had read my name on my lunch box and knew who I was.

I look at my watch, wondering where Lorna is. We drive over here in our separate cars, and she's usually right behind me.

A woman is coming in the door. Funny how she doesn't move in and grab a table, the way the regular customers do. She just stands there, watching Zack with a question in her eyes. He nods, and she looks at me and walks toward my table. What does she want? I've never seen her before. Well, maybe I have, but she just didn't register. She's one of those plump, average-looking women wtih a bad complexion, a woman no one would ever notice once, let alone twice. She's dressed in standard jeans and a light-blue, short-sleeved T-shirt. It has a smooth, folded look, as though it had just been purchased.

She pulls out a chair and sits down, her hands trembling. Weird.

"I'm waiting for a friend," I tell her. "This is our table." She leans toward me confidentially. She clears her throat, but she doesn't say anything.

I find myself leaning toward her and speaking quietly, adopting her attitude. "What do you want?" I ask her.

4

"I'll be right with you," Zack calls from the counter. His friends turn, and their eyes slide over us, except for the big-shouldered black guy, who just stares straight ahead. I wonder what kind of jobs these men have. They always seem to be free to hang around his hamburger place on Friday afternoons. For all I know, maybe they've wondered the same thing about Lorna and me.

"I don't know what's on your mind," I tell the woman, "but a friend is coming to join me any minute and . . ."

A flicker of a smile moves across her face so quickly that I wonder if I saw it. She still doesn't speak, and she keeps twisting her fingers together so hard I imagine it must hurt.

Zack swings a leg over the nearest chair back and sits down at my table too.

"What is this?" I ask him.

"You're Christina Lattimore, right?" he asks in a low voice.

I don't like people intruding in my life, disrupting things, especially these people; so I get as cold as the nose on the stone dog that sits by the gate in front of my grandmother's home in River Oaks and say, "I beg your pardon, but I see no reason to answer that question."

"Okay, okay," he says, still bending toward me, still talking in that low voice. "This here is my wife, Loretta. You come in this place every Friday. We just thought we'd get acquainted, that's all."

I automatically nod politely toward his wife. "I really am waiting for a friend, if you don't mind."

Zack stands up, scraping his chair back noisily, and pulls on the woman's arm. Her chair falls over with a clatter, and this time everyone in the place stares at us.

"Okay, okay, whatever you say," he answers, loud enough for people to hear.

What's on his mind, anyway? Why is he acting so strangely? There has to be a purpose in this, but for the life of me I can't figure out what it is. I feel as though I were in the middle

5

of one of those audience-participation dramas little Mr. Bleims is always putting on in the drama department.

Zack walks back to the counter, and the woman scurries out the door, huddled into herself like a small brown field mouse. Lorna passes her in the doorway. What a relief. She is hurrying, but I'm the only one who would realize it. She isn't the least out of breath, and every hair is in place.

She puts her books down gracefully and glides into the chair next to mine.

"Something crazy is going on," I tell her.

"You mean the phone call? You know about it?"

"What phone call?"

"Well . . . you said something crazy was going on, and I thought you meant the phone call."

"You haven't told me *what* phone call. I don't know what you're talking about."

She settles herself with a little flutter and says, "Well, just as my last class was over, I got a note saying that I was to go to the office to accept a phone call."

"Who was it?"

"Nobody," she says. "It was the oddest thing. The operator kept trying to get the person who was placing the call, and kept telling me to hold. Finally she said there had been a mistake, and the call was for someone at a different number."

"Weird."

"I know. That's why when you said something was crazy, I thought you meant that phone call. So anyhow, that's why I'm late." She sniffs the air and makes a puckery face. "I think I'll order mine without onions today."

I shrug. "I'll get them."

Zack has the hamburgers ready by the time I get to the counter. "No onions on one," I tell him.

He lifts the lid on one of the oversize buns, scrapes the glistening scramble of limp onion slices into a pan, slaps the top of the bun back on, and hands me a tray with the two

6

burgers and Cokes on it. I put some money into his hand, and he gives me the change. Neither of us says another word to the other, but he looks at me again, knowingly. I'm really disturbed. I turn quickly so I don't have to look at him, and go back to the table.

"I don't think we should come in here anymore," I tell Lorna.

She takes a dainty bite of her burger. As usual I'm getting mustard on my nose, and a dill-pickle slice is spewing out of the top of the bun.

"Frankly," she says, "I'm glad. What made you change your mind?"

I start to tell her about Zack and his wife and the strange way they acted, but somehow it seems unimportant now, unreal, and the whole thing makes me uncomfortable to think about. So I just say, "Oh, the guy at the counter—that Zack—is creepy."

"I always thought so," she says. She sips her Coke.

"So next Friday let's go someplace else."

Lorna smiles. "Chris, why don't we go to Sakowitz's tearoom?"

They don't have mustard burgers in Sakowitz's tearoom, but Lorna has been patient with me for a long time. It's only fair that I do things her way for a while. I take a big bite, and mumble with my mouth full, "Okay."

"What did your parents say about the Summer-in-France program that Madame DeJon is planning?" Lorna asks.

This is a sore point with me. I clutch my feelings to myself, as though there were another hand inside of me, holding tightly. I try to shrug it off. "I'm just about to give up asking. I guess I'm the only one who won't be taking the trip."

Lorna looks up, immediately sympathetic. "But it's going to be so much fun," she says.

"I know. It's just that . . . well, I wish Madame DeJon hadn't arranged the whole thing around the study of the old cathedrals and Roman Catholic art. It turned my father off."

7

I pull a stiff napkin out of the chrome holder in the middle of the table and wipe my face. The napkin scratches my cheeks, but at least it cleans the mustard off my nose.

I can see Lorna searching for a comforting thing to say. "It's really very nice that your father is so religious in his own church," she offers.

"Is he?" I ask.

"Why, Chris, you know he is!" Lorna is puzzled. She has a funny expression on her face, as though she thinks I might be kidding but isn't sure. "I mean, look at how much time he gives to your church, going to those meetings in Washington and Hawaii and all those other places, and being a lay preacher and all that."

I just nod. I used to admire him too when I was little. I was always so proud when my father would hold me on his lap and show me another picture of himself in the newspaper because he had just spoken at a national assembly of churches, or vacationed with a famous church leader, or something like that. I used to be crazy about my father and love his stories and the deep vibrations in his chest as he sang to me, all curled into a secure ball on his lap.

But I have grown to see things differently. My father has a wispy, spindly secretary, Rosella, who looks up all the Bible quotations and writes his speeches in a small cubbyhole off his office in our house. And he stands up and gets praised for being a biblical authority and for his loving smile. It keeps him from having to show up at the office—where he doesn't know whether he's coming or going. And it keeps him away from my grandmother, who runs her family and her business with a strong hand.

My grandfather made the oil money and founded the company, and my grandmother operates it with terrific efficiency. My father is a vice-president and collects a lovely salary. He has a fantastic house in the best section of Memorial. He also spends most of his time being a highly respected lay preacher.

It's the best cop-out I can think of for not going to work.

"Maybe your father would change his mind if you pointed out to him that the study of cathedrals and art shouldn't bother him, because the whole world is more ecumenical now, and Catholics all over the United States even voted for a Baptist president," Lorna says.

"He's old guard," I tell her. "He hasn't reached that point of thought yet."

"Could your grandmother help change his mind?"

I think about this for a minute. "Maybe she could. I don't know."

"Why don't you ask her?"

A thought hits me, and I sit up straighter. "Listen, Lorna, I just remembered my trust fund. My grandfather set it up for me, and my grandmother holds the strings on it. But it's supposed to provide for my college and other study, and all that stuff. A trip like that's supposed to be educational. That's what it says in Madame DeJon's brochure."

"It's sort of like the old-fashioned idea of sending a girl through Europe before sending her off to college," Lorna says. "And you'll be in college in a year and a half."

I'm growing enthusiastic. "Right! And my grandmother might just go for that! And if I'm using my own money, and she talks to my father . . . You know he does anything she tells him to do."

Lorna actually clasps her hands as she smiles. "Oh, I'm so excited! I'm so glad you thought of it! When are you going to ask your grandmother?"

I look at my watch. "She winds things up early on Fridays. I could go over to her office now, and I bet she'd see me."

Lorna and I leave the hamburger place and walk to the parking lot. We talk about a lot of stuff, like getting together tonight and how I'm supposed to call her the minute I leave my grandmother's office. I get in by blue Cutlass and pull out into the traffic on the access road, heading for downtown Houston.

9

I'm sort of named after my grandmother, Cristabel Lattimore. But that's about the only thing we have in common—the first syllable in our given names.

They didn't give me her actual name, because everyone felt there could be only one Cristabel Lattimore. She's something of a legend in Houston, taking over the oil company when her husband died and making it grow twice as fast under her direction. She has a hand in Texas politics and local theater and regional art scholarships, and shows up all the time in either the society columns of the newspapers or on the business pages.

Once, when I was in second grade, I had a friend whose grandmother baked chocolate-chip cookies and told funny stories while she held us on her lap. I got so jealous of my friend that I stopped going to her house to play. I had only one grandmother nearby, and she never had that kind of lap.

I park the car in one of the slots Cristabel reserves for visitors, and take the elevator from the parking basement up to the thirty-fifth floor. The doors open without a sound, and I step onto a carpet that softly bounces me along, step by step, to the receptionist's desk.

The prim woman behind the desk smiles graciously at me and almost whispers, "I'll ring your grandmother, Christina." My grandmother spent I don't know how many hours when I was little drilling into me "A lady does not raise her voice, Christina." She must have gotten to her receptionist too. The muted silence in this place used to make me feel reverent. Now it makes me want to break the spell and shout. Maybe because Cristabel has been a woman executive during a time in which they were an oddity, she is extremely careful about appearances. No one is allowed to spoil her public image.

The receptionist murmurs into the speaker on her desk, and an answering murmur floats back. "You may go in now," she says.

"Thank you," I say quietly.

My grandmother rises behind her desk as I come in, and

10

offers me her cheek to kiss. She looks positively beautiful, as always. I don't know whether she uses color on her dark-brown hair or not. I have the feeling she simply refused to let it go gray, and it obeyed her. She is dressed in a smart gray flannel suit and a coral blouse, and I think I'd like an outfit like that as a change from the stupid blue plaid skirt and blazer we have to wear through the entire twelve years at Madame DeJon's.

Twice a year my grandmother's secretary phones someone at Neiman Marcus and makes an appointment for her. Cristabel arrives punctually and is shown into a huge private dressing room, which has been reserved with her name on the door. Then a selection of dresses, suits, shoes, bags—everything she could possibly wear for the next six months—is brought in for her to try. She makes up her mind right away, her new wardrobe is charged and delivered, and at the end of the month her secretary pays the bill. Just like that. Cristabel thinks it's efficient. I think it's dull. I'd rather spend all day with Lorna, trying to find just the right pair of faded jeans.

"Hello, Cristabel," I say. She doesn't like to be called "Grandmother." I just call her that in my mind and when I'm talking about her to my friends. If I didn't think about Cristabel as my grandmother, I probably wouldn't think about her at all. The idea makes me shiver.

"Sit down, Christina," Cristabel says, and she slides into her huge leather executive chair.

I sink back into a soft, pale-gold chair and look through the wide expanse of tinted glass over the city of Houston.

"You've got such a beautiful view, Cristabel," I say. "Why don't you turn your desk around so you can see it? You've always got your back to it."

She smiles. "I'm afraid I would only be distracted, Christina. It would be difficult to get all my work done and stare out the window too." She taps a pencil against the gigantic blotter on her desk. "Is this a social visit, or is there something that you need?"

11

"A little of both," I tell her. "I haven't seen you for weeks, and I also want to ask you about something."

"And that something might concern a study program in France?"

I blink. "How did you know?"

"Your father told me that you were unhappy with his decision not to let you go."

"Cristabel," I say, "practically everyone in the junior class is going. It's . . . well, it's educational, and . . ." I remember what Lorna and I planned for me to say. "It's like the trips to Europe that girls used to take before they began college. Very . . . uh . . . traditional."

"I think," Cristabel says, "we had better keep this matter between you and your father."

I feel tears pounding behind my eyes. Tears can hurt, and I'm hurting. "My father is a religious bigot," I tell her.

She keeps her cool, poised look, but there is a quick flicker of her eyelashes. "Christina, your father not only has strong religious convictions, but he preaches them. He has a public image. If the course of study were broader, I'm sure he would allow you to go. Unfortunately, the fact that the study will be totally concerned with the art history of the Roman Catholic faith does bother him."

"I'm not an extension of my father! I'm a person with my own rights!" I lean forward eagerly. "Cristabel, I don't even have to depend on my father for the money to take the trip. It's a study tour—right? And you could let me use some of my trust fund for the trip. It's very educational, and it isn't so expensive if you think that it lasts all summer, and when I came back, ready for my senior year, I'd be. . . well . . . so informed, so . . . knowledgeable about France . . . so. . ."

She lifts a hand imperiously and says, "Christina, when it comes to your trust fund, the answer is an unequivocal no."

"But it's for my education!"

"Your education, as I see fit. Remember, I control every cent of that trust fund and always will. Contrary to what

12

you may think, I was not sent to Europe after graduation from high school. I worked as a secretary to help put myself through the university."

"You want me to get a job? Is that it?"

"You are raising your voice, Christina."

"Even if I get a part-time job, I can't earn enough money to take that trip!"

"This has gone beyond the point of discussion, Christina. There is no question of your getting a job. Your life, for the next few years, is under my direction, and it includes the proper schooling, and an eastern university, with graduate school, if we later decide that your course of study warrants it."

I stand up. "Oh, Grandmother! Cristabel, I mean!" I catch myself quickly. "I don't know why you put that money aside for me if you won't let me use it! And if you're keeping me from going to save face for my father—well, I don't think it's fair! Don't you understand how important this trip is to me?"

Cristabel stands too, facing me across the desk. Her voice is even softer than usual, making my words seem like an embarrassing shout echoing from the pale walls. "You are still a child, Christina. At your age, how could you possibly know what is really important and what is not?"

"But I *do* know what's important!"

"Remember your manners, Christina," she says.

The hurt grows stronger. "How can you talk about manners, when you must know this means so much to me?"

"I hope you'll review this conversation later and think about how selfish you sound," she says.

The words hit me. Selfish? What is selfish? My father lives in a beautiful house with eighteen rooms and doesn't know beans about the company in which he's vice-president. I ask to use part of my own trust fund so that I can go with the rest of my class on a tour of France, and I'm selfish! I don't understand what my grandmother is talking about. I don't understand my parents. I don't understand anything.

I turn and run out of the office. I wish I had enough courage to slam the door, but I don't. I am crying now, and I don't want anyone to see me, so I charge into the waiting elevator and sniffle, trying to fish in my handbag for something to wipe my nose on. There is nothing left of the packet of tissues except the wrapper.

When I get home, I'll have to call Lorna and tell her that as far as the trip to France goes, I'm out. I'm furious with my grandmother! I'm furious with my stupid father. I'm furious with the whole stupid world I live in.

2

When I get home, I remember to leave my Cutlass on the circular drive in front of the house instead of putting it away. I'll be going to Lorna's later.

It's quiet here, away from the noise of the main streets. I stand still for a moment, aware of the early daffodil buds that look ready to pop open, and the tiny leaves sprouting on the Chinese tallow trees. A jay squawks at me and sails off in a streak of blue. It's March, and spring comes early in Houston, after a wet, cold winter.

For a moment I've been distracted, and I'm glad. I have stopped being angry at Cristabel. What difference does it make? What difference does anything make? Somehow I always either care an awful lot about something, or else I don't care at all—like being dead inside and not knowing what to do about it. I don't understand myself. I wish I did.

There is a small dark-green car parked on the street down near the garages. Probably belongs to Della or one of her friends. This is Friday, the night she leaves early. Della always lives it up on Fridays, and goes around Saturday mornings as if her head were in a basket. She tells me how she dances, and her eyes light up. She says she can sling it around better than the best of them, although I can't picture those two hundred-plus pounds slinging their way around a dance floor.

I guess that inside all that Della there is a foxy chick who comes out on Friday nights.

I run up the broad steps to the veranda and put my key in the front-door lock. There is some resistance, and I bend over to look closer. The door is unlocked, and there is a small piece of that invisible cellophane tape over the side, to keep the lock from closing. Why? Who put it there?

We're all careful to keep the doors in the house locked, because there are plenty of kiddie potheads around these neighborhoods who'll steal anything to get a few dollars to buy grass.

The tape on the door is weird, and I am suddenly alert, with a shivery feeling at the back of my neck. Is someone in our house who shouldn't be here? Could someone be casing the house? I've got to find out.

I open the door, leaving the tape in place, and call at the top of my lungs, "Della! Mother! Anyone there?"

The late-afternoon sunlight is streaming through the fanlight over the door, creating a prismatic effect with the crystal chandelier that hangs in the entry hall, splashing tiny rainbows of color over the white marble tiles and the bowl of white porcelain roses in the vase under the nearly life-size wedding portrait of my parents. It looks like a spot for warmth and peace, but that's not the way I feel.

"Della! Where are you?" I screech.

"Good God Almighty! You trying to scare me to death?" Della's face peers at me over the banister at the top of the curving staircase.

"Della, are you all right? Is everything all right?"

"Of course it is. What's the matter with you?"

"It's this door. I've got to show you something."

"Not right this minute," she says. "I've got to get these sheets and towels put away. Y'all come up here if you want to talk." Her face disappears.

I take the stairs two at a time and run down the hall to the linen closet, where Della is putting sheets in neat stacks

16

with sachet bags tucked between them, the way my mother likes them. I quickly tell her about the door.

For the first time she straightens and looks at me. "That's crazy," she says. "I've been here all day. Rosella and your mama and daddy have been in and out, but that's all."

"You didn't hear anyone trying to get in?"

"Anyone wants to get in is going to get in. Why put some of that tape on the door?"

"I don't know," I tell her. "That's what I'm trying to find out. You're sure no one was here at all—not even a salesman?"

There is a sudden awareness in Della's eyes. "There was a woman," she says. Then she shrugs. "But she was just looking for a house number, and I gave it to her, and she stayed outside the whole time."

"Tell me about it."

"There's nothing much to tell. She just came to the door and said she was trying to find somebody's house number— darned if I can remember the name—and I went to the phone book and looked it up and wrote it down for her. Then I just came back and gave her the paper, and she thanked me and went away."

"But did you leave the door open?"

"Of course I didn't. You think I'm witless? When I went for the address, I shut the door like always."

"How long ago was this?"

"I don't know. Maybe an hour. About that, I guess."

"What kind of car did the woman have?"

Della shuts the wide doors of the linen closet. She frowns, thinking hard. "I don't remember seeing a car," she says.

"Della," I tell her. "Come with me right away. I have to show you that door!"

"Okay, okay!" She puffs along after me as I race back down the stairs.

The door is shut, as I left it. I take hold of the doorknob to open it, but it doesn't budge.

"There's something crazy here!" I tell her. I turn the knob,

17

and the door swings inward. The tape that held the lock back is gone!

Della looks at the door lock and back at me. The frown is deep on her forehead. "Where's this tape you were talking about?"

"It's gone," I say. I'm trying to figure this out, and for a minute my mind is blank.

Della suddenly relaxes, puts her hands on her hips, and shakes her head at me. "Now I understand," she says. "I was telling you about that movie I saw on late TV—the one about the cat burglar, and it scared me so much I couldn't sleep. You're playing a prank on me, Christina."

Her reaction startles me almost as much as finding the tape on the door. She doesn't believe me. "Della, I'm telling you the truth. I'm not playing pranks or trying to scare you. When I got home, there was a piece of tape on this door, keeping the lock from closing. Really there was!"

"Then where did the tape go?"

I search for the answer, and it hits me so hard that it makes me gasp for breath. "Della!" I say. "I went upstairs to talk to you and left the front door unguarded. Whoever put the tape on the lock was still in the house somewhere! When he left, he took the tape off! Do you realize that all the time we were talking upstairs there was someone down here?" My voice has risen to a squeak, and Della reaches over to grip my shoulders, shaking me a little.

"Calm down," she says. "If there was anybody in this house, then we would have heard them."

"Not if they were quiet," I say. "That woman who came to the door—she could have put the tape on while you were talking to her. Did you see her hold on to the edge of the door?"

Della thinks. The blue jay scolds loudly just outside the door, and I want to shout at it, "Be quiet! Go away! We're trying to work something out!" I feel somewhat irrational. I have to know who was in our house and why.

"Maybe she did," Della says. "Maybe not. She did lean over to look inside the hallway and say how pretty it was."

"And she held on to the edge of the door to support herself?"

"Might be." Della sighs. "I just can't remember."

I step outside and lean in. Automatically I grab the edge of the door to hold. And the place where it's logical to hold is at the lock, in the middle of the door edge. "Did she do it like this?" I ask Della.

"Might be," Della says.

I glance down the street. The small green car is gone. What would a woman want in our house? Was she trying to steal something?

"We're going to have to look around and see if anything is stolen," I tell Della. "Maybe we should call the police."

She quickly says, "Not until we find out if something is gone!"

I remember that when Della came to work here two years ago she told me that her son, by her first husband, was in prison for armed robbery. When the police came for him, he was in Della's house, and things got pretty scary for a while. Della got busted herself once, when the police broke up a poker game she was in. She isn't too crazy about having anything to do with the police.

"All right. You and I will look through the house," I say. "You see if she took a radio or TV set or anything obvious that she could carry. I'll look in my father's office."

"No need to look upstairs," Della says. "I've been up there ever since she came to the door."

I go into my father's office. He doesn't have a safe. He keeps his money in the bank and uses checks or credit cards for almost everything. They couldn't be after his money. I look around his office, which I'm sure doesn't look like any other man's office. There are books against one wall, and they are all religious and psychology books, many of them reference books, which Rosella uses to write his speeches. There

19

a window overlooking the veranda, and a door on the far ‍le that opens into Rosella's little office. The rest of the wall space is covered with pictures of my father. In all the photos he is either giving a speech or getting an award. Even the picture on his desk is a photo of himself, in living color, instead of the traditional picture of his wife. He's a tall man, beginning to bald, but still handsome. Although he looks like Cristabel, he's not a carbon copy of his mother. She has a vitality that my father will never have.

My mother and father are obsessed with photographs of themselves, which they hang in every room of the house. There used to be more, but my grandmother tactfully told them the decor would be improved with some good paintings instead, so my mother hired an art dealer in New York to go to Europe to purchase some old masters. Now a few rather dark paintings hang on some of the walls. Two of them are incredibly ugly. I think my mother got taken.

Nothing on the desk or anywhere in the room seems to have been disturbed. I don't want to go through my father's desk. I'll tell him about the woman when he gets home, and he can look through it himself. I walk into Rosella's cubbyhole, but there is nothing in the room except her small desk, a typewriter, a lamp, and tidy stacks of papers. There would be nothing to steal in here.

I go through the library and the sun room, then meet Della face to face as I enter the dining room. We both jump.

"You've made me so nervous I'm late starting dinner," she complains. "And I sure can't find any sign of anyone being in here."

"Neither can I."

"Your mama and daddy will be home pretty soon. They went to a meeting of that United Church something or other. You tell them about it when they get home, and they'll know what to do. I got to get dinner started."

I go upstairs to my room and throw my blazer on the bed.

I think about reading that essay for my English class, but I've left my books in my car. So I sit at my dressing table and brush my hair. It's long and dark and straight. I wish it weren't straight. I ought to wear blue eye shadow. It would bring out the color of my eyes. I don't think Della believes me. Maybe my parents won't believe me either. But I know I saw that tape! I didn't imagine it. That woman had to be in our house. Then she took the tape off the door and left before we got downstairs again. That's how it had to be, unless I'm going crazy.

Am I going crazy? No. It's an interesting thought, but I don't think so. I wonder if I should use a blue eyeliner too. There's a litttle red spot on my nose. It's going to get huge and ugly before it goes away. Blast! Who was that woman?

I hear voices downstairs, so I drop my hairbrush on the dressing table and straighten my skirt. My blouse is wrinkled. It always looks wrinkled, even when it's fresh from the laundry. I don't know what to do about it, though it upsets my mother.

She'd like me to hang up my blazer before I come down, and I almost do, reacting automatically; but then I decide the heck with it. The blazer is out of place on the little-girl, frilly, pink-canopied bed. The room is not me. The interior decorator liked pink ruffles and dressing-table skirts, and my mother loves it. I just live here.

By the time I get downstairs, my mother and father have been talking to Della. Rosella is with them. They all have identical expressions on their faces as they watch me come down the stairs. It reminds me of the way they looked at me when I threw up at my seventh birthday party and they couldn't believe I would do such a thing.

"Della believes that you're playing a prank on her, Christina," my father says.

"When I came home, there was tape on the door, holding the lock open. It's true. Believe me."

I jump down the last two steps, which causes my mother to

wince. "We believe you, dear," she says. "It's just that Della says you both searched the house, and nothing had been taken."

"Nothing obvious," I tell her. "I didn't look inside Daddy's desk. The woman was downstairs, not upstairs, since Della would have seen her if she went upstairs; so she must have wanted something in Daddy's desk. I wish you'd look through it. I really do."

My father nods. "I'll look right away, although I have little in that desk that anyone would want."

"Any money?"

"Maybe twenty dollars or so. No more than that."

My mother and I follow him into his office. Rosella skitters along behind us.

My father goes straight to the desk and opens the top drawer. Then he looks up at me. "The money is right here. If that woman had gone through the desk looking for things, she surely would have taken the money, don't you think?"

"But then what did she want?"

Rosella has gone to check her office. She comes back shaking her head. "No one has been in there."

My mother sinks into the brown leather chair near the door. "We had better look at the information we have. We keep talking about a 'she' person who has taken something from the house. But did you actually see some woman in here, Christina?"

"Well . . . no."

"Did you even hear anyone in the house?"

"No, I didn't."

"So all we know for sure is that there was a piece of cellophane tape on the door lock when you came home, and it was not there when you brought Della to see it."

I give a long, elaborate sigh. What is the matter with the whole world? I'm not the only one in it who is all mixed up. Everyone's mixed up. Nothing is right. Nothing is normal. I saw the tape. It held the lock open. That's all I know, except that it sounds like a crazy story in retrospect. My parents believe me, but Della looked as though she thought I was lying.

"Never mind," I tell them. "I don't understand anything about that piece of tape, so we might as well forget it."

My mother shrugs. "I suppose that's a good idea. We'll forget about it for now. Let's see if Della is ready to serve dinner."

We follow her to the dining room. No one invites Rosella to stay for dinner. It's just taken for granted that if she is here she eats with us. She and my father keep strange hours, because he often wants to work in the evening. Rosella doesn't have a family. She lives all alone in an apartment somewhere. I don't even know where. I don't think about Rosella much. She's a small-boned woman with a little pointy nose and eyes that always seem to be asking questions. She doesn't talk a lot, and I guess that makes me uncomfortable. People like me, who keep their feelings inside, never feel at ease with others who do the same. It's sort of like two icebergs keeping their distance from each other, never knowing when all that hidden stuff is going to collide.

We seat ourselves at the table, and my father gives his usual long, involved blessing in the pear-shaped tones that have helped him find recognition as a lay preacher. While he is praying, I examine the bowl of pebbles and bulbs in the center of the table. The bulbs have sprouted bright-green tops, and they push through the pebbles.

I realize my father has stopped speaking, so I quickly say, "Amen," and lift my head. My mother helps herself to a chicken casserole and passes it to Rosella, who passes it to me.

"Did you have a nice day, Christina?" my mother asks. "I suppose you and Lorna went to that dreadful hamburger place you usually go to?"

"I had a pits day," I say. "Nothing went right."

23

She sighs, and before she can tell me I shouldn't say "pits," I add, "I went to see Cristabel today."

"How nice," she says. "It was thoughtful of you to visit your grandmother."

"I went to see her about using some money from my trust fund to take that summer study program with Madame DeJon," I say. "She wouldn't let me touch it."

My father stares at me. "I told you I didn't want you to take that course," he says. "I'm tired of hearing about it. That's all you've talked about for weeks."

"I know how you feel about all of this being tied in with the Catholic religion," I say. "I thought Cristabel could help me talk you into it. I think I'm the only one in the junior class who isn't going."

I don't like subterfuge. I don't like pretending things with people. I don't bother to talk about most things with my parents because they don't really understand. But when I do want to talk about something, I say it straight out. I imagine that by this time they're used to me.

"What did your grandmother say?" Cristabel always makes my father nervous. I just wish she had been on my side.

"She said she wouldn't release any of the money."

"Good. I should have known she would agree with me."

"But I don't agree!" I said. "And I told her so! I think I should go, since my whole class is going! I don't want to be left out!"

My mother leans toward me. I hope she is going to offer me some support—sympathy, at least—but she says, "Oh, Christina, I do hope you weren't rude to Cristabel!"

"I didn't try to be rude," I say, "but she does know I was upset."

"It would be so foolish to be rude," my mother says. "Your grandmother has done so much for us." She doesn't say it, but the meaning hangs in the air: *and will continue to do so much for us if you play the game by behaving yourself.*

24

"We've discussed that trip enough," my father says. "You may think that my religious feelings are old-fashioned, but I must abide by my principles." He leisurely butters a roll as though it's the most important thing he could be doing. "Suppose we change the subject."

My mother puts on her bright, conversational face and says, "Christina, did you know that Rosella is going to visit her mother next week? Her mother has been ill."

I blink at Rosella, trying to remember where her mother lives. It's hard enough to picture Rosella with a mother.

"She lives in Chicago," Rosella says, as though she can read my mind. "I'll be flying direct to Chicago from Houston on Monday evening."

"That's nice," I say. I'm sure there are other things I should babble about, like what is the matter with her mother, and all that, but the pause becomes too long, and anything I think of now would sound awkward.

Finally my father begins to talk to my mother about a lecturer who might be invited to Houston for an important seminar.

Rosella makes appropriate little noises of approval, but darts occasional glances at me. I can see she doesn't believe me about the door and is trying to figure out what that was all about. I wish she wouldn't be so obvious about her feelings.

I tune out my father and Rosella and concentrate on finishing dinner. I must get over to Lorna's house. I hadn't called her in all the commotion, and I feel like talking to her. I'm glad I have a friend like Lorna. I've never wanted many friends. I'm happy to have Lorna for all the deep and close stuff, and a few others who like to do things when we all want to go somewhere and have fun.

I wait for a pause, then break in. "May I please be excused?"

I am pushing my chair back from the table when my mother asks, "Do you have plans for tonight, dear? Do you have a date?"

25

"A date?" I'm surprised that she'd ask. "Where am I going to meet any guys in a school for girls?"

"Now, Christina, you know good and well that some of those girls have brothers who could be interested in you. Just a few weeks ago you went out with Sally Jaster's brother. Sally said he thought you were terrific, and I'm surprised he didn't call back and ask for another date."

"He did," I say, "but I turned him down."

Her mouth is a little O. "Why would you do that?"

"Because he's a drunken slob."

"Oh, come now, Christina! The Jasters are prominent people in town."

"That doesn't keep their charming son from getting drunk and practically throwing up in my lap."

"What?"

"Well, he would have, except when he started gagging I pushed him out his side of the car. And then when he finished, I helped him crawl back in on the passenger side and drove him home."

"You didn't tell us any of this," my father says.

"I didn't think it was important."

"But surely we should know if something unfortunate happens to our daughter when she's out on a date."

"I don't think so," I say. "Then you'd just worry the next time I went out. And it's over, so who cares?"

"Oh, my," my mother says. My father doesn't say anything.

"May I please be excused?" I repeat. "I want to go over to Lorna's and play records."

"All right," my father says. "Just don't be home too late."

"Meaning before midnight."

"That's it."

I'd probably argue about my curfew time, except that I've argued enough for today. I'm tired of it. I suppose I'll be glad enough to go to bed at midnight, instead of later, but it's the last thing I'd let my parents know.

I change into my old jeans and a rugby shirt and pull on an old white sweater. I cut through the kitchen on the way to the driveway. Della is just finishing up, and I ask, "Would you like a lift to the bus stop?"

"No thanks," she says, wiping her hands on a dish towel. "I got someone coming to get me."

"Big date, huh?" I grin at her.

But she shakes her head. "You run along now. Have fun."

"You too," I answer. In a few moments I'm headed for Lorna's. I don't have far to go, but as I drive through the traffic on Memorial Drive I think a car is following me. I turn off on Lorna's street, and no one else turns. I guess I'm getting spooked or something. No one was following me.

I pull up in front of Lorna's house, the porch light a bright-orange spot among the slender pin oaks that grow thickly on the front lawn. Lorna's mother went in for modern decor on the inside, and their whole house is done in tones of rust, gray, white, and black. It's the kind of thing that makes you think "Fantastic" when you first see it, but after a while you find yourself wishing someone would come in with a can of green paint, or blue . . . anything to break the monotony.

Lorna's parents go out a lot, because they get involved in causes and seminars and all sorts of things. Right now it's a marriage encounter group, and they are so wrapped up in all this new thought that they practically ignore Lorna. Lorna behaves very well about it. She says she's a stoic. Tonight her parents have already left for a party, and we have the house to ourselves, so we turn on the records at top volume.

The music gets so loud that a small print of a lion shudders and falls off the wall. It doesn't matter because the glass doesn't break. We'll put it back later.

"Why didn't you call me?" Lorna asks.

"I couldn't. When I got home, we thought we had a burglar, and that kept me busy until my parents got home and we had dinner."

Lorna looks at me with wide eyes. "What should I ask first?

Did you have a burglar? Or what did your grandmother say?"

"No," I tell her. "No, in both cases."

"Oh, Christina!" Lorna says. "I wanted you to go to France on that study program. It won't be the same without you! Is there no hope?"

"No hope," I say. Sometimes Lorna talks like one of the Victorian Gothics she likes to read. "I wish I were independent and had my own money and could do what I wanted without asking my father's permission."

I don't want to let Lorna know how upset I really feel, so I quickly say, "Let's talk about something else. Did you get that new Natalie Cole record?"

"Yesterday," Lorna says. "But tell me the rest. Tell me about your burglar."

"It wasn't a burglar. It wasn't anybody. I came home and the front door wasn't locked. There was a piece of invisible cellophane tape over the lock. So I ran in to find out what had happened, and went upstairs to talk to Della. When we came down, the tape was gone and the door was locked."

"You're kidding!"

"No, really. Don't ask me to explain about the tape, because we looked all over downstairs, and nothing was missing. And we didn't see anybody. The only person who had come to the house was a woman who asked Della to look up an address."

"Could *she* have done it?"

"Yes, I think she could. What I don't know is why, since nothing was missing."

"That's wild."

Lorna puts on the Natalie Cole record, and we listen for a while. I am still fighting the desperate mood. The room smells like upholstery cleaner and stale ashtrays, and that depresses me even more.

"Lorna," I ask, "what's important?"

"Important?" Lorna echoes, looking puzzled.

"You know what I mean. Sometimes I think I really need

28

something in my life, and then it turns out not to be important at all. Sometimes it works the other way. So how do you figure out what is really important and what isn't?"

"I don't know," Lorna says. "Maybe if it has to do with love, it's important."

"Then school wouldn't be there at all, and yet adults keep telling us that classes and grades and homework and all that are the most important things in our lives. I wonder if it means more to them than it does to us."

"I think what's most important to my father is how much money he makes," she says.

"My father likes money too," I say. "But it's always there, so he takes it for granted. I think the most important thing to my father is . . ."

"His religion," Lorna answers for me.

"No," I say slowly. "I think the religion is a means to an end. It's a way to make him somebody in his own right, a way that's different from his mother's way, the only thing in his life over which his mother doesn't have control."

"What's important to you?" Lorna asks.

I groan. "That's what I don't know yet. And I don't know how to rate things to find out."

"Maybe we could make a scale of one to ten," Lorna says.

"Except the scale would keep changing, and then the things that were important one day wouldn't be the next. Remember how it was when we were little? How we just had to go to a birthday party or ice skating or something like that?"

"Yes. I see where you're coming from."

"Right now I want to get enough money to go on that trip to France. How long is that going to seem important?"

"I thought you didn't want to talk about it."

"I don't." I get up and stretch, then pull my shirt down where it clings over my ribs. "We're running out of time. I've got to be home by midnight or my father will have an attack. What have you got to eat around here?"

29

"Not much," Lorna says. "My mother put us all on a diet."

"Why don't we cook something? How about making fudge?"

She hesitates. "It's fattening."

"Good," I say. It strikes us both funny, and we start to giggle. The giggles become strident as we hunt up a recipe for fudge, improvise with cocoa when we can't find cooking chocolate in the kitchen, and drop the vanilla bottle into the bubbling brown mess in the pan.

"We went wrong somewhere," Lorna says, fishing out the now empty bottle of vanilla. "I don't think it's ever going to get thick."

"Then let's eat it with spoons!"

We pour the fudge into a bowl, and dip in and out of it with our spoons, burning our tongues, hopping around the kitchen, and laughing like maniacs.

Worst fudge I ever ate. I'm enjoying every minute of it. Finally I look at the clock. "Oh-oh! I'd better get home in a hurry!"

"What'll we do with the rest of the fudge?" Lorna asks.

"Let's give it to someone we don't like," I answer, and this sets us off again with stomach-holding laughter.

Finally I put on my sweater and walk out to my car. I open the door, and light floods the darkness around me. Lorna waves, and closes and locks her door, flipping off the porch light.

The night is still, and the moon is just a useless sliver in a dark sky. I slide behind the wheel, automatically lock my door, and head home. Behind me a car starts, but I'm re-living the fun I had with Lorna, so I forget it, not paying much attention.

In a few minutes I pull into our driveway. I decide not to put the car in the garage. It's too lonely and dark there. I have a strong desire to get inside as quickly as possible. I leave the car on the drive, then fumble for a moment with my keys, dropping them once and fishing around in the dust until I find

30

them. My fingers tremble and my breath comes in little, quick gasps.

Someone has stepped out of the bushes directly in front of me! It's too dark to see who it is. There is just a faint glimmer of light where two eyes should be in a dark mask. I open my mouth to yell, but a hand is clasped over it. I bite down hard . . . harder . . . on the finger that slips between my teeth. The taste is salty and bitter, and the hand stinks of sweat.

There is a muffled grunt from the person behind me. I try to kick, but the figure in front of me has grabbed my arm, twisting it painfully, and I feel the prick of a needle in my arm, near the elbow.

I remember the anesthetic I got when my wisdom teeth were pulled. I could actually feel it traveling up my arm in a straight, swift line toward my brain. That's what's happening to me now. I live through a sharp instant of fear. That's all I remember.

3

I am having crazy, wild dreams, with someone humming in a rhythm that pulses and fades. I am tired and I cling to sleep, although it is so intense that my mouth is dry and my eyelids itch.

I am thirsty, terribly thirsty, and I think I will open my eyes and wake up in a hospital bed with stiff, fresh sheets, and a nurse telling me that everything went fine while my wisdom teeth were removed, and I should spit out the blood in this little pan, dear.

But I open my eyes and the light is gray and grim. I realize I am lying on a cot in what looks like a cement-walled basement, with tiny windows at the top of the walls at ground level. I cry out for my mother, but the sleep is overpowering and I drift backwards, dreaming that I called my mother's name.

I know it is much later when I can wake enough to force myself to sit up, dropping my legs over the side of the cot as though they were lead weights. My mouth is so dry that I want to gag, but there is a small table next to the cot, and a carafe of water and a glass are on it. I sip the water, remembering that it shouldn't be gulped, and try to force the mist from my mind so that I can think clearly about what has happened.

I splash some of the cold water on my face. It's cool in this basement, and I'm glad I have my sweater. I must think of what to do. I stand, but drop back on the cot. My knees wobble. I must not take this too fast.

The blanket on the cot is rough—army surplus—but I pull it around me and lean back against the wall. Last night. What happened last night?

The figure under the trees comes to mind again. I look into those dark eye sockets and begin to tremble. Sitting on the cot and realizing that I have been kidnapped, I am so terrified that I can't cry or scream or shout, held by a fear that is so penetrating it shakes me, the way a cat worries a field mouse before killing it.

Is that what will happen to me? Will I be killed?

The panic rises from the pit of my stomach. I jump to my feet, staggering, trying to focus my eyes properly. There are narrow, rough cement steps at the far end of this small room, and they lead to a door. I am going to climb those stairs and beat on that door and scream until someone hears me!

But vomit comes up into my mouth. I look around wildly and see an open door leading to a small bathroom. I make it just in time, lean over the toilet, and am very sick. There is a small washbasin nearby, and after I flush the toilet I wash my face, splashing it with water over and over until I can think more clearly.

I'm glad I was sick. It kept me from making contact with whoever is on the other side of the door at the top of the stairs. I realize that there were two people, maybe more. As my head clears, I remember the scents of the night—the large sweaty hand over my mouth and the odor of fear. Fear has a taste and fear has a smell—bitter and gagging. It surprises me. I must remember to tell Lorna about it.

The thought surfaces that I may never see Lorna or my family again, and I begin to cry. Leaning against the rough wall and blowing my nose on a fistful of toilet paper, I cry until the tears give way to a series of long, shuddering sighs.

Then, for the first time, I can think. I decide that the best thing I can do is to become familiar with the room I am in. I walk around the small basement. Aside from the steps on the far wall and the cot table, there is a huge furnace with pipes extending upward into the basement ceiling, like giant arms. It's an old-fashioned furnace with a door in the side. It's not on, and there is no pilot light anywhere around it. Are the people who live in this house warm enough in the early spring not to use the heat? Or is this house so old that it has no regular inhabitants and the utilities are turned off?

There is one way to check. I see a light switch at the top of the stairs, and I climb them cautiously, my heart pounding. If someone should open the door, I don't know what I would do. Maybe I'd faint. I have never fainted, and don't know what it feels like, but I have an idea it's something I might do.

I flip on the switch. Nothing happens. The bulb in the single ceiling socket remains blank. So what does this tell me? Not much.

Discouraged, I go swiftly down the stairs again and walk around the room. A large, shiny tree roach scuttles across a corner and into a hole in the cement near the flooring. I shudder. Will the roaches come out at night when I'm asleep? And if there are no lights, will I be able to see them? My stomach heaves again, but I force back the nausea. I must keep a firm hold on my emotions and try to think clearly.

There is one thing this basement tells me. The house is an old one. Because of flooding problems, no basements or cellars have been built in Houston for many years. And it must be a big house to have a basement and bathroom down here. Old heating system, old basement. Where would I be? The Heights? West University? Or am I even in Houston? Maybe I was taken to another town or city. I have no idea what time of day it is. I don't even know what day it is. Could I have slept over into another day? I am totally disoriented.

My watch. I see that it hasn't stopped, although as I wind

34

it, I find it was close to running down. All right. That gives me something solid. It's Saturday, no later, or my watch wouldn't be running.

Strange how I am comforted by a fact that seems so insignificant. It's just something to hang on to.

I sit on the side of the cot, again wrapping the rough blanket around my shoulders. Surprisingly, the blanket smells clean. I notice that the cheap muslin sheets have been ironed. Do people still iron sheets? The floor has been swept. The basement is very tidy, very plain, very blank. Nothing much to remember. But I am going to remember. I promise myself to remember every single detail about this place, about the people who brought me here. I am angry now. I am not going to die. I am not going to give in to them. I am going to help the police find them whenever I get out of here!

I sip some more water. I'm beginning to get hungry, and with the hunger grows the desire to meet my kidnappers face to face. They are not frightening beings any longer. They are people, and I want to know why they have brought me to this place.

I hear the muffled sound of a door closing upstairs and footsteps over my head. Have these people been in another part of the house? Or have they been out and are now returning? It's weird to hear steps over your head and not know whose they are. It's like living in a house with ghosts. I find myself whimpering. I take a deep breath. I must not let go!

There is the sound of a door being unlocked at the top of the stairs. I stiffen, every part of my body tense. It hurts to breathe.

A man dressed in jeans and a white T-shirt appears. He wears a black knit ski mask over his head. He turns and closes the door silently, then comes down the steps, deliberately, carefully. He carries a tray, and I can smell beef soup. My stomach lurches. I didn't know I was so terribly hungry.

I look into the slits of the ski mask. Pale eyes look back at

35

me. I'm not as frightened now as I was when this person was an unknown. In a way he looks comical, like an overgrown kid on Halloween. Dumb.

He puts the tray on the table. There is a thin wedding band on his left hand, and a large bandage on his middle finger. So his was the hand I bit. Good! I hope it went through to the bone!

"Do you want to know why you're here?" he asks me.

I try to recognize the voice, but I can't. I think hard, so I don't answer his question. It makes him uncomfortable.

He speaks again, a little more loudly. "Listen, girl, you got to do something."

Again I am silent, waiting for him to continue.

He sounds angry now, and his hands move uneasily up and down the legs of his jeans. "I'm talking to you, girl! I've got instructions for you!"

And now I realize where my power lies. If I am silent, I have a weapon against him—my only weapon. Before, I was only waiting to speak. Now I refuse to speak. I'll see what happens.

"Dammit!" he says. "Well, if you won't talk to me, then listen, because there is something you got to do." He walks nervously back and forth to the wall at the left, staring up at the windows, as though checking them. It is easy to see the nailheads that hold the windows tightly shut. There would be no way to climb out of those small windows anyway. My mind has somehow registered that, because I seem to have known it already.

There was no click of a lock when he shut that door. I can move faster than he can, I bet, since he's not expecting me to try anything. He's at the far wall. Maybe it would give me the chance I need. It's better than sitting here, wondering what will happen next. As his back is turned, I dash toward the door, stumbling up the stairs.

I'm almost at the top when he grabs my leg, slamming me down on my stomach on the steps. The pain makes me cry

36

out. He pulls my legs, dragging me down the stairs. I can only tuck in my elbows close to my body and try to protect my face, thankful that my sweater covers my arms so they won't be cut by the rough cement. I am furious. I am filled with hate. If there were any way I could kill this man, I would. The thought scares me enough to bring me back to my senses, and the heat of hatred drains away.

I huddle at the bottom of the stairs until he speaks to me again.

"Get up and go back to that cot," he says.

I do as he tells me. I sit and face him, staring defiantly into those pale eyes.

"You're going to have to sign a letter to your grandmother," he says.

I shake my head.

He's disconcerted, and that gives me a tiny feeling of triumph. It's as though I've won a blow in our fight.

"Oh yes you will," he tells me. "Because that's the way we've planned it. You're going to sign the ransom note we typed, and I'm going to deliver it." When I don't respond, his voice becomes wheedling. "Look, girl, you haven't got anything to lose if you sign the letter. As soon as we get the money, we'll let you go."

I continue to stare at him.

"I'm not kidding," he says. "You'll have to sign the note if you want to get out of here!" His eyes light on the tray, and he stands a little straighter. "If you want to eat, you'll have to write your name. No food for you until you do."

I am faster this time than he. I pick up the bowl of soup and throw it at him. That is my answer.

He stands there with the dark broth running down the front of his T-shirt, and he is too surprised to do anything but curse. Then he reaches out and cuffs me across the side of the head with his open hand. The force knocks me sideways, and I fall on the cot.

"Dammit! I didn't want to do that!" he shouts at me. "I'm not supposed to hit you! And you're supposed to write your name on the letter! That's how it's planned! Dammit!" He picks up the pieces of the broken bowl, puts them on the tray, and stomps up the stairs without another word.

I'm hungry! But I'm also satisfied with what I did. Maybe it was stupid, maybe not. Maybe he will come downstairs and kill me because I'm not following whatever plan he's got worked out. But I feel that for now I've won. I've had the best of him. My face stings from the slap, but I feel good inside. I'll have to give this more thought.

Always before in my life I've been able to plan things in advance, to make decisions. But suddenly I'm faced with a situation in which I have to play it as it goes, step by step. What if I make the wrong move?

What would my father do in a case like this? My mother?

I think my mother would dissolve completely. She's never had to face anything threatening in her life. But maybe I'm not giving her enough credit. I've never had anything threatening happen to me either until now. Will my children someday have any idea of what I'm like inside? Of how I think and what I'd do in a crisis? At the moment I feel close to my mother, and this surprises me. Since I was a very young child, my mother and I have not been demonstrative with each other. Is it because I feel so alone that I long to see her?

The cockroach ventures out once more, its feelers waving as it explores, looking for danger. Seeing none, it travels in a straight line to a shadow behind the heater.

I know what my father would do if he were here in my place. He would pray. I try to think of a prayer, but nothing forms in my mind except the word "please." That is not much of a prayer, but my mind is blank. I can't even remember the baby prayers I used to say at bedtime while my father listened. All that comes back to me is the line, "If I should die before I wake . . ." Forget it! That's not a thought I want to dwell on right now!

The room is getting dimmer, and I realize that it must be late afternoon. I am getting used to hearing footsteps over my head, and I try to sort them out. One set seems to be heavy, one a little lighter. Are two people there? More? I wish I knew.

My stomach is rumbling like a Honda. I wonder if they can hear it all the way upstairs. If I don't sign the note, I'll go without food. The body can live for a number of days without food, as long as it has water, and there is water from the faucet in the little bathroom. But if I go without food for too long, I will lose my strength. I might need all the strength I have to get away from these people. There is no way to know.

From what the man said, the letter is already typed and I'm just supposed to sign my name. If they'd let me write it, maybe I could work in some message to Cristabel so she wouldn't give them the money. I don't want these kidnappers to get money from my grandmother! The whole idea of their using me to take her money makes me angry again.

The door opens. This time I'm ready for him. I sit very still as he comes down the stairs. He's carrying a pad with a sheet of paper on it, and a pencil. No food.

He comes to stand directly in front of me, and I must look up at him. "Are you ready to sign your name to this letter?" he asks. His voice is angry.

I nod my head, indicating yes, I am ready, and he seems startled. Good. I have caught him off balance a second time.

"Oh. Well, all right then," he says. He hands me the pad and pencil.

I begin to read the letter, and I gasp. It begins, "Dear Cristabel"!

He laughs, his ego feeding the words. "I'm a smart guy. I know all about you, girl. I know that's what you call your grandmother."

I am trying to think this out when he says, "Come on. Speed it up. What are you doing?"

I merely glance up at the man, waiting, until he says, "Okay. Read the damn thing if you've got to."

It's a short, simple letter that sounds like something from an old television drama, saying that she will be contacted by phone, don't call the police, and all that rubbish.

Then I get to the amount they are asking for, and I give a little cry. The paper shakes in my fingers.

He laughs. "Thought that two hundred and fifty thousand would get to you!"

He rubs the finger with the bandage on it. I hope it hurts like hell.

I have my mouth open to tell him he's crazy, that it won't work. Then I remember my weapon of silence, and I close my mouth again. It doesn't matter what I tell this man. He'll follow whatever plan he's made.

"Dammit," he says. "I wish you'd talk. You got to do everything the hard way?"

They'll send this letter, or one like it, no matter what I do. I don't think Cristabel will give them the money. She can't!

As though he could read my mind, he says, "You haven't got a choice. Sign it."

His laugh terrifies me more than his words. This man is out of his mind. So I sign, misspelling my name, putting an "e" where the "i" should be. It's the only thing I can think of to do.

He takes the paper from me, reads it, and seems satisfied. "Okay, girl," he says. "I'll bring you some food in a little while, before it gets dark. There won't be any light down here while it's dark. Don't want anything to look strange to the neighbors."

He leaves, clumping up the steps. The door shuts and locks.

So there are neighbors. Can something be done about attracting their attention? I'll have to think about it.

I feel exhausted now, drained. I look forward to sleep. There's a towel and soap in the bathroom at least, but I wish I had my hairbrush. There's one in my bag. I wonder if they brought my handbag with them. It was hanging over my shoul-

40

der, I think, when they took me. Did I drop it? I must have, and I can't remember.

He's following a plan. Did he make the plan? If he did, it must have holes in it. He's too dumb to make a really fool-proof kidnapping plan. But maybe someone else made it.

I listen to the footsteps moving over my head. *Who are you?* I want to cry out. *What are you doing up there?* I shove the sleeve of my sweater into my mouth to keep from screaming. I must hang on! I've got to!

A little later I am wrapped in my blanket, leaning against the wall, breathing evenly, deeply. I try to make my trembling body relax. I start with my toes and work upward, concentrating on letting each muscle loosen. The calves of my legs are heavy, my mind croons in a soft pattern. They are heavy . . . growing heavy . . . my thighs are heavy . . . they are relaxing, relaxing . . . my legs are so heavy . . .

The click of the lock at the top of the stairs causes me to jump violently. My mental exercise has been wiped out. I wait tensely as the man comes down the stairs. He carries a tray. I smell food. Something at the back of my mind registers a remembrance of something. But what? I don't know. I lose the thought.

Without a word he comes to the table and puts down the tray. His eyes are wary. They watch me carefully, and there is a strange, alert look in them.

"Here's something for you to eat," he says. "The way I promised."

There are two plates on the tray, and a glass of milk. Both plates are covered with inverted faded-green plastic bowls. He waits and watches. I hesitate, but there is no point in waiting. Apparently he wants to stay here while I eat. Then he'll take the tray and leave me alone until morning.

Shrugging back the blanket, I lean forward and remove the bowl from the nearest plate. I shriek, and the bowl flies from my hand. On the plate is a bloody mouse!

41

For a moment I gag, my hands at my throat, my eyes riveted to the plate in spite of my revulsion. Then I realize that what I am looking at is a rubber mouse, and he has poured ketchup over it! Sick! Horrible! What a crazy, sick thing to do!

I am so furious that I jump to my feet and try to strike out at him. I try to rip that stupid ski mask from his head, to scratch, to hurt him. "You bastard!" I scream at him. It's the worst thing I can think of to call this man.

But he laughs as he grabs my wrists and holds them tightly. "I knew I could get you to talk, girl! It wasn't even that hard!"

I struggle, and he says in a deeper, more intense voice, "Don't try to take off this mask. You're safe enough now, but if you can identify me, then I might have to kill you."

I'm so angry and scared that I begin to sob, and the tears flood my eyes. He becomes nothing but a blur.

"Now, look here, don't get so upset," he says. "I thought it was a good joke, myself. Hey, girl, don't cry like that."

But I can't stop. I shake with my sobs, and it's hard to stand up. I find I am leaning against him, completely unable to do what I want to do, which is to keep cool and stay as far away from this man as possible.

He murmurs things, trying to get me to stop crying, and I feel as though I were a small child and he were my father. I am dependent on him for my life. The thought robs me of whatever strength I have left.

Finally the sobs become dry. There are no tears left. He leads me back to the cot, and I sit on it, waiting to be told what to do.

"Eat your dinner now," he says. He takes away the plate with the toy mouse.

"I can't," I whisper. "How do I know what's under the other bowl?"

"Listen," he says, "be a good sport. I owed you one for that bowl of soup you threw at me. I owe you one for my sore finger too; but if I decide to collect on that, it will come later."

He pulls off the plastic bowl and nods toward the tray. "See, it's a nice hamburger—just the way you'll like it."

And then I know.

That needle of remembrance pricks again, and the record falls into place.

The voice is the same. The way he said the word "hamburger." It's got to be Zack.

And is the one upstairs his wife . . . Loretta?

I can't let him know that I've guessed who he is. He said he might have to kill me if I identified him. I obediently reach for the hamburger, my hands shaking.

"You sure look a mess, you know that?" Zack says.

I don't answer. I take a small bite of the hamburger and chew it softly. It's delicious. How can I sit here and munch on a hamburger and think about how much I like it and be so scared at the same time? It's as if there were two of me.

"I'm not going to bother you," he says. "You just relax and enjoy your dinner. I'll come down in the morning to get the tray."

I look up at him, and he adds, "You hear me?"

"Yes," I whisper. "Thank you."

I don't pay much attention as he leaves. I am concentrating on my hamburger, trying to make it last. I finish it and drink the milk, and realize that the light is almost gone. I had better wash my face before it is too dark to see where I am going.

It takes only a few minutes, but darkness is racing me and I can barely find my cot as I come back from the bathroom.

I climb between the sheets, trying to straighten my blanket, being careful to tuck it in tightly around the edges, so that loose ends can't trail on the floor. I don't know what might come rustling out of the cracks. I have an instant of panic as I think of the large tree roaches and imagine I hear dozens of them scurrying around. But I force myself to push the thoughts away.

So many hours have passed since I last slept, and some of

43

the effects of the drug they gave me must still be with me. I am ungodly tired. All I want to do is sleep. I don't even try to plan what to do next. I don't even wonder what will happen to me. I simply roll on one side, my back against the wall, smelling the musty dampness of the basement walls and the hot-iron fragrance of the sheets, the sour smell of the fear still in my throat.

When I get the blue eye shadow at the store, I'd better get some mouthwash. The incongruity of that random thought seems so hysterical that I find wild laughter rising in the back of my throat. "No!" I command myself. "Keep calm."

Steadily I push it back, push thoughts of any kind back into a void. Soon I am asleep.

4

I dream that Zack is standing at the foot of my cot. He is standing quietly, his arms folded, staring at me. I wake with a cry, kicking out, revolted and terrified.

But no one is there.

Pale morning light filters through the dirty windows near the ceiling, illuminating the room. There is no one in this room but me.

My dream has told me something about myself. There is another reason for my fear. This man, Zack, has the power to do anything he wants to me, but my mind has been pushing this thought away. Now I analyze it. What will I do if he tries . . .

My mind won't complete the sentence. I huddle on my cot, pulling the blanket around my shoulders, and shiver. I feel cruddy, and wish I could take a bath. Maybe it's better to look the way I must look. I would like to be as repulsive to Zack as he is to me.

I get up and walk around the room. I must have some exercise. I try to do a few of the standing exercises that are the delight of our gym teacher, and which I must have done over a million times since first-grade outdoor-activity period. It does help to clear my brain as I breathe harder, and I think I must remember to tell her that the exercises really do have some benefit—especially when one is kidnapped. I giggle irrationally.

It's hard to live in a basement by yourself and wonder how long you'll be there and what will happen to you. I make myself think of something else, fearful that I'll come close to panic if I begin to understand my situation. I'll go over my French verbs. No, I won't. I hate French verbs. I don't hate France, just its verbs. I would love to go to France with the girls in my class. But I can't. Why can't I? Rosella is going to Chicago. Big deal. I wish I weren't in school. I wish I had a job so that I could earn enough money to go to France with the junior class. But if I weren't in school, I wouldn't be in the junior class. Nothing makes sense. I'm hungry.

I hear footsteps over my head. The kitchen must be over the basement. Someone is going to make breakfast. If I were at home, we'd have a big breakfast before going to church. It's seven o'clock now, and my father always wakes us early. Eggs and sausages and . . . When my father isn't being pompous about his religion, he can unbend a little. There are times when we almost come close to loving each other. Almost.

Tears are running down my cheeks, and it surprises me. I didn't know I was crying. Why is it that part of my mind seems to stay very cool and part of it is going bonkers? Do people in prison feel like this? Maybe not. At least people in prison know where they are and what's going on. If I could know that, maybe I'd be all right.

I walk to the foot of the steps and peer upward at the solid, forbidding door. What if I could force it open? Last night I went to sleep like a little kid being put to bed. Why didn't I stay awake until the people upstairs had gone to bed, and then I could at least try the door and see if it were possible to break out. What's the matter with me?

Tonight, I promise myself. Tonight I'll do it. Maybe there is something around this basement I can use to work on the door lock. The basement is as clean as it could possibly get.

It looks as though no one has ever used this room. Except for the massive heating unit at one side and the cot and table for me, there is nothing in this basement. I walk over to the furnace to examine it. There is a door in the side with a little latching kind of handle. I pull on the handle, and the latch lifts scratchily through the rust. I swing the door open and see a large, hollow drumlike cavern. I poke my head inside to look at it. The pipes lead into it, and a funny thing happens. I hear Zack talking to someone!

I pull my head out again, and the sound is muffled. Apparently these pipes lead from the heating unit to registers in the rooms. Some of the vents must be open, even though the heater isn't in use, and through those open vents the voices are carried and magnified in this hollow metal expanse.

Maybe I can find out what is happening. I need to know what they are going to do with me.

I put my head back inside the furnace and listen. Zack is still talking. I pity his wife.

"Don't tell me you're setting up that old ironing board again!" he says. "You ain't even got the breakfast dishes cleared, and you're fixing to iron. What for?"

"I want to iron," the voice comes back. "You know I like the sheets and dish towels and things ironed. It just makes me feel right." Is this voice Loretta's? She didn't talk to me, so I have no idea what she sounds like. This voice is high-pitched and slow-speaking, with a drawl. Sounds more like a southerner than a Texan. I bet she's not very bright. She couldn't have her head together if she married Zack.

"That girl down there—take her the tray," the woman says. "The stuff on it's getting cold."

"Don't rush me," Zack says. "There's still a good slurp in this coffee cup."

I shut the furnace door carefully, so it won't make a sound. I go back to the cot and sit on it, waiting patiently.

The door at the top of the stairs opens, and I tense. I try

47

to push away the thought of how frightened of this man I am. I don't want him to come near me; yet I need the food he's bringing, and I need him as a source of information.

He walks across the room, still wearing the ski mask, and puts the tray on the table. Then he stands at the foot of my cot, staring at me, looking as he did in my dream, his eyes pale reflections of my terror. I begin to tremble. I can't stop.

"Hey, girl, what's the matter with you?" Zack asks.

"I—I'm cold," I stammer.

"Well, just keep that blanket around you then," he says. "There's no way to get the chill out of this basement." He laughs heartily. "It's a really pretty, sunny day outside. Going to be nice and warm out there!"

I huddle inside myself, hating him for his cruelty. His voice changes, and there is a tone of sympathy in it. "Listen here, I was just kidding. I don't like keeping you down here any more than you like being here."

My words burst out in a shout. "Then why are you doing this to me?"

Zack folds his arms across his chest. He is wearing a clean T-shirt today, thank goodness. It even looks ironed. Surely his wife doesn't iron his T-shirts too?

He shrugs. "It's only business. Didn't you ever want to get into a good business proposition and maybe have to look the other way at some things you didn't like too much? No, I guess you didn't, being who you are."

He has told me more than he knows. He has essentially told me that someone else thought this up and he went in on the idea. It wasn't Loretta. That's for sure. So someone else planned this kidnapping. Who? Is there any way in the world I can get him to tell me the name?

I suppose not. He is keeping his own name from me—or so he thinks. It would be dangerous for me to know too much, and yet I've got to find out as much as I can without letting Zack realize he has given information away.

Trying to stay as cool as possible, I reach over and slide

48

the tray closer to me. The coffee is bitter and cold. The eggs are jelled in their grease. The toast is hard. It doesn't matter. I'm hungry, so I begin to eat.

"Have you been in contact with my grandmother yet?" I ask Zack.

He grins under that stupid ski mask. "That's for me to know and you to find out," he says.

That's third-grade dumbness, I think, remembering the age at which we chanted that at each other every chance we got. Then it comes to me that third-grade mentality is probably where Zack stopped. How do you reach a third-grader in an appeal to reason? How do you convince him that he shouldn't harm you, should let you go, should be fair?

We weren't very fair in the third grade. We weren't fair to each other at all. Things seem more hopeless than ever. I polish off the coffee and lean back against the wall. The coldness of the cement seeps through the blanket, my sweater, and my shirt. I shiver again.

He reaches over to take the tray, and I try again. "Please tell me if you've reached my grandmother or my parents. I need to know. What did they say?"

"I told you," he says smugly, "that's for me . . ."

I can't bear hearing that horrible phrase again. "Wait!" I interrupt him. I desperately try to reach through to his emotions. Maybe there is something about this man that will respond. I must find out what that is. "How would you feel if you were in my place?" I ask him. "Don't you know how frightened I am?"

"That's the way it goes," he says. "You ain't supposed to be enjoying yourself all shut up down here."

"It's like being in jail," I snap at him. "You'd know about that, wouldn't you?"

"Maybe," he says. He stands there, balancing the tray, his head slightly cocked to one side as he studies me. "You sure do look a mess, girl. Don't you want to fix yourself up?"

I can't keep my body from stiffening as he says this, and

he laughs, aware of what I'm thinking, I guess. "Don't worry," he says. "I ain't fixing to touch you. You don't appeal to me."

What he says strikes him as terribly funny, and he laughs all the way up the stairs.

I breathe a long sigh of relief and pull the blanket around me more tightly. I want to go home.

It's important to keep my mind busy, I know, so I go over what Zack has said. He's told me three things without being aware of it. The first, that someone else planned this kidnapping. The second, that things are going the way they planned them, or he wouldn't be so cheerful. And the third, that he has already been in prison. This isn't the first time he's done something criminal.

Curious, I wonder what he was arrested for. He's the type I'd think could easily get into a fight with someone in a bar. Or rob one of those small, late-night grocery stores, wearing that stupid ski mask. Or maybe burgle apartment houses when the people in the apartments weren't home. Do you say "burgle"? It doesn't sound right. I have no idea what Zack could have done. For all I know, he was in prison for murder.

Murder?

That could be me, couldn't it? The panic begins to rise again from that spot at the pit of my stomach, and I think I'm going to be sick. But the door opens suddenly, and I am startled, distracted.

Zack comes down the stairs carrying a hairbrush. He gives it to me with a shake of his head. "You really need this," he says.

I take it, wondering. It's my own hairbrush—the wooden brush with the natural bristles that I keep in the drawer of my own dressing table at home. Where did he get it? And what else of mine has he brought here?

"This is mine," I say stupidly, still holding out the hairbrush.

"I know it," he says.

50

"But how . . . ?"

"Don't ask so many questions," he says, but he still sounds good-natured, pleased with himself.

"Just tell me this," I plead. "Do you have any of my other things? These clothes . . ."

He waves a hand. "I know. You'd like to clean up. Well, give us some time. We got it all worked out."

I take a step toward him. "Please, I need . . ."

"Listen, girl," he says sharply, and I stop where I am standing. "I wasn't supposed to bring you this, even. I just got tired of seeing you look the way you look. A rabbit running through a mud puddle looks cleaner than you do."

He turns and starts up the stairs. Quickly, surprising myself, I ask, "Could I have a book?"

"Huh? A book? What are you talking about?"

"I would like a book," I tell him. "I need something to keep my mind occupied. Otherwise, I'll go crazy down here. Couldn't you please let me have a book to read?"

"Where do you think I'm going to get a book?"

"Why . . . surely you must have some books in your house."

He thinks a minute. "I'm not one for reading, but my . . . Well, I'll look around and see what I can find."

"Thank you," I say. "Thank you very much."

He chuckles. "I'm a pretty nice kind of guy," he says. "You gotta admit I take good care of you down here."

I nod.

"Say it," he tells me.

"You do. You take good care of me." Who is saying these words? This is part of a crazy nightmare.

He laughs again and goes up the stairs. I hear the click as the door locks.

I am wary of this man. He is kind only when it amuses him to be kind. If anything should go wrong, I am afraid he would hurt me with no more thought or emotion than he gave

51

to my request for a book. I don't know how to protect myself. Sometimes I feel totally dependent on him, and I don't like the feeling. I don't know what to do.

The water runs until it is hot, and I scrub my face and arms, then rub them briskly with the rough towel. It's cold, so I put my sweater back on, and I start on the tangles in my hair, brushing it so hard my scalp tingles and my eyes water. But soon the hairbrush slides in smooth strokes down my long hair, and it feels much better. I wish there were a mirror in this bathroom. I wish there were a tub, so I could take a bath. I want so badly to go home.

I turn, flipping the hair back from my face, and see Zack standing there, watching me. Before I can stop myself, I gasp. I quickly step out of the bathroom, embarrassed to be there with a man watching me.

Zack tosses a book on the bed. "It's the only thing I could find. She likes to read these books, but she takes them back to the paperback bookstore and trades them when she's finished them. This one she hadn't got to return yet."

"Who's 'she'?"

He doesn't answer my question. He says, "You look a lot better now with your hair combed and your face washed. Think I'll just let you keep the hairbrush. You'll need it."

"Thank you," I say.

He turns, and I add, "And thank you for the book."

He looks back at me when he reaches the stairs. "You sure are a funny girl with your 'thank you's' and all those manners. I sure as hell wouldn't say 'thank you' to anyone who did me the way I did you."

I have no answer, so I just watch him as he goes up the stairs and locks the door again. He's right. Why should I say "thank you" to him for anything? Do these polite responses go so deeply that they mean nothing in the long run? I must remember to tell Madame DeJon. Instead of teaching us to be so damned polite, she could add a self-defense class to the curriculum. Kicking, stomping, gouging—I wish I knew how they were done. If I ever get out of here, I'm going to learn how and . . . if I ever . . .

Fight down the panic. Switch to a new thought. Think positive. Where's that book?

I pick up the paperback and look at the cover. A girl, in what looks like a filmy nightgown, is running down a hill from a spooky-looking castle—just like all those Gothic mysteries Lorna reads. They all seem to have the same cover—just different girls and different castles. Well, now I'll find out what a Gothic is like. Lorna would be pleased. She's always trying to get me to read hers.

I settle myself on the cot with the book and my hairbrush. I keep the hairbrush on my lap as I would a security blanket. It's my link with home. I busy myself reading until I get to the heroine's second run-in with the brooding man with dark, curly hair. I think if I read "his tanned, muscular arms" one more time I'll get sick and throw the book across the room. I look at my watch. Time is going so slowly.

Outside, there are the faint voices of children playing. I wish they would come closer. Maybe I could make them hear me. But they are shouting in their play, and they must be quite a distance away. No one would hear me yelling except Zack, and I can't afford to make him angry.

The footsteps are over my head again. When they were talking earlier, they were in the kitchen, from what Zack said about finishing his coffee. Maybe I can listen in again. I might learn something.

The door to the furnace scratches and squeaks a little as I open it. My hands are damp with nervous sweat. Keep cool. They can't hear this small noise up in the kitchen.

I lean over and put my head inside the empty drum. The voices have a metallic, echoing sound. I can hear the clink of spoons and pots. Loretta—or whoever she is—must be cooking something for lunch.

If there is a third person involved in all this, where is he? Has he come to the house? Does Zack meet him somewhere else?

"How long is it going to take you to fix that spaghetti?" Zack asks.

"I'm working on it," the woman says.

"You sure are a slow one, Loretta," he says.

I nod, as though ticking off another fact. It is the woman I met. It is Loretta. And I can identify both Zack and Loretta to the police when I'm out of this place.

There is a long pause while Loretta is busy doing something up there. The kitchen noises are familiar sounds in this unreal world I'm in. I feel the way I did when I was a little kid lying on the sofa and recuperating from the mumps or flu or something and hearing someone in the kitchen making me a custard or a bowl of soup. It's a false sense of security, but the feeling comes over me, and I remind myself that I am standing in a damp basement with my head inside an unused heating unit, listening to the people who have imprisoned me here. The total thought doesn't come into focus, but it's just as well. If it did, I might start screaming.

I hear Loretta say, "Zack, I'm nervous about this whole thing. We're going to get caught."

"We're too smart to get caught," he says. His voice is smugly self-satisfied.

I keep thinking I've heard this dialogue in an old Humphrey Bogart movie. Do movies really happen to people? Is that why I'm here?

Zack goes on bragging. "The way this thing is set up, there is no way we can go to jail, even if we do get caught."

"Are you sure?"

"I'm positive. It's the most foolproof thing I was ever in on."

She grunts. "You were never in on anything good. Show me what you ever got from one of those schemes you got talked into."

54

There is the sound of a chair slamming down. He must have tipped it up, resting his feet on the table. I picture him standing up, getting angry with his wife. But the tone of his voice surprises me. There is a sense of delight and accomplishment in it.

"Listen, Loretta," he says, "I know I've given you a hard time, but this is different. When we get away from here with our share of the money, you'll see. You'll like South America. We'll get us all the good things we never had before. I promise."

"But what if we get caught?" she repeats. I notice that her voice has a constant whine in it, a twangy sound, like a loose guitar string.

"Nothing to worry about," he says. "We'll be back where we started, but that's the worst that can happen to us."

"You're sure?"

"It's all set up. I told you that."

"There ain't been a thing in the papers or on radio and TV about the kidnapping. It's creepy, like it never happened."

"The grandma's just using good sense," he says. He laughs. "Just doing what she was told to do. Now, quit worrying, 'cause I'm getting sick of it."

She gives a long sigh. "Open that jar of spaghetti sauce. Do you want to take that girl her lunch or eat yours first?"

Apparently Loretta, too, is used to doing what she is told.

I don't wait to hear the answer. I certainly don't want to get caught listening in here. Carefully, I close the door and walk back to the cot. I pick up the book and begin to read at the place where I left off.

"He lifted her in his tanned, muscular arms . . ." I wince, clench my teeth, and plod through.

Later I'm going to see if I can pull the hinge from the door of the furnace. Maybe I can use it to work the lock free on the door that is keeping me here. All I can do is try. The thought gives me something to hang on to.

55

5

The day goes so slowly. I finish the Gothic. Funny, as I turn the last page and close the book, I can't remember what the story was about. I sit on my cot, staring at the cover. Why did the woman in the story run outside in her nightgown? As a matter of fact, I don't think she really ever ran anywhere in her nightgown. Shouldn't the picture on the cover have something to do with the story?

Zack only comes to the basement once, and that is to bring me a makeshift evening meal of chili and crackers. The chili reeks of onions and grease. He says something about a television show he wants to watch, and I realize today must be Sunday. I am getting mixed up about the days, even though I haven't been here that long.

The latch on the furnace is loose. The screw that held it was stiff in my fingers at first, but after a few taps with the heel of my shoe, it began to loosen and turn fairly easily. I am afraid to remove it until tonight. Zack seems to notice everything.

Now that I've decided to try to escape, I can talk to Zack without that horrible helpless feeling that I am living just on his whim. I ask him about my grandmother, but he doesn't answer me. He still seems to be in good spirits. That's in my favor. I have to wait until they are asleep to try to open the door. But I am going to try.

I sit with my legs tucked under me, in case there are any roaches scurrying across the cold cement. It's almost too dark to see anything, but by this time I know the floor plan of this room so well I am sure I'll be able to find my way around. I don't know why I'm so tired, so sleepy. I've tried to keep up my exercises. Once, in psychology class, Miss Dobbins mentioned that sleep can be an escape mechanism. Maybe I am trying to escape that way, because it's terribly hard for me to keep my eyes open. The musty, damp smell has crept over the room again. Outside my window I can hear crickets chirping in the tangled grass and, far off, traffic, as though we are near a busy freeway.

There seem to be tiny rustlings and whisperings around me, and I try to force them from my mind so that my imagination won't inflate them into horrors that could end in a scream. I think about my family . . . about my mother.

For the first time I see what my mother really looks like. I have looked at her all my life, and it surprises me that she has always been just a face and body that I take for granted, perpetually old. Why have I always thought of my mother as an old woman? Do all children think that? But as I scan my mental image of her face, I see an attractive, middle-aged woman. Her hair, which is a light brown, not dark like mine, hangs free in a perfect cut. Her makeup covers flawless skin, which seems to glow. Maybe the bottles and jars on her dressing table are responsible for that naturally healthy look. Even her false eyelashes look real.

As I look into her eyes, I see a faint sadness there. She always seems cheerful. Is there something in my mother's life that isn't what it appears to be on the surface? I shake my head, wondering at my obtuseness. Of course. There has to be. No one is the same inside as on the surface.

My father met my mother in college. Her family was comfortably middle class, living somewhere in Iowa. We went to visit my grandmother—my mother's mother—a few years before she died. I remember overhearing her say that my mother had made a good marriage. I guess that meant she had married into the Cristabel Lattimore money. I don't think of money as making a good marriage. I think a good marriage is one in which I am terribly in love with someone, and he's just as much in love with me.

I wonder how my mother felt when she got married. Did she feel proud of herself for being a beautiful woman in love, or did she tiptoe into marriage with the Lattimore name and money, hoping she'd be worthy of the position? As I look deeply into her eyes, I think I can see how she felt, and tears burn my eyelids. My poor, poor mother. You are still afraid of them, aren't you? You expend all your energies trying to please them. A rush of love and pity chokes me. I want to tell my mother that I understand her and that I really do love her, but she isn't here.

I wipe my eyes on the blanket and gulp away the tears. It is quiet upstairs. It has been quiet for some time now. Are Zack and Loretta asleep, or are they in another room, watching television? I have no way of knowing. I have no way of finding out the time, either, since I can't see my watch. It could be eight o'clock, or it could be midnight. Existence in a black hole has no time.

But I'm impatient. I've got to do something or go bananas. So I get up from the cot, try not to think of roaches, and move slowly to the furnace, arms outstretched. When I touch it, the metal is cold, and I jump involuntarily. It's a weird feeling, touching something cold and unseen in a dark place. My fingers find the door, however, and I feel for the latch. It is quite rusty, and as I wiggle it again, it seems even looser than it was before. It's hard to tell. When I could see it, I could keep it in perspective. Without the sense of sight here in the pitch-darkness, even the size and shape of the latch seem overlarge and clumsy.

The latch fits through a groove, with a single screw holding it in place. I work the screw with my fingers, and it loosens. I am able to turn it. But it comes out too quickly, and the screw drops to the floor, the latch with it. The sound seems exaggerated—a clank that could be heard all over the house. I hold my breath and wait, but nothing happens. I exhale slowly.

I have let my fear take over again. Carefully I get down on my hands and knees and feel over the floor until my fingers touch the latch. I grip it, scramble to my feet, and move toward the stairs.

I misjudge my distance and bang my toes on the bottom step. What if Zack heard that? What if he is waiting just behind the door, at the top of the stairs? The door opens inward, into the kitchen, I suppose. Will I work and work on the lock, only to open the door and see Zack there, grinning at me?

The thought so unnerves me that I can't move from my spot at the bottom of the stairs. I can only stare up into the darkness where the door should be, thinking of that sneering grin. My hands shake, and I almost drop the latch again.

As I grab for it, the spell is broken, and I am able to function. I grope for the rough boards, which make a kind of railing, and take a step upward. The railing quivers, and I realize that it wouldn't support my weight if I should fall. I'll have to be very, very careful.

One slow step at a time I climb the stairs, occasionally stubbing a toe, since they are rough cement steps, unequal in size. It occurs to me with a burst of excitement that if there were someone in the room on the other side of the door, light would show through the cracks. It is dark. Zack and Loretta must be asleep. They have to be!

I reach the door. It's hard and cold under my hands. I find the doorknob, but what can I do now? I try to slip the rusty metal latch into the doorframe where the lock enters, but it is too thick. The hinges are on the other side of the door, or I could work on separating those. The only thing I can think of doing is to try to dig away the wood around the lock. The wood must be old, and on the basement side, where it is constantly slightly damp, it might be rotten enough to give.

I dig at the doorframe with all my strength, trying to gouge out the splinters of wood. But God knows how many coats of paint have protected this wood. It's as hard as metal, and my chipping knocks away some flakes of paint, which flick at my fingers as they fall, but that's all. Finally, sweaty and out of breath, I admit to myself that there is no way I can get out of this place.

I drop the latch into the pocket of my sweater. I feel my way down the stairs and across to my cot. I know why people die of hoplessness. It comes on like a thick blanket, smothering your thoughts, your confidence, creeping into your mind and filling the corners. I lie in the dark, suffocating under horrible despair, wishing I were dead. I sleep, then wake, then sleep. The sleep is filled with monstrous dreams that attack, cry out, and vanish, leaving me once more awake and staring into the darkness. Help me! my mind is screaming, but there is no one to hear.

Morning comes. I have forgotten to wind my watch, and it has stopped, so now I have no idea how late it is. I think I hear the voices of children again. Maybe they are going to school. Is this a school day? What day is it? I am totally disoriented. I can hear the children. If I scream and scream, will they hear me?

I pull my cot to the far wall and stand on it, trying to reach the window. At the top of my lungs I yell, "Help! Help!" Even stretching as far as I can, there is no way I can reach those nailed-shut, dirt-caked windowpanes. But I can't stop screaming and shouting, and I beat my hands against the rough walls until they hurt.

The door opens and Zack hurries down the stairs. "Cut that out!" he orders.

On command the noise stops, although it seems to be going on inside my head.

"Get off that thing," Zack says, and I climb down.

A part of me is behaving like an automaton, and another part is asking why I'm doing so.

I turn toward the cot, but he grabs my arm roughly, swinging me around. I raise a hand to protect myself, and it brushes against the rough wool of the ski mask. I begin to shudder uncontrollably until Zack shakes me so hard I cry out.

"What are you doing?" I manage to gasp.

"Trying to get you to calm down, girl," he says. He reaches up to adjust the mask, and his eyes seem faded into their sockets.

"I'm all right," I make myself say. I don't want him to shake me again.

"Go on up the stairs," he tells me. "And act like you got some brains. Don't try running off again."

I am too weak-kneed to run, but I hope he doesn't know that. My legs tremble as I climb the stairs. I am filled with relief that I am finally able to leave that horrible basement room, and at the same time I'm scared to death of what is going to happen next.

He follows me so closely that his breath is hot against my right shoulder, and it reeks of onions and stale beer. As we reach the door, I automatically stop as though I were programmed, but he pushes me roughly and says, "Go on through. Go ahead."

I step into a large kitchen. The room has the high ceiling of an old house, and the cupboards have been painted a nauseating shade of tan. Someone has applied red-rooster decals in the middle of each cabinet, and it strikes me that they are slightly crooked and off center. The linoleum is in an imitation brick pattern, also tan, and faded and worn toward the center of the kitchen. At one side is an ironing board with a steam iron resting on end.

"Get yourself a drink of water," Zack says. He stands there, watching me.

61

"I don't need a drink of water," I tell him.

His answer is to push me, and I catch my balance against the cabinets. "Open the cabinet over there," he says, pointing. "There's glasses inside. Get yourself a drink of water."

I can't figure out what he has in his mind. He acts like a person carrying out a plan. How could my having a drink of water carry out any kind of plan? If he were to hand me a glass of anything, the way he is acting, I would be suspicious and wouldn't want to drink it.

Obediently, I take a glass, turn on the faucet, and fill the glass to the brim. I begin to sip it.

"That's enough," Zack says. "Pour out the water and put the glass on the sink."

I do as he tells me, but I am more puzzled than I was before.

We move, at his direction, into a dining room, and I hear someone scuttling through the kitchen and down into the basement, making little mouse movements and trying to be as silent as possible. Could it be Loretta?

My mind is tired. That is the only word for it. I have gone through fear and anger and terror and exhaustion, and now I am blank, wondering what we are doing. I can't gather my thoughts together enough to put the pieces of this insane puzzle in place. Why would a kidnapper follow his victim from room to room in a house, telling her to pick up objects and put them down? The question floats without an anchor. I have no way of trying to answer it. I simply do as I am told.

We walk up the stairs with their old-fashioned machine-carved moldings that match the patterns in the moldings around the ceilings. I touch a wall switch, at Zack's direction, and low-watt bulbs in a multi-globed chandelier flicker on, lighting fat, full-blown, hand-painted roses from another era. I note that there is no dust, that everything is clean, even the faded brown carpet on the stairway.

At the door of the first room on the right, Zack tells me to stop. "Go inside," he says.

62

I open the door and walk into the room. At first I notice the yellowed imitation maple dresser and headboard and the flowered chenille bedspread with some of its fringe missing. But what catches my eye, and takes a moment to register, is my handbag on the dresser. Some of my things have spilled out of it—my lipstick, my comb, my toning lotion that is supposed to take care of acne and doesn't . . . but that wasn't in my handbag!

I turn to question Zack, my mind beginning to clear, but he pushes me again and again, with little nudges, until I catch myself, palms down on the dresser top for support.

"This is your stuff," he says. "And some of your clothes are in the closet."

"How did you get them?"

He laughs.

"How could you get my things out of my house?" I repeat the question.

"There are a couple of things I want you to do, girl," he says. He nods toward the far door to the room. It's open and leads to a bathroom. I can see the white tile floor and the end of an old-fashioned claw-foot tub.

"You get in there and take a bath and wash your hair and fix yourself up."

"No," I say.

"Listen, your parents aren't going to want to see you looking like such a slob." His lips stretch in a grin behind that horrible mask.

It's hard to talk, to breathe, to think, but I manage to gasp, "I'm going home?"

"Sure," he says. "Told you there was nothing to worry about. Now, you just take off those dirty things you've got on, and put them in a pile here on the floor."

Instinctively I back away from him, and he shakes his head. "You been watching too many movies, girl. I won't be here. I've got things to do. There's a woman who'll be up here, keeping an eye on you." Sternly he adds, "And don't think about giving her any trouble, because she'll have a gun. I've told her to use it if she needs to."

I don't answer. There are too many thoughts in my head to get them sorted out into words. After a long silence his tone of voice becomes wheedling. "Look, now, just play along and don't think about making trouble, and you'll be home before you know it. If you start acting up, then somebody's going to get hurt, and that somebody is you."

I find myself nodding. What he says seems to make sense. I just want to go home. That's all I want. I can't trust this man. I know that. But there are few choices, and something tells me that the best thing I can do right now is follow the rules he's set up.

I see that my suitcase is on a spindly wooden chair over at the side of the room near the closet door. Zack walks out into the hall. There are some rustling movements, some whispers, and a woman comes into the room.

She stands watching me a moment. She is wearing a ski mask, identical with the one Zack was wearing. It seems incongruous with the rest of her clothing—her wide-bottomed jeans, the pink T-shirt that clings around the pudgy bulges where her midriff should be. It's Loretta. There is no doubt about it. Her eyes are small and wary. There is a gun in her hand.

She shuts the door to the hall behind her and perches on the edge of the bed as though it were a stove heating up. Her gun hand looks awfully nervous.

"Do what he told you." It's the first time she's spoken to me. It's the same voice I heard echoed through the heat register into the basement.

"Okay," I tell her. I go into the bathroom and turn on the faucets. There's a brown stain from years of water dripping in a path down to the drain, but the tub is clean. Everything in this house is clean.

"Don't shut the door!" Her voice is strident, a little scared.

64

She doesn't like this any more than I do. I'm glad she doesn't follow me into the bathroom. I'd hate to have her squeezed in here with her jittery gun while I'm trying to take a bath.

I drop my clothes on the floor, but she calls out, "Throw those things out here!" so I do, tossing them practically at her feet. Then I put my watch on the basin. I hurry into the tub and turn off the water. It's almost at the top of the tub, and in spite of my emotional state, I still delight in the warmth around my body. These old tubs are so deep. I decide I like them better than newer bathtubs. My bottle of shampoo is propped on the soap dish that hangs over the edge of the tub. They haven't forgotten a thing.

As I soap my hair and rub my scalp vigorously, I seem to get my thoughts back into focus. The warmth, the steam, the stinging of shampoo against my squeezed-together eyelids—it helps thoughts fall back into place.

I submerge, liking the sensation, holding my breath and rubbing shampoo from my hair while I'm underwater. When I spring up to a sitting position, I can think more clearly. My hair is dripping rivulets down my neck and shoulders.

I cap the shampoo and reach for the bar of soap. It feels so wonderful to be clean again. I would like to stay in the tub all day.

Loretta's voice snaps me back to reality. "You been in there long enough," she says. "Get out now and get dried. I got your clothes laid out on the bed for you."

There are two towels hanging against the wall, both of them smelling of irons and ironing boards. I'd never want to iron towels, and I don't think anyone could make Della do it, but I have to admit that ironed towels smell awfully good and extra clean. I wrap my hair in one and dry myself with the other. I am beginning to feel renewed. I'm hungry. I might be ready to tackle Loretta, but there she sits with the gun in her hand, and it's pointed right at me.

"Put your clothes on, quick," she says.

I drop the towel and put on my bra and bikini panties. My gray slacks and red pullover shirt are on the bed. I know they were hanging in the closet the day I was kidnapped. I'm positive! Or am I? I've looked at my clothes and worn my clothes, but how can I be sure when I saw them last? When did these kidnappers get them? I must know the answer.

I straighten the shirt, pulling it over my hips, and reach up to towel-dry my hair. I wonder what happened to the clothes I tossed in here on the floor.

Loretta has moved from the bed to stand against the wall, and she waves the gun in my direction. "Sit down on the bed to do that," she says. "I don't want you to try anything funny. I really can shoot this here gun." She hands me my wristwatch.

My tongue is forming the name, but I catch myself in time, breathing quickly as I realize I almost gave myself away. "He— the man who was here . . ." I say. "He said I would be going home."

"That's right," she says.

"I left my brush in the basement," I tell her. "Can I get it? I need to brush my hair."

"It's right here," she answers. She takes the hairbrush from the dresser and tosses it into my lap.

I watch her as I brush my hair. "Where did you get my clothes?"

"It doesn't matter."

"It does to me. Was it you who put the tape on the door? Did you steal them then?"

The gun wavers in her fingers. "Don't ask so many questions," she says. "Put on some lipstick, some makeup, whatever you're used to wearing."

I don't budge. "Why?"

She leans toward me as tense as the spring that holds our garage door. "Because I said so. I don't like this any more than you do, and I'm nervous as a cat having kittens, and I'm scared I might get riled enough to shoot you if you don't do what I tell you to do! You got that?"

"Yes," I say. "I understand." I fish through the things on the dresser and find what I need. In a few minutes I look healthy and normal, but I feel like Alice in Wonderland down the wrong hole, wondering what she's doing in a place like this. I know one thing for sure. I am not going to tangle with Loretta. She strikes me as being one step this side of a nervous breakdown.

I stand up and stare at her. Her eyes are bright gleams that remind me of the tiny lights that wink on and off on Christmas trees. She looks ready to short out. "What do you want me to do now?" I ask her, trying to keep my voice calm.

She waves the gun toward the door. Dear God, I hope it doesn't go off!

"Downstairs," she says. "Get yourself to that room in back —the one with the TV in it."

I walk down the stairs steadily. I've got my bearings now, thanks to that hot bath and shampoo. I try to get glimpses of the front street as we come into the small entry hall. It's an old neighborhood, and not too tidy. Across the street there is a junk car propped up on blocks and missing its wheels. A worn-out water heater lies with some miscellaneous trash by the driveway of the house next to it.

"Don't go craning your neck to see things," Loretta snaps. "It won't make you no never mind later. Just do what I told you to do."

"How do I get to the room in back?" I ask her. "I forget."

"Just turn left and go down the hall a ways. You'll come right to it." She doesn't need to remind me, but she does. "And I'm coming right after you with this gun."

I enter the room. It has the usual overstuffed furniture and odd tables that came from another, out-of-fashion generation. In the corner, its glass like a blank face, is the television set. In front of it is a deep wing chair in a scratchy, wine-colored plush fabric.

"You turn on the TV," Loretta says, "and then sit in that chair and watch it."

67

"Watch television?" I am trying to figure out the reason for this.

"Do it!" Her voice is like a screech. She is making me terribly nervous. I wish she didn't have that gun.

Quickly I pull the television "on" knob, not caring what channel it's turned to.

The voices come on first, shouting and screaming in some television game, and I adjust the volume to low. The last thing in the world I want to hear right now is some middle-aged woman hysterically kissing an emcee because she's just won a year's supply of drain cleaner.

"Sit down now!" Loretta says.

I do, and I can feel the lumpy springs in the seat cushion. Who ever heard of springs in a seat cushion? No wonder they went out of style.

"Where are you?" I ask. The wings on the chair block out my vision.

"Right behind you," she answers.

"I wish you were sitting where I could see you."

"I got no intention of doing so."

"But it makes me nervous having you back there where I can't see what's happening."

"Just having you here in this house makes me nervous!" she says. "Shut up and watch that TV show."

"I don't even know what show it is." The remark sounds inane, but surprisingly she picks up on it.

"It's a pretty good one. Those people have to match the celebrities and get them all right or they don't win."

Cautiously, trying to keep her new mood, I say, "Do most of them lose?"

"Sure, but sometimes they win, and then they get cars and trips and all that stuff."

"Did you ever want to be on one of those shows?"

"Yeah," she says. "But there's no way we're going to get out to California, and you got to be there to get picked. Did you ever notice that the people they pick are . . ."

Her voice breaks and stops. Only the raucous noise from the set infiltrates the room. Then she screams the words, "Don't talk to me! Don't try nothing with me! He said I got to shoot you if you try anything!"

"I won't! I promise!" My answer tumbles out, and I grip the arms of the chair for support. This woman is really near the brink. I had better be very careful not to upset her.

I think about this a moment. Zack had been in good spirits. The idea of kidnapping someone hadn't seemed to bother him. But Loretta is frightened. He must be used to committing crimes. However, this might be the first time she's been involved with him in any kind of crime. The whole idea terrifies her. I heard her telling Zack she was afraid they'd be caught. Has she been lying awake at night wondering what would happen if they *were* caught? He told her it was foolproof, but she doesn't believe it. She doesn't trust him. Why? I wish I knew.

I would like to ask Loretta who else is involved. That husband of hers is too dumb to work out a complex scheme. There has to be a third person. I know there is. But I can't talk to Loretta. Not now.

There is a noise at the front door, and Loretta lets out a little scream. I instinctively duck, tucking my head on my knees, wrapping my arms around my head. "Don't shoot me!" I gasp. I think I say it aloud.

But a voice comes from the hallway. "It's me!" Zack shouts jubilantly. "We did it! We did it!"

"You got the money?" she cries.

"You bet I did. It all worked out the way it was planned."

"But you got back too soon. How did . . . ?" There is a pause; then Loretta's voice comes out higher pitched, scared. "You didn't go to the airport and leave the car and take a taxi home in case you were followed?"

"I didn't need to do all that." Zack is bragging. "There was no one there but me when I picked up the money. That old lady paid attention. She didn't call in the cops."

"But you were supposed to . . ."

"Shut up," he says. "I'm feeling good, and I don't want you to nag me out of it. We got the money! That's what counts!"

I listen intently, my body ice-cold. Now what happens? What will they do to me?

I hear his voice close behind me. "Don't turn around, girl," he says, and I shiver. "You just stay where you are. Lean back in that chair and keep on watching TV. You do that, and nothing bad is going to happen to you."

There is no choice. I respond to what he has said, gripping the arms of the chair as though they were all I could cling to.

They move to the back of the room. I wonder if Loretta still has the gun in her hand. Part of my mind is clinging to the idea of escaping, but another, calmer part tells me to sit still, to do what they tell me, and soon I will be released. I really don't think they want to kill me. I hope I'm right. I clutch the arms of the chair.

Zack is talking in a low voice to Loretta, but I can hear bits of what he is saying. "There we are—the money is divided in half, and one of the halves is ours!"

I'm right! There *is* someone else involved! Will he come here for his share? Will I find out who he is?

"I want to go with you, not by myself!" Loretta's voice is a wail of fear.

He shushes her, and I can't hear what they are saying. This damn television program! Even with the volume turned low, the maniac contestants and the emcee seem to be having a contest to see who can scream the loudest.

My breathing is shallow. I am straining hard to hear Zack and Loretta, to find out anything and everything I can so that I can tell the police when I'm safe again. I'm determined that these people will be caught and that my grandmother will get her money back!

I am living in a little ball of a world, ears tuned to the far

70

wall behind me, eyes closed, trying to shut out any part of the intruding quiz show, nothing real to me except the lumpy springs in the chair and the rough plush upholstery that is scratching my arms and back. Then the world explodes around me.

There is a smashing noise at the front door! Voices are shouting! Footsteps bang down the hallway. My heart is banging too. There is a blackness of terror that is blotting out my vision. I hear Loretta scream, and it pulls me together.

"Police!" someone is shouting in a deep voice.

"Take this!" Loretta yells in my ear. There is a thump as the gun lands in my lap.

Instinctively I clutch it and stand, hanging on to the chair back. Loretta and Zack are not wearing ski masks. They are standing at the door, hands in the air. They are backing into the room. It's all unreal in a speeded-up film. I am terrified at the quick motion, the noise. What's happening?

Three uniformed policemen burst through the doorway. One of them waves a warrant. The other two push Zack and Loretta against the nearest wall and begin searching them.

One of them yells at me, "Drop it!"

I can only stare at him. My mouth opens, but nothing comes out.

"I said drop that gun! Now!" His voice is hard. He means business.

I realize for the first time that I still have Loretta's gun in my hand.

I want to tell the man who I am, what I am doing here, but I can only stare at the gun he is holding—the one he is pointing at me!

6

I find my voice. "What if it goes off?" I squeak. For some insane reason I think about an English teacher's remark that guns dropped on floors in all those TV police shows should by rights go off and hit someone.

A tall, muscular man in a beige checked sports coat the color of his hair enters the room. He doesn't look panicky. He looks at me reassuringly.

"Christina Lattimore?" he asks.

"Yes."

He walks toward me, holding up his badge. "Give me the gun, please," he says, and in one smooth motion reaches out for it. I put it into his hand. He looks at it, checks the safety, and tucks it into his belt.

"It's not my gun," I tell him, but he holds up a hand to silence me.

"I'd rather you didn't say anything until I read you your rights."

"But I . . ."

A look from him silences me. "All of you," he says, his gaze seeming to bore into Zack and Loretta, "pay attention. I'm Detective Jason York, and I'm going to read your rights to you." He takes a small blue plastic-covered card from his wallet and reads, "I want to advise you that you have the right to remain silent. Anything you say can and will be used against you in a court of law. You have the right to consult with a lawyer and . . ."

My mind turns off. I hear the words, yet at the same time I'm not hearing them. What is he doing? I'm the one who was kidnapped. Does he think I'm one of the criminals just because I was holding the gun Loretta threw in my lap? I don't understand what this is all about! He called me by name. Surely he knows I'm the victim here! He must know!

He has finished reading and is tucking the card back into his wallet. In the quick moment of silence I say, "What are you doing? I'm Christina Lattimore. These people kidnapped me!"

Zack has not looked at me, but now he whirls, his eyes wide and scared. The policeman next to him grabs his arm.

"I'm not taking the blame for a kidnapping!" Zack yells. "She worked this thing out to look like a kidnapping! She wanted to get the money from her grandmother! You saw her holding the gun!"

They are all staring at me, and I feel as though I were out of my body, standing aside and looking at a play someone wrote, something I know can't be real. Loretta glances at the money, still in two piles on the table, and begins to cry.

"I knew we'd get caught!" Loretta wails.

"Wait!" I gasp. "Please, listen to me! This isn't true! That man is lying!"

"Do you know these people?" Detective York asks me.

"Yes," I say. Then I realize how bad that sounds, and stumble over the words in my fright. "They work at a hamburger stand beside the Katy freeway, and I go there, and . . . That is, the man does. His name is Zack, and I met his wife on Friday, when she came over to my table to talk to me."

"What did she talk about?"

"Well, nothing. She really didn't say a word. I mean . . . I know it doesn't sound right, but that's the way it is. You have to believe me."

73

Loretta breaks in. "I didn't want any part of this! She talked Zack into it, and I had to go along! It's not right for her to get out of it now!"

"I don't believe this! It's not true!" I hear myself shouting, but I begin to cry so hard I can't talk. Someone takes me by the shoulders and leads me to a chair. He keeps his hands on my shoulders, and his firm grip is reassuring. The sobs turn into snuffles and hiccups and sighs. I'm glad when I find a tissue in my hand. Through it all I hear someone else come in and say, "Those damn TV crews have just poured out on the front lawn."

One of the policeman asks, "Is that guy from New York there? That one with the glasses?"

"Yeah," the man says. "He's sure been a pain in the butt." He clears his throat.

"I've seen him around your division," the policeman says. "Told my wife about him. You know he talks all the time just the way he talks on TV? Sure is funny, hearing anybody talk like that."

Detective York comes around to squat in front of my chair, and an older man with a mustache moves to stand beside him. His jacket reeks of cigarette smoke, and there is a large brown stain on two fingers of his right hand.

"This is my partner, Detective Bill Waller," Detective York says.

I find myself saying, "I'm pleased to meet you," while a hysterical voice inside my head is asking, "Do you have to be so stupidly polite under any circumstances?"

"Apparently we've got a few things to sort out here," Detective York tells me. "I think we might talk about it now, before we go downtown."

"I want to go home," I tell him. "I want my mother and father to know I'm all right."

"They know," he says. "Bill got in touch with someone downtown, who'll contact them."

74

"I want to go home," I repeat, sounding as though I were only five years old.

"Let's talk a moment," he says. "We've got two conflicting stories we need to discuss—especially since we found you with a gun in your hand."

I tense, but he touches my arm. "Calm down," he says. "No one's going to interrupt you. Just take a deep breath and tell us what happened."

So I start at the beginning, with seeing someone in front of me with a ski mask over her head. I know now that it was Loretta. I tell him about the basement and how Zack took me upstairs so I could clean up. It's hard to talk about. Sometimes my voice breaks, and sometimes Zack yells out something, but Detective York stops him.

Finally, I lean back in my chair and let out a long, shuddering breath. "And that's all, I guess."

"You've told us all you can remember?"

"I may remember something later. I don't know."

He stands up. "We'll have to ask for your story again when we get downtown."

"Then why did I have to tell you now?"

"Because we're at the scene here. There may be something you've said that we can check out quickly—something important."

Zack speaks up now. "I can tell you something!" he says. "That part about her staying in the basement! She's crazy! There's nothing like that down in the basement. We got a cot, but it's in a closet someplace. Go check it out, if you don't believe me."

Jason York nods toward one of the policemen in the doorway, and the man leaves. I am surprised to notice how many policemen are in the room. Why do they all need to be here?

"You said they both wore ski masks," he tells me.

"That's right. They look alike. They're black with a red stripe around the bottom."

75

Zack laughs at this, but it's a humorless laugh—one with cruelty in it. "Sure, I have a ski mask," he says. "But I've just the one. It's an old thing with some gloves to match. I used to wear it when I rode my motorcycle during cold weather. Haven't done that for a long time."

"Where is it?" Detective Waller asks him.

"I dunno," Zack says. He turns to Loretta. "Where'd you ever put that thing?"

"The last I seen of them, the gloves and cap were in the hall closet on the shelf," she says.

Waller leaves, and I turn to Detective York. "I can't believe this is happening. It's like a bad dream. It's a nightmare, and I want to wake up."

"Take it easy," he says. "We'll find out the truth. That's what we're trained to do."

The policeman returns. He shakes his head as he talks. "There was nothing down in that basement except an old table," he says. "No cot, no towels, nothing."

I jump to my feet. "That's impossible!" My heart is pounding so loudly it seems to be reverberating through the room. One of them . . ." I point to Loretta. "It was you, wasn't it, who sneaked down there when Zack brought me upstairs? You cleaned up and put things away!"

"Don't say that!" Loretta screams back at me. Her face is white. She's terrified.

"But she . . ." I realize I am tugging at Detective York's sleeve, shaking his arm up and down in my urgency.

He puts a restraining hand on my arm, and I turn as Bill Waller comes through the doorway. He is holding one ski mask. "This was in the closet," he says. "Just the one. I couldn't find a second one."

"Listen, please listen," I stammer. "They might have just used one. I only saw one of them at a time. Maybe they traded off the mask with each other." I know I must be right, but my reasoning sounds lame.

76

Zack stands there, grinning at me. "You aren't going to weasel out of this one and leave us to take all the blame."

"The money is divided into halves," Detective York says. "Can you give me a reason for that?"

"Because one half was for her," Zack says.

"No!" I shout. "There is a third person in this scheme. I know there is! But it isn't me! Zack isn't smart enough to think up this whole plan!"

"Yeah?" Zack says, eyes glittering. "Then who is this third person?"

My legs suddenly feel so weak I have to sit down. I flop into the nearest chair and lean back in it. "I don't know," I whisper.

"See, what'd I tell you!" Zack crows.

"There *is* a third person," I repeat. "There has to be."

"We can take them downtown now," Detective York says to his partner. "Will you call the mobile crime lab? We'll need fingerprints, and so forth."

"Fingerprints?" I sit upright like a coiled spring that has been sprung. "My fingerprints are all over the house! Zack made me turn on light switches and touch glasses and furniture and all that! He *made* me do it!"

No one answers me. Zack merely gloats. Loretta stares at the wall, fingers knotted together so tightly that her knuckles look like bleached knobs of flesh.

Detective York issues instructions, and two of the policemen leave with Zack and Loretta. York gives Loretta's gun to his partner, who goes out to meet the crime lab. He holds out a hand to me, and I take it, grateful for the support. It's incredible how difficult it is to get up from the chair.

I look into Detective York's eyes as though I could discover what he is thinking, but his thoughts are closed. I am all alone.

"Zack and Loretta are lying," I tell him. "Somebody has to believe me!"

77

He nods slowly. He is a slow-moving, quiet man. Everything he does seems deliberate. "Think hard, Christina. Is there anything else you can tell me that might help prove your innocence?"

I try to think, but my mind is a jumble of thoughts, none of them even remotely connected. Through it all comes the whimper, "I want my mother." I'm glad I can keep it inside, to myself. What would he think of me?

"I don't know," I whisper.

"Let's go down to the basement," York tells me. "Maybe if we're there, your memory will pick up something that's important. It sometimes happens like that."

There is still a touch of doubt in his voice. I can't miss it. He is doing everything he can to help me, but he doesn't quite believe me.

I lead the way to the basement and down the stairs. The rough board railing seems more rickety than ever. "Over there . . ." I point to a spot against the wall. "That's where the cot was, and a small table too."

"What did you do when you were down here?"

"I sat on the cot, or I exercised. Zack brought me a book, because I asked him to. It's the only book they had in the house, I guess."

"What kind of book?"

"One of those Gothic romances."

"What was the name?"

I can only stare at him, my mind refusing to work. "I have no idea. I couldn't keep my mind on the story. I can't even tell you what it was about."

"Did you try to get out of this basement?"

"Oh, yes!" I tell him. "You see, I figured out who the man was, but I couldn't let him know that I knew, because I was afraid he would kill me. But I recognized his voice. Then I found out by accident, when I was examining that old furnace over there, that I could hear Zack and Loretta when they were talking in the kitchen. Their voices were carried through one of the register vents and amplified inside the heater. So I listened and . . ."

I stop. It's coming back in a rush, and I'm eager to tell him, but I want to choose my words carefully so it doesn't sound as though I'm just babbling.

"And what?" he asks.

"Loretta was scared. She told Zack that she was afraid they would be caught, and he told her it was fixed so that if they were unlucky enough not to get away with the money, they wouldn't be charged with kidnapping."

"Did he say how this was going to be accomplished?"

"No. That's all he told her. But I know there is someone else involved. Loretta said something about Zack being talked into another crazy scheme, but he said this one was foolproof. Doesn't that sound as though someone else planned it for them?"

He doesn't respond to my question. He merely says, "You were going to tell me about trying to get out."

"Oh . . . of course. The heater. I took off the latch. The screw was old, and I could take it out with my fingers. And I took the latch and waited until it was late and I thought they would be asleep. It was last night."

"What time?"

"I don't know. My watch stopped."

"It's broken?"

I automatically look at my watch. I remember that after my bath Loretta gave it to me, and I put it on without thinking. Force of habit. It's running.

He takes my arm, turning it so that he can look at the face of the watch. "I see that you've reset it."

"No. I didn't. Someone else must have. I don't know . . ." Everything I say sounds like such a dumb excuse—the kind of story little children make up when they're accused of getting into their mother's face powder, or stealing cookies, and they think they can wish the whole episode away.

"When they took me upstairs so I could clean up, they must have set my watch, and . . ." Tears come to my eyes again. What's the matter with me? I rarely cry. I hate to cry. And here I am, spending most of the time sobbing like a dumbbell instead of trying to tell this detective what happened.

I take a deep breath and wipe away the tears with the back of my hands. "I'll get to that part later," I say. "Right now I'll tell you about the latch. I got it loose and went up the stairs over there and tried to chip away at the door latch. It was hard to do in the dark; and the latch was clumsy and not sharp enough, and it didn't do any good."

"That's it?"

"There was no way out. I just came back to the cot and finally went to sleep."

"Let's go upstairs," he tells me. This time he goes ahead of me and stops at the top of the stairs to examine the doorframe.

I watch him, holding my breath, as he stops and picks up a couple of flakes of paint. He pulls out a handkerchief and folds them into it.

"You see!" I am almost shouting, and I try to get myself under control.

"I see that something has chipped away at the paint here," he says. "Where is this latch now?"

"In my sweater pocket. I took it off and . . ."

There is a long pause, and he asks, "Where is the sweater?"

"I don't know. The clothes I took off weren't on the floor where I threw them when I came out of the bathtub." Quickly I tell him what happened when Zack led me around the house and Loretta came in with the gun while I took my bath. Men are moving around. Through the partially open doorway to the kitchen I can see someone working on the kitchen cabinets. I've watched enough detective programs on television to know that he is dusting for fingerprints.

"Could they get my fingerprints from the furnace too, please?" I ask Detective York.

"Of course," he says. He motions me into the kitchen and says, "Charlie, when you're finished there, could you pick up some prints from the furnace down there—around the door especially?"

"Sure," the man called Charlie says. He looks at me speculatively. I guess everyone has heard by now what I'm accused of. Again I feel close to panic, but I fight back the terror.

"Show me the room you say they took you to," York tells me.

So we go up the stairs and to the first bedroom on the right. It's as neat as it was before, with my things still on the dresser. The dirty clothes aren't in sight.

"Maybe she put them into a hamper somewhere," I say.

"What does your sweater look like?" he asks me, and I tell him.

Detective York goes to the door and calls to a policeman at the foot of the stairs. He tells him to look for the sweater. The policeman calls back to him that they found a folding cot behind some boxes in the closet under the stairs.

"Is there anything else you've thought of that you can tell me?" he asks when he returns.

I try to think, but I'm only aware of the fact that the house has the clinging odors of stale cooking, that somewhere outside the window is a murmuring of voices that rise and fall, out of rhythm and out of harmony with each other. Footsteps plod through the rooms. It's all part of another world—not this one I'm trapped in.

"Did you overhear Zack and Loretta say anything else?"

"The first time I heard them, he was complaining about her ironing all the time. She irons everything. She even irons the sheets and towels. It's funny. Ironing the sheets makes them smell cleaner. I don't know why. It's just that I noticed it with the sheets on the basement cot where I slept."

"You didn't sleep in this bed at all?"

"No." The thought hits me. "No! I didn't! And the sheets

will prove it! Those muslin sheets get wrinkled when they're used. I can show you that these haven't been used at all!"

I get to the bed in two long strides and throw back the spread, blanket, and top sheet in one wide swoop. The sheets are perfectly smooth, with the fold lines still in them. I jump up and down like a little child, grabbing Detective York's shoulder. "You see!" I am shouting and laughing at the same time.

He puts an arm around my shoulders and says, "Calm down. It's not much to go on."

"Why? What are you talking about? It proves what I've been telling you, doesn't it?"

"It proves only one thing—that the bed is freshly made."

A policeman comes to the door, holding out a white sweater. It's mine, but it's damp.

"I found this in the washing machine," he says. "There were a bunch of things in the machine—all still wet. They haven't got a dryer—just a clothesline in the backyard."

"This is your sweater?" York asks me.

I nod. "The latch is in the pocket."

"Nothing in these pockets," the policeman says.

"Then maybe it fell into the washing machine. It's got to be someplace in there!"

"What else was in the washing machine?" Detective York asks.

"A few odds and ends of girls' clothes, a couple of sheets, and some towels."

"The things from the basement!" I say.

"Look around for a piece of metal latch," Detective York tells the policeman. "And before you go down, check the other beds upstairs. See if the sheets are wrinkled—if they've been slept in." He comes back to me. "I think it's about time we went downtown. Your parents will probably be waiting for you at the station."

I gulp. I want so much to see my mother. I'll never be able

to tell her my thoughts about her, but I feel a lot closer to her than I have ever felt before. And I want to see my grandmother to tell her I'm sorry this happened to her, that I had no part in it, and I'm glad Zack and Loretta were caught. And I want to see my father.

The policeman pokes his head back in the doorway. "Double bed in the front room was slept in. That's all."

"Doesn't that prove I'm telling the truth?" I gasp.

"It's not enough to hang a case on," Detective York says. "Come with me."

He stops to talk to some people at the foot of the stairs, then leads me through the front door. I have seen the people on the lawn without realizing we'd come into contact with each other. Suddenly they are thrusting themselves into my world, and the hubbub frightens me.

In the forefront is a face I recognize. I've watched this man on national television. It occurs to me in a split second that this is the man the policeman was talking about, and now he is shoving something into my face and talking to me.

Instinctively I stop and stare back at him.

"Miss Lattimore," he is shouting into the microphone in his resonant voice that seems to be straight out of diction school, "we were informed that you were kidnapped. Then a few moments ago we were told by two of the people being brought out of this house that you had masterminded a scheme to defraud your grandmother. Would you care to comment on this?"

Detective York takes my arm. "One side, please," he says. "Miss Lattimore doesn't need to answer your questions."

Behind the newscaster I see an extra-tall boy with freckles splattered on his face, and his red hair looks as though it put up a good fight against a comb. He has the network camera on his shoulder, and stumbles as he moves in closer. He quickly catches his balance, throwing a fast look at the newscaster, who doesn't notice.

The newscaster is too intent on getting an answer from me.

While news people from the other TV stations are crowding around, this man is more insistent than anyone else. Again he shoves that microphone into my face and shouts, "How do you feel about being in this situation?"

It's too much to take. I stop and face him. "You ask that same stupid question of everybody! Of everybody! How can I answer it? I can't! I haven't done anything wrong, and I haven't got any reason to answer your questions, and if you don't get out of my way, I'm going to sock you!"

For a moment he looks as though he has gone into shock. Then he whirls and yells, "Kelly! Back to the car!" But Kelly is standing there, camera still on, with a huge grin that makes me glad I said what I did.

Now Detective York has my arm and is propelling me through the crowd, toward his car. I haven't got time to think about the newscaster—or Kelly. Detective Waller is standing by the car. I get inside, moving quickly, and lean against the back seat, my eyes closed. I can't believe this is happening to me. Who made up this insane play and cast me in it? Was it Zack? It couldn't be Zack or Loretta. Who is this third person the police should find? I want to go home!

They take me to the downtown station, a large building covered with slabs of beige stone trimmed in highly polished red granite. It's not an attractive building, especially in back. We get into an elevator. The light-green paint is badly scarred and scratched. A short, fat woman in a faded cotton dress peers at me from a corner. A thin man in front of her wipes the sleeve of his plaid shirt across his forehead and stares straight ahead, shoulders drooping, despair in his eyes. Where is he going? What is making him so unhappy? Why should I be thinking about him? What am I going to do about my own problem?

At the third floor we get off the elevator and step into a corridor, making a sharp turn to the right. The shiny gray tiles on the walls and the speckled tan squares on the floor combine to create a drab, ugly atmosphere. No wonder the man

84

looked so hopeless. We go past a long wooden bench that could have come from an old church, and past a double gumball machine, and through a door marked "Homicide Division" on its glass window.

I look around the room eagerly, but there are only a few men in the room, some of them seated at the gray metal desks, one typing, and one using a green phone. The walls are lined with gray metal filing cabinets that stretch from door to door and from window to window, taking every available inch of space.

I touch Detective York's arm. "My parents?" I ask.

Without answering, he moves away to talk to the man seated at a nearby desk. Detective Waller sits at another desk and begins to type hurriedly on some crisp sheets of paper.

York comes back to my side and says, "Just come with me, and we'll get some of the preliminaries out of the way."

"What preliminaries?" I ask him, but he doesn't answer until we are inside a small room. He flips on a switch, and two long bars of fluorescent light flicker and catch. There are four green vinyl-and-chrome chairs opposite another of the metal desks, an identical chair next to the desk, and one behind it. He motions me to the nearest chair, and I sit down. He sits behind the desk.

I repeat my question. "What preliminaries?"

He picks up a pad and a pen and looks into my eyes. "This is called a hold card," he says.

I'm reading the card upside down. "That says, 'Arrest Authorization'! You're going to arrest me?"

"Calm down," he says. "This is just a formality."

"What kind of formality? First you read me my rights, and then you fill out an arrest authorization! What are you doing to me? I thought I showed you that I was telling the truth!"

He leans back in his chair. "Christina, it's my job to gather the facts in any case I'm on. I don't make the judgments. I present enough facts to the district attorney to help him make a case against the actor involved."

"Actor?"

85

"Our name for someone we've picked up for a crime—the person under suspicion."

"I'm under suspicion?"

"According to what Zack and Loretta Tigus said, you are under suspicion for the crime of extortion."

"But . . ."

"That doesn't mean you're guilty. You should know that from your government class in school. It just means that you are suspect."

"What about the things I told you about their kidnapping me?"

"Zack and Loretta Tigus are suspect too—at the moment for the crime of extortion. They've already been interrogated and are being booked."

"They're in jail?"

"Not yet. They're probably in the identification office right now, getting photographed and fingerprinted. Then they'll go to twenty-four-hour court and either be assigned to the county jail or be set free on bail."

"My God!" I am half out of my chair. "And all this is going to happen to me?"

I am gripping the edge of his desk, and he reaches over to cover my hands with one of his. "Take it easy," he says. "We aren't here to make it hard for you. We want to help find the truth."

"The truth is that the district attorney should bring those two horrible people to trial for kidnapping me!"

"You're a bright girl," he says. "Look at our evidence. We've got your word against theirs. We've got a couple of paint flakes from a door, and so far no sign of the latch you used to make the paint chip. We have a pair of unused sheets, but no telling when the bed was changed. No real proof."

"But Zack and Loretta have no proof either."

"Zack claims to have some witnesses in the hamburger place who saw you three planning together."

I have a mental flash of those men turning to stare at me.

I can see the afternoon sun patterns across the wall. I can smell the heavy grease and the pungent, sizzling onions, just as it happened.

"But I didn't plan anything with them. I mean, Zack made it look like that, but it wasn't!"

I remember something. "Did Della tell you about the woman who was at the house? About the tape on the door?"

"Yes," he says. "She told us about that right away, but she couldn't remember what the woman looked like, and she said she didn't see any tape."

"Somebody stole my clothes from the house!"

Detective Waller comes into the room and shuts the door. He looks down at me sternly and stares at me while he's talking to Detective York. "They traced the serial number of the gun Christina was holding. The gun belongs to her father."

I think I might faint. What happens when everything begins to come and go, and voices drone into the buzzing of bees, and dark plays with light? I feel something cold and hard touching my lips. I try to turn my head away, but a large hand has a grip on the back of my neck.

"Drink this," he says, and I obey.

Slowly the room settles down. I lean back in the chair, trying to breathe.

"Put your head between your knees," York orders. He holds my shoulders down.

I murmur in a strangled voice, "Let me up. I'm all right now."

His hand moves away, and I sit up in the chair. My hands are trembling, and I can't feel my toes, but I must tell him something. "That's what the woman stole when she was in our house! We looked for obvious things, but none of us thought of looking for the gun. My father keeps it in his desk drawer, but I don't think he has ever used it!"

Detective Waller's eyes are still on me. "You think she'll be okay now?" he asks his partner.

"Sure. Go ahead," York says, so Waller leaves.

"I'm telling the truth," I say. It's the only thing I can think of. "Please believe me."

"Christina," he says, "I promise you that I'll do my best to find out the truth in this case."

"Then it's okay," I say. "Because my story is the truth."

Waller opens the door. "Someone here to see Christina."

I jump to my feet and whirl toward the door. My arms are already lifted, ready to run to my mother's arms, but I freeze, as though in slow motion, and lower my arms gradually. A portly man, in a suit that's obviously Neiman Marcus, stands in the doorway. He doesn't smile at me. He doesn't even look at me. He talks to Detective York as though I didn't exist.

"Thank you for allowing me to be present," he says. He moves into the room, shuts the door, and places a pale fur-felt Stetson on the desk. I am entranced with the gold buckle on the side of the hat band. I know real gold when I see it.

"Mr. Hennington," Detective York says, rising. "I'm pleased to see you again."

I recognize the name—Jules Hennington. He's one of the most famous attorneys in the United States, a Houston celebrity.

They go into a few minutes of talk about cases during which they've met before, while I want to scream. Where are my parents?

Finally Mr. Hennington says, "Cristabel Lattimore is my client. On her behalf I am here to talk to you about her granddaughter."

"My grandmother? Where is she?"

He glances at me appraisingly, as though I were an unfriendly witness. "Sit down, please, Miss Lattimore."

I do as he tells me. But I must know. In a tiny voice I ask, "Please tell me. Where are my parents? I thought they would be here by now."

I've seen people look at a dead cat in the street with more interest than he shows when he looks at me now. Under the smooth polish his words are chilling. "Be reasonable, Miss Lattimore. Your parents and grandmother were apprised of the facts concerning this alleged extortion attempt. On my advice they are remaining at home. Their arrival at police headquarters would simply lead to even more damaging publicity."

I am having trouble absorbing what he is telling me. "Not even my mother? My mother isn't coming here to be with me?"

"I said," he repeats in a no-nonsense voice, "they aren't coming."

1

I can see how this man got his reputation for commanding juries. He seems to grow another foot in height as he stares at me, and the firmness of his tone forces me to cringe back into my chair and keep my mouth shut, though I want desperately to question him.

Mr. Hennington, apparently satisfied that I won't irritate him further, turns to Detective York. "My client, Mrs. Lattimore, phoned me immediately when she was apprised of the situation." He looks at his watch, and I look too, hypnotized.

"I left a very important political dinner at the River Oaks Country Club," he says. "I'd like this to be taken care of as quickly as possible. In short, Mrs. Lattimore is withdrawing charges against her granddaughter, and Zack and Loretta Tigus."

"Charges?" I can't help gasping out the word.

Detective York doesn't look at me either. "The charge of extortion?"

"Of course," Mr. Hennington says.

"Miss Lattimore claims she was kidnapped," Detective York says.

"We have no time for that nonsense." Mr. Hennington gives a peremptory wave of one hand.

"I'm inclined to believe we should check out her story."

"Mr. Hennington looks at me sharply and back to Detective York. "On what evidence?"

Detective York slowly sits down again, swiveling his chair around and leaning back before he answers. "At the moment we have very little to go on, but that's what our business is all about—detecting, investigating, uncovering the evidence."

"I have already spoken to the district attorney," Mr. Hennington says. He picks up his hat, dusting it lightly where it has touched the desk top. "You can verify what I have told you with a quick phone call."

Detective York gets to his feet. He seems angry, and his voice becomes a little quieter. My mind is going in crazy waves and strange patterns. I am afraid to ask this attorney questions, because I can't put them into words. I'm terrified that if I open my mouth to speak, I'll wail like a baby instead, so I'm awfully glad when Detective York speaks for me.

"Do you and your client realize that the media are on top of this in a big way? That they have the story now from Zack and Loretta that Christina was not kidnapped, but planned this venture to get hold of her grandmother's money? You want things to hang at this point?"

"It is precisely because of this unfortunate publicity in the news media that we want this situation to be ended as quickly as possible." Mr. Hennington's voice is formal. "Miss Lattimore should be grateful that her grandmother is not pressing charges."

I jump up. This is too much to take. "You actually believe that I was involved in this! You do!" I am shouting, and my whole body is trembling, but I can't stop. "I keep trying to tell everyone! I was kidnapped! I was kept in a basement! Why can't you believe me?"

He ignores what I say. "One of my assistants is preparing the necessary papers," he tells Detective York. "I'll arrange to take her home to her parents before I return to my dinner meeting." He looks at his watch again.

"No!" I shout. I want to say more, but Detective York, in

91

one smooth movement, is around the side of the desk and is gripping my shoulder.

He speaks to Mr. Hennington, and his voice is tight. "I don't think you'd care to wait until all the paperwork is done. I'll take the responsibility of getting Miss Lattimore home safely."

There is one instant in which I can see the hesitation in Mr. Hennington's eyes. Then he nods. "That will be satisfactory," he says. "Thank you."

As he brushes past me, I say, "If someone would just pay attention to my side of this whole thing . . ." But again he ignores me.

Detective York shuts the door and turns toward me.

"I hate that man!" I explode. "And I hate my grandmother! Why would she do this to me?"

"Sometimes it's easier not to try to understand people," he says.

"But she must know what people will think about me! Who's going to believe me?"

"Your friends will believe you."

"Do you really think so?"

He pats my shoulder awkwardly. "You're in a tough situation, Christina. I think you've got enough guts to live through it. And I'll do what I can to help."

He goes around the desk and picks up the phone, punching the numbers with a big finger.

"You mean you'll keep investigating?"

"Whatever I can. You realize that this isn't my only case? That I handle a dozen or more cases a week?"

"Do you solve them all?"

"Not by a long shot. They only do that in the movies."

He begins to talk to someone, and I sit on the edge of the chair, waiting, my back feeling as though a wooden coat hanger has been shoved along my backbone to hold it together.

When he hangs up, he shrugs. "I said I'll do what I can. I

92

don't know how much that will be. That's all I can promise you."

"I don't want to go home," I tell him. "I want you to put me in jail. I want to go to court and make people realize that Zack and Loretta are lying!"

He sits opposite me and leans forward on the desk. "Look, Christina, in the first place we haven't got enough evidence on those two on a kidnapping charge to arrest them. They had to be booked on the extortion charge. The district attorney has to have real evidence in order to prosecute them on a kidnapping charge, and to be brutally honest with you, the evidence is too slim to build a case. It comes down to your word against theirs."

"But the ransom note. I deliberately misspelled my name. That must prove something."

"It only proves that a note was sent. On the witness stand Zack and Loretta would say you had misspelled your name to make it look like a real kidnapping." He leans back in his chair again and adds, "The DA won't prosecute on this extortion thing if his plaintiff backs out. He can't waste the time or money on a case he's bound to lose."

"My grandmother is the plaintiff?"

"It's her money that was taken. Yes, she's the plaintiff—or was. Now the case is thrown out, and it's all over except taking you home."

"It's all over for everyone but me."

He nods.

"When does my nightmare end?"

Detective York stands up, and I stand too. The room seems smaller than before, and too warm, so that my back has become sticky damp against the slick vinyl chair.

"I think it's going to be up to you when the nightmare is over," he says. "Some people have nightmares that never end. But you—I think you'll make it through yours. It will just take time."

"And you'll help me."

"Whatever I can do. It won't be much."

I can't answer. All of a sudden I'm terribly tired, too tired to talk. "Can we leave now?"

I turn toward the doorway. I'm so tired, and all I want is to go home. My mother will believe me. If I cling to this thought, I'll be all right.

We go through the homicide room. Detective Waller says, "The press is downstairs by the elevator. I sent word not to let them come up here."

"Thanks," Detective York says. "We'll take the back stairs."

He doesn't tell his partner that he's taking me home. I guess he doesn't need to. They seem to work together like two people who have known each other for a long time. Maybe they read each other's minds.

He takes my arm and hurries me through the stairwell, where voices echo in hollow shouts from unseen places, bouncing against the bleak walls. Soon we are outside, through the parking lot, and in his car. No one has followed us.

On the drive home he tries to talk to me, but it's too much effort to answer. Part of my mind doesn't believe what is happening to me, and the other part is staring into a long, dark tunnel and wants to scream it open. Nothing else registers.

The car swings into the drive in front of my home. I'm acutely aware of the look of my home in the twilight shadows, as though my sense of sight has outdistanced the others. It's as though I were seeing my home after a long, long time. In a way I'm surprised that it looks the same as it always has. A fat squirrel skims the drive in front of the car in a brown flash, and I am jolted back to a sense of normalcy—whatever that has been for me.

Detective York parks the car in front of the veranda.

"Thanks," I say, reaching out to open the door.

He offers me a smile, and I accept it as something to cling to. "Not so fast," he says. "I'm coming inside with you."

"Will my parents be there?" Maybe he knows. After all that has happened to me, I don't know.

"Yes," he says. "They've been waiting for you."

"How do you know all these things?"

"Our office was in contact with them by telephone. Surely you teen-agers know what telephones are?"

I know he's trying to cheer me up, but I am not ready for cheerfulness. I open the door on my side of the car and climb out, leading the way up the steps. I see a flutter of the curtain in one of the front windows, and before I can reach the door, it is thrown open. My mother rushes out, her arms opened wide to me.

Everything spills over. I run to my mother, hugging her, feeling her arms wrap around me like protective padding to shut out the world, to keep all harm away from me. We are both crying and hugging, with nothing to stop us. Oh, Mother, Mother, Mother. I'm so glad you're here!

As though our energies are blended together, as one we shut off the tears, sniffing, holding each other tightly, fumbling for tissues. We stand back, looking at each other. My mother is still gripping my shoulders as though she would never let me go.

"Oh, Mother," I sigh. "I'm so glad to be home again."

A look of pain twists her face as it passes like a swell in the ocean. "Oh, Christina," she says, "you foolish, foolish girl! Why did you do it?"

I am numb. I can only stare at her. When I manage to speak, my voice comes out in a croak. "I was kidnapped. Don't you believe me?"

"But they told us . . ."

"Don't you know me, Mother?" Anger is bringing back my strength. "Don't you know I wouldn't do anything to hurt Cristabel?"

Her hands flutter to her face. "Christina, I was only going by what the police told us—that those . . . people . . .

95

whom they arrested said you had planned everything. That's even the way it's been told on the television news."

"But I was sure my own mother would believe me!" It's growing dark quickly, and I hear a tree frog's guttural, rhythmic mating call. The air is damp with a musty, cloying odor.

Detective York steps to my side, and I realize he has been patiently waiting at the bottom of the veranda steps. He introduces himself to my mother and says, "May we go inside, please? I'd like to talk to you."

"Of course, of course," my mother stammers. She leads the way, then steps behind us to close the door. I walk resolutely into the living room, where I know my father will be waiting. Once, when I was in the fifth grade, I was accidentally hit in the stomach with a baseball bat and lost my breath. It was an awful experience, so terrible that I can still remember how it felt. I feel the same way now.

He comes to meet me. He quickly bends his head down against mine, wrapping me in a smothering hug. But I have seen the tears in his eyes.

"We're glad to have you home again, Christina," he says.

Rosella's head is bobbing up and down like the head on a little wind-up toy. "I couldn't leave until I knew you were safely home," she tells me. "I canceled my trip."

"We prayed for your safe return," my father says. He stands back and looks at me. They are all looking at me.

"Thank you," I say. "Now will you please pray that I'll be able to prove my innocence?"

I don't think he hears me. It's as though he had worked out in advance what he is going to say. "Christina, we'll have a long talk about this situation. It's important that you make peace with your grandmother."

I have my mouth open to reply when once again I feel a strong hand pressing down on my shoulder. Detective York steps to my side.

"I think that first I had better speak my piece," he says.

"I'm Detective York and am in charge—*was* in charge—of this case before Mrs. Lattimore dropped the charges."

My father is gracious, and my mother remembers her manners. Soon we are all seated in the living room, and Detective York has turned down a polite offer of coffee or tea.

"I'm sorry that the case was closed so quickly," he tells them. "As it stands now, we have only Christina's word against the word of Zack and Loretta Tigus. If we had been allowed to dig into things, maybe my partner and I could have come up with something that would have helped to clear Christina's name."

"I don't know what to say." My father looks helpless, almost frightened. "My mother feels it's better to let the matter die down as quickly as possible. She feels this is a source of great embarrassment."

"Good God!" I explode. "I'm kidnapped and held in a cold basement, scared to death, and you say it's a source of embarrassment! What kind of father are you?"

He looks at me sadly. "Christina, please don't take the name of the Lord in vain."

There's a funny expression on Rosella's face, as though she wished she could laugh aloud, but as she sees me watching her, she quickly stares at the floor.

My mother moves to perch on the sofa beside me and pats my arm. "You're exhausted, dear. In the morning things will look much, much better. Right now it's like a bad dream, but a good night's sleep will help. Maybe your father could talk to Cristabel."

"Tomorrow the Houston *Post* will have the story," my father says. "Tonight there was just a bare mention in the *Chronicle* because of the timing, I suppose. Naturally, it was on the front page. There is no way to stop the journalists from printing the story."

Della comes to the doorway. "Mr. Lattimore, there's a reporter on the phone, and he . . ." She stops, staring at me.

Then a wide smile creases her chubby face. "Christina! Nobody told me you were here already! I'm so glad to see you back home again! We was worried to death!"

"Thank you, Della," I say.

"Tell the reporter we are not available," my father says. Della leaves, heading back to the telephone.

Detective York speaks up. "This is a difficult time for all of you, I understand," he says. "I'd like to go over the facts as we know them, to help you get a fuller picture of what happened to your daughter."

"Oh dear! I'm not sure I want to go through all that." My mother sighs.

"Please listen," I ask them.

There is silence, and Detective York takes the initiative. He goes over what I told him and what Zack and Loretta said. He tells them about the missing latch to the furnace, and the paint chipped at the door to the basement. He even tells them about the unused, freshly ironed sheets. Finally he pauses.

"But they had already divided the money into two parcels," my father says. "Why would they do that if Christina weren't to get her share?"

"Because there was someone else involved! Someone who planned it for them!" I say.

I look around the room. Rosella has a little crease of indecision between her eyes. My mother looks as though she wants to burst into tears again. My father is frowning. Della is standing in the doorway, and her face is deliberately blank. They are trying to reconcile the information we have given them with what they were told before.

Detective York gets slowly to his feet. "Our police department is badly understaffed. We don't have nearly enough detectives for a city of this size, and I'm always working under an overload of cases. I would like to help Christina, and maybe I will be able to turn up something. We never know when an informer from one case will lead us back to another case with

98

vital information. However, I'd like to suggest that if you want to help your daughter prove her innocence, you hire a private investigator who can do justice to the job. I can give you a couple of names to call."

"Oh," my mother says. "We could do that, couldn't we?" She keeps her eyes on my father's face.

"I—I think we'd better discuss this with my mother," my father says. He rises and leads the way toward the front hallway. "I appreciate your suggestion, but my mother expressly stated that it would be better to let this affair die down as quickly as possible."

Detective York's glance at me is one of pity. I smile at him and walk to his side. "May I have your card, please? I'll want to know where to get in touch with you. Because I'm not going to give up on this, not even if I have to do the detective work myself."

"I'd advise against it," he says. "You don't know how dangerous it can be working with people of this type." But he gives me his card.

Detective York turns to my father. "I understand that you do a lot of preaching."

My father perks up. "Yes," he says. "Perhaps you've been to one of my seminars?"

"No," York says, shaking his head. "I'm afraid that with my hours I don't have time for things like that."

"We can always find time to discover the word of the Lord."

Detective York nods. "I'm familiar with the Bible. As a matter of fact, I'm thinking of an apt quotation right now."

"And what is that?"

He looks my father straight in the eyes as though he would bore through to the brain if he could. "Judge not, that ye be not judged," he says. Then he turns and marches through the hallway. I hear the front door close firmly.

Della gives a snuffled snort and scurries off toward the

99

kitchen. Rosella whispers, "I'll check those papers in the office," and disappears. My mother bustles around, plumping pillows and trying to pretend she hasn't heard.

I say to my father, noting that his face has reddened, "Detective York could have given me a quotation too. One on forgiveness. I know I should forgive you, but right now I can't. I can't forgive you for not believing in me enough to want to help me."

I follow the path Della took toward the kitchen, but my father says, "Where are you going? There are still things to talk about."

"Not now, Daddy," I say. "Nobody asked me if I was hungry, and I haven't had anything to eat for most of the day."

"Oh, darling," my mother says. "I didn't think! Let me get something for you."

"I'd rather get it myself, Mother. You stay here. Daddy needs you to talk to him."

It's the first time I've ever seen anyone challenge my father. I suppose there's never been anything to challenge him about. In a way I'm delighted with Detective York for saying what he did, and in a way I'm sorry for my father, because without his façade of religion he's like a toy balloon with the air let out, that fizzles around until it lies flat and useless.

I am halfway to the kitchen when the doorbell rings, and rings again. I hear voices and my father's angry, firm voice answering that I will not speak to the press under any conditions. Oh, Daddy, why can't you say, "because our daughter is innocent of those charges!"?

Della has left the kitchen. Maybe she's gone home by now. I'm hungry and want to eat something, but now I can't. A large fist inside my throat is squeezing, and a fire is burning behind my eyelids. The pain is too much to take. For a long time I sit motionless in the darkness at the kitchen table, trying to live with it.

The light footsteps tap up behind me. Rosella whispers, "Christina, there is a boy here to see you. He says he's a friend."

"I don't know any boys," I tell her. "What's his name?"

"T. J. Kelly, he says."

I frown in concentration. "I don't know a Kelly."

"Shall I tell him to go away?"

I shake my head. "No," I say. "I'll find out what he wants. Where are Mother and Daddy?"

"In your father's office. They're on the phone with Cristabel. Your mother wants to give you a chance to relax and eat in peace. Then they'll probably want to talk to you." She looks at the bare table. "But you haven't eaten anything."

"I can't yet," I say.

"Della's left for the day," she says, "so I let this Kelly in, and he's waiting for you in the living room."

"Thanks, Rosella."

She moves away hesitantly, tossing me quick, birdlike glances over her shoulder. I stand up, steady myself, and go to the living room to see who and what this "Kelly" is all about.

As I come to the doorway, he turns, and an elbow hits a crystal vase, sending it spinning. Kelly neatly catches it in time and rights it on the table. Then he grins at me. "Hi," he says. "I don't think you'll remember me. I'm T. J. Kelly."

I remember him all right. With that wild red hair and all those freckles, such a tall guy would stand out in any crowd. But when I saw him he was behind a camera.

I take a step backward. "Oh, no. You told Rosella you were my friend, but you came to get an interview. Right?"

"Wrong. I'm just a sophomore at the University of Houston, majoring in communications and manning a camera part time to help pay my tuition. I'm not a reporter."

"Then why did you come?"

"For a couple of reasons," Kelly says. "I wanted to thank you for telling off that New York transplant who thinks he knows all there is to know about television newscasting. It was

101

time someone put him in his place. Working for him is a real pain."

"I don't ever want to see that man again."

"You won't have to."

"Well, look," I say. I can feel Rosella listening in the doorway. I should have known someone would be keeping an eye on me. "Would you like a sandwich or something?"

He holds up a hand. "Wait a minute. I didn't finish telling you the reason why I came to see you."

I just look at him, waiting to hear what he's going to say.

"I came to tell you," Kelly says, "that I believe you."

8

As my mind finally registers what Kelly has told me, my last defenses crumble. "Then you're the only one," I whisper. "You're the only one who really believes me."

I don't want to cry again, but there's nothing I can do to stop it. I cover my face with my hands and sob. I feel Kelly put his arms gingerly around my shoulders and hold me, as though he's used to breaking things and wants to be very careful. I lean against his chest until the tears dry up. I find I am using a handkerchief that smells something like gasoline, but I don't mind.

"Kelly . . ." I mumble.

"Blow your nose, so you'll stop sniffling," Kelly says.

I do as he tells me. "I'm sorry I cried," I say, embarrassed. I know my eyes are red and puffy and I must look a mess.

"It's okay," Kelly says. "I've got four sisters. I've seen girls cry a lot."

I can't help giggling, and I realize it's the first time I've laughed in a long, long time. It's been days, but it feels like years.

I take Kelly out to the kitchen and fix us some ham sandwiches. Kelly likes mustard and lots of pickle relish in his, so I make mine that way too. With big glasses of milk, they taste better than anything I've ever eaten. Maybe it's just that I'm glad I want to eat again.

"If you weren't so skinny," Kelly says, wiping pickle juice off his shirt, "you'd really be good-looking."

I think about that a moment. "Is that supposed to be a compliment?"

"No," Kelly says.

"Then what?"

"It's okay," Kelly says, taking a long gulp of milk. "If you were really good-looking I wouldn't be here. Fantastic-looking girls scare me."

I start to giggle again. "You're kind of skinny yourself, you know."

"I know," he says. "It's because I grew so fast. I'm still growing, too. It makes it hard to get clothes on sale. Not many stores carry extra-longs."

He munches contentedly on his last sandwich, and I say, "Kelly, could I tell you what happened?"

"I want you to," he says.

So I go into the whole thing, right up to Detective York's leaving our house. I leave out what he said to my father.

Kelly nods, wipes his mouth with a paper napkin, and says, "Where do we start?"

"We? You mean you want to help me?"

"Why not?"

"Why? Well, because you don't really know me."

"When you came out of that house, you looked scared to death, the way a victim looks. People who are caught breaking laws look scared too, but in a different way, a kind of defiant way."

"I'm still scared."

"It's going to be okay," Kelly says.

"Detective York wanted my parents to hire a private investigator. I'm pretty sure they won't. I told him I'd investigate this thing myself, but he said that I shouldn't, that it would be dangerous." I feel I must tell him this.

"Okay," Kelly says. "But if you're the only one who's going

104

to do anything to try to prove your innocence, then you're going to need some help. When you've got yourself put together, I'll be here."

What I feel like saying is, "Kelly, I think I'm in love with you!" But I can't, so I say, "Thanks, Kelly. I think I'm getting myself put together now."

Kelly stands up, and his head grazes the glass-balled light fixture that hangs low over the kitchen table. He grabs it and stops its erratic swing.

"I'll come by tomorrow evening, if it's all right with you," he says. "I've got morning classes and work for the station on the mobile unit all afternoon."

"I'll be here. I don't think I'm going anywhere tomorrow."

"Except to school."

"I mean school in particular. I don't want to go."

"If you don't go, they'll take it as a sign you're guilty of those charges," Kelly says. "What you've got to do is go and make the best of it."

I think about facing everyone, and I shudder. "I don't think I can."

"Sure you can," Kelly says. "You've got to. Talk to your friend, Lorna. See if she remembers anything suspicious about Zack and Loretta. You said she always goes to that hamburger place with you."

Kelly's right. I can't hide. I'd never get anything done. I walk with him to the door, and lean against it, thinking about him, after he leaves. There's one person who really believes in me— just one. My mother is wavering. My father believes what Cristabel tells him to believe. Oh, Detective York is keeping an open mind, so I can count him in a way. I wonder why Lorna hasn't called.

I go to my father's study. Rosella has left for the day, and he sits at his desk in a pool of sharp light beamed down from a crook-necked lamp. He looks old and tired. There are dark bags under his eyes, and for a moment I feel sorry for him.

105

"You and Mother wanted to talk to me, Daddy."

He looks up. "Rosella said you were entertaining a guest. There was not much point in waiting for you, since your mother had a sick headache. I sent her to bed. She's probably asleep by now."

"Rosella said you were phoning Cristabel."

"We were unable to reach her."

I hesitate. "No one phoned me," I finally manage to say. It sounds inane.

"No one could have phoned," he says. "We have the phones off the hook."

"Oh."

"Were you expecting a call?"

"I thought maybe Lorna."

"You'll see her tomorrow in school. It's best not to accept any calls tonight."

"Daddy, what was it like here while I was gone? What did you all do?"

"Do?" he echoes.

"You know. Did you call the police? Did you talk to any reporters? Did Zack bring Cristabel a note at her office or her home or what? What went on?"

He sighs. "It's hard to describe. It seemed as though everything was happening at once, but in a way it wasn't happening fast enough. There were long periods of waiting and worrying and praying, of course. And we talked to various policemen —not that Detective York, but a man with a mustache—Walker or Waller, something like that. And we held a family meeting so Cristabel could decide what we should do. We did manage to keep the press out of it. The whole thing was a horrible experience."

"Are you glad I'm home, Daddy?" His office smells tidily clean, like a mixture of lemon wax and disinfectant. He is beginning to bald. There is a shiny spot at the crown of his head, collecting and reflecting the light. Why did I ask that question?

106

The question surprises him as much as it does me. "Of course I'm glad," he says. "I just wish the circumstances were happier."

I take a deep breath and clench my fists. "It's very hard to be kidnapped under *happy* circumstances, Daddy." Quickly, I turn and go upstairs to my room. I would like to say good night to my mother, but her room is dark, and I suppose she must be asleep. I didn't know it was possible to be hurt to the point of agony, but that's the way I feel.

I automatically bathe, brush my hair, and climb into bed. I pull the blankets up to my chin and curl up on my side in my usual comfortable fetal position, which has begun to make an imprint in the mattress. This is my own bed. I am home safely, and for now that's all that counts.

In my sleep I dream that I am clinging tightly to Kelly's hand. I think I cling to it all through the night, because when I wake in the morning my right fist is tightly clenched.

But morning is so unreal. As the sun seeps through the curtains, so do memories seep into my conscious mind. It's my own bed . . . it's the basement . . . my bed. I sit up, trying to orient myself, pushing away the tangled hair that falls in front of my eyes. I have always thought it was the pits in old-fashioned books to have some character say, "Where am I?" But now I know where they're coming from. It takes me a few minutes to get myself into perspective. Same old room, same frilly curtains, same canopied bed. But not the same me. I'm a different person now. I'll never be the same again.

Della doesn't usually come this early. Often I pass her as I'm driving to school, and she's walking from the bus stop, leaning into each puffing, deliberate step. My mother is in the kitchen, making French toast. She smiles brightly at me and keeps up a happy chatter. She's making my favorite breakfast, and each time she passes me she touches my shoulder, or smooths back my hair, or pats my cheek. My mother is telling me that she loves me. How can you love someone—really love her—and not trust her?

But I badly need the love she offers me, and I take it greedily. "Mother," I say, "I thought about you when I was in that basement alone."

She sits at the table next to me, cradling her coffee cup, spots of red on her cheeks.

"It was cold in that basement, and dark, and awful scary. I could hear roaches. Did you ever hear a roach in the dark and wonder where it was going?"

She shudders. "No," she says.

For a moment we sit quietly. Then I pull my mind back to its original track. "Anyhow, I thought about you and how pretty you are. I think it was the first time that I ever really looked at you, and I was looking at you in my mind."

"Oh, Christina," she says. She pats my hand nervously, and I see there are tears in her eyes.

"Someday I'll tell you what it was like, being kidnapped. I just realized that no one in the family has asked me what it was like, or how I felt, or what happened to me."

"But . . ." The sentence dies. She presses her lips together and blinks rapidly.

I hunch my shoulders against the blow of what she would have said. "You didn't ask because no matter what you told me, there were too many doubts. You didn't really believe my story." I leave the French toast half eaten and push back my chair quickly. "I've got to leave for school."

"Don't you want the rest of your breakfast? I made your favorite."

"Thanks, Mother. It was very good. I just don't have time now."

We talk to each other in useful platitudes as I get my books together. What we have said to each other I don't know, because my mind has moved ahead to what will happen when I arrive at Madame DeJon's. It's like anticipating a visit to the dentist's when a filling has fallen out and you've got a cavity as big as the tip of your tongue. The anticipation can be torture, often worse than the reality. Maybe this will be the same. Kelly said I'd have to go to school. Detective York said I'd make it through the tough days. I guess I'll have to find out.

But it's bad. I pull into the parking lot, and two men leap toward my car.

One of them is pulling out identification and introducing himself. They're from two of the news services. They bend to peer through the car window.

"Go away," I tell them, rolling the window down another inch.

"Wouldn't you like to give us your version of the story?"

"Why should I?"

"We have stories from Zack and Loretta Tigus. Have you seen the morning paper?"

"No."

"Wasn't it a pretty desperate attempt to get money from your grandmother? Did you really think it would work?"

"I was not involved with those two weirdos! I was not trying to get money from my grandmother. Zack and Loretta kidnapped me, and they set the whole thing up so this would be their safety valve in case they couldn't get away with the money."

"You're sticking to this story?" the man closest to the window asks.

"It's the truth."

I have been trying to keep my feelings under control, but now I'm furious. I throw open the door to my car, giving his knees a good crack. He stumbles backward into the other reporter. I get out of the car, quickly lock the door, and say, "You have your minds made up. It won't make any difference what I say. Your story is going to be slanted and biased and prejudiced and a bunch of lies. My story is the truth, and that's why I'm sticking to it. Now get lost, or I'll call the police and tell them you're harassing me!"

"Now, look," one of them says. "Our jobs . . ."

But I turn and run toward the building. There are other cars arriving—a few more latecomers like me—and the girls are staring strangely at the men. As I reach the back door of Madame DeJon's administrative building, I glance over my shoulder and see them getting into their car. What good does it do to talk to reporters if they're going to write the story from their predetermined viewpoint, instead of giving the facts as they stand?

It's almost time for class, and some of the girls are busy with lockers and books and stuff as I come by. A few people I thought were my friends avoid meeting my eyes and don't speak to me. A few gulp out, "Hi, Christina," the way they'd spit pits from prunes. I keep my shoulders back and my head up, just like in the old movie where Ronald Colman goes to the guillotine. Where is Lorna?

I open the door to English, and she is there, rearranging clippings on the bulletin board. No one else is in the room yet.

"Lorna," I say, standing there, looking at her, waiting for her to react. My best friend. What is she going to do?

Lorna turns, sees me, and runs to hug me. "Oh, Christina! It was terrible, not knowing where you were or what was happening! I knew something was wrong by the way your parents acted when I phoned you, but no one would tell me what it was. I didn't know if you were terribly sick, or what in the world happened!"

"They didn't tell you anything?"

"I guess they were trying to keep it quiet. Your mother did call Saturday morning and ask to talk to you. I just figured she thought you had come back to my house. I didn't get the picture until later, and then I wondered . . ."

"Wondered what?"

"Well, I remembered how upset you were about not being able to go with the class on that trip to France, and I thought you might have run away from home."

For a moment it doesn't register. I had forgotten about the

110

class trip. It shocks me that just a few days ago it was so important to me. Now I couldn't care less. I look directly into Lorna's eyes.

"But you know now that I was kidnapped."

"Yes," she says, but there is a quick flicker in her eyes, and her gaze shifts to a spot over my left ear.

"You have to believe me, Lorna."

She moves to the bulletin board and puts in a few pins. "I've got to have this ready before class starts."

"Lorna . . ."

She turns. "Detective York came to see me last night. He explained everything that happened. He told me your side of the story, and he asked me if I had any information at all that would help. He thought I could verify what you said happened at Zack's hamburger place."

"Could you?"

She shakes her head and holds out her hands, palms up. "You know I couldn't!" Her voice comes out in a wail. "Christina, you didn't say one word about Zack and Loretta coming to the table to talk to you!"

"I didn't think it was important enough to talk about."

"But I'm not a mind reader! I wanted to help you, but I couldn't!"

"They followed me to your house Friday night, and then to my house."

"How in the world could I know that?"

I walk back to my desk and put my books on it. "Don't get upset, Lorna," I tell her. "It doesn't matter. The only thing that matters is that you believe me."

"Of course I believe you."

I turn and look at her carefully. Lorna, with all her polish, can't even tell a good lie.

"I'm glad," I say, but my voice sounds hollow.

"We'll get together after school," she says, offering what she can of her friendship. "Oh . . . but not today. I'm going

111

shopping with my mother for some shoes. Maybe . . . well
. . . we'll see how tomorrow works out."

People begin to come into the room. Mrs. Hardy bustles in
with an untidy stack of papers and is in constant motion until
the bell rings. She dives into English Lit. I can see what is
going to happen. No one is going to acknowledge that anything
out of the ordinary went on. No one is going to ask me about
what I went through. They are being polite, because I am obviously an embarrassment at Madame DeJon's, where the nicest
of Houston families just don't have daughters who get involved
in extortion. Don't they want to know the truth? Don't they
care?

The ringing of the bell comes as a complete surprise to me.
I realize I haven't heard a word of what went on in class. *What
am I doing here?*

I automatically stand, pulling my books into the ready-made
niche in my arms. Lorna moves toward me. "I tried to phone
you last night, but your line was busy."

"My father took the phone off the hook."

"I wanted to tell you that—no matter what—I was glad
you're back."

"No matter what?" I stare at her.

Lorna is flustered. "Well, Detective York hadn't come by yet,
and all I heard was what was on TV, and they didn't know
everything." She flushes, and her words are angry. "For real,
Christina, how can you expect me to know what happened
when nobody told me? And for that matter, why didn't you
call me?"

"I don't know."

"Well, look," she says. "I'm your friend. Why are you so
edgy about everything I say?"

I attempt a smile. "Okay, Lorna. I guess I'm just on the
floor. I've never felt so down in my life."

She smiles back. "I understand, Chris." People are pushing past us now, coming into the next class, and she looks at

112

them, startled. "We're going to be late! See you at lunch!"

I make it through the day. How, I'm not sure. At lunch I try to tell some of my friends about being kidnapped, and they listen with wide eyes, the way they'd watch a car chase on a cops-and-robbers television show. But they tell others, and the words gets around. It no longer seems to matter whether they believe me or not. I want them to know my side of the story. Now I'm sorry I didn't go into it with those reporters.

There's one more thing I must do. I want to talk to Cristabel. I drive to her office building, ride up the smoothly silent elevator, and enter the reception area. The receptionist doesn't smile at me this time. She looks up and blinks like an owl caught in bright sunlight.

"I'd like to see my grandmother, please," I tell her.

"Oh. Surely. Right away." She fumbles with the intercom, keeping her eyes on me. She acts as though she thinks I've come from robbing a bank.

There is an exchange of low murmurs, and the receptionist says, "Your grandmother is getting ready for a dinner engagement. She'll see you another time."

Maybe another time I would have bought this excuse, but not now. "It doesn't take her that long to put on her false eyelashes," I say. Without another word I open the door, go down the hallway, and barge into my grandmother's office.

Cristabel is standing behind her desk, looking out at the city, over which wisps of stark white clouds make puff marks against the blue sky. She whirls at my entrance.

"I thought . . ." she begins.

There are deep bluish circles under her eyes. She looks closer to her actual age.

"Why didn't you want to see me?" I ask her. "You're my grandmother, and you haven't even tried to see me after this kidnapping."

"Sit down, Christina," she says, and glides into her own leather chair. "I suppose now is as good a time to talk as any."

113

"I came because you must believe the truth," I tell her. "Those people kidnapped me. They are lying when they say I had anything to do with it."

"I talked this over with my attorney," she says. "He insisted there was not a shred of proof substantiating your claim that you were kidnapped."

"Your attorney is an ass," I say. "He just wanted to get the whole thing over with as fast as possible and get back to his dinner party."

"If we're going to talk, we're going to do it without immature emotional outbursts," she says in her controlled voice.

I nod. "All right, Cristabel. Would you believe that your attorney didn't even want to talk to me? He talked over my head to the detective. He took it for granted that Zack and Loretta were telling the truth. And he didn't want to hear my side of the story, because that might confuse him."

"Christina . . ." she warns.

"Grandmother," I say without thinking. "Will you just let me tell you what happened from beginning to end? Please?"

She winces at the word "grandmother," but says, "All right. I'm willing to listen. I'll have Eleanor take any calls that might interrupt us."

As soon as she has made the necessary arrangements, she sits back in her chair. I clear my throat and begin at the very beginning and carry it through to the moment Detective York takes me home.

"Do I have to prove that I wasn't a part of the plot?" I ask her.

She is thinking. As I have talked, she has shifted to a position with her elbows resting on her desk, her chin cradled in her hands. It's her "thinking" position, and I know she is paying close attention to my words.

"Let's take this step by step," she says. "Why was the money divided into two piles?"

"Because there is someone else involved in this."

"Who?"

"I don't know! But someone had to be! Zack and Loretta couldn't have worked this out by themselves."

"To be honest with you, Christina, your claim seems to be a bit farfetched."

"That's why nobody believes me."

"You are basing your proof of innocence on just two things—that the sheets on the bed had not been used, and that you had tried to open the basement door with a piece of metal that has disappeared. That's not much proof. It leaves a lot to take on faith."

I groan. "But that's what I want from you—faith! I'll find more proof. I will!"

"How?"

"Detective York suggested that Daddy hire a private investigator, but he didn't want to. I think if you told him it was all right, he would do it. He does whatever you tell him to do."

The look on her face is sheer pain, but she gets her emotions under control immediately. "Your father simply respects my good judgment," she says. "He always has."

"So if you tell him?" I'm scarcely breathing, living on hope.

Cristabel gets up and walks back and forth in front of the window wall of her office. I don't speak. I wait.

Finally she turns and says, "Christina, I don't know what an investigator could turn up that might help you. Your story is so terribly unsubstantiated. In the business world no one would put money into a venture with odds like that."

"But Cristabel! I'm not a business!"

"Please, Christina, let's be reasonable. Hiring someone to look for evidence would only drag this thing out. It would be best for the entire family if it were dropped."

"But I came to see you to ask you not to drop it. At this point I wouldn't even mind if you preferred charges, so that this thing could come to trial and people could find out what really happened."

115

"You'd want to be tried on extortion charges?"

"Well . . . if the truth comes out, there wouldn't be a trial. Detective York would be allowed to investigate, and he'd discover the truth."

"And what if he didn't? Have you thought of that? Really, Christina, what you are asking is horrible! To drag your whole family through months and months of newspaper publicity— all of it sensational—and to have this charge against you! No! It's out of the question!"

I get to my feet. "Then please think of some way to help me, Cristabel."

She stands too, and we stare at each other across the desk. With all my energy I am trying to match her strength. Finally she says, "I have given this much thought. Believe me, I have. The best thing for all of us is to have the publicity die down as quickly as possible."

"But people will always believe the worst about me!"

"That will die down too. People will forget."

I don't know if my anguish shows, but Cristabel loses her cool. She puts her hands to her face, covering her eyes. "Go home, Cristina," she says. "We'll discuss this later."

"Won't you help me? Do you want to let me take the blame for something I didn't do?"

"I can understand your attitude." Her voice trembles. "But I've worked with all my strength to build my position. I can't afford months of racking publicity, of gossip, of . . . I love you. I forgive you, but you should have thought. You should have known."

What she is really saying gets through to me. "You don't believe me." My voice is quiet. I am too numb to shout. What did I expect?

I don't say goodbye. I just walk out of the office, leaving my grandmother with her hands still covering her eyes, go past the receptionist, and into an elevator. The attendant in the

116

parking garage scoops my money into his grimy hand and tells me to have a good day.

A good day? I don't even remember what a good day is.

I drive around for a while before I go home. I don't feel like talking to anyone. But finally the sun spills all over the western sky, blinding the drivers who are hurrying home from downtown, and I head for home.

A car is parked in the driveway that curves through our front yard, and I stop behind it. I'm not even curious about whose car it could be. It's pretty much of a junk car, an old Volkswagen with scratched orange paint and a few dents. Our gardener uses a better car than that to carry his tools in.

Someone is climbing out of the car, long legs stretching, unbending, as though they'd been folded away for the winter. It's Kelly, and for a moment I feel a spark of joy.

I hop out of my car too, and meet him there in the driveway. "You're here," I say.

"I told you I would be," he answers. "Are you ready to get to work?"

"Doing what?"

"You've got to think ahead," Kelly says. "There's something important we have to do."

"What?"

"You talked about a third person being involved in the kidnapping. Don't you think the best place to start is to figure out who that third person could be?"

"You believe me," I say, my voice barely a whisper. Kelly can't possibly know how glad I am that he came along when he did.

"I believe you," he says, "and moving on from there, I believe the evidence. The money was divided into two equal halves, and Zack and Loretta aren't bright enough to have worked out the kidnapping plan. They talked a lot to the press after they were released. They're out of jail now with charges against them dropped—which you know, of course."

117

"Are they back in—that house?"

"Yeah."

I have to ask. "What did they say to the press? Anything new?"

"No. Same old stuff they told the police. But I'm like you. I think it adds up to zilch. Somebody smarter than they were had to figure it out. It was like an insurance policy, where if you have an accident—or, in this case, get caught with the money before you leave the country—you get off free and clear."

"Come on inside," I tell him. "We'll get something to eat, and then we'll find a quiet place to talk and see that we can come up with."

Kelly puts a hand on my arm. I like the strength in it. I like the way it feels when he touches me. "This is going to be a great experience," Kelly says. His eyes shine with excitement.

"I wouldn't call it a great experience," I tell him. "I'm a little bit scared about the whole thing. I keep remembering that Detective York said it might be dangerous for me to investigate."

Kelly runs his fingers through his tousled hair, making it look even worse, if possible. "You're scared?"

"Kidnapping is one thing. Murder is another." I shiver.

"Murder? I think you're worrying too much. But you don't have to follow through. We can let it drop."

"No way," I tell him. "I can't keep going with everyone suspecting me."

"Okay. As long as you're sure you want to get into this." He looks relieved and greatly pleased.

"I do."

"Then let's get started," Kelly says. "We'll have to work fast before . . . well, before whoever that third person is knows we're trying to discover his identity."

9

Della serves Kelly and me at the dining-room table, where we perch down at one end of the dark mahogany in an unbalanced island of white Madeira place mats and bone china.

"This is nice stuff," Kelly says. "Someday I'm going to live like this."

"Where do you live?" I ask him.

He waits until he's gulped down a mouthful of cheese omelet, and then says, "We live in a standard suburban home in southwest Houston. Looks like every tenth house on the block on the outside, all of them with about the same floor plan on the inside." He mentions the subdivision.

"That's a pretty area of town," I say politely. I'm uncomfortable because I hear my parents arguing.

"It's okay," he answers, "but for me, someday, it's going to get better."

I start to ask him what he's planning to do with the rest of his life, but my mother and father come in to say hello. They're on their way to a church board meeting.

They'd been arguing about going, and the argument droned on. When I say "droned," I mean their arguments get boring, because they try to be gentle with each other. My father felt that it was important they show at this meeting and act as though nothing had happened. My mother said she would die of embarrassment, and what would people think!

119

At one point my father referred to Cristabel's phone call, so I know she had confirmed her original decision to do or say nothing more on the subject. But neither of my parents has mentioned the call to me. Do they think if they ignore the situation it will just go away?

I know what I thought when I overheard their conversation, which I couldn't help but do, since the argument traveled from the living room to the den to my father's office to upstairs and back down again. I thought that if they believed in me, it wouldn't matter what people said or wondered. I thought that there was only one thing I could do to end this miserable situation, and that was to prove my own innocence. If I didn't have Kelly to help me, I'd have to flounder around by myself.

My mother is happily flustered to see me with a boy—any boy. She clasps Kelly's right hand in both of hers, and smiles as though she had cornered the toothpaste market.

My father talks to Kelly for a few minutes and, thank goodness, stays away from religion. He used to ask my friends if they had been saved, but he stopped when Mary Kay, who never stops talking unless her mouth is full, answered his question with a half-hour recital of how she was saved all right, when the Coast Guard pulled her out of the Gulf of Mexico after her surfboard got carried out on a fast riptide. He dropped the question after that ordeal. I've always had a warm spot in my heart for Mary Kay, who will never know what she did for me.

After they leave, we talk about the kidnapping, keeping our voices low. It doesn't add up to much, just random thoughts. Kelly says he wants to know as much as he can, so I talk and talk and answer his questions.

Finally Della comes in to take the plates. She looks at Kelly suspiciously. "We got fudge brownies. You want dessert now or later?" she asks me.

"How about both now and later?" Kelly asks hopefully.

I suppose it takes an awful lot of food to feed someone as

tall as Kelly. "Why don't we take a plate of brownies into the den?" I suggest. "Then we can eat as many as we want."

"Okay with me," Della says. "Come on out to the kitchen, Christina, and I'll fix up a plate for you."

I follow her out to the kitchen, and she turns to me. In a stage whisper that would do credit to Ethei Merman, she says, "What's that boy doing here? Where'd you meet him?"

"What difference does it make? My parents didn't even ask me that."

"It's just that I gotta leave early tonight," Della says. "I don't want to leave you alone in the house with just anybody."

"Honestly, Della." I sigh. "You are living in the past. What could happen to me just because I'm alone in the house with a boy?"

"How many possibilities you want?"

"Come off it. You aren't my mother." My words are cross, so I smile to soften them. "It's okay. You can leave early if you want to. Kelly is here just to help me work out something."

"What something?"

"What makes you so curious all of a sudden?"

Della looks at me for a moment, then says, "Oh, never mind. If you say it's okay to go, then I'll go. I don't want to miss the seven o'clock bus."

She puts the brownies on a plate, and I take them, heading back to the dining room to meet Kelly. I have the nagging feeling that Della wasn't concerned just about my being alone in the house with a stranger. She could easily have overheard some of our conversation. Did we say anything that would concern her?

The thought goes out of my head when I discover that Kelly isn't in the dining room. I go hunting for him and find him already in the den. He is at the glass case, looking at my mother's collection of music boxes.

"There's some good stuff here," Kelly says. "Valuable stuff."

"I suppose so." I put the plate down on the table near the sofa and sit down. "Want to get started? We can get some Cokes later."

Kelly turns and looks at me. "Have you got any paper, and a pen?"

"For what?"

"We want to get things down on paper. It sometimes helps. It's easier to get them into perspective. At least, it always works that way for me."

"On all your kidnapping cases?"

Kelly flops down beside me and grins. "It's a big jump from term papers to solving a kidnapping."

"I'm glad you're going to try. You don't know how much I need your help."

"So here I am," Kelly says. "Get some paper and find out where Della is. We don't want her to listen in."

I get a notebook and come back. Kelly has made great inroads in the brownies.

"Della's busy in the kitchen," I say. "She can't hear us."

"This third person," Kelly says. "For starters, let's list all the things he had to be involved in where you're concerned."

"You keep saying 'he.' Why?"

Kelly shrugs. "I don't know. I guess it's force of habit. You think it's a 'she'?"

"I don't know. I haven't really begun to think about him— her—it. Kelly, we haven't even started, and I'm already confused."

"Stay cool," Kelly says. "We'll work with 'he' until we find out different."

"So we start with a list?"

"Right."

"Better write down 'the gun.' Someone stole it from my father's desk."

"You said it was Loretta."

"But I didn't see Loretta. Della saw the woman, not me. She'd be the only one who could identify Loretta as the person who came to the door."

"Has she done this?"

"I haven't asked her, and no one's questioned anyone in the house since I've come back home."

"Loretta's picture was in the newspaper. So was Zack's. And they were on TV. Didn't Della say anything about seeing the pictures and recognizing the woman?"

"Not to me."

"That's strange. Even if the woman who came to the house wasn't Loretta, I'd think that Della would tell you that."

"You want me to call her in here and ask her?"

"Later," he says. "Let's work on the list for now. What's point two?"

"My clothes. Someone packed a suitcase and got my clothes over to Zack's house."

"Someone who had easy access to your house?"

"How should I know?"

"Okay, okay." He frowns as he writes. "Next point?"

"The typewritten note to Cristabel. Detective York said it was typed on my own portable typewriter."

"Where is the typewriter?"

"They found it in Zack's house. I suppose my father will go down to the police station and get it back, and my suitcase too. Or maybe he has already. I haven't been upstairs to look."

Della calls from the next room, "Christina, you want to come in here a minute? There's things I need to tell you before I leave."

I look at Kelly, and he nods agreement. "Della," I call back to her, "could you please come in here for a minute?"

She appears in the doorway, slowly, reluctantly. "What for?"

Kelly smiles up at her. "Della, you've seen the news stories

123

about Christina in the paper and on television, haven't you?"

"Yeah."

"So you've seen pictures of Loretta and Zack."

"What about them?"

"We need to know if Loretta is the woman who came to the house the day Christina found the tape on the door."

"I told everybody I never did see that tape on the door."

He shakes his head impatiently. "It doesn't matter about the tape. We just need to know if you recognized Loretta. Was she the woman you said came to the door that day?"

Della's forehead wrinkles like dried prunes. "I don't know," she says. "All those ladies who come to the door with Avon and *Watchtower* and all that—they all look alike to me, 'cause I don't pay that much attention to them."

"Could you think harder about it and try to remember?"

Her eyebrows wag up and down like warning flags. "No, I couldn't. I don't know who I was talking to that day, and that's all I can tell you."

"But if . . ."

"What's more," she says to Kelly, "you ain't no policeman who's asking questions for a reason, and I got to go or I'll miss my bus. Christina, you want to come in here for a minute while I tell you something?"

She doesn't wait for an answer, but just leaves the room. I shrug apologetically to Kelly and follow her. Della leads me all the way to the back door before she turns and frowns at me. "I know what the two of you are up to, and it's not good," she says. "You can't go playing policeman and not get hurt."

"You heard our conversation?"

"I heard what you said about thinking there's a third person in all of this. And I'm saying to you to let it lie. Who's this boy think he is, coming in here and getting you started on some foolish chase?"

"He's trying to help me, Della."

"Help you what? Get killed?"

It dawns on me. "Della, you believe what I told everyone about the kidnapping, don't you?"

"It's not my place to believe or not believe. I just know that if you are telling the truth, and those people find out that you're looking for them, you could cause yourself a lot more trouble than you're in right now!"

"I have to prove I wasn't stealing from my grandmother."

"You don't have to prove nothing. People will forget what happened."

"I'll never forget," I tell her, and she stares at me for a few moments, searching deeply into my eyes.

"Okay," she says. "Do it your way. Just don't say I didn't warn you."

"We need to keep this quiet, Della. You won't . . . well . . . tell other people?"

She just shakes her head and goes out the back door. She pauses long enough to add, "By the way, somebody from the police brought your typewriter and clothes back. They're up in your room." The door closes and locks behind her.

I return to Kelly.

"Sit down," Kelly says. "I've put on the list the money divided into halves, and Zack and Loretta's conversation that made you think there was a third person involved. What else?"

I work at it a minute, turning it all over and over in my mind in great snatches and scenes. "I think that's it. Should we go into the missing latch or the clean sheets or my fingerprints on the basement heater?"

"Not yet. They'd add up to zilch in the way of evidence, and right now we need to concentrate on the third-person angle."

I realize that we haven't drawn the drapes across the wide windows that overlook the backyard. A sheet of blackness that reflects the interior of the den is all I can see as I look through the windows, but I shudder. It's as though unseen eyes were peering through at me. Quickly I yank on the cords and pull the drapes shut, wrapping a woven cotton wall of security around myself.

"Sit down," Kelly tells me. "Have a brownie. There are a couple left."

His words break the mood of fear, and I join him on the sofa.

"It's pretty obvious that this third person had access to your house," he says. "Who can get in and out easily besides your parents?"

"You think someone burglarized the house?"

"Could be, but I don't know. I'm working on this angle now."

"Well, there's Della, of course, and Rosella."

"Who's Rosella?"

"My father's secretary. He works at home, and she has a little office here too."

"Does she have a key?"

"Yes."

"Is she the only one outside your family who has a key?"

"Not exactly. My grandmother has a key. She bought this house for my parents and kept a key for herself."

"Why?"

I look at him for a moment. "Don't ask questions I can't answer." For some reason I'm embarrassed. "Listen, Kelly, we can work on this project without getting into my family relationships, can't we?"

"Okay," he says. "But it is important news that your grandmother has a key."

"But she's family."

He shrugs. "What would happen if her company was having financial problems, and she could explain away a loss with money going to some kidnappers?"

"Kelly! What a rotten thing to say! Cut that out!"

"Do you want to find the answers, or don't you?"

"But my family . . ."

126

"I'm not saying your family is involved. We just have to look at this from every direction. Thinking about your grandmother as the third person may lead us to another clue that points to the real person. Understand?"

"I suppose so, but I don't like it much."

"What about someone who works for your grandmother? Would anyone else have a key?"

"No."

"Could anybody get hold of your grandmother's key?"

"Kelly!"

He leans back and smiles at me. "Don't get so shook up. I'm trying to help."

"I know. It's just that this questioning has me all mixed up inside."

"Then let's go to Della. Does she have a key?"

"Yes and no. That is, she doesn't take one home with her, but she knows where the spare key is kept, so if she gets here and no one is home, she can let herself in."

Kelly sits up and whistles. "You've got to be kidding! A house like this, and you have a spare key somewhere, so that anyone can let himself in?"

"Della's the only one outside our family who knows where it is."

"Is it a place where anyone could find it?"

"No. It's in a hidden place on top of the door frame that leads from the garage."

"Does the gardener know this? Anyone like that?"

"No."

"Tell me about Della." He reaches over and eats the last two brownies as I talk.

"She's a nice person."

"You've got to do better than that. What is she like? Does she hang out in bars? Have any vices?"

I giggle. "She's a great dancer, from what she tells me. She likes to live it up on weekends. And she gambles a little."

"This kidnapping was a gamble."

"Oh, come on, Kelly. Della's not the type."

"Let's get to your father's secretary then."

"Rosella? She's not the type either."

Kelly stands up and stretches, then walks to the fireplace and back. He shakes his head at me. "Just who do you think is the type, Christina? Somebody out of an Alfred Hitchcock movie? We're talking about possibilities. Be logical."

"Okay," I say quickly. I can tell that Kelly is exasperated with me, and I don't want him to be. "Rosella Marsh is a quiet, mousy person who keeps everything inside herself. She has worked for my father for years, and I still don't know what she's really like or what she thinks."

"What kind of work does she do for your father?"

"She does all the important stuff. She researches for him and even writes his speeches. He gets all the credit, and she does all the work."

"That's hard to take. Does he pay her enough to make it worthwhile?"

The question surprises me. "I really don't know. I haven't given it any thought."

"She knew your father had a gun in his desk?"

"Everybody knew." His questions are making me terribly uncomfortable. I wish circumstances were different. I wish Kelly and I were talking about things people talk about on dates. I wish . . .

His voice breaks into my thoughts. "Can you get me Rosella's and Della's addresses? Then I'll start the legwork."

"What legwork?" I stand and face him.

"I'll try to track down anything I can about them or their families. My connection with the TV station might help," Kelly says.

"Their families? One of Della's sons was in jail once."

"Christina, how come you didn't tell me this with the other stuff? Didn't you think it was important?"

128

"I just didn't think about it, period."

"You have to think. Go over everything in your mind before you go to sleep tonight. Think about anyone else who might have had access to your house without making people suspicious. Think about anyone who could have a motive. Anyone who could reasonably have left town without arousing suspicion. Anyone who . . ."

"Rosella," I murmur.

He stops. "Rosella what?"

"She was going to visit her parents in Chicago. She had a ticket to fly out of here Monday. She stayed because she was worried about me, she said."

Kelly gives a long, drawn-out sigh. "For real, Christina! How are we going to get anywhere on this investigation? Don't you know that's important too?"

"I'm trying," I tell him. "This is hard for me. I'm the kind of person who likes to keep things inside. I'm not used to talking to people about how I feel, or probing to see how they feel."

"That's no good," he says. "Psychology one-o-one. You've got to learn to come out of yourself or you'll end up with ulcers and migraines and all that junk."

"I can't just change the way I am."

"Sure you can. People ought to be able to change when they have to. People can keep changing all their lives."

"But . . ."

"You're changing right now. Pay attention to yourself. You aren't the same person now that you were last week at this time, are you?"

"I—I guess not."

"And you won't be the same person by the time we're through with our investigation."

I have to think about this a moment. I can't understand the person I used to be. How can I make peace with whatever I'm changing into? I'm getting a headache.

129

"I'll be going now, but I'll keep in touch," Kelly says.

"When will you call me?"

"When I find something out." He quickly writes some numbers on a scrap of paper and shoves it into my hand. "This is my phone number at home," he says. "Call me if you think of anything else, or if you need me."

I melt when he adds that last bit. He can't imagine how much I needed him, and how I was just waiting until he came around.

"What should I do?" I ask.

"We'll just take this one step at a time. Wait until I find out as much as I can. Then we'll move on to what comes next." He looks at me solemnly. "And please keep this as quiet as you can. It'll be better if your parents don't know about it either."

I nod. "Thanks, Kelly, for your help." I walk with him to the front door, see him climb into his car, which is too small for his long legs, and shut the door.

Suddenly I'm very tired. I'd like to go to bed, but it's not very late, and I've got homework to catch up on. All the daily trivia have to be replaced in my world—no matter that my life has been torn apart and put back together with some of the pieces missing. The routine goes on.

I take a bath, then prop up a couple of pillows in bed, climbing in with my notebook and my English assignment. It doesn't take long to get into it. The sooner I finish the better, so I plow away.

I am answering a question no one really cares about when I realize that I'm not alone in the house. Maybe there was the click of a doorknob downstairs. If there was, I didn't notice it. I hold my breath and listen as I become aware that softly, very softly, through the thick plush carpeting on the stairway, footsteps are padding, patting, like little slaps with a powder puff. And they are coming up the stairs!

I slip out of bed and grab the bed lamp, tugging the cord

from the wall socket. Holding it high, I move toward the doorway, standing to one side, behind the door, which is wide open. I wait.

There are little rustling movements as the person comes closer. I lift the lamp higher.

I can hear the person breathing in the open doorway of my room. One more step and then . . .

A soft voice . . . one I recognize. "Christina?"

Slowly the lamp comes down. My hands are shaking. I am trembling.

"Rosella." I sigh.

She gives a little squeal of fright and peers around the door. "What are you doing?"

"Getting ready to hit you over the head with this lamp," I tell her.

She squeals again, and I quickly add, "I didn't know who was coming up the stairs and into my room! How did I know it was you? I was trying to protect myself." I flip the wall switch that turns on the overhead light.

"I had to come here to bring some papers." She blushes. "I guess I really didn't have to come by. I could have brought them when I came to work in the morning. I really came to see you."

"Me? Why?"

"I've been concerned about you, Christina. I wanted to tell you that I'm sorry for all you've been through."

I motion her into the room and toward my desk chair. "Sit down, Rosella." I perch on the bed, sitting cross-legged.

"Would you like to talk about it?" she asks me.

I hesitate. "Not really. I've talked about it so much I'm tired of the whole story. Besides, what good would it do when you wouldn't believe me?"

"Maybe I would believe you," she says. "I don't like that Zack. I don't think you'd get mixed up with him."

"What do you know about Zack?" Why do I feel so uncomfortable talking to Rosella? There is something funny here. Rosella has never sought me out for a conversation. The two of us just come and go in the household, never noticing each other as anything more than human beings who inhabit the same planet.

She seems acutely embarrassed now. "I don't want you to misunderstand, Christina," she says. "I wasn't trying to spy on you. It's just that your mother asked me a couple of months ago to investigate that hamburger place that you and Lorna go to every Friday. She wanted to be sure it was . . . well . . . acceptable."

I groan. "How well did you get to know Zack Tigus?"

"I didn't get to know him," she answers quickly. "I just visited the place a couple of times and checked it out for cleanliness and . . . uh . . . undesirables."

"Undesirables!"

"Well, your mother wanted to protect you."

I flop back on the bed and stare up at the canopy. My mother had Rosella follow me around to make sure I was in good company? The thought angers me. I'm trying to grow up, to become independent! And she checks out a stupid old hamburger place!

Rosella gets up and comes to sit next to me on the bed. She tentatively reaches out and pats my hand, then withdraws hers as though my hand had been a prickly cactus. "Don't be upset with your mother, Christina."

"How overprotective can a mother get?"

There is silence for a moment, and I glance at Rosella. She is staring at the far wall, as though she were looking a thousand miles away. Then she speaks. "I know how you feel. My parents were overprotective too. They worried incessantly about whom I was going out with, who my friends were. It got so difficult to take that I simply stopped seeing many people. I guess I took the coward's way out."

"You're not a coward."

132

"I was. Maybe if I'd had the courage to do things on my own, to let them know—politely, of course—that I had to make my own decisions, I'd have had a different life."

"What kind of life?"

She pauses again. Her voice is low as she says, "I would like to have had a job that paid more money. I would like to have been married."

We sit there quietly. I don't know what to say to Rosella. I don't think she knows what to say to me. In all these years I've known her, this is the closest we have ever been, and yet our very closeness leads to miserable embarrassment for both of us.

I try to smooth the situation. "How is your mother?"

"Oh," Rosella says, coming back to reality. "She's fine."

I'm puzzled. Carefully, I prop myself into a sitting position, slide off my bed, and stand up, stretching. Something here is all wrong!

Carefully, I say, "Rosella, I thought your mother was sick."

She looks at me, eyes blinking again. "Oh," she says. "She was, but she's better now."

"That's nice."

"Yes."

"Well," I say, "I do appreciate your coming by to see me, and I know you probably have a million things to do."

She stands too. "You don't want to talk about it?"

"I'd rather not."

"When you came home, you said something about a third person involved in the kidnapping. I wanted to ask you why you said that."

There is a funny lump in my throat. It's hard to breathe around it. As I talk, my voice is strained and sounds peculiar to my ears. "Detective York said the case was dropped," I tell her. "We'd better leave it that way. Besides, no one believes me."

"I—I think I could believe you. I've never known you to lie,

Christina. And I think you're a fine person. You wouldn't try to take your grandmother's money."

"Thanks." I move toward the door.

"That's why I thought . . . this third person . . . well . . ."

She doesn't finish the statement, and I can't. We stand in the room, staring at each other.

I have to break the silence. It's pressing against my head, and I can't bear it. "Well," I repeat. "It was nice of you to come by, Rosella."

She smiles now, a tentative, flickering smile. I can smell the perfume she's wearing as she passes me in the doorway. It's a wild, tropical perfume, and it surprises me. She seems more the rose-garden type. Who is this person called Rosella Marsh? I tell myself the third person couldn't possibly be Rosella! It couldn't! But a flick of suspicion refuses to go away.

I walk with her down the stairway, thinking with each step that it's a long way over the banister to the white marble floor below. I clutch the banister railing with all my strength.

She pauses at the door to smile at me again, and I try to smile back. The minute she's outside, I turn the dead bolt on the front door. Then I check the back door, the side door, and the glass doors that lead into the patio. I have to make sure they are locked tightly. I have to fight back the desperate feeling that I should check them all again. I turn on more lights downstairs and pick a chair with its back to the wall. I am going to wait here until my parents return. I wish I had enough courage to go out to the garage and get the extra key, but I haven't. My God! Even Kelly knows where the key is!

I have never felt so terribly alone—not even in that basement. There, I could see where the danger was coming from. Here, the terror of someone unknown is a hundred times more frightening. This danger has invisible fingers that creep around my throat and squeeze my breath away and make my heart bang against my ribs and make my legs weak when I try to walk.

I want to scream to that unknown someone, "I am afraid of you! I am terrified of you! But I won't give up! Get out of my way, because I won't give up!"

10

I can't tell my parents I'm afraid of Rosella. They come in the door, frozen in motion like startled squirrels as they see me sitting near the door to the living room.

I yawn and tell them I was too interested in my book to go to sleep, but I know that my sagging eyelids, heavy with exhaustion, give me away. My mother accepts the words, but her eyes speak to mine.

Like a small child, now that my parents are home, I go to bed and fall asleep immediately. Do I dream of Kelly? Not tonight. Tonight my sleep erases my dreams.

Usually I am alone at the breakfast table, but this morning Della is there, bustling back and forth from the kitchen to the breakfast room like a busy freighter.

"Why are you here so early?" I ask, shaking my napkin out of its carved wooden ring and into my lap.

Della stands before me, her hands folded over the shelf of her rounded belly. "I need to talk to you, Christina."

"About what?" I am cautious, suspicious. Am I always going to feel like this in response to a simple statement? I hope not. It's not the way I want to be.

"About how you should pay attention to what people have been telling you and mind what they say."

"Sit down, Della." I sigh. "I know this is going to be more than a two-minute conversation, and it makes me uncomfortable to have you standing while I sit."

"It's not proper."

"We make our own rules. Please sit down."

She lowers herself into a chair and stares intently at me once more. "What I need to tell you is that the police detective who was here told you to just go about your business and try not to meddle; and your mother and father told you that your grandmother wanted well enough let alone."

"So?"

"So, I'm telling you that I gave a lot of thought to what you and that red-haired, spotted boy were talking . . ."

"Freckled," I interrupted, wanting to giggle. I wonder how Kelly would like being called "spotted."

She scowls at me and goes on. "Don't matter. What matters is that I know you two are fixing to poke your noses into places they shouldn't be poked."

"Della, Kelly is trying to help me."

She snorts. "Don't tell me that. I don't see that boy as a Good Samaritan. What does he really want? And where'd you meet him, anyway?"

"At . . . well . . . Oh, Della, it really isn't any of your business!" I attack my toast ferociously and gulp from my glass of orange juice.

"What you do may not be any of my business, but what I do is my business, and I feel I got to tell you to give up this thing you're doing of trying to play policeman."

"We're not trying to play policemen."

"Christina," she says, bending toward me, "you aren't thinking about how dangerous this could be. You were talking about somebody thinking out this plan and getting those two stupid people to go along with them. Don't you realize that party don't want you to find out who it is? Don't you know you could get hurt?"

I wipe my lips with my napkin and place it beside my plate, deliberately studying Della. "I think you believe me."

"I think you're too smart a girl to go around making up crazy stories, and if what you told us wasn't the truth, it would be one big crazy story."

"Della, I have to get the proof to make everyone believe in me. You know what people believe now."

She shrugs and looks away. "It's just bus gossip. It don't count for anything more than that."

"What's bus gossip?"

"Oh, you know, the things maids talk about on the way to and from work. They're the ones who drag out a story and keep it going. Folks with things on their minds got better to do than that."

"The girls at school believe the newspaper and television stories. So do the teachers."

"They'll forget about it the minute something more interesting comes along. Wait till they find out that blond girl in your class—you know the tall one with those great big glasses—is pregnant. They'll forget all about you."

"What? You don't mean Gloria?"

"Yeah, I do mean Gloria, with those big glasses."

"How do you know that, Della?"

"The girl who works at their house told us on the bus." She smiles at me. "Now, see what I gave you—a good story to spread around until they all forget about what happened to you."

"I can't do that!"

She stands, pressing so hard against the table that it seems to bend. "It's a lot better way of heading than the way you're going, with this trying to be a policeman stuff. That was a bad thing, your being kept in the cold basement of that woman's old rent house the way you say. Don't you want to forget it?"

"I want to do what I think best." I stand, too, and look at my watch. "I've got to hurry, or I'll be late for school."

"Go on then," she says. Her voice changes, softens. "But please, Christina, think about what I told you."

"I'll think about it, but I'm not going to change my mind."

"You and your grandmother, most stubborn people I ever seen."

I take a sharp breath. It hurts. "I am not like my grandmother," I say slowly, deliberately.

"Not just like her," she answers quickly, "but those times she's been here I see there's a lot of her in you—the stubborn part and some good parts too."

I don't answer. I do all the last-minute things, scoop up my books, and run to my car. On the way I remove the extra key from the doorframe and drop it in my bag. At the end of the drive, instead of turning right, I turn left. What am I doing?

A feeling inside me tells me that in spite of what Kelly has told me, in spite of what I know I should do, I am not going to school this morning. I'm driving to the Tigus house. There's something I've got to do.

What? I search for the answer, but there is only silence. Maybe the answer will come later. I hope so.

At the first shopping center I pull into a parking slot, go into the drugstore, and phone the school. I tell the office attendant I won't be in today.

She immediately says what she probably says to anyone who phones in an absence, "Oh dear. I do hope you'll feel much better tomorrow."

I didn't tell her I was sick, but I don't feel like explaining. It was her idea, not mine. I let it drop and hang up the receiver.

There's a doughnut place next door. I don't really want anything to eat, but I have to kill some time. I want to talk to Loretta, not to Zack, and he will probably still be at his house. The doughnut tastes dry and crumbly and gaggingly sweet, but the coffee is good and hot. I sip at it until I notice the counter girl glaring at me and two customers waiting for stools. I put down my change and leave quickly, embarrassed at listening

139

so hard for inner messages that I'm unaware of what is happening around me.

So that hidden part of my mind has told me to talk to Loretta. That's what I'll do. I remember the address of the house from newspaper stories. I know how to get there.

As I drive, an uncomfortable thought nags at me, but I can't put my finger on it. Something Della said . . . there was something that wasn't right—out of focus. Was it my suspicion about why Della should want me to stop looking for this third person? Why should she care? I can't believe gossip on the bus bothers her. And I really don't think she's that concerned with this "danger" she talked about. Why can't people just let me alone and let me do what has to be done? I'm glad I have Kelly on my side. How could I accomplish anything without Kelly?

The morning rush of traffic is long over, so it doesn't take much time to drive to the part of the city where the old Tigus house squats on a tattered lawn. The house needs paint, its rust-red trim faded and peeling in little curls. The upstairs windows, with their crooked, slanted window shades, give a cross-eyed stare down the pointed nose of the front porch. I park down the street, where I can watch the house without being seen.

There is a car in the driveway. Zack probably drives it to work, and he hasn't left yet. Is he still working at that hamburger place? It occurs to me that I don't know, that I really know very little about what I'm doing. Maybe I should wait and talk to Kelly. No, the compulsion is strong. I sit in the car, twisting my keys over and over in my cold fingers, waiting.

The emotions I feel as I look at this house, where I was kept prisoner, are so strong and so conflicting that I feel sick to my stomach and have to fight back waves of nausea. Down in that basement it was like being buried, and the house is the gravestone.

I close my eyes for a moment, gripping the keys so tightly

they dig painfully into my fingers. When I open my eyes, I see Zack getting into his car. He is alone. He pulls the car out of the driveway, backs with a gunning of the motor and a cloud of thick gray exhaust, and speeds off in the opposite direction from where I am sitting, watching him. Good.

I put my keys back into the ignition and drive to a spot directly in front of the Tigus house. A window curtain flutters and is still. Loretta is inside, and she has seen me drive up. Strange Loretta with her nervous dedication to Zack and her ironing board . . . Loretta, the weakest link in the chain.

I am getting out of the car when this thought hits me. Of course! Now I know why my subconscious mind sent me here. Loretta is the weakest. I know about Zack, who is all loud bluster. I don't know about the third member of this trio, but I have to assume that he—or she—has more going for him than Loretta does. Loretta is the weakest link, and I am here to see if the weakest link might break.

I walk up the steps and ring the bell. No one answers, but I can sense Loretta's presence on the other side of the door, the way a fox feels out the presence of a rabbit down his hole.

"Open the door," I say loudly, "or I will stand here and scream bloody murder until your neighbors send for the police!"

The door opens a crack. I push it open, then walk inside and close the door behind me.

"Why'd you want to come here?" Loretta is sullen.

"I didn't," I tell her. "I don't like being here at all. I came because I have to talk to you."

"About what?"

"Go into the den and we'll sit down. I don't want to stand here and talk." I find that I have taken command and Loretta is obeying me, somewhat reluctantly.

"I got to finish my ironing," she says.

I shiver as the chill of the house penetrates my blazer. Carefully I perch on the edge of one of the chairs in the den.

141

Loretta, following my example, sits on another chair, her arms folded across her chest as though she were hugging herself.

"What do you want?" she asks.

"I want you to give me some answers to questions I have."

"Zack told me I wasn't supposed to say nothing to nobody."

"Not even when your life is in danger?"

Her eyes grow wider. "What are you talking about? In danger from what?"

"Not from what . . . from whom. From that person who thought up this scheme."

"You aren't making sense. What person are you talking about? You don't even know." She attempts a sneer and brushes back a thin strand of hair, but her eyes drop.

"You're right. I don't know who this person is. I just know that someone else is involved. I came to ask you to tell me who it is."

"You're crazy!"

"No, you are, because you haven't thought ahead. If this person ever gets afraid that you'll tell his identity, then what do you think will happen to you?"

She jumps in her chair. "To me? Why not to you? You're the one nosin' around."

"I'm in danger too," I say.

"Are you talking about him killing us?"

"It could happen."

"You, sitting there so cool. You aren't scared?"

"Of course I'm scared! That's why I want to find out who this person is. Right now he thinks he's safe, that everyone has bought the story of the extortion that I'm supposed to have masterminded. But one of these days he's going to get nervous —maybe even if I let the investigation drop. Each day the thought is going to creep up on him that someone might find out, that he could be caught. I don't know who he is, so I don't think he'll be so concerned about me. But you know, and he'll be afraid that you'll talk. And some night, when it's so

142

dark that the neighbors can't see, and Zack is kept late at the hamburger place, and no one will know . . . then he'll come creeping around this house and peering in the windows until he finds you, and he'll . . ."

"Stop that!" Loretta shrieks and jumps from her chair.

I jump up too and grab her shoulders. "I'm not making things up, Loretta. That's just the way he'll think!"

She shakes herself free of my grip, turns, and bursts into tears. "Go away," she says. "I can't tell you anything! I gotta talk to Zack."

I try to reason with her, but the mood has been broken. Like an old record with a scratched groove she keeps saying, "I gotta talk to Zack."

Maybe Loretta is more afraid of Zack than of this person.

So I walk to the front door, Loretta on my heels, eager to shut and bolt the door behind me.

"I'm going to find out who he is," I tell her.

Her gaze is defiant. "You think so? Well, there's a lot you don't know!"

"What makes you think so?"

"I know so."

"Is it because I'm saying 'he' instead of 'she'?"

She blinks and stares, then says, "Go on . . . get out of my house!"

I walk to my car, wondering. Has she given away something? I can't tell. I don't know. I'm not going to give up on Loretta. I'm going to work on this weakest link until it breaks open with the information I need. I just hope I can do it before the third person finds out what I'm up to. If I just had an inkling of who it could be—some idea to work on. My guess is Rosella . . . underpaid, frustrated, in a miserable little job where her boss gets all the credit for the work she does . . . where she can't meet people, where she becomes more and more unhappy until . . . Is that Rosella? Is that how she thinks? I barely know who she is. In the daylight she is much less threatening than she was in the quiet of the house last night.

The perfume she wears . . . maybe inside she's itching to dash off to South America and live as abandoned a life as she can work up on the spur of the moment—with Cristabel's money. The image of Rosella as a femme fatale makes me want to laugh.

I start the car, with a last look at the house I hate, and at the woman, who flips back from the peephole she's made in the edge of the front-window curtain as she sees me glance that way. Where to now? Maybe I should call Kelly and ask what the next step should be. But Kelly will be in class, and that's where he told me to be. I can't go back to school yet. Right now the routine of classes is so far from my world that if I had to sit through them I would scream with frustration and probably scare Madame DeJon into fits.

Aimlessly, I drive to the parking lot next to the hamburger place, cautiously dipping into and out of a pothole as I work my way through the pits and lumps of the paving to a spot where I can see inside.

Zack's not open for business yet, but he's inside, lazily getting things ready. I watch him pour hot water into a large coffee urn. He wipes his hands on his already stained pants, then yawns widely and scratches his chest and under his armpits. Does he own this place? Lease it? Why was he ready to walk away and leave it? I've seen a couple of helpers there with him. Did they take over while I was living in the basement of the Tigus house?

I used to laugh at the little light bulbs that appeared over people's heads in comic strips when they got brilliant ideas. I don't laugh now. An idea strikes me, and it's very much like a light turning on. I know the next step. I know what to do! I'm delighted with myself for getting it together.

I start the ignition, and for the first time catch Zack's attention. He stares at the car and at me, his mouth slightly open, his lower jaw limp. He resembles a catfish giving its last gasp.

144

Ignoring him, I ease the car out into the traffic of the access road, pull into the freeway, and head toward the police station downtown.

My arrival there is very different today from the way it was when I was quickly escorted through the back door by Detective York. Today I walk up the front steps and to the information booth in the tiny lobby, where an elderly man in uniform is scanning the morning paper and rubbing his left ear.

"Where can I go to look up records?" I ask him.

He stares at me curiously for an instant. "Depends on what kind of records."

"Whether or not someone has been in jail and when. And if someone owns property or is renting. That sort of thing."

"Whoa!" he answers. "You've got a couple of places all lumped together. Aren't even in the same building."

"Well, could you tell me where these places are and how I can get there?"

He stares at me, but as I stare back, trying to discover his thoughts, he shuts them off and his eyes become little pools of cold coffee. "Tell you what," he says. "I'll get someone down here who can lend you a hand."

"I can do this myself."

"Pretty complicated business." He waves toward a chair—another of those awful green plastic-and-chrome things. "You just sit there a couple minutes. He'll be right down."

"Who will?"

But he busies himself with a phone, turning away from me. I seem to have no choice, so I perch on the chair, ankles and knees tucked together, waiting for whoever it is to come and help me.

I watch the elevator doors open and shut, swallowing assorted flavors of humanity and spitting out others. Then I see a face I recognize—Detective Jason York. He comes directly toward me, and I stand up to meet him.

"Want to talk to me?" he asks.

"I didn't come for that," I say. "I came to look up some records. I need information that wasn't in the news stories."

"I know. I was called and told you were here." He waves a thumb toward the officer in the information booth.

"But . . ." I grip my hands together, so frustrated I want to cry out. "All I came to do was check out some things."

"Okay," he says. "Come on upstairs and we'll talk it over."

"You mean you'll help me do this?"

"That's what we're here for."

Now I can smile at him. I follow him into the gaping elevator for the ride to the third-floor offices of the Homicide Division.

We go into the interrogation room we were in before, and I shiver as I sit in the same chair.

He is watching me shrewdly. "Brings back some unpleasant memories, doesn't it?"

I nod, and he adds, "You'll get over it. No matter what comes along to cut us up, eventually we get over it. How come you aren't in school today?"

"I can't go back until I find out some things," I say.

"Uh-huh. Answers you think you'll find in records."

I lean forward eagerly, pushing away the large, stinking ash-tray filled with stale butts that's under my nose. "Something bothers me. If Zack and Loretta own that hamburger stand and the house they live in, then why would they just walk away and leave them? The property would be worth enough so that it doesn't make sense to give it up. But they were planning to leave town."

"I'll pull a couple of files, and we'll see what we can come up with." He's gone for a little while, and I push the ashtray all the way over to the wall.

When he returns, he sits at the desk, going through some papers in the manila folder he has brought with him. He reads intently, picking at a little red spot that is beginning to swell on his chin. Finally he looks up. "You gave me an easy one to answer. When Zack and Loretta were in the ID department,

146

they volunteered some information as the forms were filled out. Zack Tigus stated that he was managing a hamburger stand on a lease. The lease is due to run out at the end of the month, and the rent will be raised. Loretta said she had inherited the house, but a large corporation has bought a four-block area from the owners of those old houses to develop as another shopping area. The houses have been leased back to the owners at a low rent until it comes time to tear them down."

"So it wouldn't have bothered them at all to leave the country and the business and the house."

"Doesn't look as though it would."

I sigh. Things are shaping up, coming together. So far, so good. "I had to know that," I say. "Thanks."

"How about the rest of what you wanted?"

"The information office told you what I asked?"

"About jail records? Yeah."

I lean back in my chair. The plastic is hard against my back. "I'm trying to track down an area. Could we check out some names? I'd like to know more about Zack's jail record and the people he knew in jail. I'd like to find out if Loretta was ever in jail."

He raises one eyebrow, but simply says, "Remember that I told you the tracking comes from my department."

"I know, but Kelly said . . ."

"Kelly?"

"He's a . . . a friend. He believes my story. He's probably the only one who really does, and he's the only one who said he'd help me."

"I said I'd help you."

"But that's different. You also said you had a lot of other cases to work on."

"That's right." He stretches back in his chair, locking his hands behind his head. "Three murders last night, for instance. One of them a bar brawl, where no one, including the bartender, was sober enough to know what happened or who

147

fired the gun. The other two were random killings—very little in the way of leads. And we've got some old murders to work on, and assorted robberies and burglaries and . . ." He shakes his head quickly and sits upright. "Well, enough of all that. I'm still interested in your case."

"But Kelly and I have more time to work on it."

"You and this Kelly, whoever he is, are working out a fantasy. In the world of crime, people have guns without consciences on the trigger ends. They try to take what they want, and they don't let anyone get in their way. If you're a nuisance to them, with your prying around, they could just as easily put an end to you as squash a roach."

He leans toward me, against the desk, and I can see the bulge of a shoulder holster under his coat. For some reason this scares me, and makes his words seem even more real. "I'll get someone in the department to check out the records we need," he says. "I'll get them to you as soon as I can. Will you trust me?"

"Yes."

"Going through records is a good idea. Maybe it will tell us something. Maybe it will jog something in your memory, and you'll come up with a piece of information that will help us move further."

I stand and try to smile at Detective York again. It's a shaky smile, but it's there.

He reaches out a large hand and shakes my shoulder gently. "Hang in there," he says. "Go on with your normal routine— especially, stop playing hooky from school." He moves around the desk. As an afterthought he says, "And tell this little friend of yours—this Kelly—to stop the game right now. Investigating a crime—any crime—is not a job for amateurs."

"You'll call me soon with the information?"

"I'll call. How soon I can't promise."

It's a short walk back through the Homicide Division room and down the hall and into the elevator, with its assortment of

148

talls and shorts and wides and thins, all squeezing against each other, with everything meeting but eyes.

I'll have to call Kelly and tell him what Detective York said. I don't think Kelly will agree that we should drop our investigation. I hope he won't. Maybe I'm being stubborn, but I've got to carry this through, even if I have to work alone.

11

I stop in a drive-in to get a hamburger and a Coke, then take them to Memorial Park. It's quiet in the park. A couple of women joggers puff by, their faces pink from exertion, their heavy breasts bouncing up and down under their sweat shirts. A squirrel peels itself from the camouflage of a nearby oak tree and scampers to my feet, begging for crumbs. I give him the last chunk of soggy bun and go back to my car. The sky is turning gray, and the pollen from the flowering ligustrum is making my nose itch.

It's not far to a phone booth. I have the scrap of paper with Kelly's phone number on it in my handbag, and I fish for it, banging an elbow on the accordion glass door of the booth. The phone rings and rings, and finally a woman answers it with a tired sound that passes for a "hello."

I ask for T. J. Kelly, and she says, "He's at class."

"Do you know when he'll be home?"

"There's no telling. He goes from class to the studio. If they've got a big story to work on and need his camera, then he sometimes gets home later than usual."

"What's usual?"

There's a pause. "Who is this?"

I can't seem to communicate with this woman. She must be

Kelly's mother. Doesn't sound young enough to be one of his sisters. I find I'm hesitant about giving my name, but I can't be. Kelly must call me back. So I tell her.

She doesn't react. "I'll tell him you called," she says. "I'm writing it down on the blackboard we keep by the phone in the kitchen. Kelly usually looks there when he comes home. So do all the kids. They know there's no way to remember all the messages that come in."

"Yes," I murmur.

"You said something else?"

"No."

"I didn't catch it."

Our words interlock and spin into a garble of sound, so that we can't hear one another. I keep quiet to give her a chance, and she says, "Anything else?"

"No. That's it. Thank you very much." I am prim and polite, instead of shouting, "I need Kelly! Tell him it's urgent!" the way I wish I could.

There is a click of the receiver in my ear. There's nothing to do now but wait until Kelly calls—and until Detective York calls. Wait . . . wait . . . wait. I can't go back to school. To kill time I go to the library and read all the news stories about what happened. It makes me sick to read them, but I must find out everything I can. Then I go home to wait for Kelly's call.

But Kelly doesn't phone, and he doesn't come by. The ten o'clock newscasters cover two fires by arson, four holdups of savings-and-loan offices, an angry meeting of the school board, and a flash news item about a ten-car pile-up on the 610 Loop, with films of the accident to follow. Kelly, will you get home too late to phone me?

The phone rings, and I hurry to answer it, realizing that I'm the only one who would. My mother and father have gone to a bridge party at their club.

"Kelly?" I say eagerly, but there is a long pause. "Hello? Who's there?" I ask. My throat is cold. My hand grips the re-

151

ceiver as though it could never let go. I know I should hang up, but I can't move.

Then it comes . . . a whisper. "Keep your nose out of things," it says, and it adds a string of obscenities. I can't tell whether the voice belongs to a man or a woman. The whisper disguises it completely. "Do you understand?" it asks.

There is no way I can answer. No way. Like a robot, with jerky, stiff motions, I hang up the receiver, staring at the phone. My stomach hurts. The phone rings again, but I don't answer. Should I call Detective York? Should I call my mother and father and ask them to come home from the club?

Taking a deep breath, I force myself to move away from the phone. I turn off the television set and slowly go up the stairs. I should have known it would be like this. Maybe I'm asking for it. But what choice have I got? I can't go on the other way!

In the bathroom I throw up, and the pain that has gripped my stomach begins to lessen. I put on a nightgown and climb into bed, hugging the covers around my chin. Most of the lights in the house are on. I'll leave them on.

Tomorrow Kelly will call me. I'll have to be patient until tomorrow. The phone doesn't ring again, thank God. Tomorrow, Kelly . . . tomorrow.

Tomorrow comes and another tomorrow. I don't go to school. I manufacture a sore throat and convince my mother that the light sprinkling of acne under my chin is the beginning of a rash. She keeps me in bed, and runs out to Alfred's kosher restaurant for a quart of chicken soup to go. She read in an article once that Jewish-mother chicken soup was better than penicillin, so when anyone in the family is sick, that's what he gets, although she leaves out the "Jewish mother" part when she feeds the soup to my father.

I'm grateful there are no more whispering late-night phone calls. Could the caller know I'm not home alone?

This is a quandary. I can't stay in bed forever, but I can't go to school. I went to classes that one day, and I managed to get through the day without coming apart in little pieces. But I can't do it again. It takes too much of my energy, and I want to use that energy to do all the work needed to prove myself. Where is Kelly? I wonder why he hasn't called. I can't call him back. I'd probably find myself talking to his mother again, and I'd feel like a fool.

It's early afternoon, and my bed has become hot and boring and full of little lumps I didn't know were there before. So I dress in jeans and an old plaid shirt, then go to the den and sit on the floor cross-legged in front of the television set, watching Sesame Street on Channel 8. Lorna comes into the room.

"Hi," she says in a little voice, hanging back in the doorway to the kitchen, ready to jump away as though she thought I would shout "Boo" at her.

I scramble to my feet. "Lorna! I didn't know you were here!"

"Della let me in the back door."

"Well, come in. Sit over here. I'll get us something to eat. Move those cushions out of the way." I'm babbling. This is my best friend. Why am I acting as though she were a stranger?

Lorna sits on the edge of the sofa. "You haven't been at school for three days. They said in the attendance office that you were sick."

"Uh . . . yes," I say.

She looks at me with a little wrinkle of worry branching her eyebrows. "Are you feeling better now?"

"I think so."

"I've—we've missed you at school."

I flop on the sofa beside her. "Oh, Lorna, I can't go back to Madame DeJon's!"

"You have to! No one can just drop out of school. What about graduation next year? What about college?"

I groan. "I can't even think about next year. It's hard enough to think about tomorrow."

Lorna touches my hand. "Please come back, Chrissie. I'm

153

there to help you. And you needn't mind what the others do or say."

"I can't go there and face them, knowing they believe that lie about me."

Her eyes blank over for an instant, and I wonder, with a feeling as though someone had socked me in the stomach, if she's thinking about the gossip and the lie and the people who believe it, or if she still has doubts about me too.

Lorna makes her voice cheerful and optimistic. I'm sure she's practiced the speech on the way over here, because it comes out in a polished rhythm. "Everything passes, Christina. People may gossip about you today, but there's something new to gossip about tomorrow, and then they'll forget about you."

"They'll never forget. I have to prove that I was telling the truth. Besides, there's no gossip that will be important enough to wipe out the wrong gossip they've got going about me."

She perks up, and her eyes snap. "Oh no? Wait until I tell you the latest we've found out! Everybody's talking about it!"

"What?"

"Gloria!" Her voice is almost a whisper. "She's pregnant! Can you believe it?"

Suddenly I am filled with such sorrow for Gloria that I want to hold her and weep with her. I feel at one with Gloria, yet I've never really known her well. It doesn't seem to matter. I don't really know myself either.

"What's the problem?" Lorna is peering into my face. "Isn't that exciting news?"

"No," I say. "It's sad news. It breaks my heart."

Lorna looks away, embarrassed. "Come on, Christina. Stop kidding. Don't you want to know what you've missed in class? I brought your homework assignments."

She holds out a sheet of paper, which is covered with her tiny, neat handwriting. "It's a lot to make up."

"I don't mind," I say. "I'll just stay home and make up homework forever and ever."

154

"I don't understand you," she says. "Are you trying to be funny?"

"I don't feel a bit funny, and I'm having so much trouble understanding myself, I can't expect you to understand me, Lorna."

"But I want to," she says.

"Why?"

"Because I'm your friend."

Maybe I'm becoming overly suspicious. A part of my mind is asking if Lorna would really want to remain my close friend if she had doubts that I had been kidnapped. Who'd want to have an extortionist for a friend? Lorna might. She'd enjoy being a martyr, loyal to the end, especially if it bugged her mother that she was sticking by me.

I shake my head, trying to clear away the thoughts that, like little sharp-toothed rats, are gnawing away chunks of my self-esteem. I take her friendship at face value. After all, haven't we been friends since first grade?

"Let's get some sandwiches," I tell Lorna, holding out my hand to her and tugging her up from the sofa. "I'm starving."

She smiles back eagerly. "And I can go over the homework with you! I've got lots of time. You will come back to school, won't you?"

"Someday," I say, and I laugh, which causes Lorna to laugh too, the meaning of the answer disappearing in rings of giggles.

We eat and we study, and the afternoon passes, Kelly still hasn't called. I don't understand. I thought he wanted to help me.

In the distance I hear the doorbell ring, but Lorna and I are busy, and I don't pay attention. It's Della's job to take care of interruptions.

But a voice over my left shoulder says, "Hi, Christina!" and I jump and whirl around.

"Kelly! Where have you been?"

He looks puzzled, and I realize that Lorna is staring open-

155

mouthed at Kelly and then at me, and back again at Kelly, like a spectator at a tennis match between Eric the Red and Phyllis Diller. I remember my manners.

"Lorna Darvey . . . T. J. Kelly," I stammer. As an afterword to Lorna I say, "Kelly is . . . uh . . . helping me."

"Helping you what?" Lorna asks.

Kelly moves into the room, smiling and narrowly missing the coffee table. He is taking Lorna in carefully. I don't blame him, because Lorna is good-looking—no doubt about it. I feel a tug of jealousy, and for a moment I don't know whether I want to righteously push it away or experience it and enjoy the misery. Kelly's next words distract me.

"I was hoping you'd have a few minutes to answer some questions for me," he says.

"Well, sure. That is . . . Why didn't you call me back?"

"What are you talking about? Did you call me?"

"I called you Wednesday. I said it was important. Your mother told me she was writing my name on the blackboard by your kitchen phone, and you'd see it there and call me."

Kelly groans and flops into a low chair, his long legs spread out in front of him. "I don't know why she does that to me! She's got this thing about girls calling boys being all wrong, and after that chick in my eco class last year got it into her head to phone twice a day and . . ." He breaks off. "I told my mom to let me know if you called, Christina, but she gets things mixed up sometimes. Sorry I didn't get your message. We don't even have a blackboard by the kitchen phone."

Lorna stands and begins to gather her things together. "I've got to leave," she says. "It's nearly dinnertime, and I'm going with my parents to that Russian collection on exhibit at the art museum." Her eyes are telling me, "Call me as soon as you can and fill me in on this Kelly."

"Okay," I say, giving a double answer. "I'll see you."

"I'll talk to you tomorrow," Lorna says, "and you be at school Monday . . . you hear?"

156

I smile, and Lorna makes a few polite remarks to Kelly, who uncurls himself from the low chair with some difficulty and says all the right things back to her. Lorna insists on going to the door by herself, and in a way I'm glad to see her leave. I want so badly to talk to Kelly.

For a few seconds we sit and look at the walls in silence, until we hear the back door close. Then Kelly and I turn toward each other eagerly, speaking together.

"What have you done?"

"What do you know?"

He backs off first. "Tell me why you called me. What's up?"

"I went to the police station to look up some records."

"What kind of records?" Kelly is interested.

"I thought it would be a good idea to look up Zack's police record, and also to see if anyone else we know has any kind of record—anything that could tie him in with Zack."

"What did you find out?"

"Nothing yet. I talked to Detective York. He told me he'd do it for me."

Kelly thinks hard, then says, "When?"

"He didn't make any promises. He said he'd do it when he could."

"Damn!"

"Kelly, he also said that we should stay out of the investigation. He said it could be dangerous, since we don't know who we're up against."

Kelly rubs his hands through his hair, leaving wisps standing on end. "Do you go along with this?"

"I wanted to see what you thought."

"But I asked you a question. You didn't answer it."

I sigh. "Oh, Kelly, I want so much to get to the truth in all this. I'm impatient, and I don't want to wait for Detective York to get into it on his free time."

"I'm glad to hear you say that," Kelly says.

"Then you feel that way too?"

157

He grins at me. "You know it! We haven't got that much time to fool around with."

His words puzzle me. "Why? What do you mean?"

He shrugs, and his gaze shifts to examine a large painting on the far wall as he answers. "Isn't that what you've told me? Isn't that what we were talking about before? We'd have to find who that third person was, or the trail would get cold? The more time that passes after a crime, the harder it is to discover who did it."

His words make sense, and in a way I am mollified; but something in the back of my mind nags at me. I've had this feeling before. Something isn't quite right, but I don't know what it is. What's the matter with me? Am I going to go through life being suspicious of everyone?

"Do you feel that you'd be in any danger, Christina?" Kelly's face is serious.

"I—I don't know. I don't think so." Why don't I want to tell him about the phone call?

"That's good," he says. He smiles again. "Then we'll get to work."

"Kelly . . . how about you? Do you think I'll be in danger?"

He laughs. "Not from what we've found out so far!" But he adds, reacting to the expression on my face, "Don't look so upset. We have only three suspects, and I don't think any of them would hurt you."

"Three? Where did we get three?"

We are close together now, voices low, heads almost meeting. I can smell Kelly's after-shave lotion—a woodsy kind of fragrance that seems to go with his wild red hair. I like it.

"Rosella, Della, and your grandmother."

I gasp. "I told you to forget about that, Kelly! Leave my grandmother out of it! She wouldn't do a thing like that!"

"Wouldn't she?" He fishes some papers out of his shirt pocket and unfolds them, spreading out the creases with his thumb.

"A guy I know on one of the papers got hold of some financial information for me. It seems that your grandmother's company spread itself pretty thin when it began going in for land development as a sideline. They're in kind of a bind in that department, with taxes coming on a lot stronger than sales. And they haven't had such good luck lately with their natural-gas exploration either."

I put a hand on his arm to stop him. "Kelly, it doesn't matter! What kind of woman would have her own granddaughter kidnapped? Not Cristabel, I can promise you!"

"Nobody hurt you, did they? They didn't push you around, and you got fed, and there weren't any other problems. Right?"

"But . . ."

"If we're going to do this step by step, we've got to cover everything, Christina. We can't just go on your emotions. That isn't scientific detecting."

I push back my chair, staring at my outstretched feet. "Then let's forget the whole thing."

"You're kidding!"

"I am not! Either you leave Cristabel out of this, or forget about helping me. Do you understand, Kelly?" I'm glaring at him now.

"Okay," he says, and he gives me another big, lopsided smile. "I didn't know you felt so strongly about it."

I make myself relax. I'm tired. I don't like getting emotional and spilling out all the things inside my head. All I want is a nice peaceful life in which I can find out who I am. I just want to think about me for a while. I wish it weren't impossible.

"Oh, Kelly," I say, "it seems so hopeless. We're going on the possibility that it has to be someone I know—someone who has access to the house and who knows where my clothes are and where my father keeps his gun. What if it's just a very clever person who's good at burglarizing houses?"

"Yeah. It's a possibility all right."

"So what can we do?"

"We can investigate those two, at least. If they don't tie in with Zack, then we'll have to take it from another direction."

A thought comes to me. "Then how about going from Zack's direction right from the first?"

"Like how?"

There are footsteps in the doorway, and my mother sails into the room, floating gauzy sleeves behind her. She looks surprised, pleased, and disturbed all at the same time when she sees Kelly, and it's easy to see what's going on in her mind.

"Kelly, isn't it? How nice," she says, floating toward him.

He manages the trick of unbending again, and reaches down to shake her hand.

My mother looks at me uncertainly. "Did we forget to tell you that Cristabel is coming for dinner tonight?"

"Here?"

"I thought it would be nice. We need to . . ." She stops, glancing at Kelly. She obviously doesn't want to fill him in on family business.

"I'd better be going then," Kelly says.

"No," I tell him. I turn to my mother, knowing I am breaking a hard-and-fast rule from early childhood. In front of Kelly I say, forcing my mother's hand, "Please, may Kelly stay for dinner too?"

It's hard to grit your teeth and smile at the same time, but my socially correct mother manages it nicely. "Why, what a lovely idea. You can stay, can't you, Kelly?"

"Sure," Kelly says.

I give an inward sigh of relief. I counted on the fact that Kelly would avoid reading between the lines. I know he wants to meet Cristabel, and I want to have him there so our family conversation can stay on a nice inane surface level.

"You might change out of your jeans, dear," my mother says. "I'll stay here and chat with Kelly."

So I dash upstairs, take a quick shower, and put on a dress

and as much makeup as I can to have something going for me. I come away from the mirror as about a four on a scale of one to ten, which is a lot better than the minus I was before.

Kelly looks at me appreciatively when I re-enter the den, and that's all I need. My morale goes up enough to carry me through dinner, which is a disaster.

Cristabel has made an effort to come, I'm sure, because she must feel as ill at ease with me as I do with her. But she is gracious and self-possessed. She reminds me of Queen Elizabeth at a ceremony of state. She must have the same backbone and nervous system.

My mother is in her role of effervescent and charming hostess, which she plays to perfection. My father is warm dignity in a dull gray suit. I am a dutiful and mostly silent daughter; whereas Kelly is just Kelly. He accidentally sloshes water from his goblet on the tablecoth, and drops his roll on the floor. He flatters Cristabel, and seems to enjoy himself wholeheartedly. No one told Kelly he had a part in this play.

Della serves, throwing little frowns, like darts, in Kelly's direction, but none of them hit the target. I watch the lily bulbs in the bowl in the center of the table. The sprouts are much higher, stronger. They seem to grow under my gaze. Tips of green buds are beginning to show.

Kelly makes the mistake of saying something about people who want to nationalize the oil companies, and Cristabel is off and running, not waiting for Kelly to finish his sentence so she can find out whether he's for or against the idea. For the next twenty minutes she puts on an academy-award scene that outdoes Angela Lansbury. My father finally breaks in to say that the coffee is getting cold, and wouldn't it be nice to have fresh cups in the living room.

Kelly and I excuse ourselves and wander into the den.

"Your grandmother is an interesting person," Kelly says.

"The word 'interesting' is an understatement."

"Are you like her?" he asks. "I think you are, in a way."

161

"No!" Why does this question make me so angry? "I'm not a bit like Cristabel!"

"I think you are—oh, not in looks, or anything like that. I mean that I think you've both got a lot of guts."

"Great," I say. "I needed that compliment to make my evening complete."

"Forget it," Kelly says. "I've got to start for home pretty soon. We'd better decide what our next step should be."

"Detective York said he'd get any record information to me as soon as he had it."

"But how about in the meantime? No telling how long that will take."

"What do you want me to do?"

"Talk to Rosella and Della. See if you can get any more information from them. And I've got an idea I'm going to work on for now."

"What idea?"

"I'll tell you about it later."

"Okay," I answer. I have an idea of my own, but if that's the way Kelly wants to be, then I'll keep it to myself. Besides, I'm still mad at him for comparing me to Cristabel. All I want is to be myself.

Kelly leaves. I go into the living room and say good night. It's easy. No one feels like talking to me now. I take my books up to my room, throw them on the chair, and get back into my jeans.

I've got the idea, and now is the time to put it into practice. I'm going to see if Zack can't lead me to this mystery person —the one who planned the kidnapping so carefully.

It doesn't take long to look up the number of the hamburger place. A woman's voice answers the phone, and over the noise in the background of tinny, piped-in radio music and someone shouting orders for with and without onions, she yells at me that Zack is off duty and not due in until the next morning at eleven. Good. That's what I was hoping for.

The home phone for Zachariah Tigus is listed too, so I jot it on a slip of paper, make sure I have a couple of dimes in my purse, grab a sweater, and run down the stairs. At the living room I poke my head in, say, "Gotta go out for a couple of minutes," and disappear out the front door before any of them has a chance to ask me where, when, or why.

My Cutlass is in the garage. It takes just a few minutes to pull out onto the street.

I follow the route I know over to Zack's neighborhood. There is a gas station on the nearest main street, and most gas stations have outdoor phone booths in them. This one is no exception. I keep the door open, so no light shows. I can see enough from the bluish arc light on the street corner to dial Zack's number. It's not too late. I'm pretty sure he won't be in bed yet. He'll probably be stretched out in one of those lumpy overstuffed chairs, watching television, while Loretta irons something . . . anything.

The receiver is sweaty in my hand, and I can only breathe in little, short gasps. I am counting the rings, and on the fifth Zack answers. I am so relieved I find it hard to think. What if it had been Loretta? I don't know what I would have said.

"Hello? Hello?" Zack's voice is impatient.

I whisper. I found out the hard way it makes a great disguise for a voice.

"Meet me," I say.

"What? Is this . . . ?"

I interrupt, trying to put force and power into my whisper. "You know who this is. I want you to meet me. It's important."

"Where?"

"I don't have to tell you that. You know where to find me."

Quickly I hang up, get inside my car on the run, and drive two blocks to Zack's street. I pull to the curb, down about five houses from his, and turn out my lights. Then I wait.

It doesn't take long. Zack comes out of his front door and climbs into the green car sitting in the driveway. As he backs out, he turns the car in my direction. I barely have time to scoot down on the seat, out of sight, before he passes me.

I make a U-turn, glad there are no cars parked opposite me, turn on my lights, and try to follow Zack around the corner. I didn't realize that cars look so much alike in the dark. I must stay closer to him than I had wanted to. I can't afford to lose him now.

Zack drives fast. I am having difficulty keeping up with him, yet staying far enough back so that he won't see me. I don't pay much attention to where we are going until he pulls up at a small apartment house on a quiet street, turns off the lights, slams the door of his car, and runs up the steps to vanish inside.

What do I do now? Do I follow him? Maybe I had better just wait here until he leaves, then go inside the apartment house and find out whom he might be seeing.

This apartment house surprises me. I can't imagine who lives in it whom Zack would hurry to see.

I roll down the window to get some fresh air. The night is humid and full of the smell of stale grass cuttings. A mound of large black garbage bags lies next to the curb, waiting for the morning's pickup, I suppose. Old, tired trees have cracked the sidewalk with their roots, and someone's overloud television set shouts from across the lawn.

It would be a good idea to walk to the corner, read the name of this street, and jot it down along with the address of the apartment house, I think. I am reaching for the door handle when suddenly, through the open window, an arm shoots in, and a strong hand covers my mouth!

164

12

"Don't make a sound! What are you doing here?"

I gasp as the hand withdraws and I stare into the face of the man leaning in my car window. It's Kelly!

"You scared me to death!" I tell him.

"Sorry," Kelly says. "What are you doing?"

"I called Zack. When I talked to him, I whispered, so he couldn't tell who I was. I just told him to meet me. He drove here, and I followed him."

Kelly thinks a moment, then nods his head. "Not a bad idea. So this must be the place."

I shiver. "Kelly, the third person must live in those apartments. Should we call Detective York?"

"No!" Kelly says quickly. "We have no proof. We don't even know which of the apartments Zack is in. You just told him to meet you. What if he thought you were his bookie?"

"Come on, Kelly," I mutter. An idea hits me. "Just what are you doing here, by the way?"

"I was driving over to talk to Zack," Kelly says. "I'd just reached the cross street near his house when I saw him turn the corner and saw your car behind his. So I came along for the ride."

"Why were you going to talk to him?"

"You tried talking to Loretta, and that didn't work. I thought maybe I could approach Zack through his ego, maybe lead him into giving something away."

"So here we are. Should we see who lives in that apartment house?"

"I think we ought to get out of here before Zack comes out. He's probably made his contact and is steamed about being out on a wild-goose chase. He should be storming out of there in a couple of minutes."

"If we wait, we might see who's with him."

"Go home, Christina," Kelly says. "You're taking too big a chance being here."

"Just what are you planning to do?"

"I'll tail him to his house. When he gets home, I'll talk to him. Now go home."

"Wait a minute! This was my idea! And I've got to check the apartment mailboxes and find out who lives there."

"I can take care of that."

"When?"

"After I talk to Zack."

"But . . ."

"Trust me," Kelly says. "I'll get the information for you. Now be a good girl and go home. I'll be over tomorrow."

"What time?"

"Tomorrow's Saturday, and I don't go to work until two. How about if I come around eleven?"

"All right." I turn on the ignition. That uncomfortable thought is skittering around in my brain again. If it would just hold still for a second, I might be able to capture it. I wave goodbye to Kelly and drive down the street, turning the corner.

I'm about three blocks away when I begin to wonder if Kelly will be safe. What if Zack comes out with that third person? What if they see Kelly and want to get rid of him? He might need help. I don't want to leave him in a tight situation. I'd better go back.

166

I go around another couple of corners and back to that street, whose name is now implanted in my memory. I don't park in the same place. Zack's car is still there, but Kelly's car is gone. What happened to Kelly? I thought he was tailing Zack.

I cut my lights and pull up under a sagging mimosa tree. I'm fairly well hidden here, and with the help of the nearby street light I can see anyone who might come in or out of the apartment house. I wonder why Zack hasn't left the building yet.

Suddenly the door opens, and Zack appears. Without looking to the left or right, he hurries to his car, gets in, and takes off.

Where is Kelly? I wish one of us had been able to see what apartment Zack had been in. What's Kelly up to? I'm so impatient I can't stand it.

The street is silent. It's dark. I feel very much alone. But there's no one to stop me now. I've got to do what I had in mind. I'm going into the apartment house to read the names on the mailboxes. Kelly said he'd take care of that, but I think I'd better do it just to make sure. One of those names should give me a clue. I cautiously climb from my car, shutting the door as softly as I can. I'm afraid of the darkness of the street, of the silence, but mostly I'm afraid of what I might find in that apartment house. I'm terrified that I'm going to recognize one of those names!

Up the steps and through the unlocked door I go, into a cramped lobby. There is a dusty plastic plant in a clay pot on a rickety table, and a light rectangle in the paint above it where a picture had once hung. On the opposite side are the rows of little mailbox doors—sixteen of them, each with a first initial and last name printed on cards on the doors. I scan the names quickly, but none is familiar. So I pull a pencil out of my handbag and fish around for something to write on. The back of an envelope will have to do. I copy each name as

167

fast as I can, occasionally darting swift glances over my shoulder to make sure no one has come into the lobby and is watching me.

C. Washington, F. Ferris, A. Gonzalez, K. Smith . . . I scribble the names on the envelope. The small room reeks of stale, rancid odors left by many tenants over many years. I'm eager to leave.

There is the sound of a door closing upstairs, and I hear footsteps over my head. I rush through the front door into the darkness, run as fast as I can to my car, and lock myself in. I wait, motionless, until the door to the apartment house opens and a couple strolls out. They walk down the street aimlessly, away from me. Where they are going I don't care. I'm able to breathe again, so I start the car and drive home.

I go over the names in my mind while I'm driving, and after I'm in bed, wanting to fall asleep. An idea begins to slip around where I can't touch it. I grab at it again and again, but it teases and taunts, then slithers away. Exhausted, I roll on my side, knees tucked up, arms pressed against my chest, abandoning the chase, drifting into sleep.

And it comes.

The idea, miffed at being abandoned in midchase, flings itself into my conscious mind. I am so startled that my eyes fly open and I gasp. Of course! It's the answer! It bothered me at the time it was said, but it didn't completely register. Only the person working with those people would have known about that—only that person and me. Because I know. And I must tell someone!

I phone Kelly. A sleepy voice answers, grumping around the words. "Do you know what time it is?" Kelly's mother asks.

But another voice breaks in on an extension—Kelly's. "It's all right, Mom," he says. "I've got it."

She listens for a moment, then apparently decides she is too sleepy to be curious, and I hear the receiver click in its cradle.

"Christina? What's on your mind?" Kelly asks.

"What happened after I left the apartment building?"

"Is that all you called for?" He sounds disappointed.

"Please tell me, Kelly."

"There's not much to tell. I followed Zack home, and talked to him for a while, to see if he'd give out any information."

"Did he?"

"Nothing new."

"How about the names?"

"What names?"

"The names of the people who live in that apartment house."

"Oh sure. I've got them written down somewhere. None of them meant anything to me. I'll give you the list."

"How did you know I'd talked to Loretta?" I ask.

There is a pause, and Kelly gives an abrupt laugh. "Don't you remember, Christina? You told me you talked to her."

I want to say, "Oh, Kelly, I trusted you. I wanted you as a friend. Why did you lie to me?" But instead I say, "Kelly, I couldn't sleep. I needed to talk to you."

"Well, relax," Kelly says. "Try to get some sleep. I'll be over tomorrow at eleven. Is that still okay?"

"It's okay," I answer, and I slowly hang up.

I have to make one more call. I scoot out of bed, find the card with Detective York's phone numbers on it, and climb back in bed, sitting cross-legged, the phone on my lap.

He's not on duty, so I call his home number. It's not too late, I hope.

He answers on the first ring, and I'm glad to know I didn't wake him up. I hear music in the background and some people laughing.

"This is Christina," I tell him. "I know who the third person is."

His answer is deliberate. "How do you know?"

"Something that was said a few days ago. I just realized how it fit in."

"Do you have any proof that would stand up in court?"

"No," I say, "but it's something to work on."

He sighs. "Christina, it may be a long, drawn-out process, if that's all you've got."

"There's something else," I tell him. "Some names on mailboxes in an apartment house. I'm guessing, but I think one of them will tie in to the kidnapping."

"Listen," he says, "stop doing things on your own. We'll get together and compare notes. I've got some sheets from the records department. Putting them together with what you've got may help."

"Can you come by tomorrow morning—around eleven?" I ask.

"You wouldn't rather come downtown?"

"I think it's important," I say. "I think someone will be here who . . ." I interrupt myself, pleading. "Please be here! Please!"

"Eleven o'clock? I guess I can work that in, if nothing urgent comes up."

"Thank you."

"Good night, Christina," he says, and I hear a click and a dead sound. I put the receiver in its cradle and place the phone on the floor.

I sit in the middle of my bed, my arms wrapped around my legs, my chin resting on my knees. I have to think.

For some reason I'm not as unhappy or disturbed as I thought I would be. There is a certain elation at discovering this third person, a certain disappointment in the people I trusted, and a growing self-confidence in myself as a person. It's all mixed up, but my feelings are more up than they are down.

I can't even remember the Christina who was, before the kidnapping took place, years and years and years ago. That Christina was fumbling around, following orders, doing all the right things, and wishing she knew who and what she was all about. She was a child who thought the most important thing in her life was going to be a trip to France her parents didn't want her to take.

But the Christina I feel inside me now reminds me of those potted spring bulbs with tiny shoots strong enough to break through the pebbles packed over them, strong enough to reach up to the light and grow and grow and bloom and fulfill themselves. I am the shoot . . . not up very far . . . . and I know I've got a long way to grow. But it's good knowing I've come this far. I've got a direction now. It will take a lot more thought, a lot more discovery, but I know where I'm going. That's what counts.

I roll over and go to sleep on my stomach, arms and legs flung wide. Tomorrow will come soon, and there will be some risk involved in what I plan to do. But I'm not afraid.

Surprisingly, I sleep until nearly ten. I dash into a pair of jeans and a yellow T-shirt and hurry into the kitchen to bolt down a quick breakfast. The front of my shirt has a massive lion's head covering it. Very appropriate.

"Why the rush?" my mother asks. She pours herself another cup of coffee and sits beside me. Della putters in and out from the kitchen to the laundry room and back.

"I've got somewhere to go," I sputter, filling my mouth with cornflakes and trying to talk around them.

"But where, darling?" She puts down her cup with a tiny click against the saucer. "Christina, wouldn't it be lovely if we could take a day together to shop and lunch and . . . well, sort things out? We could talk."

"About what?" The orange juice goes down in one long gulp.

My mother sighs and lightly rests a hand on my arm. "Madame DeJon phoned me, Christina. She was concerned about your absence."

"I was here," I tell her. "You tucked me in bed and brought me chicken soup. Remember?"

"She was afraid the illness was somewhat psychosomatic.

171

She was afraid you had been unhappy with the attitude of some of the students when you returned to school after . . ." My mother is unable to complete the sentence.

"She may be right," I say, putting down my spoon and facing her for the first time that morning. "It was a rotten day. It was really the pits. I didn't want to see those people again."

"But school . . ."

"Don't worry, Mother." I smile and hug her. "I've taken care of that problem. I'll be at school on Monday."

Relief smooths the tired lines from her face. "I'm so glad, Christina. I know it's difficult, but . . ."

I haven't time for a replay, so I jump up, give her a quick kiss on her forehead, and say, "But I've got to leave now, Mother. I'll take a rain check on the lunch and shopping."

I hurry out the front door, avoiding the busy laundry room, and circle around to the garage.

It doesn't take long to drive to the Tigus house. As I hoped, Zack's car is gone. Now, if only Loretta is there! She has to be! I pull my car up on the driveway, close to the back door, and hop out.

She doesn't answer at first, as I pound on the back door, but I can hear her inside, feel her listening intently on the other side of the wooden door.

"Loretta Tigus!" I yell. "Open this door, or I'll get a hatchet and break it down!"

It opens immediately and she stares at me. A little bubble of saliva begins to drip from her open mouth, and she nervously rubs a hand across her lips.

"What do you think you're doing?" she asks.

I take her arm, gripping her tightly around one wrist, and tug her through the doorway. "I'm going to take you to meet someone," I tell her.

She tries to pull away, but my determination has given me strength she'll never have. She grabs at the doorframe and hangs on with all her might.

172

"Loretta," I tell her, grunting and pulling, "I'm going to raise hell out here if you don't come with me! There isn't a neighbor for blocks around who won't come running. And someone will call the police!"

"But . . . I gotta ask Zack."

"You don't have to ask him anything anymore. I say that you're coming with me! Now, come!"

Maybe it's my tone of voice. Maybe Loretta is just used to obeying orders. Suddenly she lets go of the doorframe, nearly goes limp, and it's all I can do to keep my balance. We practically tumble down the rickety steps.

I lead her to the car and make her slide in from the driver's side. She immediately tries the handle on the passenger side, but it's locked.

"Forget it," I tell her. "It's one of those safety locks that can be opened only by the driver."

I back out of the driveway and head home. A quick glance at my watch shows me that the timing is right. I hope Detective York is there when I arrive. And I hope Kelly is there too.

I turn to glance at Loretta. She is sitting upright, her hands gripped together. Strings of hair hang around her face, loose from the rubber band she had used to tie it back. Her eyes are dull, and she stares straight ahead.

"When did you last see Kelly?" I ask her.

She looks at me, startled. She reminds me of a little sparrow that has come to snatch a bread-crumb, but flutters around it nervously, ready to fly away at the sign of a cat.

"I don't know," she says.

"You answered my other question," I tell her.

"What other question are you talking about? You only asked me one."

"Loretta," I say, easing around a repair crew that blocks half the street, "you'll have to tell the truth about what happened."

"I told my story," she says. Her lips press together in a tight line.

"Zack told your story. You just repeated everything he told you to say."

She doesn't answer.

"Loretta, we know who the third person is. We know who worked the kidnapping out and who planned all those things so that if you didn't get away it would look as though I had set up a con to steal money from my grandmother."

"You can't know." Her voice is just a whisper. "Zack said no one could find out."

"Zack isn't that bright."

"And you think you know everything?" Her voice is a sneer.

"No, but I do know the name of everyone involved, and I know that you're going to tell the truth about what happened." I tell her.

"And get killed for it?"

Loretta is really scared now, and I reassure her. "You aren't going to get killed. What makes you think you'll get killed?"

"You said I might."

"I was guessing."

"Zack said so too, when I told him what you said. He said I'd be likely to get killed if I talked about it to anybody."

"Was it you who phoned me? Or Zack? Or . . ." But I've lost her. Loretta is off in thoughts of her own—frightening thoughts, I can tell by the expression on her face.

We're close to home, and I'm nervous myself. What if it doesn't work? Then we go into the long, drawn-out investigating, maybe letting this third person escape. My plan has to work!

Loretta doesn't seem to be aware of our surroundings until I slow down and pull into the drive in front of our house. There are two other cars parked there—Kelly's little orange Volkswagen, and another car, which I hope belongs to Detective York. I've forgotten what his looks like.

"What are we doing here?" Loretta screeches. "You can't take me here!"

"You have to face it now, Loretta." I hit the brakes, and we stop suddenly. She frantically grapples with the door handle and I'm not sure I can hold her, so I lay on the horn.

In a moment the front door opens. Detective York and Kelly run outside, my mother right behind them. Detective York lopes to Loretta's side of the car. I release the door lock, so when she throws the door open she practically falls into his arms.

Loretta looks around wildly, the whites of her eyes rimming the pupils. In a way I feel sorry for her.

"Where's Della?" I ask my mother.

She looks almost as frightened as Loretta. "Why . . . in the kitchen, I guess. I don't know . . . Somewhere in the house."

"Bring Loretta inside," I shout, and run into the house. Behind me I can hear Loretta screaming, "No! No!"

It takes a few minutes to find Della. She is huddled behind the front stairway, trying unsuccessfully to compress her large body into something small and invisible. Her face contorts as she sees me. She looks as though she were going to burst into tears.

The others come up behind me, and as she faces all of us, Della straightens. "What's this woman doing here?" she asks. She avoids looking directly at Loretta.

"She came to identify you," I tell Della.

"No!" Loretta shrieks again. "I didn't say nothing! I told Zack I wouldn't say nothing!"

Della lets out a long sigh that ripples through her heavy body like ocean swells in a calm sea. "I didn't think you'd push so hard to find out," she says. "I thought everybody would just forget about it sooner or later, since Christina didn't get hurt."

Kelly is incredulous. "Della is the third person?"

"Not exactly," I tell him. I turn to Detective York. "I've

175

got that list of last names and first initials from the mailboxes in the apartment house I told you about. The address is on the paper. I think you'll find the name of Della's son on that list. He'd have a different last name from hers, so I couldn't recognize it. If my guess is right, he's the one who worked out the idea. You'll probably also find out that he met Zack when they were in jail together."

"How did you find this out?" Kelly asks.

"From something Della said," I tell him. "I didn't recognize it at the time, but it kept nagging at me. Della said something about 'that woman's rent house.' I read all the newspaper stories and couldn't find anything about their house. I realized that information wouldn't have been on the television news either. The only way Della could know this would be if she knew Zack and Loretta. That was my only clue. Then when I went into the apartment house and wrote down the names, I realized there had to be another person too—and that person was probably Della's son. He thought of the plan and got Della and Zack to go along with it.

"One more thing added up," I say. "I remembered a man in Zack's hamburger place who didn't stare at me when Zack came to my table with Loretta and made the commotion. And I realized that he didn't look my way because he knew what Zack was setting up. He was in on it. I'm sure he is Della's son."

It doesn't take long for Detective York to call in for a blue-and-white patrol car to take Della and Loretta in; and he makes arrangements for Della's son and Zack to be picked up. My mother flutters over me for a while, then goes to the den to phone my grandmother. My father is speaking at a youth group luncheon. She'll have to fill him in later.

I'm left with Kelly to talk to, and I make it short. "You ought to get an 'A' on this project," I say. "Or are you after bigger game, like a full scholarship to pay your tuition so you won't have to work while you're going to school?"

176

He opens his mouth to protest, thinks better of it, and says quietly, "Both, I hope."

"I hadn't told you I talked to Loretta. You found that out from Loretta. And you found out enough from Loretta or Zack to lead you to that apartment house. I bet that last night you were checking out names on the apartment mailboxes when Zack came charging through the front door, and you ran out the back, circling around and scaring me to death."

"I followed Zack a number of times," he admits. "Once he led me to that apartment house. I thought there might be someone living there who tied in with the kidnapping."

"You were pumping Zack and Loretta for information, and you were pumping me too. You wanted to break this case yourself."

"Listen, Christina," Kelly says, "I did try to help you."

"Yes, you did, and I'm glad you did. I might not have been able to do it alone. I just wish you hadn't used me. I wish you hadn't lied to me."

"Would you have talked to me and worked with me if I'd told you I was interested in solving the case just to get a scholarship in communications?"

"No."

Kelly spreads out his hands in an open gesture and tries to grin. "There . . . you see."

"I see one thing, Kelly—that you're an opportunist. There was a time when you could have left me shattered, but not now. I can look at you without feeling betrayed."

"Betrayed? Come on, isn't that a pretty strong word?" he asks me.

"Who cares? I don't."

I walk toward the door. Kelly follows. "Christina, I think I can get a pretty good job with the TV channel I'm working for—you know, looking ahead to after graduation—if you don't call in the press for a little while. You understand? I'd like an exclusive."

I take a long look at him. "I'm not going to call anyone in yet, Kelly. You can do what you like."

"I mean, you were eager to have people know the truth about you."

"They will."

There's a long pause. Kelly looks uncomfortable. Finally he says, "Well, thanks, Christina. Aren't you going to wish me luck?"

"You don't need it," I say. "I expect you to be very successful and get everything you want out of life. It's the people who deal with you who'll need the luck."

I stand aside, and Kelly leaves. I watch his little orange car chug down the driveway; then I shut the door.

My mother comes in and wraps her arms around me. There are tears in her eyes. "It's all over now, darling," she says.

I hug her in return and answer, "Not completely, Mother. I think I've got my head on straight now, so there's one more thing to do."

She backs off, holding my shoulders, looking at me with a puzzled expression.

"As I told you, I'm going back to school Monday," I say. "But also, Monday I'm going hunting for a part-time job. I don't want Cristabel's trust fund with all those strings attached. If it were a gift, let's face it, I'd enjoy using the money for my education. But it's not a gift, and I don't need it. Lots of people work their way through college. I can too. I'm going to tell Cristabel that I've found out that I'm really very much like her in some ways. I'm just as stubborn and determined as she is."

"But Cristabel has your schooling all planned! She won't like this!" My mother is gripping her hands together as though trying to hold something that is slipping away.

"Listen to me, Mother," I say. "I don't need Cristabel's ideas or her money. I can make it on my own. And it's going to mean more to me when I do."

178

"But Cristabel can give you so much!"

"Not as much as I can give myself."

I run upstairs, smiling a little, humming a tune off-key. I feel good about myself. I've got to tell Lorna someday that I've found out what is really important—I am. It's a great feeling.

